PRAISE FOR M. L. BUCHMAN

Buchman has catapulted his way to the top tier of my favorite authors.

— FRESH FICTION

One of our favorite authors.

— RT BOOK REVIEWS

Buchman has catapulted his way to the top tier of my favorite authors.

— FRESH FICTION

A favorite author of mine. I'll read anything that carries his name, no questions asked. Meet your new favorite author!

— THE SASSY BOOKSTER, FLASH OF FIRE

M.L. Buchman is guaranteed to get me lost in a good story.

— THE READING CAFE, WAY OF THE WARRIOR: NSDQ

I love Buchman's writing. His vivid descriptions bring everything to life in an unforgettable way.

— PURE JONEL, HOT POINT

Nonstop action that will keep readers on the edge of their seats.

— *TAKE OVER AT MIDNIGHT,* LIBRARY JOURNAL

M L. Buchman's ability to keep the reader right in the middle of the action is amazing.

— LONG AND SHORT REVIEWS

The only thing you'll ask yourself is, "When does the next one come out?"

— *WAIT UNTIL MIDNIGHT,* RT REVIEWS, 4 STARS

The first…of (a) stellar, long-running (military) romantic suspense series.

— *THE NIGHT IS MINE,* BOOKLIST, "THE 20 BEST ROMANTIC SUSPENSE NOVELS: MODERN MASTERPIECES"

I knew the books would be good, but I didn't realize how good.

— NIGHT STALKERS SERIES, KIRKUS REVIEWS

Buchman mixes adrenalin-spiking battles and brusque military jargon with a sensitive approach.

— PUBLISHERS WEEKLY

13 times "Top Pick of the Month"

— NIGHT OWL REVIEWS

Tom Clancy fans open to a strong female lead will clamor for more.

— DRONE, PUBLISHERS WEEKLY

(Miranda Chase is) one of the most compelling, addicting, fascinating characters in any genre since the *Monk* television series.

— DRONE, ERNEST DEMPSEY, AUTHOR OF THE SEAN WYATT THRILLERS

(*Drone* is) the best military thriller I've read in a very long time. Love the female characters.

— SHELDON MCARTHUR, FOUNDER OF THE MYSTERY BOOKSTORE, LA

Superb!

— DRONE, BOOKLIST, STARRED REVIEW

A fabulous soaring thriller.

— *TAKE OVER AT MIDNIGHT,* MIDWEST BOOK REVIEW

Meticulously researched, hard-hitting, and suspenseful.

— *PURE HEAT,* PUBLISHERS WEEKLY, STARRED REVIEW

Expert technical details abound, as do realistic military missions with superb imagery that will have readers feeling as if they are right there in the midst and on the edges of their seats.

— *LIGHT UP THE NIGHT,* RT REVIEWS, 4 1/2 STARS

THE COMPLETE HENDERSON'S RANCH

A MONTANA BIG SKY ROMANCE COLLECTION

M. L. BUCHMAN

Buchman Bookworks

Other works by M. L. Buchman: *(* - also in audio)*

Thrillers

Dead Chef
One Chef!
Two Chef!

Miranda Chase
*Drone**
*Thunderbolt**
*Condor**
*Ghostrider**

Romantic Suspense

Delta Force
*Target Engaged**
*Heart Strike**
*Wild Justice**
*Midnight Trust**

Firehawks
MAIN FLIGHT
Pure Heat
Full Blaze
*Hot Point**
*Flash of Fire**
Wild Fire
SMOKEJUMPERS
*Wildfire at Dawn**
*Wildfire at Larch Creek**
*Wildfire on the Skagit**

The Night Stalkers
MAIN FLIGHT
The Night Is Mine
I Own the Dawn
Wait Until Dark
Take Over at Midnight
Light Up the Night
Bring On the Dusk
By Break of Day

AND THE NAVY
Christmas at Steel Beach
Christmas at Peleliu Cove
WHITE HOUSE HOLIDAY
*Daniel's Christmas**
*Frank's Independence Day**
*Peter's Christmas**
*Zachary's Christmas**
*Roy's Independence Day**
*Damien's Christmas**
5E
Target of the Heart
Target Lock on Love
Target of Mine
Target of One's Own

Shadow Force: Psi
*At the Slightest Sound**
*At the Quietest Word**

White House Protection Force
*Off the Leash**
*On Your Mark**
*In the Weeds**

Contemporary Romance

Eagle Cove
Return to Eagle Cove
Recipe for Eagle Cove
Longing for Eagle Cove
Keepsake for Eagle Cove

Henderson's Ranch
*Nathan's Big Sky**
*Big Sky, Loyal Heart**
*Big Sky Dog Whisperer**

Love Abroad
Heart of the Cotswolds: England
Path of Love: Cinque Terre, Italy

Other works by M. L. Buchman:

Contemporary Romance (cont)

Where Dreams
Where Dreams are Born
Where Dreams Reside
Where Dreams Are of Christmas
Where Dreams Unfold
Where Dreams Are Written

Science Fiction / Fantasy

Deities Anonymous
Cookbook from Hell: Reheated
Saviors 101

Single Titles
The Nara Reaction
Monk's Maze
the Me and Elsie Chronicles

Non-Fiction

Strategies for Success
Managing Your Inner Artist/Writer
Estate Planning for Authors
Character Voice

Short Story Series by M. L. Buchman:

Romantic Suspense

Delta Force
Delta Force

Firehawks
The Firehawks Lookouts
The Firehawks Hotshots
The Firebirds

The Night Stalkers
The Night Stalkers
The Night Stalkers 5E
The Night Stalkers CSAR
The Night Stalkers Wedding Stories

US Coast Guard
US Coast Guard

White House Protection Force
White House Protection Force

Contemporary Romance

Eagle Cove
Eagle Cove

Henderson's Ranch
Henderson's Ranch

Where Dreams
Where Dreams

Thrillers

Dead Chef
Dead Chef

Science Fiction / Fantasy

Deities Anonymous
Deities Anonymous

Other
The Future Night Stalkers
Single Titles

CONTENTS

ABOUT THIS SERIES

Come ride beneath Montana's Big Sky.

Where you'd expect a rancher, you'll find a retired US Navy SEAL.

A disabled war dog handler finds a new dog and new lease on life.

A New York chef finds a cowgirl with a knack for building everything except her own dreams.

A reporter, after a life "on the outside" tries to make sense of being welcomed inside.

A former dog handler who never wants to see a dog again, but gets little choice in the matter.

A ranch origin story for a former SEAL and the woman who has shared his life.

A Christmas story and a super secret bonus tale.

And finally a new home for a wounded war dog and for the woman who wouldn't let her die.

CHRISTMAS AT HENDERSON'S RANCH

Chelsea Bridges' *first trip to Montana lands her at Mark Henderson and Emily Beale's family ranch. In the past she pursued adventure from hiking the Continental Divide Trail to trekking in Nepal, but a horse ranch provides whole new world of wonders.*

*   ***Doug Daniels*** *spent three tours in the Navy before he became foreman at the ranch. He has finally found his home.*

*   *Nothing prepares them for the surprises that await during: Christmas at Henderson's Ranch.*

CHAPTER 1

"*This isn't right!*"

Chelsea Bridges leaned forward to see what Emily Beale was looking at. Chelsea didn't see a thing wrong, but then she'd never been to central Montana before. Out the small plane's front windshield were miles and miles of rolling green prairie. Streams crisscrossed the grassland in a bewildering maze. The backdrop was the foothills of the Rockies breaking the skyline with their snowy peaks and conifer-clad sides. The westering sun silhouetted the hills, but lit their tops with gold.

"It's absolutely gorgeous!" Then she clamped her mouth closed. She was trying to reel it in. Emily was always so even-keeled and understated that Chelsea was constantly stumbling to be less... Chelsea. Emily was this perfect woman with a drop-dead handsome husband and about the cutest kid on the planet. Chelsea had only been their daughter's nanny for a few months, but she'd seen the deference and respect that everyone at Mount Hood Aviation's firefighter airbase paid Emily. In return, the woman was kind, courteous, and utterly terrifying. Chelsea wouldn't mind being all of those things.

Her husband Mark, who sat up front in the other pilot seat of the small plane, wasn't much more effusive—except around his daughter. At least he had a sense of humor, though not as much a one as he thought he did; an observation Chelsea kept carefully to herself.

Chelsea looked over at Tessa who was strapped in beside her. She had her tiny version of her mother's elegant nose pressed up against the window. "Green," she announced. Out her window was nothing but the rolling grasslands of eastern Montana.

"It's wrong," Mark agreed solemnly but turned enough to wink at Chelsea, or at least she presumed that's what his cheek twitch was indicating at the lower edge of his mirrored Ray-Bans. "Not much snow in the hills. Means another drought year next summer."

"That's not the problem," Emily responded. "Okay, drought is a problem. But that's not the real problem."

"What is, Emma?" Again the sassy wink that said he already knew what his wife was talking about. It was amazing that the man had survived this long. Chelsea would never dare tease Emily Beale; she could probably kill with a glance if she ever took off her own mirrored shades.

"It's December," Emily took one hand off the plane's wheel—if she was on board, she was the one doing the flying—and waved it helplessly at the stunning scenery before them. "We came to Montana for a white Christmas."

"I thought it was to see Mom and Dad."

"It's still supposed to be white," she grumbled and set up to land the plane. It was as much emotion Chelsea had seen in her entire two months with them. Emily Beale was never unkind, but she was cold. Or at least chilly. But that wasn't right either. The woman was frank and forthright, as much with her daughter as with her husband. Yet Tessa was often in her lap, welcome not as child to adult, but rather as a piece of Emily that was simply back in the place where it belonged. The mother and daughter weren't close; they were simply one when they were together. It was about the most incredible thing Chelsea had ever seen. It made her ache for a family of her own; not a familiar feeling.

Again Chelsea strained up against her seatbelt to look down. A herd of horses startled and looked up at them as they passed by. They didn't scatter and run, but they eyed the low-flying plane carefully.

"Horsies!" Tessa declared delightedly when Emily shifted her flightpath so that the herd was visible outside her daughter's window. Not cold at all, just…inscrutable.

"Yes," Chelsea encouraged the toddler. "Those are horses. Aren't they pretty?"

"Pretty!" Tessa burbled, and they laughed together with delight.

Chelsea had never seen a whole herd of horses before. There were at least fifty in the group of every shade imaginable: grays, browns, whites, blacks, and mixes in patchworks, dapples, and who knew what all. They were gone behind the plane too fast to distinguish more. She tucked away the trail mix snack they'd been sharing to make sure Tessa's blood sugar was up.

Even after two months, Chelsea wasn't quite sure how she'd ended up in this situation. Not that she was complaining, Emily and Mark were great parents and it showed in their total sweetheart of a daughter. And flying with Mark over forest fires was often very dramatic.

It had started with Aunt Betsy who was a cook for the Mount Hood Aviation helicopter and smoke jumping firefighters. When Chelsea's degree in psychology hadn't led to any kind of a useful job, her aunt had asked if she liked to fly. She'd shrugged a yes because she'd flown in passenger jets any number of times to visit grandparents, and a trip to Nepal for a backpacking gap year.

She'd now spent most of the last two months sitting in tiny planes of six or eight narrow seats and been paid to enjoy the scenery and play with a baby girl. Best job she'd ever had by a long way.

Tessa was a fixture in Mark Henderson's plane when he was flying as the Incident Commander high above the fire. What was surprising wasn't that they'd added a nanny, but rather how he'd done the job for so long without one. Tessa was a pretty low maintenance kid, but she was also eighteen months old and quite intelligent.

It was a late fire season, Mark had said, and MHA had still been flying fire in the Southwest. But, finally released from the summer contract, they'd come north for a vacation and brought Chelsea along with them. She sure as hell wasn't going home. They'd known that.

As they flew closer to the ranch, more and more fences became visible, cutting the prairie into smaller pastures and training rings. There were several barns, smaller residences, and cabins surrounding the main residence.

Emily flew once over the grand log-built ranch house and waggled the plane's wings in a friendly wave.

Chelsea pointed to out to Tessa, "Isn't it amazabiling?"

"'mazbling!" Tessa called out happily. Emily sighed audibly as she circled wide of the barn.

Chelsea wondered if Mark's habits were rubbing off on her, but she couldn't resist messing with Tessa's rapidly developing language set. They landed on a gravel strip that ended close beside the house and a large out-building that turned out to be a hangar.

A big man strolled out to meet them, still buttoning up his sheepskin jacket. He was an older version of Mark; just as tall, just as broad-shouldered, his light hair going silver. But Mark's face was different. Darker, broader, and his hair was thick, straight, and almost midnight black, sharing only his father's gray eyes.

The clouds of mist puffing about with each breath of Mark Senior —Mac, she reminded herself, they'd said he liked to be called Mac— had Chelsea bundling up Tessa before the plane came to a halt in front of a hangar. The ground might be snow free, but it was far colder here than Oregon where they'd boarded the plane.

D*oug Daniels had stuck* his head out of the barn when he heard the plane come over low. The trademark gloss-black-and-red-flame paint job told him who was aboard. Some part of him had been alarmed that a client was in-bound for a ranch vacation even though they hadn't taken any Christmas reservations this year. But it was just Mark and his knock-out wife. He liked Mark fine, but he had trouble speaking around Emily Beale. It wasn't just the beauty, he knew how to talk to pretty women just fine; it was the fierce level of competence that she demonstrated at every turn.

He finished helping Logan pitch the hay into the stalls' feedboxes before heading out to greet them. The air had a sharp bite to it, wholly different from the horse-and-straw of the barn, but no moisture. As he stepped out of the barn, he noticed that there wasn't even a hint of cloud in the cobalt blue of the late afternoon sky. The temperature was already dropping though it was still an hour to sunset. It was going to get cold tonight.

Doug stuck his head back inside. "Hey, Logan. Open up the gates. If the main herd has any sense, they'll be coming this way by sunset."

"You bet, boss. Any horse that stays out there tonight needs his horse-sense meter checked."

Doug went out to help stow the plane. There was room in the hangar because he'd moved the helicopter tight to the side after the morning's flight to check the main herd and make sure there were no stray or injured. He hadn't been able to get an accurate count, but it had felt low and that was bothering him. Happened all the time. Still, it worried him.

He ducked through the hangar's side door, popped the release, and slid open the main door from the inside. It rattled and boomed in the cold air. A sharp squeal in one of the wheels had him adding "needs grease" to the infinite mental checklist that was running a working dude ranch.

Just emerging from the plane was a figure wrapped deep in a parka, with the fur-rimmed hood already raised as if it wasn't a merely brisk day, but rather a north polar night. She, for there was no chance of a guy wearing such tight jeans and making them look so good, carried an equally bundled child.

He came up and stuck his nose right into the child's hood, "Tessa, my love! Give us a kiss!"

"Kiss!" the little girl squealed and kissed him on the nose.

Then he rubbed noses with her until she was giggling before he pulled back. He'd ended up standing very close to the woman holding her. He could just see brilliant blue eyes, a freckled nose, and a bright smile in the narrow opening of the hood.

"Do you greet all the girls that way?" Her tone was light, almost musical.

"Sure." Never one to back down from a challenge, he stuck his face right into her hood until their noses rubbed and cried out, "Give us a kiss!"

Unlike the little girl, there was no squeal. Instead, there was a quick squawk of surprise.

Way over the line, Doug.

But before he could retreat, she gave him a quick kiss. Unlike Tessa's it didn't land on his nose, but right on the mouth. There and gone, but the lips were warm, soft, and tasted of peanuts and chocolate.

Once he was clear of the hood, the gloved slap that he expected to follow, didn't. He glanced again into the tunnel of the raised hood.

The bright blue eyes caught the low sunlight and weren't round with shock or narrowed with anger.

"Well," she blinked in slow motion, "okay then."

He laughed, he couldn't help himself.

Now that was his kind of woman.

CHAPTER 3

Chelsea **had no idea** what had come over her. She didn't randomly kiss men, even tall handsome ones who adored small children.

Men who then scooped a little girl out of her arms, slung her around with the ease of long practice until she was riding piggy-back, and—while Tessa shouted, "Horsie!" with glee—galloped about the yard with a protective hand wrapped awkwardly behind him. The man shook back his collar-length, sun-streaked hair the color of worn leather so that it brushed in Tessa's face. He let out a fierce whinny escalating her giggles of delight.

He trotted up to Mark and Emily then stopped with a sidle and a stomp that was thoroughly horselike and delivered the child to Emily. Then he and Mark made quick work of pushing the plane back into the hangar.

Chelsea was still standing shocked into place when they'd finished and the men had returned carrying the luggage.

"A field pack, very practical," the man who'd kissed her held it aloft as if it contained only air rather than most of Chelsea's worldly belongings. Her camping gear was stashed at Aunt Betsy's and a dozen boxes of books at Mom and Dad's, but the rest of it was in that pack.

"It's my hiking pack, but I use it for everything. Really practical since I hike a lot," she was rambling; time to cut that out. She sniffed at the air and the cold made her nose hurt on the insides, "At least when it isn't sub-Arctic."

The man's jacket was fleeced-line denim, but he hadn't even bothered to button it against the frosty day. He smelled of hay and his kiss had been warm and fresh with the outdoors.

Mac greeted his son with a firm handshake, but gave Emily a deep hug that surprised Chelsea almost as much as being kissed by a total stranger. What had happened to the woman's backbone of steel? Emily leaned into Mac's hug as if she was the one related by blood and was happily come home. Then he led them toward the house, leaving Chelsea and her luggage bearer to trail behind.

"Do you have a name or should I just shout 'Sherpa!' when I want your attention? Or perhaps *daai?*"

"*Daai?*" he led her onto the wide porch and held the door for her to enter the mud room. There they shed boots and jackets. She was glad she'd been wearing a thick sweater against the damp chill in Oregon and kept it on for added warmth.

The others were talking happily enough together to be lost in their own conversation as they too stripped off the outdoor gear and pulled on slippers from the large basketful of them close by the inner door.

"*Daai* means *older brother* in Nepalese," she explained softly. "A sign of respect. Better yet, *bhaai* for *younger brother* as who knows if you're worthy of respect."

"You kiss me and question whether I'm worth respecting? That doesn't bode well for the morning after."

Chelsea was preparing a comeback, for she certainly wasn't the one who had done the kissing...or had she been, when she turned and saw the look on his face.

"What?"

He shook himself like a horse again. "If I'd known what was under that hood, I might have spent longer kissing you."

"Skin deep, *bhaai.*"

"Yes, but what a nice layer it is."

CHAPTER 4

D

oug knew he was staring, but how was a man supposed to not? Thick waves of red hair cascaded down to her shoulders. Her cream-and-freckle skin only highlighted the brilliant blue eyes that were presently rolling at him. Her sweater must have been custom-made because it traced and enhanced the slender woman within. The rich green was finished with red zig-zags at wrists and waist. A small but elegant snowflake had been knit right over her heart.

"Frozen heart?" He teased to hide his suddenly dry throat.

She looked down where his attention had strayed. "I called this one White Christmas, *bhaai*. And watch where you're looking."

"I am watching where I'm looking, and very glad to be doing so," his made his voice pure tease. Then he wondered, "You name your sweaters?" Could he sound much stupider?

"Sure. At least the Christmas ones."

"You knit it yourself?" Apparently yes, he could sound dumber. But there was something about this girl—woman. She *liked* hiking? Major understatement. Her pack looked like it had been carried by an entire Army brigade, worn shiny in a hundred places. A very well-used piece of top quality gear. She knew terms of respect in Nepalese and could knit sweaters that made her look like a Christmas delight.

"I—" they stepped out of the mud room and into the living room. Her gasp of amazement echoed that of all who came here. Every ranch guest who entered the main house couldn't help but stumble to a halt.

"Quite something, isn't it?"

"It's gorgeous! A little daunting, but..." she did a slow twirl to take it all in. "But this is right out of a magazine. It's unbelievable!"

The large river-stone fireplace was a showpiece, big double-length logs crackled away on the grate. The flagstone hearth was surrounded by plush chairs and inviting sofas. An upright piano stood by a corner window overlooking the horse pastures and snow-capped peaks. And the high-beamed cathedral ceiling made the twelve-foot spruce that he and Mac had felled up on the northwest slope fit right in. The Hendersons always really did up Christmas. Coils of holly were draped from mantel and piano. Wreaths, garlands, winter-themed quilts on the walls...

"Quite the spectacle, isn't it?" And this nameless woman in a sweater named White Christmas fit right in.

"It's fabulous! My family does a totally lame Christmas, as in almost not at all. Once I got to college, I discovered it and turned into the Christmas loon of any group. You should have seen this poor pistachio tree I decorated one year in Puri."

"Puri?"

"India. On the east coast. I spent a couple months traveling there by train after I left the Himalayas."

Himalayas? Right, well, that explained where she'd picked up the Nepalese. What hadn't she done?

"I try to do up my place, too," he answered. "Same style of construction, but cozier. Bet you'd like it too."

"You do, huh?" Something was amusing her but he couldn't quite think what.

"Sure. I live on the far side of the meadow. I'm the ranch foreman."

"Your...place."

"They gave me a sweet little setup. Two bedrooms. Looks a lot like this, just on a smaller scale. A ranch house in miniature."

"You bet I'd like it?" Her tone had gone impossibly dry.

And her meaning finally sunk through his thick skull. "I didn't mean—" He'd just invited a woman whose name he still didn't know back to his place for a quick— Someone should just take him out to pasture and shoot him.

A wicked smile crossed her features. "Sure know how to make a girl feel welcome, *bhaai.*"

Little brother. Suddenly that really wasn't the role he wanted to be cast in. Not even a little. Because he could certainly picture her clearly in that cozy little log house of his.

CHAPTER 5

Chelsea *was curled up* in one of the big chairs by the fire with Tessa on her lap. The girl was fading, but not out yet and Chelsea felt completely content working through the thousandth iteration of *Carl's Snowy Afternoon* picture book.

Mark's parents were relaxing comfortably in side-by-side armchairs. It was easy to see where Mark had gotten his good looks. His father had passed on his physique and kindly eyes. His mother Ama was half Cheyenne and had passed on dark skin and hair to her son. The three of them together were stunning.

Mark sat on an oak-trimmed leather couch and Emily was curled up against him with a woven throw of geometric tans and dark reds across her legs. She looked as sleepy as their daughter while the others talked about the ranch, and fires that MHA had flown to this season. Tessa had her father's gray eyes and her mother's fine features and blond beauty. When Tessa was grown, the three of them would make an equally stunning trio.

It was so unusual to see Emily relaxed, that it made Chelsea content to remain as long as she could in the room. Emily, the successful senior helicopter pilot of Mount Hood Aviation, the woman always in absolute control of any situation, lying against her husband like...well, like a woman in love. It was surprising and wonderful. Yet another thing that Chelsea put into her Someday List. Lie before a warm fire with her arms wrapped around a man she loved.

No. Scratch that. With *the* man she loved. She still had plenty of time to find him; she hoped. Mr. Wonderfuls weren't exactly hanging about for the picking, but it was a nice image.

It wasn't hard to picture what the man would look like in her fire-warmed daydream. He'd have casually long rough-cut hair, worn-leather brown just like—

There was a soft jolt in her lap. She looked down to see that Tessa had landed face first and fast asleep with her nose on Carl's finished snowman.

Chelsea slipped from the room with her and decided that it was time to put both Tessa and herself to bed before she became any more ridiculous.

Still, it was a nice image as she curled up in a guest room with Tessa on a low trundle bed beside her.

Doug Daniels was a *very* nice image.

CHAPTER 6

"C an't sleep all day, c'mon."

Doug went for brash to cover his initial reaction to seeing a sleep-tousled Chelsea hunched at the breakfast table. He'd come in to refill his coffee and check up on her as Emily had asked. It looked as if he'd surprised the sleeping lion in her den.

Wrong image. Chelsea didn't strike him as dangerous, just enthusiastic. Like an Irish Setter. The dark red hair color wasn't a bad match. Except at the moment she looked like she'd been run over by warm bed and a soft pillow, and would still be a while recovering. Or like he'd want to sweep her right back into—

Cut it out, Daniels. But he'd lost a lot of sleep over her last night and her current state wasn't helping matters.

Chelsea was clutching a mug of hot chocolate like a lifeline. She wore a gold-colored turtleneck that proved the sweater hadn't lied last night. It revealed strength aplenty to carry a hiking pack and curves to...

He sighed at his libido's nudge-nudge, wink-wink.

"Where's Tessa?" she looked up at him through a screen of unkempt hair that she didn't bother to brush aside. The ten-foot distance from the coffee pot to where he could brush it aside himself was a good thing.

"They all went into town; took her with."

"I should wait for them."

"They won't be back until dinnertime."

She squinted up at him again. "Where the heck is town from here?"

"Choteau is only thirty miles out, but there's not much there unless you fancy a good steak. They're headed into Great Falls which is eighty each way."

"You sure?"

"There's a note from Emily by your elbow."

She twisted her head to read it without relaxing the death grip on her mug. The long line of her neck was…something he shouldn't be thinking about. Mark and Emily might not be his bosses, but this was their guest. And thinking hot thoughts about Tessa's nanny was wrong in so many ways, not the least of it being that they'd be gone soon. Christmas was just the day after tomorrow; they'd be gone the next day.

"You eaten yet?"

She nodded.

It took him a moment to spot the pan and dish, already washed and perched in the drying rack. Neat and respectful too.

"Good. Dress warmly. I'll meet you at the hangar in five minutes. I need to go up."

"Or I could just kill you and go back to my cozy bed."

"You'd do that to *younger brother?*" he asked in horror.

"Absolutely," but he could hear the grin in her voice even if he couldn't see it clearly through her shield of hair.

"You'll miss a beautiful helicopter ride."

"*You* know how to fly one?" She was quick enough to take in that he must be the pilot and turn it around into a tease.

He didn't even condescend to answer as he headed for the back door. "Four and a half minutes."

CHAPTER 7

Chelsea *made it in* four and had spent three of that whipping up some instant hot chocolate in a pair of steel travel mugs.

"For me? Thanks."

When he reached for one, she pulled it away. "Mine. Two-fisted drinker."

It earned her that good laugh of his and she handed one over.

Doug had a pretty little Bell JetRanger pulled out of the hangar and was going over it carefully. Chelsea was taken aback for a moment. Two months ago she knew helicopters were the ones with their propellers on top instead of pointing to the front; now she recognized a JetRanger on sight. Furthermore, she thought of it as small compared to the massive Firehawk helicopter that Emily flew for MHA. When had that happened to her?

The pilot-plus-four-passenger craft was clean, but well worn. It looked well-maintained but hard used.

"I've never flown in a helicopter."

Doug looked at her aghast. "You work for two of the best helicopter pilots the Army has ever produced and you haven't been up in one?"

"I—" Chelsea hadn't known that about them. But rather than look foolish for the lack of knowledge, she just shrugged. "My job is to take care of Tessa. Mark is the Incident Commander Air"—she hadn't even known he could *fly* a helicopter—"so I fly with him and Tessa in the ICA plane."

"A helicopter virgin. Well, you're in for a thrill, honey."

"Watch it, *bhaai!*"

Again the merry laugh as he escorted her into the left-hand seat and made sure she was buckled in.

The ride was a real joy. The cabin heater kept the chill air at bay as they roared aloft. Headsets with boom mics made it easy to hear him as he pointed out the features of the ranch.

He let her look her fill, but she didn't know if she'd ever get enough. The green prairie stretched smoothly to the hills. The mountains broke from the grassland as if someone had drawn a line on the ground and said, "start them here." It was an abrupt and visceral shock. Only as they flew closer did the illusion start to break; secluded valleys intruded deep into the hills with small rivers sliding between sheer headlands.

"I love this land," Doug whispered softly after she'd finally managed to voice her awe at the rugged beauty. "It can be a hard land, but I never tire of looking at it."

"I wouldn't either," she said with a sincerity as if she was making a promise.

"Now who's being forward?"

She hadn't meant to be. Then she realized that she hadn't been. It was just Doug Daniel's mind twisting in…she sighed…much the way hers had been.

But the ranch was one of those places that simply felt right. Chelsea would start helicopter lessons tomorrow if it meant she could fly here. Doug flew with such an easy confidence.

"You've been flying for a long time," she finally turned her attention to the fine scenery inside the cabin.

"Navy. Did three tours, six years. That was enough for me and then some. A SEAL buddy hooked me up with Mac."

"A SEAL buddy? Like the diver guys?"

"Sure, Mac was one too," Doug shrugged easily. No wonder he flew with such ease and confidence. Except he didn't look confident; he looked worried.

"What's wrong?" She checked the narrow dashboard that rose on a pedestal between their feet. She recognized about half of the instruments that were like the ones in Mark's plane, but nothing looked wrong on them and nothing was flashing red.

"Lucy didn't come back to the barn last night. And she had a late season foal, so I'm a little worried about them."

Chelsea looked out the windshield but couldn't imagine how to spot a horse in such a vast area. Now at least she understood that Doug hadn't been sweeping back and forth over the ranch and the prairie simply to show it to her; he'd been quartering and searching the ground. She'd done search and rescue for lost hikers, but that was tromping through woods and over rough terrain.

"How do you find a horse in thousands of acres?"

"Well," he pointed down at a lush, pocket-sized meadow around a tiny lake. "I was hoping she'd be here. It's a favorite of the horses. Hold the collective a minute."

"The what?"

"The control on the left side of your seat. Just hold it steady, don't worry, you can't crash us."

She tentatively wrapped her hand around the control, until she had a firm grasp. "Okay," she barely dared whisper it.

Doug took his left hand off his matching control and reached back to scrabble around behind the seat.

Daring greatly, she pulled up on it ever so slightly, and could feel the helicopter rise. She eased back down until the altimeter said she was back at the starting level.

"Here," he dropped something heavy in her lap. "Put that on, would you?"

She opened the case and looked down at the contraption, for that was the only word for it. There were straps to hold it to your head. It looked like a pair of goggles from one side, and like a half-unicorn, half-bug-eyed monster monocular protruding from the other.

"What is it?"

"Night vision. Lucy and the foal will be significantly warmer than the background. She'll show up clearly. Mark gets us the best toys."

Chelsea straightened it out and leaned over to put it on Doug's head.

"No," he stopped her. "You wear it."

CHAPTER 8

Doug was amused by her exclamation when she got it turned on. Chelsea took such pleasure from everything about her. The countryside, the helicopter—rather than showing fear she'd proved she had a good and light touch—and now the night vision was tickling her fancy. Last night he'd left early. Partly because it was a time for the family to be together, but also because the vision of Chelsea with Tessa in her lap had been so powerful. She'd made it too easy to imagine a red-headed girl sitting right there, curled up by his fireplace.

For the next two hours, he flew and she scanned. He filled the time with learning about her background. Deeply independent—with parents who had little interest in an intelligent child filled with dreams—she'd forged out on her own. Six years to get her degree because she'd spent two years traveling and hiking; first walking the Continental Divide Trail from New Mexico to Glacier Park, and then all over the Himalayas.

It both amazed and saddened him. She was incredible, had a much clearer view of the world and herself than most people. But he'd found where he wanted to be and she had adventure deep in her blood. She'd never be satisfied with…stupid fantasies of a demented ranch manager.

"There," her shriek almost blew his eardrums. Close beside the farthest fishing cabin, Lucy and her foal were huddled up against the side of the building. Lucy was lying down. Not a good sign.

He landed as close as he dared and rushed out to the mare. He'd brought a handgun, but not wanting to jar Chelsea's sensibilities, he'd left it stowed on the helo.

"We won't have to shoot her, will we?" Chelsea was right beside him.

Okay, so much for that worry. "Let's hope not."

Lucy was down, but had raised her head to watch his approach. Her whinny of greeting was encouraging.

He talked to her as he checked her out. No complaints as he tested for broken limbs. Same for the abdomen. Then she coughed in his face, a dry, hacking cough. He felt under her jaw and found swollen lymph nodes.

"Oh, crap!"

"What?"

"We vaccinated her against this."

"What?" Chelsea sounded deeply worried.

He sighed, "She has the flu. I can't do much for her here. She needs a warm barn and some rest. I'll have to ride back out, bring some high energy food and probably start her on a round antibiotics against secondary infection. With a little luck, she'll come back if I guide her. It will be a long slow ride."

CHAPTER 9

They flew back, and when Doug saddled up a horse, she'd insisted he saddle two. She'd never ridden a horse, only a very recalcitrant mule when she'd sprained an ankle coming off climbing Imja Tse. She could have hobbled out faster than that Nepalese mule had carried her.

At Doug's guidance, she'd packed a pair of saddlebags with a change of clothes and several days of food. He packed clothes, camping gear in case they were caught out, horse meds, and a twenty pound sack of oats.

He led off at a light trot and she let him. Her horse, a big dapple gray male called Snowflake, looked at her strangely several times as she struggled to imitate Doug's easy saddle position. Every now and then he'd glance back to make sure she was still with him, and she always managed a plucky wave or nod as the saddle's hard leather slowly beat her to death.

They were about an hour out when he happened to look back during one of her barely-still-on-the-horse moments. Doug twisted his mount in a tight circle like it was the easiest thing in the world. He twisted again until they were side by side. He leaned over to grab Snowflake's reins and everything came to a blessed halt.

"Haven't you ridden before?"

She could only shake her head, because if she opened her mouth she might start crying from all the places she'd rubbed raw.

"You're either incredibly brave or ridiculously stupid!"

"Mostly," she managed through gritted teeth. "Except you got the adjectives backwards." Being at a blessed standstill gave her some tiny sliver of ease. "According to my parents, I'm ridiculously brave and incredibly stupid."

Doug regarded her for a long moment, then glanced in both the direction they'd come and the one they were headed, considering the options. If he tried to send her back, she'd…she didn't know what. But she hadn't gone through this much pain for nothing.

"Okay," he shook his head. "I've seen that look on plenty a stubborn horse and don't want an argument. Stand up in your stirrups, if you still can."

She managed it without crying out.

He unrolled an extra blanket he'd had tied to the back of his saddle. He folded it in quarters, tossed it over her saddle, and then pressed her lightly on the shoulder until she eased back down carefully. It wasn't too painful, and far better than it had been.

"I lead probably a hundred trail rides a summer, Chelsea. You know how many beginner riders could have pulled off what you just did?"

She shook her head.

He held up his fingers and thumb, tips together to show a zero.

"I deserve a prize then."

Chelsea only had a moment to see his grin before he leaned in and kissed her. This wasn't some quick peck through the shield of her parka.

Doug leaned into the kiss and, fool that she was, she welcomed it without even a little protest. He provided plenty skill and heat, but that wasn't what she was really noticing. What riveted her attention was how absolutely her body was galvanized by the simple act. Actually, ungalvanized. She melted against him despite the two horses that separated them. Leaning as far as she dared, she hung tightly onto the saddle's pommel with one hand and his jacket with the other and pulled them together. The kiss ran right down to her toes and made them curl in her riding boots.

When he finally eased back, Doug Daniels looked awfully pleased with himself. Of course she was feeling much the same way.

"I'm not sure," Chelsea was amazed she could even speak, "which of us you were just rewarding."

"At least you won't be *bhaai-ing* me anymore," his laugh was even more self-satisfied than his expression. "Now, let's teach you how to ride. First, take your reins like this."

She did her best to follow his instructions and pay attention, but he'd made a warm buzz between her ears despite the cool day only now breaking above freezing.

Doug Daniels was many things: handsome, male, and a heavenly kisser being only three of them. But *younger brother* he definitely wasn't.

CHAPTER 10

It *was four hours* to the last turn up to the fishing cabin, less than
an hour later than he'd planned. Chelsea was the most apt riding
student he'd ever taught, and while Henderson's Ranch might be a
working one, they made the majority of their income from all of the
city folk guests who wanted a week or two of "country." Chelsea took
to it as if she'd been born in the saddle…though she'd probably be too
stiff to walk right for days. It had been cruel to keep going, but he
couldn't afford the time to escort her back even if she'd have let him.
He'd bet the chances of that were close to zero, yet another thing to
appreciate about the beautiful woman. Tenacious as hell.

As it was, they'd be staying in the fishing cabin tonight. The sunset
was only a few hours off and Lucy wouldn't be able to move quickly.
It would be a far slower ride back tomorrow. On top of that, keeping
Chelsea in the saddle through the night's journey back would be a
cruelty, even if Lucy was up to it.

The final lap to the cabin at their quick walk should take about
half an hour. Then Doug glanced back over his shoulder—more bad
news. A squall was inbound. Blocked by the height of Wind Mountain, and the twisting trail up to the cabin, he hadn't seen it coming.

He stopped them long enough to haul on ponchos, but he knew it wouldn't be enough. They were about to get drenched.

They'd galloped briefly on the flat trail, but they were now climbing up a harder route. The way wasn't dangerously narrow, but it would be far more challenging. Another eye at the rain front, now a gray curtain sliding down the mountain face, had him changing plans.

"Ease up out of the saddle a little bit," he told Chelsea. "Lean forward. Loosen the rein. Good!"

And he smacked Snowflake hard on the butt.

He nudged his own mount forward and in moments they were galloping together up the valley. The way narrowed and steepened until they could no longer ride side by side. Doug didn't dare lead from where he couldn't see her.

"Ride on!" he shouted as the first crash of lightning struck the mountain top and thunder rumbled down upon them, amplified by the echoes off the high rock cliffs.

Bless Chelsea, she leaned into it and flew up the trail. He watched closely, but she stayed solid, didn't even a grab the pommel. Her legs must be screaming fire, but she rode, if not like an experienced horse-woman, then plenty close.

The icy rain broke over them, but the trail was solid and drained well, so he left them at the run.

In five minutes they were drenched, but the cabin was in sight. He shouted ahead and they eased down through canter to trot and arrived at the cabin at a walk.

"Down you go," he slid off and helped her down from her horse. "Take their reins and walk them back and forth. It will do all three of you good. Slow is fine, just keep moving." He stripped the saddle bags and tossed them into the cabin. He heaved the saddles inside moments later, then waved her, holding their mounts' reins, down the valley.

Even aching and saddle sore the woman had a walk that stirred his blood. *Ridiculous!* That's what he was being.

He grabbed his medicine bag and the oats and circled around to Lucy who was thankfully back on her feet, but hanging her head miserably in the rain. Her foal was cowering against her. She'd been ten feet from the overhang and the big box stall, but had been too dazed—yet another symptom—to walk under cover.

He guided them in and checked her. He couldn't do anything for the flu, which was viral, but he gave her antibiotics against secondary infection and a booster shot of vitamins. She perked up a bit for her oats and water. He got blankets over her and the foal about the time Chelsea staggered back up to the stall with their mounts plodding along behind her.

"Is this enough?"

He ran a hand over them. No longer breathing hard, not hot. "You did good Chelsea. Go inside. I'll be in as soon as I get these two settled with the mare."

When he entered the cabin a few minutes later, Chelsea was on the floor in a fetal position.

Shit! He was an idiot.

CHAPTER 11

Chelsea *had been this* cold before, she was sure of it. Like when she'd camped above snowline at the base of Chulu West and the zipper on her sleeping bag had broken. But in her memory it didn't feel colder. And when her knees had knocked together high in the Himalayas, she'd laughed at the novelty. Now she fought not to cry as the insides of her legs, rubbed raw by the saddle, sent shivers of pain right along with the cold shakes.

She opened her eyes when Doug entered the cabin and immediately began cursing. He looked furious! His dark hair matted flat and black with the rain, water cascading off his poncho. He hauled it off with a yank and dropped it on the rough wood with a wet splat.

Chelsea wondered if he was about to tear her to shreds because she'd collapsed, then realized she wasn't the one he was swearing at. He dropped to his knees beside her and began calling her name loudly.

"I'm c-c-c-cold, not d-d-deaf," she managed through rattling teeth.

"I'll start a fire," he jumped up toward the iron woodstove in the corner.

She tried avoiding the hard "c" of close, but found the "sh" sound little easier. "Sh-sh-shut the door first, you big lummox. R-raised in a b-b-barn."

Doug closed the door and then redeemed himself with his efficiency in building the fire.

"Heat? How long?" she managed.

He looked uncertainly from her to the stove. Not soon enough.

She tried to remove her poncho, but her hands weren't under her control anymore. This was bad.

"C-c-clothes. Off. B-b-bed," she instructed.

He stripped off the outer layers and hesitated until she stuttered out a series of curses at him. She cried out when he peeled her jeans.

Then he began cursing all over again.

She looked down. Her legs' normally pale skin had gone white with the cold, except for the insides from boot top to panties were livid red with abrasions. No wonder they hurt.

The goofball stopped at her soaking wet turtleneck as if embarrassed.

"C-c-come on. You know you want to s-s-see me naked."

He grunted and had the decency to try and look away as he finished the job and then scooped her up like a feather hard against his soaking wet jacket.

"Eww!" Yet even the tiny bit of heat that escaped through the denim felt so good.

The cabin was simple. Three bunk beds, several couches and plush chairs that had seen better days probably back at the main house, and a small corner kitchen with an impressive collection of cast iron pans appropriate for frying fish. Doug dropped her in one of the lower bunks and began piling blankets over her. She couldn't even clutch the blankets to pull them tighter.

"S-s-strip!" Chelsea ordered.

"But…"

"C-c-come on. You know I want to s-s-see you naked," she did her best to stammer it out the same way she had the first time. "I need heat."

He began peeling down and Chelsea watched as much as the shivers would allow.

"Wow! C-c-cowboys *are* built pretty."

He smiled at her for the first time since finding her on the floor. "This is a horse ranch. Not a cattle ranch."

"So get your fine butt in here, horseboy. Before I f-f-freeze to death."

He hesitated at shedding his underwear, someone please explain men to her, then turned away as he finally stripped off that last piece. His butt really was fine; topped by a narrow waist and broad shoulders with muscle that rippled across them with each movement.

Doug slid in beside her and, after a moment's hesitation, pulled her against him. His skin was so warm compared to hers that it burned, but she leaned into it as hard as she could.

"Christ! You're freezing!" He began chaffing those big hands of his up and down her back.

"D-d-duh!" Chelsea managed to get the covers completely over her head and concentrated on soaking up Doug Daniels' warmth.

Doug held her until the shivers stopped. With his arms still around her, he could feel her breathing slow. Once she was deeply asleep in exhaustion, he slipped out of bed and dug out fresh clothes from the saddlebags, hanging the others to dry. He stoked the fire, made hot chocolate and wished for coffee, but the latter would make him even more awake than he already was.

A quick radio call back to Logan told him that the Hendersons weren't back from Great Falls yet. Logan wasn't a pilot so he couldn't bring the helo to fetch Chelsea. With the shakes gone, she probably just needed sleep…and time to heal. Gods but she was tough.

The windows were dark with the fading light of sunset happening somewhere beyond the heavy overcast. Lightning still shimmered through the heavy rain, though far enough off that the thunder was a rumble rather than a crack. The weather was still too nasty for a flight even if Mark was back. He had Logan leave a message on the kitchen table so that they wouldn't worry when they returned and found no Chelsea.

"Doug," Chelsea's voice was a whisper barely louder than the crackling flame from the glass-fronted woodstove. "Come back to bed." The firelight caught the blue of her eyes and the tip of her nose from where they peeked out of the blankets.

"You trying to kill me, girl?" Yes, he'd wanted to see Chelsea naked, from the first moment he'd spotted her climbing down out of that plane in those deliciously tight jeans. Even shuddering with the leading edge of hypothermia, she was beyond spectacular.

"Not girl. It's woman. And I think you trying to kill me once already today should be enough for both of us."

"I didn't—" But he had. He'd taken her skills for granted when she climbed up on the horse. And led her on a grueling ride through a storm. Sending her out on a cool-down walk in the freezing rain was about as dumb as it got.

Unlike so many of the guests who came to the ranch, Chelsea radiated skill. She'd triggered none of his high-season alarms that told him who to watch out for. Though she was certainly triggering other reactions.

"I don't think that's a good idea."

She rolled her eyes at him. "Get your warm butt back in here before I have to climb out and kick it. I ache right down to my joints."

Which told him just how dangerously cold she'd gotten.

Once again he stripped down, far more conscious of the woman who now wouldn't turn away than the earlier one whose eyes had been partly rolled back into her head.

She went to throw a leg over his, but jerked back and hissed at the pain.

"God I'm so sorry. Let me get some horse liniment," he climbed out of the bunk.

"Hello! Not a horse."

He grabbed a bottle from the kitchen shelf and returned to stand over the bed. How was he supposed to...

"Here," he held out the bottle. "Trust me. It works great."

CHAPTER 13

Chelsea felt as if she was being a total wanton. She was in a cozy little cabin with no distractions of electricity. A very handsome man, momentarily unaware of his own nakedness, stood close beside her lit by the soft firelight that filtered through the woodstove's glass-paned door. And he was holding out the horse liniment the way you hold out a mouse for a dangerous viper to snack on.

The normal version of herself would have taken the liniment and tried to slather it on under the covers.

Instead, she watched Doug's face as she slipped a leg out from under the covers and twisted to turn it, inside-thigh up. His eyes didn't narrow suspiciously, instead they widened in alarm. She'd watched him handling the horses with a gentle but firm hand. A half ton of horse flesh didn't bother him at all, but the inside of a woman's leg had him totally flustered. Damn but he was cute.

"Come along, horseboy," she coaxed him in the same tone he'd cajoled the colt to follow its mother into the stall.

His gaze snapped from her leg to her face, and then his nice deep laugh rolled out. "Okay, you got me. I'm dying to slather some liniment on those fine legs of yours." And he knelt on the wood floor beside her and smoothed some on.

It was cold and sent a shiver up her leg. But the warm steadiness of his hand stroking in the thick liquid calmed the convulsive response before it could turn back into the shakes. She could feel his hard calluses and easy strength, but was surprised at the gentleness of his rough hands. Within moments a numbing warmth spread up her leg in a wave of relief.

"I'll smell like a horse," she complained to cover a moan of delight. The camphor was sharp in the cabin's warm air, but her attention was nowhere near her nose.

"A sweet smell to a rancher."

"How about to a horseboy?"

"Lady," he didn't even bat an eye. "You smell incredible to this horseboy, with or without the liniment."

There was no sign of any embarrassment by the time he'd ministered to both her legs and tucked them once more under the covers. He'd somehow transferred all of it to her. As he slid back under the layers of blankets, Chelsea was intensely aware of the narrow bunk and the warmth of his body pressed against hers. She was more of a long t-shirt gal, but it would be stupid to ask for one with a man she'd lain naked against for most of the last few hours.

Unable to find words, she simply nestled inside the curve of his arm. Then, against the fiery tension building so high that it roared in her ears, Doug began talking. He told her about the birth of the foal, who slept even now in the nearby stall with Lucy. He talked about the ranch and the spring wildflowers that colored the prairie like a paintbrush.

She fell asleep with the sound of his love for his life rumbling from his chest directly into her ear. It was the sweetest, safest sound she'd ever heard.

He'd offered to call the helo a half dozen times this morning, but Chelsea had turned him down cold, despite hobbling about like a geriatric case. Another round of liniment helped some, but he knew she'd be stiff for days.

Doug finally gave in. Partly because he knew Lucy wouldn't be up for more than a casual amble and partly because he wanted every single minute with Chelsea that he could get. He'd held her throughout the night, marveling at the rightness of it.

It had been like that when he'd arrived at the ranch fresh out of the service. After three full tours, most of them spent on ships in the Persian Gulf, he'd been sick to his heart of the unending heat, the limitless steel, and the noise—for a Navy ship was never silent. He'd been on the ranch for three years now and could still feel the Persian dust in his pores. But the ranch had fit him since the first moment he'd stepped on the soil.

He'd ridden plenty as a kid at his parents' place in Wyoming. When he didn't re-up, SEAL Commander Luke Altman had sent him up to see his own former commander outside Choteau, Montana. Mac had shown him around Henderson's Ranch and Doug had decided on the spot that he never wanted to leave. Mac and Ama had been looking for a foreman. Together, they'd transformed the aging ranch into a showplace tourist destination.

He'd worried a lot about "the son" coming home, until he'd met Mark and Emily. Mark had taken one look at the transformation and thumped him hard on the shoulder before walking away without a word.

It was Emily who'd translated for him. "He was so worried for his parents. You've really touched him." Then she'd kissed him on either cheek. "You done good, Doug. Keep it up." Then she'd gone after her husband. That's when he'd set his sights on the kind of woman he wanted. One just like Emily Beale.

And he couldn't have found one more different than Chelsea Bridges if he'd tried. Oh, a lot of the things that were right with Emily were just as right on Chelsea, especially her absolute fearlessness—the image of her galloping through a thunderstorm on her first ride still fired the imagination.

But where Emily was quiet, thoughtful, and soft spoken, Chelsea spoke her mind and laughed with a bright joy—even when on the verge of succumbing to hypothermia.

He imagined it would take years to fall for the right woman once he met her, because his ideal woman didn't fall that quickly. At least so he'd thought until he'd rubbed noses with Chelsea inside a parka hood and received a kiss for it. Now he was crazy about a sassy redhead who'd slept in his arms like she'd always been there.

Slept. And that was all she'd done. Hard to blame her, as her body had been through a lot of extremes yesterday. But the only extremes he'd been through had been treating Chelsea as if she was his injured sister. Everything had been perfectly chaste last night, if you didn't include his thoughts.

"Storm has passed," he did his best to distract himself. "Temperature is falling and there's another front moving in. Let's get ahead of it."

"Sure," she gamely picked up her saddle, that probably weighed half as much as she did, and headed for the door.

So much for a morning tumble, or even a kiss.

He'd escaped her bed early—because it was either that or he was going to do something wholly inappropriate—and bundled up to go tend the horses. Lucy had perked up overnight enough to greet him. She was still snotty with the flu, but it was clear so no secondary infection yet. Her breathing also sounded clear enough for the walk back to the ranch. The foal was more cheerful than the night before, which he'd take as a good sign regarding his mother's condition. By the time he was back inside, Chelsea was dressed in warm clothes and had made the bed. Oatmeal and coffee were simmering on the woodstove.

She'd looked as natural here as no paying guest ever really did.

They'd had breakfast together; Chelsea going on about the upcoming ride...and he hadn't jumped her. What was up with that? There was decent and there was ridiculous, and he'd definitely crossed that line somewhere in the night.

Then she'd washed the dishes, grabbed her saddle, and gone.

He'd already taken his own saddle out. So, he gathered up their saddle bags, double-checked that the woodstove was secure—the few remaining embers would burn themselves out—and gave the cabin one last look. All shipshape...damn it. Not a single tousled bed sheet. He hadn't brought any protection with him, but that didn't mean there weren't other options. But had they used them? Nope! Not a single, damned, inappropriately pleasant fondle had passed between them.

Closing the door, he stomped around to the horse stall and ran head on into a kiss.

This wasn't some little kiss through a parka or a taste of wonder when they were both up on horses. Chelsea wrapped herself around him and had him backed against the rail fence. With her arms tight around his neck, she was rapidly killing off fantasy after fantasy. Who knew it was possible to pack so much joy into such a simple act? Apparently Chelsea did.

When Snowflake came over to snort in his hair across the fence, Chelsea flapped a hand at the horse's nose.

"Busy here," she mumbled at the big gray.

Damn straight! was all Doug could think. All that soft and gentle warmth of last night had been replaced by the lively redhead who'd teased with him since the moment of her arrival. She didn't play coy or tease now; she delivered a kiss with her entire body. It left him shuddering with need when she abruptly released him and, as if his world hadn't just been spun around and dropped on its head, strode into the stall with one of the saddlebags that he'd dropped when she'd jumped him.

Unable to trust his voice, he focused on saddling them up. No need to rope Lucy or the foal. Lucy, he knew would follow them, and the foal would follow his mom.

Placing his hands around Chelsea's waist to help her up into the saddle was almost his undoing. With her arms raised to the reins and pommel, her jacket slid up and her waist was slender and warm in the circle of his hands.

Her smile was mischievous as he climbed up on his own mount.

"What?"

"I just wanted you to know, that kiss wasn't a thanks for how wonderfully you took care of me last night."

"Then what was it?"

She turned Snowflake and with a skilled nudge, sent her down the trail at an easy walk. "That," she called back over her shoulder, the only sound in the still morning other than the clopping of the horses' hooves. "That was just a preview. Like coming attractions at the movies."

Any ability to speak that Doug thought he'd regained was washed away. If that was a preview, he couldn't wait for the main feature. But the ranch was a long way off.

He looked back at Lucy and her foal who'd fallen in behind. "How fast can you walk?"

The horse declined to answer, instead settling into a slow shuffle.

CHAPTER 15

"*So, the lost is* found," Mark greeted her cheerfully as Chelsea entered the ranch house kitchen.

"Seems so." It had taken seven hours to walk Lucy back. A long cold ride, but under a broken sky rather than a freezing rain. It was now mid-afternoon and the sky was once again darkening beneath an overcast. At least she'd be cozy and safe for the next storm.

"Tessa's down for her nap, so you can just relax. Where's Doug?"

"He's out at the isolation barn. He wants to keep the three horses and foal away from the herd until he's sure that they're not contagious."

"Good man."

"The best." Chelsea knew she'd never met a better one.

Mark looked at her curiously, and then headed for the door. "I'll just go and check on him."

"Do you know *anything* about horses?" She didn't know where the tease had come from. Women didn't tease men like Mark Henderson. But Doug had told her how Mark loved to fish, and almost always used an ATV rather than a horse to get there, so she couldn't resist.

He just winked at her and was gone.

Chelsea took a quiet minute to heat some leftover beef vegetable soup before sitting with it at the big kitchen table. It could seat a dozen without crowding. The kitchen was on the border between a generous farm kitchen and a small commercial one. It was cozy but also designed to feed a hungry hoard. She could imagine dinner parties here filled with laughter and good food.

"What would it be like to live here?" she asked the quiet kitchen. "How happy would it be?"

"Quite happy."

Chelsea startled and almost lost her soupspoon to the floor. For a startled second she thought the kitchen had answered her.

Then she spotted Emily Beale sitting quietly in a deep chair by the kitchen fireplace, a book in her lap. She rose smoothly and came to sit just around the corner of the table from Chelsea.

"The first time I came here, I was in absolute terror."

"You, in terror. Like I'm going to believe that."

Emily's smile was always a surprise and it was this time as well. "Seriously. I was engaged to my co-commander of an elite U.S. Army helicopter team—seriously bad from a regulation point of view—and about to meet his parents, one of whom had served twenty years as a Navy SEAL. I'd never gone fishing, never seen a horse up close, and never been to Montana."

Chelsea toyed with her soup. "This place is so amazing though; that must have helped."

"It did. Though not as much as realizing that Mark knew as little about horses as I did." Now Emily's smile turned rather wicked. "Mac and Ama bought the ranch after Mark had gone to West Point."

"So?" Chelsea tried to picture Mark not perfect at something and wasn't coming up with a good image.

"Let's just say that he ended up head over heels in the river and I didn't."

Chelsea held up a hand in salute, but was shocked when Emily actually high-fived it. "Women rule," Chelsea added weakly.

"We do," Emily agreed and offered her a smile of companionship that felt as crazy as everything else that had happened in the last two days.

"I've been very happy here," Emily continued though more as if she was speaking to herself. "It's a good place, as good as any I've ever been."

"I'll miss the ranch when we go."

Emily nodded, but was studying Chelsea carefully.

"What?"

Emily shook her head.

"Nope." Chelsea grabbed onto her bravery. "You don't get to do that."

"Do what?" Emily pretended all innocence.

Chelsea aimed her soupspoon at Emily, "Have that clear a thought and then not share it."

Emily considered for a long moment and then nodded at how that might be a reasonable demand. "Just remember."

"What?"

"You asked."

Chelsea swallowed hard. Why didn't she think she was going to like what came next? She nodded for Emily to go ahead anyway.

"It isn't the ranch that you'll be missing."

Her soupspoon slipped from nerveless fingers and landed in her bowl with a splash.

"Thought so," Emily remarked drily.

"Couldn't you at least have made it a question?"

Emily shook her head. "Why would I, when it isn't one."

"But we haven't even—"

"Doesn't matter. When it's the right one, the particulars don't matter. Trust me, I know."

"The right what? But—" Chelsea managed weakly wondering why she was trying to argue. She'd never met a man like Doug Daniels, a man who simply shone with the love inside him. He had such a passion for the land and the horses.

During the long, cold ride back from the fishing cabin, she and Doug had warmed the time with stories. He'd told her about his experiences overseas, so different from her own tramp abroad. In all of her travels, she'd never found anyone so easy to be with.

And the way he'd knelt before her in the cabin, naked and beautiful and so worried about offending as he treated her abraded legs with stinky liniment.

The way he'd held her last night. There couldn't be another man anywhere who wouldn't have taken advantage of the situation. But not Doug with his soldier's honor.

"I—"

But Emily was no longer there to explain things to. In the big kitchen was only the warm crackling of the fire, Chelsea, and a bowl of soup.

Doug was slumped on his couch. The grumbling in his stomach complained about missing dinner up at the main house; too frustrated to whip up something in his own kitchen. He hadn't been able to go because of what else he'd find there. What he was wanting so badly.

The knock on his front door had him racing to answer it. "Is Lucy…o…kay?" The only knock he'd been expecting had been Logan's if Lucy had a relapse. His nervous system was not ready for the vivid redhead standing on his front porch.

"Hi!" Her smile was big and again mischievous.

He had the feeling that he was suddenly in deep trouble.

"Do I get invited in? If not, I'm taking Emily's special homemade pizza back with me. She said that it's one of your favorites."

That's when he focused on the large covered tray Chelsea was carrying. Emily was an amazing cook, had won the hearts of Mac, himself, and every one of the ranch hands with a beef stew on her first visit to the ranch. But it was her from-scratch pizza that blew Doug away.

"Uh—" He looked back up at Chelsea. "I'd like to invite you in, but I don't think that's the best idea. Because if I do—" If he did, he couldn't be accountable for keeping his hands off her a second time. Last night he'd liked the brave and competent woman, and lusted after the redheaded knockout. On the long ride back, he'd also come to admire her deeply. She'd made some hard choices on her path, who hadn't. But hers had always come straight from the heart.

"—If you do invite me in," Chelsea picked up for him as she eased him slowly backward with the leading edge of a tray of pizza, "we just might enjoy ourselves beyond all imagining."

"Something like that," he managed.

"Good. I'm counting on it." She kicked off her boots, and carried the tray through his living room and into the kitchen as if she'd always lived here. "You were raised in a barn. Close the door; it's cold out there."

Helpless to argue, he did as she suggested and followed her into the kitchen.

"I'm sorry," she set the tray on top of the cold stove.

"Sorry for what?"

"The pizza and the tiny ranch house tour are going to have to come later. I can't wait any longer." She shed her gloves and jacket and dropped them to the floor. Then she walked straight into his arms.

They had cold pizza while sitting among their clothes on the kitchen floor. Doug reheated some after they'd made prolonged use of the living room sofa; long enough to have to restock the fire. They finished the last of the meal on their way upstairs when she went hunting for the bedroom; a search that was gloriously rewarded.

"Did we miss anywhere?" Chelsea lay sprawled over him, sore in so many wonderful ways. She'd never done anything like this. Never had so much fun having sex either. Doug's blend of powerful yet gentle, of roughly needy and deeply giving had enthralled and sated her like no one before.

"Uh, big bathroom, second bedroom, home office."

"Oh." They'd probably kill each other if they tried for all of them tonight.

"Back porch lit by June moonlight," he mumbled on. "There's a set of waterfalls with a hot spring about a three-hour hike above the fishing cabin that shouldn't scare off a woman who had hiked in the Himalayas. The open prairie on a warm May afternoon where you'd outshine the sun. I'll show you—"

She put her fingers over his mouth to stop him and he kissed the fingertips.

"I like your imagination," she propped herself up on his chest and looked down into his dark eyes. "So the sex is good."

"Incredible," he agreed.

"You love what you do?"

"I do," he agreed just as equably.

"And you've spent two days and two nights fantasizing about having me beside you forever."

"Yep."

She waited for it. Perhaps it was unfair. Giving a man his favorite food then making love to him multiple times; his defenses were pretty much gone.

But there was no shock of recognition at what she'd just said. No startled disclaimer that he wasn't dumb enough to extrapolate two days into a lifetime.

"Whoa there!" It was supposed to have been a tease.

"As the lady once said," he grinned up at her. "Hello! Not a horse."

"Hold on."

"The way I figure it," she could feel his chest rippling against hers as he spoke, "it's actually been two days and three nights. I think we're closer to sunrise than sunset. So, we've already made it twenty-five percent longer than what you said."

"Douglas," she warned him.

"Just Doug. Nobody calls me Douglas, not even Mom."

"Douglas!"

"Yes, Chelsea?"

"Does it make any sense?"

"Nope. Not a bit," and his voice remained merry.

"Aren't you even a little surprised?"

"Nope."

"Why not?" Chelsea's own thoughts were in such turmoil, they might as well be a wheeling herd of horses.

"Got over it in the barn while taking care of Lucy."

"A *horse* told you that we'd be spending our lives together? Even from horseboy, I'm not buying that one." *Spending our lives together* and still no flinch on his part. She checked in with herself. Even stranger, there wasn't a flinch on her part either.

"No, from Mark."

"Mark?" was all she managed.

"Yep! I was out making sure Lucy and the other horses were all settled in, when he came out to the barn."

"What did he say?" Chelsea was pretty sure she didn't want to know. She went to roll off Doug's chest, but he trapped her in place with a hand resting lightly on her hip. Just enough to tell her she was retreating, not enough that she couldn't get away. *Fine!* She could take it if he could, and rolled back into place.

"He said that you were one of the nicest young women he'd ever met and I'd never find any better. That part I agreed with readily enough," Doug nodded emphatically as if marking such an outrageous statement as simple truth. "And if I was too stupid to see that you were already in love with me, he'd be glad to pound some sense into me."

She let his "love" statement go by for the moment.

"Do you think they set us up?" She wasn't sure if she'd be angry or not, but wanted to know.

"My question too. Mark said no. Emily's not much sneakier than he is, so I'm guessing the answer there is also no. I suspect that we did this to ourselves."

"We...what?" But it was lame and she knew it. Emily had said the same thing, or why else was Chelsea here in bed with Doug?

This time when she pushed away, he let her go.

Chelsea wrapped a blanket around her shoulders and moved to look out the window. The yard rolled away into the darkness. Faint lights marked the barns, a lone porch light up at the main ranch house.

Could she be happy here? Working horses, sharing this gorgeous land with visitors? In a heartbeat.

With this man?

Doug slipped up behind her and wrapped his arms across her shoulders.

How was she supposed to know something like that so quickly?

Even if she already did?

Emily had said she recognized that he was the right one for her. As if she knew what love looked like. Well, if any woman did, it would be Emily Beale.

Chelsea leaned back against Doug—and the rightness was there. It ran so deep that she couldn't imagine being anywhere else.

"So I was thinking," he whispered in her ear.

She hummed with pleasure, couldn't help herself.

"How about we just try each other on for size? You and me."

"And the horses."

She could more feel his laugh than hear it.

"And the horses. We'll agree to make no decisions at all until the snow melts."

"But there isn't any snow," she waved a hand toward the window.

He didn't speak, instead he pointed. In the faint lights, she could see the first flakes spinning down out of the sky.

"A white Christmas," she managed on a tight breath.

He wrapped his arms around her a little more tightly.

Doug was right, they needed time to decide if what was between them was real or not.

But she knew. Her wandering days were done.

A white Christmas together.

Chelsea turned in Doug's arms and kissed him. She knew right down to her heart that this was only the first of so many to come.

REACHING OUT AT HENDERSON'S RANCH

A Navy SEAL without an arm is as useful as...

Stan Corman *hates waking up each morning to discover he's lost an arm, his war dog, his teammates, and his calling. The only thing worse? Going to sleep to face the nightmare of that single, life-changing moment.*

Mark Henderson sends Stan to his family horse ranch beneath Montana's Big Sky. Not even a shard of hope remains until Bertram, a Malinois puppy left on his doorstep, has different ideas about Reaching Out at Henderson's Ranch.

CHAPTER 1

He reached to console the frightened villager child.

Stan Corman knew it was dangerous, but he couldn't stop his hand. His left hand kept moving closer though some part of him screamed for it to withdraw, to fall by his side.

The boy, no more than five, could have been his nephew Jack. They had the same tousled dark hair, though Jack's skin was far lighter.

His hand continued to reach.

Deep inside himself, Stan cursed and fought, but his arm moved without his willing it.

No control.

Except his eyes. Though his hand remained out of his control, he could see with his eyes.

Stan could see the little boy's fear—his eyes so wide that the dark irises were almost lost in the vast field of white. He'd knelt so that they were eye to eye. Then Stan looked down and he could see his dog Lucy abruptly sit, close in front of the boy.

Lucy wasn't supposed to sit without a command unless—

Stan's hand brushed the boy's arm.

Lucy whined.

She was a military war dog and was trained to sit and be still when she smelled—

The boy disappeared in a cloud of light that slammed Stan into the void.

The scream tearing out of his throat ripped him from nightmare to darkness.

Absolute darkness…except for the afterimage of an exploding boy etched so deeply on his retina that it was all he'd been able to see when he woke in the hospital.

Now, months away, he tried to rub at his eyes as his pulse peaked somewhere past skyrocket and began a slow fall that Stan knew from experience would banish any hope of sleep for hours.

But there was no hand to rub his eyes with, only a fleshy stump remained of his left hand. His other hand was tangled in the sheets and for a long awful moment he was sure he had lost that one as well. Before he could scream again, he managed to pull it free and pressed his hand to his face.

Five.

He counted four fingers and a thumb pressed from jaw to forehead. Flesh and blood. He could feel them. Five. His right hand still remained intact.

As did the image of the exploding boy.

Stan's life had been saved because the boy's parents—or whatever total bastard had wired the kid up—had rigged the explosives too low. The alignment of explosive and Stan's life had been almost entirely shielded by Lucy's body.

The helmet had protected his head, the goggles his eyes, and except for nasty scarring on his left cheek, the rest of him had been behind armor and dog. Lucy had taken the hit and like a nuclear blast burn image, the shape of her had been imprinted on his lower face and chest in blood and bone fragments. The rest had healed: the dozen broken ribs where parts of Lucy had slammed into him, the concussion from the wall he'd been thrown into so hard that even his helmet hadn't saved him from that. They'd managed to save his left calf and knee with screws and titanium plates, but had warned him it would always be fragile. Just what every SEAL wanted to be labeled: fragile.

He lay in a cot. His pulse had slowed enough—though the rate of his breathing hadn't yet—for him to feel the hard chill of the cabin. The fire had gone out, which meant it was past three a.m.

It was a good sign. Usually the nightmare woke him by midnight in plenty of time to restoke the small cast iron woodstove for the long, sleepless dark watch. He considered waiting until dawn under the covers, but experience also had taught him to get up and build the fire now or the cabin would stay frosty until midday.

A North Carolina boy, his only experience with true cold before now had been on assignment. The Afghan winters had been brutal, but that's where Special Operations said to go—so he and Lucy went.

Lucy. Shit. They'd been together for two years in-country. She was six months dead and he still missed her every damn day.

He snapped on a flashlight, for all the good it did him. All he could see right now was the little Afghan boy etched in light. The doctors insisted that it was psychosomatic rather than retinal damage because doctors made shit like that up when they didn't know what was going on. The only part of his vision that he could use for the next hour would be in the one dark, dog-shaped patch that had been Lucy in the lower right corner of his vision.

He swung out of his bunk, tipped his head back and to the side so that he could see where he was going, and crossed to the woodstove. Grabbing the handle without a hot pad had him yelping again—not pain but a sharp, panicked sound that rang harshly in the small cabin. If he damaged his right hand he'd be beyond fucked. It was all he had left. He sucked on the slight warmth on his palm as if it was a second-degree burn, cursing the damn stove for still being hot to the touch, but not heating the cabin.

Reaching with his other hand didn't help. The paired titanium hooks of his prosthetic arm didn't care about the heat, but he hadn't pulled the rig on and all he had to wave about was his fucking stump.

Fumbling toward the woodpile, which was on the side he couldn't see, he found a small log and used it to whack the metal handle upward and swing the door open. For its duty and fine service, he chucked the log onto the few remaining embers inside.

Raising one knee, he propped a small bellows on his thigh and pinned its lower handle in place with his stump. With his remaining hand, he worked the upper handle until he coaxed a small snap of flame to life. It was bright enough to shine through the boy's afterimage. Carefully stoking the fire, he watched the flame grow as the boy faded.

The stove wasn't throwing much heat yet; all of the iron had cooled…except the goddamn handle. But he didn't move away. His bare skin rippled with goosebumps, but he remained to watch the flame.

When he'd first come to this small cabin in the Montana foothills, he'd spent many nights contemplating throwing his fake arm into the fire and then himself. At first he only resisted because he knew he'd piss off the ranch owner, and you didn't piss off a man like Mac Henderson or his son Mark.

Mac was a former SEAL—except he'd done his twenty years and retired. Being a SEAL, it was an easy bet that Mac would have followed Stan straight into hell and dragged him back to whup him good for throwing away the gift of life.

Gift of life, my ass.

It was early April. Back in North Carolina, the Sweet William would be blooming right now. The cherry blossoms would have already had their spring and the young cottonwood leaves would be unfolding to seek the sun.

Instead, he was squatting in front of a cold fire in a ramshackle cabin on the edge of the Montana wilderness surrounded by snow. It wasn't the life he'd pictured. But the life he'd pictured had thrown him out on his ass. When he'd gone home, his mother had burst into tears every time she looked at him. His fiancé hadn't even bothered to Dear Stan him. True love hadn't even lasted out the month for the half-man he'd become to make it out of the hospital. His sister had forced Stan's brother-in-law to offer him a pity-job at the bank, as if Stan would be forever helpless.

Besides, there was no way he could ever survive working indoors. And young nephew Jack had taken one look at his steel hooks and run away screaming in terror—as terrified as the little boy in the Afghan village.

Then one day he'd gotten a call from his former CO to come over to Fort Bragg. It was the last place in the world for a one-armed former SEAL to be, but saying no to Lieutenant Commander Luke Altman wasn't something a man did.

Altman had met him at the gate, which was a real favor. It saved him having to kill every damn grunt who stared at the hooks sticking out of his shirt sleeve and gave him that you-ain't-a-soldier-no-more look.

"Got someone I want you to meet."

"I don't need another goddamn therapist or perky wounded warrior volunteer to tell me how to live with myself."

Altman had merely looked over at him in that long, quiet way he had and Stan shut up. Altman took him to the SWCS dining hall. It was strange to be back on the JFK Special Warfare Center and School grounds and not be ragged from their typically brutal training scenarios. He hadn't let himself go after getting released, but he hadn't done a decent work-out either—not with one fucking hand. The month on his back had cost him a lot of muscle and the PT hadn't really put it back on—weird to trade the military's Physical Training acronym (or Puking Torture depending on who was leading the drill) in for medical's Physical Therapy, which told him just how civilian he'd become.

They grabbed trays and went down the line. Stan had learned enough about working his hooks to not need any help. Actually, having been left-handed before the injury, he was almost better with the hooks than with his clumsy right hand. It had become almost natural that when he extended his arm, or flexed his opposite shoulder, the two hooks separated and when he withdrew or relaxed they clamped together tight. Stan used them to load up on he didn't care what and went to sit with another pair of civilians—the ex-military kind by the look of them.

"Stan Corman. This is Mark Henderson and Emily Beale. Former Night Stalkers who founded the 5D."

Okay, that got Stan's attention. The Night Stalkers Special Operations Aviation Regiment specialized in helicopter transport for soldiers like him—like he'd been. He'd flown with SOAR plenty of times, but never with the 5D. They were practically legendary and were always with the very top teams, Delta and DEVGRU. He hadn't known one was a woman, but nothing surprised him about the 5D. If these were the founders… But shit! They were still intact. What was their goddamn excuse?

"They," Altman was still yammering, "have a place that they're going to tell you about. His dad runs the ranch and Mac trained me back in the day. Stan, you're going to shut up and listen."

Shutting up and listening had never been his top skill, but not arguing with his CO—former or otherwise—had been too ingrained, especially when it was SEAL Commander Luke Altman.

And that meeting had led to him squatting naked in front of a woodstove at the far corner of Henderson's Ranch in snowy April.

The dawn had happened at some point while he watched and fed the fire. The purging by flame no longer beckoned to him, but its warmth didn't comfort him either.

He was never going to fit back in. His dog was gone. Two of his team also had been close enough that they'd gone home in a box. The other two had gone down in a hail of crossfire that filled two more boxes. Left for dead; he'd been the "lucky one."

The lucky one.

No team. No unit. No longer a soldier. He'd lost fiancé, family, and town.

There was no one who wanted him. No place he belonged. The dead end was staring him in the face and there was no reverse gear out of it. His future was bricked in as surely as the sides of the glowing iron box filled with ashes and fire. Who would give a shit if the flames did consume him? Easy answer. The future held noth—

A knock sounded on the cabin door. The sudden sound where there shouldn't be any sent him diving for cover behind the woodpile.

All it earned him was a couple of splinters before he recovered and remembered where he was.

Furious with himself for sliding back into the black hole of panic and depression, he strode to the door and reached for it with his stump, then yanked it open with his right hand and a snarl.

Ama Henderson stood there with her horse tethered to the porch rail behind her. Mac's wife was a tall, magnificent woman. Her skin was still dark and smooth, but her hair had turned that dark steel-gray that was so unique to her Cherokee heritage.

"May I come in?"

It was a several-hour ride from the main house to the cabin that they'd given him; a damned cold one. The sun...he'd lost time again. It was a couple of hours above the snowy horizon in the crystal blue that was a Montana winter sky.

He held the door wider and the chill wind wrapped around him and reminded him that he was naked.

"Shit! Excuse me." He left Ama to close the door as he dragged on some clothes as well as he could. They were icy cold because he'd dropped them on the floor last night rather than on the chair by the stove. Without his arm on, it proved impossible to pull on underwear and pants.

Hating it, he stood there naked and dragged on a t-shirt first. He couldn't stand people seeing him put on his arm—not even the docs who'd fit it and trained him—but he had no choice. He found the thin cotton sock and pulled it up over his stump, careful to smooth out any wrinkles despite his haste. Then he unsnarled the harness, slipped his stump through one loop and into the socket of the prosthesis. With a practiced lean, he managed to get his good arm through the harness' other loop on his first try, thank god, and shrug it on. Now able to control the spring action of the paired hooks, he was able to drag on underwear, socks, and pants. A heavy jacket against the still cool cabin —he hadn't closed the woodstove's door and damped the fire to get good heat from it—and then he jammed his feet into his boots, though he'd be damned if he'd demonstrate for anyone how clumsy he still was at lacing them.

When he turned back, Ama was sitting at the small table looking down into a bundle she'd been carrying. Kind enough to offer him privacy while he struggled.

"Sorry, Ama. Can I offer you some coffee?"

He kicked the woodstove door shut, almost losing one of his unlaced boots into the fire in the process.

"No. I have come to offer *you* something."

As he'd learned was typical with her, she didn't say much but when she did, there was no point in either interrupting or attempting to hurry her to the point. So, he sat in the other chair and waited.

She looked at him with her intensely dark eyes. "You have decided that you don't want to stay at the main compound. I can respect that. There are times that a man must face his future alone. But there is also a time for that to end. My husband would leave you until spring to stew in your own thoughts. By then the pot will boil over. I do not choose to leave you so long."

He readied his protests that he wasn't fit to be neighbor to man or beast. His screams alone as he rose from each night's dreams were proof enough of that. What if they never ended? What would he do then?

Apparently done with what she had to say, she stood and headed for the door leaving her bundle on the table.

"Ama. I—" he called after her, but the bundle on the table moved. In the moment of his distraction, she was gone out the door. He knew that even if he rushed after her, she would somehow be gone, departing as quietly across the snow as she'd arrived.

The bundle moved again.

Then a nose stuck out the top.

It sniffed the air once, twice, then the rest of the head emerged and the puppy turned to look at him. Its dark face wore the goofy grin that could only be a Malinois—the same breed as almost every war dog. The same breed as Lucy.

Stan stared at it in horror, not even able to tear his eyes away to look at the door where Ama Henderson had left him.

A dog.

He couldn't even care for himself; how was he supposed to care for a dog?

The puppy yipped at him and he flinched.

It wasn't fair. He would end up killing it just as his one mistake had killed every other good thing around him.

CHAPTER 2

Freshly weaned and only partially housebroken, the dog soon had Stan far more occupied than he'd been on any day in his three months at the cabin.

His usual day's activity was to work on fixing up the cabin—that's how he was paying his rent. It was a fishing cabin in the summer for tourists and it showed. Years of wear and tear had battered the place hard. He'd started with the kitchen. Figuring out how to hold a measuring tape had been a challenge at first but was trivial compared to saws and hammers. With practice, he was getting the hang of it and had made slow but steady progress. Something that had been one motion might now be three, but there was no rush. And once he figured out how to do each task, he moved along well enough. Except the screwdriver was going to send him to the nuthouse; he just didn't have the manual dexterity retrained into his right hand yet.

But the first thing the puppy did once he'd lowered it to the floor —Stan used the blanket the pup had come in so that he didn't have to touch it—was to race around the room about twenty times and then pee on Stan's only clean pair of socks. A second later, the furry whirlwind had chomped down on the leg of a pair of Stan's jeans and begun wrestling them into submission.

He'd forgotten what an insane chewing machine a young Malinois was. He spent the next half hour racing to keep a step ahead of the puppy. He'd pick up one thing and the puppy would discover another. His hand was as big as it was or he'd have swatted the damn thing aside to just give him a single goddamn moment of peace. When his leather tool belt had become the next great find, Stan gave up and let him have at it.

Him. At least Ama had given him that bit of kindness. If it had been a female Malinois, he didn't know if he could have looked at it without breaking down. But like Lucy, it had classic markings. A little smaller than a German Shepherd, instead of a black Shepherd back, it had a black face. And instead of growing into its paws, a Malinois grew into its upright ears and this dog was going to be big—which meant the puppy looked like he was half rabbit.

When the puppy had finally convinced the leather tool belt just who was the king of the cabin, he ambled over and plunked his bottom down beside Stan's boot and began tipping its head one way and another as it inspected the laces.

"Oh no you don't," he stomped his foot, sick of the damn thing.

The pup looked up at him and back down at the boot without startling away.

That gave him pause. "What do you think of this?" He rapped his hooks sharply on the table top.

The pup looked up at the underside of the table for the source of the noise and then its eyes tracked back and forth between him and the table.

Stan rapped again.

This time the puppy watched him instead of the location of the noise.

"Smart little fella, aren't you?"

In response to his compliment it jumped up and yipped in delight. Then it raised a leg to pee on his boot.

In a single motion, Stan scooped it up with his good hand, two steps to the door, and he tossed it into a snow drift.

That turned into another excuse for a dozen circles and then it peed where the front porch post disappeared into the now yellowing snow. It eyed the low steps with some confusion, but had soon struggled back up onto the porch. Once it reached him, it sat and tipped its head as it stared up at Stan to see what he would do next.

Stan looked down at his good hand and flexed his fingers against the strangeness. It was the first living thing he'd touched since the Afghan boy. He tried to wipe off the sensation on his jeans, but the warmth wouldn't go away.

Stan spent some time gazing out at the hoof prints in the snow that proved Ama Henderson had indeed been here and he hadn't imagined her. He looked down. He hadn't imagined the goddamn dog either.

CHAPTER 3

S tan reached out.

The little boy looked so scared.

Five Special Ops soldiers were enough to scare anybody. It was kind of the point. Lucy, fifty pounds of war dog, was no less daunting a sight. Her body armor included goggles against wind and sand, and a Kevlar vest that also sported a camera that could feed visible and infrared imaging directly to a screen that Stan wore inside his wrist. She also had pouches for food, water, and doggie first aid. To the little boy, used to painfully lean feral mutts, she probably looked as alien as the soldiers did. She could work on or off leash, but in the village he kept her on the long lead, more for the villagers' peace of mind than for any real need.

The boy sidled closer as the team eased forward across the village square. It was the edge of evening, the worst visibility for the locals. There was a rumored Al-Qaeda nest two blocks up and one block over. Their team was being sent in to roll it up and look for any intel.

He and Lucy worked to make sure there weren't any IEDs in their path. Check that—they *knew* there were IEDs; it was up to him and Lucy to tell the team where.

The boy came closer, desperately clutching a toy truck. He was close enough for Stan to see that it was a real toy, not just some piece of scrap metal turned into a pretend truck. He knew that was a clue of something, but he couldn't come up with what.

To get down to the boy's height as he edged closer, Stan took a knee—placing one in the dirt, his other raised with his foot planted so that he could push off into a sprint if called.

He reached toward the boy, saying meaningless noises to calm him.

Take them back!

But he kept murmuring.

Shoot him! Chase him away! Scare him! The boy was on the edge of running away in fear as it was.

Instead he beckoned, calling the boy closer, easing his fear rather than adding to it.

No! Run! Hide!

Lucy stepped up close, sniffed the boy, and planted her butt down between them.

He'll kill me!

Lucy whined.

The truck is a bribe! A real toy as a gift to make the kid overcome fear!

And in that instant, something landed on his chest like a hard punch.

Stan swung at it and missed.

Stump. No hand.

He pulled his other hand free of the blanket and grabbed hard onto whatever had hit him.

A sharp yip of surprise and pain. For a brief instant he held a handful of struggling fur.

Fur far softer than Lucy's.

A puppy's fur.

He let go and could hear it scrambling away across the cabin.

Shit!

Stan struggled up from the bedding. The cabin was still warm. He hit the flashlight and checked his watch.

It was one the same wrist as the hand holding the flashlight.

Twenty-two hundred. The dream had given him less than an hour of sleep this time.

But he could see the cabin without tipping his head like the goddamn dog. No explosion apparently meant no afterimage. That was a first.

He went searching for the puppy and finally found her cowering under one of the bunks he hadn't fixed up yet. He had to lie down on the rough wooden floor, which was not all that warm, to reach in and snag the pup.

He nipped Stan's hand, but didn't even break skin. Stan had enough scars from training Lucy and other dogs that puppy teeth didn't phase him.

Sitting back down on the bed, he calmed the pup. Telling it he was sorry. Gods, he was sorry for so much. The puppy forgave him quickly enough, planting both front paws on Stan's chest to reach up and lick the bottom of his chin.

If only Stan could forgive himself.

CHAPTER 4

Early April had melted into mid-May before there was another knock on the door.

It didn't send him diving for the woodpile this time. It also explained why the pup had gone up on point, but remained dead silent—just as trained. He took to instruction quickly. Usually the first couple years were about little more than socialization and basic behavior. The pup had taken to commands as if born to them.

He bent down to pat it on the head which was now up to his knee rather than at mid-calf where he'd started.

"Good boy." He really had to name the dog, but that would make him too real, too important. Besides, with only the two of them in the cabin, it wasn't as if there was any confusion about who was talking to who.

Stan pulled open the door and Mac Henderson was standing on the other side of the threshold. He was a big man, still powerfully built though he was in his late sixties. His hair, unlike his wife's dark steel, was almost pure white. It gave him a grandfatherly look, but his handshake was still a force to be reckoned with.

"So," he looked down, "that's where Bertram got to."

"Bertram?" Stan asked the dog and the quick thumping of its tail said that the name had found the dog already.

"Ama brought him by."

Mac winked. "Ama's a sneaky one, isn't she?"

"No, she's..." Then he started thinking about the person he'd been six weeks ago compared to the one now. No diving behind the wood-pile. Half of the time the pup—Bertram—woke him before the nightmare could take him back under. A couple nights he'd actually just slept through. On the nights it did strike, he rarely woke screaming, though the shakes and adrenaline were still there. He'd snap his fingers and the pup would hop up and join him in the narrow cot and sometimes he could even get back to sleep. Maybe Ama was sneaky.

"Told ya," Mac nodded with satisfaction. "Let's see what you've got done." They spent about half an hour touring about the small cabin. Stan had done more than merely resetting drawers and renailing ladder rungs up to stacked bunk beds. He'd sanded and refinished all of the trim. The kitchen shone. The fine oak that he'd discovered on the bed rails now had a warm glow to them. The gray patina of old wood that had built up over the years had been banished. There was still more to do, plenty more, but he was pleased and so was Mac.

The friendly thump on his back, despite the reminder of the criss-cross of his prosthetic's harness, was appreciated.

"I can see that I need to maroon more SEALs in remote cabins around about here."

Stan decided that it had certainly worked for him, when he was sure that nothing else would.

CHAPTER 5

I t was the end of May when the storm hit.

Stan and Bertram had gone for a final hike up into the hills.
Two more days and he'd have to move out. The cabin shone, ready for
the paying customers to feel they were roughing it out here.

Funny, Stan had just assumed they'd keep him on, give him a place
to fit in. In his mind, he'd been sure of it. The itch between his shoulders? Not so much. Could he make it back in nowhere, North
Carolina? No. That home was gone. He'd have to find somewhere
fresh. Start over. Start over with Bertram? The dog belonged to the
Hendersons and was showing real potential.

Shit! Once again he was a half-man with no future. Would he ever
find a road to a whole new life? One where he wasn't himself? Apparently not. He had to laugh.

"Too damn scared to try," he told the dog. "Wouldn't that just piss
off Altman?" Oddly, Stan realized he would piss himself off too.
Maybe, just maybe, he could do this. Find some place…God knew
where.

He chucked a stick for Bertram, who raced off through the tall
meadow grasses to kill it and drag it back. At first he'd been as clumsy
throwing with his right arm as a teenage girl *trying* to look helpless.

But he'd slowly gotten the knack of it—the dog had been willing to help him get plenty of practice.

About an hour later, far up beyond the cabin, and the fishing stream that ran close behind it, a long set of falls climbed to an upper lake. They weren't one single drop, but a series of cascading white water separated by brief pools. Bertram loved to plunge into those, despite the glacial-fed chill, and they came up here often.

Today they'd reached the lake for a last look around. A pair of elk, mother and calf, were feeding along the lake shore. He called Bertram to heel. The pup obeyed, though he quivered with excitement as they watched the two goofy looking animals drink and then amble into the freezing lake as if it was a warm bubble bath.

A chill across Stan's shoulders had him turning from watching their play.

The sky to the west had turned dark, almost black. He blinked at it in momentary confusion. To the east, the Montana skies were still a brilliant blue. The cabin was a cheery spot far below. He'd even gotten a fresh coat of paint on it, sky blue with dark green trim, so it really stood out in the meadow of spring grasses and wildflowers.

Back to the west, the darkness was boiling closer and the temperature was plummeting. He hadn't even brought a jacket, just thrown on a t-shirt and gone walking.

Time to get his ass moving. They were at least an hour from the cabin and the storm would be on them in minutes.

Another glance filled him with disbelief. This wasn't some rainstorm, the ground below the leading edge was turning white. Snow at the end of May? It didn't make any goddamn sense, certainly not in North Carolina or Afghanistan. Sensible or not—it was coming.

He was halfway down the steep path along the falls when it hit. The blizzard slammed into him with hard winds. In moments, it was a whiteout.

Keep moving.

"Only dead men stop moving," one of Altman's favorite phrases.

Bertram was doing far better than he was. Atop his thick fur Stan had fashioned a vest in roughly the pattern of a war dog's armor. It carried water, dog snack, and first aid—a good training tool that was now buffering him from the elements.

The path was soon obliterated and he had to slow his pace. His instinct to chafe his arms proved stupid. Rubbing his left with his right, all he felt was plastic and wire. When he tried the other way, all he got were freezing metal hooks scraping up and down his good arm.

Useless.

Broken half-man.

At the third waterfall, he must have veered off the path. He didn't even have time to cry out before he was plunged into freezing water. The only thing that kept him from going over the biggest drop of them all, were his hooks.

His right hand was already numb from scrabbling through the snow. But the metal hooks didn't care about temperature and instinct had him jamming them into a crack in the rock. There was no screaming strain on his arm muscles either. The harness took the load and distributed it to the straps across his shoulders. They were narrow and bit in, but they held.

Forty feet of tumbling waterfall crashed loudly on the rocks below. Even if he couldn't see the bottom through the snow, he could hear the water pounding on the jagged rock fall. As he clung there, it struck him just how easy it would be to give up—just...let go. Then it wouldn't matter that he had no place he belonged, he'd be gone.

Then Bertram whined at him.

And for the first time outside his dreams, Stan knew fear. Real fear.

He'd felt anger at everything he'd lost. He'd felt betrayed by his family and by the military. But to die now? To leave Bertram? To not look at the cabin again—a job well done—or heave a branch for the dog to bring back? That would be a tragedy.

He dug in, hauling himself up through the freezing water, mostly with his hooks. He found a purchase for a boot, and felt blessed that he'd finally gotten good at tying laces.

When he eventually rolled up onto the trail, he knew he was screwed. Still half an hour to the cabin even under normal conditions, soaking wet and shivering in the snow. He was going to die of hypothermia right here.

He started to laugh. It was a crazed, hysteric sound, but he couldn't stop it. He'd survived SEAL training. He'd survived being blown to pieces in a remote Afghan village. And he'd survived his own self-destructive thoughts.

A late snow on a Montana ranch was going to be what killed him. Fucking snow.

Bertram licked at his face as if he wasn't already wet enough.

"Why can't your name be Lassie? Then I could say 'Get help' and you'd race the miles back to the ranch in time to save me."

Stan tried going fetal to conserve what little warmth he could, but the plastic arm didn't help.

Then something tugged at his belt.

Bertram. He'd never gotten over gnawing that first belt into submission.

The dog yanked at him again.

"Go away. Now isn't the time to play."

Bertram answered with a hard growl and tugged at the belt hard enough that Stan actually slid a foot down the trail.

"Goddamn it! Cut that out." Stan waved an arm at him.

When the steel connected with dog, he yipped in surprise, then answered with a hard snarl and clamped down on his forearm with a fighting hold.

If it had been his real arm, he'd have torn muscles and streaming blood from the force of the attack.

"Release!" He shouted through the roar of the storm's wind. Great. Snow wasn't enough, he needed a wind chill to make sure he was a goner.

Bertram let go, but didn't back off.

When he didn't move, the dog took a step in again.

"No you don't!" Stan forced himself to move.

"Only dead men stop moving." Goddamn Altman.

But he *was* moving which meant he wasn't dead. For the first time in far too long he really didn't want to be dead.

He flailed out with his hooks, and this time managed to catch the lift-loop he'd stitched into the back of Bertram's vest. It was used when a dog had to be lifted and carried, or winched up into a helicopter. He'd made the loop strong, the one surviving portion of the leather tool belt that a new puppy had defeated on his first day.

"Go," he croaked out the command. "Cabin."

Bertram turned and dug in. He wasn't big enough to make much difference, but he was still a force in the right direction as long as Stan didn't unclamp his hooks from the lift-loop.

At first, he could do little more than crawl as Bertram dug in with all fours. But he finally found one foot and then the other.

He wished he could say he didn't remember the rest of the trip back to the cabin, but he did, every grueling second of it.

His morning cooking fire had kept the cabin warm. And even that remaining bit of warmth was enough to sustain him through restoking the fire, stripping, and crawling into bed.

Unable to snap his fingers, he stuttered out the dog's name and Bertram climbed in beside him. He too was shivering.

Stan held him close, hard against his chest, but the dog didn't complain.

He buried his face in the dog's fur and knew he could never let go. He and Bertram were a team. They would find a way through, together.

Bertram licked at the salt running down Stan's cheeks before they both fell asleep.

CHAPTER 6

"I had this crazy idea."

Stan sat on the verandah of the big house, a beer bottle pinched securely between his hooks, and his good hand rubbing Bertram's ears.

Mac sat on the dog's other side and they both faced out across the ranch. It was now busy with the first of the June tourists trying to prove they could ride a horse around the corral and being shocked as shit that they actually could.

"Let's hear it," Stan was open to any ideas at this point.

"Back in my day, we didn't have the dogs. Left them behind in Vietnam and didn't need them again until Iraq and Afghanistan."

Stan knew about that. The entire program had been lost for thirty years and had to be rebuilt from scratch. Same thing had happened between the World Wars and again until Vietnam. The military swore that wasn't going to happen again, but he knew the main training center down at Lackland Air Force Base was already feeling the budgetary pinch with the supposed end of Iraq and Afghanistan.

"Now the Special Ops dogs, they're special, aren't they?" Mac asked it as half a question. Clearly he already knew the answer.

"Sure. They're trained by select contractors rather than going through the standard Lackland program. We—" Stan practically choked, had to sip his beer to clear his throat. "They, the Spec Ops, need dogs with more skills than the standard program gives them, no matter how good it is."

Mac nodded sagely. He gave Bertram a rough rub on the head and the dog sighed happily.

"Takes a lot to run a ranch. A lot to keep it afloat."

"Hell of a spread you've built here," Stan agreed going along with the subject change. He'd spent the winter and spring out at the fishing cabin. It was only now that he was seeing the horse wranglers, the recreation directors, the kitchen staff, and all the others it took to run the place.

"Still haven't figured out what I'm going to do with that patch of pasture," Mac waved off to the south of garage. "There's also a lot of room to try crazy ideas."

"Such as?" Stan still didn't see where the old man was heading.

"You trained Bertram up a treat," which sounded like another subject change.

"Thanks," Stan wondered when the man would find his point, but he was just as wily as his wife on working his way there, so Stan waited a little longer.

Mac stood up and stretched. Finished his own beer and tossed it in the small bin on the porch with a sharp rattle of glass.

Stan watched him walk down the front steps and head for the horse barn.

He could barely hear Mac's final words as he walked off toward the barn, "Bertram has five brothers and sisters. Come along if you want to look 'em over." Then he kept walking.

Five brothers and sisters? A whole litter of Malinois? And enough room to train them. He looked at the south pasture again. There was plenty of space for him to build an obstacle course for the dogs. Maybe even a training center for the handlers. Stan could see it clear as day.

He looked at the old man and then down at the dog who had tipped his head to watch Stan and see what he'd do next.

"Bet they barely know how to fetch. What do you think? Want to train up your litter mates?"

Bertram leaning in for another head scratch was all the answer he needed.

He tossed his empty, rolled to his feet, and slapped his good hand against his thigh. Bertram leapt down the steps and they headed out to the barn together to see what the future looked like.

NATHAN'S BIG SKY

When Emily Beale and Mark Henderson retire to the family ranch in Montana, they enter a whole new world. Meeting all new people.

Chef Nathan Gallagher's *escape from New York City lands him in the most unlikely of places: Montana. With his past dumped and his future unknown, he seeks something new. If only he knew what.*

Julie Larson, *former rodeo star and born-and-bred cattle rancher, loves the prairie and the horses. The cattle ranch work with her three brothers? Not so much. The local cowboys labeling her as a Grade-A Prime catch? Even less. When she rescues Nathan from a near-death experience, her future and her heart alter past all imagining.*

The only place a New York chef's future and a Montana cowgirl's heart can thrive? Under Nathan's Big Sky.

CHAPTER 1

The silence was deafening.

Nathan gripped the crowbar-handle of his car's jack so tightly that it hurt his hand but he couldn't ease up. It was his sole hope of survival.

The only sound for miles on the emptiness of the Montana prairie was the hot-metal pinging of his cooling Miata sports car, lurched awkwardly to the roadside by a flat tire. The chill of the cold April evening almost hurt his lungs. The sun hadn't quite set; instead it illuminated the clouds of his own breath like some horror movie with a fog machine turned on too high.

How was it that he'd come to this place to die?

Chefs were *not* supposed to die alone in the forsaken wilderness; they were supposed to have a butter-induced heart attack in the middle of a meal service. But the safety of his New York kitchen lay an impossible distance behind him. He'd bolted forty-eight hours ago, sleeping only a few fitful hours in Chicago before punching west as if all the hounds of hell were after him.

And they'd caught up with him in the form of a monster.

Two days to cross most of the country and now, like a gunslinger fated to his doom, he was going to be murdered in the emptiness of the Montana wilderness by the largest cow ever born.

It put Paul Bunyan's mythically massive blue ox Babe to shame.

Purest black, it was an inkblot on the continuance of Nathan's life.

Horns the length of a New York cabbie's woes sprang from either side of its head, ending in points that looked sharper than his finest boning knife.

He'd hit Choteau, Montana, in the late afternoon for directions, as his little brother's instructions had turned out to be utterly useless: "Henderson's Ranch, just west of Choteau." There wasn't a single app on his phone that told him where the ranch might be. There'd also been no answer on his brother's phone, but he was used to that. Apparently most of the ranch was beyond the pale of civilization and didn't have reception. His brother had always been useless about answering the phone anyway, unless you were a pretty girl—them he'd always had a sixth sense for, even on a blocked number.

Maybe Patrick's directions sucked because he was messing with his big brother. Or maybe it was because he assumed Nathan would never cross west of the Hudson River—which historically was a reasonable assumption—so it wasn't worth the effort to be more descriptive.

A Choteau (*Cho-toe* that was almost *Sho-toe*) local had known the name, however. In a town only three blocks long, it made sense that he did. "Just go down the highway apiece until you hit Anderson's farm. Can't miss it. He has the last big white cow barn this side of Augusta. Take a right on the main road and go on until you've just about hit the mountains. Out onto the dirt a ways. That'll set you in the right place."

The "highway" was a narrow two-lane called Montana 287.

By the time Choteau was two miles behind him, he'd passed two Andersons, an Andersen, and an Andreassen. This driveway had no mailbox that he could see, but it had a big white barn and a road along one side of the property. The map on his cell phone said that Augusta was fifty miles ahead. Telling him "the last big barn before Augusta" counted as a local having fun chapping his ass. He must have taken one look at Nathan's two-seater Miata and painted a little mental target on Nathan's forehead—just as the monster cow now had one painted on Nathan's life.

The turnoff road was a lane and a half wide. Nathan guessed that in its favor, it was paved and had an actual stop sign where it met the "highway." Sunlight was streaming out the backside of the sign through several bullet holes. He wondered if someone was going to shoot him for being in a sports car instead of a pickup with a gun rack.

Did upstate New York even have roads like this one—not even two lanes wide and with no painted stripes? Or was that only legal west of the Mississippi? Manhattan and Long Island certainly didn't. During his five years in Paris, he'd rarely been farther out than the Metro could carry him.

For thirty miles past the white cow barn, he drove unknowingly toward his doom as the mountains drew closer and closer. He kept assuming he'd reach them in another few miles and they insisted on teasing him just like his brother. After the unremitting flatness of the Great Plains, they had loomed tall and rough to the west as seen from Choteau. Now he was discovering that Australia wasn't the only place that had an Outback.

The peaks kept growing bigger and climbing higher but the land remained flatter than the ocean off Coney Island on a hot summer's day. The peaks' jagged flanks were shrouded in snow despite it being April. He turned on the Miata's heater as the sun settled toward the west, but he left the convertible top down because the view was so amazing. The blue sky arced forever over him until the mountains sliced it off like a kid's construction project: sharp, jagged, unreal.

Each time he'd passed a ranch, he checked the name, but none said Henderson. He even pulled out his phone to check that he'd remembered it right—and almost drove his car into the gaping ditch. Not a good idea. For all he knew, there might not be another person down this road for a week. He'd seen a few tractors—which were far bigger than he thought they would be—far out in the fields, but no one else on the road.

With a crash and thud that made him check his rearview to see if he'd left an axle on the road behind him, the pavement ended.

"Out onto the dirt a ways." Maybe the old-timer in Choteau hadn't been completely chapping his ass.

He slowed down to preserve his suspension. A cloud of brown dust obliterated his past. If he wanted to turn around, he'd have to eat his own dust. That sounded like a properly cowboy-like metaphor for the last decade of his life. Two days ago he'd cut every tie to that past. If only he could figure out how that had led him to the Montanan Outback, he wouldn't feel quite so overwhelmed at the moment. Twenty-eight years old and his life fit in a two-seater sports car—with room to spare. That might not be right, but it didn't make it any less true.

For the last ten miles he'd been hoping to meet someone on the road to ask directions again. Or maybe how to escape, little knowing it would soon be too late.

The dirt road narrowed and then he actually hoped he didn't meet anyone because he'd have to crawl to the side to get by them. Out here he wasn't threatened by ditches anymore, they'd disappeared along with the pavement, but instead by barbed wire running close down either side of the dirt track. Not a chance that his Soul Red Metallic paint job would survive the encounter.

After a few miles of dodging potholes and gritting his teeth over washboard ripples, he started looking for a place to turn around. The road wasn't wide enough to be sure he could turn even his small car without dinging it up.

He'd been climbing slowly since Choteau, and spring had turned back into winter. There was a bitter snap to the evening air that promised what looked like snow and ice up ahead...really *was* snow and ice up ahead. By this point the mountains were so high they looked as if they were going to roll over and land on him.

Manhattan didn't have places like this. Neither did Paris, where he'd done his time at Le Cordon Bleu and three years servitude for

Chef Guevarre—may his brutal training and magnificent palate both be in hell by now. There was something wrong about the flatness behind and the impossible mountains ahead.

Then, topping a low rise, facing straight into the setting sun, he was confronted by the beast from hell that was going to kill him.

He'd slammed on the brakes, skidding sideways on the washboard gravel, and barely managed to avoid hitting the cow. A tire caught in a pothole where it had blown with a loud bang that scared him almost as much as the creature of his doom had.

Now he stood in the middle of the road between his crippled car, pinging the last dying notes of its hot-metal song, and the monstrous black cow that was about to charge him. The damn thing didn't so much as blink its malevolent eyes, as if it was trying to hypnotize him.

His only weapon choices were his chef's knives, which would be very useful if the cow was already dead and butchered but not until then, and his car's jack handle. Retreating into his car and pulling up the convertible's roof would be pointless—this monster was so big it could practically step over the Miata. And the tips of its horns were actually wider than the car itself.

His ears rang with the silence, now broken only by a scuffing of one New York metro bus-sized hoof as the cow prepared to charge. Nathan had served a thousand roasts, ten thousand steaks, and this meal-still-on-the-hoof knew it. It had come to exact revenge for all of its spiritual forebears...fore-steaks?

The last thing Nathan was going to smell was the crackling dry grass of the prairie, the biting chill of the fast-approaching night, and the hot breath of the demon cow so big it seemed to block out even the vast expanse of the Montana sky. There had been fourteen hundred miles of flat since Chicago, but here, with his back up against the mountains, the vast horizon seemed far bigger than should be possible. His last-ever vision would be to actually see the curvature of the earth.

Then, impossibly, as if it wasn't bad enough that his epitaph was going to read: *Here a once-decent chef was trampled to death by a cow—*

trampled sounded like a marginally more pleasant way to go than gored—he heard a clip-clop sound coming from behind him.

He didn't dare turn, because he knew the beast-cow would charge the moment he looked aside.

Still, the sound behind him grew.

Unable to stand it any longer—the sound was so close—he spun and raised his foot-long jack handle in one last desperate bid for life.

Backed by the sun, a silhouetted cowboy sat up on a horse even taller than the cow and looked down at Nathan from under the brim of his cowboy hat.

"What are you doing out in the road?"

Not cowboy, cowgirl. A soft voice, but no less disgusted for all that. Against the dazzling sun he could see that she wore cowboy boots, a heavy leather jacket, and had a rifle tucked close to hand.

Hope?

Maybe she could shoot the demon cow before it trampled, trompled, gored, or whatever demon cows did.

He tried to speak, but his throat was clogged dry with fear and road dust. The air was so dry it seemed to suck the moisture right out of him.

She rode around him and his car as if he wasn't even there. "Go on now, Lucy. Scoot!"

A hell-beast named Lucy?

He'd had a great Aunt Lucy, but she hadn't been very fierce—more the quiet and retiring type, which was perhaps inevitable beside her husband's garrulous stockbroker charisma.

The woman rode her black-and-white patterned horse up to the "monster cow from hell" before he could warn her off.

Yet, in a startlingly sudden surrender, the gigantic animal turned and ambled back through a broken gap in the barbed wire fence that Nathan hadn't noticed. As it walked, he recognized the scuffing sound that he'd thought proceeded a deadly charge—it was just the sound the cow made by walking.

After riding her horse through the gap as well, she then swung a long leg over the back of the saddle and came down out of the sky.

Paying no more attention to him than if he was a bump in the road, she pulled out some tools and walked up to the fence.

He could only watch—numb with his unexpected last-second stay of execution and the biting cold—as she repaired the fence. It was only the work of minutes before she had three fine strands of barbed wire strung back up between the posts; her and the cow on one side and he and his broken car on the other. The flimsy wires had no chance of stopping a baby cow, never mind the hell cow Lucy, currently tearing at the low dead grass.

The woman had been towering in the saddle; on the ground she was still tall. Perhaps slender beneath the heavy leather jacket. Straight, light blond hair fell past her shoulders. Her cheeks were rosy with the cold, which he'd always thought was just a saying.

When she finished, he finally found his voice before she could disappear back into the landscape as eerily as she'd arrived.

"Excuse me, can you tell me how to get to Henderson's Ranch?"

"I can," he could just see her eyes beneath the wide brim of her cowboy hat. They were as brilliant blue as the sky and seemed to be laughing at him, though her mouth wasn't. What was it with locals chapping his ass today?

"Would you mind telling me?"

"Not a bit," and she let it hang long enough to make him sigh.

The failing sun caught the cloud of his breath in the chill air.

"You're standing on Henderson land."

"I am?" he looked down at the road, but it was keeping its secrets to itself. "This doesn't look like a ranch, it looks like a whole bunch of nothing."

"It's two *ranches*," she sounded miffed by his description, which, he decided on review, hadn't been the most tactful thing he'd ever said. "You're standing on Henderson's, but your passenger seat is on mine —property line runs up the middle of the lane. You've been on Mac and Ama's land for the last five miles or so. If you'd like, I can chop your car in two and then you'll be off *my* family's land."

"That's okay. I like my car the way it is."

"Even with the flat?"

"Okay, except for the flat." Was this what passed for a sense of humor out here, or was she about to pull the rifle hanging on her horse's saddle and make good on her offer—maybe shooting his poor car for trespassing before skinning it? Perhaps it would be safer if he kept her talking. "What are you doing way out here?"

"Riding the fence."

He assumed that meant something to someone other than him, but he couldn't figure out how to ask what. Her horse stepped up to her and rested its chin over her shoulder. She reached up a gloved hand and patted it on the cheek a couple of times.

"I was looking for different," and it didn't get more different than the woman in front of him.

"Thought you were looking for Henderson's."

"I was. I am," and he was on the verge of being turned into a babbling idiot. He'd left New York looking for a change. For something he'd never done, someone he'd never been. Couldn't get more different than a burned-out New York chef and a tall, blond cowgirl out "riding a fence" who had a horse for a pet.

"Their drive is another mile yet, on the left. Can't miss it," she tipped her head toward farther down the road. Then, in a move so smooth she might have been doing it since birth, she stepped one foot up into a high stirrup and swung atop the tall horse. He'd briefly dated an American Ballet Theater dancer—sleeping through her performance had not earned him many bonus points—who didn't have the grace or posture of this cowgirl. Cow-woman. Was that a real phrase? She stepped once more into line with the low sun and he lost her in the glare.

"Thanks," he called out. One of his more charming lines.

"Need help with the tire?"

"I can change a flat."

Her blinding silhouette nodded as if that might be a miracle worth witnessing, then she tipped her hat and turned to ride away. He couldn't argue with that conclusion, but it would be too embarrassing to admit his gross incompetence.

"Will I see you again?"

"It depends," she spoke over her shoulder without fully turning.

"On what?" Nathan had to call more loudly as she headed away perpendicular to the road.

"On how long I can avoid you."

Unwilling to turn, Julie Larson kept an ear out. It took a bit, but then she heard a soft laugh.

A minute later, the rattling sound of someone jacking a car—a sound far enough away to be no louder than the ticking of a lone cricket. Anything else was lost beneath the sound of the last of the dry winter grass swishing against Clarence's hocks, but that laugh intrigued her. She didn't know why the man made her more prickly than a stinging nettle.

This had been the last stretch of the fence line. There were a half dozen places where the winter had snapped a post and occasional runs where wood rot had finally taken down a whole stretch of wire, but nothing bad in the entire run. In the morning she'd grab one of the hands and a truck; they'd have the spring pasture put together before the cattle were ready for it. Old Lucy had somehow slipped in early, but she'd been a certified escape artist since her third day afoot.

Will I see you again?

"Not a chance, city boy. I've already got my big strong man. Don't I?" she leaned forward to scrub at the side of Clarence's neck as his ears pricked back to listen to her. What was it with city boys and a woman on a horse? For that matter, what was it with cowboys and a woman on a horse?

Number One question: *You aren't married?* (delivered with an astonished gasp). Twenty-six and single was definitely a crime. Or at least a freak of nature.

Number Two question: *Wa'll how about me, darlin'?* (as if a lame Texas accent worked wonders in the Montana Front Range).

I was looking for different.

What had he meant by that? Didn't matter—he was Mac and Ama's problem now.

She leaned in just enough for Clarence to lift up to a quick trot. It was still comfortably above freezing, but there wasn't a cloud in sight so it would chill down fast once the sun hit the horizon. Even now the long shadows of Old Baldy and Rocky Mountain stretched across the prairie leaving her in a narrow slash of red-gold sunlight across the still-brown prairie.

Julie resisted Clarence's urge to gallop. She didn't want him to get all heated before a cold night in the barn.

Different. The city boy had that right. A sports car in the land of pickup trucks. A convertible in a place where rocketing winds and plunging temperatures defined seven months of the year. He had tousled dark hair, warm eyes, and an easy smile that seemed to be aimed first of all at himself.

Different. She looked at the sweep of land around her, the Larson barn, house, and sheds coming into view, and wondered at it. There were so many things to love here, but different wasn't one of them.

Clarence asked again with a shift in his stride. She eased off and let him slip into a canter. Even big, handsome boys like him deserved to have some fun. She tugged down on the brim of her hat to make sure she didn't lose it and decided that she deserved some fun, too. She gave Clarence his head and between one stride and the next he took her to the pure exhilaration of a full gallop over the rolling pastureland.

Why anyone would want *different* when they could have this, she didn't know.

In New York, turning onto someone's driveway said that you were close to the house. Out here it apparently meant only that you were in the same time zone.

At the turnoff, the first one in miles, a big arch of wood weathering to gray crossed above the dirt drive—no smaller than the road he'd been on. The headlights barely caught the carved "Henderson's Ranch" in big letters with a horseshoe nailed in at either end.

It had taken forever to change the tire. Thank goodness the manual had pictures or he'd still be out there wondering what a lug nut was. Though a flashlight certainly would have helped. He'd been able to see the manual in the dome light, but he'd finished hanging the wheel in darkness by feel alone. Even with the top up and the heater on high for the last stretch, he wondered if his fingers would ever recover.

A mile or more up the lane and around a low hill he spotted a porch light and had never felt so like he was coming home. To his left were several big barns and sheds. A few small houses lay beyond them. The main house, the one with the ever-so-welcoming porch light, was a big, two-story, log cabin structure. The foundation was stonework and the roof disappeared steeply into the night. There was a real elegance to the place—no less than a Long Island mansion, but in a style all its own.

When he'd finished changing the tire, he had stood up—and was utterly alone. The only sound was the chattering of his teeth. He'd swear he could hear the starlight puncturing brilliant holes through the ice-cold air.

Where was the stunning blonde now? Had she ridden off into the dazzling sunset and gone back to some Montana fairyland in the sky? He could almost believe it. She'd galloped away so fast into the orange sun that it was as if she'd sucked the light out of the sky with her slipstream.

He'd never had a pet and the women he'd dated never had anything bigger than a cat, but the cowgirl made a horse seem like such a natural companion that it was hard to imagine her with anything less.

"Not going to find a welcome there," he told the night.

She'd ridden away from him without a name or a backward glance.

Had her driveway been around the next bend, or was her family ranch so big that he'd need to set his watch ahead an hour in order to find her?

Well, he was here. Finally. Unsure where else to go, he climbed out of the car and stumbled up the ranch house's broad wooden steps onto the deep porch that ran off either direction into the darkness. The door was a warm red with a semicircular arch of glass above that glowed with a soft light.

He knocked. Waited. Knocked again harder. If he had to camp in his car on this Arctic night, he was in deep trouble.

The door creaked open and a tall woman with dark, Native American features and waist-long straight hair—black and shot with steely gray—looked at him eye to eye. She wore jeans and a simple flannel shirt. She was positively majestic, except for her pink bunny slippers.

She noticed the direction of his attention, "A Christmas gift from my daughter-in-law. She has a curious sense of humor." The first words spoken between them. She had a warm, steady voice, as if nothing in the world could ever surprise her.

Then she looked right at him for a long moment as he shivered on the threshold.

"You are lost," she said simply and stepped aside, then waved him in.

"No," Nathan stepped into the firelit warmth chaffing his hands together. "If this is Henderson's Ranch, I think I'm found."

If the woman smiled, it wasn't on the outside.

"Sorry, best line I've got after the crazy evening I've had."

She turned and walked away without another word, but he had the impression that he should follow.

He almost lost track of her when he stepped forward. The entryway gave way to a massive great room. Cedar finish, gigantic beams, shining hardwood floor, and a towering stone fireplace: it was an absolute showpiece. But it was also much more than that. Red and brown leather couches were gathered in comfortable groupings. Geometric throws of strong colors were draped over the backs of the couches.

"This is like a cliché out of Montanan Architectural Digest." His tact-o-meter had never been high but tonight he seemed to be hitting new lows.

"Yes," her voice echoed from somewhere back to the left.

He tracked her through an arch into a large dining room, with a rough wooden table that could seat thirty or more family style, and into a kitchen.

"It is what most guests expect when they come to vacation on a working ranch. It makes them happy when they find it just as they'd expect. It has been three generations since my family wove Cheyenne rugs. But I researched and studied the techniques and now teach classes for guests because they expect it from someone like me."

"I suppose that's irony at its finest." A weaving class taught by such a striking and regal Cheyenne woman, he'd sign up for that class in a heartbeat. "Do you at least enjoy it?"

"Very much, or what would be the purpose?" This must be the Ama of "Mac and Ama's" that the blond cowgirl had referred to.

He meant to ask some polite question next, perhaps even introduce himself, but that thought was gone the moment he looked about the kitchen. The chef in him almost drooled with envy.

It wasn't a commercial kitchen, not really, but neither was it a residential one. There was a large prep island with a wide array of cast iron and copper pans hanging on iron hooks above. Below were sheet pans, cutting boards, and a dozen other handy containers for large-scale meal preparation. The gas range had a dozen burners, and there was a broad griddle plus three ovens. A pair of big Sub-Zero side-by-side refrigerators dominated one end of the room. And it wasn't merely the space: it had the best of everything from its borderland between residential and commercial. The pair of the largest residential KitchenAid stand mixers, a big Cuisinart, a Vitamix blender and juicer: everything a chef could need to have unlimited options. The cabinets were bright oak and the counters dark granite. It screamed cozy efficiency.

At the other end of the room was another dining table, this one for a dozen at most. The family dining room. There was also a single gathering of chairs and couches around another stone fireplace. So, not just the family dining room, this was the part of the house used by the family, whether or not there were guests.

"Can I stay forever?" He meant it as a joke but the woman, who had yet to introduce herself, simply put on the teakettle and pulled out a drawer with a dozen flavors of tea for him to choose from. He selected chamomile because his nerves definitely didn't need caffeine at this point.

As he watched the kettle not boiling, Ama set about other tasks. By the time he had his tea, a steaming bowl of vegetable beef stew and a slab of homemade bread were waiting for him on the big table. He dipped the first slice and tasted the stew. Carrot, sweet parsnip, chunks of potato, and long-cooked beef in a thick gravy that was so good it was dribbling down his chin as he tried to eat it too fast. Thyme and bay, salt and pepper, and a dash of...not hot sauce... Worcestershire Sauce. The beef was tender and rich—definitely grass fed to get that degree of flavor with a moderate Burgundy red wine.

"Now I'm definitely found!" If this was farm cooking, he was all over it.

The woman tipped her head as if to say maybe.

"I'm Nathan Gallagher, Patrick's brother."

She nodded as if that much was obvious, even though he and Patrick looked nothing alike. Sons of different fathers—his own hadn't stuck much past conception. Patrick's had arrived before Nathan's birth and raised them both as his own.

"Is my little brother around?"

"He is in Great Falls, then Bozeman, making deliveries and getting a load of supplies. He should be back tomorrow night, maybe the next. Your bedroom is through there," she pointed to a door off the kitchen. She couldn't have known he was coming, he barely knew he was coming himself until he arrived here. Yet she'd said *your bedroom* not as if he was a visitor or guest, but as if he somehow belonged here.

Though it would only be for a few days, Nathan welcomed the *suggestion* of stability. The world's rug had been yanked out from under his feet in the last few days and even a moment's respite was welcome.

He really was in heaven. Another taste of the stew. It was simple, rich, but there was one flavor more that he couldn't quite identify. "What's—"

But he was alone in the kitchen as if it had always been that way. He never heard her leave on her bunny slippers and now he wondered if he'd dreamed her, just like the cowgirl and her two-toned horse.

CHAPTER 2

J ulie dreamt of clowns.

Small ones. Tall ones. Wide and narrow. All driving teeny, tiny cars and brandishing teeny, tiny steel bars at one of the gentlest cows on the range.

And all making her want to smile. Not at their ludicrous gestures and overblown reactions, but because they all smiled at her as if she was something special.

The only clowns she was used to were the ones at the county rodeos to distract the bulls after the rider was thrown. On this cold April morning, the summer rodeos were still too far off for even dreaming. She hadn't decided if she'd sign up this year or just go and watch from the stands.

She rolled out of bed in time to help Ma with the cooking. Dad and her three older brothers came in from the barn as they were finishing up, with Dad handing out orders like usual.

"Matthew, get that bale stacker greased and going by noon. The cows aren't going to feed themselves for another month yet. Mark and Luke, check the Poplar Creek pasture. They're dropping their calves like hotcakes right now; bound to be a couple in trouble out that way. Julie—"

She always wondered how much it irritated her father that he'd had a girl instead of a boy that he could name John, but he was such a stern man that she'd never dared ask. At least he'd resisted naming her Johanna. That would have made it even more of a slap in the face.

"—finish riding the spring pasture fence line today."

"Already done. I fixed a lot of little things yesterday. I'll take the F-150 and some posts. I'll have the whole spring pasture clean and tight by midday."

"Good girl."

"Then I'm switching over."

That just earned her a grunt.

She had her own business to run, no matter how busy the spring season was on a cattle ranch. Frankly, if she never saw a birthing cow again, it would be too soon. It was freezing April and they were as likely to drop their newborns on a wind-torn snowbank as a soft bed of winter grass in a sheltered hollow. Cows started out dumber than most sheep, but the more trouble they were having, the dumber they became. The twins, Mark and Luke, were likely to find a hard birth in the middle of a stream where the cow could also fight the battle of hypothermia and drowning, as if giving birth weren't a challenge enough for a woman.

"Don't forget we've got a party tonight. I expect you all to be clean and presentable," her father rode over her reminder that J. L. Building was launching its second year tomorrow—its first full year if she could find the contracts.

Wait. "What party?"

Her father's scowl said she should have kept her mouth shut and asked Ma.

But May Larson saved her only daughter, something she didn't do much for the boys. "Hendersons. Mark and your friend Emily are moving back to the ranch."

"Oh, that's tonight?" She barely remembered it as news at all. She didn't know Mac and Ama's son particularly except that he was ex-military of some sort. Julie had met him a few times, but the guys tended to cluster around the "military man" so she'd had little contact with him.

She knew Emily a little better and liked her well enough. She was a stern, taciturn blonde—an incredibly striking one. On the rare occasions they were together, they drew puzzled looks. Other than her white blond to Emily's golden, folks who didn't know them seemed split on asking if they were mother-daughter or sisters. Probably because she was an Easterner, it was impossible to tell what Emily was thinking and Julie had always been a little uncomfortable around her. Julie would never label her as a friend.

Dad's scowl said exactly what he thought of Julie not keeping up on such things. And probably a hundred other things wrong with her, like her still being single rather than bringing another man into the family to work the ranch. Oh! Which was exactly why her father wanted her to be excited about tonight's party. It would be the first gathering after the hard winter snows and hands would be coming from all the ranches around. The place would be packed with eligible bachelors.

Someone please shoot her now. She'd rather spend the night with Lucy out in a cold camp.

Then the last piece connected.

J. L. Building's one contract for work was at Henderson's, enough to last her through the first month or more. And that's where that guy in the tiny clown car had been headed. With the way her luck ran with men, he'd be on the ranch the whole time she was working there, underfoot and in the way.

The local boys had learned not to mess with her. A hand on her ass was likely to earn a slicing swing with the short end of a hard lariat rope across theirs. That settled most of them quick enough.

But city boys were like puppy dogs—she never quite had the heart to shoo them away so harshly that they'd actually remember it.

She suspected that she'd have to make it extra clear this time.

Nathan hadn't thought to close the curtains so he woke when the sunrise pounded into his face. He could have slept a dozen more hours. He'd barely slept in his final week in New York—being a chef at a high-end restaurant like Vite, sleep wasn't a big part of his life. Then the two-day mad dash across the country.

He tried pulling the covers over his head, but the room was freezing. He peeked out and saw a thermostat on the wall. He hadn't noticed it last night. With the bowl of warm stew inside him and twenty-two hundred miles behind him, he hadn't noticed much of anything. The thermostat's little handle was slid all the way to the left.

He bolted from the barely warm covers and into icy clothes that had him rushing into the kitchen praying for a cup of hot coffee. At sunrise he expected to be alone. It was an hour he was wholly unfamiliar with except as the time of day for that brief excursion to do the day's shopping for the restaurant at the fresh markets.

His normal day started in late afternoon, ran through dinner service, a couple of bars, half a night's sleep, a few hours of shopping if he couldn't palm it off on some other chef, more sleep, and waking in time for a late lunch before prep began for the next dinner service.

He stepped into the gorgeous farm kitchen now flooded with early morning sunlight. The dark granite warmed. The rich oak glowed and the burnished steel did some other welcoming adjective that he'd think up after he had some caffeine flowing through his system.

Ama Henderson was at one of the counters greasing up a pair of big waffle irons.

Nathan found a mug, filled it from the round glass pot on the commercial dual-bay coffee maker. A brief search turned up cream and sugar.

He didn't see any batter going yet.

She made no comment as he pulled out a steel bowl and a basket of eggs. They were dirty, like they'd been rolled in mud. He carried the basket to one of the sinks and began to wash them off. "Do your store your eggs in mud puddles?"

"Chicken shit," she didn't look up.

For a moment he wondered why they would do that. When the

obvious reason registered—because that was the other thing besides eggs that was under chickens—he lost control of the egg he'd been washing and it hit the bottom of the sink with a sickening splat. In his world eggs came from clean little cardboard cartons, not from…chickens.

Ama might have been smiling as she passed him carrying a large plastic container filled with sausage meat. It didn't look as if her sausage meat came from neat little Styrofoam trays covered in plastic wrap either.

Once the rest of the eggs were clean, he began cracking them into the bowl. "How many?"

"A dozen eggs should do."

From that scant clue as to how many they were feeding, he began building a waffle mix. She didn't tell him where things were, leaving him to discover that milk was in the steel jug in the dairy fridge, and which cupboard held the baking powder and flour. When he didn't have enough flour, she pointed him toward another door.

"Oh. My. God." This time he could feel her smiling at his back, though he didn't turn to see.

The door led to a pantry that could feed an army. There were walls of staples. Lidded plastic buckets on the floor were labeled: rice, lentils, red beans, black beans, and more. There was an entire wall of shelves dedicated to canned goods. Not canned like from a store, but canned like the glass jars that cost him ten or fifteen dollars apiece at Dean and DeLuca's in SoHo. Asparagus, beans, corn…the whole alphabet of vegetables was represented. Jam jars nudged up against quarts of cherries and tomatoes—maybe he'd died and gone to heaven. A massive chest freezer was packed solid with bags of frozen fruit. Another with cuts of meat wrapped in brown butcher paper.

It was so overwhelming that he had to look at the empty container in his hands to remember what he'd come in to find. Flour. Right. He dipped a couple of scoops from a fifty-pound bag into the container and wandered back into the kitchen completely dazed.

Ama had taken over the waffle mixing. His delay would have put the meal out of sync if she hadn't.

Rather than switching back, he handed off the flour and took over the sausage. She'd made patties and dropped them on the griddle. He knocked off a cooked bit and tasted it. Pork, heavy on the salt and light on the pepper.

Nathan ducked back into the pantry and grabbed an onion and a jar of roasted red peppers in oil. He diced both down quickly and got them running on the griddle. Thyme and a shot of Tabasco. More pepper, but no more salt. Soon the kitchen was thick with the smell of good sausage, fresh butter sizzling on the griddle, and hot waffles.

People started coming into the kitchen through the back door. They brought a wash of cold air and the smell of dry grass and sunshine in with them. Wow. He wasn't first up, he was last. Minutes past sunrise and they'd all been outside working. That explained the two pots of coffee that had been going.

As each person came in, Nathan dropped an extra egg on the hot grill. Another taste of pepper-onion mix, then he added a touch more hot sauce and a pinch of tarragon.

No one spoke to him—they'd all know who he was by this point— but he could hear them chatting about the morning's work. Horses, farm equipment he'd never heard of, and cabins under construction— a lot of discussion on that last point. But he was too busy cooking to let it be more than a wash over him.

Ama began handing him plates with a trio of giant waffles on each. Big appetites here.

With a broad spatula, he dropped a sausage patty beside the waffles, smothered it with the onion-pepper mix, slipped an over-easy egg on top of it, then handed off the plate. Finally, no one arrived to take the next plate.

In confusion he slipped out of the zone and discovered that he had no more eggs to serve either—the last one was crowned over the sausage on the plate he was holding.

He turned and everyone was sitting at the kitchen table. They all had plates before them and were busy dressing the waffles with butter and syrup.

The transition was always hard, but this one was stranger than most. He generally made a point of cooking the staff meal himself. Before the day's dinner service began, he would serve everyone a plate, and himself last. They always ate together before the night's mayhem began. Even Chef Guevarre, despite all of his control freak madness, always sat and ate with the crew—though he'd never cooked for them as that would be a "waste of his time and talent."

But this was no table with hungover chefs, predatory sous chefs, and waitresses dressed far more to please with their bodies than their personalities.

Mac and Ama sat at either end. Six others sat scattered along the length. A striking redhead was leaning in to tease a guy with brown hair down to his collar. There was a huge guy with a buzz cut and paired steel hooks sticking out of one cuff, a sharp contrast to his other big powerful hand of flesh and blood. Two of the men, both sandy blond and rancher solid—and alike enough to be twins—rounded out the crowd.

Ama patted the spot by her side and he slid into it gratefully.

He picked up a fork, then set it back down when he noticed no one else was eating. They were all looking at Mac.

Mac's glance traveled around the table, stopping on each of them. Nathan found that his own was doing the same. The big hard guy with the hooks to his right, Ama to his left.

No one spoke. No one closed their eyes or mumbled prayers. There were looks and smiles and nods around the table.

It lasted only a second or so, a few moments of acknowledging that these were the people whom they were breaking bread with. Before it could get weird or uncomfortable, Mac declared "Hooyah!" from the other end of the table with some kind of military call. It rippled like a wave around the table and then they began eating and talking all at once.

Nathan sat a moment longer appreciating the feel of the moment. He wished he'd thought to do something like that at his restaurant. If he ever spoke to his buddy Estevan again, he'd have to suggest it.

Nathan was the last to pick up his fork.

"Wow!" the redhead exclaimed. "That's some seriously good

sausage. You can cook for me anytime. I'm Chelsea, by the way. I married-in last spring," she hooked a thumb at the man beside her. "Doug was just too good a package to leave on the shelf. He can even kinda cook, which is good because I'm totally hopeless despite my mom being a cook for a whole bunch of Oregon firefighters ever since before I can remember. Doug is the ranch foreman and never speaks."

"Sure I do. I just can't ever seem to get a word in edgewise. It's Stan who never speaks."

"Give me a reason to," the big guy with the hooks for a hand grunted out. He looked rough, but not angry. More like the guy you wanted on your side in a brawl.

"He only talks to his dogs," Chelsea explained.

"At least they listen," Stan shot back.

"You know Mac and Ama, of course," she continued the introductions as if Stan hadn't spoken at all. Maybe he spoke plenty and she just never heard him. Or maybe she was teasing him.

As to Mac and Ama, not at all and barely. But as it was obvious there was no stopping the speeding train of Chelsea, he simply nodded. The big guy at the head of the table offered him a wink as she turned to the last occupants of the table.

"These two we call Tweedledee and Tweedledum. They aren't twins, they only look that way."

"I'm Dee. He's Dum," the not-twins said in practiced unison, aiming a forkful of waffle at each other.

"Actually I'm Fred and he's George," one said.

"Can't be," Nathan was getting the hang of their conversation.

"Why not?" the other asked.

"First, are either of you magical?"

"Like a fairy? Sure, Dum is. Magical like a giant? You're talking to the main man." Even though he was slightly the shorter of the two.

"Your hair isn't red."

"Depends on the day of the week."

Nathan couldn't help but laugh. He'd wager that the two of them never gave a straight answer to anything.

"Maybe you're the twins from *The Parent Trap.* Then you could both be impersonated by a young Lindsay Lohan." His suggestion started them off on using little-girl voices.

The rest of the meal carried on the same way. They teased him some about his sports car. Dee and Dum, whose actual names he still wasn't sure of, wanted to take it for a spin.

"Found these still in the ignition," Doug reached into a pocket and tossed him the keys.

Nathan must have been even more out of it than he'd thought to do that. Very *not city* of him.

"I moved it into one of the garages, what with the storm coming in tonight. Stacked your gear inside the front door." His smile said he might have taken it for a quick spin on the way. Chelsea's smile confirmed that he had and she'd been along to enjoy the ride.

If this was New York, he'd be pissed that someone had taken liberties with his Miata. Here it didn't seem such a big deal. "Careful, there's no spare. I had a flat about a mile from here last night when I nearly plowed into a sky-tall cow from the underworld named Lucy. I thought I was a goner until an angel on a horse rescued me. Where's the nearest station to get that fixed?"

"Choteau."

Thirty miles to the nearest gas station? Where the hell was he?

"But I can patch the tire for you if it's just a puncture. Not a chance I have a spare of the right size lying around for something that small."

Nathan didn't know how to answer that. Full or flat he knew. Puncture vs...what? He hoped for the former and just nodded his thanks to Doug.

"Lucy spooked you off the road?" Chelsea had a bright, merry laugh so he played it up. The saga of the mighty horns and the nostrils streaming with fire in the evening light. When he got to the part about the angel on the black-and-white horse, they all nodded.

"That'd be Julie up on her Clarence," Dee said.

"She loves that painted horse," Dum replied with a sad sigh that said he'd found no luck with its rider.

"*Really* loves that horse," Dee's sigh said that he too had failed there.

At least he now had her first name.

Thankfully no one pushed him about why he was here. There were some things he wasn't ready to explain to anyone, not even himself. Or how long he'd be staying, which was awfully polite of them—especially as he had nowhere else to go.

Instead the talk turned to the plans for the spring.

Apparently the cowgirl's ranch had cows, thousands of head of them. Mac and Ama had a horse ranch. They were a guest ranch, so fixing up and expanding the cabins before "the season" started really was a big priority.

"You have any carpentry skills?" Mac asked, then sighed when Nathan merely shook his head. "This spread lay dormant for years. Been a load of work knocking it into shape. Last year was the first we actually turned a profit. A whole lot of it is in hay. Still lease about a third of it as grazing land to Nils Larson across the road."

Larson. Julie Larson. Now he had both her names—though Nathan wasn't sure why he cared or what good it would do him.

There was also talk about a celebration dinner tonight. Before he even finished helping with the cleanup, Ama began cooking. She made it easy for him to pitch in.

"How many are you expecting?" Nathan asked as she hauled a gigantic roast out of the meat fridge.

Ama shrugged, "Most of the ranches hereabouts. It's coming up spring. People are tired of staying in." And that was pretty much all she had to say as they worked through the morning.

Julie had been on a winning streak all afternoon, no sign of city boy. Not even his car. As a bonus, the two cousins who looked like twins, Devin and Drake, were nowhere about, though she almost had them trained into treating her like a person. And Patrick—who she couldn't seem to train at all—was off on a supply run.

It had just been her and Mac all afternoon. He'd named the five cabins for the local trees: Douglas, Lodgepole, Larch, Ponderosa, and Aspen. They went through each one making notes. Douglas would just be a matter of fixing some blown shingles, and Larch had a cracked window. A fresh coat of paint on all of the doors and trim would make them feel well maintained, but the wood siding was left weathered to give the rustic, Montana Ranch experience. Ponderosa was a much bigger job; it was the oldest cabin and the bathroom predated the dinosaur bones that Jack Horner became famous for unearthing at nearby Egg Mountain.

Aspen was a little sweetheart of a cottage and had always been her favorite. It was off by itself a bit and sheltered by a small copse of aspen. It didn't need much work to merely be ready for guests, but with a little attention it could be a real showpiece. If it was hers she'd — There was a pointless train of thought. If she didn't get her business going she was going to be living on the Larson spread for the rest of her natural-born days.

The first guest wasn't booked for a month, so she had plenty of time to finish all this work herself. She'd fix up the easy ones right away so that Mac could take advantage if someone called in.

"It's the delay on the new cabins that worries me, Julie. I had twice the calls last season than I had the guest housing for."

Last fall they'd sited-in the plumbing and electrics, burying them deeply underground—well below the freeze and frost heave line. Mac had loved the excuse to give his backhoe a workout, but an early and hard storm had frozen the ground and stopped them before they could dig in the basements. That was a problem of a different scale. Their plans to start building atop the basements while the ground was still hard hadn't been possible.

"We need to get down deep and I don't have time for that now," Mac sat down in the clearing for the first cabin. They could probably dig now, there'd been enough warm weather. But even if they started today, it was too late. It would take a month of hard work to even get ready for the foundation pour; the cabins wouldn't be done until the fall. And that was only if she could find enough crew to hire on during the busy summer season. While she'd welcome the steady work, it wasn't going to help Mac at all.

Julie sat beside him, the grass crunching slightly after the chilly night—the remainder of last night's snow hadn't melted yet—and looked out at the land. It was an ideal setting. The main house was perched on the south side of a broad rise, sheltered from the hard northerlies that slammed down off the Arctic and the Canadian plains in the winters. Below, in a protected swale: horse barns, shops, lodging for the hands, and the foreman's house.

The guest cabins were upslope from the main ranch house, circling the crest of the rise. They had commanding views in every direction, yet were close by the main house for meals and evening activities. This new cluster was to be on the next rise, another hundred yards away from the others. They'd be for those guests who wanted the extra feel of privacy.

For a while they talked ideas back and forth.

Forget the frost heave and let the cabins "float" on heavy footings with adjustable jacks? It meant more maintenance every year. Cut in just two basements this year? That would leave those two cabins feeling remote and lonely, rather than adventurous in a group. Nowadays, with instant reviews up on travel websites, the experience had to be perfect, right from the beginning.

But for all his worry, Mac was easy with taking the time to just sit and chat about it. Her father would have mandated "get it done" and stomped down the slope, the same way he stomped down every obstacle that rose in his way. She didn't like how much she was like him in that respect, but no matter how she looked at this problem, she couldn't seem to bludgeon it into submission.

"Something will come to us. We don't have to solve this today."

"But—"

"No, Julie," Mac waved to encompass the landscape lying before them. "This isn't some battle scenario. Nobody dies if we don't solve it until tomorrow."

"Maybe not, but it feels that way. I've been thinking about this all winter. If we don't solve it today, it could be next winter before we do."

"No, it doesn't feel that way. Not really."

That's when she remembered his background. He'd been a Navy SEAL for twenty years.

And his son and daughter-in-law had spent nearly as long in the Army, a lot of it in Special Operations.

"You're looking forward to them coming here to live, aren't you?"

He nodded. "A father worries. Can't tell his wife or kid, because it's up to him to be the strong one. But trust me, he worries."

Julie wasn't so sure about that. Her father might worry some, but it would be about his cows first, his male children second, or maybe third after his standing in the community. Her mother next, and then she was somewhere far down on the list of things Nils Larson worried about.

"Yes, it will be good to have them home. Miss the grandkids, too. Having Mark and Emily fighting wildfires was bad. When they were in the Army before that, it was worse. I lost count of how many times they were shot down. Twice on national TV for Emily; once for Mark. Damned hard to watch, I don't mind admitting. At least to you. They will probably never tell me all the times it happened."

Julie looked out again at the view. The house and ranch buildings tucked safely below. The massive Front Range of the Rocky Mountains sweeping up out of the Great Plains in a grand gesture of towering rock. The fierce snow-covered mountains soared to the west and the limitless horizon of the grasslands to the east. Big cumulus were moving south out of Canada, one last snow or else a freezing rain. There wasn't a rancher who wouldn't prefer the snow—a chill rain killed animals far more quickly.

"It's such a beautiful place. I hope they love it here," Mac's voice was barely a whisper on the soft breeze.

Julie heard the new worry in his voice and felt foolish for her own petty concerns. Mac and his family had risked everything for their country. Risked and made it through to the other side.

What in the world had she ever done? Lived her entire life on a cattle ranch, scrabbling for the thin line that meant success each year and hating the struggle.

Off in the far distance, she saw a tiny plume of dust out near the horizon. Someone on the road.

"When are you expecting Mark and Emily?"

"Any time now."

"Then I think you'd better head on down to greet them," she pointed out the far-off blemish. A small cloud of dust rose way out along the line of the road in from Choteau.

Mac looked for a long moment. "You've good eyes, Julie. Notice detail. That's important. No wonder Emily likes you so much."

"Emily doesn't like me."

Mac simply smiled without quite facing her.

"You'd better get a move on, old man, if you're going to meet your son."

He nodded and rose to his feet, brushed himself off. Rather than teasing her back, he reached down and scrubbed the top of her hair to mess it up. "You'll find him, Julie."

"Find who?" She flipped her hair back into place with a shake of her head. She'd thought they were talking about Emily.

"*Him.* Trust me. You're too good a girl not to."

He started down the path.

"But I'm not looking for anyone," she finally told the big sky long after Mac passed the lower cabins.

Maybe his years in the Navy and then worrying about his son had made him some kind of a romantic.

She was a practical kind of woman. Had a business to get going and that required solving the problem of Mac Henderson's cabins. It was her company's first big job. If it didn't happen, then her company probably wasn't going to happen. Slinking back into the cattle ranch life was *not* an option. Landing once more in the role of the daughter who should marry another strong farm hand into the family was *absolutely not* going to happen.

But sometimes she would just watch Henderson's Ranch like she was now, or ride Clarence to the remote corner of her family's property where she could just see the main compound. She would sit and watch the comings and goings, or just listen to the meadowlarks as the cloud shadows slipped over the waving fields of hay. She never thought much about it, but just liked the way it looked.

Stan working with training his dogs.

Chelsea and the other three men tending the horses. Late in most afternoons of the spring through fall, Mac and Ama would take off riding. Their property ran almost twenty thousand acres and backed up against two million acres of the Flathead National Forest. They could ride a half dozen miles in a straight line west or south and not leave their property. Or plunge into the primitive area and not see a soul for weeks in any direction.

Soon they'd hire in the summer help. The horses were foaling and the tourists were coming, the ranch would be more than this crew could handle alone. Mark and Emily would be welcome assistance, even if it was only sitting around evening campfires and telling stories. Though they were such active people, it was hard to imagine them coming to any sort of a stop.

Julie looked at the storm rolling out of the north. It wouldn't be here until evening, but she'd best take Clarence back before then. It would be hammering across Larson land before it reached the Hendersons.

As she stood and began heading down the trail, someone came out of the back door of the main house. The kitchen was the closest part of the house to the barn buildings and the guest cabins—the working entrance to the big house.

In a second she knew who it was—clown-car boy. He looked about him as if he'd never seen the sky before. Montana's Big Sky did that to newcomers. Did it to her often enough and she'd grown up here.

Then he looked down from the heavens and spotted her. He gave a cheery wave. She wasn't close enough to see his easy smile, but knew it was there.

She raised her notebook in a "Howdy" gesture. Then she cut off the path and over the meadow, down toward the horse barn where she'd left Clarence napping in a stall.

His hand lowered uncertainly, making her feel bad.

"How hard would it be to be polite?" she asked an early crocus shoot that had fought its way through the hard soil.

She held her focus straight ahead.

Apparently too hard.

CHAPTER 3

The crowd was so thick that Nathan retreated to the kitchen. Actually he hadn't left it except for the occasional run at the sideboard groaning with food. The families and hands of all the ranches for miles around had come by. In addition to the monster roasts and dozen pies he and Ama had made, everyone brought a dish big enough to feed ten or more. They'd have excess food for days. Maybe that was the plan. Though his brief foray for seconds revealed that the crowd was able to inflict a serious amount of damage on the spread.

He had no reference for this. New York wasn't big on potlucks. Sometimes a group of chefs would go out together to try a new restaurant, then spend the evening confirming that it was no threat to any of their own, no matter how good it was. Other times they'd all gather in one chef or another's kitchen where they'd cook outrageous creations and old favorites, and drink until they could no longer stand up.

That was his circle of friends.

Friends?

Most of them would barely note that he was gone. "Did you hear about Nathan? Another one bites the dust." The only message on his phone during the whole drive out was from Estevan, and Nathan hadn't returned it because he had no idea what he'd say. When the nights were quiet and all that was left was the drinking, the two of them would talk about opening their own place together. Their menu, their way. Always a dream, never quite coming together.

Didn't seem to matter now.

This Montana potluck was so completely different from any of that. It was busy with talk of weather and cattle. Some women wore nice dresses, but others were dressed in jeans and denim or flannel shirts like most of the men. No one seemed to care one way or the other. Cowboy boots outnumbered everything else combined, by a fair margin—enough that he was actually self-conscious of his sneakers whenever he ventured out of the kitchen.

He hadn't even met the guests of honor yet, though he'd seen their arrival...at the same time Julie Larson had given him the polite version of "Go to hell and do it quickly." He'd known it was her the first instant—too far for any details, but he'd known.

Normally he could gear up and be gregarious enough to join any crowd, but when out filling his first plate, he'd seen Julie Larson. Her back had been to him, but he'd known it was her in the first instant— and not only because the setting sun was dazzling through the window behind her. She glowed. It was as if she had made a special deal with Mother Nature to always have a solar backdrop.

Apparently her idea of dressing up was changing her scuffed brown cowgirl boots to ones with pretty stitching around leather of red and gold. Her jeans were as worn as any high-fashion boutique could provide, a blue flannel shirt made her ramrod posture look soft, and her straight blond hair fell to the middle of her back like the smoothest fall of sunshine.

A whole cluster of cowboys was gathered close about her.

A glance around the room revealed that the redheaded Chelsea, just by her very nature, was also charming a whole circle of big ranch-hand types even as she was sitting beside her husband. Stan was nowhere to be found. Ama must be with her son...

The kitchen was his exclusive domain and his retreat.

It wasn't like him to hide away, but the quiet was comfortable. And there wouldn't be any uncomfortable questions about what he did for a living…nothing at the moment. Or what he was doing in Montana… he didn't have a clue. He could hear the buzz of the crowd beyond the door and pretend that it was a crowded dining room—a world separate from the kitchen. All he lacked were a sous chef, a grillardin, and the half dozen others necessary to make a dinner service. Mix in a clattering dishwasher and a small flock of waiters and he'd feel right at home.

Except he didn't feel at home there anymore—one of the many reasons he'd bolted from the city.

The echoing silence of the ranch kitchen was wrong as well. He shifted from the kitchen to the family dining table. And from there to one of the big wing-backed armchairs by the fire where he settled deep into the soft dark leather. Not being able to see the kitchen helped some. He wasn't all that far from retreating right out the back door to freeze in yet another Montana night.

Then he heard the door swing open and shut again followed by a deep sigh.

"Dear Lord above. Spare me from such men."

Julie Larson. It was a voice that had ingrained itself in his soul the minute she'd rescued him from the demon beast.

He should reveal himself, the wings of the big armchair blocked his view of the door, but after her brush-off of a simple friendly wave this afternoon, he remained hidden, hoping she'd leave quickly.

Nathan traced the track of her footsteps as her boot heels paced over to one fridge, then the other. After a long pause, they tromped toward him.

She plummeted into the next chair with a loud exclamation of, "Refuge. At long last."

"Perhaps I should go," he said softly to not startle her.

By Julie's squawk of surprise, he'd totally failed. She nearly lost the plate that held a big sandwich apparently scavenged from the refrigerator. And if she hadn't plunked the beer bottle down on the coffee table before she sat, she'd be wearing it.

"Sorry," he started to rise.

"City boy! You scared half a life out of me."

"Where's the other half?"

"I'm like a cat. Nine lives, and I'm trying to conserve them." It was a good thing she didn't smile, she was already far too pretty without it. The blue flannel accented her blue eyes. Seeing her without a horse, a monstrous cow, or a barbed wire fence, he could appreciate why she might need refuge. Up close she was even more stunning than his memory of her.

"I'm Nathan," he had to do something to break his own desire to stare at her. She was like a breath of fresh air. Chilly Montana air, but still incredible.

"Hi, Nathan. I'm Julie. You can stay as long as you promise not to act like you're a white knight, a shining prince, or a rutting cowhand."

"So I can *be* one as long as I don't act like it?"

She eyed him as she took a sip out of her beer bottle. "Let's see. I don't think that a white knight or a shining prince would be so scared of a cow as gentle as Lucy that he'd wave his little jack handle in the air."

"Which leaves me the category of 'rutting cowhand.' I'll pass."

"Good," she bit deeply into her sandwich. "Or I'd whack you with something a lot bigger than a car jack," she spoke around the mouthful.

"No food out there?"

"I couldn't get near it without some hoot-n-hollerer saying, 'Let me help you with that, Julie. I'll set you up a plate just the way you'd like it.' As you said—"

"You'll pass." Nathan slouched deeper in his chair and considered the fire while trying to think of the next thing to say. "Only cows I've met before have already been butchered. Those I know what to do with."

She managed a garbled exclamation around her next bite, but it sounded disbelieving.

"Very few unbutchered cows in Manhattan."

"Manhattan, like New York City? Why would you want to live there?"

Nathan decided that if he slouched any lower he'd be on the floor and his feet would be in the fire, but he couldn't find the energy to prop himself back up either. "Can we skip that question for now?"

"Okay." He could feel her looking at him. "I already know why you're here, so that shoots down the next question."

"You do?" He turned back to her and she was studying him with those impossibly blue eyes. Even at night by firelight they spoke of the sky. "I sure as hell don't."

"You're looking for something different. You told me so yourself, so I figure it must be true."

"I suppose." He had said that. He returned to his former slouch.

"New York and the Montana Front Range, couldn't get much more different than that."

"The Arctic," he mumbled just to be contrary.

"Sure, though in winter the temperature here is about the same. Make sure you're gone by September if you don't like the cold."

He shrugged. He didn't really expect to be here more than a few days to see Patrick. Though he didn't care much one way or the other about the weather. If the city scorched in a heat wave or bogged down under a foot of chill slush, it never affected him one way or the other.

"You've really never seen a cow?"

"At a distance out of a car window, but never up close and personal. Their horns don't look so big and dangerous when you're doing seventy down the interstate."

"Lucy's breed is called longhorns for a reason."

"Sure, for scaring the crap out of chefs. I think you bolted extra-large horns on her when you saw me coming."

"Right," that detail had slipped her mind. "I forgot Ama said you were a chef. You sure made a hit with your roast."

"Did you like it?"

"Couldn't get near the thing." She'd grown up on a farm and could skin a cow or butcher a hog as well as the next man, but wielding a knife on a roast was clearly beyond her. It had been a close thing, not taking her own knife to the Olsson brothers.

When he didn't offer to go get her some, Julie actually appreciated it. "You're not acting much like a city slicker."

"I'm not a city slicker. I'm a chef."

"You drive a fancy sports car."

"Not very. It's Japanese, not a Porsche or a Ferrari or anything. It's cheaper than a truck."

"Not mine." Her business couldn't afford a decent truck and there wasn't a chance that she'd ask Dad for the use of one of the farm's vehicles to get her business going. She'd scraped up enough for a 1959 Ford F-250, which was a whole lot of rust from being a classic. But it was all hers right down to the last worn ring and gasket leak. If she could just solve Henderson's cabin problem, maybe she'd have enough cash to rebuild the engine. She only needed a couple hundred bucks in parts and a week of peace and quiet—though not a chance that was going to happen this side of winter.

He shrugged again.

"Why are you hiding in here?"

"Tired I guess. I practically drove straight through to get here."

There was something more than that. Julie had no idea why she wanted to pry—she'd spent her whole evening trying to avoid men— but she was curious. Drove straight through? As if something had been after him.

"Why—"

"Sanctuary!" Someone cried out as she entered the kitchen.

Julie leaned out of the chair far enough to see Emily Beale leaning with her back against the door as if she could bar anyone else from following. She had her newborn cradled in one arm, though there was no sign of her three-year-old girl.

"Hey, Emily." The woman unnerved her, but not enough to deny her an escape. "You're safe enough in here. What are *you* escaping from?"

Emily hit the fridge. "I would kill for a beer, but I don't need a drunk newborn." She came over carrying a ginger ale, but didn't seem to know what to do with Belle. As if even her own child was too much to handle at the moment.

Julie reached out and took her; she was fast asleep and too cute for words. Just a few months old, it was easy to see that she'd gotten her mother's delicate features. Only time would tell if she'd take on her mother's incredible strength of character as well.

"Thanks," Emily sighed as she dropped down on a couch.

"Too many people! I know five and there must be a hundred out there. They all think that my sole value is that I've made two babies. And conversations! I haven't had to talk that much in a year. Is he safe?" She nodded toward Nathan.

"Not sure yet. Are you safe?" Julie couldn't resist prodding him. She enjoyed babies, and this one was a sweetheart—at least while she was asleep. It would be a long time before she had any but if she did, she'd gladly take one like this.

"Me?" Nathan looked back and forth between them. "Do you think I'm dumb enough to take on two dangerous blondes? Is the kid blond? That makes three. Ama told me you're a warrior," he nodded to Emily, then turned to her. "And I've already seen you ride down a *longhorn* hell-beast—"

"He met Lucy on the road last night," Julie filled in with a mock-panicked look that stung even more than an eye roll.

"Not a chance I'm going to tangle with any of you," Nathan concluded. "The kid could probably throw me down already since she's yours."

"I've met Lucy," Emily shuddered. "Never seen anything look so big in my life. Mark had taken me out to a fishing stream one of my first times on the ranch. I was sitting there not hurting a fly, just reading a book. Then this huge cow came out of nowhere and tried to eat my straw hat while I was still wearing it. My scream spooked Mark face-first into the stream—didn't seem to bother Lucy a bit."

Julie laughed. "Hard to imagine anything scaring you."

"I'm not some superwoman. Just an Army pilot now retired. I grew up in Washington, DC. Very few giant cows except in the Capitol Building."

"Ask her what she hasn't done," Julie prompted him. "Go on. Ask her."

Nathan blinked at Julie, feeling no sharper than a cow. He was still trying to get over the two women sitting with him. Both were tall, blond, fit, and couldn't be more different if they tried.

Emily Beale looked the warrior. Narrow face, jewel-blue eyes, and her hair sliced sharply at her jawline. She wore a black turtleneck, a fleece vest, and khakis with sneakers. Julie's hair was a lighter shade that fell well past her shoulders in a soft flow emphasizing her open face. The blue flannel shirt accented her sky-blue eyes and the worn jeans that he'd admired earlier were no less admirable up close. Her fancy-stitched cowboy boots really were nice work. It was the first time he'd ever seen cowboy boots that made sense—in New York they'd always looked incongruously ridiculous worn with skin-tight leggings by the city's trenders.

He didn't know what to make of Julie cradling a baby. She made it look like the most natural thing, whereas he'd never really seen one from so close before. Patrons of high-end restaurants hired babysitters. A few of his staff had reproduced over the years, a very few, and the babies were rarely more than a briefly flashed photo on a phone's screen that always seemed to blank to black the moment it reached him.

Again he was staring as he tried to puzzle her out. Had to stop that, at least the staring part, no matter how pretty she was.

"Okay," Nathan forced himself up straighter and faced Emily. "What haven't you done?"

Emily rolled her eyes as Julie answered for her.

"She was a military helicopter pilot for some secret Special Operation types—the first woman ever. And a major, too, which is awfully high up. Then she led a fleet of the best heli-aviation firefighting helicopter pilots around. I know they're the best because they stopped a monster wildfire from escaping the primitive area and overrunning all the ranches hereabouts. She has a gorgeous husband—"

"I do," Emily admitted finally.

"—and two of the cutest girls you can imagine," Julie actually cooed at the one sleeping in her arms. "She makes me feel inadequate just by walking into the room."

"I do?" That had Emily sitting up. "No I don't."

Nathan didn't know whether to mediate or to egg them on and see where it led.

"You sure do," Julie insisted.

"This from a woman who can herd cattle, has won a string of state rodeo ribbons, drives a combine, and rebuilds tractors when they act up."

"That's just ranch stuff," Julie protested around the last of her sandwich.

"Can't do a one of them," Emily tipped her soda in a salute.

"I can cook," Nathan put in his grand bid for fame, but couldn't think of anything else to add.

"That roast was you? What did you do to it?" Emily redirected her bottle toward the dining room.

"Nothing fancy, just lending a hand."

He saw Julie eyeing the door, but he understood the issue. "I could use some more. Anyone else want something from the spread?"

Julie eyed him now like she didn't trust his motivations, which was a good bet. He didn't want someone else snagging her attention. In addition to her beauty, she was also skilled and dryly funny. He had a weak spot for funny.

He took her indifferent shrug as a yes.

Most everyone had migrated out to the great room, leaving the dining room empty except for a couple of hands obviously going for fourths. No one paid him any mind as he loaded a platter with several slices of roast and a nice-looking beet salad. He filled another with three different slices of pie: rhubarb, apple, and one he wasn't sure of, but the crust looked golden and flaky.

The three of them ruled their corner of the kitchen until well into the night.

It was the first thing in Nathan's life that had made sense in months.

Julie stood out on the porch, surveyed the empty driveway, and wondered who she needed to kill: Dad or her three brothers? Marooned.

By the time the Henderson's hands began bringing plates back into the kitchen, she'd learned a lot more about Emily and decided that maybe she could like her even though she became more daunting rather than less with each story.

Nathan had continued to be surprisingly tolerable as a fireside companion. His depth of cluelessness about Montana was so awesome that she wondered how he'd survived the trip from the barn, never mind Choteau. It was like he'd found the fourth largest state in the nation by stubbing his toe on Wyoming and landing in Montana face-first.

Beyond that he'd spoken plenty but said little. He was the one who had teased stories out of Emily and, now that she thought about it, out of her.

It was only as she had followed Nathan to lend a hand with the cleanup that she realized she still knew little more than he was a New York chef and his little brother Patrick was a pain in the ass. She knew that herself. Patrick was a nice enough guy, but he was *so* full of himself—even more than most locals. And he was always trying to find a line on her.

A New Yorker turned ranch hand was not what she wanted, no matter how painfully persistent. What did she want? *That* was a mystery that eluded her with even more skill than Lucy.

Now, she was out on the porch. It was pitch dark. Well below freezing. And *both* of the family trucks were gone. The storm that had threatened this afternoon had passed through quickly and left a veneer of white snow on everything. Already the clouds were shred-ding enough to reveal the starry sky—the temperature would still be headed down. It would be a very slippery walk in leather soles unless she cut across the rough pastures in the dark.

"Something wrong?" Nathan stepped out onto the porch behind her. He wore only a light turtleneck. He hadn't lied about not caring about the cold; he didn't even ram his hands into his pockets.

He wasn't startlingly handsome; she kept expecting that from him, but he wasn't. He was average height and build, his brown hair seemed tousled by its very nature. His face would have been plain without the easy smile that reached his eyes most every time. The only really exceptional thing about him was his hands. She could see the chef in them whether he was offering her a choice of pie or picking up a beer bottle. They weren't rancher weather-beaten, but they were strong and callused—even if it was in ways she didn't recognize. They implied that he worked long and hard at his cooking.

She'd never seen that before. Ma cooked. Ama did too. But that roast had been different somehow, as if she'd never really tasted beef before. There were cowhands and there were real, honest, born-to-the-saddle cowboys. There were cooks and there were…whatever Nathan was.

"Thinking mighty hard on something, Julie," Nathan's comment brought her back to the present and the complete lack of any vehicles parked in the Henderson's driveway.

"I'm going to jail tomorrow for killing a family member. Nothing new," she turned back to the night in order to not think about how nice Nathan looked. He looked…normal, in a way no ranch hand ever did. Not with some "get the gal" agenda. Not with an ego saying "look at how impressive I am." He was just…Nathan.

He looked out at the empty driveway, "No car." He also wasn't slow.

"No truck actually, but same result. Going to be a long cold walk, and then I'm going to kill someone with my bare hands." She flipping up the collar of her sheepskin jacket.

"How far?"

"Three miles by the road, two by the pasture."

He held up a finger telling her to wait and went inside. He was back a moment later in a heavy jacket and a woolen hat. "Ride or walk?" He held up both car keys and a flashlight.

She almost called his bluff, then decided maybe it wasn't. "Do you even know how to drive on snow, city boy?"

"Sure, you take the subway. Easy-peasy." He appeared to be serious, but his eyes gave him away.

If she had her work boots, she'd walk and see if he was for real. Instead she looked around, "Don't see a car either."

"It's in the garage…" he tapered off as he looked about the farm. "At least that's what Doug said. Any guesses on which building that is?"

"That thing you said about not being a shining knight…"

"Tell me about it," Nathan sighed a big plume of cold air. "Actually don't. I've known it for years." He made it easy to share a smile.

"The Hendersons have a couple of garages," she led the way off the porch and into the darkness.

The family garage had a couple of pickups, including Mark and Emily's, which was robin's egg blue. According to Emily, Mark had mounted a major campaign to repaint it black and, for that reason alone, Emily had said she was having none of it. "He thinks he's still Mr. Macho Military, not the guy who agreed to be the fishing guide for his dad. I have to retrain him on that. Not much hope, but I do what I can."

When Nathan had asked why he wasn't leading hunting parties, she'd said that they'd both seen enough blood to last a lifetime, which had silenced their conversation long enough for the fire to need tending. Julie had had to tell him how to do that as Belle was still asleep in her lap and Emily had no more of a clue than he did.

Nathan's sports car wasn't in the equipment bay either. It was funny to watch his eyes bug out. The Hendersons weren't farmers, except for a big kitchen garden, so mostly it was just a hay mower and rake, a baler, and several work trucks. He looked at them as if they were alien spacecraft. The ranch's helicopter and a small cluster of ATVs were parked down at the end.

She knew that Doug's garage didn't have space except for his own truck, which left her wondering if she was going to be walking home after all.

"It seems unlikely, but let's check," she led him through a door into the main horse barn. "God but I love this smell." It was hay and horse and leather. The Hendersons were doing some horse breeding, but most of it was lessons and guest rides.

"Really?" Nathan rubbed at his nose with the back of a glove. "It smells…horsey."

"You thought pretty horses were going to stink like cattle?"

"Cattle stink?"

"You have no idea." Actually, he probably didn't. Most of the horses were asleep, but a few stuck their heads out over stall doors to inspect them as they walked by.

Parked in the last stall at the end, complete with a rope halter fashioned around one of the tires, sat his little car.

When Julie stopped laughing, she helped him get it out of the barn. Not wanting to pump exhaust into the horse's faces, they pushed it out of the stall and back up the long central aisle of the barn. Now all of the horses were awake. They looked out of the stalls, nickering and snorting between themselves as if his car was the funniest thing they'd seen in a month of Sundays.

"I'm guessing that my next move would be to pay Doug back somehow," Nathan tapped on the brake when they reached the main door.

"Absolutely pay him back," Julie started laughing again.

"Any suggestions?"

"Pepper in his shorts? I'm sure Chelsea would be glad to help you out there."

"I'll have to remember that you have a low sense of humor, Julie Larson."

"I'll take that as a compliment." She slid the main barn door sideways and he gave the car a final nudge out into the chill darkness of the barnyard.

With the top up, they were suddenly very close together. The smell of horse lingered until the heater finally kicked in. Then a richer but gentler scent filled the car.

"You smell like Montana." Nathan knew that he should have kept his mouth shut, but he hadn't been this close to her before. Practically shoulder to shoulder in the car, she seemed to fill the space.

"I what?"

"Fresh and, I don't know, spring-like?"

"Keep your nose to yourself, buster."

"Not much choice. It came attached as standard equipment at birth."

Julie glared at him for a moment—which seemed to be her standard expression for covering a laugh—then pointed down the driveway. "Left at the end."

Nathan eased down the driveway. There were a dozen sets of tire tracks through the snow. He'd heard the secret to driving on snow was no sudden moves, so he stayed in first gear.

"Walking would be faster."

"I put the car in a ditch and you'll get that option." He'd been half hoping that she'd opt for the walk. It would be worth facing the cold to walk with her. Emily had led a fascinating life, but it was Julie's stories that had really captivated him. She'd slowly painted a picture of a day-to-day life like none he'd ever imagined. She almost made him want to learn to ride a horse just by the way she described it.

She didn't say anything during the short drive. He gained enough confidence to shift up to second, which had him arriving at her front gate far too soon.

"Double-L?" Nathan looked at the big arch over the driveway.

"Founded by Lars Larson a hundred and fifty years ago. Thanks, Nathan. Here's fine. I'll just hop the gate and walk up to the house.

Besides, it looks like Lucy escaped again and I don't want to force you to face the 'demon beast'."

In the glow of the headlights, he could see the cow watching him through the gate. She didn't look one bit smaller than she had last night. He could only see the house beyond as a vague, dark outline against the starry sky.

"Do you have your keys?"

"My keys?"

"To unlock the door?"

Julie gave him a puzzled look. "Why would we lock the door out here?"

Nathan didn't have a good answer to that one. His apartment door in New York had had three locks—deadbolt, door handle, and jammer—and that was inside a secure building.

"So you're okay from here?"

Julie looked at him for a long moment. He really could smell her, like the promise of spring.

Then, without any words, she leaned toward him and kissed him lightly. "Don't read anything into that. You're just a good guy." Then she was gone.

He watched as she climbed over the gate rather than swing it open. Her long legs and fine physique were caught for only a moment in his headlights before she crossed over.

Through the slats, he saw her pat Lucy the death cow on the flat spot between her eyes before heading toward the house. The last he saw of her was a quick wave and his headlights catching a flash of her bright blond hair.

He drove back to the ranch just as slowly, not because of the snow, but because he wanted to imagine Julie still sitting beside him.

Julie had the Douglas cabin fixed up by midday. The winter had been kind to this one and it would have to be a little warmer before she could paint. It was warm enough that last night's snow had melted and she was able to work in a light jacket, but not a chance that paint would set up properly.

She had the measurements for the new window for Larch called into town, which she would pick up over the weekend. Harvey promised to throw it in his pickup on Sunday, and she'd transfer it over at church.

Aspen would be the last one she'd work on. It didn't really need much, but she didn't think that Mac would complain if she spent a day or two sprucing it up. She wanted to hold off on it as a treat to herself.

Ponderosa. Just like the tree, this one was going to be a *big* problem. She spent a grim hour pulling out bathroom fixtures. The sink had a bad crack. The toilet definitely had to go. Yanking that revealed rotten flooring. The monstrous clawfoot tub had punched one leg down through another board because a hundred years ago no one had thought to place a support under where the heavy iron feet landed. It was not one of those charming old tubs that leant character. It was a big, ugly, heavy lump. Even in summer, no amount of hot water would make the cast iron comfortable to sit against.

Mac had taken very little convincing to replace it, but now she had to get it out of here. She could either cut out the side wall, cut down a couple of trees that were in the way, leverage it onto her pickup, and turn it into a water trough somewhere, or she could bust it up in place and haul it to the landfill.

"Sledgehammer, definitely."

In a minute she was back with a sledge, dust mask, goggles, and kitted up in heavy leather chaps and jacket. Busting up cast iron was nasty work.

Julie raised her big twelve pounder and gave it a hard swing. It bounced off the side of the thick tub. On the fourth swing, it finally did what cast iron does—it didn't crack, it shattered. A one-by-two-foot chunk broke free and slammed into the open door, missing her shins by inches and making a deep gouge in the doorframe she'd now have to fix as well. That would have hurt despite the leather.

There was a yelp of surprise close behind her.

She spun around to see Nathan Gallagher standing in the doorway, his eyes wide with shock as he inspected the chunk of tub mere inches from his toes.

"What in the world are you doing?" He eyed the sledge that she'd swung up to rest on her shoulder.

"Breaking up a bathtub."

"You look dangerous as all get out."

"Normally I only pummel on something that ticks me off."

"Remind me to never do that."

"Deal. What are you doing here?"

He held up a cloth sack. "Lunch. When you didn't come down to the main house, Ama worried."

"I was supposed to...?" Of course she was. On a ranch you fed everyone working on the property.

Nathan looked past her at the mess of the Ponderosa bathroom. "This looks ugly. You need a break. It's sunny and almost pretending to be warm on the front porch."

She really wanted to keep moving on the project, but it was hard to resist Nathan when he was in one of his coaxing modes, as she'd learned last night. Actually, he was quite charming about it. A shining prince was supposed to be tall, strapping, and blond. Nathan was her height, comfortably built, and had medium brown hair with eyes to match. But giving her the ride home, asking after her keys instead of just dropping her off or making a grab for her, and now bringing her lunch, he was definitely delivering on the charming.

Before she knew quite what was happening, they were out on the porch swing, looking down over the ranch. The chains creaked annoyingly at the first rock. She eyed them and saw that one of the eyebolts was wearing out. She made a mental note to replace that.

"I wasn't sure what you wanted, but you opted for a sandwich yesterday, so I went with that. Did you get inside okay?"

Julie opened the cloth bag he handed her, but had to take off her goggles and mask to look down into it. After shedding her leather gloves, she pulled out a monstrous sandwich. Not a bit of *a woman should only eat a dainty amount* from Nathan. This was a feast on a bun for someone who'd been burning calories all morning. Still in the bag was a can of pop and a plastic bag of—

"What's wrong with the potato chips?"

"Nothing. They're homemade."

"You know how to make potato chips?"

He shrugged as if such magic was nothing.

She tried one. Thick, crunchy, and heavy on the salt with just a hint of something spicy. Several more followed the first before she recalled the sandwich in her hand. Julie bit in and sighed: last night's roast, thick brown mustard, winter spinach, and pepper jack cheese.

"This is so good," she took a second bite before answering his question. "I got home fine, but you were right, I needed my keys."

"You did? Now I feel awful for leaving." He actually sounded upset, as if he could have helped.

"My brothers aren't the smartest cattle on the ranch. They locked the doors to prank me, but Mark and Luke left their window unlocked. They're both sound sleepers…until I dumped a five-gallon bucket of snow all over them." Their shouts had woken the entire household, but she'd slipped back out the window before they found the light switch and climbed up the outside of the porch into her own second-story room without anyone else the wiser. She'd locked both her window and the door to prevent retaliation.

Nathan's easy laugh had her smiling back at him. "Promise you'll never teach your vengeful tricks to Patrick. I'm the only brother he's got and I'd rather not wake up with snow in my bed."

"You make me another meal or two like this and you have a deal." Julie wondered just what he did like in his bed and then was aghast at her own thought. She went back to eating her wonderful sandwich.

"Done. You say when and I'll gladly cook for you."

Nathan couldn't stop smiling as he watched Julie eating his food with such obvious pleasure. He couldn't remember the last time he'd simply watched someone eat his food. He liked the kind of deals he was making with Julie. They were easy, comfortable. They didn't feel like the *quid pro quo* of the infinite tally sheet of the city. *Sure I can lend you an extra eight lobsters, but you'll owe me ten back.* He always knew who he'd borrowed what from and what favors were outstanding when— Nathan wasn't missing that at all.

He also liked that she made no affectations about who she was. There wasn't a woman in Manhattan that wouldn't have checked her hair or brushed at her jeans if caught in mid-project the way he'd caught Julie—as if the city women he'd met would ever tackle such a thing. Instead, she'd been completely unapologetic about the mess she was. She sat there like a leather-clad warrior and not the sexy, Xena Warrior Princess kind. Julie looked impossibly real in her working gear.

This is who I am, deal with it.

And he was good with that. She had such a refreshing honesty. "I like that you don't play games."

"Sure I do. Wait. What kind of games?"

"Passive aggressive-ego manipulating kind of games."

"What would those be?"

At first he thought she was joking, but maybe not. "Saying one thing. Meaning another."

"Give me an example."

"Last night when you kissed me," and then he wished he'd started anywhere else. It had been a means-nothing kiss of thanks that had cost him half a night's sleep.

"I told you not to read anything into it. I just..." and then she shrugged as if she wasn't sure what she just...

"I'm not. That's my point. I mean, sure I'd like to kiss you again and do it like we meant it. But you meant it as a thanks and then you made sure that I knew that's all it was and that it wasn't a come-on or a tease or any kind of a future promise, it was just a friendly kiss and Christ but I'm babbling. Shutting up now."

She ate a couple more of the potato chips he'd made specially for her. "No. I don't play those kinds of games. Half the ranch sons around here think I do, but I don't. The other half think I'm a stuck up witch just because if I say no, I mean it."

"Same thing when you say yes?"

She nodded.

"Damn, I could really get to like you, lady."

"Don't!"

"Why not?"

"Because at some point you're going to go back to your big city. I'm not a country-girl-for-a-fling sort."

"Never thought you were," Nathan couldn't imagine anything further from who she was. But she was right about him going...even if he didn't know where. "You strike me more as the one with the club."

"The club?"

"Conk the man over the head and drag him back to your cave?" He could imagine her very easily in the role—right down to the leopard skin dress that she'd killed and cut herself.

"Might be," she nodded as she finished her sandwich, then chips, then soda in methodical order.

"Well, there's an image for me."

"If you're picturing me in animal skins—" she left the threat hanging.

"Bet you'd look good in them," but he was unable to avoid the blush at being caught.

"Be glad the snow already melted or you just might find a bucketful down your shorts. Cool down, city boy."

"Yes, ma'am," Nathan offered his soberest tone, then decided his libido needed a subject change. "What are you working on?"

"Fixing up these cabins for guests. First ones will be here end of month. Mac hired my company to fix windows, replace a bathroom, things like that."

"You own a construction company? Emily was right, you *can* do anything."

She was shaking her head. "I can't fix the problem with the cabins we started construction on last fall."

"What problem?"

In minutes, she'd shed most of her leather protection and was leading him past the cabins and up the hill in a light jacket and worn jeans that he was starting to think of as one of her trademarks. It was a trademark that, on her fine figure, he wholly approved of.

He looked around for a distraction just as they were passing the last older cabin in the row.

"Hey, I like this one."

"It's my favorite. Its name is Aspen."

He didn't know exactly why he liked it. There was just something about it. It looked…cozier than the others. It was two stories, set into the side of the hill. The only one with a porch on both floors.

"It's solidly enough built to ride out the winter without trouble and it's tucked in a nice little shelter of its namesake trees. I also like the proportions. Come inside, it gets even better." She looked a little surprised at her own suggestion, but he followed.

The cabin was a single room deep. Either side of the main door was a living room and kitchen/dining room. Up the heavy-tread stairs was a pair of snug bedrooms and a small office, all facing the southern view. It was done in the same style as the ranch house: heavy timber beams and hardwood floors. But that was where the similarities stopped. It was cozy rather than majestic. The layout was for three or four people (plus a few sleeper couches for extra guests), but not forty.

After the tour, he gravitated back to the kitchen. It would take very little to make it an ideal space for testing new dishes or cooking for a family. He'd add an island with an extra sink and maybe a wok burner. Enough width for a couple of stools at the island so that stormy-day meals could be eaten at the counter while looking out the big windows.

"I love this place," Julie's voice was unexpectedly soft.

"It's easy to imagine you here." And it was. Her beloved Montana out the front door, but safe and warm within. Horse barns only a few hundred yards below.

"What about you? Can you imagine yourself here?"

Julie was aghast at her own question.

She could picture Nathan here. Right here. Beside her.

That simply wasn't possible.

He leaned on the sink counter and stared out the window for a long time.

Unable to retract her question, her only choice was to wait.

"I don't know what I want anymore," his voice was rough; harsh in a way she wouldn't have thought him capable of.

"Something different?" Julie prompted him when he again fell silent.

"All I know is that I don't want what I had. I'm almost thirty. I had an executive chef position at a top restaurant called Vite. It means 'breeze' in French—not like a wind, but like an easy motion. Could have had my own restaurant in another year or two. Guess that I could have a couple years ago, but for some reason never got around to it." Then he looked down at the sink and appeared to be holding onto the edge with both hands as hard as he could.

She wanted to apologize for asking. For breaking whatever shield of lightness that he'd been projecting. She had the sudden suspicion that his problems were far worse than her own.

"I've done nothing but been a chef for over a dozen years. And then one day, I was making my eight millionth *steak au poivre* with a side of tiger prawn-stuffed mushrooms and it was all so meaningless. I finished the dinner service, packed my knives and my car, left a note for my landlord, and hit the road by two a.m. Slept a night outside Chicago in a goddamn yurt in some screwed-up kind of hippie motel along the interstate. Now I'm here and I'll be damned if I know why."

Something tugged at Julie, made her want to go to him, but she didn't know what she'd do if she went. Consoling a horse was one thing. Consoling a man? She didn't have a clue.

"Sorry," he stood up and wiped a hand down his face as if brushing off his past. "My shit. Shouldn't be making you wallow in it. Let's go see your new cabins." And he was out the door before she could think what to say.

He was well up the trail by the time she caught up with him.

"Nathan, I—"

"No. Don't say anything. You're right. I'm probably going back to the city someday. I don't know why I would, but it's where I've always been. And I sure as hell can't imagine myself anywhere else, though I keep trying." Then he stopped so suddenly that she almost ran into him, and he took a deep breath. "I *can* see why you might love this though. There's nothing here and it goes on forever. It's like there's no pressure."

"No pressure?" Julie practically screamed at him in her own shock. "My entire company, getting out of my psychotic house, depends on this working. Do you think I want to live with my father and three brothers the rest of my life?"

He turned and blinked at her in surprise.

Julie wanted to pound a fist into his smug face.

Except it wasn't smug.

Instead it had that worried look again, like when he was asking if she'd be okay getting home fifty paces from the house she'd grown up in.

"You're right," he said in a tone of apology. "I don't know anything about living out here or what you're dealing with. I'm just a lost city boy. Sorry."

And he looked doubly sad.

Julie searched for some calm and wasn't having much luck. This *had* to work. She'd never had so much riding on a single problem. If she could beat the basements into the ground with her fists, she'd do it.

"Sorry," he shrugged an uncomfortable apology. "Maybe we'll get together and have a mutual whining session about it some time."

She felt the bile knot up in her stomach at even the thought of failure.

"Or maybe not."

Her expression must have been dire for him to be backpedaling so fast.

"For now, tell me about your cabins."

Julie managed to rein in her fears and worries. This must be how Nathan felt only moments ago, holding on to that sink for dear life.

He retreated a step and she felt bad for it.

"I get it now. My shit. Shouldn't be making you wallow in it." Her simple repetition of what he'd said brought a soft smile of understanding to his face.

He brushed a warm finger down her cold cheek as if signing a pact between them to set all that aside for the moment. The gesture was both surprisingly intimate and infinitely kind.

The combination took her breath away for a moment.

"Where are these cabins?"

"You're standing in one."

He looked down at his feet in puzzlement and then back at her.

"Snowberry, Ninebark, Wood's Rose, Beargrass, and Meadowrue," she pointed as she named them. "The downslope cabins are the trees. This cluster are to be named for the bushes and grasses."

"Still not really seeing it, Julie."

She sighed and looked at the grassy slope. "Neither am I. That's the problem. An early freeze last fall meant that we didn't get the basements cut into the soil before the ground froze too hard."

"The ground freezes basement deep here? Patrick said it got cold, but I never thought he meant that cold."

"It can freeze down a couple of feet. We have to go down to five or six to avoid frost heave. But if I build the basements starting now..." she struggled against the ill feeling.

"There won't be any way to get the cabins built by summer for them to pay for themselves," Nathan finished with deep insight. "Don't look so surprised. I've run a number of different restaurants. I know how to run a business."

Julie sighed and sat down on the grass—and regretted it immediately. The snow had melted, but the ground was still too frozen for the water to go very far. Her butt was instantly soaked.

"Don't!" But Nathan had already landed beside her.

"Thanks for the too-late warning, cowgirl."

"Anything for a friend, city boy."

"So, since neither of us is smart enough to stand back up..."

"Yep."

"What if you didn't dig the basements?"

"The buildings would tend to shift around. Buildings don't like that."

"Big pilings?"

Julie tried to picture it. Pilings would probably take more concrete than a basement, but there would be savings in the digging. Could run the utilities up in an insulated box. And the cabins had no use for a basement except as a support. "Maybe..."

"Can you do that and still have time to build the cabins?"

"Not even with a crew." So much for hope.

"What about those temporary things?"

"Tents?"

"No, yurts. It didn't look as if there was much to those."

"Yurts?"

"Sure. Like that one I stayed in outside Chicago. They were mighty proud of it; told me that state parks are using them all over the place. Little ones, big ones. It was kind of nice, once I got over the strangeness of it. I liked the domed skylight and all of the wood lattice work inside. I don't know anything about yurts or building, but it looked like the only built structure was a circular deck for a floor."

"Would they survive a winter?" Julie was liking this idea. Liking the glimmer of hope even more. A cluster of yurts could really be attractive here. She'd put down some extra pilings for outside decks to open up the view of the ranch. From up here she could even see Larson's Double-L Ranch and was surprised that at enough distance, even it looked picturesque. Far more importantly, pilings and yurts could be fast.

"Do you need them for guests in the winter?"

"Winter guests are rare, but—" And then she saw it. If they went up fast, it meant they'd also go down fast. Up in the spring, down in the fall. Drain the utilities and leave the decks in place. Maybe with a protective cover.

Julie grabbed onto his arm. Hard. She was far stronger even than she appeared.

Nathan could see her thoughts were churning. "More adventurous than the cabins. 'Stay in a yurt on the Montana Front Range.' It even sounds adventurous."

"And you could upgrade them to cabins later, then shift the yurts into another section as the place grows. Could even do a communal bath and showers like a campground so there's only one set of utilities to put in this spring. Microwaves and water coolers in the cabins."

She began shaking him back and forth by her grasp on his arm.

"I take it you like the idea."

"Like it? Like it! That could actually work. You're brilliant."

"No, I just passed out in one near Chicago is all."

"Cut it out," she shook him again. "This is good. I've got to go run some numbers. I have to find Mac. This could really do it."

Nathan liked how she looked when she was excited. There was more than beauty, there was joy, and it looked really good on her. He hoped that it worked out.

"You're a lifesaver!"

"Great!" Her change in mood was incredible. It was easy to feel swept up in it. "Do I get a prize?"

"Sure!" She let go of his arm, grabbed him by the lapels of his jacket, and pulled him into a hard kiss.

His thigh squished into the cold mud as he rocked toward her.

She didn't just make it a short, hard smack. In moments she was leaning into it as hard as he was. He got a hand around her back, though he wasn't sure which of them he was steadying, and gave back as good as he was getting. As with everything else she did, when Julie Larson kissed him, he knew that, by god, he was being kissed.

Then between one instant and the next, she leapt from his arms up onto her feet.

He was far too dazed to follow.

"I've got to go," she started off, displaying a perfect muddy imprint on her butt.

"Hey, cowgirl!"

"What?" She stopped ten feet away and turned back to him. Her dazzling blue eyes, her blond hair caught in the light breeze, her unthinking stance of grace and power: she looked like a miracle.

"I just want you to know," he'd meant to make it a question, but that wasn't how it was coming out. "I am absolutely going to be reading something into that kiss."

"Why?" A look of uncertainty slid across her face.

"Because it was absolutely lethal. That's why."

"Lethal, huh?" Her smile lit her up brighter than the sun playing across her hair. "I like the sound of that."

And then she was gone, practically skipping down the hill.

CHAPTER 5

Nathan sat in the chill mud with the taste of spring and brown mustard on his tongue.

He'd had his share of lovers over the years.

The ones who weren't chefs never lasted through the maddening hours that consumed his life.

The ones who were chefs never lasted through the maddening hours that consumed *both* their lives. Or the job would tear them apart: competition, opportunity elsewhere, there was always something. For a while he'd been screwing a sous chef fast and hard in the walk-in refrigerator. There was a fantastic synergy when they cooked together and it was the only bit of privacy where they could burn off the mid-dinner-service heat that consumed them in a flambé-towering burst. There was a hostess-floor manager who he'd had every night for months, but only in the back booth of Vite after everyone else had gone home. Then Nathan had learned that she had a husband—when he came to the restaurant with some business partners and wanted to meet the chef he'd heard so much about. That was the end of that lifestyle.

For the last year since then, he had cooked. He had just put his head down and worked.

And now he had a wet butt and had been kissed in a Montana field by the poster girl for wholesome blonde.

What the hell?

As Julie hurried down the trail, Nathan spotted a big truck that had just pulled up into the main yard by the barn. The driver climbed down and tried to slow Julie's passage, but she blew right by him.

Despite the cowboy hat, Nathan knew his walk as well as he knew his own.

"Patrick!" His shout must have carried down the slope because the big tall cowboy turned to look and then waved both arms.

Nathan hurried down across the meadow, following far less nimbly in Julie's path.

They slammed into each other and pounded one another on the back.

"Is it the apocalypse?"

Nathan looked up at his brother. He himself wasn't short, but Patrick took after their dad, both of them hitting six-three. "Apocalypse?"

"It must be for you to just up and leave New York. I was bettin' on that happening this side of never." Patrick had picked up a cowboy twang that sounded unnatural compared with the other people Nathan had met here, even more unnatural considering his Suffolk County, Long Island upbringing.

"Maybe it was." A personal apocalypse would explain a lot. "Honestly I still don't know what happened. One moment I was cooking in a top Manhattan restaurant and forty-eight hours later I was eating Ama's stew."

"And kissing granite lady."

"Who?"

"Granite lady. Julie Larson: stone hard, stone cold."

Nathan would never apply any of those adjectives to her.

Patrick sat back on the big truck's bumper and leaned back against the front grill. "You sayin' that you wasn't just kissin' Julie?"

"I'm thinking that's between the lady and me."

"Crap, Nathan. You're such a stick in the mud. Is that what it takes to get to her? She won't give me the goddamn time of day, though the lord knows I try some fair bit. I'm gone for a couple days and you're all over her."

"I'm not all over her." He sat down on the bumper beside his brother.

"I just can't believe you'd cut me out like that."

"Cut you out? I'm not cutting anybody out."

"You kissin' Julie Larson is gonna piss off a whole lot of boys around here. You're my brother so I'll give you a pass. But it's a close thing, I can tell you."

Julie stood close by the truck's door, just out of sight of the two brothers.

She'd caught up with Mac in the barn and he had loved the idea of the yurts. Now she'd doubled back to tell Nathan before hurrying off to do more research.

And he and his brother were talking about her as if it was up to anybody other than her who she kissed. As if she was a commodity for exchange like a side of beef.

Anger built in her until she was shaking with it; it wasn't an emotion she was used to. Just moments ago life had been so good. The solution of replacing the cabins with yurts. The bone-melting kiss Nathan had delivered almost made her think something good could happen with a man, no matter how little time he was going to be in Montana.

And now—

She turned and was stalking away, she didn't know where, when Emily stepped out of the barn and flagged her down.

"I had a question for you..." Emily trailed off. "But I'm guessing this is the wrong moment."

Julie swallowed down her fury, blinked away the burning sensation in her eyes. "No, now is fine." Her throat felt as if she'd been chewing glass.

Emily's eyes called *Bullshit!*

"I'm fine. What's up?"

Emily scanned around, caught the two voices at the front of the pickup. Julie couldn't hear what they were saying at this distance, but she could still hear the bantering tone they'd been using to talk about her. Emily's sigh was sufficient. It *was* nice to have another woman around.

Ama was so reserved that she rarely spoke, and Chelsea was so young that she did little else.

Emily looped her arm through Julie's and guided her away toward the barn.

She braced herself for some conciliatory talk or empty reassurances that she had every right to be mad. Instead, Emily was quiet as she led Julie into the warm, horsey air of the barn.

She would *not* remember the easy fun of finding Nathan's car corralled down at the end of the row, or the consideration he'd shown for not wanted to start the engine inside the barn. Last night he'd been intriguingly different. Now he was just like all the other cowhands, though he'd gotten further than most with that kiss. He could read anything he wanted into it now, she was a closed book as far as he was concerned.

At the center of the building was a built-out set of rooms. To one side, two large tack rooms were filled with neatly arranged saddles, blankets, and halters. On the other side was a room filled with brushes, hoof picks, and a locked cabinet with all of the medical supplies necessary when the nearest vet was thirty miles away, and an office. Chelsea was there keeping up the paperwork on all of the horses.

"Hey, girlfriends. What are you two up to? Ooo, sad face," she scrambled out from behind the desk and gave Julie a surprising hug. "I saw that kiss," she pointed toward the window in her office. "You're not supposed to be wearing 'sad face' after a whopper like that. Was Nathan a bad kisser? I thought he was kinda cute. I had hopes for him. Or is he leaving already?"

Julie couldn't even catch her breath under the barrage. Any

thoughts that her private life was somehow…private died fast deaths.

"What's up with him anyway? Is he—"

"Chelsea," Emily sad softly, which ground Chelsea to halt.

"Oops! Running off at the mouth. I've really got to watch that."

Chelsea's preferred mount, a big dapple gray named Snowflake, stuck her head out the first stall by the office at the sound of Chelsea's voice. Without hesitation, Chelsea shifted over to scratch Snowflake's cheek and straighten her forelock. Julie could forgive her a lot for that thoughtless bit of care for her horse.

Julie stepped over to greet Snowflake and to let Chelsea know it was okay. But she definitely needed a subject change. "Emily, you had a question?"

Chelsea jumped right back in, "She wants an office out here in the barn, but I need mine. We could convert one of the stalls, but I'd hate to lose the horse space, that's already at a premium. How much space do you need, Emily?"

"It's not a question of space really. A couple of chairs, a few computers. It's a question of security."

"Security?" Chelsea seemed glad to carry Julie's half of the conversation as well.

"Sound and electronic. I want to run a small but secure communications center."

Julie resisted the urge to ask why and looked about the barn.

For once Chelsea was stymied as well. Emily shared a smile with Julie at that.

Julie nodded and looked around again. "What about up there?"

A narrow stairway led up between the two tack rooms across the main aisle from Chelsea's office. On top of the rooms was the big open loft close under the barn's roof. It was filled with the normal detritus that accumulated around horses: worn leather that might still be useful someday, ropes in need of splicing, old saddles that someone hadn't wanted to throw out, buckets of rusted horseshoes and nails. Once the three of them had climbed up to survey the space, it was clear that most of it was crap that simply hadn't been dealt with.

"Really?" Chelsea held up a rusty pitchfork missing a tine and a shovel with a broken handle. She tossed them back down in disgust. "I can clear all this in an afternoon. Well, most of it." There were some things worth keeping.

Julie paced out the space atop one of the tack rooms as well as she could, threading her way through the debris. "What if you boxed in an office on top of this room? On top of the other one, you could build a couple sets of shelving and hooks to organize the rest of this."

"Works for me," Chelsea shrugged.

Emily stepped over as if entering her new office.

"It's close under the slope of the roof, but you'd have full height for most of the space," Julie could see it taking shape. "Insulate the roof here. Maybe punch through a skylight down here on the slope so you'd get sunlight as well as a view out over the property. And if you want a more open feel, a couple of windows inside overlooking the barn as well."

Julie liked the view from here. She could look down into a dozen or so of the horse stalls. Some were sleeping, some tugging at the hay in their feeders, one or two watching what the three women were up to so high in the air.

Emily followed her gaze. "You really love the horses."

"Born to them," Julie shrugged. "Never was much of a one for the cows. That's my dad and brothers. They'd just as soon use an ATV as a horse—they see them both as just tools. I'll take Clarence any day of the week."

"Yet you've never come here, to a horse ranch, to work."

"Sure I have. In fact, I should be working now. I've got to do some research and then get back up to Ponderosa. That bathroom won't fix itself."

"I meant to work with the horses."

Julie shrugged. Mac was a great rider and Ama rode like a dream as well. Doug had been born to horses as much as she had and Chelsea was a natural athlete at anything having to do with the outdoors. "The ranch has always had all of the horse people it needed."

Emily kept whatever her next thought was to herself, which was just as well. Instead she took one more tour through the junk, then nodded her head.

"So, you like the idea?"

"Yes," Emily nodded. "When can you have it finished?"

"Excuse me, what?"

"I don't have the skills to build it."

"Me neither," Chelsea agreed. "Though I'd be glad to help if you need an apprentice. Always cool to learn how to do something new."

"I was just helping you figure out what you needed," Julie wasn't sure why she was protesting. She didn't have any other work lined up after the cabins for Mac. She'd rather hoped that the work and his recommendation would generate some more business at other ranches around.

Time to change her tune if she was going to make a go of it as a contractor.

"Building a space is easy. I can build you a space. Sound insulation is no problem; good ventilation and heating isn't hard. I can run in any power you need, but I don't know anything about electronic security."

"I have some friends who can help us there. Let's worry about physical security. A stout door, with a good locking mechanism. Your job if you want it," Emily finished.

It was a simple structure. A couple of walls. Windows and a skylight. A subpanel for the electrical, maybe with a battery backup of some sort or a small generator. Better yet, solar on the roof. She'd been dying for a chance to tinker with solar. And with Chelsea's help she could knock out the shelving on the other side in a couple of afternoons.

"Okay," Julie took a deep breath. "How fast do you want it built?"

Emily's smile was as close to a laugh as Julie had ever seen on her. "Imagine me, retired, leading people on fishing trips."

Chelsea actually snorted out her laughter.

Julie smiled back at Emily, "So, that would be soon?"

Over the next couple of days, Nathan couldn't get near Julie.

She was in some kind of a whirling dervish mode that was worthy of a New Yorker. One minute she'd be ripping the floor out of the Ponderosa cabin's bathroom. The next she'd be loading a dumpster in the barn. When he tracked her to the equipment shed, she and Mac were so involved in hooking up a nasty piece of spiral-shaped steel auger, two-feet across and a person tall, to a backhoe that she didn't even notice him there. Then they were up on the hill punching holes into the ground with it. After that she was back to ripping out the broken window on Larch. She was working sunrise to sunset and often as not Mac or Emily took her a lunch. Mark was soon involved as well.

And Nathan could feel his welcome growing thin.

His few attempts to get near Julie had been met with a reaction he couldn't quite understand.

She mostly appeared to be too busy to stop when he was around, but every now and then he'd catch her *getting* busy the moment she spotted him.

The longer it went on, the more sure of it he became.

Patrick was no goddamn help. "Granite lady. Like I told you. She's as hard as those hills," he pointed at the snow-shrouded peaks of the Front Range.

It was almost a stumbling shock when one day she simply wasn't there. He was on his twentieth foray from the kitchen to see if she'd arrived, when Emily came walking along the path from the barn to the house.

"Have you seen Julie?"

"Not today."

Nathan sighed. "I'm starting to think she's avoiding me."

"Starting to?" Something in Emily's tone confirmed the worst of his fears.

He'd spent most of the week trying to figure out if he'd done something wrong. It wouldn't surprise him, but he had no idea what it could be. They'd kissed, and then she'd gone invisible with no apparent transition in between. The word "flighty" had fit other women in his past, but not Julie. Moody too didn't seem to be her style, based on what little he knew of her. The only option that was really left was pissed—but he couldn't think of why.

"She's not avoiding you today, if that makes you feel any better."

"How do you know that?"

"It's Sunday."

"Oh," he'd lost complete track of time here. He'd arrived... Monday, Tuesday...he wasn't sure. It wasn't like when he was a chef with every night blending one into the next until there was no difference. Out here each day was so distinct it could have been sliced from the sky in discrete chunks. But which day it *was* seemed to have little meaning. Horses and ranch hands had to be fed. Today there was less of the frenetic pace that seemed to fill the rest of the week, but not enough to really stand out. So this was Sunday on a ranch.

"I expect she's at church with her family."

"Where's the nearest—" but he knew, it was the same as everything else out here.

"Choteau," he and Emily said in unison.

"Do you have any idea...no, sorry. I told her I didn't want to drag her down with my own worries. I'm guessing that you don't want to be dragged into this either."

"Can't say that I do," but Emily waved for him to follow her into the barn.

He hadn't been out here since the night he and Julie had found his car together. He wished he could find some way to rewind to that night.

Emily led him up a flight of stairs to a set of framed walls covered in bright plywood. He didn't remember this being here.

"Her work?" He didn't know enough to tell if it was good or bad, but it looked solid.

"She's building me an office," Emily sat down on a saw horse in the middle of the space.

Nathan sat on one opposite her.

"I can't tell you what, but I can tell you when."

He really didn't want to put Emily in the middle of it all, but was helpless on what else to do.

"She was standing beside the truck when you were talking with your brother shortly after his return. I've seen warriors in combat who looked less furious."

Nathan tried to recall the conversation.

Patrick had been talking about Julie like she was a side order dish on the menu.

And if she'd thought he was doing the same…that would explain a lot.

"But I wasn't," he said it aloud without meaning to.

"But she thinks you were, whatever it is. And right after you kissed her."

"She kissed *me*," not that it made any difference.

Emily glanced out one of the windows at a horse's nicker. "So she likes you?"

"I like her, too. For all the good it's going to do me."

"Do you want some advice?"

Nathan shrugged, "Couldn't hurt anything at this point."

Emily smile was brief as a New York cabbie's as she rose to her feet, "Remind her of that."

Julie liked seeing Emily up in her office. She'd been pushing hard to keep all three projects moving, which is why she was back after church. That and she had a fresh load of supplies from town. In addition to the window for Larch, she had all of the glass and skylight for Emily's office.

As she came up the center aisle of the barn, Emily descended and nodded a good afternoon. Then she nodded up towards the office as if warning her there was someone else up there. As if—

Oh no!

Emily's third nod confirmed her guess.

Nathan.

Julie was not ready to deal with him yet. But Emily repeated her signal with a commiserating shrug of her shoulders. How did she communicate so much without speaking? Julie would almost swear that there was another implied level saying, *give him a chance.*

She'd come here to work, not to… But Emily was gone before she could protest.

Fine. She'd fix this fast and then get to work on things that really mattered.

She tromped up the stairs, the treads creaking badly. They were stout enough and served their purpose well enough for a storage loft, but for an office space, she needed to pop them up, then glue and screw to kill the squeaks. Another task on her already overwhelming list. Maybe she should just pop off all the treads and maroon Nathan up here by himself.

He was sitting on a sawhorse facing her when she walked in.

"What is it with you, Nathan?" Not the nicest of greetings.

"I like you, Julie."

It took her a moment to shift gears. She wasn't expecting such a simple statement from a guy. "You've got a damn weird way of showing it."

"Wasn't me. Just my brother. I never could beat decent manners into him."

"He wasn't the one bragging about kissing me."

"Neither was I. *He* was complaining that he hadn't and I had."

"But I heard—" What had she heard?

"He saw us. And I couldn't get him to shut up. Has he really been coming on to you like you were a side dish?"

"More like a slab of female first course."

"I should pound the shit out of him," the look of anger that suffused his face only fit Nathan if he really was the white knight. She'd never met one. Didn't even believe in them since she'd been groped at ten by an eleven-year-old Danny Andersen. Julie had thrown every single one of her cherished princess and fairy tale books in the manure pit that day. It didn't seem likely that a New York chef could actually be a white knight, but he was doing a fair imitation.

Either he was better at it than most others—because at least he was trying—or maybe it was one of those sneaky games he'd mentioned.

"If you do decide to beat him up, I'll be glad to help. I've tried most everything else to get him to back off."

"There won't be anything left after I strangle the little shit." Nathan was still angry enough that he looked ready to spit out horseshoe nails.

"Are you now doing some macho, she's-mine, kind of crap?"

"No! It's just not the way you're supposed to treat a woman," then about half his fury dissipated when he looked up from the hole he'd been trying to glare through the floor. "You mean like some hound dog pissing on his turf?"

"Exactly like that."

Nathan actually looked puzzled as he inspected her, the floor, the ceiling, and then her again. "No, I don't think so."

"You don't *think* so?" She finally sat on the other sawhorse.

"Never thought about it really. But I don't strike me as the guy who does that kind of thing."

"All guys do that kind of thing." At least all of the guys she'd ever met.

Nathan just shrugged.

He was silent long enough for her to become aware of the dust motes in the air and the occasional huffing sighs of horses perfectly content to be inside on a chilly day.

"As I said, I like you. But I'm not stupid enough to think that a kiss, no matter how spectacular, makes you *mine* in any way. The only claim I can make on you is that I like you. I seem to keep saying that. I guess because Emily said I should."

"Emily said you should keep saying that you like me? You asked her for relationship advice after a single kiss?" Julie didn't know whether to go back to being furious or to laugh.

"Not exactly. She said that I should remind you that you like me. And no, I didn't ask for advice. I just asked if she knew where you were."

"She thinks that I was so angry because I'd forgotten I liked you?"

Nathan shrugged a yes.

That tipped her over into laughter.

"What?"

"So much for the infallible Emily Beale."

Nathan tentatively matched her smile, but he didn't get the joke yet.

"I got so angry because I *do* like you. Now get out of here, I have work to do."

He nodded and rose. He didn't go for a kiss. Didn't even hesitate to see if she'd offer one. He just took her at her word, rose, and left.

If he wasn't the strangest thing in the history of Teton County, she didn't know what was.

CHAPTER 6

As soon as Nathan knew what was going on, he had a plan. It couldn't be sneaky, instead it had to be utterly blatant or it might just irritate her again and there'd be no predicting the end result.

The plan was so clear in his head that he hadn't even thought to kiss her when leaving Emily's loft office until he was out of the barn and most of the way back to the house. It was just as well, he didn't want anything messing up his plan.

He couldn't do anything about it that night, except a bit of prep. Sunday dinners were apparently a big deal on a Montana ranch. Emily helped him and Ama with the cooking, others chatted from the fireside or were recruited to peel or chop.

Julie was her usual all-over-the-place on Monday, which worked well for him. Unexpectedly she came down to the house for lunch—which he still couldn't get straight in his head was supposed to be called dinner. Her arrival almost screwed up his preparations, but he managed to hide the ingredients he'd been assembling without having her any the wiser.

Only Ama knew what he was up to and she didn't say a word.

Patrick and the not-twins were merely *moderately* obnoxious to their unexpected lunch guest—at least they weren't downright offensive. He didn't dare jump to her defense because that would just egg on different rumors. Emily shut that down hard when she joined them, though. Hard enough to earn his appreciation of her, even if no one else at the table appeared to notice. Maybe it had been just normal teasing. Julie had certainly handled it as such, but he still didn't like it.

After lunch (dinner), she headed up onto the hill.

Perfect.

He carried his first load of supplies up to the Aspen cabin as soon as he and Ama had lunch put away. Julie was right, of course. If he had to choose any cabin of the five, now that he'd toured them all, it would be this one. The others stood together on the grassy hillside. Aspen's treed cloister cut down on the vista to either side, but it made it private and cozy. Once inside, he fired up the cabin's heat and the oven.

Julie answered his casual wave with a nod from where she, Mac, Doug, and Mark were auguring piling holes up at the new cabin sites. They had giant cardboard tubes that they slipped down into each hole as soon as it was dug out.

His hands were full on the next trip as he brought up most of the rest of the cooking supplies. She was driving her truck down for more of the tubes as he walked up the trail from the house, so this time it was his nod to her wave.

Last night he'd set a pair of steaks in marinade made mostly of red wine. The wine pre-digested the meat just enough that it would be fork tender by the time he cooked it. He started in on German scalloped potatoes, done in a vinegar-bacon sauce rather than a cream one.

As he worked through the warm afternoon, he was pleased to discover that he still enjoyed cooking. He hadn't been sure if that was something else he'd left in New York. Helping Ama prepare the meals for the family and the ranch hands had been pleasant, but it wasn't *real* cooking. This was, and it was fun.

He used a cookie cutter to make sure that each circle of puff pastry was exactly the same size for the tiny puff pizzas which he would garnish with roasted pepper, a sauce he'd spent all morning building on jarred tomato, and identical slivers of caramelized onion cut on the bias to make each piece a curling arc around tiny cubes of roasted winter squash and Ama's sausage.

He'd had to discard a dozen different dessert ideas due to lack of ingredients before he'd decided that simpler was better. Fresh vanilla bean ice cream on individual-sized huckleberry and candied ginger pies.

The sun was headed down when he made his last trip to the house for a bottle of wine and a couple of glasses. He'd purposely left it behind because he wanted to pique her curiosity with another back-and-forth.

The work crew knocked off about the time he returned to Aspen cabin. His timing was perfect.

He checked on everything that was cooking, poured two glasses, and headed out to sit on the porch swing.

By the time Julie rolled her truck to stop on the dirt track below the cabin, he was relaxed and enjoying the last of the sun's warmth before it ducked down behind the mountains.

"What have you been up to all afternoon, city boy?" she called from her open truck window.

"Come see for yourself, cowgirl." He picked up the second wine glass and held it aloft as an offer.

She cut the engine and eased out of the cab with the care of someone who'd been working hard all day. "All I want is a hot shower and a beer."

"Damn! I didn't think to turn on the water heater." She looked just fine to him in dirt-spattered boots and jeans. Her fleece-lined denim jacket, a yellow bill hat with a blue Ford logo on the front, and her hair pulled into a ponytail through the back loop were also just what he'd expect of a woman like her. Utterly practical.

"Do you even know how to turn on a water heater?" She came up on the porch. "Are you trying to seduce me?"

"Probably not."

She eyed him strangely.

"I mean the water heater."

"So, you probably *are* trying to seduce me? Fair warning, it's not going to work."

"No, I know. I just wanted to cook for you. We had some bargain about me having to cook for you."

"So that I don't teach my evil ways to Patrick."

"That was it. I think he has enough of his own already. He *is* a good kid, you know. Even if sometimes he doesn't show it so well."

"Sure," Julie agreed as she finally unwound enough to sit down beside him and take the glass of wine. "Or maybe he will be if he ever grows up."

Nathan decided that both parts of that statement bore a lot of truth.

"So what did you cook for me?"

"Dinner. Or I guess you call it supper."

"I've never in my life had a meal like that." But it seemed that she certainly should have. Food was normally just something to be eaten, but not Nathan's supper.

Through each course he'd explained how, when there was time to make it properly, a meal should unfold in layers of flavor. The tiny shredded pork ravioli were swimming in a broth that she could gladly have bathed in it was so tasty. He'd explained how the meal would have shifted if he'd followed with a fish course rather than a winter greens salad with walnuts and a mustard vinaigrette.

The night of the party, when he'd said he could cook, she'd foolishly thought that meant he could "cook." Maybe at one of the fancy hotels in Great Falls, which served scallops and fancy fish from Alaska. She'd had king-crab-stuffed sirloin once and it had been… good. She'd thought it had been great, prior to this moment.

Now all she cared about was how glorious she felt. The flavors, the preparations, she'd never cut a two-inch steak with just the edge of her fork before. And it had practically melted on her tongue.

The company had been shockingly pleasant as well. The warm fire, which Nathan had built tolerably well, made Aspen even more welcoming than she'd ever imagined. There was no candle on the table, which she realized was *not* an oversight. Nathan really didn't seem to be running a seduction here. Instead they ate by the light of a single lamp—the table so friendly that there was no motivation to leave it for the living room. The meal itself seemed to have wandered forever, meandering down odd conversational lanes into strange and dusty corners that were always interesting.

"How can you know so little about the world? You live in New York."

Nathan shook his head as he nursed a cup of tea and took a final scrape of melted ice cream. "I live, lived, in a kitchen. My world is ingredients, not..." he flapped his hand outward, "...all that noise."

"Sherlock Holmes," she said, wondering if he'd get a literary reference.

"Right. The case of the... I can't remember... *A Study in Scarlet.* Sherlock complains when Watson tells him that the planets orbit around the sun. That fact was irrelevant and useless to his purpose of solving crimes. He didn't wish to have it cluttering his thoughts. Works for me."

Julie tipped her head back and forth studying him. "You're a very strange person, Mr. Gallagher."

"I could have told you that much. Why this time?"

"As far as I can tell, you haven't done a single thing to try and impress me."

He laughed, "I told you that I only had one skill. I know how to cook. If that didn't impress you, I've played the only card I've got. Shot my full quiver."

"Impress me? *That* was not cooking—I'd call it delirium, it was so good. Not what I meant anyway. I mean, you aren't trying to show off your knowledge, or how good you are at something. Not how many cattle you can brand in a single hour, or your epic ride on the latest rodeo bronc, or even how many prize belt buckles you've won."

"There's such a thing as a prize belt buckle?" He sat forward shoving aside some plates and dishes so that he could lean on the table. But it wasn't as if he was leaning in to get closer to her. He was just being comfortable.

She laughed because she couldn't help herself. She was very proud of the ones that adorned her bedroom wall.

"There are even things called Buckle Bunnies. They're women who wear cowboy boots and painfully short shorts."

"Let me guess. They go to rodeos and try to trip cowboys."

"Bingo."

"Any boy buckle bunnies trying to trip cowgirls?"

"Nah. Just—"

"Rutting cowboys," they said in unison and she laughed again. She could feel the attraction across the table—a very nice bit of sizzle. But Nathan had none of the aggressiveness necessary to be a rutting cowboy. Overall, though, he was still climbing on both the prince charming and white knight scales.

Nathan sobered, "As to how many of those things I can brag about? That's easy. Does zero count as an answer?"

"It does. I'm not particularly sure what to do with it. But it counts. I think."

"I can't wrangle a cow. I can't build a cabin. I can't train a dog or ride a horse. I'm—"

"Wait a second. Back up there, city boy."

"A dog? I was watching Stan out there working with those military dogs he's training. I see why he doesn't talk to people; his main language is dog. And he's good at it."

"Not that. You can't *ride a horse?*" Julie didn't know if she'd ever actually met someone who couldn't ride a horse. Even the most incompetent city guests who came to Henderson's Ranch were coming to ride horses. "Tessa is three years old and can ride a pony just fine. Though it spooks Emily every time she does. Belle will be three months in a little bit. Definitely time to get her up on a horse."

Nathan looked aghast, exactly as Julie had planned.

"In someone's arms. She can't even sit up yet. You let go and she just tips back over and giggles. Cutest kid you ever saw." And how she'd ended talking babies with Nathan Gallagher, she had no idea. She gunned back for the prior topic. "Really, really never ridden?"

Nathan just shrugged. "They rent horses up in Central Park. At least I think they do, but I never hired one."

"You can't ride a horse."

Nathan looked around the room. "Strange echo in here. Never heard a delay like that one before. Never pet a horse either. Don't think I've so much as touched a horse. Or a cow. Well, you know, not before it was butchered. No interested in petting Lucy, just so you know."

"Oh, city boy. We really are gonna have to fix that. Soon."

He squirmed uncomfortably in his seat.

"Not an option, city boy. It's just too sad for words."

"Yeah, that's me." The way he said it stopped her.

There was something more behind that, something she'd caught a glimpse of earlier in the week—sad and painful. But it was clear he didn't want her prying. And after the amazing meal, she decided that kindness was something she could give him, tonight anyway. But it was the second time she'd caught something wrong and she was going to have to dig it out; it was bugging her like a stone in Clarence's shoe.

She went searching for a different topic—and spewed out pure stupid.

"So what's the course after dessert? Is this when you try to seduce me?" Talk about giving him an vast opening. Bad move. Very bad move.

Nathan smacked his forehead with his open palm. "I knew there was something I was supposed to be doing next. I've got to run down to the main house and get some bedding. Could you check upstairs and see if the mattresses are musty? Probably should have scattered rose petals up the stairs and into the bedroom. You don't have any rose petals handy do you? Crap!" He started patting his pockets as if he'd find them. For half a second she thought he was going to actually rush out for sheets and blankets and, god help her, rose petals.

Then the joke caught up with her. "You run a crappy seduction, city boy."

"Special for you, cowgirl," he dropped back in his chair as if exhausted by all of his momentary flurry. "Actually, I thought that maybe just getting to know you a bit might be fun. That, and find out if I can still cook."

"Put a big check in that last box, Nathan. It was truly amazing."

He was nodding to himself as if he wasn't so sure.

"Okay. Spit it out. Enough of this sad dog act."

"Spit what out?"

But he didn't deny the sad dog part of it.

After a moment he raised both hands in resignation. "Not tonight, okay? Not over my food. Maybe over someone else's."

"Well, don't be looking at me. I can cook on a grill or a campfire well enough to not poison most folks, but I'm all thumbs in a kitchen."

"I'll keep that in mind for the future. What are my survival odds? Fifty-fifty? Sixty-forty? Still might be worth the risk."

"Might end up accidentally knocking your cowboy hat into the fire," she made it a threat.

"Don't have one of those either."

"Oh, city boy," she sighed.

She'd helped him clean up, which wasn't much. Nathan always ran a clean kitchen: washing up as he went, reusing what he could. But they'd fallen into an easy synchronicity even over that simple task. With him washing and Julie drying and putting away, they'd cleaned up the Aspen kitchen in record time.

He closed up the cabin and walked her to her truck by the moonlight shivering down out of the crystalline dark sky.

"You really weren't running a seduction on me, were you?" Julie hesitated with one hand on her truck's door.

"Seems to me, way too many guys have been trying to run that game on you just because you're nice and you're pretty."

"Most of them don't care about the nice part," the chagrin sounded as if it came from deep experience.

"So, here's my deal with you—seem to be making a lot of those. No games. I cooked for you because I wanted to. As a bonus, I enjoyed this evening even more than I expected to, which is saying something. You make a great dinner companion."

It was only a quarter moon, but it seemed so close here, much closer than in the city. There were more stars in the sky than at the Hayden Planetarium on the Upper West Side. The light caught her hair, though not her expression. Her breath into the chill air sparkled for a moment before dissipating.

"Also, there's a lot to like about you. The fact that you're gorgeous is definitely on the list. But so is your competence, your quiet sense of humor, and your incredibly positive attitude." He knew he was getting too serious. "Though your misplaced belief that you can teach me to ride a horse definitely makes your common sense suspect."

She looked up at him from under the brim of her hat for a long moment. "That's a kinda long list from someone who claims he isn't trying to seduce me."

"No games. No lies. I've had enough of both to last a lifetime."

"You're walking a thin line there, Nathan."

"What line?"

"You cook like a dream. You're thoughtful. You think your brother is a better man than he is, and you just might prove you're right and he's wrong someday. You've got this sort of sad little corner that makes a girl think about taking you home and feeding you a bottle of warm milk like a sick calf."

"I could have done without that last image." Being pitiable wasn't exactly the trait he wanted to be known for by a beautiful woman.

"It works on you." Then she took her hand off the truck's door handle and instead slipped her chilled fingers around his neck and kissed him. It wasn't the hard smack of their last kiss. It was soft, warm, and slowly eased into full body contact.

Even on this cold winter night in early April, she tasted of spring. Warm, lush, and welcoming. Neither of them hurried through it, nor did they cling afterward.

Just as he'd thought of her since the first moment they'd met, Julie's kiss was exactly what it was—a really amazing kiss. No promises of tomorrow. No offer to share her body. No teasing rub together hinting that there might be more if he did everything "just right." It was simply and thoroughly a kiss.

He managed not to ask if all Montana women kissed that way after she climbed into her truck and slammed the door shut herself.

"'Night," was all she said through her open window as she started the engine.

"Goodnight," was all he managed before she rolled away into the night.

CHAPTER 7

"Rise and shine, city boy." Nathan jolted awake when Julie kicked his bed.

Damn but he'd looked cute all curled asleep in his bed. Cute, hell, she was more than half tempted to wake him with a kiss and see if last night's had been as real as she was remembering. While they'd kissed, he'd just held her. Not groped or even gone for a quick "accidental" feel. He'd just snugged his arms around her waist and held her tight. It had felt mighty good.

He blinked at her in sleepy surprise and pulled the covers up tightly around his neck. By the neatly folded clothes on his chair, she could see that he didn't even wear underwear to bed, unless he was a pajama man. He didn't strike her as a pajama man.

"Wha'?" he mumbled as he twisted to look toward the window—it was still pitch dark. Then his clock—the hour on it seemed to surprise him some.

"Enough of you sleeping in 'til all East Coast kind of hours," she gave it a good country drawl. "If you're gonna be on a ranch, it's about time you shift over to ranch time. Besides, now is the only time I've got. I'm busy the rest of the day. You've got five minutes. Meet me in the main barn. Dress warm and wear boots, if you've got any."

164

"I have boots."

"Wear 'em."

He nodded, but made no move to get out from under the covers while she was still in the room. Definitely not a pajama man.

Julie turned on her heel and, after a brief stop for coffee, headed out to the barn.

Nathan was there in close enough to five minutes, but he'd clearly skipped a lot of things to make it. His softly curling hair was more uncombed than usual and his night's beard showed a stronger chin that one would expect of him at first glance. There was a little toothpaste caught at the corner of his mouth that she didn't comment on but he eventually licked away. His boots looked like they'd come out of some New Yorker-in-the-snow movie—soft rubber with a furry lining. Something else they'd have to fix if he was going to stay in Montana for any length of time.

She wasn't going to think about her own reaction to that thought. Why should she care if he stayed or went? They'd shared a great meal and a spectacular kiss. That was all.

"Let's start with the basics," she walked up to the stall Chelsea had set aside for Clarence. He popped his head out over the half-height door when she approached. "This is a horse." She scrubbed a gloved hand between Clarence's eyes.

"Ha. Ha. Ha."

"Well, you thought Lucy was a savage animal. I figured I should start simple."

He didn't bother to repeat himself, just stood there looking grumpy. He had his fists jammed into his jacket pockets and his head still hung with being only partially awake.

Julie took pity on him and handed over her half-finished coffee.

"That helps some. Thanks."

She handed him a couple of sugar cubes.

"No thanks, I don't use it. Though some cream next time would be nice."

Julie sighed. "Starting with *this is a horse* maybe was the right place. The sugar isn't for you, it's for him."

Clarence was watching it with great interest.

Julie showed Nathan how to hold palm and fingers flat so that Clarence didn't accidentally chomp down on them.

"That tickles," Nathan smiled as Clarence lipped the cubes eagerly off his hand, then crunched them loudly. She wasn't sure how she felt about her horse receiving Nathan's first smile of the day rather than her. He finished her coffee and set the mug aside.

Step by step she led him through all of the beginner stuff that she didn't remember learning. There was more than she'd thought and it took some effort to unravel it for him. His instincts around animals were nonexistent—maybe Lucy had spooked him for real.

No sudden moves, keep your toes well clear of the horse's hooves, speak to him as you move, and so on.

He laughed at how Clarence's skin rippled wherever Nathan's hand traveled. Julie had been trying to teach him how to let the horse always know where he was by trailing a hand over him, but Nathan's touch was so tentative that Clarence's nerves treated it like a fly and kept trying to flick it off.

"No," she clamped her hand down over his, pinning it against the warm, bristly surface of Clarence's shoulder. "If you're going to touch a horse, really touch them. Make your presence and confidence clear."

"I'm guessing just the opposite works with you," he brushed a finger of his free hand so lightly down her cheek that it utterly took her breath away. She was suddenly aware that pinning his hand to Clarence's shoulder also had them holding hands—at least hers holding his.

"Don't do that," she managed on a whisper. She didn't have the ability to twitch her skin like a horse to shoo him away. Julie also didn't like what his gentle touch was doing to her knees. Her knees and her heartrate were *not* supposed to be connected to her cheek.

"I've been thinking about last night's kiss."

It had been an amazing kiss, though she kept that thought to herself. Nathan was a man who looked like a comfortable, average man, but under the surface had a startling intensity. She saw that now in the way he cooked, had felt it in the way he'd kissed. Now, he seemed to be trying to hypnotize her.

It was working.

She couldn't shift a muscle as he leaned down to kiss her again. Just a brush of the lips. Just a taste of the possible. Just—

Nathan jolted and yelped right in Julie's face. He yanked his hand free and slapped it on the sharp pain in his ass as he turned to see who had attacked him.

Clarence snorted in something that sounded very like a laugh.

A sound that Julie clearly echoed from close behind him.

"Well done, Clarence!" Chelsea was leaning on the stall's half door. "High five, buddy." She held up her hand and Clarence nosed forward enough to accept her affectionate pat.

"What the hell just happened?"

"Clarence doesn't like you kissing his girl," Chelsea explained. "Pity. It looked like it was gonna be a really good one."

"But—he's a horse!"

"Doesn't mean you didn't deserve a nip on the ass for manhandling Julie."

"I wasn't—" he didn't even know why he was trying. He checked his butt. No tear in his jeans and he didn't feel any blood. "Do I need a shot or something?"

"For what?"

Julie was still laughing, her amusement sliding into a giggle that would have been charming under any other circumstances.

"I've just been bitten. Am I going to get rabies or something?"

"Hey," Julie shoved against his shoulder to get between him and her horse, which was fine with him. "Clarence is a clean, healthy horse. Don't you malign him."

"Malign him? Malign him!"

Clarence eyed him warily.

"He bit me!" The next biggest thing that had ever bitten him had been a mosquito. And his brother had then read aloud a whole website entry on the different diseases that a mosquito could carry and all the symptoms that Nathan now had to watch for. If a mosquito had all that, he couldn't begin to imagine what something as big as a horse had.

"It was just a nip," Chelsea and Julie said together in a unified defense of the perpetrator.

"Just a nip? Why I oughta—"

Clarence raised one hoof and stomped it down hard. The stall's floor was just dirt, but Nathan swore he could feel the ground-shock up through his boots.

How low did a man have to go to have a horse get impatient with him?

Pretty low he supposed. He rubbed his butt once more and decided that maybe—just maybe—it was merely a nip; the pain had mostly faded while he was busy ranting.

"Pretty damn pleased with yourself, aren't you?" he asked the horse.

Clarence jerked his head up and down through a three-foot arc that was disconcertingly similar to a human nod.

"He's my guardian angel," Julie confirmed as she leaned back against the horse's shoulder and the perpetrator turned to snuffle at her. A great blast blew her hair aside. He'd been left the option of "rutting cowhand" and her damned horse got "guardian angel."

"Yeah," Chelsea still leaned on the stall. "Next time you want to manhandle your woman like that, I wouldn't do it near this horse."

"I wasn't—" What was the point? Arguing with a redhead, a blonde, and her horse struck him as a losing proposition.

"His *what?*" Julie's shout had even Clarence stepping aside as much as the stall would allow. Without his shoulder supporting her, Julie almost went down on the straw bedding. "I'm *nobody's* woman except Clarence's."

"No secrets up in the big house, Julie," Chelsea was enjoying this more than any of them. "Fancy dinner—at least the list of ingredients sounded fancy to me. Do you have any idea how long it takes to make puff pastry? I didn't, but Emily filled me in. Then lights on up in the Aspen cabin until mighty late with your truck out front. Was it sweet or romantic? Did it get steamy? Oh, I really hope it got steamy; I love steamy. Give me the details, girlfriend."

"I'm not *his woman*," Julie ground out the words.

"Why not? A cute man who cooks and owns a hot sports car? That would be more than enough for me."

"Chelsea! You married a ranch foreman who owns a pickup and can barely fry an egg."

She nodded, "But there are other things he does so...very...well." Her smile said exactly what some of those things were.

"Enough!" Julie cried in defeat, pushed out of the stall, and she and Chelsea were gone in a moment.

It took Nathan several heartbeats to realize that it was just him and Clarence alone in the horse stall. The horse was eyeing him suspiciously.

"Her guardian angel, huh?" The horse did a headshake that flopped its mane neatly into place. It might have been a yes or a no...or maybe a "look out, bub."

"I guess if I'm going to go after your girl, I better be nice to you." Was that what he was doing? To what end? Wasn't he leaving soon?

Clarence had no comment.

There was only so long he could freeload off Mac and Ama. She'd ignored him when he tried to pay for the ingredients for last night's dinner. Yes, he helped in the kitchen, but she didn't really need him.

"Well, there comes a time in every man's life when he must..." but Nathan couldn't remember the rest of the quote. "I guess...when he must take his life in his own hands and suck up to a horse."

Make your presence and confidence clear, he reminded himself silently. That's what Julie said was the secret to handling a horse.

He stepped up to Clarence, gave him the best imitation Nathan could conjure of a manly thump on the shoulder, then stepped confidently—and quickly—out the stall door.

There was a sharp clack of horse teeth close behind him, followed by a whinny that he was simply going to pretend he hadn't heard.

Julie's protest that she "didn't want to hear it" was about as effective on Chelsea as could be expected. Finally resigned to her fate, she followed Chelsea into the barn's working office and closed the door.

It was a good space. She'd helped Chelsea rearrange it last fall and Chelsea had made it her own since then. Like everything else in the barn, it was clad—floor, walls, and ceiling—with heavy lumber gone dark brown with age. A big roll-top desk sat up against one side wall. Out a big window in the back one, Chelsea had a sweeping view of the property up toward the ranch house and the cabins.

All around the desk and on the other side walls were photos of happy families and couples up on their horses or camping up by the waterfalls on the far side of the Henderson property. There was also a big monitor hanging on the wall, which at the moment was showing the information on her laptop's screen: every horse broken down into...

Julie hadn't seen a rating like this before, but once she figured it out, she couldn't help but laugh.

"I know, right?" Chelsea looked pleased.

The columns headings weren't: OK for beginner, intermediate, advanced rider only... They were: easy-going, opinionated, *really* opinionated, and downright ornery. There were only a couple of names in the last column, and Doug—the best rider on the ranch— was working with those. Julie wouldn't mind doing some of that work herself, though it wasn't as if she had the time.

"I'd always thought Clarence was, like," Chelsea tipped back in her chair and stared at the chart, "—easy-going. Something about Nathan really sets him off, right up into *really, really* opinionated."

Julie had to grant that. She'd never seen Clarence act up so around a man. Not even when she lost her virginity right out by Henderson's waterfalls. He'd just munched away on the high summer grass as if nothing of interest was going on. Regrettably, Clarence's sense of what was happening had been more accurate than her own.

With her desk to the side, Chelsea could swivel her chair to face a small couch and a couple of other chairs so the big desk wouldn't sit between her and the clients. Julie sat on the couch and thumbed through the magazines sprinkled across the coffee table: *Western Horseman, American Cowboy, The Trail Rider, Young Rider,* and a couple of rodeo and barrel racing titles she hadn't read in far too long. She had to remember to hang out in Chelsea's office more often. *American Farrier's Journal* and *Equine Wellness* were lined up on a shelf above her desk—of less interest to a ranch guest but still looking well thumbed, probably by Chelsea, who inhaled knowledge about horses.

"You've really settled in well here."

Chelsea shrugged. "What's not to like? I was always an outdoors kinda gal. Thought I might spend my days out trekking. I loved the Himalayas. Decided I was going to do all the long trails. I was most of the way up the Pacific Crest Trail, my first one, when I stumbled on Mark and Emily's firefighting outfit in Oregon. Kinda needed a break and they took me on as Tessa's nanny. Didn't last long 'cause they brought me here. Met Doug a year ago Christmas and now can't recall what I was walking so hard and fast to get away from. Pure bonus, I get all of these sweetie pies to take care of," she waved a hand at the wall of photos.

Julie wasn't sure if she meant the horses or the guests. With Chelsea's big heart, she probably meant both. Julie flipped through the magazines again.

Chelsea's laugh stopped her.

"What?"

"You know that you're gonna have to spill at some point."

"What are you talking about?"

"Duh! Me or Emily. At some point you're gonna have to talk about it or it'll just build up in you until you don't know what to do with it. I guess you could talk to Ama, but she still spooks me what with her see-into-your-soul bit and then pointing out the shit you didn't want to see with, like, one word or a well-timed shrug."

Julie had always rather liked Ama—a woman of few words. Though talking to her about relationships did sound a bit dangerous; Ama would be sure to point out something Julie didn't want to hear.

She didn't exactly like getting advice from a twenty-two year old either—no matter how ideal Chelsea's and Doug's relationship appeared to be.

"Everything's fine. There's nothing going on."

"Sure," Chelsea leaned back in her chair and propped her cowboy boots on a copy of *Barrel Horse News*. "I believe you. Even if neither Clarence nor a blind man would."

Julie made a show of lying sideways on the short couch, propping her head on one arm and her calves on the other. "Go ahead, Dr. Chelsea. Try me. I dare you."

Chelsea made a show of tugging her long red hair back into a tight ponytail and trying to look severe, then gave it up as a lost cause.

"Nah! I'm gonna leave you to Emily. She's way better at this kinda shit. Besides, it's time for breakfast…if Clarence let Nathan out of the stall alive so he could go cook it."

Julie found it easy to laugh with Chelsea as they double-checked that there was no body on the floor of Clarence's stall before heading up to the house together.

Nathan didn't go back to the house.

Instead he tracked down his car.

It had become a game and locking it up didn't help.

One day it had been put out to pasture along with the horses, along with its own burlap feedbag. The time that he'd finally tracked it down in the hay loft, he'd simply turned away—no idea how they got it up there and no idea how to get it down. Waiting out the jokers seemed to be his best strategy at that point.

Sure enough, yesterday it had been an element of Stan's dog training obstacle course. The memory still made Nathan smile.

"Unarmed explosives," Stan had explained when Nathan had asked why the dogs were sniffing his car so intently. "Stashed some for them to find in door panels, the trunk, and so on."

For over an hour he'd watched Stan working the dogs. It was a small litter, just six animals, but his patience with them was remarkable.

"They're really too young for this work," Stan came over to the fence after telling the dogs to go play.

He leaned against one side while Nathan leaned against the other. The way the dogs collapsed to the turf convinced Nathan that Stan wasn't the one who needed the break.

"This is more about me practicing my training methods. Lackland Air Force Base trains all of your standard military war dogs. But the ones for the Special Operations teams—SEALs, Delta, even Rangers— they're trained up by contractors to different standards. This litter needs another year of aging and then we can start their real training. Mac has a long-term view, sees what this can be in a couple of years. Gave me a shot to prove it." It was clear by his tone that he worshipped the old man.

"If they're too young," they looked full grown to him—like black-tinted German Shepherds. They were beautiful dogs. "What about him?"

Stan looked over to a small pen just inside the fence where a puppy lay napping with his chin resting on a small stuffed animal. "Vizsla. Hunting dogs. Picked him up in Choteau. Shouldn't have, but have a friend back east thinks they'd be good military war dogs. Promised Mary I'd try one and there he was, so I had to get him. She named him Gibson."

"Friend back east…" He was so gruff that it was hard to imagine Stan having a girl.

"Retired librarian. Funny lady."

Okay, so much for that idea. Nathan nodded back toward the resting dogs, "Is there a star of the group?"

"Bertram there," he pointed at the pack with his hooks, which told Nathan nothing. "Far and away the smartest of the lot. Watch."

Stan picked up a ball, then a second one. All of the dogs were instantly on their feet, ready to play—except the puppy still asleep in its pen. Stan heaved the first ball high. Five of the six dogs raced after it, striving to grab it out of the air. The sixth dog still sat on its haunches, looking from Stan's face to the ball in his hand.

Stan winged it low and fast. Before he even released it, Bertram was on the move. Reading Stan's body language on the throw, he snagged it out of the air before it had traveled fifty feet, despite the wide angle and high speed that Stan had heaved it at. He dropped the ball at Stan's feet while the other dogs were still wrestling over who could keep the first one.

The two of them had settled into a game of catch of their own—a game that had shown so much of how Stan felt about his "best dog" that Nathan had felt he was intruding to watch more of it. Rather than retrieve his car, he had left the two of them to their game.

That had been yesterday. Today, of all odd places (one of the last he looked), Nathan found his car in the dim confines of the garage—no daylight yet through the windows. His Miata was parked among the ATVs that weren't all that much smaller. Doug had made good on his offer and the flat tire was repaired and back in place.

The gas was full.

It was all set to go.

Julie was always thrown when she ate at Henderson's. The contrast was so sharp to her own home experience that it almost gave her a sense of vertigo—like she was barrel racing and hit the turn wrong.

At home, no one interrupted Dad during a meal. Matters unrelated to the farm or an upcoming rodeo were rarely discussed. The latter was the only time she had a real place as she was by far the best rider in the family and her display of ribbons and prizes were a point of family pride. There was a gap there that continued to irritate her father: the Miss Rodeo Montana award. Or even—never said aloud of course—the coveted Miss Rodeo America award.

She hadn't cared about manners and world affairs and "representing fine American traditions". Instead she'd gone for the only prize she really cared about, and come closer to winning than she'd ever expected. She'd taken home Third Prize for Barrel Racing at the Calgary Stampede. The foot-tall bronze statue of a cowgirl and her horse carving a hard turn around a barrel held the place of honor in her bedroom. She'd beat out any number of professional riders for that coveted win. When she died, she was taking that statue to the grave with her.

At a Henderson's Ranch meal there were so many conversations that she didn't know which to follow. Topics ranged all over the frontier from lame horses to the tourist economy to international news. Devin and Drake were either a goldmine (or maybe they were a landmine) of Hollywood celebrity gossip—at least about who was sleeping with who. It was both funny and just a little creepy. No one could ever pay her enough to put up with that. Being three-time top rodeo rider of Teton County had gained her far more notoriety than she liked. She had sight-unseen proposals from as far away as Bozeman and Missoula—not to ride, but to wed.

Mac Henderson didn't even make any attempt to corral the conversations. It was just crazy. Though the guys, even Patrick, were better behaved around Emily, which Julie appreciated.

But the most disorienting thing of all was Nathan's absence. The straw wasn't deep enough for her to have missed him on the floor of Clarence's stall. If he wasn't here, where had he gotten off to? She wanted to ask Ama, but she was at the far end of the table taking care of one of her granddaughters. Emily too was at that end.

Patrick and the non-twins were busy dissecting Tom Cruise's latest *Mission Impossible* performance and debating that if he got to choose any one of the female costars, which one should it be.

Chelsea was teasing them about which man the female costar

should choose, and how it shouldn't be Tom because "he was getting so old. Still cute, I mean I'd trip him if I hadn't met Doug, but seriously? If you guys want to pretend you're over fifty and would have a tenth of the chance that Tom would, go for it."

Mark and his dad were discussing possible fishing trip plans for guests. For a change, Mark's ever-present mirrored Ray Bans were dangling from his shirt's collar rather than hiding his steel-gray eyes.

"For the back-country fly fishers, there're several fine spots up towards the falls. Stan did a great job fixing up the fishing cabin last winter," Mac said in his easy manner.

Stan, as usual, made no comment though he was listening in. He wasn't a fisherman, that she knew of, but he appeared even more bored by the on-going Hollywood discussion than she was.

Mark's speech was more clipped, more...recently ex-military. "Need to look into back-country permits. Helicopter them in for a true wilderness experience. Scout some lakes, fish them a bit to see what's biting."

Mac had slapped Mark on the arm knowing exactly what his son was up to. "You never were made for just sittin'."

"Except along a trout stream."

Julie had never been one for "just sittin' " herself. And she realized that's what she was doing, even though breakfast was already done. Another very non-Larson style activity, still at the table after the meal was eaten.

She rose to her feet and cleared her place over to the sink. Still no sign of Nathan. It wasn't as if he was duty bound to show up. And it definitely wasn't that she wanted to see where that first hint of a soft kiss might have led if Clarence hadn't taken exception to him.

It definitely wasn't that.

Mac flagged her down halfway to the back door.

"We need to talk, girl. Come along to my office." He led her back through the ranch house and to the grand double staircase that swept up from the front entrance. The sunrise was shining in through some of the high windows, lighting the big foyer like a cathedral.

She'd never actually been upstairs in the house since the Hendersons had taken it over.

"We used to sneak in here when we were little kids," she told him to hide her nerves. "Big, spooky old place to a little girl, but I always liked it, too. Even then I could see the house's bones were good under the age."

Mac nodded. "Bart Sr. offered it to me when I retired. How could I refuse? I'd saved his son during Desert Storm when we were forward deployed past Saddam's lines. Nothing Bart Jr. wouldn't have done if our positions had been reversed. But his dad was—still is—one of the big ten owners in Montana. Legally made this place mine as long as me or mine are working it. Can't sell it except to him, and only for any added value. Fair a deal as I've ever been offered."

Almost a tenth of Montana private lands were owned by ten major holders. She'd always wondered how the Hendersons had afforded such a big spread. Neither theirs nor the Larson land was anywhere near the top ten category, but they were two of the bigger ranches around for a long ways. Her family had done it by moving onto the land back when Custer's Last Stand at Little Bighorn and the Great Sioux War were passing into history. Back when no one had cared about this stretch of the Montana Territory except the "injuns"—who long since had been moved onto reservations or forcibly relocated.

"It had gone fallow," Mac continued telling his ranch's recent history she barely recalled. "Only thing that saved the place is how remote it was. 'Fix it up however you like,' he told us. Five years back, he brought his grandkids out to ride horses. They were our first clients, insisted on paying. 'Don't give anyone no charity they haven't earned,' was one of Bart's rules."

At the head of the stairs, the transition was dramatic. She vaguely remembered cobwebbed corridors and a long attic of weathered gray wood.

The attic was now a big airy room with five big pedal looms and a couple of smaller ones. Dark cherry wood and bright maple, they stood on a floor of polished oak beneath large skylights. Tall windows, glowing with the morning sunlight, offered a sweeping view only a little less spectacular than the one from up at the cabins. The walls were hung with Cheyenne weavings: deep red, black, tan, and gray. Some were bright and new, probably Ama's work. Others looked to be museum-quality heirlooms.

"There's such a sense of belonging here." Julie wished she could somehow wrap this space around her and hold it inside so that she'd know it was always there. Mac gave her the time to walk through, brush her fingers over the rich colors and tight-woven geometric shapes, and pretend for a moment that she had such a depth of history.

The Larsons were Minnesota dirt farmers who followed the cattle west in the late 1800s. They'd only arrived in Minnesota after working their way across from some long-lost Scandinavian famine. Their history hadn't moved with them. Ama's had; Julie could feel it in the air.

"Thanks for that, Julie. We've worked hard to create that," Mac sounded as if he still didn't believe that they had. She remembered what he'd said about how a father worried, at least some fathers.

Taking his hand for a moment, she looked at his lined face. "Your son and his wife could have chosen anywhere in the world to live. They chose here. You done good, Mac."

He nodded, looked aside for a long moment, then nodded again. "Come on back," his voice was rough as he guided her along the corridor.

To the other side of the main stairs from the majesty of the weaving, a door led to a cozy hallway adorned with family pictures and a few smaller wall hangings. This was the family's private space, separate from all of the splendor downstairs. The dimensions were smaller, more human. The architecture simpler. This was their home.

How did that feel, having a home? She had the house she'd grown up in, the bedroom that had been hers since the day Grandma had passed when Julie was four. But this was different.

Home meant someone to live with, didn't it?

"You're going to be a 'hard woman' soon," her father had taken to saying. A hard woman: unmarried, alone, bitter. Too hard for any man to want her.

It wasn't true. She knew it wasn't. But sometimes she worried that it was.

And then Nathan had cooked for her and done it like she was special. Kissed her softly as if that's how she *deserved* to be kissed.

For the first time in years, perhaps ever, he made it possible to imagine "home."

Nathan sat on a hay bale in the equipment garage and looked at his car parked among the ATVs. In front of him was a helicopter. Behind him, an entire array of machinery that he couldn't begin to name. The metallic red Miata MX-5 fit in here just about as well as he did—not at all.

It had been a crazy purchase for someone who so rarely left the city limits. He'd put more miles on it the two days of coming here than he had in the year before, maybe the two years before.

And now?

He should get in the damned thing and just drive away. Just go. Don't even go up to the house to get his knives or his clothes, because she was up there.

Just slide open the big door and fire out of here.

What the hell was he playing at anyway?

Julie was a startling woman. A breath of fresh air that he liked more with each passing moment. But how fair was what he was doing?

To either of them?

She was right. He'd be gone. Sooner or later, probably sooner, and then where would he be? Where would they be? They'd both be even more miserable than if he left now. Just toss the dice and start over.

Somewhere.

Seattle or Portland? They were supposed to both be hotbeds of foodie innovation.

So was Brisbane, Australia. But he didn't *want* to go to Brisbane, Australia.

Back to the city?

He'd go insane.

And if he stayed here? Great Falls or Boise? Or was Boise in some other state?

Even crazier.

Maybe he should just drive until he ran out of gas, or money, and start over wherever chance landed him.

Not cooking. He'd liked cooking for Julie. He liked watching her eyes slide shut as the flavors overwhelmed her.

But a restaurant? Never again. He'd sooner herd cattle from hell.

He stood up.

That's what he'd do.

He took a step toward his car.

"I'll just start the engine and go. See where the road leads me."

It was good. It made sense.

He reached for the door handle.

It was the right thing to do, for him. For her. Cut it off before he did more than kiss her. Before he fell for her like he'd never fallen for a woman before.

He could see that, too. Really falling for her. And *then* having to go.

Best to just do it now.

Best to—

"There you are."

Nathan almost shouted in pain at the interruption.

If Mark Henderson noticed anything out of the ordinary, he didn't comment on it.

"I'm going up. Want to come along? Help me roll this out." Mark opened the equipment bay door in front of the helicopter, letting a slash of hard sunlight slice through the air. He signaled for Nathan to help push without waiting for an answer.

Not knowing what to do, or even how to speak at the moment, he pushed where Mark said to push. Together they rolled the helicopter out of its garage bay and into the brilliant morning sunshine radiating from low in the east.

The sky was shockingly blue, horizon to horizon it looked like spilled paint.

———

Halfway along the upstairs corridor, Mac led Julie through a doorway into a small office. It was almost comical it was so plain. Two steel desks, a couple of big file cabinets, and a view back into the sloping hillside. One desk was neat as a pin, the other looked as if it had been through a train wreck—a wreck that was still in progress.

"Didn't want this to be nice. Get work done, then get out in the sun where I belong. That desk is for doing the books," he waved a hand at the neat one. "This one here is for thinking."

She suddenly felt uncomfortable. Why were they meeting in his office? Was there something wrong with her contract? Or with her work? She needed this to succeed.

"I figure that running a ranch should be done out on a ranch, not locked up in some pretty office," Mac had read her surprise at how plain and cramped the space was in the otherwise expansive house.

"Dad's the same way. I think his office might have once been a broom closet. We kids always clear out when he goes in to deal with the paperwork because he usually comes out in a foul mood."

"Happiest when he's out and about," Mac nodded and sat down at the "thinking" desk, which she'd take as a good sign, and indicated for her to sit across from him.

Julie tried to shunt the huge wall of worry aside and answer Mac truthfully, which wasn't a very comfortable feeling when it came to her family.

"I'm not sure happy is a word I'd ever apply to Dad, but *content* might work." During rare moments.

"That's something you learn in Special Operations. You work hard, you train hard. But there is a time when you have to celebrate being alive. Really let your hair down and kick it out a bit. You ever do that, girl?"

The only image she could conjure up was galloping on Clarence over the empty fields. She wasn't sure if that counted, so she shrugged uncertainly.

"You should do it, Julie. I'm serious. Take that young man you're so worried about and go play."

She wasn't worried about Nathan. Not really. Though she wished she knew where he was.

Mac fished around on the desk until he unearthed a pen and a pad of paper. He made a clear spot by shoving some of the journals, notes, catalogs, and a couple of books about snipers over on top of more of the same.

He plopped the pad down on the desk and raised his voice to carry over the helicopter that was passing close over the ranch house.

"So, here's the problem I'm thinking on."

Nathan tried to remember how to breathe, "I thought you were going to hit the house."

"Not a chance. I missed it by over twenty feet," Mark actually swooped back down toward the ground on the back side of the big ranch house until they were skimming mere feet over the grass. "God it feels so good to fly again."

"How long has it been?"

"Days, maybe weeks. How about you?" Mark swooped low over the cabins.

"I flew to Paris about a decade ago and spent five years there."

"Airliners don't count. Sardine cans of the sky."

"Then," Nathan swallowed hard and hung on to the edges of his seat, "never."

The Bell JetRanger had three seats in back and two in the front. Mark sat in the right-hand seat and Nathan had the left. The clear plastic window offered him a fantastic view—a clear vision of whatever Mark was about to ram them into. But each time, at the last moment, he swooped aside. Not in hard, panicked moves, but as if it was the most natural thing in the world.

The engine and rotor were so loud that he could still hear them despite the heavy headset Mark had given him.

"Do you always fly so close to the ground?"

Mark's laugh was bright over the intercom. "Depends on the mission. You fly a firefighter helo a hundred feet above the flames, give or take. I've spent most of the last five years up in a command plane. To you that would be two engines with propellers on fixed wings. About a dozen seats, but I needed it for speed and range, not for people-carrying. I flew that within a thousand feet or so of the fires. Far enough to stay out of the way of the helos and airtankers."

"There's no way that we're a hundred feet above the ground," their flight path slewed across a broad pond just over the rise behind the cabins that Nathan hadn't even known was there. It looked as if there was still ice around the edges. There was also a sagging dock that was going to need some work before it could be a decent swimming hole.

"Do you skate?"

"Like Rockefeller Center? Ice skating? A couple of times, if she was cute enough to talk me into it. Fell down a lot."

"Midwinter there's good skating on this pond. I'll get you some hockey skates and we'll have a game," he climbed up the far berm and headed out over the fields.

"Sounds good." And it did sound good. Too bad he wasn't going to be here by then. Nathan actually shivered when he thought about how close he'd come to not even being here by lunch. It had been a close call. Whether that was good or bad was a question he couldn't deal with, especially while occupied with hoping he'd live through the next thirty seconds.

"On a mission, trying to stay out of sight, we'd be more likely to fly here," and Mark carved a turn around a tree, then slid down until it looked as if the skids were brushing the grass.

Mark's smooth moves still appeared casual, but Nathan could feel the silence of intense concentration settle over him. Nathan looked over but Mark's mirrored shades reflected the racing prairie as if the landscape had become his actual eyes.

"It takes a lot of control. Have to think without thinking. Every movement is critical." He narrated between shifts and jogs as he cleared the ground by feet and hummocks by inches.

Nathan felt a little seasick when he looked down. The window by his feet was so close to the rushing ground that all he could see was a blur—except when he blinked. Then, like a freeze frame, he felt as if he was standing on no more than a stepstool above the ground—the moment before it *rushed* out of sight underneath them.

"Goddamn it, Lucy!" Mark cursed sharply and did something to the controls that jerked them harshly upward.

They cleared the cow's massive horns by inches.

Far out—on Henderson land—Lucy was grazing on winter grass.

Mark circled her once from a couple of stories higher in the air. The cow watched them balefully, but kept chewing on her latest mouthful.

"It's the curse of the demon cow," Nathan shuddered. "You shouldn't have brought me along. She seems to know where I'm going to be and just shows up."

"Nah, I needed you as a second set of eyes."

"To avoid stray cows?"

"Need to scout out some fishing trips. Promised Dad I'd lead one now and again. Do you fish?"

"I cook."

Mark gave him a long, assessing gaze. "Heard some about the meal you made for Teton County's most eligible."

"Did she like it?" Nathan knew she had, but couldn't help himself. He was so pitiful. Hadn't he been on the verge of leaving for her own good just a few minutes ago?

"Mom said a real lack of leftovers came back from the dinner. So I'm guessing the answer is yes. Don't you know?"

Nathan decided to keep to himself how truly pitiful he was about wanting to please Julie. Actually, it was something of a surprise *quite* how important that was.

Mark swooped low over the broad pastures that looked to go on for miles. The mountains that had loomed so close all week were getting even closer. Thankfully they now flew several hundred feet above the rolling prairie.

"A chef really only lives for two reasons. If he's insanely lucky or practices for a lifetime, he may create a new flavor or a new dish that will outlive the moment of creation. The other reason is to make people happy with his food. Regrettably, knowing that he'll probably never achieve the former, he is constantly convinced that he can never achieve the latter."

"You really need to get a life, Nathan."

"Tell me about it."

Mark laughed easily enough.

"Instead, tell me what we're doing out here."

"We're on a fishing expedition."

"Fishing for what?"

Mark's sigh was unexpectedly deep. "Fishing for a way that I can survive retirement."

For over an hour, Julie worked with Mac on the future of Henderson's Ranch. First, they'd verified that all the orders were in place for the yurts: bunks, fixtures, bathrooms, and the yurts themselves. They'd opted for all five the same, the medium-sized twenty-foot diameter ones which could comfortably handle up to six people with a cozy sitting area for rainy days—though the main activities on those days would be down at the ranch house.

There was already a shower at the back of the main house. It had been for the hands to clean up back when the place still ran cattle. Mac added fixing that up to her to-do list, which had saved the size of the bathroom building up on the slope, though Julie wasn't sure about that choice yet—when you had children with you, a shower close to hand seemed preferable. The spring workload was shaping up well for J. L. Building.

Then they'd looked over some of the ranch's prime recreation spots. They both knew the good trails that were a mix of prairie to gallop on, woods to mosey through, and the occasional vista. But there was only the one remote fishing cabin out by the waterfalls.

"I'd like to add one a year. First, maybe a hunting cabin back against the primitive area."

"Next, out by Old Baldy," she tried to be careful about not overstepping her place. But each cabin would be a couple months of good work for her if she did well on these first jobs. "There are some great trails back there. The guests pay for the ride out to the cabin, then the horses get a day or two of paid rest while they hike themselves up the trails."

"Make them happy to spend more for something that costs us nothing extra but some feed and a guide. The businessman in me calls that a win-win."

"Nothing comes for free." Then Julie nearly choked on her own words, because they were her father's.

"Nothing but the best things. Those are always free." So not her father.

Julie didn't know what to say to that, so she kept her thoughts to herself. It sure wasn't part of her experience. There was a cost, a trade-off to every decision in the Larson household. Pursuing her own future also earned her the brunt of Dad's disapproval. While her brothers seemed to appreciate his focusing on her for now, she sure didn't.

After she and Mac mapped out a couple more ideas—she was pretty pleased at coming up with geocaching of historical sites and especially spectacular views. Once the course was set, it would be a whole day horseback quest that didn't even need guides except as protection in case they spooked a bear. Could even change it up each year with new sites and new routes.

Finally Mac tossed down his pen and pad, then pulled out a desk drawer, leaned back, and propped his feet on it.

"Like the way you think, girl. You know this land better than I do."

"No, I don't."

"Ama and I have been here for just over fifteen years now, you've been on it your whole life."

"I spent most of the time over there," she pointed in the direction of Larson land.

Mac rocked his chair back on its hind legs and looked straight at her with steely gray eyes the same as his son's. Other than that and his powerful build, they barely looked related. Mark had Ama's dark straight hair rather than Mac's graying blond. Though Mac still looked dangerously military, there was a soft kindness to his face that balanced him out. Mark's steel-eyed gaze unnerved her even more than Emily's used to.

"That's not my point. You know the land, the Big Sky country. I came from Chicago. No way you'd ever guess how I became a SEAL, so I'll just go on and tell you."

Julie kept her smile to herself. By his casual manner and willingness to take the time to tell a story, he fit right in. Somewhere along the way he'd become Montanan, whether or not he knew it.

"I was headed to California to become a surfer bum. Fresh out of Oberlin, liberal arts education in French literature, and absolutely no skills."

"You're telling me you got Ama because you were a surfer bum turned SEAL?"

"No, I met Ama before I did either of those. My car broke down in Cheyenne, Wyoming, during the Frontier Days, so I wandered to the rodeo while they were replacing my starter motor. Ama was a native performer there and I'd never seen anything so amazing in my life as that tall Native American beauty. I was done and gone before her dance was half over. She'd never traveled but wanted an adventure, so she went to California with me on a whim. We both sucked at surfing, but I can't begin to tell you how good that woman looked in a bathing suit."

Julie tried to picture Ama Henderson as a bikini-clad surfer babe and simply couldn't conjure up the image. She was still beautiful, but she embodied the serene matron of the spiritual connection to the ranch as if she'd never been anywhere but on this land.

"While we were surfing off Coronado," Mac was tipped back and studying something far beyond the ceiling. "I'd watch the SEALs run on the beach during the day and sweep up all the great women in the bars at night."

"But you already had Ama, right? She doesn't strike me as the type to get swept up too easily."

"True. I had her, but I wanted to keep her, too. That's how I became a SEAL. Did it for her, and whenever I had to dig down and find that extra motivation, just thinking of her did that for me. We made a good life together. She and Mark joined me overseas whenever it was safe. Neither of us knew crap about ranching before Bart gave us the place to run. Learned a lot, but we weren't born to it the way you were."

"Well," Julie thought about the ranch house, the property, the cabins, the horses, and the plans they'd just been working on for the future. "I think you've done a fine job of it, Mr. Henderson."

"Thanks, Julie. Means a lot coming from you," he thunked his chair down into place. "Enough jawing, as they say. Let's go get 'er done."

"Sure thing," Julie rose to her feet.

As Mac led her back along the corridor and down the stairs, he muttered as if speaking to himself, "Whole life changed because of a shorted-out starter motor."

Julie missed a step and might have tumbled to the bottom if it hadn't been the last one.

All because his car broke down.

"Now this *is* a sweet spot." Nathan lay back in the grass and watched a lone cloud slipping through the blue sky like a giant cotton ball.

Mark had landed them by a high lake well to the south of the waterfall. With the excuse, "Just need to see what's biting here," he pulled out a fishing pole he'd stashed aboard the helo and was soon casting a line out over the pristine water.

It was a fair-sized lake, wandering back into the deep trees for almost half a mile. While Mark fished, Nathan had explored. A lively creek drained to the north. He pulled out his phone and snapped a couple of pictures of Mark casting, thinking he'd send them to his friends still in New York—they'd never believe where he was—except he'd have to wait to send them until he found a signal again.

"Welcome to the wilderness."

He'd finally returned to the helo, grabbed a horse blanket from the supplies in the back, and lay down on the grass to watch the day. He hadn't truly stopped since getting here. Cooking with Ama to feed the hands. Talking to Julie. Kissing her. This morning's pre-sunrise "horse" lesson, provided equally by both the woman and the horse in question. Except for his sore butt, he thought it had gone well. Clarence wasn't nearly as intimidating close up as he had been in the evening light out on the road.

Nathan was utterly exhausted by the uncertainty of his life. His struggle to leave this morning without even seeing her one last time had almost broken something inside him. He had nowhere to go. Nowhere to be. Whatever came next—

Mark's soft whistle from fifty feet along the bank had Nathan looking back down from the sky. A trio of the ungainliest animals he'd ever seen had wandered down to the lakeside not a hundred years away.

"Moose?" he whispered. He'd never seen a moose.

"Elk," Mark whispered back. "I think. Not a lot of either in Iraq or Afghanistan."

The trio ignored them as they waded into the frigid water. There was a baby that was nearly as big as Clarence, a monstrous bull with a rack of horns which might even be bigger than Lucy's, and the mama in-between. "What do they call the mother?"

"A cow. Bull, cow, and calf."

"You're closer. Does she look demonic? I have really bad luck with cows." They'd been slowly raising their voices toward normal speech, but the elk's, or moose's, reactions were only a twitching of the ears.

"Usually people worry about the bull," Mark checked for him. "Looks more like she's just happy to be in a bath and away from

Junior." The young one was playing in the shallows, barely in the water up to its knobby knees.

"An elk family," Nathan sat up and shot a photo with his camera so that he could ask Julie when he saw her. If he saw her. If he didn't just grow a pair of balls and climb in his car to go as soon as Mark flew them back. He took another, this time of the angler and the critters together. Actually, that one would make a great publicity shot; he'd even caught the nose of the helicopter in the frame. Even if he left, he'd send it to Ama for the Henderson's Ranch website.

"Or moose. I'm really not sure."

"Maybe it's some kind of weird crossbreed that only happens in Montana. A melk?" He could picture it being a melk.

Then with a flick of water, Mark's line snapped tight. In moments it was racing off his fishing reel.

"Grab the net!"

"Don't you have to land it first?" But he tossed the horse blanket back in the cargo hatch and dug around until he found a net.

Mark was slowing the spool, but the line was still growing longer. Nathan didn't like the angle.

"It's going straight for the moose, or elk. Don't let it—"

But it was too late, the racing fish had dragged the fishing line across one of the moose's legs. The big bull levitated straight out of the water with a loud sound that was half bray and half honk.

When it landed back in the water, it glared in their direction.

"Uh-oh!" Nathan began edging back toward the helicopter. "I've had some experience with this. If Lucy had looked like that, not even Julie could have rescued me. Let's go."

"But I've got a fish," Mark's voice was nearly a whine. But he too began backing away. As he did, it must have moved the line, this time the big bull didn't levitate, he roared.

"Mark. Forget the damned fish." Nathan had reached the passenger side of the helo and tossed the net into the foot well.

"Aren't you supposed to face down wild animals?" But Mark didn't sound so sure even as he said it.

"Haven't you ever seen the videos of moose crashing into each other with their antlers?"

"Forgot about that." Mark made some decision, then hurried up to him. "Take the pole. Don't let go." Then he raced around the other side and climbed in. Within moments, the helicopter's engine whined to life and the rotors began turning slowly. Too slowly.

Nathan climbed in on the passenger side, feeling like a complete idiot for still holding the pole out the open door.

The moose twisted in their direction, bellowed again, and began clambering up toward the shore.

"He's coming this way, Mark. Get a move on."

When the calf tried to engage his dad in play, the bull nipped him sharply on the butt and the calf squeaked in pain and surprise.

"I know how you feel, buddy."

By the time the bull reached the shore, Mark had the rotors going.

There was some momentary slack in the line. Nathan prayed that the line had simply broken. He fooled around with the handle until he figured out how to wind in the line.

As the rotors wound faster, so did he.

The melk (eoose? whatever) also took that as his cue and moved more quickly along the shore in their direction. The closer it came, the bigger it looked. Its huge rack of antlers were massive curved plates big enough to serve a suckling pig on, with sharp points sticking out from them. Its bulbous nose pulled back over bared teeth as it bellowed out a warning that seemed to shake the hills.

The line snapped taut and the pole bent, the sudden tension almost yanking it out of Nathan's hands.

"Let out line. Let it out! That button on the right. Press it!" Mark shouted over the blast of engine and rotor noise that was now beating on him.

Or was it the noise of the moose's pounding hooves as it shifted from a walk to a trot after it reached the grass?

"Damn! That thing is huge! It's coming our way. Get us out of here!"

"Almost..." Mark was doing things to the controls, but none of them were getting them aloft. "Don't touch the spinning reel with your bare hands, you'll get a bad slice. Ease on the brake. Not hard or you'll snap the line."

That last sounded like a good idea to Nathan, but he did as he was told.

The moose went from trot to run. Then it lowered its head to ram them just as Mark got them aloft. The moose's blow caught the skid squarely on Mark's side and knocked them through the air toward the lake. The impact had Nathan whiplashing against Mark and then being almost ejected, along with the fishing pole, out the door on the other side. No time for a seat belt.

Mark managed to get a little more height and turned the nose to face the angry bull. The second blow shattered the small window by Nathan's feet when the moolk rose on its hind legs to pound home a final blow.

Again they were pushed toward the lake.

Mark finally was able to lift them out of the moose's reach and get them out over the water.

The bull stood at the lake shore looking big, dangerous, and triumphant—which it should, because it completely ruled the lakeshore. The cow had herded the calf off under the trees somewhere farther along the shore.

"Do you still have it?" Mark shouted.

"What? My heart? My life?"

"No! My fish."

Nathan could only stare at him.

"Reel in. See if you've still got it."

Nathan cranked on the reel until the line went tight again. "It's still there."

"Good," Mark looked at the tip of the pole and flew sideways in the direction it was pointing, easing along just ten feet above the icy water. "Keeping reeling it in."

"I can't believe we're doing this."

They crisscrossed back and forth above the lake, chasing the fish as Nathan kept shortening the line until finally the line was straight down into the water and he could see the fish struggling and splashing just below the surface. Then Mark descended as Nathan reeled until the helicopter's skids were in the water.

"Hey!" Lake water was splashing in through the shattered window and soaking Nathan's sneakers.

"Sorry, forgot about the window." Mark eased up a few inches, which didn't help much. "I need two hands to fly."

Nathan could barely hear him over the rotor's roar. Neither of them had a free hand to pull on the headsets.

"So pole in one hand, but don't lose it. Grab the net with the other."

It took Nathan a couple of tries, but he finally snagged the fish in the net. It was big for a rainbow trout—longer than his elbow to his fingers. He'd never seen a live one. It was beautiful—nothing in common with the ones in the New York fish market. He finally understood why it had been named rainbow: color glistened down its side, especially an iridescent pink.

For lack of anything better to do—at Marks' instruction—he grabbed it by the tail and brained it against the edge of the door.

"Dinner!" Mark sounded utterly delighted. Though Nathan suspected that he'd be the one who had to cook it. Maybe he'd do a simple white wine and thyme poach, let the gentle fish speak for itself. Though browned in clarified butter with a sage-mushroom-cream sauce, using wild mushrooms and farm fresh cream, also sounded good.

Nathan tucked the pole, the net, and the dead fish back between the seats, then closed the door and pulled on both of their headsets and his own seatbelt. As the adrenaline drained away he realized that he was actually happy.

Mark circled back up over the still-glowering moose, standing with its feet just into the lake as if ready to come after them at the least sign of weakness.

"At least I know what a truly angry animal looks like now," not that a soul back in New York would believe it. Then he started laughing.

"What?" Mark was smiling.

"I never knew why they call it fly fishing."

Mark guffawed as they turned back toward the ranch, the chill wind whistling through the shattered window and over Nathan's soaking wet feet.

"What the hell did they do to my bird?" Doug was scowling at the sky.

Julie looked up just as the helicopter passed by low overhead. There was a big crease across the nose and one of the windows was broken out. Nathan waved cheerily from the passenger seat, but they were gone before she had a chance to respond.

At least that explained where he'd been all morning.

She didn't know why she cared.

No. She *did* know why she cared. Some terrified corner of her heart had feared that he'd gone. Over dinner last night she'd heard his love for New York City. He didn't miss it, or he didn't seem to, but he knew its terrain as intimately as she knew the Montana Front Range. It was a part of him.

There hadn't been time to hunt him down or his car—the hay loft had been her idea, but she didn't know what the boys had done with it last night. So all morning she'd worried over it. There'd been no sign of him in the kitchen or crossing the yard. Not once had he appeared to scan around for what she was doing—something he'd done constantly, even when she wasn't speaking to him.

Preparing the holes for the yurt platforms' concrete footings, ones that would be stout enough to support full cabins in the future, was a three-person job. And she had to take advantage of the help while she could get it rather than hunting for him.

Mac was on his backhoe operating the big auger. It crunched through the last of the frozen ground like it was shaving ice at a county fair for snow cones, then quickly cut down into the rich soil.

She and Doug concentrated on bending and wiring up the rebar internal framework, then placing them in the finished holes and slipping sixteen-inch cardboard Sonotubes over that to define the post for the concrete pour. She'd gotten everything pre-staked and run one of Mac's flatbeds all the way into Great Falls to get the rebar and Sonotube she'd needed. Splicing in a temporary power pole, they had the juice they needed to run saws for slicing the tubes and cutting the rebar.

At this rate they'd be ready for concrete in just a few more days. Then she could start on the yurt platforms.

And what had Nathan been doing? It wasn't that she expected him to be working. He was…she didn't know what he was. He wasn't on vacation. He was helping Ama with the cooking and had now gone somewhere with Mark. But he also wasn't leaving.

Doug held a freshly bent length of rebar in place and she wrapped a thin wire around to secure it.

What *was* Nathan up to? With his fine food and his soft kisses. He wasn't trying to bed her, or if he was, he was going slower than molasses in January.

More to the point, what was *she* up to? She never let a man close unless she knew what she wanted from him. But she had no idea what she wanted from Nathan Gallagher. She—

"Don't need to strangle the poor thing," Doug interrupted her thoughts. She'd wound the wire so tightly around the next rebar joint that it was never getting away.

"Maybe it deserves it. Besides, I don't want it going anywhere." Though it definitely hadn't needed the three extra wraps before she twisted it off.

Doug bent and placed the next piece before speaking again, barely louder than the steady grind of the big auger chewing up the next snow cone layer before getting down to the dirt.

"I'm maybe not the best person to speak to about these things, Julie. But I'm willing to try if it'll help."

"What things?" Another piece of rebar cinched down within an inch of its life.

Doug sighed, "And Chelsea wonders why I leave her to do the talking."

Julie was irritated with herself for any number of reasons, prime among those being caught thinking about a man when she should be thinking about work. After they dropped the rebar cage into one of the holes and slipped over the piece of Sonotube, she made a show of pausing, going to the cooler, and getting them each a bottle of water.

Mac eased the auger to a stop and clambered down off the backhoe to stretch for a moment and drink some water with them.

Suddenly she had an audience when she really didn't want one.

Down by the garage, she could see Mark and Nathan closing the equipment bay door after tucking away the helicopter. He waved with one hand and held up a dinner-sized trout with the other. She didn't want to draw everyone's attention down there, so she just gave a nod that she hoped he'd be able to see, then returned her attention to the project.

"Making good progress," Mac started the conversation.

"Seem to be," Doug agreed and emptied half of his bottle of water.

"Slow but good."

"Uh-huh."

It wasn't slow at all. They were well ahead of her planned schedule. To make sure, Julie began mentally counting number of footings to go in her head when she happened to look up and see that neither man was looking at the worksite progress. Doug was avoiding her gaze and Mac seemed fascinated by the two men and a fish that were headed into the house.

"I'm talking about the foundations," Julie kept her tone business-like.

"Sure," Mac agreed but she knew better than to trust that.

"Seriously, that's all *I'm* talking about."

Doug harrumphed.

Mac looked down at the latest hole fully prepared for the concrete truck. "Well, then I'll change 'slow but good' to 'incredibly faster than expected' but work isn't what any of us are talking about."

"I am," Julie tried, but knew it was lame. "Okay, I'm so not." Some part of her was near to panicked over Nathan's sudden disappearance and she didn't like that one bit.

"Now you're talking," Mac agreed.

"No, she isn't," Doug idly kicked some dirt back in around the outside of the Sonotube. "Now she's just feeling helpless. That one I know. Chelsea bowled me over in the first ten minutes."

"First two minutes," Mac corrected him.

"Maybe not even that long," Doug agreed. "Damned if I knew what to do about it though."

When had she *known?*

Julie swallowed hard and bent down to strangle a fresh piece of rebar with a tie-wire.

She didn't *know* anything. Because there wasn't anything to *know.*

CHAPTER 8

It took them three hard days of labor to get the rest of the footings in place and Julie could feel the ache in every muscle.

No morning horse trainings because that precious hour before sunrise was one of the few chances to calculate what other supplies were needed. No pleasant evenings over a fine meal, because that's when she was able to work on Emily's office. No time for Nathan—which sounded like a good thing, but didn't feel that way at all.

The midday temperature was up into the fifties, which reduced them all to shirt sleeves. Her hands throbbed from working the rebar despite the heavy gloves.

For three days she'd worked like a mad woman and successfully avoided three things: the question of her attraction to Nathan, Nathan himself, and sleep. Her mind had become an endless churn of why Nathan hadn't tried to seduce her after that dinner and what was she going to do about it.

That night, she wouldn't have gone with him even if he had tried. She was still fairly certain about that. But for three days now he hadn't done a single thing except be friendly and make Ama's ranch food—which had always been a treat—even better.

If he were to ask right now, she just might go willingly. Perhaps even very willingly.

There was a round of silent nods with her, Doug, and Mac after they finished the last footing prep. A careful scan of the hillside revealed six clusters of footings springing up through the grass and mud—five for the yurt platforms and one for the common bathroom. Not a single marker stake left, every single one had been augered, rebarred, and Sonotubed.

The three of them began cleaning up the site. Restacking extra supplies. Moving the heavier tools like the rebar bender and cutter, both of which they were done with for now, into the bucket of Mac's backhoe so that he could drive them down to the barn.

She paused to slam back half a bottle of water that did nothing to soothe her parched throat.

And then it struck her: had Nathan been playing some kind of waiting game? Knowing that she was churning away inside and it was going to twist her up? But even as she thought it, she remembered his promise: *No games.* Besides, it didn't sound like something Nathan would do.

Let your hair down and kick it out a bit, Mac had told her. Maybe he was right.

She looked down at the main ranch house and recalled how Nathan had looked that morning—three days and forever ago—sleepy and holding the covers tight about his neck. How could so much be packed into a single morning? A horse-interrupted kiss, the fear of him leaving, and her impossibly huge relief to see him flying by overhead.

Only now did she admit to herself that she'd had an image of another way to wake him besides kicking the foot of his bed. For just a moment, less than a second, she'd had an image of sliding under those covers with him.

Take that young man you're so worried about and go play.

What if she did? She had an errand down Great Falls way. She'd been planning to make a morning run—down and back in one shot. What if...

"Go, Julie."

"What?" she looked at Doug but he wasn't explaining himself.

"Get yourself moving, girl. Doug and I've got this," Mac gave her a small shove to get her moving. She barely managed to hand off the last spool of tying wire and the cutters before she headed down toward the house, still unsure of what she'd do when she got there.

Nathan was slicing a loaf of fresh-baked sourdough, while the stew he'd made for lunch bubbled away, when Julie came striding through the back door of the kitchen. She wore her Ford baseball hat and was covered in dirt as usual. Heavy leather gloves clasped a half-finished water bottle like she could do war with it as her sole weapon.

She looked absolutely fantastic.

Meeting her halfway between counter and door, he did the only thing he could think of: he wrapped his arms around her and kissed her. He hadn't even recalled sleeping last night, not with Julie and his own future both all stirred up in his thoughts.

Having decided not to leave had opened something in him. For three days he'd wondered what fit there. It was an open spot that Julie slid right into.

She made a pleased "Mmmm" sound and wrapped her own arms around his waist. Had a woman ever felt so right in his arms? She fit there like…like…the trout had fit in an amandine sauce.

When she broke it off, his head was spinning from the impact. His nervous system had just been hit by a stampeding herd and showed no sign of recovering.

"Come with me?"

"Anywhere." He needed her. Now. Blindly. He didn't care what or where or how. He wanted to be beside her. To touch her hair. To watch her blue eyes slowly shift when a reluctant smile finally reached them. To take her body with his until they both cried out like—

"I have to run into Great Falls."

"That's…" he tried to remember his route here, but couldn't. Great Falls was somewhere beyond Choteau. It was, "…a ways."

"Yep. Couple hours either way."

"Love to." As long as it was Julie Larson leading the way, he'd follow.

She nodded, then started for the door. Halfway there, she looked down at herself. "I need to go home and change."

"Should I bring anything?"

"Your car keys if you're willing to drive." Then Julie hesitated for a long moment before continuing softly. "Might bring along a toothbrush too."

Nathan grabbed that as well as a jacket, a fresh shirt, and a small box of protection he'd left in his suitcase. He stuffed them into a knapsack and hurried out to hunt down his car. This time, it was oddly parked in its own bay of the garage, just sitting there ready to go. He followed Julie's truck over to her ranch.

It wasn't a big place, and definitely not a showpiece like Hendersons. But it looked homey. A comfortable two-story. Maybe a little small with four grown kids, but it was pretty with the sky blue siding and white trim that seemed so popular along the Front Range.

Julie tried to have him wait in the front drive, but he figured that wasn't fair. He didn't want her to face her family alone while a "young man" sat waiting out in his car. It simply didn't feel right.

However, he hadn't counted on meeting them all at once. It was only when he and Julie walked into the kitchen at the end of the Larson's lunch (which locals called dinner) that he remembered the stew bubbling away on the kitchen counter. Well, it would be found and consumed shortly, so no need to panic there.

Introductions were made. "Nathan has agreed to drive me down to Great Falls for a morning meeting. I have to go change." It didn't fool anybody.

"I'll be quick," she whispered and disappeared from the room like a shot.

Five sets of eyes turned on him and their reactions were all different.

Mom looked pleasantly surprised.

The twins looked ready to rough him up, maybe just for the sport of it.

Nathan had expected Julie's father to be the worst of it, but he was all polite manners: shaking Nathan's hand in greeting, offering him dinner even though it was clear they were already done, and giving him a glass of lemonade when he turned down the food.

It was the oldest brother, Matthew, who looked the most displeased. He rose silently from the table and stood just as silently with his arms crossed until he looked bigger than Lucy or the moolk that he and Mark had barely survived out at the lake.

"I don't think we've met," her father started off the conversation. Which was better than the "Who the hell are you?" that Nathan had been expecting.

"I'm staying up at Henderson's. You may know my brother, Patrick, sir," Nils Larson was definitely a *sir*. "I'm out visiting," though he decided to leave out that he was from New York. From Julie's comments he'd guess that while an outsider might be unwelcome, someone from New York City or Los Angeles would be considered certifiable. Or perhaps eligible for target practice—Matthew certainly looked at him that way.

"How are you liking the ranch lifestyle?"

"I see much to recommend it. Except for an," he made a guess, "elk that Mark Henderson and I ticked off the other day."

"Good man. Served his time and then some. Have you served?" But Nils glowered at his sons. Apparently none of them had either and that looked to be a bone of contention.

Matthew opened his mouth and Nathan hurried his answer to keep the peace.

"No, sir, I haven't," Nathan changed back to his earlier topic quickly. "The elk took exception to Mark's fishing methods and head-butted our helicopter before we could escape aloft."

"Head-butted a helicopter?" One of the twins remarked in surprise.

"Great big antlers," Nathan held his arms out wide. "Like great curved platters with spikes."

"Moose, not elk," Matthew growled out.

"Oh. Thanks. I've lived most of my life in cities, so I wasn't sure. Mark's fish dragged the line across the bull's legs while it was browsing in deep water. It was very unhappy about it."

"Do you fish?"

"No sir. I cook."

"Like at a restaurant?"

"I did. Not anymore." Could he sound more useless if he tried? "I'm helping Ama Henderson while I'm here."

There was a shift in the room and Nathan could feel it. It was like when a star reviewer was spotted in the restaurant. Everything shifted. Tension went from typical service-scaled worry to full-blown flambé. The only step beyond that would be fire-in-the-kitchen panic.

"And what are your inte—" Matthew had been leaning back against the kitchen counter, but now stood straight to tower over Nathan. Maybe there was a step beyond fire-in-the-kitchen panic—something like *Oh god! Oh god! We're all going to die.*

"We've got to run," Julie breezed into the room, now carrying a small backpack. She'd changed and washed her face, but he could still see the dirt line along her neck. Thankfully riding to his rescue rather than wasting precious moments to shower.

"Did you eat yet?" Nils Larson's manners stepped back in.

"We—" Nathan started, but Julie jumped right in.

"Ama fed us. We're all set. Come on, Nathan. I've got a whole list of errands in the city."

"The city?" That only had one meaning to him—New York.

"Choteau is the town, Great Falls is the city. Helena is the capital and Bozeman is too far away for anyone to think about," she was speaking fast, obviously trying to hide her nerves. She turned to her family, "Nathan wanted to see some of Montana while he was here so I agreed to play tour guide if he'd help me with my errands. Gotta go. C'mon, Nathan."

She was halfway to the door before Nathan had time to turn and shake Nils hand again. "Pleasure to meet you, sir. I look forward to a chance to talk."

"You may count on it, young man."

Matthew made the moose look timid.

Julie couldn't breathe. Couldn't move fast enough.

Nathan pulled his keys out as they crossed the front porch and she grabbed them out of his hand.

"Get the gate. Make sure it latches behind you." The top was down so she vaulted over the door and slammed into the driver's seat.

Then couldn't find the key hole.

Nathan leaned over the passenger door and pressed a big button marked "Engine Start" and it purred to life.

She didn't need purr. She needed *roar*.

He strolled to the front gate as if he had all day and her family wasn't at the windows, breathing down her neck. She never should have brought him here. She never should have brought him with her. Was it too late to pull out? Leave him back at Henderson's?

But as she rolled through and he (finally) closed the gate behind him, her truck was now home and she wasn't. There was no way she could take Nathan's car without him and she actually did have to go to Great Falls.

"Take a breath. First gear. Clutch out with a little gas." Nathan had climbed into the passenger seat without her noticing. "It's fine, Julie. Let's just get some distance so that you can breathe."

She managed to get them moving, working her way up through the gears until they were flying down the road—washboard and pothole nothing more than low spots to fly over. She finally caught her breath when they reached the pavement and she could really open up the little car's engine. She still needed *roar* but it was too well mannered an engine for that. However, the speedometer said they were doing eighty (a speed far beyond the one at which her truck would try to shake itself to death) and she felt much better.

"They seemed nice enough," Nathan was the first to break the silence.

"Ha!"

"I mean for people who didn't know what to do with me. Your big brother—at least I assume that's who he was by his sheer size, almost as big as Mark Henderson—couldn't decide what kind of machine to feed my soiled remains into: a combine, a scythe, or a shredder. Your father would make a fair job of auditioning for the role of a space alien bearing nasty body probes and a memory eraser—except without the memory eraser. Thankfully his manners were too good to start right away. I think the twins would help hold me down for either of them."

"Matthew?" Julie puzzled at that one. "He's always been the only one I could ever talk to. Not even Mom, who is like a straight line to Dad. You actually talked to Dad?"

"Let's just say that if I ever have to meet him alone, I want Stan to show up in my place."

"I can't believe you met them at all. That definitely wasn't part of the plan."

"We were just supposed to sneak off to Great Falls and have amazing sex?"

Julie could feel the heat rising to her face and couldn't do a thing to stop it.

"Wow! Brighter red than the rising sun."

"When did you ever see the rising sun?"

"When someone kicked me out of my bunk in the middle of the night to go be bitten by a horse."

Julie stomped on the brakes, skidding the car to skewed halt.

"What?" Nathan had one hand braced against the dash and the other at the center of her chest as if to protect her. His touch calmed her like a bucket of cold water.

"Clarence," she felt foolish for startling Nathan. "I forgot about Clarence."

"Julie," again he used that calm-down-a-riled-bronc tone of his. "I'm sure Chelsea will pamper him plenty."

Chelsea would. Julie had taken to keeping Clarence there because it was the only way she got to see her horse. She was rarely home while the sun was up—there was just too much going on at Henderson's. She glanced at Nathan then turned away. Way too much...yet also not enough or why was she here.

She looked back the way they'd come, four long black skid marks that would have everyone down this way talking and wondering for months to come. "How could I forget about my horse?" It was no longer a worry, but still, it just wasn't like her. She turned to Nathan, "How did I do that?"

Nathan's soft laugh made her feel more at ease. "I never knew quite how good a compliment could feel. I'm so distracting that Julie Larson thinks of me even before her horse."

It was true. He leaned over for a kiss. This time his hand traveled up her ribs, caressing, testing, until it reached her breast. Her soft moan matched his.

The car jerked when her foot slipped off the clutch and then the engine died. He held her for a long moment before collapsing back in his seat.

"Gods but I need to get you in a hotel room soon."

She couldn't agree more. Her hands were still clenched on the steering wheel and the gear shift, though her body was humming and she could still feel the imprint of his hand on her breast. "Not in Choteau. Everyone there knows me and reports would flow back to my family so fast it would make our heads spin."

Nathan groaned dramatically, "I'm supposed to keep my hands off you until Great Falls? How far away is it?"

"How fast is your car?"

"What about the speed limits?"

"This is Montana. Those are really just suggestions."

"Even with New York plates?"

Julie laughed, finally feeling like herself for the first time since Clarence had nipped Nathan's butt. "Oh, city boy. There are so many things to fix. Are you really worth the trouble?"

"Let's get to Great Falls and find out."

CHAPTER 9

"The Hotel Arvon?"

"It sounded nice." Nathan had never heard of it, but once they were in close enough range to get a phone signal, he'd done a quick search. All, absolutely all of the other top-rated hotels in town were the big chains. It didn't bode well for the city. But the Arvon was a recent restoration of the original 1890 hotel and sounded promising. Even more promising, they'd had a room available on a half hour's notice.

Julie had done an impressive job of finally proving exactly why he'd bought a sports car even though he rarely left the city and never broke the speed limit. With the top down and the wind in her hair, it was hard to believe he was cruising through Montana and not a car ad. Truckers had popped their horns in loud blats of appreciation for the vision as Julie whipped past at speeds he hadn't known his car could go. With the heater on and the growing warmth of the afternoon, it was a very comfortable ride.

"Nice?" Julie protested. "It's the best hotel in town. Can you afford it?"

"I never spend money except on cooking. That plus a rent-controlled apartment for five years. So, a lot of it ended up in the bank for some reason. Besides, I'll be damned if I'm going to take you somewhere less than the best."

"Oh, Nathan," she said it on a happy sigh.

It wasn't New York, but it also wasn't New York prices.

The block it was on wasn't very impressive and that worried him. The hotel itself was a three-story, chunky brick building; only copper decorations along the roofline that were long gone green gave it any relief. Or maybe it was green paint. It was sandwiched between a used furniture store and an electrical supply, but the hotel frontage itself looked cheery and welcoming. There was nothing else particularly attractive in the area except an old railroad station a few blocks away. The main street they'd come in along was a mix of old brick and modern that lacked the frontier-town feel that he'd been expecting.

Once inside, the hotel was a welcome mix of modern with red leather furniture and Western art on the walls. Julie was practically vibrating with impatience while they checked in. The clerk didn't even blink at the small knapsacks they were carrying instead of luggage.

When they hit the room, Julie hit him.

Full body slam!

Arms, legs, lips—she was everywhere at once. It was like being attacked by a whirlwind of spring and sunshine.

Nathan tried to slow her down a bit.

It wasn't working.

There was a frantic edge to her that had him trying to ease back even more. She had his jacket off and his turtleneck as well. Her flannel shirt was wide open, revealing a flat stomach, a fit body, and a very nice pair of breasts in simple white cotton.

"Julie."

She didn't respond, just continued her attack.

"Julie!"

Still nothing.

He hooked his hands under her arms, lifted her up, and set her back down with a little space between them. She was nearly as tall as he was, so he didn't get her moved far, but it helped.

"Julie."

"What? I thought you wanted to have sex," her eyes were narrowed in confusion.

"With you? Absolutely."

She tried to surge at him again, but he kept her at bay. "Then what's the problem?"

"With *you!*" Nathan couldn't believe that he was holding off a gorgeous woman who was throwing herself at him.

Julie merely looked bewildered.

He took her hands in his and led her to a couch. She tried to protest as he pulled her down beside him rather than toward the king-sized bed. He resisted the urge to close her flannel shirt. Her body was a hell of distraction, but he guessed that pushing her away a second time would be a bad idea.

"Julie. Talk to me."

"About what?"

He laughed. "That's a good question. Talk to me about...why you're here?" She'd been manic since she'd walked into the kitchen in the middle of his lunch preparations.

"I'm here to..." But she stalled out. "Because...I'm so sick of being a good girl!"

That came out with a blast of anger he wasn't ready for.

"I'm starting my own company, which my father hates. I won't sleep with every man who thinks I should, which they hate. I won't marry someone I don't care about, which my father (again) hates because he wants the help on the ranch. Cattle are more work than you can imagine. Mac and Emily and Chelsea all want me to be madly in love with you. And they—"

"Wait, what?" He almost missed it going by in the tidal wave of angry words she was suddenly flooding out.

"*You'll find* him, *Julie. Remind her that she likes you, Nathan. Isn't he just the cutest thing?*" She did a fair running imitation of each of the three in turn. Then she huffed out a hard sigh. "Then—" she shrugged.

"Then you decided that if you just screwed me and got it over with, they'd all leave you alone and you could go back to work."

"Yes. Maybe…I don't know." Then she thumped her forehead against his bare chest and left it there. Then she groaned as if in pain. "Real nice for you, huh? I'm sorry, Nathan. You deserve someone better than me."

"That's hard to imagine, anyone being better than you."

"Ha!" But she didn't raise her head and it was a bitter sound.

He slipped his arms around her and brushed his hand down her smooth glory of hair and onto her back. "I'm serious."

"So am I," she mumbled against his chest.

He tipped her back until he could see the blue of her eyes. There were tears lurking there. Of frustration, of rage, of sadness? He didn't know, but he didn't like them.

Brushing gently at them only made them start to flow. Crying woman. What to do with a crying woman?

Nathan kissed her on the forehead and then on each salty eye.

"Julie?"

"Yep. Julie the mess here." She didn't even appear to be aware of the tears.

"What the hell have the men of your past done to you?"

"Screwed me and done," the harsh edge in her voice cut at him. He knew men like that. Too many. Braggarts in the kitchen about what babe they'd scooped up at some bar. He figured that both sides got what they deserved out of those kinds of places—he'd done it more than a few times and could never seem to scrub off the feeling afterward. Not who he was anymore and *definitely* not who Julie was.

"I want to make love with you."

"But you just said—" she blinked at him in confusion.

"Do you want to make love, *with me?* Not some male, but with me?"

"Oh!" She patted a hand on his chest a few times, the warmth of her fingers trickling over his skin just like the tears still sliding down her cheeks. "With *you?*"

"Uh-huh."

She looked him in the eye, really looked at him for the first time since the horse stall three mornings ago. Apparently not trusting herself to speak, she finally nodded.

He'd prefer the words, but didn't want to push his luck. Besides, she was more of an actions-speak-louder-than-words gal.

So, he scooped her in his arms—and almost dropped her on the floor when he stood. Sweeping a grown woman into bed always looked easier in the movies. Julie was giggling by the time he deposited her on the mattress.

Not exactly the reaction he'd been hoping for.

No one had ever carried Julie anywhere. No one except Nathan the White Knight. It was simply too funny that all of her childhood princess dreams were coming to life with a New York chef. That he wasn't carrying her across the room to save her, but rather to ravage her willing body only made it all the funnier. White knight with a tinge of the rutting cowboy—which actually got him into the quarter-finals for prince charming, maybe the finals.

He stood, looking down at her for a moment. Not cowboy-working man buff, just a good solid man. One whose dark eyes were watching her, asking permission one last time.

In making it wholly her choice, even with both of them already half undressed, she knew what she had forgotten. She didn't want a man—she wanted *this* man. The one who somehow already knew her well enough to understand that she'd lost that distinction. Well, with his help, she'd found it again and she knew the real answer.

Taking his hand in hers, she tugged lightly. "Yes, Nathan. With you."

He huffed out a big breath like he'd just finished a cross-country cattle drive. "Well, that's good news." Then rather than lying down upon her or undressing her the rest of the way, he sat down on the edge of the bed. Men, Montana men, always seemed to know what they wanted and simply took it. Happily along for the ride, she'd almost always enjoyed herself. At least the act itself, though the after-math was typically far less charming.

Nathan instead brushed lightly at her hair, then trailed his curled fingers behind her ear and down her neck, watching his own hand. When he finally leaned down to kiss her, it was with that same impossible gentleness that he'd demonstrated before.

"Nathan."

"Uh-huh?" he shifted his attention to her neck.

"I already said yes."

"Uh-huh." But he didn't speed up any.

She half feared he never would. Sex wasn't supposed to put a girl to sleep. It was—

Then he kissed more deeply. And then more. He built slowly from an arroyo trickle into a melt-out torrent. One strong arm about her waist, the other lifting her from the bed until she was as much in his lap as lying beside him.

"It's been a long time, Julie. I don't want to scare you or mess this up."

"You couldn't," and in that moment she knew it was true. Both parts were.

And he didn't.

Being made love to by Nathan wasn't about *to*—it was all about *with*.

It was impossible to ignore the joy he took from every caress he gave. His joy at every one he received was equal. It unleashed something inside her.

She wasn't some horse being ridden, no matter how expertly, by a cowhand.

When it came to making love, Nathan made it as perfect as the best horse and the best rider flying along in unison. One moment he was the one in control, the next it was her, and there was no break of stride as it shifted back and forth between them.

The lines and roles blurred so thoroughly that it was mere chance that she was one who landed astride him for the final race to a glorious finish. Together they rose and clung, gasped and moaned. Most importantly—absolutely the first time ever for her—they both gave.

When Julie slowly fluttered down upon him as gently as a leaf caught in the lightest of breezes, Nathan wondered if now *he* was going to be the one to cry.

How had he missed this? How had he gotten so far in his life and never had an experience like this one? Her body was a work of art: strong, lithe, and masterfully formed. Julie was painted in the fairest of shades except for the alarming intensity of those blue eyes that she didn't close until the very final throes shook her. The woman within was both sweet and fierce, with a big dollop of impossibly dynamic—all at once. He'd never had so much fun having sex or been wracked by such a powerful release.

Thinking that he knew who Julie Larson was, ranked as perhaps the most presumptuous thought of his life. She tasted of salt tears, warm skin, and—he buried his nose in the crook of her neck...and sneezed—dirt.

She looked down at him curiously as he sniffled.

"What? Are you allergic to me?"

"No," he couldn't help sniffling again. "Just to the places you didn't wash off in your hurry to scoot me out of your kitchen."

"You mean my hurry to rescue you from my family?"

"Oh, absolutely. Life and limb at risk. Dead without you. Which actually may have been closer to the truth than I'd like to think about."

She held up an arm, which sported a ring of dirt where glove would have met sleeve. "Not exactly charming."

"Utterly charming." It made him like her even more. Julie wasn't the sort of woman who felt a need to primp. Again, she was just so absolutely herself.

"I need a shower."

"I'll help." Then that charming blush of hers lit her face. "Never showered with a man?"

She shook her head, unleashing a cascade of hair over his face. "Skinny-dipped, but that's different."

"Skinny-dipped. Like outdoors with no clothes on?" He pictured

Julie instead of a long-legged moose stepping into a mountain lake. "I definitely have to give that a try."

"You've never done it?"

"Well, the problem was we could never agree on where to go. The Jacqueline Kennedy Onassis Reservoir in the middle of Central Park seemed disrespectful, even discounting the thousand-odd member audience you'd have on any typical day. The Conservatory Water was always a possibility, but the model-boat sailors have rules about these things. There's a very nice fountain at Lincoln Center, but would upset the opera patrons something awful. And in the East River or the Hudson you'll just get run over by a Circle Line tour boat if you aren't poisoned by whatever is floating down the river."

She propped her chin on her palm to look down at him.

"You have sharp elbows."

Julie didn't apologize or move. "I don't get you, city boy. How have you lived your whole life like that?"

He shrugged, which only let her elbow dig in a little deeper. "Born and raised to it."

She shrugged as if it didn't make any sense to her. Then she pushed off and rolled out of bed. The scenery in this hotel was really excellent.

When he finally mustered the energy to follow her, he realized it was even better than he imagined. The shower was separated from the bath by floor-to-ceiling glass. He checked the slowly fogging mirror. Yes, it was definitely him in it. He looked back through the glass. There was definitely a drop-dead gorgeous, all-American blonde in there. He just couldn't reconcile the two being in the same place.

Once the mirror fogged out and he'd joined her, it was less hard to imagine.

"That. Was. Spectacular!" Julie eased down into a back booth at the restaurant. Her body was still splendidly liquid. "I knew that chefs were good with their hands, but what you did in that shower, that was almost better than that meal you cooked me."

She could still feel the heat. The man-in-control that she hadn't met in bed had definitely entered the shower. If she didn't know him so well, he'd have looked dangerous as he stalked into the glass enclosure. Never once speaking, he'd manhandled her in the most incredible ways, making her body arch and shudder with just a washcloth, soap, and hot water. Her release hadn't been as big as the wonder of having him inside her, but it was a good thing he had strong shoulders to hang on to or she'd have been down on the tile floor while she begged for mercy. Or begged for more. She couldn't remember which she'd asked for.

"I didn't even know there were things like that to feel."

"Better than riding a horse?" Mr. Dark and Sexy hadn't completely gone away yet.

She threw up her hands. "Okay, you got me. That was *at least* as good as riding a horse. Even at a full gallop during a summer sunrise."

"I guess that's as high as a mere man can aspire."

Julie laughed. She couldn't seem to stop smiling around Nathan, even when he was being a little grumpy. No man had ever affected her that way. She hadn't even paid any attention to where he led her.

"Hey, this is nice."

"Welcome to the Celtic Cowboy. It's what sold me on staying here. Nathan Gallagher and Julie Larson—umpteenth generation Irish and cowgirl. Seemed like a natural."

Julie was on the verge of commenting about how *natural* had nothing to do with the heat they'd generated between them, but the waitress arrived and she'd save those thoughts for later. Like when she had enough blood sugar to go another round with Nathan upstairs.

She checked the unlikely name on the menu that the waitress—wearing cowboy boots and an Irish green polo shirt—delivered. The downstairs restaurant at the Hotel Arvon really was called the Celtic Cowboy; Nathan hadn't been fibbing. A dark walnut twenty-stool bar commanded one side of the room. It had at least that many beer taps down its length, the wall of bottles behind were mostly whisky, and the four big screens were running basketball and rugby. Tables clustered beneath Western-style lights and a band was setting up in the far corner with a harp, fiddle, and a keyboard.

It was early evening; they'd spent almost an entire afternoon in bed or the shower. A dozen or so patrons were scattered about the room and more trickled in from the fading day.

"Can I start you with something to drink?"

"A pint of Ivan the Terrible."

Nathan looked at her strangely, "Excuse me?"

"Beer. Stout, a good one."

"You drink a beer called Ivan the Terrible? What the hell planet am I on?"

"Montana," the waitress glared at him in mock disgust.

Julie tried to explain, "Big Sky Brewing Company. Great beer. Used to ride rodeo with the daughter of. They have beers like Pygmy Owl, Slow Elk…"

The waitress added in, "They also have specialty beers like Olde Bluehair and Buckin' Monk."

Nathan looked as if he was being cornered. "How about a whisky? Something Irish?"

"Chicken," the waitress laughed at him. "Sure you don't want a glass of Moose Drool? It's a very smooth brown ale."

"No, I've had enough to do with mooses to last me a good while."

"The plural of moose is meece or meeces," Julie corrected him incorrectly. He'd told her the story of the Great Moose Encounter, and if the moose could mess with him, she didn't see any reason not to do so herself.

"I've got just the thing. And I've always used meeces for the plural," the waitress said perfectly deadpan and was off without giving Nathan a chance to choose his liquor.

"You do things differently here in Montana," Nathan was watching the fine things that heeled cowboy boots and tight jeans did to the waitress' retreating figure.

"Hey!"

"Like the way you make love, Julie Larson," his dark eyes turned back to her and she wondered if he'd even been conscious of where his eyes had tracked. He now looked at her with an intensity that almost made her look away and definitely drove some heat to her cheeks. "Never experienced anything like it in my life."

Neither had she, but she couldn't think of what to say to that. Talking about sex was another thing she had no experience with beyond, "That was good." The nicer guys would eventually think to ask, "Was it good for you?" Though she doubted if they ever heard her reply.

"Women usually…" he ground to a halt. "Shit! I'm sorry. I seem to say the clumsiest things around you."

The waitress was back with a beer and a whisky. She thumped them down on the table, then put her fists on her hips and looked down at Nathan. "Try that."

"Told you," Nathan winked at Julie. "Montana is very strange."

"Ignore him," Julie told the waitress. "He's a city boy."

Nathan sipped his whisky, closed his eyes for a moment, then sighed happily. "Now *that* is a fine bit of Irish—even if I'm not familiar with it."

"That," the waitress was beaming, "is Logan Bar twelve-year-old. Distilled by Bridget MacDeaver…right here in Montana." She turned back to Julie. "Just flag me when his jaw stops flapping in the breeze and you're ready to order," then she sashayed off.

Nathan sniffed at the glass again, shrugged, and then raised it toward her in a toast. "Seems there are several things to like about Montana." He made it sound as if he was talking much more about her than the liquor.

She tapped her glass of stout to his tumbler and looked down at the menu. Any other man saying that line would have been talking more about the whisky than the woman. Had her bar really been set so low that someone less than the wonderful Nathan Gallagher, from New York City (the good lord save her), could step over it? Sadly, past experience already answered that. Wasn't going to ever happen again though.

Nathan sipped the whisky. He rarely drank it anymore—it had been his poison as a young chef. But he'd learned a lot about them in his younger days and this was a fine one indeed.

Montana. He didn't know what he'd expected, but this certainly wasn't it. A Celtic Cowboy bar, a truly fine single-malt, and Julie Larson.

He had only begun to learn the curves that made up her body. They were enough to make a man go mad. It practically had. *Women usually—Idiot!* But it was true. All the women he'd ever been with, from high school to the Cordon Bleu to the hostess in the back booth at Vite had a *studied* beauty: plucked eyebrows, makeup, carefully stylish clothes. Even the sous chef he used to screw in the walk-in fridge wore a tailored blouse and lacy underwear while they worked together over the cook line.

Through the glass of the hotel's shower enclosure had stood Julie Larson—a woman who was nothing more (or less) than she appeared to be. She worked hard, got dirty, and had the incredible body to prove it.

He'd bet his last bottle of Château Margaux Bordeaux 2005 that she'd actually meant it when she said she didn't know what passive-aggressive games were. They were part of every interaction in the restaurant business. Piss someone off, and the fish arrived to the line overdone, forcing the whole table to be refired so that everyone could be served together. Break up with someone and you could find that your lockbox of truffles was "accidentally" put away in the freezer.

Julie was as straightforward as she appeared. It had overtaken him as he moved to join her in the shower. Maybe he'd gone in hoping to prove that she hadn't just negated the value of every single relation-ship in his past by shining such a bright light on the present. Instead, she'd responded with such an absolute honesty that he'd sought to do for her what she'd done for him—purge her past until it washed down the drain.

How could the prior men in her life not see her for how incredible she was? How many men were like his fellow, bar-hopping chefs, or worse yet his little brother?

Damn it! She deserved better than that and he'd done his very best to give it to her.

Now, across the rim of a whisky glass, he studied her while she read the menu. Her pale blonde hair fell in a smooth cascade down either side of her face. She wore a flannel shirt that was just open enough to provide a splendid view of her collarbone. The curves below were lost in shadow and closed buttons. No coy games. No teasing cleavage.

"What are you looking at, city boy?" she didn't raise her head. "Because you sure aren't looking at your menu."

"Prettiest woman who ever let me take her to bed."

"Skin deep, Nathan."

"On most women I can tell you that's far more true than you think." Even the nice ones. There was always a deeper layer with a hidden agenda. "You, I'm thinking your beauty goes all the way to the core."

"Pretty speech. If you're trying to get me back into bed with you though, it's not going to work."

"That's not what I was say—"

Then she looked up and grinned at him. "Not until I've had something to eat anyway. But keep trying, Nathan. I'm discovering that I like the way it sounds."

She flagged down the waitress.

"I'll have the Ploughman's Lunch. And I don't think my friend is quite awake from his afternoon endeavors, better give him the Irishman's breakfast."

"Need him to wake up some, honey?"

"Don't know as I'd survive if he woke up more, but I'm willing to risk it. Maybe I wore him out."

"Not a chance. Around you I've got plenty of..." Nathan then glanced up at the waitress' knowing smile and shut up.

"We've got one more stop before we leave town," Julie settled into the passenger seat of Nathan's car. It might have looked like a clown's car to her, lurched sadly sideways on the road that first night, but it had a solid, comfortable feel that she could get used to in a hurry. It also didn't rattle as it labored along. Instead, as Nathan eased it through Great Falls, it slid along smooth and quiet.

He looked good. Their first stop had been at Hoglund's. First they bought him a good denim shirt and jacket, and a decent pair of work boots. Not even cowboy boots, just some good leather Red Wings that he could tromp through the spring mud or ride a horse with.

Her attempts to get him a decent hat had been thwarted when he reached into a small cubby behind his car seat and produced an Indiana Jones-style hat. He'd tugged it on and given her a smile that was at least as charming as any Harrison Ford look. She'd tried on a Falcon hand-tooled leather hat—perfect for going about fancy—but her budget couldn't justify it.

"Someday we'll get you a real hat and boots."

"Sure thing, lady," with a brim-tug right out of the movie. He made it funny, but she found it harder to laugh this morning than she had last night.

Last night.

When did a girl ever have a night like that? Yes, they'd made love again and it had been as tender as the earlier time had been wild. Then he'd held her and they'd just talked. That was something that was wholly outside her experience. A couple times she and her big brother had run into each other during a late night raid on the ice cream and talked about nothing much through a bowl or two, but never a lover.

She was a ranch girl—up before the sun and gone to bed not long after it set. If she and Nathan had slept more than a few hours last night, she'd be surprised. Instead, she'd spent the night curled up against the man who could make her feel...she didn't know what. Cared for? Important? Lucky?

The problem with Nathan wasn't that he didn't talk. Most men— now *she* was guilty of the same kind of generalities that Nathan was always making, which made it easy to forgive him—didn't talk about how they were feeling. Growing up with three older brothers and a passel of field hands, she'd learned to read men. Men not like Nathan anyway.

Nathan did talk—and about what he was feeling. Sometimes he did it too well.

Over dinner, and afterwards as he nursed his lone whisky, he'd finally told her about New York. The amazing restaurant scene and all the wonders that the city had to offer. But also the disappointment, the loss, and the confusion he felt were all laid out on the table for her to see. He'd never been anything but a chef.

"Cooking for you was the first meal I've cared about, really cared about in months."

If she hadn't already been soft in the head for Nathan Gallagher, that would have done it.

Once through Great Falls, where the two-story brick of Old Town gave way to suburbia and strip mall, he followed the signs for Malmstrom Air Force Base. It was only a mile or so before the houses became closer together as they neared the base.

It was that hint of sadness in him that she'd spotted before, that loss

of joy in cooking. It was also her own revelations about her upbringing, about her marginal value in the Larson household and finally realizing, as she told the story, that she'd started J. L. Building as an escape
plan that had made them especially gentle with each other last night.

Afterward, curled up, Nathan had told her about being a young
chef. A multi-generation Irishman who cooked fine French food in
Paris and New York.

That had been the problem that she didn't know how to wrangle.
It was so easy to hear his passion for cooking and for the energy of the
city. Somewhere in the night she'd finally understood. Someday,
perhaps someday soon, Nathan would be gone—back to his beloved
city.

Then Julie Larson would be down the shitter. One choice was to
push away now, hit the ground hard and let the bronc finish out its
dance alone. The other was to hang on and enjoy the ride as long as it
lasted.

She never knew when to let go, or even how to. Not in rodeo, not
in work, not in relationships—even the marginal ones. Without
asking, she knew that she'd be holding on to Nathan Gallagher until
the last possible moment.

The trick was figuring out how to make sure the fall didn't break
her at the end.

Nathan had followed Julie's directions to Malmstrom AFB. Apparently there was some delivery to pick up for her loft office project
with Emily. They had taken turns on the drive down making up
bizarre possibilities from a science fiction plasma rifle to a personal-
sized ICBM—Minuteman missiles in their silos was the whole
purpose of Malmstrom. Getting to know Emily, none of the ideas had
sounded quite as implausible as they should have.

The gate guard looked very serious and very armed when they
rolled up in his red Miata.

"We're here to pick up a delivery."

"Post office is back that way half a mile," the guard indicated with his rifle, not quite raising it all the way to point but making it clear he didn't have time for this shit.

Julie leaned over, "I was told to ask for Quartermaster Belkin precisely at eleven o'clock." The clock on the dash read 10:59.

"Stay here." The guard retreated to his shack and the phone.

"I think we're in a movie," Nathan teased Julie. He'd hardly gotten a laugh from her all morning, probably because she was tired. He was used to short hours, but that didn't explain how he was feeling. There was a euphoria that was hard to deny.

To hold her close all through the short night had been more than a gift. It had been a chance to pretend that there was something in his life that could be normal. That maybe there was a future even if he couldn't see it. He'd been at the ranch for a week (about five days more than he'd expected to be welcome), barely seen his brother, slept with the most incredible woman, and cooked. By god, he cooked. He'd enjoyed himself more making breakfasts with Ama than he had in his last six months at Vite.

And her laugh. Julie Larson had been so serious when he met her, like it had been driven into her soul. Every laugh he'd been able to elicit had been a glimpse of simple, purest joy.

The guard came back, looking pissed. "Through the gate. Stop there," he jabbed a finger at the spot next to his Humvee. "Do not get out of the car. Do *not* piss me off. Someone will be here in five minutes."

The thrum of a helicopter sounded low overhead.

"What the hell?" the guard was looking up at the big aircraft with two sets of rotor blades.

"What's wrong?" Nathan wished he hadn't asked when it drew the guard's attention back to him. The man's rifle looked far more real and dangerous than on some movie screen.

The helo slewed around and began to settle inside the perimeter fence, just beyond the parked Humvee.

"We don't have any Chinooks here. Just Hueys. And Air Force birds are gray, not black."

"Whose are black?"

The guard just scowled again, raised the gate, and waved them through.

Nathan looked at Julie, but she had no more of a clue than he did. He didn't know about helicopters and apparently neither did she. He eased his Miata forward.

After it landed, a rear ramp opened and lowered to the ground. A woman in uniform walked down the ramp and waved them forward.

Nathan checked the rearview. The guard had at least transferred his scowl from them to the big helicopter. There wasn't a marking on it. No white star. No numbers. Just pure black.

The woman didn't just wave him to the ramp, but up onto it.

Julie shrugged and they rolled forward. The inside of the helicopter was two Miatas long and there was at least a foot to either side of his car. Every surface was covered with a pipe, a cable, a piece of shining equipment, or a warning sign. Just past the nose of his car was a pair of mounted machine guns that looked as long as a person, thankfully not pointed toward them.

"Howdy y'all," a tall blond man in a cowboy hat strolled into the cargo bay while the ramp closed behind them. "My name's Justin and you must be Emily's contractor. Not quite what I was expectin'. Good choice in hats though."

Flummoxed, Nathan just hooked a thumb toward Julie. "She's your man…so to speak."

"Howdy, ma'am. Not *a' tall* what I was expectin'. Though not any big surprise with the stories I've heard about Emily Beale."

"Pop your trunk," the woman in uniform told him.

He did, but when he went to get out of the car, she just shook her head.

Justin and Julie were talking horses at some sort of esoteric level that sounded like a foreign language.

The woman and another crew member piled several boxes into the back. He could feel the car settle—they might be small, but some of them must be heavy. Another crew member started chatting with him about how he liked his car and how it handled on the open road, making it so that he couldn't follow what else was going on.

Less than two minutes later, the ramp was lowering and he was being guided backward down the ramp and into the real world of bright sun and scowling gate guards.

"Next time y'all are in Austin, you just call the ranch and we'll show you some *real* horses," the big guy doffed his cowboy hat to Julie, then strolled back to the cockpit.

The rear ramp closed and the big rotors, which had never stopped spinning, hammered the air down on them hard until he backed far enough away. Then they were gone back into the sky.

"You've got to be asking yourself, 'So, who are we'?" he asked the glowering guard as they rolled out through the gate. He answered his own question before he slipped out of earshot. "We're just folks."

Julie's laugh cheered him immensely as he headed toward the highway.

"So," he asked once they were on their way, "who were those folks?"

"No idea. But if we're ever in Texas and want to go to one of the top horse-breeding ranches in the country, Justin just gave us an invitation."

Nathan turned to look over his shoulder as if he could see what's in the trunk, "Any guesses?"

"Emily told me she had some friends who could help with electronic security for her office. I guess she meant the US military."

"This happen to you much? Is Montana really like this?"

"Oh, sure. All the time. You should stick around, city boy."

The warm fun of cuddling together, going into a cowboy outfitter like he'd never seen before, and cruising with Julie beneath the sunshine, ripped away in the chill air that seemed to descend on the car as they reached the highway.

Stick around. It was the one thing he couldn't do and they both knew it.

CHAPTER 11

Their escape ended the moment they crossed back onto Henderson land. They'd been gone less than twenty-four hours and Julie felt as if her entire world had shifted.

A huge load of supplies had arrived, including all of the material for the yurts' platforms. For the last eleven miles back to the ranch, they'd eaten a cement truck's dust on its way to pour the pilings for the yurts and the common bathroom.

When they arrived, Chelsea, Doug, and Patrick were putting the saddle horses through their paces, shaking off the excess energy of a lazy winter so that they'd settle down for the tourist season. She envied them that. The non-twins and Mac were rebuilding one of the truck's engines. Stan was doing what he did every day, working with his dogs. Ama had updated the website and was taking reservations.

And she and Nathan had somehow forgotten how to speak to each other. They'd each tried to start conversation on the drive back, but nothing had caught.

Emily met them at the barn. "Sometimes, the best way to move very valuable equipment is in plain sight." The two of them helped her carry everything up to her unfinished office—it had walls, windows, and a secure door, it just didn't have an interior yet.

When she went to check on Clarence, Nathan followed her into the stall. As he held and kissed her, Clarence didn't make any comment. Which was good, because she was too busy melting against Nathan's wonderful body to protect him from her horse. Then, still with no idea what to say to each other, Nathan rubbed Clarence's nose and left the stall.

"What's happening to me?" she asked Clarence as he nuzzled up against her. She hid her face in his mane for a long moment before going to snag a treat from the bin in Chelsea's office.

She was thankful for the quiet moment she had with Clarence while he crunched on a couple of sugar cubes and a carrot. It would be her last for a while.

Julie threw herself into the work. When the first of the summer's guides and a maid had arrived, Julie sicced them on the cabins. First they painted the doors and trim while she finished out the Ponderosa's bathroom. Then they cleaned and prepped them for the first guests. One of the guides was a contractor during the winters and along with the twins, once the truck was running again, they tackled the decks.

Over the next few weeks there were only rare occasions that she saw Nathan. He would smile and wave. On the rarer occasions when they got close, there was a hug and a kiss. In those moments, she could rarely do more than cling to him.

"It's just a busy time," he whispered.

All she could do was nod before rushing off to whatever crisis called next.

When the yurts were delivered, they performed exactly as promised. The first one went up in half a day. The others took even less time now that she'd figured out the tricks.

The first time she saw Nathan up on a horse, it almost killed her. He and Mark were soon trotting around the corral, even a brief canter. She could only watch out the Larch cabin window; watch as her heart ached.

"He rides well," she told no one before going back to tackling the busted pipe under the sink. And he did. She could see from up here that he sat the horse solidly. And they'd put him up on Red, rather than an old-timer like Daisy. Red was an intermediate horse, but still Nathan looked comfortable. Then she noticed that he was wearing his Indiana Jones hat and for reasons she couldn't explain to herself, she started crying.

"Morning, Julie," Mac blustered into the cabin.

She turned away and wiped her face but not fast enough. She couldn't stop the tears.

"Easy, girl. Easy."

"I'm not some damned horse, Mac," but her voice choked and stumbled.

He fumbled about for a moment, then held out a paper towel at arm's length as if she was a pissed-off grizzly. She used it to blow her nose into and wipe her face.

When she'd cried at the hotel, Nathan had held her. And the memory of that hurt all the more.

She ran a splash of cold water, then regretted it when she heard it splattering inside the cabinet where she'd removed the busted U-joint.

"Something you want to be talking about?"

"Not really."

Mac watched her in silence as she sponged up the freshly spilled water under the sink and squeezed it into the bucket she'd prematurely moved aside.

She slipped on the new joint and tightened up the fittings. Then she wiped everything down with her tear-stained paper towel and turned the water back on full. She let it run for a full minute, checking for drips or water squeezes around the plastic washers. Nothing, all good. She stuffed her tools in her tool belt, dumped the bucket's contents down the drain, and turned off the water. One last check, the U-joint and her face were both dry now.

Mac was still there, leaning back against the counter. "Think we need to talk some, girl."

"I don't have time."

"Fine. You're fired."

"What? But I—" she waved a hand helplessly at all of the unfinished tasks.

"Until you talk to me some, girl, you're off the clock. Period." This wasn't his friendly rancher tone. It was his retired Navy SEAL tone.

She covered her eyes for a long moment. "I really don't want to talk about this."

"Tough."

Julie turned to stare out the window.

Nathan was following Mark out of the corral and into the first pasture. At an easy jog, they soon disappeared over the first rise.

"That was supposed to be me."

Mac was nodding when she turned, "Wondered what was up with you two. Looked like that trip to Great Falls didn't go so well so I decided to keep my trap shut."

"No, Mac. No. It went…" how was she supposed to put words to it? It was the best memory, maybe ever, in her life. "It was perfect."

"Then, pardon my language, what the hell, Julie?" He folded his arms over his big chest.

"You know his background?"

"Some fancy-pants chef in New York. Damn good one according to his brother."

"I went online and looked up the restaurant he used to work at. Top twenty on almost every website, top ten in some. That's in New York, Mac. He's one of the best chefs anywhere. There's not a chance of him staying in Montana."

"And if you went with him—"

She tried a scoffing laugh to hold back the tears. It worked, barely. "I'd wither and die."

He nodded slowly, "Yes. I kind of imagine you would. Even your father isn't rooted to the land the way you are. That's the thing about you that so confuses the young men who come sniffing around. None of them understand that about you."

"Nathan does. He's going back to New York and he didn't even ask me. At least he could have asked." And she had to turn away because the tears were back and she couldn't stop them.

"He is? He never said."

"No. Not yet. But it's obvious. I can't imagine it will be long now."

"Fight for him, girl."

"How?"

Mac was silent long enough for her to wipe her face again and look over at him.

"Am I supposed to go out and become a Navy SEAL?"

"Now you're trying to steal my tricks. They're the sort that will only work for me. We're just going to have to find you your own."

"I won't trick him," her protest was sharp. That had been part of what he liked about her. No games. Not even if it broke her heart.

"Wouldn't be you to use tricks," Mac confirmed. "We'll just have to think on it a bit."

"Better hurry," she waved a hand out the window. Two tiny figures on horses topped the next rise, then disappeared out of sight.

Nathan alternated between having the feel of the trot and then completely losing it.

In one moment he understood why Julie talked about Clarence the way she did. Red would be striding along, following the line of a small stream that wandered down out of the far hills, and it would feel as if he could sink right down into the smooth leather of the saddle. The horse's muscles working in perfect sync with his own.

Then it would all go to hell and he'd be bouncing so hard that he could barely stay in the saddle. It was a miracle that his tailbone didn't break as the powerful horse slammed up against him every billionth of a second. It was only after the fifteenth or sixteenth transition that he caught on to what was happening.

Red was toying with him. Red was shifting his stride on the sly, hoping to abuse the beginner. A couple more changes that Nathan managed to catch onto more and more quickly, then Red settled down. The glance that the horse cast back at him looked very amused.

"Ha. Ha. Ha." He told the horse. Just as he'd told Julie when she'd started her lesson with *This is a horse.* She felt so far away. He knew she was busy, but that wasn't all of it. He should turn back, track her down, and ask what was going on.

Ask her to go with him? Go where? New York? She'd shrivel and be bitter the rest of her life. She was the one with a business, with family and a place. Not something he was going to find out here. He'd barely talked to his brother in all of his weeks here. They were friendly, easy enough with each other to joke around, but they weren't friends. That had been a hard discovery. He and his little brother had so little in common anymore. The decade apart—him in his restaurants and Patrick on Montana ranches—had put so much distance between them.

But there was something, even if he wasn't sure what, that he and Julie had to talk about.

He looked around and he wasn't so sure that he could find her even if he wanted to. He and Mark were out on the open prairie. The mountains were ahead of them, but behind him there was no track through the winter-dead grass. Because he'd been preoccupied with Red's games, he hadn't been paying attention. This wasn't New York where, if he got totally turned around, he just had to walk to the next street corner and read the signs.

He'd never been so far from everything. Out here there were no fences, no ranch house or cabins. There was just brownish-green grass with the first hint of purple flowers, soaring mountains, and the biggest sky in the world. Except it wasn't far away, it was somehow strangely all...closer. As if he could reach out and touch every piece of the most expansive place he'd ever been.

He wanted to stop and appreciate it, but Mark had kept them moving at a trot for a while now.

"What's the rush?"

"Just passing on the favor, buddy."

"What favor?"

"My parents took over this spread when I was a 'cow'—means it was my third year at West Point. Their first ranch hand was a real old-timer. Crotchety son of a bitch, must have been eighty if he was a day, but that man could really ride. I came out for my first visit to see the place, so impressed with my hot school and that I'd be a 'firstie' soon —a senior at the best military academy there is. I *knew* I was hot shit and could do anything."

"Is that where you met Emily?"

"No. I missed her somehow. She was a freshman plebe my senior year. Damned woman did what I couldn't—was made First Captain her senior year, top of the school. Only woman so far to pull that off."

Nathan sighed with relief when Mark eased them back to a walk and his butt could start recovering. Though now there was a side-to-side roll that started sandpapering his inner thighs.

"That old bastard put me up on the orneriest horse on the place and made me ride him. Looking back, he was probably no worse than Red there, but I'd never so much as seen a horse. I can tell you that I fell off a bunch more than the one time you did."

"How many times did Emily fall off?"

"Never," Mark sounded totally disgusted as they continued along the stream up toward the mountains. From that one helicopter flight, Nathan had enough of a feel for the size of the ranch that he doubted they'd reach the hills today. "What's your secret?"

"Julie said it was about confidence. She told how horses aren't *thinking* critters, they're *feeling* critters. So I'm trying to be confident. I also don't want her laughing at me if she sees me riding."

"Impressing a woman is a good tactic. Did that by rescuing Emily from a bunch of Thai hill-tribe opium runners."

"I'll make that my Plan B."

Mark turned them back toward the ranch, then rode up close beside him. "Ease up on the reins a bit. Make sure you stay solidly in your stirrups. Even looser on those reins."

It felt wrong. Red would be breaking back into a trot if Nathan didn't rein him in soon. He wasn't ready for more of that yet.

"Lean forward a bit. Perfect," Mark drifted back a couple feet.

Out of the corner of his eye, he saw Mark whip over the end of his reins, smacking them hard against Red's rump.

"Go on!" Mark shouted as Red leapt straight into a gallop.

Nathan took one glance at the greening grass racing by without the relative safety of a helicopter wrapped around him and knew he didn't stand a chance if he fell off.

Confidence. Like seasoning a dish with panache. It wasn't about the carefully measured spoon, it was about having confidence.

Red stretched out his stride and the world moved even faster. The horse's ears—what Julie had called the windows to a horse's emotions—slowly swung from back hard the moment Mark smacked him, to forward as he lowered his head and they sped over the prairie. Up one rise and down the back side. Sweeping by a family of small deer too startled to run and a wild rabbit that shot away fast enough to avoid being trampled.

He eased up in the saddle a little more, gave his hat brim a tug to make sure it stayed in place, and it felt like he was flying.

It wasn't as good as making love to Julie Larson, but it was right up there.

Julie was up on a ladder with her head sticking out of the central hole of the yurt when she heard the thunder. She checked the sky, stark blue except for a couple of cumulus bumpers too small to hold any water.

Steady thunder. Not big enough to be a stampede, but plenty to be—

Two cowboys shot up over the back of the rise. With a swerve and a *Whoop!* they swung to either side of the yurt. One had been wearing a black cowboy hat, the other...an Indiana Jones one.

"Nathan!"

At her shout, he turned to look up at her and that was his undoing.

Red carved a hard turn to the right to match Nathan's weight shift. Except Nathan didn't lean into the turn. Instead, he continued in a straight line as the horse ran out from under him. He was pitched down the slope, which was all that saved him. Instead of going splat onto flat ground, he rolled and tumbled and spun until he came to a stop well down the slope.

She slid down the ladder, raced outside, vaulted over Doug working on the porch, and was at Nathan's side while he was still just blinking in surprise.

"What happened?"

"You fell off."

"I know that. I thought I was doing so well. How did I screw up?" He sat up slowly, testing himself as he did so. She sat close by him, ready in case something was really wrong. But other than a few winces and groans, he appeared unscathed.

"You okay, buddy?" Henderson trotted up close beside them; he had Red's reins in one hand.

"Idiot!" Julie tried not to yell, but watching Nathan fly through the air and tumble like a broken rag doll really threw her. She'd seen more than one rodeo rider broken or crippled by less.

"Which one of us?" they asked in unison.

"Both! You," she aimed a finger at Mark, "for teaching a beginner to gallop."

"He didn't teach me. He just whacked Red with his reins. Why me? All I did was fall off."

"You," she couldn't help herself and hugged him because she was so glad he was okay. "For being stupid enough to go riding with Mark on your first time out."

"It's a mistake I won't be making again," Nathan glared up at Mark, who just grinned.

"Next time, it's with me or no one."

Nathan looked at her. That smile of his slid to life, then he leaned in and kissed her on the nose. "That's a deal."

Julie had no idea what in the world to do with him. She wanted to smack him, hug him, and take him right here and now. Most of all she wanted to keep him as close as she could for as long as she could.

CHAPTER 12

The next day the yurt topping-off party was a big occasion. He and Emily chased Ama out of the kitchen and spent all of that same afternoon creating a feast.

"You really cooked at the White House?" Nathan had never actually met one of the White House chefs and it took him over an hour to stop feeling clumsy beside her.

"For just a few weeks. Private chef to the First Lady," Emily didn't make it sound like a very nice experience, but he had to ask.

"What's she like? The First Lady?"

"I've known three of them. The last one and the new one are both wonderful. I cooked for the one before that." Her tone put a clear, end-of-discussion period at the end of it. She'd cooked for the one who'd died at the White House—that must be a bad memory indeed. He remembered it only vaguely; he'd been surviving his Parisian servitude at the time.

What he discovered as they cooked together was that she was an unconventional chef, clearly with no formal training—with an exceptional palate. That was the one thing that was hardest to teach, but Emily didn't need any instruction there. Her looser style forced him to adapt. It was fun, especially working on the flavor profiles together.

As executive chef at Vite, he rarely cooked *with* anyone. They cooked *for* him. Tasting and seasoning with Emily was a reminder of what a joy it was to work with a truly talented chef who was more of a partner than an underling. He hadn't had that since he and Estevan had worked together at the ill-fated *Le Carte Blanche* just off Wall Street.

Because the day was plenty warm for eating outside, Chelsea improvised a horse cart for them and they hooked up Red—one of the few horses also trained to a full harness. Reconciled to his bumps and bruises, he let Red know that there were no hard feelings with a carrot *and* an apple.

"Gonna spoil that horse," Chelsea chided him.

"That's the plan," Nathan agreed.

By keeping a weather eye out the window, he could gauge when the last yurt would be done. They made a pretty little cluster atop the hill. The mountains, their ice-capped peaks glowing in the afternoon sun, shone in a brilliant backdrop. The tourists were going to love it from their very first sighting. They might end up even more popular than the cabins.

Timing it right, they delivered the feast up to the yurts just as Julie slid the last acrylic skylight into place and secured it in position.

All the ranch hands came up, even Stan with his favorite dog Bertram.

Nathan helped Chelsea drop the sideboard on the wagon and turned it into a serving station. They uncovered platters of pasta with meatballs, pesto chicken skewers, and shish-kebab veggies still hot off the kitchen grill. Sometimes comfort food was called for, but he and Emily had elevated it a couple notches while they were about it.

Nathan had even tracked down a case of Moose Drool in the pantry and loaded it into a cooler of ice.

He'd also seen to one other detail for later. Thankfully, Patrick had been out on another supply run this morning and had been able to bring back the one special ingredient he'd been lacking—which Patrick had delivered with only a brotherly ration of grief. Nathan couldn't resist peeking in his pocket to make sure it was still there.

The party quickly settled down to a lot of weary people sitting on the edge of porches that still lacked railings or chairs but had a view to die for.

He sat next to Julie, trying to hide the winces from yesterday's fall that aspirin had been unable to relieve.

"You load up a fine chuck wagon, Nathan," Julie spoke as she devoured her meal like the hungry worker she was.

"Glad you like it. Emily might have helped some."

"Best meatballs I've ever had."

Nathan tried not to cheer, those were completely his—except for a bit of the spicing in the red sauce, but he wasn't going to mention that.

Mac thumped a hammer on the porch a few times to call everyone's attention. Even though there were only ten or fifteen of them, it took them a while to settle down. The sun was bright and warm, the new spring grass was brushed with the purple he'd only noticed this morning. Ama had said that within a week the prairie would be purple, gold, and red with wildflowers. That's a sight he wouldn't mind seeing.

Mac thumped his hammer one last time, then tossed it down on the decking.

"First, thanks go to Nathan and Emily for this fine feed."

"And Red," Chelsea called out, slipping the horse a palmful of carrot sticks.

"And Red," Mac agreed happily.

"I hooked up the wagon."

"Shutting up now, Chelsea."

"Yes, boss."

Nathan liked how easy they were with each other.

"Next, I want to thank you all for busting your asses to get this ranch ready for the spring."

"You mean *you* busting *our* asses," Tweedledee shouted out.

"Mine's still broken," Tweedledum agreed.

"Hush or I'll bust 'em again."

"Too late," Dee. "Still busted," Dum.

"But the one person I want to thank more than any of you lot is the lady who really made it happen, Julie Larson," and Mac started the applause that swept through the crowd.

"Long way to go yet," she muttered under the applause. Her face was brightly flushed.

"But where would they be without you?" Nathan couldn't believe that she didn't see how little would have happened without her skills and drive. "Remember that, Julie."

She nodded uncertainly.

"Don't you see the value you're bringing here?"

A shrug.

"Crap, woman! I bet Mac wishes he could find five more just like you, or even one more. Except there isn't anybody like you."

The applause ran long but finally tapered off some time after she'd gone from flushed to beet red. She didn't speak again until other conversations resumed and some of the hands went back to the cart for thirds.

"Stop selling it, Nathan. I can get that out of the back of a horse anytime I want." Then she grimaced, "Sorry. I just have a mental to-do list in my head that could kill a Triple Crown Winner."

"A Triple Crown…"

"Kentucky Derby, Preakness, and Belmont Stakes," Julie explained with her *oh-city-boy* sigh. "If you get a horse in a decade who can win all three, you've got something really special."

"Come by Aspen around sunset and I'll show you who I think is so special."

"You looking to get laid?"

He reached into his shirt pocket and handed her a single, perfect, red rose petal.

Julie arrived at the Aspen cabin just as the sun was shifting behind the Front Range crags. Getting past the steps was hard. She wanted to protect her heart, but—she had to admit as she ascended the steps to the front porch—she wanted Nathan more.

Inside, there was a cheery fire. Though the evening was warm enough that it wasn't really needed, it looked mighty cozy. No Nathan in the kitchen. No food on the table, which was just as well. She'd barely worked off the fullness from the amazing spread Nathan and Emily had delivered.

Then she spotted a yellow flower petal in the middle of the floor—a daffodil—and another. Not red roses, but sunny, spring daffodils. She never told anyone that they were her favorite, but somehow Nathan knew…or just got lucky. The trail led to the bathroom where a towel and a fresh bar of soap had been laid out on the counter. The shower ran hot when she tried it. She managed a laugh past the tightness in her chest, wondering who had helped Nathan turn on the water heater.

It felt so good to be clean that she stayed under the spray far longer than she normally would have. She let the water run hot until she knew she was avoiding whatever came next. With a slap, she stopped the water and dried off. A terrycloth robe hung on the back of the bathroom door. It felt sinful to pull it on over bare skin; she'd never worn a bathrobe at home.

She ventured out of the bathroom, still holding her one red rose petal, and spotted a second trail of yellow daffodil petals leading up the stairs and into the main bedroom. Whatever thin temptation lay along the first petal trail, leading to escape, wasn't enough to pull her aside.

Upstairs, unable to believe what she was seeing, Julie stopped at the threshold. Nathan sat in a comfortably worn armchair beside the bed, reading a book. Looking as if that was simply where he belonged, at home, waiting for her. The room was lit with candles and a single oil lantern dialed barely bright enough to read by. The light curtains had been drawn over the last hints of the sunset. The pictures of the ranch and Montana history blended into the shadows. The big bed had been made up with spring green flannel sheets and one of Ama's showpiece Cheyenne blankets.

The daffodils led to a vaseful of red roses on a small table at his side. No one had ever given her flowers, never mind roses.

Nathan's smile was brighter than the lantern. He closed his book, reached out, and missed dropping it on the table by more than a foot. When it hit the floor, they both jumped, then shared a laugh in surprise.

"I've imagined you here so many times since that dinner," his voice was rough as he clambered to his feet.

"So have I," but she couldn't get herself moving again. Across this threshold would be an incredible night. And then what? The lost chef —spooked by a cow and never ridden a horse—him she knew. The man who galloped across the prairie, laughed with the hands over a beer, and now waited for her with a vaseful of flowers and a smile full of promises—him she didn't know at all. Who would he be in the morning? Worse, *where* would he be?

He rose and moved until he stood just over the bedroom's threshold from her.

"What is it, cowgirl?" Nathan tucked her hair behind her ear.

Not trusting herself to speak, she let the warmth of his touch pull her into the room, into his arms.

She could feel Nathan's strength and his confidence as he pulled her against his chest. It was as if their awkwardness with each other since the trip to Great Falls had all been in her imagination. He held her more tightly than ever before, practically crushing her against him.

His kiss made it impossible to remember the world outside the bedroom door. In here there was only him. And he made it clear that, as far as he was concerned, there was only her.

Julie took a brief side trip to bury her face in the roses. They really did smell utterly incredible, just like in the novels and movies. She set her one petal close beside the vase.

Nathan led her to the bed and it was a hundred times more momentous than leaving with him for an out-of-town tryst. She didn't help him undress, but she couldn't look aside as he did. He'd become stronger, more solid in the weeks that he'd been here. More real. The last of his clothes hit the chair, except for one sock that landed on his forgotten book on the floor.

Never had she been so aware of a naked man. His unthinking power, his confident stance, his *incredible* maleness. How had she ever pictured him as belonging in a clown car? His presence filled the room and chased away shadows.

When he brushed her robe off her shoulders, it wasn't with greed, it was with reverence. He didn't untie it or tug it down to expose her breasts. Instead he nuzzled one bare shoulder, then the other. He eased it off her in such small stages that she couldn't place the moment when she transitioned from dressed to naked, from hesitant to gasping. Not until the robe lay in a pool about her ankles did he stop uncovering her inch by inch. Then he looked up at her with those dark, hungry eyes from where he knelt before her.

"You are the most beautiful thing I've ever seen."

"Thing?" Julie was amazed that she could still speak.

"Better than any sunset or the finest meal at Le Bernardin."

She had to laugh, though it was hard to find the breath to do so. "I'm guessing that last one means something."

Nathan smiled. "Best restaurant in New York. It's one of only six Michelin three-star restaurants in all of New York. One of the very best in the world. If I could be anyone else, I'd be Eric Ripert—the head chef. But if I was, I wouldn't be here with you."

She wanted to look aside from the intensity of his gaze. Needed to look aside. But couldn't. Nathan Gallagher of New York City might well be the best *thing* she'd ever seen as well.

Without breaking eye contact, she eased backward onto the bed and under the covers. He followed her slowly.

Each place he touched her, she placed a wall around—to both preserve it and keep it safe against the unknown future. His hand, endlessly tracing the curve of her hip until it was sealed as surely as the prairie by a winter's hard frost. Where his head lay between her breasts as he listened to her heart until the sound was swallowed by the vast emptiness of the Montana prairie.

And when he finally took her, when he filled her heart like no one ever had or could again, that too she locked away behind the hard mountains of her soul. She locked it away though it was bigger than the Montana Sky.

When his ringing phone woke her, the world was still dark beyond the curtains.

"Murmph," Nathan said into his phone once he recovered the screaming thing from his discarded clothes.

Julie checked the time. Too close to sunrise to sneak back home and pretend she hadn't just spent the night on Henderson's Ranch. Not too late to snuggle back under the covers with Nathan for a few minutes.

"Who?... Estevan, you asshole... What's wrong with me? It's the middle the night is what's wrong with me... What do you mean what time zone am I in? Montana. Whatever zone that is... I know. Crazy, right?"

The more Nathan woke up, the farther away Julie felt. Estevan was clearly a friend. A friend Nathan had never mentioned. From a past that was suddenly in bed with them.

She slipped from between the covers and out into the chill morning air. The cold bathrobe brought goosebumps, though none as much as Nathan's loud exclamations.

"You did? You actually broke off and started your own restaurant? Who's your backer? Oh, she's good. What's your take on it? Sounds fair... No, French puts you right up against Vite. You need your own voice in there..."

She closed the downstairs bathroom door, which reduced Nathan's voice to a distant rumble. A quick shower to wash off the night muffled him briefly. His questions had turned to excitement in just the two minutes she'd been under the water. On her way through the kitchen, she spotted a small bag of bagels. Where in Montana had Nathan found bagels? Oh, it was Nathan. He'd probably made them himself. There was no jam or butter in the fridge. The only thing there was cream cheese, which her mother had only ever used for making cake frostings.

Nathan's laugh boomed through the bedroom door and down the stairs, "No, shit? How is this my fault?"

She was almost out the door—chewing on her first bite of the dry, oddly dense bagel—when she heard the one thing she'd been hurrying to escape.

"You need me in New York by when?"

***

Nathan was still scratching his head when he hung up the phone.

"Can you believe that bastard went and—" He turned, but Julie wasn't there beside him to hear what he had to say. Not her, not her bathrobe. But he could smell her, could feel her. It was the best night of his life: making love to her, holding her while she slept upon his shoulder. He'd spent hours imagining them like this, night after night. Waking together morning after morning.

Even asleep, he could feel her strength where his arms hooked lightly around her. How could someone so strong be so womanly at the same time?

And now all trace of her was gone as if she'd never been here.

No—she'd left her roses.

Maybe she was downstairs eating breakfast. He hadn't set up the coffee machine, but he should have.

Dressing quickly, he tossed the Zane Grey western back on the bookshelf, swept up her vase of flowers, and trotted down the stairs.

No clothes in the bathroom. No sign of her at all, except that on the kitchen counter there were only three of the bagels he'd made for her. Not four.

He stuck his head out the door; the sun was just putting the first hints of pale blue into sky—only a few stars struggled on. Down below, he could see Doug and Chelsea turning the horses out of the barn and into the pasture. Stan was feeding his dogs.

And the bright *whirr* of a screw gun told him that Julie was already hard at work up at the yurts.

He had cursed Estevan for calling so early and now he cursed himself for not waking up sooner. He'd missed his chance to see Julie Larson wake. To make love to her as the sun rose over the distant horizon.

Turning back, he cleaned up the cabin quickly. The only thing he couldn't quite figure out was the untouched cream cheese. Why would she eat her bagel dry?

Out the front door, he turned to head up to the yurts. To at least say good morning or...but he saw the backs of the non-twins and a couple of the other hands already past Aspen on the trail up to the construction site.

Instead, he tossed Ama's Cheyenne blanket over one shoulder, picked up his bags of supplies and laundry, and turned for the main house and the kitchen.

The kitchen.

Two weeks from take-over to open. No wonder Estevan was panicked. He had plenty of connections to staff up. The money woman was a responsible one and had taste. The front-of-house renovation would be a real pinch, but that was a given on a fast open.

It was an idea he and Estevan had figured out over a bottle of wine and three a.m. pasta a couple years back.

"How can we open a place and not bleed capital for three months while we build it out and get everything in place?"

They'd chased Estevan's question for half a bottle and straight into leftover chocolate-and-Courvoisier mousse before Nathan had finally seen it.

"Do a pop up!"

"Feh!" Estevan had been disgusted. "I don't want a pop-up restaurant—there one day and gone the next. I'm talking about a permanent, fine-dining, linens-and-wine steward sort of place."

Nathan recalled he'd been tired and drunk enough to barely hold onto the idea, but he'd managed. "I am too. You pop-up in your future space one night, and then you don't tear it down. Make improvements every day, but cook and serve every night. It gets the cash moving."

Estevan's askance look had motivated him.

"Get the customer involved. Give them little feedback cards with every meal. And not just on the food, but on the décor, the attitude, what wines and liquors to stock. Even if you ignore them, they'll feel like they helped make it what it is. We'd get customer loyalty out the wazoo. And they'd forgive a lot of the mistakes that usually happen with a new place."

Now, after all this time, Estevan was really doing it. Doing it, and told Nathan that he was expected to show up and help. It would be his kitchen as well. The old dream of running their own restaurant was finally coming true.

Nathan got everything put away at the ranch house and was toasting a bagel by the time Ama came in.

"I was thinking cheese-and-mushroom open-faced omelets and Potatoes O'Brien," he told her while he watched the coffee pot fill. The ranch hands had emptied it and not bothered starting a fresh pot. They'd be back from their start-of-day chores for breakfast soon.

"No bagels?"

He split another of the ones he'd meant for Julie and slipped it into the toaster for Ama before pulling a whole bag of them out of the bread drawer. She smiled and began washing and cracking eggs. What he wouldn't give for some lox, capers, and slivered red onions right about now, but the nearest supply of those was two thousand miles away.

Two thousand miles.

He began washing and dicing potatoes.

Estevan was choking on the menu ideas. Nathan could feel it. He was going to serve the same things they'd cooked at Vite. He was a creative chef, but didn't trust that. Any pressure and his friend scampered for familiar ground.

This is all your fault. Nathan's fault because of his dropping off the face of the planet—as Estevan had called Montana—had put a different kind of fear into Estevan. A fear that he would never have the guts to open his own place and would then end up feeling as lost as Nathan had.

Estevan had begged him to come back and help. "At least through the open. I've got a couch. Come on, man. Together we can build the menu the way it should be. You owe me, bro."

And he did. Estevan had gotten him through the door at two different restaurants before Vite. Had listened and commiserated each time another relationship had collapsed. Nathan was far closer to Estevan than his brother. Who seemed just fine out here in Montana. He'd never fit anywhere in New York, not the way Nathan had. Ranch life really did fit his little brother.

The next thought should be that it didn't fit himself.

He diced up some onions, tossed them on the griddle...and nothing happened. He'd forgotten to turn it on. Chef's rule Number One: first thing you do on entering the kitchen is fire up all of the ovens and burners you're going to need. He lit the griddle and shifted over to rounding up the spices while it heated.

Ranch life didn't fit him. He wasn't a rider...he'd proven that yesterday. It had been exhilarating; with practice it might even be fun. But he could see the natural riders and the trained ones. Julie, Doug, and Chelsea all rode as if born to the saddle. No one else on the ranch, not even the two summer trail guides rode the way they did.

Everything here was foreign. He'd asked for different, but frankly, he was having trouble keeping up with it. For the first week, well... He'd been such a wreck that it shouldn't be a surprise that he'd been going through detox—not from drink, just from the standard chef's high-adrenaline, sleep-deprived lifestyle.

The only times he slowed down, felt as if he really belonged anywhere, were with Julie. But the morning-afters were proving to be rough.

You gotta come back and help me, man. I signed everything this morning. You're my first call. I open in fourteen days.

Fourteen days. He could do that, then come back to...somewhere he didn't belong in the first place. He'd only been here...

"What day is this, Ama?"

"Wednesday."

"No, what date?"

She didn't look up from the grill that he'd completely forgotten he'd fired off. The onions had added a bright sizzle and tangy bite to the air. In chagrin, Nathan got the peppers and potatoes on the grill before turning to the omelet pans.

"April 30th."

"It's..." *what?* This time he almost lost the whole bowl of eggs to the floor. Hadn't he left New York in the first week of April? A month. Somehow he'd come for three to four days and been here a month. The way the time had slipped by, he couldn't account for it. A week until that first dinner up in Aspen. Another several days had led them to Great Falls. Had he really let two weeks of busy go by before last night? Apparently he had.

He couldn't keep floating through life on someone else's charity. He had to find a city and a restaurant where he could earn his way. Where he belonged rather than out on some Montana Front Range spread beneath a sky so big that it still shocked him every time he looked up.

"Here she is, Ama, just like we promised." The non-twins came in through the back door making a show of escorting Julie between them. "She resisted."

"I already had a bagel," Julie's protest didn't make the non-twins release her.

"Without any cream cheese," Nathan teased her.

Tweedledee looked at him through narrowed eyes, "Why would you put frosting on a New York doughnut?"

"Heathens," Patrick said coming in behind them. "I warned you, Nathan. These guys are nothing but heathens."

"I have work to do," Julie cut for the door, but the others grabbed her.

"If you work on this ranch," Ama said quietly, "you eat in my kitchen."

Nathan figured it would take a braver man than he was to argue with Ama when she used that tone. Maybe she'd gotten it from her SEAL husband.

"But—" Julie was apparently impervious to even that.

"Girl! Sit!" Maybe Ama had *given* that tone to her husband so that he could become a SEAL.

Julie sat, then wished she could switch sides, but it was too late.

It was hard watching Nathan as he moved about the kitchen. Something was wrong. He usually looked so smooth, as if he was dancing. This morning something was distracting him badly…and it wasn't her.

He'd teased her—which she'd let slide off—but he hadn't really looked at her. Not even his usual easy smile. He was thinking hard about something that wasn't her.

She sat and watched her worst fear come to life across the width of the Henderson's kitchen. His friend's phone call this morning.

A chef calling from New York.

It was like the call of milking time. All of the beef cattle could spend the entire summer wandering aimlessly over the prairie and rarely be seen until roundup time. But the hundred head of dairy cattle trooped to the barn twice a day like clockwork to be fed and milked. You had to go.

The call had come. Nathan would be gone. Very soon.

All through the meal she did whatever was needed to appear normal. Growing up with three big brothers and her father, she'd learned young how to keep everything inside.

After the meal, Nathan caught up with her just outside the door. She didn't even give him time to speak—didn't know if she could bear to hear his voice saying those fatal words.

"If you're going, Nathan, then go. I heard the call. I know what it means. Have a good time." She searched for one more thing she could say without revealing the pain, the flaming geyser of agony. *Have a good life? Go to hell for breaking my heart? Ask me to go with you?* She couldn't do that last one. She knew that.

But he could at least ask!

He didn't.

"Thanks," was all she could manage past the layer of rock she had wrapped around herself last night to keep her heart safe.

"Hey, Julie," Emily passed them on her way toward the barn. "Can you give me a hand with something when you have a chance?"

"Now's fine," she needed to run, far away. "Bye, Nathan."

Then she turned and walked toward the barn. No one would be able to see what was going on inside her. Not even Emily.

CHAPTER 13

Nathan made the mistake of turning the car right when he hit the main road and going to Helena. He'd figured the state capital would have the best flight connections. Besides, it wouldn't feel right going to Great Falls without Julie.

At least he got to prove that the last big, white cow barn on the road from Choteau to Augusta was indeed the one at the turn toward Henderson's Ranch. But that wasn't the mistake.

His real mistake was not checking the flight booking more carefully. Great Falls had a one-stop flight to La Guardia, six or seven hours depending on the layover. Helena's only real choice was to fly the wrong way first—through Seattle. It was twelve hours, two stops, and no better connections. He'd driven an extra forty miles to end up with a flight that was going to take double the time. For reasons that completely eluded him, he had to travel a thousand miles further west to Seattle to get back to JFK.

And he spent the whole time puzzling over what Julie had meant with that deadpan, "Bye, Nathan."

Not, *See ya, city boy.*

No, *Come back fast.*

Not a hug. Not a smile. Nothing except, "Bye, Nathan."

As if he'd been a nice screw, she was done with him, and she'd really meant goodbye. But it didn't make any sense.

Unable to sleep on the redeye—how was he supposed to sleep as he was flying over Montana again—he began working on a menu. Something had to distract him.

Nathan started with a classically French menu. He made a dozen different attempts to veer that one way or another, but couldn't seem to find it. Estevan, like most of New York's finest French chefs, was Hispanic—one of the weird truths of haute cuisine. The flavors of Estevan's youth had no place in a French restaurant...but what if they did?

Nathan began listing ideas, crossing out more than he kept. Snails in salsa was ridiculous, but a slow-simmered pozole beef stew reworked with a Burgundy wine had possibilities. Coq au Vin, made with a yellow Oaxacan mole. Instead of Courvoisier-chocolate mousse, a chili-chocolate one.

Mexican-French Fusion. He paid for some airborne internet time and did some searching. There were a couple people trying it, but none in New York and none doing it high-end. Of the few he found countrywide, most were panned. But there were a couple good ones. Someone had proved that it worked, but it wasn't even enough to be a trend yet. Estevan was a good enough chef that maybe he could turn it into one.

By the time Nathan reclaimed his knives from checked luggage and the cab got him to the city, it was eight a.m. Six a.m. back in Montana—time to get up and cook. He headed straight for the restaurant.

He found Estevan crashed out on a sagging settee at his new place halfway between Ripert's Le Bernardin and Keller's Per Se, and not too close to Hell's Kitchen. It was an amazing location... and a total wreck. It looked like a cattle stampede had come through.

"Hey!" He kicked the settee just as Julie had kicked his bed a lifetime ago to introduce him to her horse.

"Buddy, you came," Estevan's groan was dramatic. "What time is it?" He looked at his watch then collapsed back onto the broken settee. "Wake me some time past noon."

Nathan kicked the settee again, which may have been a mistake as he was still wearing the heavy boots that Julie had made him purchase in Great Falls. Standing in the heart of Manhattan, it was hard to believe that he'd ever shopped at a place called Hoglund's.

The heavy blow was too much for the settee. Something inside cracked, then the whole thing gave way, ejecting Estevan into a line of chairs that weren't much better than the settee.

"What?" Estevan yelled without opening his eyes as he rubbed at his banged elbow.

"It's time to cook."

"It's eight in the morning."

"Exactly," Nathan could get to enjoy this. "Let's see the kitchen."

Estevan staggered to his feet, lurched into the kitchen, and punched the coffee maker—literally. It seemed to be a random act until Estevan did it again and the power light flickered on.

"Cold or hot?" Estevan held up half a pot of blackened sludge.

"I'll wait."

Estevan poured one chipped cupful, looked around the wreckage vainly for cream or sugar, shrugged, and took half of it in one swallow like bad medicine. Behind him, the machine cycled to life and began dribbling hot coffee onto the empty burner. The reek of burned coffee filled the air before Estevan could dump out the half pot of cold and slam it back into place.

"Time to cook?" he looked at Nathan through the one eye that might have been starting to wake up.

Nathan knew how to cure that. He handed over the stack of recipes he'd spent the last half of the flight writing down.

Estevan grunted at the first, went quiet by the third, and by the fifth was starting to smile.

"Amigo! *Muchas gracias!* But why not espazote leaves here in the Tarte Flambée? It would go well with the bacon and onion."

"Because I didn't think of it."

Estevan grinned at him. "You and me. Two weeks. This will be spectacular. Mexican-French fusion, but all the way high." He wrapped Nathan in a bear hug and pounded on his back as if he wanted to break some vertebrae.

"Simple ingredients," Nathan managed once Estevan released him. "But perfect preparations."

"Yes. Yes. Haute cuisine, but with a big punch of Mexican flavor."

Nathan looked around the kitchen. "Where are we going to cook? We need to test this."

Estevan kicked an oven—the door fell off with a crash. "The crew hits in an hour. By tonight, we'll have enough of a kitchen to start testing. By three days, the kitchen will be done and they will start out front. I *knew* you would come back. Help me start breaking down this old equipment. The Irish owner was so cheap that he never fixed anything. I have to replace it all."

"Hey, I'm Irish," Nathan couldn't help laughing.

"Get some whisky in you, then you will be." They went back a long way, long enough that they'd helped each other dry out before they became true chef-alcoholics.

"It's a good space. Show me your layout."

Estevan found a magic marker and began drawing directly on a countertop. They soon scrounged up a tape measure and were making adjustments to the layout of the cook line.

Open in two weeks.

You and me.

I knew you would come back.

Nathan didn't know quite what was going on. Except that he knew Estevan would never get this place open in time without him.

"Montana? Really?" Estevan began throwing rusted and broken utensils into a huge garbage can.

Nathan didn't want to talk about it. "It's where I ran out of road."

CHAPTER 14

Julie stood in front of the last yurt and looked around her, unsure of what to do next. Every bunk was in place, every heater tested, every screw tightened. Ama had done one of her Cheyenne patterns in tile for the communal bath and showers. That alone was so beautiful that the yurts could well become the preferred rentals.

There were already tourists in three of the cabins—she'd finished the Ponderosa bathroom with only a day to spare. Next week, the first of the yurts would be occupied.

Down in the big corral, one of the summer guides was doing a basics class for the new guests. The kids were making better of it than their parents, but she could hear their laughter.

The ranch was waking up, but the springtime was slow. The local farmers were starting to worry and the part-time Montanan preoccupation with the weather had taken on a full-time chokehold. The spring rains had yet to come. The doomsayers were already calling for a dry year, her father was on the fence, and Mac was still hopeful.

She had another day or two of work on Emily's office. A few touchups where Patrick had backed the baler into the corner of the barn.

But nothing major.

Nothing to hold her here.

She'd been too busy to line up other jobs. For the last two weeks since he'd left, she'd purposely kept herself too busy to think. Except at night, after driving past the darkened Aspen cabin, to go home and lie in the silence of her bed.

"Damn you, Nathan."

He had given her so much in so little time. The way he saw her: more beautiful, more capable, stronger than she could even imagine. The way he'd held her. The way he'd loved her.

But not enough to stay. Not enough to ask her to go with him. Could she survive out from under her Big Sky?

She'd never be able to leave Clarence. So what would he do? Become a stabled New York horse, only allowed to see the sun when trotting slowly through Central Park? She could see him even now, pastured in with the other Henderson horses. She'd barely ridden him in the last hectic weeks and it had seemed too cruel to leave him alone on the Larson ranch. And that would be far less cruel than some big city stable.

Mac came up the hill with another group. Only Aspen and Larch were still empty. Not able to bear it if they were headed for Aspen, and definitely not able to bear any more of Mac's gentle probing, she tossed her tool belt in the back of the truck and drove down the track to the barn.

The sooner she finished Emily's office, the sooner she could get off Henderson land and away from all of the reminders of what she'd had here—however briefly.

But today, she couldn't even face that.

Instead, for the first time in weeks, she went up to the corral. She didn't even need to click her tongue to call Clarence over; he spotted her and cut through the herd at a brisk trot.

"Just you and me again, my big man," Julie scrubbed at his nose, then apologized for not bringing a carrot. "Stay there."

She doubled back to the truck and grabbed an old horse blanket she'd been using when she didn't want to scuff up the new flooring with her tools.

Clarence followed her on the other side of the fence until they reached the gate. Once he was through, she tossed the blanket over him, then climbed the first couple rails until she could hop on bareback.

She gave him a nudge with her knees.

His ears twitched forward and in moments they were off.

CHAPTER 15

"**D**os artichoke empanadas and *tres* crispy duck quesadilla," Estevan called out the firing order.

Nathan slapped three duck legs on the big griddle. Miguel began on the empanadas.

"I swear to god, *mi amigo.* You ever get tired of this, you should become fancy pants consultant for opening of restaurants. You can charge a ton. *Si?*"

"*Si,*" Nathan agreed because it was easier than arguing with Estevan.

"And 'meals half price while under construction.' Brilliant, Nathan. F'ing brilliant. At the real open, there won't be any sticker shock at the real prices."

They had a packed house on the first day. With the open kitchen plan—it had taken an extra two days to knock out the wall but it was worth it—they could hear the excited buzz. It wasn't just French-Mexican fusion cuisine, it was French-Mexican fine dining. Tall walnut tables and minimalist chairs, set in a space with twinkle lights and still untouched bare brick walls. Next week they'd clean up the brick. After that, add fine linen and better service ware. Then...

The upbeat energy of being able to see the kitchen played off the attentiveness that even a French *maître d'* wouldn't be able to fault.

Rather than a breadbasket, every table was started with quail-and-black bean grilled jalapeño poppers with just a little of Estevan's killer-good secret salsa recipe. It was served in classic dimpled French escargot plates of the finest porcelain.

There were some fine wines coming out of Mexico and one of Estevan's more comely cousins was also a top-notch *sommelier*. The beautiful steward—as well-versed in beer as in wine—was proving to be very popular. Like so many Mexican restaurants, Estevan had made it a family operation as much as possible. But he ran them through hard-core training on proper deportment and fine service, right down to the daily lecture on dish ingredients and the best ways to describe each one. The typical Mexican casual was replaced with elegance.

"C'mon, *amigo*. Give," Estevan called out between orders.

"What?" Nathan tapped one of the lobster tails but decided it needed another thirty seconds in the pan.

"I know what you are thinking of when you go quiet."

"Shut up, Estevan."

"*La mujer bonita. La jolie femme.* The pretty lady cowgirl."

"I should never have told you anything. Leave it." One late night, so late that he knew Julie would be waking up soon, he'd told Estevan just a little.

Some of it had sounded stupid, sitting here half drunk in a Manhattan restaurant. The way she looked when she rode. Her easy confidence around the cows and horses. The way she had seemed so a part of the land.

Nathan stayed focused on the six sauté pans lined up in front of him, each with a different order. He was having a hard time keeping them straight. It was as if the edges were blurring.

Was he so out of practice? It had been years since he'd even had to think to keep a dozen separate orders all firing at once, just at this one station.

And now all he could think of was the way that a blonde cowgirl had smiled at him while eating a meatball.

———

After curry-combing Clarence and getting him settled back in the Henderson's barn, Julie headed home. It was after dinner, after dark, even after Dad had finished the books and gone in to watch a game on the TV along with his sons.

Julie dug around in the refrigerator and unearthed a piece of meatloaf and some leftover mashed potatoes. She didn't even bother with the gravy, just nuked them in their plastic containers and sat down alone at the dinner table.

She was halfway through the meal before she became aware that she wasn't alone. Her father was leaning against the doorway, just like the weary cowboy that he was. He was tall, taller than Nathan, almost as tall as Mark. She knew he was impossibly strong, but he wasn't built big. She'd gotten her leanness from him.

"Can see you're unhappy, Julie." It was so rare for him to actually call her by anything other than "girl" that she didn't look away. In a house full of men, "girl" had always been sufficient. "Anything I can do about it?"

She shook her head. "I wish there was, Dad." She looked back down at her plate and really wished there was.

"Got to do with your little company?"

She shrugged. "Not really."

"'Cause I was chattin' with Vern about the kinda work you're doing for Mac. He sounded mighty interested. You should give him a call."

Julie looked up at him. She'd hoped for recommendations from Mac, but never expected one from her father.

"Their property is off a ways. Not sure if that's a good thing or a bad."

Vern's spread was as far the other side of Choteau as they were.

Sixty miles by the crow from here. Well clear of the Front Range. Well clear of the memories. She liked…and didn't like that part of it.

"Got to do with that young man."

He didn't make it a question so it was hard to shrug it off.

"He worth it?"

She could only nod.

"He's gone back to New York?"

Even the nod was beyond her.

"Not coming back."

Again not a question.

"Shit!" Then after a long pause, he spoke softly. "I'm real sorry, Julie."

By the time she could trust herself to look up, her father was gone.

The next morning Mark nearly steamrollered her into the ground as she came into the barn and he was headed out.

"Hey, Julie! Help me roll out the helo." It wasn't a request, it was an order.

In five minutes, with hardly another word, Mark was in the air and headed East—fast.

Emily was waiting for her when Julie reached the new office. It had changed a lot over the last six weeks. The battered loft filled with the unwanted refuse of a horse barn was now unrecognizable.

Up the stairs above the two tack rooms and to the right was a set of cubbyhole shelves and hanging pegs for coils of rope. Leather strapping had a different shelf for every gauge. There was even a big bin of old horseshoes to be given to eager kids to hang on their walls at home.

To the left was one of the strangest rooms Julie had ever been in— never mind built. From the outside, it looked wholly innocuous. She'd sided it with old barn lumber and normal-looking windows. But she'd found (and Emily had been thrilled with) special glass that looked mostly black from the outside—as if the lights were always out inside the room—but offered full visibility from within.

The parts she'd picked up at Malmstrom AFB with Nathan offered an entire layer of electrical silencing. Nothing done inside the room traveled out except as an encrypted signal up to satellites via a few small antennas she'd mounted beside the solar panels. No emissions to detect. Even the fresh air system was a crazy collection of electronic filters and wave disruptors that she didn't begin to understand, but the installation instructions had been clear enough for her to install them.

Inside, Emily' seat commanded a jet black cocoon of enough electronics to make an alien spaceship look average. What made it even stranger were the views out the windows overlooking the horse stalls, and the skylight on the sloping ceiling that allowed a view of the fields and sky.

When she'd asked, Emily had laughed. "Nothing mysterious. I do tactical consulting on complex missions for my old unit. Since I refuse to leave my children in order to do that—the whole idea behind leaving the Army in the first place—they built me this. Well, you built it, but they paid for it. It's a tactical command center."

Which had prompted Julie to add a small wooden plaque outside the door which read "Tac Room" to go with the two larger "Tack Room" signs below.

The door was open when she reached the top of the steps.

"I like my sign," Emily greeted her and waved her to a chair.

"I hoped you might."

"What's left?"

Julie ran down her punch list, which was actually depressingly short. She'd be done with all of her Henderson's Ranch contract work by midday.

Emily nodded, "Good. There are some people who want to talk to you."

Some traitorous part of Julie lit a brief candle of hope—that she squashed as fast as she could.

"No, not Nathan. I'm sorry."

"That's okay," Julie got her stone walls back in place around her heart. "Who? Certainly not Mark. He lit out of here like his hair was on fire."

"I sent him on a mission."

Julie eyed the darkened computer screens behind Emily.

"Not that kind of mission. He'll be happier once the tourists are here. He's better with the kids than I am. Little children, fishing trips on horseback, the helicopter tours that Nathan thought up—"

"That Nathan thought up?"

Emily nodded, "We're also going to start offering, for a fee of course, heli-transport from Great Falls International Airport to the ranch. It's not a Black Hawk, but Mark will welcome the air time. I think I've probably flown enough for this lifetime. If it goes well, I might get him a bigger helo that can take more than four passengers. But then again, more trips will help keep him busier."

Julie was still pondering Nathan thinking up helicopter tours.

"Are you ready?"

Julie shrugged. "Since I don't know what for, bring it on. Is it something else to fix?"

Emily smiled, which Julie was learning to be a rare enough occurrence to be noteworthy. "In a way. Chelsea, you're up." Emily called out one of the inside windows after opening it.

There was a very Chelsean cheer, and then the pounding of booted feet up the stairs. "You're finally done?" She burst into the room with more energy than Julie would ever have again.

Julie nodded. Most of her words had flown away with Nathan.

"Yes!" Chelsea did a fist pump followed by a little clog dance around the room before plummeting into a chair. "Please say yes. Please. Please. Please! Please…PLEASE!"

Julie almost laughed, another thing that— She chopped off the thought. "To what?"

"I need an advanced rider."

"For what? A pony express run? Closest point of the old route is probably Big Sandy, Wyoming. That's a ways off."

"Oh, wouldn't that be so cool if the Pony Express had run through here. We could offer Pony Express rides and—"

"Chelsea. Focus," Emily not only smiled but might have been fighting a laugh.

"Right. Sorry. We're trying to draw an expert-level crowd. That's a new market segment for us. The only person we really have to lead those kind of rides is Doug and he needs to be here to run the ranch. Mac said that I had to wait until you were done with the spring work because your brain might explode if we gave you another thing to think about, but now that you're done you can think about it. Right?"

Julie tried to absorb the strangeness of the request. "How often?"

"One a week, probably three-four days each trip—right through the high season. You know this country better than anyone. Ama wants to do more riding, too. The two of you could scout together, maybe lead them together sometimes. When you're here, well, Doug said he's never seen anyone better at talking down the feistier horses and he wants you to work with them when you have time. Then there's the breeding program we want to start up and— Oh crud! Doug wanted to talk to you about that later. But that's in there too."

"I have a business…" though Julie couldn't imagine anything she'd like to do more. Working with the horses was beyond a dream come true.

"That's my part of it," Mac was leaning on the door frame.

She hadn't heard him come up the stairs behind her. Maybe she should have left a squeak or two in the staircase. Though Mac had been a Navy SEAL, so it might not have made any difference.

"The management of Henderson's Ranch," Mac pointed at himself and then up toward the house, indicating Ama. "We're thrilled with the work you did, but we can't afford you full time."

"That was my point," Julie hoped she could make one now that Mac's presence seemed to have silenced Chelsea. "I need to go find some work. I've gotten a good taste of building and find that I like it. Though a less crazy schedule wouldn't hurt me none."

Mac smiled. "Yep! This spring was a real stretcher that I don't want to repeat either. What I meant to say is that we can't afford you full-time as a building contractor alone. But if you wanted to mix that up with the trail rides and horse work," he gave one of his eloquent shrugs. "I think we can make that work."

"Full-time? Here? At Henderson's?"

Mac nodded, "Got a place picked out for you, already know you like it." He nodded up toward the cabins on the other side of the barn.

Julie looked out the skylight window. She was glad it faced away from the cabins—away from Aspen where…

He couldn't mean that.

If he did…

No! Impossible! She never could.

The skylight faced toward Larson land. And somewhere far to the east, a construction job on Vern's ranch. He was a good man. His older son was married and Julie liked his wife well enough when they met at church socials or the county fair. The younger son wasn't a complete troll either.

"I—"

"We're going to clear out of your way," Emily stood up and made shooing motions at the others.

"You get the trim and such finished in here. And just think on it."

She really didn't need to. What she needed was to be far away, but she nodded. Emily Beale wasn't the sort of woman to argue with.

Mac gave her a nod and a smile, then departed, probably assuming that of course she'd take the offer.

Chelsea made praying motions and whispered, "Please, please, please," another half dozen times as she backed out the door. Chelsea, at least, knew it wasn't as sure a thing. Though Julie had rebuffed her attempts to talk about "things" several times since Nathan left, she would miss Chelsea.

"Two nights, Julie," Emily said when it was just the two of them. "I want you to sleep on it for two nights. Because I know that's all it takes to change a person's life."

When she was gone, Julie couldn't find the energy to move.

Two nights.

Exactly the number of nights she and Nathan had had together.

She'd wait because Emily had asked, but then she was gone.

"What the hell, buddy?"

Nathan startled up as the big voice boomed forth in the restaurant.

All other conversation immediately died and the patrons were all staring at the big guy in a jeans jacket.

"Mark?" Everyone in the restaurant wore upscale chic, even the tattering of some patron's clothes had been done by a designer. Mark Henderson looked big, burly, and completely out of place in his ranch attire. "What are you doing in New York?"

"Damned if I know," Mark brushed by the hostess and the waiters. Somewhere along the way he acquired a beer. He plucked an empty stool from one of the high-top tables just as its occupant headed off toward the restroom. Mark carried it to the center of the servers' station and dropped onto it.

It was the exact busiest point of the entire restaurant. It was where the three different legs of the cook line came together in front of the expeditor—which was Estevan because they hadn't found a good one that they could afford to steal yet. The expeditor finished the plating and made sure everything was perfect before sliding it across to the waiters. Sliding it to exactly where Mark had unknowingly parked himself.

"Hey. Get out of the way," Estevan flapped a hand at him. He couldn't do more because every patron was staring into the open kitchen to see what happened next.

Then Nathan recognized Mark's look, the look of a man who had just been head-butted by a moose and still kept his wits about him regarding his precious fish.

Mark knew *exactly* where he was sitting.

Nathan tipped his head to come back into the kitchen.

Mark sat through another long sip of his beer just to make Estevan crazy, then came around the side, still carrying his stool. He plunked it down just barely out of Nathan's way.

"What do you mean that you're damned if you know why you're in New York?" Nathan dropped three salmon fillets in butter with just a sprinkle of fresh-ground guajillo red pepper.

"Emily told me to come. Not a chance I'm going to argue with that woman. One thing I've learned about her over the years, she has a habit of always being right. I don't mess with that."

Nathan nodded as he spooned the butter up over the fish in fast little strokes to keep it moist. Too much liquid escaped from the first layer of the flesh if he didn't. The goal was a perfectly seared finish on one side, and a consistently moist bite from top to bottom. The butter gave a more luscious mouthfeel than white wine. It also played better off the artichoke salsa served alongside it.

Then he remembered Julie crowing with delight over proving Emily fallible.

I do like you!

He accidentally splashed a scoop of butter onto the burner rather than fish. Someone, probably him, was going to have to clean that up after the stove was cold. The butter smoked and tickled his nose as it burned off. Almost made him sneeze like that time with Julie when—

"So what did Emily have to say?" Because he certainly wasn't going to ask after Julie.

" 'Get on a plane, go find Nathan, and fix this.' I think those were her exact, and only, words. So what the hell am I fixing? And why did I have to fly two thousand miles—on a commercial jetliner, for cripe's sake—and track you down to do that?"

"How *did* you track me down?"

"Emily did one of her things with your phone's location from up in that room Julie built for her. Said you've barely been out of this building for two weeks."

Nathan cracked his neck. His shoulders hurt like hell, which they hadn't since he'd quit and driven to Montana. Hunching over a hot cook line did that to a guy.

"Where's my fish?" Estevan managed to keep it below a shout.

Nathan looked down. Scorched and dry. "In the crapper." He began knocking pans into the waste bin so that he could refire the whole order. In the process, he accidentally grabbed a duck confit and knocked it into the trash as well, which was going to screw up a whole other table's sequencing.

"Basket case," he called out. There were nights when a chef turned all thumbs. There were only two approaches that Nathan had ever found would work. One: plow mindlessly ahead while the disaster rippled through the service for an hour or more, all the way out to the tables, before it finally tapered off and resettled.

Or two: cry "Basket case" and get the hell off the line.

Estevan was muttering foul imprecations as he juggled the line in order to take over the position himself. "Get out of here, Nathan. And take this asshole with you."

"Sorry, man."

Estevan shrugged. It happened, just never to Nathan. He'd set up the system at Vite, but he'd never had to call it on himself.

He returned the stool to the perplexed patron who had only just returned from the restroom.

Nathan swiped a beer from the bar and led Mark out the front door. It wasn't a warm enough evening for New Yorkers to use the outside sidewalk tables, but after Montana it seemed almost balmy.

"Find me and fix this?"

"That's what she said," Mark toasted him and drank. "Any idea what it means?"

"Yeah," Nathan sighed, then returned the gesture and drank himself. "Yeah, I think I do."

CHAPTER 16

Julie hadn't been able to stand it. There wasn't a way she could stand waiting a whole second day.

Dad had silently lent her a hand loading her truck. There wasn't that much to load. She couldn't take Clarence, not until she knew the lay of the land at Vern's ranch, so it was just her work clothes and her tools. The old Ford cringed under the load, but stood staunchly by. She had the money in her pocket to rebuild the engine—Mac had paid her off yesterday afternoon—but she didn't have the time.

When everything was loaded, they stood awkwardly in the front yard close beside her truck.

"Mac called me about the offer couple days back," her father finally grumbled out. "Told him I hated to lose a hand as good as you, but it sounded like a better fit than this place will ever be. Or Vern's. You sure you're making the right decision in turning him down? He's a good man. Good spread. I know your mama would like having you close to home."

Julie studied her father's grim face. It was perhaps the longest speech she'd ever heard from him. And it was definitely the closest Nils Larson had ever come to saying he'd miss her.

It touched her that he tried.

"I'll still see you and her at church, Dad, and the Choteau socials. First rodeo coming to Great Falls is but a handful of weeks off. Besides, I'm just sixty miles off." Not New York or some other impossibly faraway place. "Have to come back and get Clarence at some point."

"You thinking of taking up racing again?"

Julie shrugged. She'd liked barrel racing. It tested a horse and rider's cooperation like no other rodeo event. The men's event of bronc riding and tie-down roping was as much about raw nerve and real guts as anything else. Women's barrel racing was about pure horsemanship.

"You were good, Julie. I was sorry to see you quit after that third you took up in Calgary."

"The pro riders, Dad. The ones who don't have to work for a living. Can't go up against them."

"S'pose so," he shrugged, but it was more like he was sorry she'd quit. "Well, you take care, Julie. You need anything, give a call."

"You too, Dad."

He wrapped his arms around her for a moment and patted her on the back.

She breathed him in deep so that she could keep that memory close. As close as those memories she'd kept of Nathan. The problem was that after two long weeks and starting a third, those memories were already starting to fade.

Julie was losing him and couldn't bear it.

Her Dad let her go.

They exchanged nods, then she climbed in her truck and headed out. He opened the gate, where Lucy stood waiting to get back in.

He shooed the cow into the yard, then closed the gate behind her after she pulled out.

He didn't wave.

———

Julie was less than a dozen miles of dirt from Vern's ranch when a helicopter came in low and fast from behind her.

It swooped by so close above her truck that she ducked even though she was inside the cab.

Then it soared upward until its nose was almost straight at the sky. The tail kicked around, and it dove to land not a hundred yards directly ahead of her.

Julie slammed on the brakes to avoid ramming it before she recognized the crease in the nose. The passenger's foot window had been replaced, but the moose's dent in the nose definitely marked it as the Henderson's helicopter. Which now completely blocked the dirt one-lane.

She knew that Mac couldn't fly anything like that.

There was only one person aboard—though she didn't know why she'd expected anything else. Emily or…

Mark Henderson climbed out before the rotors had fully stopped. He stalked up to her truck window and rapped his knuckles on the glass.

The window crank had fallen off while crossing all of the rough roads and gone somewhere under the seat, so she opened the door wide enough to be heard.

"Go away, Mark."

"Not a chance. Turn this truck around."

"Not a chance."

He looked up at the sky and growled. Then he yanked the door open so abruptly that her hold on the inside handle almost tumbled her to the ground. Once she had her balance back, she reached back into her tools and grabbed the first thing that came to hand.

A crowbar. God was definitely laughing her butt off over this scenario.

"Out of my way, Mark. I mean it," she brandished it high, just the way Nathan had waved it at Lucy that first evening she'd met him.

He sighed, then made a sudden move to grab it. But she'd outmaneuvered enough cows and fought off enough rutting cowhands to not be such easy bait.

She dodged clear, but not before she whapped his butt a good one with the side of the bar.

"I have had enough of this shit!" Mark shouted down the long stretch of empty road. Then he spun too quickly for her to follow.

He swept her legs out from under her so fast that she had no way to recover. She landed hard, flat on her back. When she managed to open her eyes, she lay in a cloud of dust and Mark was tossing her crowbar back into the toolbox in the truck bed.

Just for fair play, she spun around, hooked his ankles with hers, and sent him toppling as well.

"What the—" Mark snarled from the dirt.

"Three older brothers," she sat up and rested her elbows on her knees. "You?"

"A whole line of Army hand-to-hand combat instructors that I'm going to have a hard word or two with next time I see them." He sat up opposite her and began dusting at his arms and legs. Even his sunglasses had a patina of dust on them.

"I can't go back, Mark. I just can't face it. Your dad, with the best of intent, was going to offer me Aspen. I can't go there. I can't stay there, can't even look at it. There were too many good things in that cabin."

"Yeah, a certain hospital bed comes to mind," Mark smiled to himself.

"A hospital bed. What was the other one?"

"The other what?"

"Emily said there were two nights that changed her life. Mine were a Great Falls hotel room and the Aspen cabin."

"She said that?" his smile looked awfully pleased. "Back of a Black Hawk helicopter would be the other."

"Should have guessed that one." Julie shook her head. "But you two got the end of your story. How do I go back when the rest of my story isn't there? I want that job. I want it so much. I love your ranch. And the people. The horses. It's all so perfect and it's all so ruined," her throat cracked hard but she couldn't stop it.

"You never give the hell up," Mark practically shouted. "I should have lost my commission for the hospital episode and we both should have for the second one. I lied my way into the White House to get her and almost got us both killed. You never give the hell up."

Julie cringed under the tirade Mark unleashed on her. But he was right. She had given up. Maybe too easily. She'd quit the barrel racing because of the truly exceptional women who were full-time riders. It wasn't that they were just the pro riders who didn't need to work. They didn't need to work at anything else because they *were* the top women's pro riders. And she'd finished third against them. If she'd been willing to give up everything else, she could have been as well.

But she was giving up the sweetest job offer there ever was because she couldn't face all the *good* things that a man had given her. That was so wrong.

And if she wasn't going to give up the job at Henderson's...

Then she certainly wasn't going to give up so easily on the best thing to ever happen to her. She stood and dusted herself off.

Mark eyed the hand she offered him carefully, then grabbed ahold and rose as well.

"If he's not in your helo, then where the *hell* is Nathan Gallagher?"

Mark's smile was radiant. "I dropped him at his car in the airport parking lot, so he's about an hour behind me. Or was before I had to come chasing after you."

She climbed up into her truck. "Get out of my way, Mark."

He held up both hands in mock surrender and backed away while she maneuvered a five-point turnaround on the narrow dirt lane. And headed back.

She worked the truck up into third gear and wished for a fourth, fifth, and sixth while she kept the pedal down hard. Let it rattle and moan.

He didn't drive to New York. He flew.

Mark had had to go and get him, so he'd probably dug himself in pretty deep.

But he left his precious car here.

Maybe he'd thought that he'd fetch it later like she'd thought of fetching Clarence in a few weeks.

But he hadn't taken it with him. Some part of him had known he'd be back.

Just like some part of her had known not to move her horse.

She leaned low over the driver's wheel, hoping that would get her a little more speed back to Henderson's Ranch.

CHAPTER 17

Nathan sat on the porch of Aspen and watched the weather rolling in, darkening the afternoon. He didn't know where else to go. The last twenty-four hours had been so strange. In a way, the least strange thing had been Mark hunting him down all the way to New York City.

For the entire trip back he'd been obsessed with that one little phrase of Julie's, her confession of: *I do like you!* Somehow, that seemed bigger than their trip to Great Falls or even making love here in the Aspen cabin. Emily had told him to remind her that she liked him—and to not let her forget. Somehow he had been the one to forget and now it was time to remind them both. If she gave him the chance.

Nathan was now betting every single choice on that memory—thank god Mark had come to New York to knock some sense into him.

But the mad race back to the ranch had run into a major issue: Julie was nowhere to be found. Not even all of Emily's military equipment could find her, probably because Julie was somewhere that didn't have cell reception.

While Nathan drove, Mark had flown his helicopter from the airport. Once it was determined Julie was gone, Mark had tracked Nils to the Larson's calving barn and found out where she was headed. Emily called Nathan to report that Mark had taken off in the helicopter to chase Julie down at about the same moment Nathan turned off the highway at the big white cow barn. He'd almost run into the gun-shot stop sign.

He didn't know the roads well enough to chase after her on his own. If she came back, there was only one place he could be sure she'd eventually go, and that's what drew him back to Aspen cabin.

Nathan had raced the Miata along the highway, but the washboard roads from Choteau forced him to what felt like a painful crawl—no matter what the speedometer said otherwise. It was the longest thirty miles of his life.

Now, at the cabin, holding his breath, all Nathan could do was wait.

Emily had locked herself in her office and was probably doing marginally legal things to track Julie for Mark to intercept. Mark hadn't called to report his success or failure. Chelsea had swung by with Doug to offer him a few words of hope that he'd barely been able to acknowledge. Nathan managed to wave back when Mac and Ama looked up toward him from the main house's back door. He'd have to go far to find stauncher friends.

Nathan spotted the returning helo first, a small white dot against the heavy gray clouds. He stood and watched, holding onto a porch post because he didn't trust his knees.

He felt as out of balance as that moment last night sitting with Mark outside Estevan's restaurant when he realized his mistake.

Being a New York restaurant burn-out had sent him scrambling to Montana in the first place. And in just two weeks of helping Estevan, he'd gotten sucked right back in like some sick drug addict. Didn't even see what he'd done until Mark pulled the plug on him. Estevan's restaurant was on its legs, the friendship debt was paid, and his job was over.

At the next revelation he almost laughed—would have if he wasn't so scared: if he never cooked in Paris or New York again, that would be fine with him.

From Aspen's porch, Nathan saw the helo land, shut down—but Mark was the only one to climb out. He was too far away to see clearly, but Emily came rushing out of the barn. She threw herself at him and he swept her tight into his arms.

Nathan would take that as a good sign. Surprising, but good.

An even better sign, he spotted the dust of a vehicle far out along the road that ran between Henderson and Larson land.

In minutes the dust cloud resolved to reveal an ancient beater of a pickup racing toward the ranch. Unable to stand any longer, he sat down on the top step and waited. His hands ached with how tightly they were clasped, but he couldn't seem to let go.

Closer. Definitely Julie's truck. It disappeared behind the bluff for an agonizing couple of minutes, then came racing up the main drive.

It didn't slow through the main yard, which sent Patrick skittering aside when he foolishly tried to cross the open expanse.

Without a single hesitation she roared up the frontage road by the cabins, sliding to a barely controlled halt in front of him.

He couldn't stand.

For a long minute she sat there, looking at him through the closed window, her hands clenched on the steering wheel.

Unable to tolerate it any longer, he managed to rise and walk down the steps.

She watched him as he stepped up to the truck's door. Still held the steering wheel tightly.

He opened the door as the first drops of rain pattered softly on the roof of her truck.

She was covered head to toe in dirt.

"Hey, cowgirl." She looked incredible.

"Hey." No "city boy". Bad sign? Definitely not good.

"You're all dirty again. What happened?"

She shook her head. Not relevant. Right. Time to talk about what was important.

"A friend called. He needed help opening a new restaurant."

"So you just…went?" Her fury sounded deep, but he could read the hurt behind it. Nathan had no idea how he'd ever done this to her. He could only shrug. However, pointing out that she'd told him to go wasn't likely to help anything.

Instead he tried to explain. "It was a dream he and I used to have long ago. I owed him. Even more, I owed the dream."

She watched him with those impossibly blue eyes.

"I almost got lost in it again. So dangerously close. But one thing stopped me."

"Mark."

Nathan laughed and shook his head. "Not even close," he reached out and tucked her hair behind her ear.

She leaned into it a little, but didn't let go of the steering wheel.

"All Mark did was remind me that Emily can be wrong."

"What does Emily have to do with this?"

"You said, 'I *do* like you.' You said that Emily got it wrong and that you do like me. Is that still true?"

After a long moment she nodded.

"The piece I didn't connect was that I like you, too."

"Well, that's convenient."

He laughed at her tone. He now knew a Julie Larson-tone when he heard one. He thought he'd figured out a way around that, but he wasn't quite ready yet. It was the chef in him. A meal had an order: a build, a fullness, until the final validation at the end. In a meal it was called dessert. Here in Montana, beneath the roiling clouds of the Big Sky, it was called the rest of his life.

"Will you come sit on the porch with me, Julie?"

She eyed the porch over his shoulder, then nodded cautiously.

It was hard, but she managed it. Nathan offered his hand, but that was asking too much. She flipped a tarp over her tools in the truck bed to protect them from the increasing rain and then climbed the porch steps beside him.

Aspen cabin. It was so thick with memories, with feelings, with hope and despair. He was here, but she didn't dare let the hope out. If she was wrong, she would never rebuild the walls holding her together.

"How are you here?" *How* was as far as Julie dared go. She didn't dare guess *why*. It was too risky.

"Mark and I got drunk last night, very drunk."

"That explains the bloodshot eyes."

"Actually, we got drunk last night in New York. So I think that the bloodshot eyes is more from having a hangover during the flight back. Don't ever do that. It sucks."

"Does this have a point?" Nathan was here. In Montana. Why was she complaining?

"It does actually. Usually drunk equals stupid—sometimes really stupid. I lost a couple years' worth of brain cells to being a stupid chef. Then I quit, cold turkey on my own, and became a slightly smarter chef. For some reason, last night, for once in my life when it really counted, drunk equaled smart."

"What were you smart about?"

"Mark and I came up with an idea. It sounded beyond stupid at first, but we were just drunk enough to chase it around a bit. Once we had, it sounded smarter. Then a lot smarter. Mark called Emily to roust Mac and Ama out of bed because we were so excited about this crazy idea. It was past midnight here, but they said yes before we had it half explained. *That's* when we got stupid and *really* drunk. Celebrating."

"Celebrating what? You draw this out much more, Nathan, and I'm going to have to commit more bodily harm on you than I already did on Mark." The rain began pattering on the porch roof.

"I'm sick to death of New York, Julie. It's not just because of you. Actually that part isn't you at all. I'm tired of the grind and the way it chews up good people until there's nothing left of them but a palate and knife skills. I spent the last year having no life outside the kitchen—a whole year of my life. It's not how I *want* to live. Yet cooking for you, I was reminded how much I love to cook. Just as you reminded me every day what it looked like to be intensely alive."

"And…" she meant it as a growl, but she was too keyed up for it to come out that way. It explained so much, right down to the whisky he'd never quite finished at the Celtic Cowboy, proving to himself exactly who was in control.

"Cooking classes."

"Cooking classes?" What did they have to do with anything?

"Uh-huh. Cooking classes at Henderson's Ranch. They have that magnificent kitchen. And there are bound to be guests who aren't so hot on horses married to ones who are. Also Ama wants to cook less. So, Emily and I will step in there together. And I was thinking to rebuild that wagon we used for the yurt-raising party. You and I could fix that up as a classic chuck wagon. Then Red and I could deliver dinners to remote campsites. Set up someplace a couple hours' ride away as a kids' camp and serve them meals from a chuck wagon. Give their parents a little alone time in the cozy cabins. We can offer fully catered ranch weddings. We'll get some great photos when a couple of Mark's old firefighter friends get married out here this summer."

He kept spinning ideas as fast as Chelsea had, just…yesterday morning.

"During the winter season, I'd get guest chefs out here and we'd do two-week pro-level master classes. During harvest we could—"

"And you'd be happy doing this?" She cut him off before he completely overwhelmed her with his words.

He nodded.

"Here?" she felt the cabin behind her but couldn't turn to look at it. She couldn't manage more than a whisper, barely louder than the steady rain.

"What's with all the rain? I've never seen a drop since we got here except that first night's bit of snow."

Julie hadn't really focused on it. What about her question? Was he avoiding it? Her heart was feeling too jumbled to hold focus on that, so instead she answered his question. "It's the first heavy spring rain. Everyone has been waiting for it. If it holds for a couple of days, it will be a good year along the Montana Front Range. Another major dump in August and it will be a great year."

Nathan rose and walked away from her to hold his hand out past the edge of the covered porch. "It's warm."

"We call it the 'Million-Dollar Rain'. It sets the crops, fills the reservoirs, and changes the prairie from struggling to lush. In a couple days, you're going to see wildflowers like you never imagined in your life. The entire prairie blooms purple, red, and gold."

"I'd like to see that." Then he turned back to face her, nodding toward Aspen's cabin door showing that he hadn't forgotten her question. "Yes, right here. One condition."

"What's that?"

"You said that you like me, cowgirl."

"I think we already covered that."

"But do you love me, Julie? I couldn't go through that door ever again without you beside me."

She turned from Nathan and those dark eyes that looked at her with such sudden hope. She finally looked at the front door of the Aspen cabin.

Could she live here? With Nathan? With their children?

Looking out over this beautiful land?

She finally faced Nathan once more but could only nod. The answer to every single one of those questions was yes.

He knelt before her.

"Then will you marry me, Julie? Because I can't imagine life without you."

A nod was too little. Not nearly big enough to explain the protective walls around her heart that were crumbling to dust. Washed away by a million-dollar rain and the love of a chef. Then her freed heart found what to say.

"Oh, city boy. Yes."

They were the happiest words she'd ever spoken in her life.

WELCOME AT HENDERSON'S RANCH

*Freelance journalist **Colleen McMurphy** finds her Irish penname far more professional than the Kurva Baisotei her Japanese parents perpetrated upon her at birth. Her "itinerant writer" role fit her deliciously single lifestyle, until an assignment sent her to Montana's Big Sky Country to write an article about Henderson's Ranch.*

***Raymond Esterling,** summertime cowboy, gratefully forgets his life beyond the prairie, at least for those precious months beneath the Big Sky. But when he meets Colleen, he can't help but make her Welcome at Henderson's Ranch.*

CHAPTER 1

Dateline: August 15, Henderson's Ranch,
Bloody Nowhere, Montana

Colleen McMurphy could write this article in her sleep, with her keyboard tied behind her back, and…

"The wife and I had such a splendid time there. You simply must go and write us an article about it." For some reason Larry always went old-school English whenever he got excited—which coming from her Puerto Rican boss who lived in Seattle seemed to be almost normal for Colleen's life.

He, of course, was too busy being Mr. Hotshot Editor to write it himself. That and he couldn't write his way out of a martini glass. He was one of the best editors she'd ever worked for—and as a freelancer that had included a suckload of them—but his twelve-year-old daughter could write new material better than he could. Hillary was named for Sir Edmund of Mt. Everest fame and just might follow her namesake at the rate she was being amazing. She was a precocious little twerp who was so delightful that she made Colleen feel grossly inadequate half the time and totally charmed the other three-quarters.

So, off to Montana it was. Magazine feature article—she was on it.

The most recent in a cascade of ever-shrinking planes banged onto the runway in Great Falls, Montana clicking all Colleen's vertebrae together with a whip-like snap that surprisingly failed to paralyze her. A Japan Airlines 747 had lofted her from the family home in Tokyo to LAX. The smallest 737 ever made hopped her up to Salt Lake, and a wing-flapping 18-seater express fluttered as hopelessly as a just-fledged swallow to Great Falls. If there'd been another plane that was any smaller, they were going to have to put her in a bento box.

But finally she was here in…major sigh…Nowhere, Montana.

She'd used this job as an excuse to cut the two-week trip home in half. Two weeks! *With her family?* What *had* she been thinking? She was going to have a serious talk with her sense of filial duty before it dragged her from Seattle back to Japan again.

Outside the miniature plane's windows the airport stretched away pancake-flat and dusty. Four whole jetways, the place was *smaller* than a bento box. But their plane didn't pull up to any of them—because it was too short to reach. Instead, it stopped near the terminal and the copilot dropped the door open, filling the cabin with the familiar bite of spent engine fumes and slowing propeller roar. She'd spent the whole final flight glaring out at the spinning blades directly outside her window, waiting for one to break off, punch through the window, and slice her in two like one of Larry's martini olives.

"Enough!" she told herself so loudly that it made the fat-boy businessman—who'd made the near-fatal mistake of trying to chat her up across the tiny aisle—jump in alarm. Twenty hours and nine minutes in flight didn't usually make her this grouchy. Her parents did though.

"Why did you change your name?" *Because everyone in America would laugh their faces off calling her Kurva—for the Hokkaido mulberry tree you conceived me under, much too much information by the way. It especially doesn't translate so well for a girl who is Japanese flat. Besides there isn't an American alive who can say* Baisotei *properly.* Kurva Baisotei was not a moneymaking byline.

Then, not "When are you going to get married?" but rather "Why do you not give us grandchildren like your sister?" *My sister has three. How insatiable are you as grandparents?*

"Why do you not return home?" *Because you live here.*

"Ma'am?" Fat-boy was waiting for her to get out of her seat first. Maybe because he needed the full width of the tiny plane, or maybe he was just being nice. She was about to step back on American soil—even if it was Montana—so she gave him the benefit of the doubt and offered a "Thanks" with a smile that hopefully he didn't read as encouraging.

The air outside the airport smelled strange. It definitely wasn't Seattle, which had an evergreen scent that wrapped itself around you like a warm, though often damp, welcome home. Her best girl Ruth Ann always met her when she landed from trips to Japan to drag her to their favorite dive, the J&M in Pioneer Square, and make sure that she got safely drunk within an hour of landing. It was doubly strange to arrive somewhere else without Ruth Ann's patiently sympathetic ear.

Montana was dry and, despite the warm afternoon, somehow crisp. In Seattle there were a gazillion things sharing the air with her: Douglas firs, seagulls, dogs playing in the park, ferry boats—the list went on and on. Here it tasted more rarified. More...special.

Also high on the *special* list was the guy leaning comfortably on a helicopter with "Henderson's Ranch" emblazoned down the side like it had been branded there with a flaming iron. He already had one beaming couple beside him with Los Angeles cowboy written all over their Gucci. He towered above them: six-two of dark tan, right-out-of-a-romance-novel square jaw, and mirrored shades for a touch of mystery. His t-shirt was tight and his jeans weren't bad either. And—crap!—ring on his finger. Fantasy cowboys weren't supposed to have rings on their fingers, but she wasn't going to complain about this piece of the Montana scenery just because of the "Back Off" sign.

Another couple joined them. First-timers by their lost look.

"Hi!" He even had a nice deep voice to go with that big frame. "I'm Mark Henderson. Climb on aboard," and he was helping the two couples into the back seats.

Handsome guy who flies a helicopter. Sweet! Maybe Montana

wasn't going to be so bad. Ruth Ann was gonna be wicked jealous. She snapped a photo of him just for that purpose.

"Looks like you're up front with me, beautiful," he aimed a lethal smile directly at her.

She returned the smile, feeling pleased. Then lost it when she realized the implications.

Two happy couples in the back.

Handsome married dude in the front.

And that's when the background research she'd done on their website finally made a horrible kind of sense. Weddings this. Couples that. Family horseback rides the other. Larry should have sent Colleen's perfect sister's family, not her.

She was a single Japanese chick, with an Irish name she'd taken from the old TV show *China Beach.* (She'd always liked the main character—strong woman back when that wasn't a very popular thing to be.)

Be strong now!

She was going to a couples' paradise. This was going to be worse than the parental purgatory.

She'd be pleasant. Polite.

And as soon as she got home, Larry was a dead man.

CHAPTER 2

Montana greets visitors who fly in with the dullest landscape imaginable. Rulers are tested here for an accurate straight edge by laying them on the ground.

But fifty miles to the west, the Rocky Mountains soar aloft, forcing the eye to constantly scan upward to the bluest sky imaginable. Henderson's Ranch lies nestled in the softly rolling country at the base of these majestic peaks.

A night's sleep and Colleen felt much more human this morning, even if she couldn't make sense of what lay outside her cabin window. To the south and east, the land stretched so far away that she felt as if she was perched atop an infinite cliff and at the least misstep might tumble down forever. A person could get vertigo here just sitting still.

To the west, the mountains punched aloft in bold, jagged strokes with little of the softness that Washington's forests provided to Seattle's peaks.

There was a wildness that confronted her every time she looked at these mountains. Her inner city Tokyo childhood, her rebellious escape to the community of fifty-thousand students at the University of Washington, Seattle's million people—none of it prepared her for this stark emptiness.

Here along the Front Range, aside from a few dozen guests and another dozen ranch hands, there might not be a soul for twenty miles. It felt like a thousand.

Down the slope, a tall woman stepped out of the back door of the main lodge and rang a giant steel triangle just like in an Old West movie: *clangety-clangety-clangety-clang.*

Families and couples streamed out of the other cabins and headed downhill toward the massive two-story log cabin structure that looked like one of those Depression-era lodges. Huge, powerful, unmoving.

A quick survey showed that she was the only singleton—if she didn't count kids, and even they seemed to come in packs. Almost everyone was dressed in K-Mart Western, or some designer version that looked no more likely.

There were breakfast fixings in her cabin, and she was tempted to retreat there, but she was here to write a travelogue article. For that she had to experience the experience.

She was last down the trail to the big house. The guests were all guided along the wrap-around porch to the front entrance into the big dining room she'd seen on last night's welcome tour. Thirty people could eat communal style at the long table.

However, a few others were coming around to the kitchen door. They were dressed far more casually, and far more authentically. Cowboy boots, dusty jeans, a variety of hats—some battered cowboy, some baseball-cap redneck. The women were dressed much the same.

Not really paying attention to what her feet were doing, she fell in with the ranch hands and found herself in a massive and beautiful kitchen. The hands were making use of one of the sinks before gathering at a smaller version of the big communal table out front.

"Mornin', Colleen. Not up for our 'Happy Couples' breakfast?"

Mark the pilot greeted her with an understanding smile, reading her too easily.

Time to gear up the pleasant-reporter face.

He wasn't any less handsome this morning, but a stunning blonde kissed him on the cheek as she topped up his coffee, confirming that the ring wasn't just for show.

"Not so much, if that's okay."

"Take a seat. Dad's this one, Mom's the other end, when she bothers to sit down. The rest are up for grabs."

She took a seat almost, but not quite, at the middle of the table on the far side. It gave her the best view of what was going on and would let her hear most of the conversations without being the center of them. No one so much as blinked an eye as she joined them. A pretty redhead gave her a South California, "Hey!" Her husband was more the quiet-nod type.

Another long blonde gave her a very authentic sounding, "Howdy!" just as the male cook (with a Brooklyn-tinged "Hello and welcome") came and set a plate in front of the blonde, then kissed her on top of the head.

Shit! She was in Couplandia here as well. Finally some more guys came in until there was a fair balance of single men. More what she'd expected.

Her goal of keeping track of the conversations went out the window in the first ten seconds. They were talking about the day to come and what they knew about the guests, but doing it in a handful of simultaneous discussions: "Most of this lot we won't get out of the corral for a couple days." "Did you see that absolute babe from England? Never saw a woman sit a horse so *purty*. She'll ride far and hard." His companion—alike enough to be his twin—gave him a knowing smile that was all about the woman and not so much about how she sat.

Colleen stayed focused on her meal and her article. The food was incredibly good despite how basic a hash brown-and-ham scramble with a biscuit buried in gravy sounded. Article ideas were perking up as she enjoyed the camaraderie around the table. These people liked each other. Liked working together. And whatever else they were saying about the guests, none of it was bitter or caustic. She'd expected some derision of "city cowboys" but nothing even remotely like that came up in any of the several threads she was able to follow.

She wondered what they'd be saying about *her* behind her back.

"I like the way you listen."

It took her a moment to rewind the comment because it was only the last word that actually caught her attention. She finally traced it (nearly accentless) to the man across the table. He wasn't a big man—Colleen had an absolute weak spot for big men, who thankfully often had a weak spot for petite Japanese women—but he had a nice smile so she wouldn't hold his normalness of height and build against him.

"Uh-huh," her cordial-meter was still running below normal, but then no one was supposed to see through her pleasant-reporter face. She really needed another mug of tea.

"Heard you just arrived from Japan. Family there?"

"Uh-huh," her cordial-meter bottomed out. That was a reminder that she didn't need.

"Apparently the wrong question."

"Uh-huh," she dialed up her emphatic-sarcasm mode to full.

"Do you ride?"

Her first temptation was to go to "uh-uh" but she already was being subverbal far beyond her norm. Besides, it was the easiest response. Like writing, the easiest word (the first word she thought of) was rarely the most precise or evocative one. Good writing required avoiding the obvious while still telling the story—whether it encapsulated what it was like to work on the Boeing manufacturing line like her last article or the current purgatory of Couplandia.

Her interlocuter (yes! her vocabulary was finally coming back online) looked like a nice enough guy. Cowboy lean with a pleasant smile. She supposed that she'd have to ride a horse to get the full "Henderson's Ranch" experience and a private lesson sounded far better than shaming herself in public.

"Not yet," she added a smile which she knew was one of her strengths. The guy returned with a powerful one of his own.

It was only then that she noticed Mr. Handsome-with-a-ring Henderson rolling his eyes at her—at least that's what she assumed he was doing behind his ever-present shades.

Okay, maybe she could have been a little more subtle. But he said he liked the way she listened—one of the skills she was most proud of. That bit of insightfulness was going to earn him a lot of leeway.

CHAPTER 3

Colleen turned on a light against the fading day and flipped back through her notes again. Where had Day Three gone? Where had Day Two gone for that matter?

She finally found Day Two.

Mac Henderson, technically Mark Henderson, Sr. and almost as handsome as his son, had been thrilled to have her on the ranch. Apparently she was their first journalist, so their resort had a lot riding on making her happy—though he acted as if he was simply glad *she* was here, not several million readers AAA magazine would be sending this out to. Which was sweet of him to pretend.

On Day Two, he'd toured her about: cabins, yurts, cooking classes, weaving classes, horseback riding, even a military dog trainer named Stan—a big, gruff man with a hook prosthetic on one arm who only spoke to his dogs.

As the day had progressed, Mac had grown more and more excited about showing her around his ranch until he was as wound up as one of Stan's puppies. A former Navy SEAL in his sixties who almost wriggled with delight. She'd always thought SEALs were supposed to be broody and stoic, but Mac was a thoroughly pleasant guy who clearly loved this land with a passion.

What she'd found truly unbelievable was the amount of work it took to run the place, and Mac made sure that she had a chance to meet and chat with every person of the staff. The redhead who ran the barn was so voluble that Colleen couldn't have gotten down one word in ten no matter how fast she took notes—and she was fast. Her husband, the ranch manager, was laconic to the point where Colleen wondered if people catnapped between his sentences.

It took her a while to catch on that he was teasing her with it.

Day Two afternoon: Mark's wife Emily took her on a solo helicopter flight over the ranch that was stunning in both its expansiveness and its variety. The softly rolling landscape around the buildings gave way to rugged prairie, patches of pine forest, and even waterfalls along a small river that ran down out of the hills. A group of horses out at a remote fishing cabin revealed that at least some riders had made it past the corral.

The cook wasn't a cook at all—he was a dropout New York chef... one she'd actually heard of.

She was getting why Larry and his family had gone nuts over the place, but that didn't explain what had happened to her notes. She was sure she taken more of them.

Day Three's notes were definitely not here. Then she remembered...

Raymond Esterling, her Day One breakfast companion.

Who liked the way she listened.

That's what had happened to Day Three.

...and most of Day Four.

Colleen sat down abruptly on the bed in her small cabin. She ran a hand over the bedspread: Cheyenne weaving done by the owner's wife. She was one of those tall, majestic Native American women that never actually existed in real life. The blanket's geometric reds and golds were as warm as the campfire they'd all sat around while burgers were cooked over open flame on a heavy iron grill earlier this evening—some of the best beef she'd ever tasted.

Whatever in the wide, wide world of Montana was happening to her? A good girl's education in being Japanese hadn't prepared her for this place. Nor a journalist's.

Her ears rang in the silence. No cars at night, no planes. Not even the ocean when she vacationed down at Cannon Beach, Oregon and could pretend the waves were actually the low rumble of I-5 that was never silent in Seattle—easily audible from her apartment on the other side of Lake Union.

A soft whinny drew her back to her feet and out onto the cabin's porch.

Raymond sat astride a big roan—as she'd learned to call his cream-colored mount with dark legs and mane. The sunset lit his gentle face.

He'd "happened" to more than her notes. He was happening to her and none of her training, neither as Kurva Baisotei nor Colleen McMurphy, was ready for it. Not even the city pickup bars had prepared her for him—not even the good ones (if there was such a thing).

Worse, Raymond hadn't resisted her journalistic inquisitiveness.

(*Anta, sensakuzuki,* her sister would curse under her breath—*you are always so nosy,* with the *anta* insult thrown in.)

Raymond hadn't resisted it because she hadn't unleashed it on him. Which was totally unlike her. But he had impressive listening skills as well.

To his credit, after his horseback riding lessons yesterday and today—in between the lessons he was giving to others—she had a good feel for riding. This afternoon she'd joined a trail ride for beginners and even cantered once; which had been both exhilarating *and* nearly scared her back into the womb.

But she knew so little about him.

He didn't seem to mind talking—he wasn't a reclusive *hikikomori* or even a male jerk "not in touch with his feelings." But it was as if his life beyond the boundaries of the ranch stretched as empty as the scrub prairie.

She knew that was total crap—he was a summer instructor and trail guide, no more. But every time she got ready to pin him down on what he did the other eight months of the year he'd smile at her, adjust her "seat" position, point out an eagle soaring on a thermal, anything to distract her…without appearing to distract her.

Now he sat astride his horse not five feet from the porch of her cabin, looking the quintessential "cowboy in the sunset."

"You can't be some mystic cowboy forever, you know?"

"Evening to you too, Kurva." Somehow he'd gotten that out of her. He also managed to say it like it wasn't a comment on her figure, or rather lack of one, so she let him use it. Instead, he turned her name into a tease, a friendly nickname that didn't chide her for choosing another.

"Evening to you, Raymond. What are you doing up on a horse at this hour?"

"Hoping to take you on an evening ride and see the stars. It's a warm night, but you might want a jacket." Never quite a question, yet not a statement either. As if coaxing her along like a reluctant horse. She didn't appreciate the metaphor but couldn't find the urge to fight it either.

Her own mount, a patient bay named Gumdrop of all silliness, trailed behind him on a lead. Colleen was really getting the vernacular down. She wanted to do a little horse-words rap there on the porch but resisted it. Instead she grabbed a polar fleece off a hook inside the door and climbed up into the saddle.

> *Seattle girl in the saddle girl*
> *Astride some rawhide like a way cool—bri—No!*

Her mind nearly strangled itself when her inner rap artist cast up "bride" for worst-rhyming-word-choice-of-the-century award. Definitely not!

The vertiginous Big Sky of Montana expanded even more as they rode up past the cabins and over the rise at a lazy, side-by-side plod. Gumdrop's head bobbed easily, no longer nearly jerking Colleen out of the saddle each time the horse leaned down to crop some grass as they went along.

In the sky, golds found reds.

Reds hinted at impending purples.

Soon Raymond reined to a halt and pointed to the west, "Venus."

Colleen didn't know where to look.

Raymond pulled his mount close beside her so that she could easily follow the line of his pointing arm.

It took her a moment to pick the sparkling point of light out of the red-gold sky, then she had it. It hung above the silhouetted-black mountains like a diamond.

"Planet light, planet bright, First planet I see tonight, I wish I may, I wish I might, Have this wish I wish tonight." Ray's voice was as soft as the call of a passing bird. "Meadowlark," he filled in for her.

"This seems to be the sort of place that wishes come true." It really was. The pale dry grass lay in golden waves over the rolling prairie. Far below—she didn't realize they'd wandered so far as she had watched the shifting light—lay the cozy cluster of ranch buildings: lodge, barns, and cabins. The next farm over, a big-spread cattle ranch, was just barely visible and looked homey as well.

"What do you wish for, Colleen Baisotei?" He said it right. It was as if he couldn't quite leave her names alone but had to play with them like cat toys. It seemed to make him happy to do so and, curiously, it didn't bother her. Words were her toys as well. She liked that in a man.

"What do I wish for? Not this."

"You don't?"

"Not really. The beauty here is like a drug. Perhaps in small doses, but I'd miss the city too much as well."

"I know," his voice was as soft as the night. "I come here for the summers, retreat to my city in the fall. But I don't think about that now. Now, I am simply here."

"A cowboy."

"They let me play at being one."

Colleen liked that about him, too. He knew what he himself was, even if she didn't know what he was in the real world. And now she understood why. Whereas she— "Huh!"

"What?"

"I'm…not sure what to wish for." Peace with her parents? There was a greater chance of a forest fire in Antarctica. Finding… Colleen didn't know what to plug in there. That bothered her. She really should know.

Sure, she was doing fine. She had good friends in Seattle, whether for a quiet dinner or to go out dancing: square dancing at the Tractor, Britpop Thursday at the Lo-Fi, or bottom-trawling at the J&M. Her job sent her traipsing up and down the Northwest until she knew it like the back of her hand, but kept discovering new things there anyway. Men were pleasant and easy. She knew there was a type of man who looked at her and melted, and she didn't mind that either. Slim-Japanese-with-dark-hair-well-down-her-back slayed them… another advantage to America over Japan where she was just another potential housewife. Dressing in a tight tube-top at least doubled her yield.

But what to spend an actual wish on…

She turned to him, "What's yours?"

"I would think that was obvious from the moment you walked into the ranch kitchen, Ms. McMurphy."

And when he said it, it was.

She turned from the diamond light of Venus to inspect Raymond Esterling, itinerant horse guide and otherwise unknown. He was what she wasn't. Melting-pot American versus pure-blood Japanese. Sandy blond and fair skinned. Easygoing to her own hyper tendencies— though those seemed to go quiet around him.

"I didn't come here looking to be a summer cowboy fling." Yet he'd grown on her enough over these last days to make it a reasonable consideration.

"Can't say that I've ever been much for flings myself. Every time I try them, I get burned."

"But you're willing to try me? I burn men baaaad! Just warning you."

"I expect, despite my mortal fear of fire, that you are well worth the risk." He also knew how to slay her with a simple piece of flattery. It might be a line, but it was a good one.

"Let's find out."

CHAPTER 4

Dateline...uh...unknown.

Lying naked in the bed, the cool Montana morning washes in the open window and over my body raising goosebumps. The crickets called through the night, singing a chorus of heat that had indeed scorched between the two highly-compatible humans. Now the siren call of the rising sun drags me back to the present.

For five more fun-filled days, and five enchantingly rigorous nights, Henderson's Ranch had delivered. She'd fished, learned to cook her trout on a heated rock by a wilderness campfire (though she'd passed on learning how to gut and clean the fish), gone horseback on a wildlife photo safari (she'd bagged a fox, two elk, and a rare bobcat with her camera), and even discovered some skill with a bow and arrow.

She'd also unearthed a bottomless need for how Raymond Esterling could make her feel.

Feel?

Dear gods, it was like she hadn't known the meaning of the word. Her body had responded to his in ways she'd never imagined. His hand on her calf as he checked her stirrup was enough to wrap her entire body in a warm heat. Even now it burned through her memory despite his having left her bed to start his morning chores.

And what she felt inside was equally foreign.

Demanding that her journalistic objectiveness chronicle what was happening to her resulted in—no answers.

Instead, like the splash of cold water that sent her scrabbling for the covers, she was reminded that her idyll was done. This was Last Day, Departure Day.

By this evening she'd be at SeaTac airport, waiting for her best friend Ruth Ann to pick her up and get her good and drunk. Except she didn't feel the need to. Ray had somehow purged her soul of her parents far more than the most exotic cocktail. Going trawling for a bedmate at the J&M, after she'd had a taste of what Ray could make her feel, would be beyond pointless.

Yes, he could make her feel. And by his desperate groans and happy sighs, she knew she did the same in return.

They'd started their final night together with another sunset ride. This time he'd brought a blanket and they'd made love together under the stars. Once before, she'd done it outdoors, fast and desperate on Golden Gardens beach at a college bonfire party, the fear of imminent discovery adding to the hurry.

Last night had been a slow, languid adventure under a brilliant canopy of starlight. When the half moon rose, it had turned the prairie pale yellow and was more than bright enough for them to appreciate each other visually as well as physically. She'd come to like the way Ray looked, a great deal. He was lean but strong. And only six inches taller meant that instead of her face being crushed to a man's chest when they embraced, she could lay her head on his shoulder and nestle against his neck.

She was a journalist because she loved learning new things.

The things Ray had taught her she could place in no article, but they'd been written indelibly upon her skin and emotions.

But now it was time to go. Showered and packed, she was surprised at the hugs she received after breakfast. The women in particular made a point of saying how glad they were to have met her. It felt genuine.

There! That was the hook on her travelogue about this place.

It didn't feel genuine—it *really was* genuine.

She might have become closer to the staff than the tourists, but as they all gathered together for departure, there were many warm farewells.

Colleen stood in the midday-flight time group, waiting for the helicopter to return from the morning-flight group. New arrivals were inbound for their own adventures, welcomed, and were escorted to their freshly cleaned cabins.

Then Ray arrived and cut her out of the herd. She went willingly until they were alone with the horses in the barn.

"Kurva Colleen. May I see you again?"

"Gods, please, yes. But I'll be in Seattle."

"So you said. I'll come looking for you there when I'm done being a cowboy."

"You'd better."

His kiss made that promise as the distant thrum of the helicopter approached to whisk her away.

CHAPTER 5

Dateline, done.

Larry loved the piece. For the first time, it passed beneath his evil editor's pen without a single tick-mark or correction. Her next assignment started tomorrow, learning about building boat sails. There were several premier sail lofts in Seattle and she had a very nice contract to write a multi-page marketing-promo article about them for one of the glossy magazines.

But she didn't care about any of that.

She cared about the simple text message, "J&M, 8pm. R"

It would be good to just sit with Ruth Ann, drink a Mai Tai or a Mango Daiquiri, and catch up. She'd been back two weeks. Back? As if time was now measured in distance from Montana.

Out of habit and the lingering Seattle summer heat—rather than thinking about attracting men—she wore a clingy tube-top, short shorts, and sandals, and brushed her hair out long. For once it wasn't about torturing men or even finding one.

She'd already found one, and was discovering that she wasn't getting over him as she'd expected. Her sometimes-cowboy was persevering in her thoughts—like a good story that was hard to forget.

Somehow, she couldn't quite remember how, she'd let him slip away without any way to contact him. He was always good at using distraction. Perhaps he hadn't wanted to keep in touch.

Colleen had considered calling the ranch, but he would be gone soon. The short Montana summer was ending. With the start of school, their number of guests would plummet and the extra hands wouldn't be needed. Yet some part of her waited.

She went with the familiar J&M daiquiri for coolness. She also managed to snag her and Ruth Ann's favorite table. It was small, but close by the door. It offered a good view of the male wildlife down the long bar as well as at the small streetside tables outside the windows. A hundred-and-thirty years of drinking had happened here (with a one-year hiccup in '09 that had been devastating until a new owner was found), and she could feel the history every time. It was deep and solid.

The band in the back was just getting rolling. Country-rock tonight. In another hour, conversation would approach the impossible and everyone would move onto the dance floor. For now, shouting was only necessary in the deeper sections of the bar, and the dancers still had room to do some moves.

The parade of men and women through the door barely registered on her. She could see that she was registering on them, but that was the point. Dates were having to poke their men in the ribs, some of them sharply, to keep them moving.

Then one man arrived by himself—which wasn't unusual.

Dressed in typical Seattle: sneakers, jeans, and a UW Huskies t-shirt.

But his gait was odd.

As if he'd just...gotten off a horse.

Ray smiled down at her as he strode up to the table like he was still roaming the prairie.

"You're not 'R.'" But he was. Not Ruth Ann. Raymond. She hadn't even looked at the sender on the message.

"You told me you liked this place."

"I do," then she caught herself and patted the seat beside her. "Now

I really do."

"And I thought you were dressed that way for me." He sat beside her.

"No, just to torment passing strangers."

"I'm hurt. But it definitely works. You're absolutely killing me."

"What are you…?" His t-shirt registered. "Huskies? You're an alum?"

"Not exactly."

She knew there were adult students, but he didn't act like a student.

He cleared his throat as if preparing to lecture.

He worked there!

"UW Professor Raymond Esterling, specializing in advanced robotics, particularly communication protocols with natural language. That means how robots and people speak to each other."

"You like the way I listen," she recalled the very first thing he'd ever said to her. Of course he would appreciate that.

His nod was easy as he ordered a beer from a passing waitress, as if it was as natural as could be. Of course, she liked the way he communicated too. Except when he evaded her.

"You knew all that time that I was from Seattle and you didn't say anything?" A part of her that had been strangely quiescent over the last two weeks stirred to life. Like one of the Front Range's hibernating bears starting to wake up. She didn't know yet if she was of the angry variety.

"That's a separate part of my life. My days in this life are pretty intense. All indoors, a lot of computer code, with some mechanics and theory stirred in. For three months every year I get to ride horses and look at the horizon."

"And snare willing ranch guests."

"Tally of one so far. But based on that narrow statistical sample, I'd say it was absolutely worth the risk. Don't you agree?"

The last, gentle words were so soft they barely cleared the noise level that the J&M was pumping itself up to.

Raymond Esterling. Robots and horses. He took her hand and the warmth ran up her arm and wrapped around her. Not just her limbs, but that strange place inside where no man had ever belonged.

Belonged.

Something she'd never done. Not in Japan, not really in Seattle. Always a barfly never a…she let the next word come after only briefly shying away. Never a bride.

Yet whether enjoying each other's bodies, riding through the sunset together, or just sitting here knowing they'd be on the dance floor soon, she now knew what the belonging meant.

For outsiders, Henderson's Ranch was about welcome—maybe having a place for a week, or a summer. But with Ray, he made it easy to imagine so much more. There was an absolute rightness that was undeniable.

She leaned in to kiss him. Just before their lips met, she whispered.

"Now I know what to wish for. And yes, absolutely worth it."

BIG SKY, LOYAL HEART

Major Emily Beale struggles to excel in her new role as both mother and wife.

Colonel Michael Gibson's career reaches a crisis, not that he's talking about it.

Trainee military war dog **Rip** naps—he was named for Rip van Winkle, after all—while awaiting inspiration.

Film student turned cowboy **Patrick Gallagher** just keeps riding through life...until the woman of his dreams threatens to ride off into the sunset without him.

Recently retired Delta Force war dog handler, **Lauren Foster** sets herself a simple mission: forget about the Army, get back to New York City, and try to be a civilian.

But first, Lauren must escape Montana before she gets caught by the Big Sky and a loyal heart.

CHAPTER 1

The Montana Front Range was breaking upward, shattering the flatness of the plains.

When the helo pilot announced they were nearing the ranch, Lauren Foster stared down at the flat prairie. The whole transition happened in a matter of ten kilometers—or rather *six miles* as she was a freaking civilian again. In a matter of *six miles* the flatness of the Great Plains gave way to the abrupt jolt of the Rocky Mountains.

Henderson's Ranch lay as a narrow band between the two of gentle hills, abrupt valleys emphasized by the low angle of the morning light, rich grasslands turning brown with the late summer heat, and patches of trees so dark and thick they could be the forest primeval. All the land features were jumbled together as if God had been playing a game of pick-up sticks.

Definitely not the Big Apple, girl.

After far too many deployments into Iraq, Afghanistan, Somalia, and every other hellhole that Delta Force inhabited, she'd been so ready for a dose of the best city in the world. New York was calling. She'd planned to start at Katz's with a pastrami sandwich slathered with sharp mustard that bit the nose even harder than the tongue, and a root beer that tickled the throat. Every one of the stupid, touristy things that no local ever did, she wanted to do. Visit the top of the Empire State Building. Take a freaking Circle Line boat trip around Manhattan. Maybe she'd go around twice or three times, just sit with her feet propped on the rail and watch The City go by. Get off downtown to chow down some fresh dim sum with a cold Tsingtao at Jing Fong before she...

Instead, she was a hundred klicks—sixty freaking miles—into the Montana wilderness without flying over a single rinky-dink town since Great *Podunk* Falls. The grass was unending brown. The cows they were flying over were brown. The buildings were brown. None of the vibrant neon and shining glass of the big city.

It wasn't as if Great Falls, Montana, was anything more than the closest airport. It was the same twenty-two square miles as Manhattan—and if she stacked twenty-seven Great Falls on top of each other, she'd get the same population density as the Big Apple but still a millionth the character. The Big Apple had started cooking its own unique blend of city in 1624 and no Montana-come-lately could ever hope to compare.

Also, nothing smelled right here.

The air from the helo's vent system smelled fresh, filled with early September promise rather than pastrami on rye. Though it also didn't smell like Dustbowl Afghanistan, stinking goat Iraq, desperation Somalia, or any other screwed-up desert she'd patrolled over the years, which was a relief. Even the helo itself smelled fresh-washed with a hint of leather seats—not splashes of Jet A fuel matched with the hard stench of burnt cordite and stinking soldiers who'd been too long in the field. No coppery after-hint of spilled blood either, another plus.

"This is all your fault, Colonel."

Colonel Michael Gibson, seated beside her in the back of the helicopter, didn't bother to respond. He rarely did, but he didn't have to. When the best field operator in all of Delta Force said, "You're with me," you went. Even if she wasn't in the military anymore, she went.

"I was within easy windage of a Nathan's hot dog!" Coney Island Boardwalk was calling her, too—even now from two thousand *miles* in the wrong direction. She'd had a ticket home in her hand and a spot all picked out on her brother's couch. She'd done her fifteen years and was out. Way out.

"Get a grip, Foster." The colonel's command was stated with the same calm he always used, whether in the briefing room or under heavy fire.

Get a grip? Yeah, my hands around your throat! But she kept the thought to herself. Besides, it would just piss off his wife sitting copilot. And Lauren liked Claudia Jean, even if she talked almost as rarely as the colonel. Kind, beautiful, blonde, a red-hot helicopter pilot with the Night Stalkers—what wasn't to like. Her deep-bred warmth a sharp contrast to Gibson's chill factor. No, that wasn't right because the man wasn't unkind, he was just...austere. Like looking up at the Empire State Building until your neck hurt from trying to see the top.

The pilot who'd picked them up in Great Falls was the poster boy for tall, handsome, and retired military right down to his mirrored shades and cheeky grin. Somebody Henderson. Her blood sugar had crashed along with missing a night's sleep. She only remembered his last name because "Henderson's Ranch" was plastered across the side of his little Bell JetRanger helicopter along with a painted team of running horses.

He flew like retired military as well. She wondered if he flew this way when he had a load of tourists aboard. She hoped so—especially if he had footage of their faces.

The number of things that civilians didn't understand about the military, and about what women like her had to do to serve there, made her completely crazy. No matter how she tried to explain, they looked at her as if she was either a cold-blooded killer or a lunatic. The only person she wanted to kill in cold blood was still stationed who-knew-where. He was still on the inside and she was now on the outside, which was just fine with her. Having the civilian-military divide between them provided yet more distance—none of it comfortable. As to being a lunatic? Wouldn't find her denying it.

Guess what, folks? Out there, life comes by a different measure. Which definitely was going to make *her* the crazy person in the ever-so-normal civvie world, rather than *them* being the strange ones so secure beneath their hard-won security blanket, double-shrouded in purposely-head-in-the-sand, ostrich-style naivete.

Thankfully, there wasn't a person on this flight she had to explain shit to; not even why she'd left. Fifteen years in, eight of it attached to The Unit (as Delta Force called themselves) was enough wear and tear on anyone. The pointless loss of her military war dog had been one straw too many.

Even now she could feel Jupiter resting his head on her thigh. Instinctively she moved her hand to pet the Malinois and stroked... nothing but air.

Shit!

Two months and the reflexes weren't going away.

Gibson saw it of course, the man missed nothing, but he was smart enough not to say anything.

For sanity, she brushed her fingertips over her pant's belt and found a little peace there. She'd made it from Jupiter's last leash.

"Welcome to my family's ranch," the pilot boomed out cheerfully over the intercom. "Our land runs from the Larson cattle ranch directly below us—"

And the helo's vents offered solid proof that they were flying over a lot of cattle. Lauren had to sneeze to clear the smell.

"—right up to the two and a half million acres of the Flathead National Forest wilderness area. Don't want to go riding into there without a guide I can tell you."

Lauren scanned the ranch. How would she track across such land? Even the central compound? It was all spread out with no encircling protective wall, not even a gate that she could see. Any fool could just walk in.

Would she lead a patrol along the ridge where they were exposed and easy to see, or along the valley where they could be ambushed from above? And the big ranch layout would be a nightmare to secure. Three barns, multiple corrals, a monstrous main house in the I-was-a-log-cabin-as-a-little-girl style, outbuildings, cabins up among the trees...

A hundred places for a trap.

A million ways for the enemy to—

She recognized the pattern in herself and wrestled it back, fought it down with sheer willpower.

Lauren no longer led patrols. Jupiter, what she'd been able to find of him, was buried in Afghan hell and was never coming home. All of Delta Force had only nine dog-handler teams who could hit The Unit's standards, and she and Jupiter had been the best. Until… Until they only had eight.

But there lay another, far deeper trap. There lay the fury that still ripped her apart every time.

She glared out the window of the helo as it circled and she leaned into the laser-like focus brought on by the rage.

The big house was a grand two-story timber lodge with a deep and welcoming wraparound porch. It sat slightly above the other main buildings of the compound; only the guest cabins up the hill ranged higher.

The main barn connected to several large corrals. Even now, seven horse-and-rider pairs were working their way through a jump course in one of them.

There was something odd about the roof of the barn. There was a single large skylight midway along the roof. Near it, where she expected a little cupola would normally be perched, stood a trio of high-gain satellite antennas. The helo circled low enough to see that they were military grade. On a ranch in Montana?

Closer to the ground, she again scanned for how she'd approach the area.

There! That's where she'd start a scouting patrol.

She'd start at the back corner of the farthest cabin. It perched at the crest of the hill in a small wood, overlooking the entire ranch. No one could surprise her from there. She liked the safety of the position, even if it would be more exposed to the weather from the north. From there she'd range downslope and—

"Remember to breathe at some point."

She *hated* that she'd been caught. Though nobody ever slipped anything by Colonel Gibson. Carefully, consciously, she took a breath. Two more before she turned to face him.

They weren't coming in hard to a browned-out LZ in an armored Night Stalker Black Hawk. They were sitting in the back of a little Bell JetRanger, civilian version. Cushy seats. Even a small drink cooler at their feet, for crap's sake.

"Why?" Breathing just meant another day of remembering the pain. *And* doing it without a Nathan's hot dog or a plate of dim sum as an analgesic.

The colonel merely quirked a fleeting smile. So he *could* smile. That was news. She'd been on countless missions with him over the years and hadn't known he had it in him. Then he looked down at the fast-approaching ranch and grimaced darkly.

Now *that* made her feel better.

There was something eating his behind as well.

Good!

Mark's usual flight approaches never bothered Minotaur. The American Paint gelding was typically rock steady, even when Patrick Gallagher had been a total greenhorn—three years back as the ranch's newest hand.

The horse had actually been named Minnie, but no self-respecting cowboy would ever ride a horse named Minnie, much less a male one. His splotchy coat was red-brown with white spots that could almost be a red polka dot dress. From the rear haunches down, he was as white as Minnie Mouse's bloomers—the little hussy. And the same white from the withers up, to where more red-brown made a bow like Minnie's on his face that masked both of his eyes. A few more polka dots there made the horse appear to be looking about with more than the usual two eyes.

Patrick supposed that the name had been inevitable, but he preferred Minotaur—the monster in the labyrinth, thankfully without the attitude. He'd changed the gelding's name and no one had argued with him. Probably because Patrick had never really told anyone other than the horse and the dude ranch's guests—the horse didn't seem to care in the least and ranch guests were gullible enough that they believed anything you told them.

This time, however, Mark flew the helicopter like he was still some crazy military pilot. He swooped so low over the barn that he could have cleaned the gutters. He zipped close enough over the path between the paddock and the barn where Patrick was currently riding that he could taste the hot carbon of the exhaust. Mark pulled up hard at the last second to thump down on the dirt in front of the garage as if this was the team insertion scene from *Black Hawk Down*, not an ideal setting for *The Horse Whisperer*. Minotaur was not happy about it and reared up in protest. Patrick was no longer a greenhorn, but there were still a few tense moments before he managed to get secure in his seat.

Once Minotaur had returned to a standstill, the corner of the big garage blocked his view of the newcomers so he leaned sideways out of the saddle enough to see what tourist distractions Mark had been fetching in from Great Falls. Long legs exited the rear door of the JetRanger. Legs were followed by a sleekly lean frame in a leather bomber jacket, finally topped by a movie-star profile framed in light-brunette waves down to her shoulders. Not as tall as his own six three, but well on the way. Definitely worth checking out.

A tough-looking guy, maybe old enough to be her father, came out the other side. No problem. Patrick had plenty of practice cutting pretty young things out of the herd. He knew his slightly shaggy dark hair and bright blue eyes had power over female ranch guests seeking adventure. Cowboy strong—plus boots and hat—didn't hurt either.

Just as she turned to face him, Minotaur took a sudden step sideways in the wrong direction.

There was a weightless, Wile E. Coyote moment before Patrick plummeted down to land face-first in the puddle made of last night's brief rain and his pride. At least the morning sun had warmed it.

If the sleek woman laughed before she turned away, she hid it well.

Minotaur nuzzled at him in surprise.

"Some help you are."

Minotaur puffed out a big, hay-flavored horse breath that knocked Patrick's Stetson into the puddle for good measure before moving off to crop some grass.

"Little early for a swim," Stan commented as he came out of the garage through a nearby door. He shifted some paperwork he'd been carrying between the parallel hooks of his missing left hand to his good right one, then offered his hooks for Patrick to grab.

"I was getting hot." Patrick supposed the stainless steel hooks would be easier to clean than Stan's other, flesh hand. Since the woman's back was still turned, Patrick gratefully accepted the help.

"I saw," Stan glanced over toward the helicopter. "Nice first impression."

"Thanks. I try." And usually it worked out just fine. He knew how to play his tall height and good looks to win, especially now that he was cowboy strong from three years of hard labor on the ranch.

"I was talking about *her* first impression. *You* should keep trying," Stan chuckled, then snapped the fingers of his good hand. One of his dogs, who'd been busy marking a fence post, trotted over...and kept right on going. "Rip. Heel!"

They stood side by side, Patrick in the mud puddle and Stan on dry land, but Stan wore a look of total surprise on his face as if he was the one at sea.

"Rip!" Stan called out again.

But the dog kept going; nose first, he was on some scent. He trotted up close behind the tall brunette, then sat abruptly.

"I thought he only did that for explosives?" Patrick always enjoyed watching the former Navy SEAL dog handler training up a pack of hopeful military war dogs.

"Uh-huh," was all the response Stan managed.

"Don't the dogs usually look back at you after they sit? Doggie pride or some such thing you once said?"

"Every time. They want their toys as a reward for making the find."

"He's not turning," and Patrick didn't blame him. The view from behind was as nice as from the front on this tourist despite the battered leather jacket masking certain details. The war dog training was a separate part of the ranch operation from the dude ranch's guests and rarely mixed.

Stan started walking over to see what was up with his dog. Patrick hesitated only long enough to flip Minotaur's reins around a fence rail near a deep patch of grass and retrieve his hat from the puddle before following along. No way was he going to be cut out here.

Mark, climbing out of the pilot's seat, saw him first and burst out laughing.

Okay, definitely not his best first impression.

The brunette very studiously didn't turn, keeping her fists in her jacket pockets. The old guy looked over at him, then looked away as if he was of no consequence. A light blonde came around from the other side. She was absolutely majestic—just how a woman *should* mature.

Patrick liked his women young and frisky, though he'd outgrown coeds a number of years back, at least mostly, but the older blonde was well worth a second look. Up close, there was also more to the old guy than at first appearances—all wiry and hard muscle. His look clearly said, *Do* not *meet me in a dark alley.* Like Tom Berenger in *Platoon.* The guy must have seen some serious shit, but that would be in his younger days. Now he had some salt in his longish dark-brown hair. The light-blonde stepped up close to him, close enough to be a couple. Her smile at Patrick was amused and, perhaps, a little sympathetic for some weird reason.

Then the younger brunette with the long legs turned, the slightest hint of smile on her lips more cutting than a laugh at his expense. For the briefest moment, her unexpectedly light brown eyes regarded him —rich as the amber of red clover honey.

Then she glanced down at the patiently waiting Rip.

She screamed and dropped like she was about to be run over by a cattle stampede.

In a moment of shocked silence, everyone, including Rip, just looked down at her curled up on the dirt.

Then the old guy spoke softly, "Oh, shit!"

"I don't know what happened." Lauren was a little surprised to find herself sitting with a cup of hot tea cradled in her hands, hanging onto it for dear life despite the warm morning. She sniffed at it carefully. Peppermint with honey—she could deal with that.

She hadn't been aware of much since seeing Jupiter impossibly reincarnated and sitting at her feet. She'd never fainted in her entire life. But all she remembered after seeing him were like brief snapshots. Being carried, tight against a well-muscled chest. Bright blue eyes crinkled in worry. The door into the big log-cabin style house. Inside had been all space and light. Modern furniture mixed with rustic decor. Then a dining room that could seat forty at a single long table and through to a kitchen big enough to feed them.

Now she was in an armchair at one side of the kitchen. There was a big stone fireplace, unlit, and a ring of comfortable leather chairs and sofas. It felt safe, but could she trust that? It had also felt safe to step from the helicopter onto good old American soil for the first time in far too long. Fort Bragg soil didn't really count, but she'd thought Montana would be safe.

So not.

She looked around carefully. Listened.

No dog.

Working up some nerve, she checked around her feet and the other side of the chair. Still no. Should she be relieved that she was merely hallucinating? Or was that worse?

Surreptitiously, she rubbed her fingers over her belt. Yes, it was still Jupiter's leash. Around her waist rather than attached to some hallucination turned far too real.

Close beside her sat the colonel's wife, Captain Claudia Casperson, and another woman Lauren didn't know who might have been Claudia's twin sister—at least in some ways.

"Who are you?" It came out rude, but her nerves weren't steady enough to fix anything.

"Emily. Mark's my husband. Old friend of Michael as well."

Michael? Oh. First name basis with Colonel Michael Gibson. He didn't strike Lauren as a man who made many first-name friends.

"Do you feel up to talking about it?"

She shook her head, but Delta wasn't about avoiding hard truths. A deep breath to gear up didn't help at all. Lauren finally gave in and asked the question that was scaring her the most.

"Was there really a dog?" Though she didn't know which answer she'd prefer.

Claudia nodded.

"A nearly pure black Belgian Malinois?"

This time Emily nodded. The two tall blondes shared straight, long hair cut neatly at their shoulders and piercing blue eyes. But after the first impression, they looked less and less alike. Claudia had a softer, Nordic face, but her soldier strength showed in powerful shoulders. Emily was pure Anglo-Saxon melting pot and look lean and fierce enough to take down a Russian T-14 Armata main battle tank—bare-handed. Lauren liked that in a woman.

"Okay, that makes me feel a little better." *Not* Jupiter reincarnated.

"Why did Rip surprise you so much?"

Rip, not Jupiter. She sipped her tea. That, too, seemed real. "How about a different topic?"

"Well, you certainly scared the daylights out of Patrick," Emily looked amused.

"Hooks or klutz?"

"Hooks belong to former Navy SEAL Stan Corman. He was also an MWD handler, now a trainer."

"TMI." *Way* too much information. Lauren didn't want to know anything about any military war dog handler. That was the *last* person she wanted to talk to or about. Jupiter was too recent. His eyes—

No dogs.

No. God. Damn…

And there lay the yawning hole once again. She sighed, then clawed her way back out. Again. At least she was getting good at that.

"So Patrick is the klutz," she confirmed.

"He's actually a surprisingly good horseman, considering his background, but—"

"He fell off a stationary horse into the only mud puddle in the county."

"He did," Claudia confirmed and sipped her own tea. "Guess it's hard to blame him."

"Why?" Lauren could think of no one else at fault than the man himself.

Claudia and Emily shared a look that Lauren couldn't interpret, then both turned back to her.

"What?"

Emily rose to her feet, crossed the kitchen to rinse her mug at the sink and toss it into the washer. The room was high and airy, filled with light from the big windows. Hardwood flooring, vast counters, and all the equipment necessary to feed a ranchful of guests. Close by the back door, a kitchen table of thick slab fir had a dozen chairs clustered around it. There was a hint of a recently finished breakfast on the air, but the room was immaculate.

"Your room is over there, just off the kitchen," Emily pointed in the other direction where a small hallway passed between two monstrous silver-faced refrigerators. "That way you won't have to deal with the ranch guests if you don't want to. Stan, the guy with the hooks for a left hand, brought in your duffle."

"Not the klutz?"

"Nope," Emily confirmed. "Now I have to go find out why Michael showed up here unannounced since Claudia won't tell me."

"I would if I knew, Emily. He's not even talking to me on this one."

"Likely story. You're the only person he's ever talked to." Emily left by the back door.

Lauren turned back to face Claudia. "Surely it wasn't Colonel Gibson who carried me in?" She couldn't imagine the humiliation of having him carry her in here. It was so bad to have collapsed in front of him that maybe she should just catch a night horse to New York right now so that she didn't have to face him ever again. Easy to get lost and hide in the Big Apple—from anyone other than Colonel

Gibson. He could track anyone anywhere. There'd been missions with him where she'd wondered why she and Jupiter were along at all. Fieldcraft wasn't something he knew; it was something embedded in his DNA at birth, then honed like the finest knife.

"No, Michael didn't carry you," Claudia confirmed. "Nor Major Mark Henderson."

Major? Major Mark Henderson? The ranch pilot had been a full major before retiring? That would have been almost as embarrassing as being carried by the colonel.

"Hold it."

Claudia simply smiled at her before rising to rinse her own mug.

"*The* Major Mark Henderson?" Lauren twisted around to look at Claudia.

She nodded without turning and racked her mug.

"That means that was…" Lauren turned to face the chair. Finding it empty, she swung to look at the back door where Emily had exited. If the pilot had been Major Mark Henderson, then "Emily" was the *legendary* Major Emily Beale. The two best pilots that the Night Stalkers of the 160th SOAR had ever put at the controls of a Special Operations Forces helicopter. Both were retired, but they were the standard measure of everyone who followed in their flightpath—the standard no one ever matched.

It knocked the wind right out of her.

First name basis with Colonel Michael Gibson and his wife? Of course Major Beale would be. There were few better warriors in any military. Had *she herself* called Major Beale "Emily?" That would have been presumptuous and incredibly embarrassing, but she didn't think so—she'd only been horridly rude in her first greeting. *Strike One, Foster.*

"She couldn't be the—" But Lauren was alone in the kitchen. Claudia had gone as well.

She went to the sink herself and looked out the big picture window as she finished her own tea. To one side there were definitely horses. To the other was a hillside peppered with guest cabins tucked invitingly into pines and aspen. Some had people sitting on the porch, other folks were on the move toward whatever event was next.

The farthest cabin, the tiny one she'd picked out as the best from a tactical standpoint, peeked out between the trees. It looked nicely cozy. And out in the distance, towering mountains shot up out of the Plains with a suddenness so abrupt that it was like waking up in the midst of a freefall parachute jump.

Definitely Montana.

How in the world had she ended up here? Colonel Gibson still hadn't explained the *why* either. He was such a "forthcoming" guy—never spoke two words where none would do. How had a man like that landed a woman like Captain Claudia Casperson? Simple, by being the very best there was. Truly exceptional would work for her as well—if she ever met one who was single. And her own age. And who never wanted to own a dog—ever. And…

Lauren had the answer to another question as she rinsed her own mug in the sink. One whole side of her clothes were lightly coated in drying mud as if she'd been cradled against someone's chest—their muddy chest. On her jeans, a big dirt handprint curled around from the back of her thighs to confirm that she'd been held close by a man without hooks for his left hand.

The tall, lean klutz with the nice chest had carried her to the kitchen.

Patrick.

And alongside the handprint…a big paw print on her thigh.

Neither one would brush off when she tried.

It was such a warm day that Patrick just rinsed himself off at the horse trough. He dug a couple of hatfuls of water and sluiced them over himself. It did nothing to help cool him down.

Lauren had felt so fragile and helpless. She weighed almost nothing despite her height and it felt as if he could have carried her all day. Rip had been almost frantic with worry when she collapsed. He himself had jerked forward like a roped calf until he had her scooped up in his arms. By then Emily had appeared from her secure office in the barn and led the way to the house.

Her eyes had fluttered open a few times, but he didn't think that she'd actually seen him.

When he'd tried to stay with her, Emily had shooed him—and everyone else—away like stray barn cats. As if. Of course, even Mark didn't argue with Emily. The woman was a primal force.

Patrick had things to do. He knew he did.

"C'mon, Patrick, think," he muttered to himself.

"Like that's gonna happen any time soon," Stan was watching him again. He had some kind of weird, built-in stealth mode despite being such a big guy. Probably came from being a Navy SEAL.

"That was my internal dialog, Stan. You're barely in the cast, so you shouldn't be able to hear it."

"Film nerd," Stan sneered, knowing Patrick's obsession with movies. No point in arguing against the truth.

"Totally! But you're not helping any more than my horse." His bunkmate slouched against the fence where Minotaur was still grazing. Rip sat at his feet. "I see that your dog is back. Too bad he fell for another woman. Musta hurt."

Stan grinned down at the dog. "Better her than some girly boy like you."

Patrick couldn't help but like the man. Stan had showed up on the ranch about the same time he had. Stan had technically arrived first, spending a Montana winter living in a remote fishing cabin for reasons he never explained. Of course, Patrick had never asked.

He himself had answered a ranch-hand job ad on a whim, trading in his aging Camaro on a used compact pickup to fit in better before driving across the country from Long Island. He'd been razzed endlessly about it by the other ranch hands. How was he supposed to know that his little Ford Ranger would be a reason for ridicule in the heart of Dodge Ram 1500 Crew Cab pickup country? Then there were the 3500s with rear duallies which made his truck look even more pitiful. He'd have been better off keeping the Camaro.

The timing of his and Stan's arrival had made it natural for them to bunk together.

He'd never had a military friend before, never mind a retired SEAL. Yet somehow they'd hit it off—once Stan got over his role of being so taciturn that he rarely rose above a grunt. Even total guy-guys in film had more dialog and emotional range than Stan initially did in real life.

Rip, barely out of puppyhood, had liked Patrick right away and that had helped break down the walls. *Good dog.* Stan's favorite dog, Bertram, had been slower on the uptake, but warmed to him over time.

Patrick had felt as if it was the beginning of one of those buddy movies: the Army vet and the man from the Big City.

"He did more than like that lady," Patrick nodded down at Rip, looking for a way to redeem himself from Stan's "girly boy" crack.

"Yeah. Weird, huh?" Stan folded his arms—always an odd sight as his left one was mechanical all the way up to his biceps. Stan had gone Terminator rather than cosmetic in any way. *I yam what I yam said Popeye the Sailor Man.* And Stan's remaining arm was muscled enough to play the role without any CGI.

Together they inspected Rip, who wasn't saying a thing about his own behavior.

"It's not like she was wrapped up in explosives," Patrick kept digging.

"I know. Have to check that out some," Stan rubbed the dog's head with his good hand.

"Hey, you're the dog trainer. If you keep your eye on *him,* maybe you'll figure it out." The last thing Patrick wanted was Stan keeping an eye on the pretty brunette. She was the best thing to hit the ranch since Julie Larson had ridden in from her family cattle ranch across the road this spring. The fact that she was marrying Patrick's older brother next weekend was just the worst kind of unfair.

"I don't know," Stan scratched at his short beard with the rounded tips of his hooks. "Might have to look pretty careful at what's going on there."

Patrick had never known Stan to go after a woman on the ranch. Sometimes he wondered if Stan's arm wasn't the only thing blown off in Afghanistan, but there were some questions you didn't ask a guy who could bench press you one-handed. Stan might be only six one, but he was powerfully built and square-jawed in a way that Patrick knew women liked.

Stan burst out laughing. "You should see your face, bro. You should absolutely get a mirror. Have at her and good luck. Woman looked like she had brains, which puts you out of the running." He double-clicked his hooks and Rip popped to his feet and hovered in the "heel" position at Stan's left side.

"Shithead," Patrick put a laugh rather than any heat behind it. He headed over to gather Minotaur's reins; maybe the horse would remember what they'd been doing before the helo brought... *Damn it!* He didn't even know her name.

"Want my guess?" Stan called back as he walked back toward the dog kennels where the rest of the pack would be waiting to start the day's training.

"No!"

"Way out of your league, bro. Classy dame. Damned classy."

"You sound like you're in a 1930s noir film."

"You'd know, bro." And Stan moved out of earshot.

Of course he'd know. He'd graduated from NYU's renowned film school. Even worked on a couple of indies that, sadly, no one outside of immediate friends would ever see. He'd thought they'd been pretty good, but the speed at which they were rejected by film festivals he'd submitted them to had been alarming.

Then, thinking that being a Montana cowboy for a summer would give him some good creative grist, he'd come west. An incredibly visual land. The ranch manager had worked his ass off, and for some reason Patrick had loved the first hard work in his life. He'd stuck around after the season was over and the summer hands headed off to warmer pastures. Every single day working with the horses and fixing up the old ranch had felt more real than the thousands of hours he'd spent behind the camera or poring over some script.

Film school. Wow! Now *that* was a flash from the past. It felt like another Patrick entirely.

He swung into the saddle and looked up. The Big Sky shone—a brilliant blue bowl overhead stretching on forever. One side of it anchored by the infinite Great Plains and the other end skewered into place by the majestic Rockies. That sky had to be part of the reason to film here—it was like nothing he'd ever seen. He could feel himself settle more solidly into the saddle just by looking at the perfect, screen-test consistent blue.

"Hey, Pat." Patrick looked down to see his older brother coming toward him.

"Hey, Nat." Nathan had a pair of heavily loaded saddlebags slung over one of his broad shoulders.

"Got these for you."

Patrick wasn't sure why, but he helped Nathan set them over Minotaur's hindquarters and secure them to the saddle.

"Looks like you've been swimming."

"Looks like you're a lovesick bull calf." Howard Keel in *Seven Brides for Seven Brothers*. Now there was a good leading man's role.

"Getting married to the most wonderful woman ever in seven days. That's not lovesick, that's lucky."

"Turd," was the best comeback he could find—not very Howard Keel at all.

Julie Larson, the hottest cowgirl in any parts, hadn't even given him the time of day. Three weeks after meeting Nathan, they'd gotten engaged and been living together for almost six months up in one of the cabins. He liked those little cabins. Wasn't hard to see himself in one with…somebody. As long as it wasn't anytime soon.

"How did a lousy chef from New York land the leading lady of Montana? Can you explain that one?"

"Brains and personality, Pat. Brains and personality. And if you had any brains, you'd be getting your trail ride organized."

"Trail ride?" Then he remembered. That's where he'd been headed when the nameless woman had dropped out of the sky and into his arms. That's what the saddlebags were filled with—lunch. Nathan had found his role as the ranch's chef.

He spun Minotaur about, give him a light kick and a soft rein. His horse shifted from a standstill to a fast canter without any apparent transition—one of his tricks—almost leaving Patrick in the mud puddle once more.

His brother's laugh followed him past the garage and most of the barn.

He rode into the corral just as Chelsea was helping the last of the ranch guests up onto their mounts. A quick glance. A dozen riders. Five obvious greenhorns (looking down in surprise at how far away the ground now appeared from atop their horses, even though they'd already done four days of corral riding), three overeager kids, and four who clearly thought they had it down now but didn't know one thing about how to sit a saddle, much less hold the reins.

A beginner trail ride.

Worse, he remembered, an *overnight* one. *Oh, man!* No chance to see the brunette again.

"Hi, y'all!" He knew it was wrong as soon as he said it.

Chelsea smirked at him, piling her assessment of him on top of Stan's sneer and Nathan's smug superiority.

"*You guys,*" she corrected him in her typically cheery tone, "are in good hands now, even if Patrick showers with his clothes on."

Patrick looked down. He was still damp from rinsing off the mud at the horse trough. A couple of the women were looking at him with particularly nice smiles. Maybe he should arrive wet a bit more often.

"Patrick knows some great places to ride. Remember, if you want to take a picture, be sure to stop your horse first and never completely let go of the reins. When you reach camp, the famous Henderson's Ranch Chuck Wagon will be out to set up a real feed. Have a great time."

Famous. The marketer in him thought it sounded ridiculous, but she wasn't bragging. Big brother Nathan had been a top New York chef before bailing out. His chuck wagon had been written up in a half-dozen different foodie magazines—big ones with national circulation—further increasing the ranch's reputation. Patrick was never disappointed with what Nathan sent out to trail ride camps. Which *almost* made him forgive his brother for snagging the hottest cowgirl in the entire Montana Front Range as his bride.

Patrick normally helped get everyone saddled, starting to know them in the process—when he wasn't being distracted elsewhere.

"Thanks, Chelsea. Big hand for her!" He clapped his hands together. The others joined in, half of them dropping their reins on their horse's withers to do so. The ranch hands had long since learned to tie the rein ends together for beginners for just that reason. Oh, this was going to be *such* a fun ride.

"Nice of you to show up," she whispered merrily as she came over to check on the saddlebags that held the group's trail lunch. He was just lucky that she didn't have a mean bone in her body.

"Got delayed up ta the big house, little lady."

"Your John Wayne is showing again," she was always putting down his attempts to sound more Western.

"What's a Long Island boy to do?"

"Embrace your inner Billy Joel?"

She'd teased him before with the song line about a boy from Long Island with a six-pack in his hand. And that's about how naive he'd been when he first arrived here. He was a good rider now, but he still couldn't get the Western accent down.

He'd wanted to be a film writer and director, not *actor*, but here he was, stage center in his own life. Weird. No mood lighting. No perfect romance on the horizon. Just a bunch of beginning riders and sun so bright he wondered what had happened to his shades—they'd been perched on top of his hat before, well, before he'd nosedived into a mud puddle. They were either in the mud puddle or at the bottom of the horse trough now.

He looked around, but it was definitely himself playing himself in this surprising role. Too bad. He'd much rather be Sam Shepard in *The Right Stuff*, about to race his horse through the desert after the laughing Barbara Hershey the night before breaking the sound barrier.

Chelsea waved the closer riders toward the gate.

He nudged Minotaur back a few steps and pointed the way so that the first of the riders would lead the way westward. A spunky thirteen-year-old black girl looked at him like she was going to be definite trouble. They still always seemed to like him and it often took some tactful work to keep the teen girls at bay without upsetting them.

"Watch yourself out there, cowboy."

"Yes, ma'am."

"That's Chelsea to you, you goofball."

"Yes, ma'am, Chelsea, ma'am."

She slapped Minotaur hard on the rump. "Get along, Minnie."

The horse knew exactly who doled out the hay and oats in the barn—and who to listen to. His horse once more went from standstill to canter in a single motion and only the saddlebags of lunch fixings—now slightly flatter—kept him in the saddle. Several of the other horses tried to follow and, for an instant, the entire beginner's trail ride hung in a fragile balance. He immediately reined in and talked down the other horses before they tossed their riders in the hopes of a good run.

He ended up having to catch the reins for a woman who must be the thirteen-year-old's seriously hot mom. If the girl grew up like her mother, she was gonna be even more of a man-killer. Mom's smile declared that she had man-killer down cold already. No ring. *Single* mom.

It was going to be a *very* long ride.

CHAPTER 2

Lauren nosed cautiously out of her room. It was a lot nicer than her brother's sprung living room couch. Queen-sized bed, a woven blanket in some Native American style, horse photos on the walls and a view similar to the one out the kitchen window. It also had a shower that she'd spent a long time under, trying to soak her arrival out of her system. Oh-four-hundred this morning she'd been standing in the hot pre-dawn darkness of Pope Airfield, Fort Bragg, North Carolina, and headed for New York. Now thirteen hundred hours—it actually took her a moment to convert that to one o'clock—and she was in Montana.

Soft voices sounded from the kitchen, so she followed them.

She was a step into the kitchen when a burst of laughter cascaded about the room. Hooks was telling a story and made a sweeping gesture that could only be Patrick the Klutz nosediving into the mud puddle. The laughter climbed, holding everyone's attention on Hooks and away from her. Over a dozen people were gathered around the big table kitchen table. Most looked a little trail worn—these were the ranch's working hands, not a guest among them. Far more people than she was ready to deal with.

"Want some dinner?" A guy in a chef's apron was bustling about and was the only one to notice her entrance at the far side of the big room. Handsome, dark hair.

She double-checked her watch—still thirteen hundred hours. She sighed. Still just one o'clock. Her life was moving very, very slowly. "Dinner?"

He grinned hugely and made a show of coming over to shake her hand. Chef strong hands. "East coast or west?"

"Uh, east."

"Awesome. Welcome aboard. We'll swamp these Great Plainers and their midday dinner yet. *Lunch.* Would you like some lunch?"

"I guess," her retreat cut off, she could only scout ahead.

"Head on over."

She eyed the table again.

"They don't bite."

"You sure?"

"Relatively. I'm Nathan Gallagher, by the way."

"Lauren."

"Go get 'em!" Then he hurried back to whatever he'd been working on. A big stack of raw steaks lay on the counter. She hoped that was for the evening meal, whatever they called it, rather than lunch. Maybe that's how they ate their meat out here in the Wild West.

She reached the table just as most of the group stood. They delivered their plates and tableware to the dishwasher, then headed for the door.

Hooks—*Stan*—eyed her as if she might be a closet terrorist before heading out with the others. Before the back door closed, she caught a glimpse of the black Malinois that had been waiting outside. It jumped to its feet to follow Stan. The dog *was* real, not a hallucination. That was a relief at least, but she was glad both of them were gone.

No sign of the klutz.

"Feeling better?" Claudia patted a seat next to her.

Lauren sat cautiously beside her, across from Major Beale, just as Nathan set a big bowl of stew in front of her. "Hope you're not vegetarian."

"So not."

"Good. Dig in! Don't miss the bread. Fresh this morning. Anything else for you, Emily?" He was on a first-name basis with Major Beale.

When she shook her head, he returned to the working part of the kitchen.

She took the thick slice of crusty sourdough that Claudia had cut off a big loaf for her. Lauren dunked it in the steaming stew, then took a taste.

"Holy shit!"

That earned her the attention of both women as well as Michael and Mark, sitting over pressed cider—so fresh its appleness still tickled her nose—and brownies at the other end of the otherwise empty table.

"You like it?" Major Beale looked pleased. "Nathan's an exceptional chef, but we worked on this one together." Of course Major Emily Beale wasn't just beautiful and a legend, but she could cook too.

"*Like* it?" She dunked the bread again and bit off another dripping chunk though she wasn't finished chewing the first. "This ain't no MRE," she mumbled with her mouth full.

A laugh from the whole table. All military. She liked not having to explain herself.

Meals Ready-to-Eat would keep you alive in the field, but they were no treat. Even discounting her recent return to the U.S. biasing her toward any American food, this was probably the best stew she'd ever tasted. She ducked her nose down close to the surface to breathe in the richness until it seemed to fill her.

"How?" She waved her bread to indicate their shared background in the Armed Forces.

"Not intentional," Emily assured her. "Mac, Mark Henderson Sr., is a former SEAL. He and Mark's mother, Ama—she's Native American, which is where Mark got a lot of his good looks—are off on a vacation. The high season is tapering off here and, with Mark and me here full time now, it's their first break in years. Most here aren't former military: us, Stan, and you. Ranch manager did three tours, but he was regular Navy, so I'm not sure he counts. Mac does make it easy to not have to conform to some set of civilian-boss expectations."

"Why am I here?"

"You don't know?" Major Beale barely blinked before she looked past Lauren at Colonel Gibson. "Why is she here, Michael?" Emily Beale had targeted him as quickly as any threat to her legendary helicopter.

"That's for her to figure out," he pointedly returned to discussing the tactics of some recent mission with Mark.

"Well, that's no help," Emily grumbled. She had shifted to "Emily" in Lauren's thoughts—though she'd be careful not to use it aloud. Still, it was hard not to like the woman. Despite being a legend, she was unexpectedly real.

"Men so rarely are," Claudia concurred. "Too bad we love them so much."

"Too bad," Emily nodded.

"Did you ever get him to talk about why *he* is here?" Lauren nodded toward Colonel Gibson. If he overheard Lauren's question, he gave no sign of it.

"Not a word," and both women sighed.

Lauren tried to slow down from total-wolf mode on the stew, but it was hard. She couldn't cook squat, but even her lame palate could appreciate the spoon-soft braised beef, the freshness of the vegetables, sage she decided...maybe, and perhaps some red wine. She didn't even feel the need to dump in a load of salt to give it some *real* flavor. Whatever it was, she'd gladly bathe in it.

Which brought to mind the cowboy diving into the mud puddle. It had been her first smile in so long that it had been like a sharp pain in her chest and she'd had to turn away even as he looked up at her from the depths of his puddle. Piercing blue eyes in a handsome face. Hair curling down to his collar, a nice length for a woman to play with. And... She shook her head to clear it, but instead it dislodged a memory that she'd buried deep.

The last time she'd really smiled, Jupiter had done something similar.

She had chucked a Frisbee for him that had found extra lift on an unexpected breeze. Jupiter had spun and leapt at least five feet clear into the air to nab it—the moment before sixty pounds of Malinois had crashed into the set of makeshift clotheslines at the forward operating base. The entire FOB's laundry had been flopped down into the dirt, tangled around her dog. The Army grunts stationed there had cried out in dismay. Jupiter had finally emerged from the snarl with a huge doggie grin around the Frisbee still firmly clamped between his teeth. She'd helped the guys redo and rehang their laundry.

They might have grumbled, but they'd also laughed and petted the Malinois.

The next day he'd been gone.

"Wow! That was an ugly thought, Lauren."

She ignored Emily's comment and kept her attention on the stew. Subject change. Need a—

"What's the klutz's story?" Not that she really cared, but hopefully it would deflect the topic.

"The klutz?" The chef…Nathan, that was his name—always worth remembering the name of a man who could cook like this—dropped down in a seat beside Emily with a can of Coke in his hand. He bumped his shoulder into Emily's. "I think she likes our stew."

Lauren looked down. The bowl was mostly empty.

They shared a close smile before he continued.

"You must be talking about my little brother. What did Pat do this time? Has he found yet a new way to besmirch the Gallagher name?"

"Nosedived into the only mud puddle in the yard the first time he saw Lauren," Emily said it like a flat statement. But there was some tease in there that Lauren didn't understand—as if the two events were somehow related.

"Really?" Nathan sipped his Coke. He squinted at her for a moment. "Yeah, I can see how you'd be his type—more than most of the ones he goes for. He's really into old movies and you've got that classic beauty."

Yet there was no vibe at all in the chef's manner. It was just an utterly ridiculous statement of fact. Was he somehow focused on the major? But she was married to Mark, who was sitting just down the table. What was it with men who—

"Ignore him," Emily dismissed Nathan. "He's getting married next weekend. Can't even see another woman."

"Nope!" Nathan agreed happily, then bounced back to his feet with an energy more appropriate to a New Yorker than the slower moving Montanans she'd seen so far. He hurried back to his steaks.

"Is he always like that?" She whispered to Emily. She wasn't sure if she was questioning his behavior with Major Beale or his East Coast energy.

"No, he's usually worse. He was a top chef before he showed up on our doorstep. Fell in love with the cowgirl next door, but that hasn't slowed him down at all."

"And Patrick?" she dropped "the klutz" because it was getting a little strange to think of him that way—too...personal. She didn't want to be anyone's *type*. Yeah, being forward deployed with Delta Force meant that it had been a long dry spell and that every single man in The Unit hoped that he was her type. But for whatever reason she was here, spreading her legs for a cowboy wasn't on the list. Once she'd done whatever Gibson had brought her for, she'd head back to New York and start figuring out the rest of her life.

If Patrick had fallen into a mud puddle because she was "his type," that was his problem. He *so* wasn't hers...at least she didn't think so. Lauren wondered if she had a "type" anymore. She couldn't come up with one. The fantasy of that had died when she'd caught her "perfect match" fiancé having "one last fuck" with Lauren's maid of honor. That Lauren had been Lynn's maid of honor just three months before didn't seem to bother either of them. Lynn's husband had merely shrugged when she'd told him. Lauren had demanded the diamond ring he'd been holding onto as best man. It had been a long throw, but she'd managed to chuck it into the East River from their venue on the high perch of the Brooklyn Bridge pedestrian walkway.

"Patrick joined the ranch while I was still flying firefighting helos," Emily kept going as if that wasn't a whole conversation in itself. "But Chelsea—our horse manager—said he fit in from Day One, once he learned to ride a horse. Who would expect a boy from New York to slip into ranch life so smoothly?"

"You flew firefi—" and the gears in Lauren's head jammed. "Wait. New York? As in Upstate or as in The City?"

"Long Island," Nathan said as he cleared away her empty stew bowl and topped up Emily's lemonade. "Suffolk County out near Stony Brook. Mom and Dad are both professors there."

She hadn't really tasted the last half of the stew and regretted missing out. It wasn't weird enough that Colonel Gibson had brought her to some retired military horse haven in deepest, darkest Montana. Now there were two guys from The City, or close enough. What else was whacked about this place?

"Do you fish?" Henderson called from the other end of the table.

Apparently a lot else.

A quick glance at Emily and Claudia made them both raise their hands in a "no way" gesture. She was about to side with them when she saw the Colonel's intent look. If she wanted to get to the bottom of why she was here, she knew that she was going to have to confront him before she'd be free to go back to New York.

"Fishing?" She grabbed the last brownie off the plate, which Nathan immediately swooped in and cleared away. "Sure. Those little carnival machines where you plug in some quarters and fish the little crane around the glass box to snag a stuffed animal? I'm a pro. Got a whole collection." Or had once. After fifteen years in the military, her parents retiring to Florida, and her brother moving in with some guy much to everyone's surprise except hers, she wasn't sure if she still owned anything other than the contents of her duffle. She didn't even have a POV because what use did a girl from The City have for a personally-owned vehicle?

The colonel's eyes crossed trying to figure out how to answer her explanation.

But Mark Henderson grinned happily, "Perfect. Let's go."

And that's how she ended up alone in the back of the helicopter ten minutes later with Emily's good wishes, three fishing poles, and a box of tackle.

One minute everything was perfect.

After a big picnic lunch from a sunny vista, Patrick had scouted out a small herd of North American elk and brought the trail ride up to them along the riverbed from downwind. The river here ran just thirty feet wide and a foot or so deep—a rushing burble over rounded boulders. There was a smooth ford about a mile upstream that they'd be crossing for the excitement of "crossing a river." Here, protected by high hills to either side and a bend in the river, it made a secluded spot for grazing and bathing that he knew the local herds favored.

He'd led the trail ride group through the woods and stopped just at the edge of the trees with the river and the herd revealed close in front of them.

Camera shutters were snapping faster than upstate New York mosquitos. Most of the riders were still dropping their reins on the horse's withers. But the horses Chelsea had chosen were sufficiently mild-mannered that all they did was graze where they stood while the ranch guests ignored their mounts.

The elk, in turn, were used to the trail ride horses. As long as they were downwind, the elk tolerated their presence. The head bull, a five-pointer, had a decent harem of a dozen cows and nearly as many calves—though most were big enough that they'd be heading out on their own soon.

Then, without warning, a roar of fury sounded from beyond the trees they'd just ridden through. Not a bear, though out of instinct Patrick laid a hand on the butt of his rifle sticking up out of his saddle's scabbard. He'd never had to shoot one and they were mostly busy feeding on fish at this time of year, fattening up for hibernation, but they could need some scaring off. He also had a bear-sized can of pepper spray on the other side of his saddle.

But it wasn't a bear.

The Henderson's Ranch's helicopter cleared the treetops with only feet to spare. It flashed by directly overhead, swooped down to race low over the river, and shot westward. By the way it flew, Mark would be the pilot. He probably hadn't even seen Patrick's group hanging close by the trees.

The elk scattered.

The horses jolted a few steps with surprise, dropping several of the riders abruptly to the soft grass. But the animals were used enough to the helo for them to stop close by and return to grazing once they remembered that they weren't afraid of it.

Except for Rolo. He decided to take the pretty single mom for a fast ride downriver.

Patrick kicked Minotaur into a gallop and raced after her—she was far less sure of her seat than her daughter. No grab for the dropped reins or any attempt to slow Rolo's run, which the horse took as permission to stretch his legs for a change. She clutched the saddle's pommel with both hands. Down, around the bend in the river, he closed on the racing pair. Rolo plunged into the water just steps before Patrick could reach the dangling reins.

Rolo wasn't a fan of running water and jerked to a halt. The woman flew up and over his head in a high arc before plunging into the river. It had narrowed and so ran deeper and faster here.

Patrick didn't slow Minotaur for a moment, instead jumping the horse straight into the current. He managed to arrive far enough downstream in time to scoop her into his arms the very first time she surfaced. Minotaur liked the water and gamely swam them back to a shallower area as Patrick settled the woman across his lap.

"You okay, Clara?" Her name had been easy to remember. Even if she had African rather than English ancestry in her coloring, she had the same beauty and athleticism of Clara Bow, the "It Girl" of Roaring Twenties Hollywood. Horses just weren't her thing apparently, whereas Clara Bow had been an expert horsewoman.

"I think so," she clung to him. "Most of all just surprised. The river's so cold."

"Glacial melt, even in September."

"Brrr!" She gave a mock shudder as she clung more tightly to him. Her very fit figure pressed harder against him. The river water soaking through his shirt was chilly, though he was finding it hard to complain. She might be a mom, but she was a very pleasant armful—and her loose blouse, now plastered to her body, declared she'd still be a top contestant in any wet t-shirt contest. The early afternoon sun was warm and they'd both dry quickly. Hopefully not too quickly, the wet look was very nice on her. Maybe after everyone—especially her daughter—was asleep tonight, they might wander off to watch the stars together for a bit.

He rode back along the bank while she remained clinging to him. He gathered up Rolo's reins—he'd stopped to graze on the bank, all content after enjoying his run—and walked them back around the river bend to where he'd left the other riders.

The helicopter had landed a couple hundred yards upstream. The elk were nowhere to be seen. Mark, the old guy, and the amazing brunette were mingled in among the riders. He could hear by their tone that they were making sure everyone was okay and getting some laughs. Good. He'd worried about the mood. Ranch guests didn't much like being dumped out of their saddles, especially not the beginners. A more advanced rider might grumble a bit when tossed, but they took it much more in stride.

It was only as he rode up to them that the brunette turned to look up at him. Again, he had no idea how to read her expression.

Then he spotted the devastated look on the face of Clara's teenage daughter. That had him looking down in surprise at the woman cradled in his lap.

Oh.

He just wasn't going to catch a break today.

Lauren had caught Emily and Claudia's hints that Patrick was taken with her. Couldn't have missed them any more than a runaway train coming into Grand Central Station.

Yeah, right.

So taken with her that just a few hours later he was cradling a very pretty black woman tightly against his chest in much the same position she must have been.

Men never changed. She supposed it was a good thing as it made them predictable.

At first, Patrick had looked quite noble. Mark hadn't seen the trail ride clustered close against the pines as he overflew them, but from the back of the helo, she certainly had. Horses jolted and riders tumbled even as she shouted to Mark to ease off—too little, too late.

Then one mount had raced off with its rider in tow.

Patrick had ridden after the runaway in a flash, flying across the deep grass at a full gallop. As Mark had slowed and circled back, she'd just been able to see Patrick make a fantastic jump—his horse launching from the edge of the bank and plunging into the river with a huge cloud of spray. Impossibly, he and the horse had emerged from the water still together, even his cowboy hat in place. He'd gathered the rider out of the river before the spray even had a chance to settle. *So* not the klutz. He'd looked magnificent as he'd ridden to the rescue.

Why magnificent? What was it about a tall cowboy in a Stetson that made a woman get all mushy? Well, maybe a little weak in the knees. Mushy wasn't in her repertoire. No, not even weak knees! Especially not on a day that *already* included her fainting in front of Colonel Gibson.

As soon as the JetRanger was down, they had all hurried back to help the remaining riders. And then Patrick had reappeared with his arms full of very attractive and very clinging woman. Maybe that was his *thing*. Gathering helpless females into his arms.

Since she didn't remember it—and rather suspected that she'd been more sack-of-potatoes than possessively clingy—she didn't see any point in being jealous of her own moments in his arms. Instead, she turned to console the woman's upset daughter. The girl's sad face almost made Lauren smile.

She herself had once had a huge crush on Brad Pitt after seeing *Fight Club*, then been devastated by his wedding to Aniston while Lauren had still been a high school sophomore. She'd never been a big fan of movies after that—not that she had been much of one beforehand. She'd rather be playing Ultimate Frisbee in the park or volleyball at school anyway. With her height, she was a major asset at the net. Not All-State or anything fancy, but the Vanguard Panthers had ruled the Upper East Side her last two years on the high school team.

By the time Brad moved on to Jolie, she was over him. She was already an MWD handler for the US Army 75th Rangers by then and Brad was welcome to screw whoever he wanted to. Though she still never watched Aniston in movies or *Friends* reruns, not even when looking for a late night distraction.

Lauren helped the girl down from her horse and walked her over to the riverbank while the others were getting organized. No flat rocks here for skipping, she selected a round stone and arced it out where it landed with a barely audible *plonk!*

"It was never going to happen, you know. I'm Lauren, by the way," she kept it easy, off hand.

"Mirisa," the girl sighed deeply. "I know. He's too old. But he's *so* totally handsome. And he rides a horse named Minotaur—he controls *the beast.* Just like Theseus, the beloved of Ariadne. I just adore Greek mythology. Imagine Patrick Gallagher the cowboy as the hero of the Cretan labyrinth," she said the last like a headline and followed it with another heartfelt sigh.

Lauren tried to remember what she had loved at thirteen. The New York Yankees' box scores. That was another thing to hold against Colonel Gibson, dragging her two thousand miles from Yankee Stadium. She hadn't seen a game in so long that she barely knew the roster anymore, never mind their stats. It was September and their season would be ending soon. Each game she missed was one she'd never get back.

"Greek mythology? What are they feeding you kids these days?"

Mirisa stuck her tongue out at her, which Lauren took as a good sign.

"You see his horse?" Lauren leaned in and whispered confidentially to the girl.

"Uh-huh," Mirisa looked over her shoulder. She still had some things to learn about subtlety.

"Notice anything about its coloring?"

"Not really. It's all reddish and spotty."

"A lady named Chelsea told me that his horse's real name is Minnie, because he looks like he's wearing Minnie Mouse's dress." Chelsea had casually cornered her as Mark and Michael had been gathering the fishing gear for the helicopter. She was the ranch's horse manager, and had ever so casually told her about Patrick's horse. At the time she'd thought the cheery redhead was just making conversation, but she was less sure now.

Mirisa slapped a hand over her mouth to cover a bright squeal of delight. "Oh my *gawd!* He *totally* does. A horse in a mouse dress!" A storm of giggles slipped out. She recovered a little, then looked over her shoulder again, once more bursting into giggles.

Lauren followed the direction of her gaze, figuring it was safe as their cover was completely blown.

Patrick now stood on the ground, shed of the clinging woman (at least temporarily), and holding Minnie's reins. He was looking right at them with a very perplexed look on his face, as confused as if he'd just risen from the mud puddle once more.

His cowboy shirt clung damply to his chest.

Mirisa might now be giggling at him and his horse, but Lauren was finding it hard to look away. Colin Firth in the *Pride and Prejudice* lake scene came to mind. Her mother's kind of movie rather than hers, but they'd watched it on TV together when it was first broadcast in the US back in the '90s. She'd already been enamored of Brad back then, but the wet-shirt scene was *very* memorable.

Patrick looked even better.

She turned once more to face the river, selected another stone, and heaved it high and hard.

***

Patrick puzzled at Mirisa's excessive cheerfulness—without any more long looks and deep sighs—that had continued throughout the afternoon.

And then there was Lauren's look, which he also couldn't unravel. By the time they reached camp a couple hours after the helicopter incident, all he could conclude was that some women were very unpredictable. At least he'd found out Lauren's name when Mark had called to her that it was time to go catch some fish.

Lauren Bacall made her a no-brainer to remember, as if he'd forget. That same elegance and impossible beauty. Would a smile light her up like it had Bacall in *To Marry a Millionaire* or would this Lauren always be the cool and emotionless Bacall in *Key Largo?* Bacall was known for her wildly emotional marriage with Bogart, both the fighting and the loving—but she was often a different woman on screen. Did this Lauren have that heat hiding away inside her? It was hard to imagine. He suspected she was much more the *Key Largo* Bacall—the one that had the director, John Huston, actually twisting her arm painfully up behind her back in one scene, trying to make her show any emotion at all.

Devin and Drake had driven out with the chuck wagon—stocked with some of Nathan's marinated steaks and other treats—by a much shorter road than their own round-about trail ride (though it would take a sharp ranch guest to figure out how little distance they'd actually traveled from the main house). And tomorrow's route back would be even longer. The cousins had set up the tents already and had a campfire going. It made for happy arrivals of the beginner-stiff riders, despite the mild walk-trot pace he'd set throughout the afternoon. He, and the cousins who looked and acted like twins, showed the campers how to tend and picket the horses.

Then, despite their groans and complaints about aching muscles, he walked the guests up to the top of a small knoll for the view. It was a planned event, because otherwise they'd seize up and be unable to move the next day.

The knoll also offered an incredible vista to the north and west. The beauty of the Front Range and the wildness of the Rockies. And, just at the base of the far side of the knoll, was one of the best fishing streams on this end of the ranch. Maybe, if the gods were with him, he could spy out the fishing party.

The oohs and ahs, soon followed by the electronic shutter clicks from everyone's cell phone cameras that could never really capture the Big Sky country, told him of the success of the first purpose. He held back, giving the guests the front-row positions.

And down below the small JetRanger helo, emblazoned with a herd of running horses—like right out of the final scene of *Hidalgo* —told him of the success of his second ploy.

If Mark, Lauren, and the old guy were camped there overnight, would he be able to make an excuse to leave his group and go over? Just to check in and make sure everything was okay, of course.

Then a hand slid into the back pocket of his jeans. He wasn't the only one who'd decided to stand at the back of the crowd. He looked down at Clara in surprise and found it very hard to look away. She'd changed out of the loose blouse, which had long since dried and would have been fine. Now she wore a form-hugging t-shirt with a low V-neck. He was at the perfect angle to see that she wore nothing beneath it, and her wet t-shirt contest assets were definitely in the prize-winning category.

***

"There are good days," Lauren lay back in the sweet-smelling grass along the riverbank. "Then there are better days."

"Beginner's luck," Mark groaned as he cleaned the last of the four fish—the three cutthroat trout and the mountain whitefish that she had caught for their dinner.

Michael was building a small campfire to cook them. They'd both been skunked and she'd declared her part of dinner prep done.

There are good days, then there are better days. How long since she'd even thought that? She wasn't sure, but too long. Since before Jupiter's death. Maybe a long time before. Lauren kept her next thought to herself. *Was I past ready to get out of the military and Jupiter was only the final straw?* That was a new thought.

"What kicked you out?" Mark washed his hands in the stream, then sat down beside her. No question what he was talking about. Out of the military. She didn't appreciate the mindreading.

Death of my dog. But she wasn't ready to say that. Had said it too many times in the past.

"Sometimes you're just in for too long," which oddly *was* true now that she'd given a voice to it. She'd seen so much of awful. It was alarming how willing people were to kill each other, even booby-trapping toys to injure children and increase the burden on the enemy. If she never saw any of it again, it would be too soon. "How about you?"

"Emily came down with something incurable: pregnant with our first, Tessa." And his face went soft, which looked strange on the tall, powerfully-built soldier. Though he might be retired, he hadn't lost any of the attitude.

Would she, over time? Probably not. She hadn't been exactly known for her "mellow" in high school either. And kids? Not likely.

"I found something even more important than flying for the Night Stalkers: being alive to watch my family grow. Knocked us both for a loop, but it's the best decision we ever made other than joining in the first place. That and getting together. You got a man, Lauren?"

"I had a dog," it surprised her when that slipped out. "And The Unit. Until recently that was enough." And now she had neither.

Michael kept tinkering with the fire, squatting over it and adding one stick here and a twist of dry grass there. It smelled of crackling pine one moment, the wide prairie the next, and somehow also of the slowly heating circle of stones. There was a reality to it. A weight of presence that eluded her. Even the fire and the stones belonged close beside the quiet bubbling of the nearby water over the river rocks.

"You look like you're praying, Colonel Gibson." And like he was hiding something, but she knew the direct approach wasn't going to uncover it. Emily had already tried that and reported failure.

His shrug wasn't a denial on either account.

Mark fished three beers out of a cooler and handed them around.

A small group of ducks floated down the river, occasionally ducking their heads underwater to snatch some plant or tiny fish, but mostly taking a free ride through the quiet of the evening.

"Proposed to Claudia over a fire even smaller than this one," the colonel's voice was barely louder than the crackling wood and a brilliant blue bird that perched on a nearby bush to call loudly once before continuing south.

A glance showed that Mark hadn't heard this story. So they both kept quiet and sipped their beers.

Michael tipped his head back and looked up. "Sky as big as this one, just different. Arizona desert. Dry. Softer blue. Taste of creosote and flint on the air. Coming up dawn rather than an hour to sunset." So many words at once appeared to exhaust him and he fell silent again.

Already the long shadows of the mountains were stretching across the prairie toward them. Blinks of light attracted her attention to the east. A line of people up on the ridge behind them, taking pictures with the flashes on automatic despite it still being daylight or she might not have noticed them. The trail group, now off their horses.

And half a head taller than most, a man in a cowboy hat. Patrick. Close at his side—very, very close—the woman he'd rescued from the river.

Have fun, Patrick.

She didn't doubt that he would. And she had no hold. No claim. She'd be gone back to New York soon enough anyway. It might have been fun to play with a cowboy for a few days, but apparently that wasn't going to happen.

Even as Lauren watched him, he looked down at the woman beside him, and didn't look back up. *Yep! Got your answer, Foster. Not for you.*

Not that she cared.

"You got problems with Claudia?" Mark asked it softly.

"What? No! What makes you say that?" Colonel Gibson's response was as close to shock as she'd ever heard from him.

Lauren laughed (she *actually* laughed, even if it was barely a quick bark of it). *Would wonders never cease?* "You're clearly sitting on something uncomfortable, Michael," she accidentally took the liberty of using his first name and wasn't rebuked for it. She was a civilian now after all, so maybe it was okay. "Something even *Emily*"—that too felt all right, mostly—"couldn't pry out of you. You've got your wife good and worried."

"She could never doubt how much I care about her."

"And when was the last time you told her that?"

Michael looked at the sky, back down at the fire, and over toward the setting sun.

"Michael?" Even Lauren knew better than that.

"Shit, man," Mark groaned. "You don't reassure them at least once every couple days—women get antsier than horses."

"We do not."

"Do!" Mark rolled his eyes at her. At least she assumed he did behind his mirrored shades.

Michael inspected the sky once more, then rose to his feet abruptly and crossed to the helicopter. He pulled his cell phone out of his pack.

"No signal out here," Mark whispered to her with a soft laugh while Michael stood glaring at his phone.

Not to be defeated, Michael dug once more into his pack and pulled out a military satellite phone.

"Bet he was a hell of a Boy Scout," she whispered back to Mark.

"Best soldier I've ever met," no joking in his voice this time. "Even better than Emily."

Lauren wondered what it would take to have someone talk about *her* like that. Well, first it would require her being someone a lot finer than Lauren Foster. Military retired. No dog. No job. No life. Not even a cowboy to play with.

Michael's soft voice carried from the helicopter, "It's me. I just…"

"I was just thinking of you," Lauren called out softly.

He didn't even turn as he repeated her words.

"Now I'm a goddamn relationship ventriloquist," she told Mark.

"Shush, I'm busy listening," Mark sipped his beer.

"I…" Michael stumbled to a halt once again.

"Tell her that you love her," she called out.

Mark choked and sputtered as he tried to pass his beer through his nose.

"I just want you to know…" Michael trailed off again.

Lauren considered going up to smack him.

"Yeah. I miss you too… What? … Oh… Yes. I feel just the same."

Lauren sighed. It was both sad that he had to be prompted…and impossibly sweet.

"Uh-huh. We're camping here…"

News to her, not that she had anywhere better to be.

"Right… See you tomorrow." Michael tucked away the phone, then came back to sit by the fire.

For a long time they listened to it crackle and pop. He arranged the fish on a couple rocks as the mountain shadows overran their position and the sky shifted from blue to gold.

"Thanks," Michael said so long after the phone call that it took Lauren a couple minutes to connect that he was addressing her.

"You bet."

Before the fish was done, Mark had dug some paper plates out of the helo's baggage compartment, but couldn't find any utensils.

Both she and Michael watched Mark as he struggled to eat the fish with the thin curved boning blade. He kept cursing as he burned his fingers on the hot flesh.

"You really *have* gone civilian," Lauren teased him, feeling that just maybe it was okay to do so.

Michael offered one of his quiet smiles that was apparently his version of laughing aloud. He pulled out a Cold Steel SRK six-inch blade and a Gerber Multi-Plier for dealing with any stray bones—both black anodized so they wouldn't catch any light.

"Okay, Foster," Mark hissed in pain and sucked his fingertips again. "Show us *your* shit."

She wished she had something else to show, but she didn't. So, as casually as she could, she pulled up the leg of her jeans and slid her Extrema Ratio Glauca B1 out of its leg sheath.

Michael stopped with a speared flake of fish on the tip of his SRK and inspected her carefully.

Mark just whistled. "I thought only the French GIGN had those."

France's elite counter-terrorism group—the closest thing they had to Delta.

Lauren used the folding blade to brush back the crispy skin with a single long sweep. "Their lead dog handler liked me." Georges Marchand had liked her a great deal. They spent four weeks in a cross-team training program together, and then a week with just them and their dogs at a Tunisian beach resort. His parting gift had been his Glauca.

"I wish someone liked me enough to give me a five-hundred-dollar knife."

"Dream on, Major."

"Maybe I'll just steal yours."

"You're welcome to try."

He grunted, "Could get to like you, Foster." Then he tossed his own knife aside and began picked at his fish again with his bare fingers.

Fresh-caught, campfire-cooked, eaten among friends... Or at least military friends, which was a different category but still counted for a lot. It was some of the best trout she'd ever eaten.

She kept a casual eye to the east, but no cowboy came riding over the hill. Even after dusky red had gone to full dark filled with glittering stars, she caught herself glancing to the east though there was nothing to see.

Patrick had solved his problem of what to do with Clara by sticking close to the thirteen-year-old Mirisa. He still didn't understand why the girl kept giggling at him rather than sighing, but she was soon entertaining everyone with the Greek myths and stories. She had an unending supply of them, but told them with a sophistication that seemed unlikely for her years. She also pointed out the various star constellations that went with each story she told.

It kept the entire group well entertained until it was time to bed down. He asked the best of the riders—a seventeen-year-old boy—to help him check the horses over for the night. Partly as a reward and partly so that he didn't ask Clara, then somehow forget to come back.

He also made a point of telling them not to wander off into the night, because there might be a bear out feeding somewhere. He'd patted his rifle to emphasize the point.

"Don't keep any snack food with you tonight. Not even sealed in plastic. I think bears can smell right through it."

Drake and Devin had ridden off with the chuck wagon and the scant remains of a steak and fire-baked potato dinner a few hours earlier. They'd finished with s'mores made with some gourmet chocolate from a Seattle boutique shop called Chocolaterie Bosco with which his brother had make a special mix for the ranch, including dried black huckleberries and a hint of ginger. No other s'mores anywhere would taste like the ones at Henderson's Ranch, which Patrick supposed was the point. The breakfast bag—strung up high on a line between two trees well clear of the campsite—was filled with Nathan's awesome homemade cinnamon rolls.

"And don't be wandering off farther than the outhouse," which was tucked a little way into the grove of Rocky Mountain maple.

It was only as he said it that he knew he was trapped by his own words. It was his job to stay in the camp and make sure everyone was okay. Just happening to mosey into Lauren's camp as if everything was normal—like Mel Gibson in that Old West gambler movie with Jodi Foster, wasn't going to happen. What was it? He never forgot titles, but he couldn't bring that one to mind. No leading man getting a feisty blonde Jodi. Instead he kept picturing Lauren's thoughtful gazes and minimal gestures.

He sighed as he curled up in his bag close by the fire. A few of the more adventurous were camped out with him. Clara retreated to the tent she shared with her daughter with a sad look on her face.

Patrick offered her an apologetic shrug to let her think that it would have happened if it had been in his control. It cheered her up some, and she returned the shrug in a friendly enough way as if saying, "Oh well. Too bad."

And it wasn't in his control. His imagination was busy wandering over to the other side of the knoll, still wondering how to turn this into a leading man moment.

CHAPTER 3

"Not ready to face the humiliation?" Lauren folded the blanket she'd slept under, still reeking slightly of horse—which she probably did now as well—and stowed it back in the helicopter.

"Didn't bring any breakfast supplies," Mark's grumble greeted her tease. One glance at him told Lauren that this was a man who *needed* his morning coffee. The sky was pink with the pending sunrise. The bright spot of Venus, the morning star, had faded from sight less than ten minutes ago.

"I'm glad to catch breakfast," not that she really wanted more fish.

"Careful, or I'll make you deliver on that boast rather than flying us back to the ranch." Mark was doing the preflight inspection of the helicopter.

Michael was using a Henderson's Ranch ball cap he'd found under one of the helo's seats to transport water to douse the fire's ashes, not that there was a wisp of smoke when he stirred them with a stick. Still, he methodically doused and stirred to make sure the fire had truly died overnight. The horse blankets, apparently kept in the aft hold for emergencies, were all that any of them had needed for bedding. She'd slept in much harder holes than on a cushy grass bed watching the stars turn through the night sky—though that queen-

351

size bed back at the ranch felt awfully inviting when she'd woken up at the crack of dawn, chilled by the heavy dew.

"We could always go over the hill there and raid that tourist camp," she nodded toward the low ridge. "Bet they have food. Probably still sleeping so we can catch them by surprise."

"What are you talking about, woman?" Mark didn't look her direction as he wiggled the helo's tail rotor in a way that probably told him a hundred things about its condition and merely told her that it wiggled.

She pictured their relative positions last night: Michael tending the fire, Mark busy cleaning the fish. She was the only one who'd been turned to see the line of guests atop the vista point.

"Just do them a favor, *flyboy*," a deep insult to any Army pilot—that's what the Army called a pilot who could only qualify for the Air Farce. "Don't pass over the other side of the hill on departure."

Mark and Michael at looked each other, then at the grassy hill, then at her. Some look passed between them. As if Michael said, "I told you," and Mark replied, "Guess so."

"What?"

No response. They were having some stupid-ass, guy-speak moment and it didn't take a genius to know it was about her. But neither one was volunteering the contents of the first half of their conversation.

Carrying her blanket, she passed close behind where Michael squatted over the remnants of his fire. She shoved firmly against his butt with a knee.

Rather than tipping forward into the ashes as she'd planned, Michael snaked out a hand. He caught her behind the knee, swept her other leg with a swing of his own, and rolled so that when she slammed down onto the ground, he was poised atop her to strike with his fist.

He might have surprised her, but with her left hand she had grabbed his knife from its sheath on his right leg as she went down and landed on her back with the breath knocked out of her. She held his own SRK blade steady to his throat.

It earned her a small smile before he pinched a nerve on her arm—his hand had been perfectly pre-positioned so all he had to do was squeeze. The blade tumbled from her suddenly limp fingers. It sliced through the grass with a slight *swish* sound before digging in point first close beside her ear.

"She *is* good," Mark sounded wide awake.

Michael grunted, then rose to his feet, retrieving and resheathing his blade as he did so.

Lauren rolled, swept his feet out from under him, and continued the roll to get well clear before he could recover. At the moment Michael hit the ground with a surprised grunt, she rolled over the folded blanket she'd dropped. She clutched it to her chest as she pushed to her feet and began walking over to the helo to stow it as if she hadn't even broken her stride.

Mark's laugh lit up the morning.

Michael's grunt sounded more thoughtful this time as he climbed to his feet.

Why did they need her to be good? What kind of a test was this?

"No longer in the military, jerkwads."

Neither man answered.

Yesterday had been a fog. Too much had happened. Her final flight home from Afghanistan, mustering out, then standing on the tarmac with her duffle and her DD 214 Honorable Discharge form. Fifteen years in. Army, Rangers, Delta. Three dogs. All done.

For fifteen years, the US Army had provided everything: housing, food, and plenty of action. She was done with them. Only respect for the rank of the out-processing officer had kept her from chucking the re-up offer in his face. Instead, she'd stood in front of the offered chair she hadn't taken and shredded the form into confetti, then scattered it over his desk before returning to parade rest.

She'd been awarded too many medals and commendations for him to change the "Honorable Discharge" to "General" or worse, but she could see his pen hesitate over Box #24 "Character of Service." He'd finally signed her DD 214 and practically thrown it in her face.

"You're belt isn't regulation." *Damn straight.* It was refashioned from the tubular nylon dog leash she'd been holding coiled in her hand when she'd let Jupiter scout ahead off-lead. If she'd needed evidence that she was stateside again, that was it. Next he'd be asking where her reflective exercise belt was—the first garbage can she'd found in Kandahar after it had been issued. She'd walked out of his office before she could earn a dishonorable discharge for taking down a superior idiot.

There she'd stood, out in the early morning light of Pope Field, Fort Bragg—knowing it was her last military flight and she'd never be back—blinking hard against the bright dawn that was making her eyes burn. She didn't have a single friend outside the military...and the wall of a DD 214 now stood between her and her friends on the inside. Her first step off the plane when it reached New York would be into a world she couldn't imagine—a world she'd departed straight out of high school and never looked back at.

Then Colonel Gibson walked up to her with his wife Claudia, each bearing a light pack, and led her toward a different plane. Somehow, she'd ended up in Montana.

Now she had some sleep—at least enough to be coherent and stop fainting, though not enough to cure crossing a dozen time zones in the last forty-eight hours. She could finally think again. That was some progress.

Today she was going to get some answers or by nightfall she'd be headed to the Big Apple—even if she had to walk to get there. If she was stuck on the outside, it was time to start learning how to live there.

Patrick didn't hear the helo start, but he heard it pass well to the south. No startled horses this time. No runaway Rolo forcing him to gather a snuggly woman into his arms.

He'd spent a third of last night thinking it had been a *bad* decision to put Clara off. It wasn't as if Lauren was just waiting to fall into his arms—again—after he'd plunged into a mud puddle, then been caught cradling another woman. Some movie star hero he was. More in the untrustworthy playboy role. Maybe he was Tom Cruise in *Top Gun* in that part of the film *before* he fell in love with Kelly McGillis. That was a little more promising, but as he was most of a foot taller than Tom...

"That is definitely a wrap," he muttered to himself. End of any film with himself as the hero.

He really was in the role of plucky comic-relief sidekick and couldn't see any way out of it. If Stan or one of the other hands was suddenly cast in the leading hero role, he'd have to shoot himself. And miss, of course, because it was bad form to kill the plucky comic-relief sidekick.

Then he'd spent at least half the night thinking it had been a *good* decision to put Clara off and "save" himself for Lauren, just in case. There was something about her beyond merely stunning looks. Maybe it was a Florence Nightin-guy effect. She'd felt fragile in his arms as he'd carried her to the house unconscious. But it had also felt right. For at least that one brief moment, he *was* the romantic hero in the movie.

Somewhere near dawn he'd decided that he'd cast himself as the hero in the movie that was his life from now on. He liked the sound of that. Time to take the reins of his own life. A cowboy metaphor. Even better.

And the few remaining minutes of the night, he might have slept. Or he might have spent it trying to dig out the rocks that insisted on poking through his bedroll despite the camping air mattress.

Trying to be entertaining and attentive to the ranch guests this morning, while being barely conscious, was proving a challenge. Coffee with extra sugar didn't help nearly enough.

Not thinking about Lauren was proving impossible.

Regrettably, staying in his saddle when Minotaur decided to walk under a low, stout branch on a Douglas fir tree was also out of the question. It swept him backward, over Minotaur's hindquarters, and left him lying on his back in a pricker bush. He lay there, trying to redraft the scene in some way that wasn't just plain embarrassing as the horse whickered a laugh at him. Minotaur had known exactly what he was doing.

Mirisa's bright giggles weren't helping him shed the comic-relief sidekick role one little bit.

"What the hell?" Lauren had only ducked into her room long enough for a combat shower and a change of clothes. In the four minutes she'd been gone, the breakfast table had changed from packed solid with joking field hands to empty. And Mark and Michael were nowhere to be seen.

"How do you like your eggs?" Nathan was the only one left in the kitchen.

"Couldn't care."

"I'm a chef. You've got to do better than that, First Sergeant."

"Don't call me that!" It came out with a snap he didn't deserve. She grimaced an apology. "I'm on the outside. Retired. My name is Lauren Foster. That's who I am now."

"Sorry. I heard Colonel Gibson refer to you as First Sergeant. The way he said it, I'm guessing that's good."

"For a female dog handler, I suppose so." Actually it was good and hard won. "But—"

"Oh, you're like Stan."

"No," she wasn't. Not anymore. "Yes," because it *was* what she had been. "I—" she didn't know what to say. "Scrambled is fine."

"Scrambled it is," Nathan turned to the stove.

"Where are those two assholes?" She was going to get to the bottom of their plans if she had to take them all the way down herself —or maybe she'd enlist Emily and Claudia and do some serious damage.

Nathan laughed easily.

She supposed that Emily was right, Henderson's Ranch had learned to be tolerant of ex-military personnel and their moods.

"They decided to go into town for breakfast and some errands."

"When will they be back?" How soon could she throttle them? One or both. She was past caring.

"Hard to say. They drove and it's over thirty miles to Choteau, which is the nearest place. More like eighty each way if they run in to Great Falls." Nathan served her up a plate...no, a platter thick with toast, bacon, hash browns, and scrambled eggs. "Hope this is okay, the guys wiped out all the sausage I had made up."

"You make your own sausage?"

"Sure."

"For sausages I usually hit a sausage, pepper, and onion cart in Central Park or over at Riposo on 72nd." She took a piece of bacon with her fingers and crunched down on it. Just fine with her.

"I prefer Faicco down on Bleeker, but I was always a downtown sort of guy."

Lauren leaned back against the counter and ate one-handed, occasionally pausing for some coffee.

"You're a southpaw."

She waved her fork at him left-handed. He waved back with a chef's knife in his own left, then they traded the silent smile that left-handers always had for each other.

She'd shoveled down half the plate before she caught herself. If she ate fast, then there was nothing waiting for what to do next. And it was food worth tasting. Even Nathan's scrambled eggs were worth slowing down for.

So, to give her mouth something to do other than eat, she started asking questions about New York—she'd barely been back in fifteen years and would soon be living there. She'd never heard of either of his restaurants, but she'd wager that her brother had. His crowd was into the whole foodie thing, even if they couldn't afford the upper tiers of it. She'd have to ask. No rush. She hadn't even told him yet that she was out. Just showing up was more her style and he'd always been fine with that—which made him a perfect brother, even if they weren't overly close. He was...comfortable. More than either of their parents had ever been, so she wasn't going to Florida. Comfortable was about all she could handle at the moment.

Kind of like standing here chatting with Nathan was comfortable. He was pleasant, an easy man to talk to.

"So where's this amazing woman I can see that you're dying to tell me about?"

She couldn't have gotten a much bigger reaction with a Taser.

He' been puttering around the kitchen, fussing over a marinade for a tub of chicken and answering her with just as little brain as she'd been using to chat with him about New York.

Suddenly she had his full attention.

"Julie's out on a trail ride. I try not to worry. She takes the advanced riders out into the Flathead Wilderness, right up into the heart of the Rockies. She's taken me there, but only the easier places. She's the best rider the ranch has—I sometimes think she was born on a horse. Or maybe she's part horse. I've asked her but she thinks I'm just being silly. You know, she placed third in barrel racing at the Calgary Stampede. She's thinking about getting back into it next year. Anyway," he waved his hands long enough to catch a breath before plunging back in. "We schedule really high-end riders together, into every other week over the summer. This is the last one. The risk of a heavy snowfall becomes too much any later in the season, especially up in the Wilderness. It's already not good. Storms blow out of there with so little warning."

"Yeah, the Khyber Pass in the Hindu Kush has fast weather changes like that." That earned her a blank look. Right. Her past was now irrelevant. Civvie-world was looking harder and harder with each passing moment. She'd been fine camping out with Mark and Colonel Gibson. But each time she dealt with a civilian, the conversations kept having these dead moments when things like foreign places came up that weren't in France or Italy—or, god help her, Canada.

"Uh-huh," Nathan made an agreement sound, but too little too late. "Stan nearly got himself killed up at the waterfall above a fishing cabin out there in a freak spring snowstorm. He says he'd be dead if it wasn't for Bertram saving his life."

"Who's Bertram?" Then her throat went dry as a brownout dust storm.

"That's—"

"One of his dogs," she managed to choke out.

Nathan nodded, then returned to the subject of his bride-to-be and high country rides as if Lauren hadn't just stepped on the worst kind of land mine.

It wasn't some IED—improvised explosive device—that went off when you stepped on them that were the worst.

Nor the engineered Bouncing Betties—designed to pop up to waist-high after you stepped off them, then release a lateral explosion to cut down a whole squad.

Her demolitions trainer had called the worst ones HSE mines— Hollywood Special Effect—because they didn't really exist out in the battlespace. Step on them, and there's a loud click. "Everyone" knows that stepping off them is what blows them up. So some unlucky sod just stands on and on, with nothing his buddies can do to save him.

"Strictly Hollywood," her trainer had sounded disgusted and moved on.

But here she stood, in the warm, sunny kitchen of Henderson's Ranch, with her foot firmly down on an HSE mine and wondered just how soon it was going to kill her.

Did she dare lift her foot?

Don't think.

Did she dare breathe?

Did she dare even blink?

A dog trainer saved by his dog. A man who said his life had been saved by a dog... Then she thought about Stan and his hooks—he'd clearly been through some shit worse than she had. Which meant that if he said Bertram saved his life, the Malinois had.

She didn't want to think about dogs. Especially not trained dogs. Was this why Colonel Gibson had dragged her across the country? To be "cured" about dogs?

Lauren handed her half-finished plate to Nathan and walked out of the kitchen while he was still in mid-sentence about something. She'd apologize later. If she survived.

Out of the back door, she tried to breathe but couldn't find any air.

She leaned back against the lumpy log siding, gasping like the fish she'd yanked out of the stream last night. The sun was still on the far side of the house, the air here on the west side was cool, damp, cloying. It stuck in her throat until she feared she would choke.

Was this PTSD?

No!

She'd met the wrecks that had once been soldiers. She wasn't one of those. No ruined shell of a soldier plagued by nightmares until they couldn't function. She'd walked out of the Army standing tall, not carried into some VA psych ward strapped on a stretcher. No negative psych eval on her DD 214, despite shredding the re-up offer on the personnel officer's desk—she'd still count that as a healthy choice.

Covering her face with her hands, she screamed into her own palms in frustration.

"It doesn't help, does it?"

This time Lauren yelped as she spun to face Emily. She was leaning one shoulder against the lodge's wall about ten feet away.

"How…"

"Nathan called. He said you just blanked out in mid-sentence."

"Shit! I'm fine!" At least she would be if no one was watching her.

Emily just nodded. "The screaming doesn't help though, does it?"

"Tenacious bitch," Lauren tried to keep the mumble to herself, but it didn't work. *Strike Two, Foster.*

"That's what Mark keeps telling me, though he uses kinder words."

Lauren considered apologizing, but didn't feel like it.

Emily pushed off the wall and strolled out of the lodge's shadow. The sun caught her light hair and lit it like a beacon. "The problem is that the scream doesn't tell you if you're still sane or not."

Lauren cursed, carefully to herself this time, then hurried over to fall in beside Emily. There was a heat to the sun, despite the coolness of the early September air. Maybe that contrast was what made it taste like fall.

"Doesn't even let off the steam behind it."

"Then what does help?" Which of course implied that there was a problem. But there wasn't…but there *was.* Maybe it was just jet lag. Or being in Montana. Or…

"You'll hate the answer."

"That's okay. I already hate the question."

Emily offered one of her ghostly smiles. "Patience."

"You shitting me with that lame-o answer?"

"Nope," Emily guided them around the main lodge, then crossed the broad sunlit patch of the main yard. All roads met here: the one up from the ranch entrance, branches off to outbuildings, barns, and even up to cabins. A dozen cars, a pair of horse trailers, and a tractor were parked in various places. A classic chuck wagon, complete with wooden wheels and a hooped red-and-white checked canopy was backed into an open garage bay.

Lauren hadn't had a chance to explore anything yet—not that she wanted to. She wanted to curl up on her brother's couch, watch bad cable, and…go quietly insane in private.

"Patience isn't something I'm real good at."

"Delta? Dog handler? Those didn't teach you patience?"

"I may have been accused of being as hyper as my Malinois."

"Restless or hyper?" Emily led her into the biggest of the barns.

"Wow! This is different," Lauren stumbled to a halt. She'd never been in a big horse barn before. Or a cow barn, for that matter. It was like a kennel on steroids. But instead of a long line of chain-link gates blocking concrete cells each with a dog bed, a chew toy, and a hyper-driven war dog, it was all wood and shadows. The sun's heat had been chopped off behind them, but rather than being cold, there was a warmth—a warmth that smelled distinctly horsey, but was welcoming nonetheless. The wide central aisle was lined with wooden stalls that looked as old as the hills. The wood was dark and weathered, scuffed with years of hard use. But not beaten and battered. Instead it felt better cared for than a new-built military kennel.

Many of the stalls were open—horses out on rides or grazing in the pasture. But every now and then, the half-height door was closed and a horse would peek out at the two women who had suddenly entered their world.

At the center of the long barn was the only break in the aisle of stalls. Offices to the right. To the left, a large space filled with saddles and bridles. The sign above it said "Tack Room."

A steep flight of stairs led up to another room with large windows that she couldn't see in. She scanned the length of the barn. No skylight. One her way in, she'd spotted a skylight at roughly this location. Near the three rooftop satellite antennas.

She shifted enough to see the door. Biometric-coded lock. She'd bet the windows were one-way glass as well or she'd be able to see the brightness of the skylight. A small sign said, "Tac Room." Without the k.

She looked back down to see Emily watching her closely.

Lauren stuffed her fists in her pockets and shrugged, *Ain't seen nothing.* Except a military-grade installation in the middle of a Montana horse barn where it made absolutely no sense. She'd seen similar installations in war zones, usually CIA command-and-control rooms.

She glared her knowledge at Emily: *I can see your shit, woman, no matter how blind and dumb everyone else around you is.*

Emily kept her thoughts to herself as she stepped up to a stall close by the stairs.

A horse the color of mahogany stretched out particularly far.

"Hello Chesapeake," Emily moved in to rub the horse's nose, which made it sigh happily.

"You ride horses, too. Any show ribbons?" Because there was nothing Major Emily Beale didn't do well.

"No, that's Julie—Nathan's intended. Has a whole wall of them. But riding is part of living on a ranch. Chesapeake and I had our first ride together the day before my wedding. Went well, didn't it, pal?" She addressed the last to the horse. The horse made a happy sound, with extended neck and awfully big teeth exposed.

"Is that a laugh or is he about to eat you?"

"A laugh. Besides, horses are vegetarians. It wasn't one of Mark's better days. He made up for it the next day though."

"When he married you."

Emily held up her left hand as proof. The ring's stone matched the color of her eyes.

"Nice," she was never sure of what else to say when someone did that. The one time she'd held a ring it had seemed so light and insubstantial—the moment before she'd chucked her dreams into the polluted river.

"Tell me about your—"

"Oh, shit! I knew it!" Lauren should never have followed Emily. It had been part habit—because Major Beale, retired or not, was a superior officer. It had also been because she was desperate. But she wasn't that desperate.

"—your life," the major continued as if Lauren hadn't spoken, "back in New York."

"Oh. Thought you were going to dig into the mess I am now. Do you have any suggestions on how I can get my foot back out of my mouth?"

"You mean your hoof?" Emily's slight smile was understanding and washed the last of "The Major" out of Lauren's vocabulary.

"Not a whole lot to tell. Decent enough parents who were more interested in their careers than their children. A gay older brother. Being so tall and built like a stick, I played a lot of volleyball. Nothing much of interest." And her ex-fiancé could die along with the rest of her past, she wouldn't bother mentioning him.

Emily merely nodded and leaned back against the half-height door.

The horse rested its head on her shoulder and they both watched her.

Lauren sat on a nearby hay bale and tried to explain herself—something she rarely even bothered to do to herself.

"I guess I was never what you'd call a deep thinker. That was my brother, always asking me what I thought or felt until I wanted to pound on him. He had the empathy gene even when he was a little shit. Never wanted it myself. Never missed it."

Claudia, Michael's wife, and Chelsea, who'd told her about Minotaur's real name, came out of a nearby room that must be the barn's working office.

"My Doug is dreamy that way," the redhead effused, stepping right into the middle of their conversation with her tight jeans and cowboy boots. "He's always thinking about things like that. Me, I just blunder ahead until I run into something I have to climb over." She sat on the bale beside Lauren, pressing their shoulders together as if they were already friends. Chelsea hooked a thumb at Claudia. "She told me—"

Oh man!

"—almost nothing at all about you. Why are you dressed that way?"

Lauren looked down. She'd just grabbed the first clothes that came to hand. By ingrained training, she wore Army boots, camo pants, a black t-shirt, and her Glauca knife in the leg sheath. Wearing no sidearm felt weird, but she'd turned that in to the quartermaster before her departure from Pope Field. She'd have to get a personal weapon at the first opportunity.

These clothes defined the person she was. Civvies could never hold a candle to this.

"You say you go *over* things?" Lauren faced Chelsea going for a subject change.

"Sure! Right over the top!" She smacked her palms together and then shot one upward like plane taking off. Her long hair flounced with the power of the motion. Her face was mid-twenties, innocent, happy, though definitely not simple. "Best way!"

Lauren smiled softly. "Me? I go *through* them." She stomped a boot, making Chesapeake jolt back a half step.

"Perfect!" Chelsea wasn't to be slowed down. "Let's team up. I go over them. You go through them. Emily outsmarts them. And what do you do?" She aimed the last at Claudia.

"I sic my husband on them."

Colonel Michael Gibson was a formidable asset indeed.

Lauren didn't laugh with the others, but she could feel the smile. It didn't hurt as much this time.

Halfway back to the ranch, Patrick had the sickening thought that maybe Lauren would be gone before he got back. No one had said how long she was staying. She'd only arrived yesterday, but if she left without him seeing her again he'd… He didn't know what, but he'd *definitely* do something. As soon as he thought of what it was.

He brought the group out onto the unpaved road a mile down from the ranch. From here, the beginners could risk a canter to get them back to the ranch in style. Rolo, of course, needed no coaxing to run, and Clara was game enough to let him do it—though she kept control of the reins this time.

With them in the lead, her daughter let loose her own reins and shouted a *"Yee-haw!"* like a cowboy in a movie—completely forgetting to kick the horse. But with the barn so close, her mount didn't need more coaxing than that. In moments they were all at a canter, or at least a fast trot.

A dozen horses thundered down the road, the Larson's cattle fields to the left and the wide pastureland of Henderson's Ranch to the right, with only a lone longhorn cow grazing where it wasn't supposed to be. He waved to Lucy, who they couldn't seem to keep out of anywhere. The cow watched him briefly as she chewed, then ducked her massive head back into the unharvested field of Henderson hay.

He galloped to the head of the group to make sure they didn't miss the turn up the ranch's driveway. So he was the first to see the spectacle as they pounded triumphantly into the main yard.

Four women played at the grassy volleyball court that had been set up near one of the corrals. Chelsea's bright red hair waved like a flag as she raced to return a ball. Emily took the pass and leapt high at the net to fire it across. The older blonde wasn't looking so old as she dove and saved the spike. Despite the dive, she made a near perfect setup at the net.

Except there wasn't anyone to take advantage of it.

Then, rushing up from the back court, a vision sprinted ahead. Five great strides across the grass with her incredibly long legs moved Lauren from the back line to the net. She leapt into the air until it appeared she was floating there and looking down from above onto all the others.

He nearly choked as he simultaneously tried to gasp with relief that she was still here and also hold his breath pending her play.

She swung an arm down in a spike so hard that he could hear it over the sound of the hooves pounding into the yard behind him.

The ball didn't cross the net. Instead it blazed a trail as if it were a comet descending from orbit. It pounded down between Emily and Chelsea before they could even blink and he was surprised it didn't just keep going and plow its way to China.

Lauren turned to slap a high five with the blonde as Chelsea and Emily groaned in frustration. That's when Patrick finally registered that Lauren wasn't wearing a shirt. Bare feet, camo pants, and a black sports bra. She might be all leg, except she was tall enough that she was all torso as well. He couldn't look away.

Minotaur, however, knew his post-ride duties and turned to follow the last horse in the group over to the corral where Doug was waiting to help everyone dismount. Patrick kept straining to watch as Lauren moved to the service line at the back of the court, catching the ball with a complete surety that only happened on ESPN.

Just before she served, she glanced for a moment in his direction.

Then she tossed the ball high in the air, jumped up, and pummeled it into the net.

"That's one," Emily called out.

Lauren caught the ball as Claudia tossed it back to her. She wasn't sure what had gone wrong with the first serve. Sometimes you missed. That's just how it went. But for her, a miss was an inch outside the back line, or a bright tick on the top of the net as it went over. Emily and Chelsea had learned to respect her serves.

Instead she had nearly pounded it into the back of Claudia's head.

"Maybe you should come over to our side, Claudia," Chelsea heck-led. "You'd be safer over here. C'mon, Lauren. Another net serve! Let's go!" No matter what she might say, Chelsea crouched in preparation.

Lauren twisted the ball until the air hole was in her palm and the manufacturer's label was right side up and facing her. She'd done that the same way since her very first serve back in junior high. Knowing it was wrong, she thought about her prior serve rather than her present one. Had she under-lofted the ball? Or jumped so high that she'd over-topped it? The volleyball court had always been one of the few places that she could take on Delta operators woman-to-man. That and tracking with her dog—with Jupiter.

Then she'd watched Patrick turned nearly backward in the saddle as his horse ambled away without any control from him.

She tossed the ball, then jumped.

Even as she hammered down on it again, she knew what she'd done wrong. Too high, and turning just enough to see if Patrick was still watching, she slammed her serve square into Claudia's butt.

"Hey!" Claudia stumbled forward and had to grab the net to regain her balance. "Ow! That hurt!"

"Yes!" Chelsea's cheer turned into some sort of a dance as she tromped about, thumbs tucked in her armpits, and her elbows flapping like a chicken's wings.

Claudia was now retrieving the ball as she rubbed her backside.

Emily simply watched Lauren through the cage of the net.

"What?" Lauren mouthed.

Major Emily Beale was back. Her face remained utterly passive as she offered the smallest nod toward the departing cowboy and his mouse-dress-colored horse.

When Lauren shook her head, *no freaking way,* Emily offered another of those fleeting half smiles.

Chelsea's serve hit her square in the chest. Without thinking, Lauren caught it.

Chelsea added ecstatic clucking to her victory chicken-dance as Lauren tossed the ball back to her.

"Did you see that?" Patrick whispered to Doug as the ranch manager helped him shoo the riders and their horses around the ring one final time. Freed of saddles, curried down, they were walking off the last of the run—both rider and horse.

He could have had them walk the last half mile to the ranch for the cooldown, but that would ruin the triumphant return. And after two days in the saddle, it was good for the tourists as well.

"Made it impossible to get decent work out of anybody around here for the last hour," Doug grumbled. But he had a dreamy look that said the other ranch hands hadn't been the only ones watching the game. As long as none of them were thinking about Lauren, maybe it was okay—though he envied them the hour.

"You know," Doug leaned close, "that Lauren is the only single gal of the four."

Which meant that *every* single male hand on the ranch had been thinking about her rather than the other three. Doug, on the other hand, was like some campy Hugh Grant lead every time someone so much as mentioned his wife Chelsea.

"Heard how you carried her up to the house," Doug continued after they'd gotten the horses back in their stalls and sent off the riders for well-deserved showers and a reminder to not be late for a fried chicken lunch in the big dining room.

"Might have." They wandered back out to the corral and leaned on the fence, which offered them a good view of the game.

"Doesn't exactly look like the frail, fainting type."

She didn't.

Emily and Lauren were facing off, clearly outclassing the other two players. They were well matched. Lauren had an inch or two of height and more reach, but Emily was so fast that she could make up for most of it. Emily was down to a sports bra as well and their bodies glistened in the sun like some ridiculous '60s beach movie.

Mark's big, baby-blue pickup rolled up the drive and eased to a halt near the court. Three years and he'd never found out why it was baby blue—Mark just snarled anytime Patrick asked. He could see

Mark and the old guy looking at each other, then they both climbed out, shed their shirts, and strode over to join the play.

"Think maybe we should go even up the odds?" Patrick asked, but Doug was already on the move.

Patrick didn't need a horse to kick him to tell him it was a chance to actually be in the volleyball scene from *Top Gun.* "Am I Maverick or the Iceman?"

Doug laughed as he pulled off his shirt and kicked away his cowboy boots.

"Remember Merlin?"

"The goof played by Tim Robbins?"

"Bingo," Doug slapped him on the shoulder and sent him over to Lauren's team before stepping to the other side and sweeping Chelsea into a steamy kiss.

Patrick stumbled to a stop close in front of Lauren. "Uh…hi." *Great opening line, dude.* Oh, god, maybe he was Anthony Michael Hall in *Sweet Sixteen,* trying to be friends with the outrageously cute Molly Ringwald and never succeeding.

"Can you even play volleyball?" Lauren scoffed.

"Just you watch." He'd played plenty on the sand at Long Beach Park as a kid.

An hour later Patrick stood in the shower and wondered if he'd ever move again. The game had raged back and forth. No score kept, each serve and volley a triumph of its own. Each change of service a major victory.

He'd given everything he had. And if that meant grinding his chest into bare grass in a diving save, then he'd done it. The stains felt as if they reached all of the way down to the soles of his feet…from the inside. Of course, his feet were also stained on the outside.

But his stains hadn't begun to match Lauren's scars. Stan had told him that every military war dog trainer had scars—though he'd lost his worst ones overseas along with his arm. He said there were bites that somehow always found the hole through the protective layers of a bite-training suit, claw scrapes as the animal fought for a purchase on an "attacker," and being knocked into innumerable unforgiving objects by seventy or eighty pounds of racing military war dog.

Lauren's body bore those scars. A slice of four parallel white lines where a rear claw had raked down her thigh. Tooth marks on her upper arm and shoulder. And other injuries that looked as if they'd hurt like mad, but weren't in any pattern he could imagine a dog making. Two were ominously round, like bullet holes.

Somehow, the scars had added to, rather than diminished, her perfection. She wasn't some movie star. She was a powerful, real woman. For the hundredth time, he wondered what had made her faint that morning, but he just couldn't imagine.

He cranked the shower another notch hotter, letting it soak into his muscles, but he knew that he'd be sore anyway.

There was no way that a game of v-ball to match this one had ever been played. By the end, Doug had upgraded him from Merlin to Goose—as if that was such a major improvement. At least he was one of the main characters now and married to Meg Ryan. Except he got killed off deep in the movie despite being in the "best buddy" role. That didn't bode well.

No matter how he tried to cast Lauren, he couldn't find a role that put him in the leading man position beside her. For each time he threw himself into the hard ground, Lauren had already been in the right position to make the perfect tip, save, or spike. It was like watching Doug or Julie ride—they'd been born to horses and it showed.

She'd been thrown off her game when the men joined in, but she soon settled down and proved that she was truly lethal on the court. No idle chatter for her—Lauren was a hundred percent about the game.

"What else were you born to do, Lauren Foster?" Patrick asked the shower wall he was leaning against.

It didn't answer.

"Fine. Be that way."

He'd figure it out himself. She'd been Delta Force. There were never any women in Delta Force movies. Just macho dudes blowing shit up. Those flicks were low-brow, fun, and Chuck Norris had ruled. But there were no women.

Except Lauren.

He shut off the water and wondered if he had the energy to eat any of the fried chicken at lunch. It was his brother's recipe, so he probably would. He was half out of the bunkhouse door before he remembered that maybe he should dry off and get dressed first.

It was after dark and Lauren sat out on the unlit porch of the big log house, no wiser than she'd been this morning. And no closer to leaving for New York, which surprised her. The Adirondack chair was big enough for her to slouch in. The wooden slats were more comfortable than she'd expected, but she was looking forward to the queen-sized bed tonight.

Between the jet lag, sleeping out under the stars, and the volleyball game, she felt pleasantly wrung out—without going for a 10K run. It would be tough to do that in The City. Central Park had a 10K outermost loop, but it was almost impossible to really run it between joggers, walkers, moms with strollers, horses, and all the other noise. Out here she could choose a direction and probably run 50K without bumping up against much of anything.

No cities, barely towns.

Montana was a strange place.

Also no machine gun nests, no Taliban with AK47s, or ragheads who'd rather see her dead than walking tall with her dog on point for a military patrol. No parched desert that would kill for even a single mistake, without the aid of fanatics.

"It's different, isn't it?" Colonel Gibson slid silently into the chair beside her—a shadow against shadow. She hadn't heard him approach, not that it surprised her. He probably had some mental map of every creak and loose board on the entire porch tucked away in his head somewhere. She considered for a moment. She only had it about half mapped so far—an unconscious habit.

"More than a little different. Off into bizarre-land." Afghanistan might be more the latitude of Texas than Montana, but she'd seen plenty of the sky. And after dark there should be even less difference to observe.

Yet being here on the ranch was like being on a completely different world.

A hoot of an owl. The heavy flap of wings counterpointed by the high chirp of crickets. The chilly night air was now scented with wood smoke drifting from the cabins. She stuffed her fists deeper into her jacket's pockets.

"Why am I here, Colonel?"

"You'll figure it out. You never give up, Foster. I've seen enough who have, to know. You don't. So you'll get there."

"Asshole."

His silence felt as if it was wrapped around a smile. He certainly didn't contest her accusation.

"Fine. Why are *you* here?"

And the silence shifted and changed. No, it warped. One thing a Delta learned was how to listen. Everything from direction of fire to tracking a sniper by his breathing. She didn't need the twitch of her dog's ear to tell her something had shifted in the man beside her.

"Do you even *know* why you're here?"

Again that long stretch of cricket-filled silence before he answered. "I know why I came."

"That's more than I've got. Puts you ahead of the game."

She could imagine his shrug even if she couldn't see it. *Why* he came, which he wasn't saying anything about. But not why he was *here?* What brought a man like the colonel to a ranch in the Montana Front Range?

He was already married to a Night Stalker captain. Claudia Jean

Casperson was almost as impressive as Emily Beale. Despite her quiet manner, she evoked a knee-jerk respect that couldn't be denied. He had to know that he could trust her, but whatever was clawing at him, he wasn't telling even her. And he hadn't told Emily either.

"Was that what yesterday's fishing trip was?" She looked over at the shadow beside her. By the faint starlight glimmer, she could see by his profile that he was staring out into the night.

"What?"

"Was it you getting away from the ranch to avoid Emily's and Claudia's questions? Or were you looking to get off alone to talk with Mark and I got in the way?"

"You weren't in the way."

"Which means yes to the first question."

He grunted. "Sometimes I forget that I'm not the only asshole here."

"Proud to be. Is it me you're looking to talk to?" There was a scary thought. She was a first sergeant (retired) with fifteen years of service. He was a colonel with something like thirty years in.

His snort of a laugh answered that one.

"You know, you are going to have to talk to someone at some point if you want an answer. You do know that, right?"

Again the silence of an unvoiced shrug.

Who was *she* going to have to talk to? The colonel wasn't giving her any clues. It had better not be Stan and his dog, because there was no way that was going to happen.

She liked Emily well enough—as well as she could like someone so terrifyingly competent. Beautiful woman, two kids, handsome-as-hell husband, illustrious military career, retired to a sprawling horse ranch after four years of flying firefighting helicopters. But Lauren couldn't imagine actually talking to her about anything important, even if she knew what she was supposed to be talking about. It would be like telling the high school beauty that you didn't feel pretty—it was a pointless conversation because the HSB would have no point of reference to give advice from.

Well, she certainly wouldn't be looking for advice from—

"Hey, there!" The porch lights blazed on. She threw an arm over her eyes to cut the glare.

Patrick.

"Sorry."

She risked peeking out and the dark had returned once more, but she still had afterimages of a brightly lit cowboy, complete with hat, blotting out the stars.

In retrospect she recalled that she'd heard his boot heels coming across the stone foyer inside the house. But she'd felt safe enough to not bother tracking it consciously. That was a dangerous precedent for only being two days out of the service. Unless the precedent had been recognizing Patrick's walk. Her subconscious was busy thinking other thoughts, safe in knowing it was him.

He'd looked amazing on the volleyball court. Shirtless, he was even more impressive than merely wearing a wet one. And he had thrown himself into the game with a passion, something so few others besides herself really did. Yet he'd also brought a cheeriness that almost matched Chelsea's—an innate positivity that made him everybody's friend. A skill she'd certainly never had.

"Nathan said he thought you were out here. What are you doing on the porch all alone?"

All alone? She hadn't heard Colonel Gibson depart, but his stealthy departure wasn't any more of a surprise than his silent arrival.

"Mind if I sit with you?"

"Free country."

She was getting back her night senses and could feel his hesitation.

"Sure. Sit where you like."

He fumbled his way along the porch. Only a quick pulling back of her legs kept him from stumbling over them. He discovered Gibson's chair with a barked shin and a soft curse that brought the klutz moniker back to mind.

Did he notice the wood's unusual warmth from it being recently occupied? Or was Gibson so stealthy that he didn't even leave behind a heat imprint? Lauren decided that it was better not to ask.

"Pretty night," Patrick said after a long silence.

"You can do better than that."

"What are you talking about?"

"Patrick, if you're trying to start with a pickup line, 'Pretty night' is pretty lame."

"McCoy in *Streets of Fire.*"

"What are you talking about?"

"Amy Madigan played McCoy in the movie *Streets of Fire.* An obscure little cult classic. You're like that."

"Never heard of it," which came out ruder than she meant it. "Why am I like her?" Not that she was really interested.

"She's this ex-soldier. Always says what she's thinking flat out. No games. You remind me of her. Except that she was short and blonde. She was really rough around the edges."

"Gee, thanks. You really know how to compliment a girl."

"No. Wait. That's not how I mean it. I—"

She let him flounder for a while to see how long it would take him to dig his way out of it. It soon became obvious that if she didn't toss him a hook and line, he'd be lost in the stream for a while. "Thanks for…" *carrying me* was too weak, "…helping me out yesterday."

He stumbled to a halt, apparently relieved to escape his own meandering monologue. "Sure. You okay?"

She shrugged, then remembered that he wasn't Delta and probably couldn't read it in the dark. "I suppose. Never passed out before, but I hadn't slept in a couple days. Or eaten much." Neither of which had anything to do with it. You couldn't be Delta and not take such things in stride. Seeing the spitting image of her own dog resurrected at her feet… She shuddered against the chill night.

Patrick blinked his eyes hard, trying to see something of Lauren. He wished he'd left on a hall light inside, so that it would have at least partly lit the porch.

There had to be some movie like this, but all he could think of was an old saying.

"I was blind but now I see." And that's what it felt like. He'd been just riding along through life. First behind a camera and then on a horse. All of it soft focus—preamble blur under the credits that no one really paid attention to. Then Lauren had stepped in-frame and everything snapped into sharp focus. The director's name scrolled off the screen and the real movie had begun.

The visual impact of Lauren stepping off the helicopter. Her warmth and smell as she'd been cradled in his arms, her head on his shoulder and her arms tucked together between their chests as if an innocent child. And then the shining woman in camo pants and a black sports bra against tanned and battered skin, slicing a volleyball across the net as if it was a weapon of war.

"What are you talking about?" Lauren's voice had none of the soft warmth of a romantic heroine. It was the gruff McCoy of *Streets of Fire* all the way.

"What do you mean?"

"Are you addled? You said *I was blind but now I see.*"

"Uh," he didn't really want to explain that, but he didn't see any easy way out of it. Maybe he'd take a lesson from McCoy and just speak what he was thinking. "I've never seen a woman like you."

"Emily's a retired soldier."

"She's also married to my boss."

"So the fact that I'm single makes me unlike anyone else? What about that mom you were carrying back from the river in your lap?"

"You're jealous of Clara?" *Really?* That gave him some hope. Maybe Lauren *was* attracted to him.

"Why would I be?"

"Okay, so much for my ego." He kind of hoped for a laugh, but didn't get it. Maybe she was smiling in the dark—at least it was nice to think so.

"Are you telling me that you didn't take her out for a tumble in the tall grass last night?"

"No."

"Why not? She was more than willing. Saw the way you couldn't look away from her."

"Because she wasn't you," then he felt the heat flame to his cheeks and was thankful that there wasn't any light at all on the porch.

"You've got a mighty strange view of the world."

Patrick tried, but he couldn't detect any reaction to what he'd just said.

"Is that the Long Island or the Montana part of you?"

"Both! Neither!" Then he gave up. "I'll be damned if I know. I just know that since you showed up, I haven't been able to think of much else."

"I just know that since I showed up, I can't wait to leave."

"Ouch!" And he'd been worried about her going. But that she couldn't *wait* to go was a whole different level of suckitude. The problem, he realized, was that for the first time (perhaps ever), he was looking for something more than a fast tumble in the hay loft. If she went back to New York, would he leave the ranch to follow her?

And the only thing surprising about that thought was that it didn't even surprise him. Maybe he could pick up the filmmaking from where he'd dropped it. But it never worked in the movies. The heroine, because it was always the "hopeful female" trope, followed the hero out of her native element and became resentful at what she had to give up. Of course the hero always won her over to their new life...

He loved ranching.

And Lauren couldn't wait to leave.

"Something wrong, cowboy? I can feel that you just bit down on something nasty."

"How did you know that?"

"Silence isn't just silence, Patrick."

"I like that. It's a neat way to explain things. I've studied directors who aren't afraid to use silence in their films, but I never thought about the different textures of silence."

"Clearly you've never been in Delta."

"You were really in Delta Force?"

"I truly was."

"And a dog handler like Stan?"

"Until my dog was killed." She bit that off hard. He could feel the silence fill with pain.

"Wow!" It was all he could think to say. He'd only had a moment to scan the online entry on them before dinner, but he got the impression that Superman would need to do some serious prep if he wanted to audition for a role in Delta. Though he was pretty sure that Batman would be a shoo in.

"I guess that means that I'm sitting here with Wonder Woman. That's even more daunting then when I thought you were just Lauren Foster."

"*Just* Lauren Foster? I wonder who the hell that is."

He couldn't think of how to answer that, so he went against his nature and kept his mouth shut.

There was one of those long, strange silences that she'd mentioned. He tried to sense the quality of it. Tense? Pensive? Bored? He just wasn't sure, but he was leaning toward some form of tension, as if the air was vibrating in some new register.

Then he heard her rising to her feet. He stood as well and actually bumped elbows with her.

They remained without speaking for several long moments. Tentative? Questioning?

"You actually didn't sleep with Clara in case you got a chance to sleep with me?"

"No. I didn't do anything with Clara because it felt as if I'd be dishonest with her if I did. It wasn't her I would be thinking of, so I didn't..." Patrick trailed off, unsure what else to say. He was supposed to be Robert Redford smooth. Instead he was fast winning the footrace with Hugh Grant for most awkward actor in history. The only step worse was Woody Allen, and he refused to go there.

Another silence, then a soft creak of one of the porch floorboards.

The next moment his world blanked. Lauren shifted against him until he couldn't help but wrap his arms around her. Her kiss started soft. Her lips just the slightest bit cool from the night. But she flowed against him and the kiss heated fast until he wondered if the fire in his brain was glowing through his cowboy hat.

This wasn't a Houston bar in a film. This was Lauren Foster at Henderson's Ranch and nothing else in his experience compared.

She slipped her hands down into his back pockets and yanked their bodies together.

Her hum of pleasure tickled his throat as the fire plummeted out of his brain faster than a descending comet. She was just three inches shorter than his six three and no woman had ever fit against him like this. So long and so lean that he could wrap his arms right around her. And so strong that he doubted he'd be able to escape if he wanted to.

Which he didn't.

Lauren let herself be held. Let herself feel just how amazing a man's body was. It had been a long time and his cowboy-strong shoulders filled her arms as nicely as any soldier she'd ever dallied with.

His kiss was a bone melter. Whether she was the heroine in some movie in his head or herself merely standing in the Montana night, it didn't change a thing. She wanted to touch, feel, hold, take, sate her body until something in her life stopped being a clusterfuck of confusion and even just one thing made sense.

She pushed Patrick back against a post holding up the porch roof in order to gain some leverage. It was so good to just feel. To hell with propriety. Who cared about meaningful or not? Morning-after could deal with itself.

And Patrick wasn't holding back either. She managed to hook a leg over the porch rail and pull them together harder.

He moaned with his need, which was pretty cute.

He also smelled wonderful. She'd become impossibly aware of him during the volleyball game. Each pair a married couple except for the two of them. When he'd peeled his shirt, it was almost impossible to look away. She'd thought only soldiers had that kind of strength, but working on a ranch clearly had its benefits. He was lean, but his body rippled with muscle. Whether facing her to set a spike or showing his back as he leapt high to hammer one down himself, he'd been an amazing sight.

And now she could feel it. One of his big hands against the small of her back more than strong enough to hold them together so tightly it was getting hard to breathe. The other stroked over her. Digging into her hair one moment, sliding down her side and hip to run over her leg and tracing where her knee hooked over the rail the next.

Sure, she'd be gone soon, but why would she care? For one night, let her body plunge and buck to its heart's content. Tomorrow she'd worry about consequences.

And just that fast she was out.

"Damn it!" Lauren buried her face against Patrick's collarbone. "I'm sorry." Tomorrow wasn't the problem. It wasn't the only problem.

He still held her tightly, but his hands had stopped roaming while he waited. Which, in addition to being damned decent of him, also showed that he understood more about silence than he thought.

She wanted to pound her fist against something in frustration. Something hard. But doing it to the luscious man presently wrapped around her would be even less kind.

"What is it?" Patrick's voice was hoarse—hard to blame him.

"I'm a fucked-up mess is what," she eased back against his protests. "I was all set to just use you, even though I'm leaving. I don't even have the decency you showed to Clara."

"Please. Use me!"

She'd laugh if she didn't feel so awful. "You're sweet, Patrick."

"Curse of my life."

"What the hell am I supposed to do with sweet? You know what I'm thinking about right now? When I should be thinking about how amazing you were making me feel?" She tried to back away, but Patrick stopped her with a gentle hold. It wasn't the hard clench of moments before, pinning them together. Instead it was a request. A question. So she stayed in place.

Patrick offered his silence, which was all that let her keep speaking.

"I'm thinking about tomorrow. I'm thinking about being out of the military. It's been my life since high school graduation," plus two weeks of wedding prep she wasn't going to think about. "Before that actually, because I knew by junior year that's what I was going to do. Half my life." She lay her forehead against his shoulder. *Half?* Her *entire* adult life. "I just don't think I could handle another variable right now without going Section 8."

"Section 8?"

"Discharged as mentally unfit for duty."

"Oh, right. Like Corporal Klinger in *M*A*S*H* always wearing dresses."

"Well, I haven't worn one since—" *my aborted wedding* "—a long time, so I might be considered unstable if I wore one now."

"Bet you'd look nice in one."

She leaned back enough to look at his face, but his head was just a silhouette against the stars with a porch-post shadow sticking out of the top.

"A classic," he continued. "Tight waist, pleated skirt," his hand was delicious as it traced down over her hip. "Maybe just above the knees," he traced a line of fire where her leg still hooked over the rail. "Or maybe a men's dress shirt turned blouse," waist and up ribcage to rub against her t-shirt collar, "and a mid-calf skirt that teased and hinted at good legs. I bet you have great legs, Lauren."

"I do." Enough soldiers had told her so when she wore shorts and went out for a run.

He made a thoughtful *hmmm* sound.

"Get that image out of your head, Patrick."

"Nope. Not working. Seems that I'm gonna be stuck with it. Not that I'm complaining."

She swung her leg clear and pushed off his chest until they were standing a little apart.

"Now I *do* have something to complain about." His hand lingered on her hip for a moment before sliding free.

"Sorry," and she actually was. The chilly night air slipping in the front of her jacket only emphasized how good he had felt pressed against her.

"You could make it up to me."

"Why doesn't this sound good," as if turning down a nice man once in a night wasn't enough.

"We've got a hunting party going out tomorrow. It's sort of a yearly celebration around here. Get some elk and maybe even bear meat for the freezer. Come with us."

"Hunting."

"Sure. We've got this guy comes in each year who likes going after the elk—his favorite game. He's a good guide and it has sort of turned into a thing each fall for the two of us and anyone else who's in the mood. You should come."

Lauren felt as if she was walking into a trap, but couldn't quite see her way out of it. Though she could use some time out in the field. One last walk into the wild before heading back to the concrete canyons of New York.

"What do you say?"

"I'd say that I don't trust your motives, cowboy."

"Wa'll ma'am," he did a decent John Wayne—even she knew who he was imitating. "Ain't none in these parts is gonna call you dumb. Leastwise not in my presence they ain't gon' dare." He ran his hand down her waist and hip to make his motives absolutely clear, but he didn't grab for her breast or try to pull her back in, which was in his favor.

"So you have nefarious and evil designs to have your way with me even though I'm a royally screwed-up mess?"

"Yes, ma'am." Still John Wayne.

She placed a hand on his chest to keep him in place while she brushed a light kiss across his lips. "I'll think about it."

"Think on it hard, Lauren," Patrick was back and surprisingly earnest. This wasn't the sound of simple lust. He meant it.

"I will."

"Promise?"

Again that laugh that almost tickled its way free. "Sure."

"Say the words."

"I promise," but they didn't slip out as easily as she'd thought they would. Needing distance, she stepped away quickly and headed inside. Closing the door softly, the ongoing hum in her body made her thankful that Patrick was now on the other side.

A single light was still on in the kitchen when she passed through, a reading lamp over in the seating area by the fireplace.

Lauren debated seeing who else was still awake. A part of her voted for hiding under the covers and ignoring the unexpected flare of need that Patrick had awakened in her.

Her feet apparently decided this wasn't a democracy and headed toward the light in search of a distraction from exactly those kinds of thoughts.

"Out kinda late for a cowboy, cowboy."

"Maybe I found some nightlife," Patrick ignored Stan. He was stretched out on the lower bunk, reading the latest Lee Child thriller. He had a bit of rubber clamped in his steel hooks to help him turn the pages.

"Not that late. Which one dumped your sorry excuse for manhood? Clara or your movie fantasy chick?"

"Were you always an asshole or is that Army training?" He shucked down to his underwear and grabbed a toothbrush from the sink. The bunkhouse had four double rooms and a shared bath, but each room also had a private sink, which he appreciated.

"Born this way. Refined by the best trainers anywhere. And that's *Navy,* you idiot. SEAL? Remember?" There was no heat behind it. He barely glanced away from his book.

Patrick offered him a toothpaste grin. Of course he knew SEALs were Navy after two years of living together. Which made it a perfect target. That, and Lauren had the US Army on his brain. For all the good it was doing him now. Instead of continuing the fiery kiss as a fantastic tumble together, he was back in the bunkhouse with a one-armed Navy SEAL.

The building was old, but in good shape. He liked the old plank wood walls of knotty pine. It was everything a ranch bunkhouse should be, right down to the Cheyenne tribal-style blankets that Mark's mother had woven for each bed. Brightly colored, the geometric shapes added a real character and warmth. The space was too close to shoot film in, even with a Red 4K digital camera, but it was like living in a movie set. Hard used, but still cozy.

Yeah, a great place, except for the grumpy one-armed dog trainer rather than the lithe, sexy Delta operator.

"Asshole," Stan muttered under his breath as he turned the page. He never liked being caught rising to the bait.

Patrick spit into the worn porcelain sink and studied his reflection in the small medicine cabinet mirror.

So…was he the hero? She'd kissed him as if he was. Like she really meant it. *Meant it? Shoot!* Lauren had kissed him in a way that no previous lover had ever prepared him for. Unleashed, intense, no hesitancy at all. It was an all-out kiss of hot passion that still had him tingling from head to toe. *Figure out how to capture that on film and it would be a sellout.*

"I'm guessing by how late it *isn't*," Stan didn't look up from his book, "that the sultry Clara turned you down."

"Didn't even go there."

"Seriously?" Stan looked up from his book for the first time, narrowing his eyes as if Patrick had somehow changed. "You really do have that Army dame on the brain, don't you?"

"That Army dame was a Delta Force soldier."

"They're called operators," he tossed aside his book and released the straps of his prosthetic arm.

Patrick filed that away for later use. "Worked with dogs, like you. Maybe that explains the way Rip reacted to her."

"Maybe… No dog ever reacted to me that way."

"Well, if you took a shower once in a while."

Stan stopped working on his arm for a moment to give Patrick the finger. Then he got the arm off and slid it under the edge of the bunk. He unrolled the protective sock off the odd stump that Patrick had never quite grown used to, so he looked away. It seemed politer to do so.

"Said she was a handler. Until she lost her dog." Patrick decided his grass-stained jeans were past redemption and chucked them in the laundry pile. However, the shirt was clean since the volleyball game and smelled slightly of Lauren. He tossed it over a chair for tomorrow.

Patrick turned for his bunk and froze.

Stan stared at him—the color leached out of his face.

"What?"

"She lost her dog?" Stan's voice was rough.

"It's not like she misplaced it somewhere." Stan didn't get to be pissed at her. It sounded like she had enough on her plate. "Said it was killed."

Stan, Mr. Unflappable SEAL, actually flinched.

"What?"

"You see this?" Stan waved his stump at him. "Really look at it."

Patrick did. Stan's arm had been cut off mid-biceps. The flesh folded strangely at the end of the stump. Stan's big shoulder muscles tapered to nothing at the end of his stump right where his other biceps bulged. He looked at his own arm and tried to imagine what it would be like if three-quarters of it was gone, and couldn't. It was too much a part of him.

"This is nothing—*Nothing!*—compared with losing a dog. God damn it! Don't know why I didn't see it. Thought she was weak when she fainted. But turning around to see Rip sitting at her feet... Shit! I really should have seen it. No wonder Colonel Gibson is hovering over her so much."

Stan's face was a study of pain and fury that made Patrick both wish for a camera and be glad he didn't have one. It was such a pure emotion, but it was also far too personal to try to use.

He aimed his stump right at Patrick's face, making him take a step back. "You don't treat her right, cowboy, and I hear about it—you're fucking toast. We clear on that?"

"Uh, sure."

"Sure," Stan scoffed. He flicked off the light. "Get some sleep and do your best not to be your usual self around her."

Patrick found his way into the upper bunk in the dark.

Stan didn't have to worry about not treating her right. She'd already walked away from him and left him standing in the dark.

But Stan was wrong about Lauren being fragile. She'd said she was a mess, but that, too, was part of the leading lady's role. A mess, but already so magnificently strong that the audience could only hold its breath, awaiting the moment when she'd discover that inner truth.

And Lauren hadn't exactly turned him down. There was still a chance. A chance that would be vastly improved if she came out with the hunting party.

And the hero settles in, excited by the possibilities of what tomorrow will bring.

But the possibility of what? Normally he'd be shrugging off his disappointment that some female ranch guest hadn't been as willing as she'd first seemed. He knew he was good-looking enough that once things started, they rarely stopped, but it happened.

This felt different. He wanted…

He wasn't sure what he wanted.

A chance to play with Lauren's fantastic body? The way they'd been pressed together, there was no question about the visuals not matching reality—he'd never held any woman who felt like that.

He wanted…

More.

Real deep there, Mr. Gallagher.

That didn't tell him *what* he wanted more of. He…liked her. Her fierceness on the volleyball court and in his arms. Her quiet, observer silence at other times. Her honesty and integrity in not wanting to use him, no matter how willing he'd been to let her.

She was a fascinating character with richness and depth. She had secrets and internal conflicts that showed only briefly above the surface of her Delta cool. Her beauty hadn't gone to her head; she acted as if it wasn't a magnet for every eye in the vicinity.

He wanted...Lauren Foster. Not just any woman. He wanted *her*. And not just for some fun.

Well, that was new as well.

Now that the hero has plotted his course...

If only he had a clue what was going on with the heroine.

"You're up late," Lauren said softly so as not to wake the baby asleep in Emily's arms.

"Uh," Emily barely managed a response. She sat in one of the deep leather wingback chairs wearing a bright yellow terrycloth bathrobe with her slippered feet propped up on an ottoman. Her own head was back as if exhausted, but her arms were rocking the baby. She looked so unlike the powerful woman Lauren had met on her first arrival that she half wondered if Emily had a twin.

"Like your slippers."

"Mark's idea of a creative Christmas present," Emily blinked at her blearily. The slippers were shaped and colored like the ugliest trout imaginable, with big smiles and googly eyes.

"Not surprised. You should have seen him when I was the only one able to catch any fish." Lauren settled into the chair close beside Emily. The baby had Mark's dark hair and built-in tan coloring overlaid on Emily's fine features. "She's cute." Unlike most babies in Lauren's limited experience, this one actually was.

"Cute. Let me tell you about cute. I was fast asleep and then Belle started fussing. I didn't want her waking Tessa, my four-year-old, so I brought her out here. Cute? Never have two kids together. You might skip having even one."

"Then why are you looking at her like that?"

"Like what?"

"Like you couldn't love her more if you tried?"

Emily grimaced but it did nothing to change her expression. "Maybe I do. But at the moment I'd rather be asleep. I think one of my arms already is."

"I could hold her for a while." And where had that come from? Lauren had never held a baby in her life.

"Would you? I really need a moment to not be Mom."

And before Lauren could so much as blink, she had an armful of blanket-wrapped child. Once she got over the initial nerves, she could only look down at it in surprise. "She's so small."

"Won't last," Emily stood and shook out her arm. "Motherhood changes you in so many ways. Good ways, but it never stops. Tea?"

"Sure." Lauren leaned close over the baby. A whiff of talcum powder and... "Oh, my god!"

"What?"

"Belay the tea. We have a DEFCON 2 nasal alert going on over here."

Emily groaned. "I'll be right back." True to her word, she was back with a big carryall before the vapors emanating off the child had quite melted Lauren's face off.

"How can you sleep through that?" she asked the child.

"Wrong question," Emily set out a plastic sheet on the ottoman. "The real question is how she does it so constantly. Tessa went through less than half the diapers. If I'd known what a blessing that was, I might have appreciated it more at the time...though I doubt it."

Despite her complaints, it was under two minutes flat that the rebundled baby—who'd barely roused for the procedure—lay once more in Lauren's arms, smelling mostly of talcum powder this time as Emily bagged the poop explosion.

"Thankfully it wasn't a bad one."

"That wasn't a bad one? Oh, my god! Sign me up for no kids. Definitely."

"You'll change your tune once you find the right man," Emily returned to making the tea and had it done before Lauren had quite adapted to the tiny child in her arms. "It's some sort of a curse—a foul magic that radiates from him that makes an otherwise rational woman want to bear his child." She slouched back in her chair cradling her mug of steaming chamomile tea like a lifeline. But she had a soft smile as she looked down at her child asleep in Lauren's arms.

"Maybe I'll just swear off men." The right man? What man would make her want to go through all of the pain and trouble? Though Belle did look sweeter than a Peanut Butter and Banana Cream from Doughnut Plant in the Hotel Chelsea. It was easy to imagine a child with Patrick's softly curling hair and easy smile.

And it was easy to imagine that she'd completely lost it and belonged in a psych ward—Section 8 and all.

"Doesn't work, does it?" Emily was smiling at her over her tea mug.

"What doesn't?"

"Pretending to ourselves that we aren't thinking about them."

"I—" Lauren shut her mouth. Being Delta, she'd learned to keep her mouth shut when she didn't have anything to say. But she should be able to come up with some good defense, argument, or at least a decent denial.

"I spent months trying not to think about Mark. First he was my commanding officer, but years before that he saved my life. Fished me out of a jungle hellhole in the wrong part of Thailand. He's the reason I applied to the Night Stalkers—gunning to be beside him. Never figured on a man that amazing noticing me, but at least I'd get to serve with him."

"What happened when he did notice you?"

"I honestly don't remember. I remember his kiss because it was impossible to forget *that*. Men are not supposed to have that kind of power over my body—but he did. He claims that I slammed him head-first into a dining table on an aircraft carrier, then climbed in as passenger on an F/A-18F Super Hornet, but all I remember is that kiss. Came out of nowhere and almost knocked me on my ass. One moment he was raging at me and the next we were in full lip-lock."

"Well, that wasn't quite my reaction…" All she'd done was melt against Patrick while her body begged him to ravage her past all reason.

"Thought so," Emily was nodding as if she'd just won a bet with herself.

"What?"

"You don't strike me as a woman big on fooling herself, Lauren."

"I'm not."

"Then don't."

"But I'm—" not... Except she was. She was thinking about when was her next chance to test herself with Patrick. A chance to find that inner part of her that had indeed gone soft and mushy as he held her. She blew out a hard breath that briefly unsettled Belle, who gurgled, then turned her face into Lauren's breast and went back to sleep. What would it be like to have her own child do that?

Her *own* child?

She quickly shuffled the baby back into her mother's arms. "What are you trying to do to me, Emily?"

"Nothing intentional," she said softly. Emily rose, offered a nod and a yawn, then shuffled from the room in her trout slippers without another word.

Lauren trusted her words, but she wasn't so sure about trusting Emily's silence.

"Where's Claudia?" Lauren missed her at the breakfast table. Mark was gone as well. Only Emily and Michael remained. No kid. They sat alone, yet in silence. It didn't feel awkward. It also wasn't filled with questions like Emily's silence last night. It was simply...silence—silence with coffee mugs. Neither of them talking and neither one uncomfortable with that.

Lauren had risen with the sun, but the ranch hands had already eaten and cleared out. No sign of Patrick, but she wasn't going to satisfy Emily's knowing look by asking about *his* whereabouts.

"Claudia was called back in. Mark's flying her to Great Falls airport right now."

Lauren vaguely remembered the sounds of a departing helicopter as she'd woken. The little JetRanger was so quiet compared to a Black Hawk that it definitely wasn't what had dragged her from sleep.

No, it was the rather lurid dream. A lurid dream that had prompted a long cold shower and made her miss the others at breakfast. It didn't include Patrick's face... But it might have included the feel of him and she most definitely was not comfortable with that.

"But you weren't called?" she asked Michael as Nathan delivered one of his breakfast platters and a steaming mug. The caffeine slammed her hard—hard enough to pretend the dream hadn't been quite the serious breach of internal security that it had felt like in the first place.

Michael shook his head. "I was ordered to take a leave of absence."

Emily's mug, which had been raised high to empty the dregs, fell to the table and shattered against her heavy stoneware plate. She goggled at Michael but couldn't seem to speak. Which meant that it was news of an unprecedented scale.

"I take it that doesn't happen to you much?" Lauren asked, enjoying her own serene calm in the face of Emily's shock.

"Last time was the week before I was engaged to Claudia."

"Sounds more like a vacation than enforced leave. Though it's a story I'd pay to hear." Not that there was any chance of Michael spilling a single detail. Claudia she might have been able to get some juicy tidbits from, but not Colonel Michael Gibson.

"What? You mean tell you what happened after I proposed?" And Michael's expression actually softened at whatever that memory might be.

"I'm guessing that included great sex and a remote location. I meant you proposing, because I'm sure that you did it without saying anything."

"We've both always had a preference for remote locations," Michael's infinitesimal smile said that he too was enjoying the banter and Emily's complete discomfiture. And his shrug about a silent proposal was eloquent. Maybe for the first time in his career, Michael was on inactive status until *someone else* said he was back in.

"Are you hurt?"

He just shook his head. No *wonder* Emily had been so shocked. Now she was starting to feel it herself. What was going on that the Delta commander had taken Michael, his Number One field operator, off the front line?

Emily finally managed to gather the broken chunks of her mug, dump them on her empty plate, and shove the whole thing aside. "Does Claudia know?"

"This morning. Before she left." Michael shrugged.

"Did you also tell her—"

"Yes," Michael's growl told her to keep her mouth shut, which had Emily looking back and forth between the two of them. Lauren was down with that, so kept her thoughts about gruff men telling their wives that they loved them to herself.

"So you filled her in and then shuffled her off to keep Emily and me from questioning her?"

"I think my wife is made of sterner stuff than you think."

Lauren glanced over at Emily. Their shared look said that, between them, they could have gotten around Claudia's defenses.

But there was no chance of getting around Michael's.

Emily opened her mouth to try anyway when a gurgling sound came out of her phone. She was on her feet and gone before the sound rose to a questioning cry. Baby monitor app.

Michael looked down at his empty mug, then over at Lauren's plate. Once again, she'd eaten Nathan's food without really tasting it. Damn! It was a soldier's habit—and she'd make sure that it was one of the first she broke.

He rose, and Lauren knew by his look that she was supposed to follow.

As Patrick waved at the Mooney M20E Chaparral circling down to land, he was sorry to have missed Lauren at breakfast. The single-engine airplane circled once more before lining up to land on the roadway. The dirt and gravel road was broad enough to be a landing strip for small planes. It ran between the fences that separated Larson and Henderson pastures and led to both of the ranches' driveways. A bright orange windsock fluttered slightly in the gentle morning breeze.

It was shortly after sunrise and it was a fine day. Mack Bryson, the pilot, knew the routine and had radioed ahead so that Patrick would be waiting to drop a section of the fence line. Touchdown kicked puffs of dirt off the three wheels, then the plane slowed abruptly. In moments, the pilot had taxied through the gap in the fence into the lower field with a throbbing roar of the three-bladed propeller, then shut it down in the tall grass.

Mack had taken him up in it last year and Patrick had decided that having a horse as his primary mode of transportation was just fine. The Chaparral was the fastest production single-engine airplane of its day and still moved fast enough to give him the willies.

"Hi, Mack," Patrick called out once the engine went silent and the pilot's door swung open.

"Howdy, youngster," Mack's reply was cheery and his handshake enthusiastic if not the strongest. Of course the guy was old and even thinner than a young Jimmy Stewart, though with none of his height. He looked about as heavy as a feather, but Patrick had learned over the last couple years not to underestimate him when he was on the trail of an elk.

"Growing shorter, Old Man." Mack didn't even reach Patrick's shoulder and was probably older than his grandfather, though he'd never asked. The word *wizened* didn't fit someone so impossibly cheery.

"Still on the right side of the ground, youngster," he was wholly unflappable.

At first, Patrick had doubted Mack's memory, but over the years he'd proven it was just fine—he simply labeled all men under fifty, maybe sixty, with the same moniker.

"Tie her down for me, would you? I don't bend so easy anymore."

"Sure thing, Mack." There were a couple sets of iron rings anchored in concrete pilings that they kept Weed Eatered for fly-in guests. He ran a pair of ropes up from the rings to the loops on the underside of the low wings as Mack unloaded his gear. Just being around Mack made Patrick feel as if he was in a May-December buddy film. He'd asked around and Mack Bryson made everyone feel that way.

"How are the elk running this year?"

"Saw a herd up by the Miller campsite two days back."

"Lowlanders. No real sport in picking off from a lowland herd. Up into the hills, boy. That's the ticket." Then he winked. "Unless them lowlanders need some thinning."

"All looked fine and healthy to me."

"Into the Flathead Wilderness it is. Grab the pack for me." Mack took his rifle case, which was almost as long as he was, and strode off through the tall grass.

Patrick always looked forward to this trip and he wondered who else would be along for the ride. He could always hope…but he wasn't taking any bets on whether or not Lauren would be along. She'd already been camping one night and he didn't know if she'd want to go out again so soon. Some guests wanted to spend as much time in the wild as they could, others didn't like leaving the cozy security of their cabins and the main compound. Except she wasn't a guest. She was… He didn't know what.

She was a mystery.

He'd signed up to be the guide with Mack again this year, but that was before he'd met Lauren. Before he'd *kissed* Lauren. Before he'd spent half the night wondering where she'd been all his life, when he already knew the answer.

Sergeant Lauren Foster had been in the Army: Rangers and Delta.

While she'd been in the military, he'd spent a couple of years doing crap jobs before going back for his film degree. Then a couple of years making films and supporting himself with odd jobs in theaters, mostly as a sound or props guy in off-off-Broadway productions. Then he'd come west. He supposed it was possible that he could have gotten further away from a military career path, but he wasn't sure how.

There was no question about Mack and a cozy cabin. The old man must have been up seriously early to fly in from the Oregon Coast—crossing the Rockies in the dark—but he headed straight for the barn with a spring in his step, raring to get out into the wilderness.

The layout of the entire compound had been clearly mapped inside Lauren's head since their aerial arrival, though she had yet to scout it out on the ground to align purpose with layout. She told herself that's why she didn't quite connect where Michael was leading her until it was too late. It was either that, or she *wanted* to go there—and she didn't like that possibility one bit.

They circled around the back of the main house, including past her bedroom window. The place was bigger than it looked. The upstairs, where the family lived, was actually bigger than the main story, by jutting out over the back porch. This would be a good spot to sit and watch the hills on a hot summer's day. It was oriented northeast and would be warm in the morning and the coolest spot for the rest of the day.

There was a freshness to the air that she hadn't run into in very many places. Lackland Air Force Base—the main center for military war dog training—lay baking in the semi-arid scrubland of central Texas. She'd spent the most of her time at Fort Bragg, North Carolina, or the Dust Bowl hell of America's two wars in southwest Asia. The year she'd spent on Libyan patrols was best not remembered. New York often smelled amazing, and occasionally very nasty—impossibly thick with the richness of people, food, and commerce.

Here, under the everlasting blue bowl of the sky, it tasted as if the air had swept down out of the Canadian Rockies arriving washed, tumbled, and dried straight from the Arctic and the Canadian tundra. It was still cool with the morning, but it felt so good that she kept her jacket in her hand rather than pulling it on. It tasted as if the last one to breathe this air might have been a polar bear. Or maybe—

She yelped in surprise as they stepped up to a fence line just past the garage. They'd broken into the sunshine at the edge of the west pasture. She didn't need to see the occupants of the corral to know what it was.

Half of the area was open field, but the other half was the most impressive dog training agility setup she'd ever seen off a military base. Slalom gates for side-to-side work. Long, snaking, eighteen-inch-high tubes that taught a dog how to race low and fast. Staggered hurdles to be cleared clean, and high walls that would require a dog to plant its paws on the top to haul itself up and complete the jump.

Ladders led to either end of a narrow ledge fixed high above a splash pool to ease the dog's fall if it stumbled. There were even old cars and SUVs with the side windows down to teach them how to leap into a car in full attack mode to take down a driver.

Beyond the corral was an old RV, a decrepit bunkhouse, and a few other outbuildings given over to dog training. She'd wager that somewhere in the hills, well away from any skittish horses, would be a crash-and-bang field to inure the animals to the sounds of gunfire and explosives.

At length she managed to focus through her overwhelm and see that the course wasn't empty. Stan had six dogs leashed to stakes in a line. Two merely watched the seventh dog running the course. Two others looked to be eagerly awaiting their turn. It would take time to determine if they were overly aggressive or had that fine balance of patient-but-also-a-hard-charger that made a good MWD. There was one small scruffy mutt, but he appeared unselfconscious about being half the size of his mates.

The last Malinois was asleep and probably didn't have what it took to make the grade.

Or so she thought until suddenly its head popped up and twisted in her direction. The dog leapt to its feet and charged. He hit the end of his leash so hard that it yanked the stake right out of the ground and the dog kept coming. She wasn't wearing a bite suit. This was going to hurt like hell.

With a quick flip, she spun the jacket she'd been clutching in her hand around her forearm and presented it crosswise at chest height. The dog would naturally go for the raised forearm. She shifted in front of Michael to protect him and braced herself for the impact.

The dog's racing stride—stretched to its limit—crossed the space in seconds.

In her peripheral vision she saw Stan turn. Assess. Shout.

Too little, too late.

The big, all-black Malinois had already launched. His paws barely touched the top rail as he cleared the four-foot-high fence.

Rather than taking the bait of her raised forearm, he punched into her with all fours, two on her shoulders and two on her thighs. She crashed backward, knocking Michael aside as she did so.

She tucked her chin, hoping against any hope to protect her neck from being torn apart by his powerful canines.

He let out a loud bark that made her ears ring and then licked her face as Stan hustled up to haul him off.

The dog sat on her knees, keeping his forepaws firmly planted on her chest, one quiet painfully on one bruised breast.

"What the hell, Rip?" Stan snarled—more surprise than anger by the sound. He had his real hand around the leash, but didn't haul the dog clear.

She reached up to shift the paw off her breast, which the dog used as an excuse to lie down on her—paws on either shoulder and his head tucked up under her chin hard enough to choke her if she'd been able to breathe with eighty pounds of dog on her chest.

"I think he likes you," Michael dusted himself off as he rose to stand beside Stan.

"Off!" Lauren managed to grunt by hardening her diaphragm against the weight.

Rip popped to his feet, once more driving his claws painfully into her skin, then moved off to the dirt close beside her and sat.

She pushed herself up to sitting. She and the dog were face-to-face.

"What?"

Rip merely offered her a goofy grin, then licked her face again.

She scratched the dog's ear. "Huh!"

"What?" Stan still had a tight hold on the leash.

"First time I've touched a dog since…"

Stan nodded. "Know what you mean," he held up his hooks to say just what had happened between his last dog and the present one. Then he turned and looked at the other Malinois that had followed him over from the obstacle course and now sat at *his* side.

She could see the hard-faced man soften impossibly. It was a change that absolutely identified him as a born-and-bred dog handler.

"You've got something, Lauren Foster. Rip's got a ton of potential, but I've been wondering if he cared enough to really make the grade. Can find the explosives just fine, but not real motivated about it. However, he definitely sees something in you."

"Rip?" The dog's ears perked up. "Thought he was going to rip my throat out."

"Nah," Stan chuckled. "He's named for Rip Van Winkle. Even as a puppy he'd do that asleep one moment, at the ready the next moment trick."

It felt strangely as if she'd been the one asleep. She climbed to her feet. Patted the dog once firmly on the side to let it know it wasn't the dog's fault before she turned and walked away.

"Hey, Lauren. You look like you've seen a ghost." Patrick had rushed out of the barn when he saw her walking across the yard. He had the distinct impression that if he hadn't spoken, she'd have run squarely into him without noticing.

"I did," her voice was soft and dreamy, but not in any way he'd been hoping for after last night. "At least I think so," she turned and looked about her feet as if expecting to find something there, then looking up at him in confusion when she didn't find anything.

"You okay?" She looked as fragile as the moment *after* she'd collapsed on her arrival.

"So not!" That sounded more like her. "Let's get out of here."

Us? That sounded awesome to him. "Sure, where?"

"Couldn't care. Away."

Then he remembered Mack's trip. "How about there?" and he pointed toward the mountains.

She followed the direction of his arm like a sleepwalker. "Sure. That works just fine."

"We leave in twenty minutes. Grab some clothes and foul weather gear just in case. Figure on two or three days. I'll take care of throwing together a kit for you: bedroll, food, and so on."

"Uh, sure." She headed off in the direction of the house. All her sharp edges were gone. He had the impression that if he'd told her to walk straight into a rushing river, she'd have done so with just as little emotion.

But he didn't care. It wasn't quite the leap into his arms and drag him into the hay barn he might have been hoping for as a morning-after-the-first-kiss moment. Not even a decent smile. Or one at all, really. But she was going with them and that counted for almost everything.

"She okay?" Michael came up behind him.

"Looks fine." Who was he kidding, she looked incredible. "But didn't sound very happy."

"Huh," Michael's grunt was thoughtful. "Overheard the last of it. Where are you going?"

"Hunting up in the Flathead. Room for more if you want to join in." He wished he'd kept his mouth shut, but it was ranch policy. Always encourage adventure. He didn't know what their relationship was, father-daughter-but-not in some strange way. He'd rather have Lauren to himself, away from Michael's watchful eye, but it was too late to take it back.

"Who else?"

"Small party. One guest. Emily said she'd come. Something about leaving Mark with the kids for once. Though they have a nanny too. Normally Mark Sr. and Ama come along, but they're still on their vacation. Julie, my brother's fiancée, is just back from leading a trip into the Flathead and wants a few days off before her wedding."

Michael didn't look at the Rockies or Patrick. Instead he kept watching Lauren as she reached the house and climbed the front stairs.

Patrick supposed that it was trudging for Lauren, but she was so damned graceful.

"Target?"

For a second Patrick wondered if Michael was asking if Lauren was the target. She was definitely his target, but... "Elk. For the freezer. Maybe some bear."

"Always heard that hunting for bear is just plain dumb."

"We don't go looking for them, but up in the Flathead, they aren't shy about looking in on us."

Michael nodded. "Let's see what you have for weapons."

"Don't you want to get some gear?"

Michael looked down at his clothes—boots, pants, t-shirt, and jacket—then back up at Patrick. He offered a shrug. "Have a rain slick I can borrow?"

That's when he figured out who the guy was. He'd imagined Lauren walking into the wilderness with nothing but a dog. The scars on her skin said she could survive anything. This "old guy" must be another one like her. He didn't look like much, but Stan said he was Colonel Gibson, which sounded pretty high up. If he was also Delta Force, it would explain a lot about him.

Maybe he was Lauren's commanding officer, which explained even more. Now their odd interdependence made sense.

As he led Michael into the barn to review Chelsea's arms locker, Patrick tried to imagine what their relationship would look like if that was the case. Part father. Part guardian. Part judge. *Are you good enough, Sergeant Foster?* Protective, yet a harsh taskmaster. The father figure to the soldier woman who'd lost her dog.

Cool! He really *was* living out a film role in real life.

Patrick glanced up at the casting director in the sky, sending aloft a silent request. *Please give me better casting today than being the sidekick.*

CHAPTER 6

Lauren eased herself out of her saddle and wondered if the insides of her legs were ever going to recover. They'd ridden straight through the morning, crossing the full breadth of the ranch.

The character of the ground had changed as they neared the mountains, but Patrick led the way with the surety of someone who'd come this way many times before. What had started as cantering across the broad grasslands of the lower ranch had turned into carefully picked out routes along the base of scree slopes and following winding deer paths through deep forests.

Bypassing a quaint fishing cabin that already had a riding party in residence, they finally stopped for lunch at the base of a powerful waterfall. What would it be like to have your own private waterfall that cascaded in tumbling cataracts over fifty feet of combined drops? Closest thing to that in the Big Apple was the Lincoln Center fountain, which wasn't on quite the same scale. Or the same solitude.

"Morning," Patrick strolled up to her showing none of the effects of the long ride.

Lauren glanced up at the sun, "Afternoon."

Patrick checked his watch, then shrugged easily. He took her thoughtless insensitivity in stride rather than throwing it back at her. He *had* left much of New York behind. More than she was ready to do.

"Nice waterfall," she tried to make it up to him as he lashed her mount's reins to a log hitching post clearly placed for just such moments. Collette was a dog's name in her experience, maybe for a French poodle. But the tall Montana Traveler—nearly pure black with just a hint of dark red that caught the sunlight—was so even-tempered and surefooted that it was easy to imagine her indeed having French blood. Chelsea had made a big deal in the barn of choosing this particular horse for her. Lauren didn't know why it mattered, as she'd be gone soon enough, but the herd manager had said it was important and delayed the whole party while she'd considered the options and finally selected Colette.

Lauren did like that the horse's ambling gait was quick enough that others had to occasionally trot to keep up, except for Emily's tall Chesapeake. She'd looked forward to riding beside Emily, and she had —before the trails narrowed to single file. There hadn't been anything to say, but Lauren enjoyed the companionship nonetheless.

"It *is* a nice waterfall," Patrick tipped back his cowboy hat to survey its full height. He tucked his thumbs in his belt as if he'd been personally responsible for it. "Only one more than a few feet high on the whole property. Nice big lake up above with plenty of fish in it."

"You told me a story about a waterfall..." Then she remembered what it was and wished she'd kept her mouth shut.

Patrick was still looking up at the falls, so he missed her grimace of pain. "Up there past the top," he pointed. "Stan was out hiking in the spring and, trust me, the falls are truly amazing when the spring runoff is slamming out of the wilderness. Got caught in a t-shirt during a white-out blizzard. Apparently he fell part way down the falls, but managed to crawl off to the side, about there, I guess."

Lauren surveyed the steep rocky slopes to either side. Today was warm and sunny, and she wouldn't be comfortable climbing to that point without a rope and some gear. Stan had done it while freezing to death in a white-out.

"Said he was ready to give up right there, but Bertram latched on to his false arm and wouldn't let go. Half gone with hypothermia, he barely knew where he was, but Bertram led him all the way back to that fishing cabin, if that ain't the damnedest thing."

Lauren looked back down the valley but couldn't see the cabin they'd left far behind. It must have been pure hell. No wonder Stan credited the dog with saving his life—there was no doubt that Bertram had.

How many times had the dogs saved her life? Max and Rex? Max she'd left behind because he was a regular Army asset, not trained to Special Ops standards when she'd started scouting for the 75th Rangers. Rex when she'd made the cut for Delta and he'd retired into old age. And Jupiter. Jupiter, who she'd left behind in a shallow grave in the Afghan desert. Her dogs had warned her of IEDs, hunted down hostiles, even leaped to the attack to protect her.

And what had been her reaction to Rip's unlikely greeting? She'd staggered back to her room lost in some zombie haze. It had taken her thirty seconds to assemble her gear for the ride—and ten minutes kneeling over the toilet puking her guts out until she was stopped by the sheer agony of being convulsively sick long after she'd emptied out her breakfast.

She still felt light-headed despite the long morning's ride.

"Just glad it wasn't me," Patrick was still surveying the cliff as if trying to figure out how to film it for one of his movies. "Don't know if I'd have survived it."

Lauren looked around for somewhere to go, but it was just the five of them, their horses, and miles of wilderness. If her life came down to a moment like that, would she have survived? What had it taken Stan to face *his* dog again? To trust his very life to Bertram?

She couldn't imagine how he'd done it.

Lauren wasn't avoiding him, but neither was she cozying up.

That wasn't how the script was supposed to run. Patrick decided that the bright side was that he'd been right about not going after

Clara. That one single moment with Lauren had brushed aside any doubt.

And dropped a new load of doubts in its place.

By editing out the one scene and inserting another—another cheery romp in the high grass with a cheerfully willing ranch guest traded for a single kiss from the taciturn, emotionally chaotic heroine—he'd changed the entire course of the story. With a single gesture, he'd tossed out the familiar script of his life. So what came next?

He'd turned from telling Stan's story of the waterfall adventure—which was so cinematic that he'd written it as three full pages in the Montana ranch screenplay he was no longer writing—to discover that he'd been talking to himself. Lauren had moved away to stand by Mack, the lucky old coot. They were chatting away about horses as if it was the only thing happening in the world.

He didn't worry about Mack stepping into the hero role. First, it would be beyond a May-December romance and second, he knew that Mack and Nancy had been happily married for fifty-five years. But that knowledge didn't harness his rampant imagination.

All through lunch his inner scriptwriter tried to stage a *Harold and Maude* moment, when it should be seeking an original story.

As they rode deeper into the Flathead Wilderness, he realized that had been the problem with his earlier films. They were all derivative. *The African Queen* and *E.T.* weren't derivative. So how had Huston and Spielberg done it? Even Ron Howard's *Apollo 13*—taken straight from real life—had avoided that curse.

Was his entire life derivative?

Billy Joel: just another boy out of Long Island.

Failed filmmaker: so utterly cliché.

Off-off-Broadway stagehand: never aspiring to the big houses around Times Square.

Right out of a John Denver song: seeking a Rocky Mountain High.

And finding it.

He loved the ranch. At least that didn't feel derivative.

He looked around and couldn't imagine being anywhere else. He was presently leading the ride up the North Fork Deep Creek. Boulder-strewn, a couple of dozen feet wide, they were beyond trails. He led them time and again into the water when forest and cliff left him no choice.

Mack was the only other truly skilled rider, happily astride his favorite sorrel Morgan, Rambler. Emily wasn't far behind, though it was clear that she hadn't been born to horses. Of course neither had he, that's how he recognized Emily's few shortcomings.

Lauren had adapted so quickly that it was easy to discredit his first impression of her marginal competence. Michael rode well, but not happily. Still, when the trail opened up a bit, Patrick kept the pace slow. Riding hard over rough ground would be a skill neither soldier had yet learned.

Not another soul for miles around. Just the five of them and the wilderness.

In that moment, breathing in the pure air, listening to the creek bubbling its way down a small rapids, he knew that he'd never be leaving here. It wasn't even a revelation, but rather simple truth.

And what did that mean about Lauren?

Back to New York. She'd made that goal absolutely clear.

The joy of the day slammed out of him. Yes, he loved the wilderness, but without Lauren in the heroine role, it would be such a disappointing ending.

Fix that, Mr. Director.

They were a mile farther upstream when the next piece finally connected.

Don't be derivative.

"Always wanted to meet a woman like you," Mack was smiling at Emily across their small campfire, the sole light other than the Montana stars. The sparks flicked briefly upward mingling smoke and the scent of pine into a heady mix.

They'd built the fire close beside a big boulder. A few convenient logs had been kicked into place as benches, but Lauren sat on the dirt with her back against the boulder and her legs stretched out into the darkness.

Then he turned to Lauren.

"Now I've met two right here. Can't tell Nancy, even if she's not the jealous sort."

"Two of us?" Lauren knew Emily was special—didn't take a genius to see that. But she couldn't imagine why anyone in their right mind would compare the two of them.

"Young, beautiful, competent—"

"Both of them a foot taller than you, Old Man," Patrick teased him. It was clear that the two of them truly enjoyed each other's company. Whatever else she might think of Patrick, he was a superior horseman. He also had that gift that she'd always lacked, an innate kindness that everyone could see so clearly that he was everyone's instant friend.

She was no one's friend. Service buddy, sure. But as a female dog handler in an all-male squad, that was the limit on the depth of her interactions with other Delta. There were female Deltas—a few of them—but they were more typically on undercover missions, pretending to be part of a couple. She and Jupiter had been embedded with a combat team. She'd never actually met another female Delta despite The Unit's relatively small size. Delta Force conferences weren't exactly a thing—no parallel equivalent to the Navy's notorious Tailhook parties.

"A foot taller means there's all the more of them to appreciate," Mack continued unabashedly. Yet his eyes didn't trace down either of their bodies. Instead, he aimed a saucy wink in her direction that Lauren didn't know what to do with.

Like Patrick, it was impossible to not like the old man.

Like?

Is that what she felt for Patrick? If so, it was more than she'd felt for any particular man in a long time. She respected Michael, but the colonel was so daunting that *like* didn't seem a fitting word. She liked Mark well enough, what little she knew of him. It was as if that segment of her emotions had been on hold for the duration of her military service.

She'd slept with men. Even enjoyed their company on occasion. But *like?* That was something else again.

She forced herself to look at Patrick. It wasn't until that moment that she realized she hadn't—not all afternoon. Or through their slow evening in the makeshift camp beneath the stars.

His head was back, laughing—another emotion she'd lost track of somewhere overseas. He was telling some joke about an Irishman, a Jew, and an East Indian jumping out of a plane that even had Michael chuckling. Emily's rare smile shone brightly. And Mack's encouraging, "What then?" fed the story.

The four of them in some perfect tableau out of one of Patrick's movies. And now *she* was doing it.

He'd spent much of their dinner of a kielbasa, cabbage, and potato fry-up talking about being so immersed in movies that he'd lost track of real life. He'd spoken about it as if it was a fresh concept...and he was perfectly willing to share it—just laying his innermost mistakes out for all to see.

"I've spent so much of my life trying to cast myself into my own life that I have to wonder how much of real life I missed."

She'd had so much of "real life"—soldier-style—that she wondered if she'd ever find her way back. Somehow sitting around a tiny campfire in the depths of the Flathead Wilderness only epitomized that. She had shared nothing with anyone. Not in years. Not since her arrival here. Last night, Patrick's kiss had offered so much more, and she'd backed away.

Why?

Too personal? Too "real" but in some context she wasn't familiar with?

She'd never backed away from anything in her life.

Until Jupiter died.

Now she backed away from everything.

She'd left Delta, the finest place a soldier could ever hope to serve.

She'd left behind the dogs. She'd left Patrick on the porch last night because she couldn't face whatever "more" might be.

It was like there was a black-ops, eyes-only mission briefing folder that was her life and she hadn't dared open the cover. What lay inside? Her hopes—if she even had any left. Fears—of which she had too many.

Herself?

She'd lost her way in there. Died along with her dog due to some asshole's order that—

"No!" It heaved out of her like the sickness that had wracked her entire body this morning.

"No what?" Patrick asked in the sudden silence broken only by the soft crackling of the fire.

They were all looking at her. Caught mid-pose. Frozen except for the shifting surprise on their faces. Except it wasn't all surprise.

Patrick, again in mid-story, indeed wore a look of simple surprise. Though it was fast sliding toward concern.

Mack, well, nothing startled him after all he'd seen. He simply raised his eyebrows at her in question.

Michael's surprise had a certain *"Finally!"* quality to it. That she just might have to beat out of him later.

And Emily...once again Emily wore an expression from the first day they'd met. This time Lauren understood at least a piece of it. Encouragement.

Lauren wasn't used to having someone on her side. Yet she knew, right down to her boots, that Emily was completely in her corner.

"No what?" Patrick asked again.

How could she answer that? It was too big. Too unwieldy. No matter what Emily offered.

Patrick had shared something important about himself. Something core.

"How did you do that?" She managed to choke it out without heaving up her dinner into the burning coals.

"Do what?" As if he hadn't laid out his heart for all to see. His life was as open as the starry sky arced above them. Hers was buried beneath a scree slope at the foot of a mountain.

"Just…say all that stuff that you said?"

"When?" Patrick's brows knitted together under the brim of his cowboy hat. "Oh! That?" Then he actually looked embarrassed and spent a few moments poking at the small fire with a branch he held. "I was kind of hoping that no one had noticed. Pretty dumb, huh? Thinking that living a movie role was more important than…" he waved his stick enough to indicate the wilderness around them, but not enough to risk poking anyone.

She liked that he didn't have the words. That was a good sign.

"I dunno," Patrick shrugged.

For some reason that simple gesture brought back the memory of how it felt to be embracing him far more than watching him ride all day. On a horse, he was a competent cowboy, tracking into the wilderness, taking care of his charges. But with that negligent shrug, lit by the warm glow of burning logs, he was close and very, very real.

"I just sort of said it," then he looked up at her. "Is it what I said? Or is something worrying at you, Lauren?" There was concern there. As if she hadn't walked away from him last night. As if he couldn't imagine that she had any problems even though she was a complete and total disaster.

She wasn't ready to talk about that. So instead—

"My dog was murdered by a one-star general who never should have been allowed out of the Pentagon. Never, ever should have been overseeing a combat operation."

Michael would know the story, at least parts of it. Emily would understand it. For Mack and Patrick, especially Patrick, she had to find some way to explain what had happened. She sat on the hard ground, hugging her knees tightly to her chest, and tried to explain her way through the events that had ended any desire to continue in her chosen career.

"A Spec Ops dog and their handler," how could she have started there of all places? Unable to stop herself, unable to deny Patrick's concerned silence, she forced herself over the precipice. "It's not a normal dog-owner alliance. You train together. You eat together. You sleep together. The dog will do anything to protect the handler. Anything! It also trusts the handler to do the same. It's a special bond that I can't begin to explain. Bertram saving Stan's life is just one small piece of it."

Her breath was fast, shallow. She could feel the bile rising again and clamped her jaw against it. Her head swam badly enough that she had to close her eyes as she began rocking back and forth.

"What happened?" Emily's voice was so soft, so sympathetic, that Lauren latched onto it like a lifeline.

"I— He— We were on forward patrol. A big, combined forces operation. I was— *We*—" it came out somewhere between a gasp and a choke, "were point on a mixed team of Delta, Rangers, and combat controllers out of the 24th STS. A company-strength team of regular forces secured the perimeter—no back door escapes this time. We were in there to shut down the enemy once and for all. All under the command of Brigadier General Complete Asshole."

She fought the nausea down again. She couldn't even say his name, though she'd never forget him standing toe-to-toe with her, screaming an order that she *knew* was wrong. Lauren knew she should have refused the order and faced the court-martial for doing so. Or even the firing squad he'd threatened her with for refusing a direct order in a combat situation. At least then Jupiter would be alive and she'd be at peace.

"He gave me a direct order that I never should have followed. And Jupiter trusted me. Did you know there's a bounty among the Taliban for each military war dog killed? Ten thousand US and up, twenty if you get the dog handler as well," she thumped her fingers into her chest hard enough to hurt.

She supposed it was a good sign that she no longer wished that they'd earned the double bounty.

"I signaled Jupiter ahead. He knew it was wrong too, I could see it in his eyes. Then he hung his head and went. It was the last thing he ever did for me. *I'm* the one who killed him!"

She wouldn't cry.

She held herself tighter.

No way!

She'd shed her last tears months ago over the makeshift grave with the Delta squad formed up to either side as an honor guard. She'd *watered* the grave with her tears, knowing that nothing would ever grow from such harsh soil, and right there she'd sworn she would never cry again.

Unable to hold it in any longer, she bolted to her feet and ran off into the night.

Patrick was on his feet before she reached the edge of the darkness. He paused only long enough to grab the rifle Mack held out before racing after her.

She moved so quietly that the moment's delay was almost too much, but he managed to track her by her ragged breathing. She led him far enough away that he wondered if he'd be able to find their route back to the fire, but he didn't have time to worry about that.

Lauren finally stumbled to a halt against a tree, a Douglas fir by the rough bark, its huge trunk at least ten feet across.

He whispered her name as he set the rifle close to hand against the trunk. This *was* bear country, after all.

"Go away!" Her voice was so low and hoarse that it barely sounded human.

No dumb movie roles this time. He knew what he had to do, even if he could easily guess at the consequences.

He stepped in and wrapped his arms around her.

Sure enough, she pounded the side of her fist against his chest. Hard enough to really hurt despite how close together they were.

He held her tighter.

Lauren hit him once more before collapsing against him.

"An RPG," she groaned against his chest. "They killed my dog with a rocket-propelled grenade. You use that to kill helicopters and airplanes, not a sweet dog." Then she simply wept.

He held her close. Felt the dry sobs rippling through her slender frame as if they'd shatter her. But he knew how strong she was. Had felt it. Had seen it. Even if she didn't appear to know that about herself.

"Did they get the bastard?"

Lauren finally shrugged, then shook her head.

"Shit!"

She slowly quieted.

"You do know that you didn't kill your dog?"

"I—"

"No!" He cut her off. It wasn't like him, but he could feel a certainty, a rightness to what he was saying. "Blame can be pointed in a dozen different directions, but that dog loved you. Would do anything for you. You don't get that kind of loyalty if you aren't the kind of person who deserves it."

"But I—"

"No, Lauren. It's a wrap. That film shoot is in the can," he managed to gentle his voice this time. It was hard. He wanted to hunt down this general and hurt him badly. Patrick had never even been in a fight as a kid, but he was warming up to the idea. "I know what you're thinking, but it's just plain wrong. You're too good a person for that to be true. I'm sure that you did everything you possibly could."

He could feel the doubt. It was a tension across her shoulders, a stillness where her face still pressed hard against his shoulder.

"Look around you. Michael is hovering over you worse than a whole coop full of mother hens. He's made me worry more than once about getting anywhere near you, half afraid I'd wake up dead or hanging by my toes with my head in an anthill or something. While it's really clear from watching him that he doesn't ride or like horses, the instant I told him you were coming with us, he insisted on joining us."

Lauren didn't respond except to grow a little quieter.

"And Emily. She's ready to go all mama bear for you, which, I can tell you from experience, isn't like her. She takes care of the women around her, but she clearly thinks you're something special."

Through the next long silence, he could feel her shoulders finally let go and she slumped against him. He tightened his arms so that she didn't just slide bonelessly to the ground.

"Just so happens I think you're pretty special, too."

"More like you just want sex."

"With you? Don't need to ask this boy twice. But that doesn't begin to cover what I think is special about you."

Lauren considered asking Patrick if he'd lost his mind.

"Sure. Because I'm *so* attractive at the moment." She was snotty, shaky, and thankful for the dark because she was probably red-eyed as well if the burning sensation was anything to go by.

"You don't know the half of it," Patrick kissed her atop the head.

"You're nuts!" She was a screwed-up mess on a grand scale.

"You don't know the half of that either," he agreed with an easy laugh. A laugh that made her smile against his shoulder in the dark despite how awful she was feeling.

How was she supposed to face the others after her outburst? How was she supposed to face Patrick? She didn't even dare unbury her face from his shoulder for fear of what he'd think of her the moment that she surfaced.

Maybe she'd simply stay here. Not in Montana, of course, but just hiding against a strong chest, wrapped in a man's arms.

He leaned back against the rough tree bark and let her simply lie against him. It was a very nice place to be.

"Violet is Level Six," he whispered.

"Uh-huh… Wait. What?" She raised her head just enough to see the hint of his face where the moonlight hunted its way down through the trees. A bat fluttered by. There was a distant laugh slipping through the woods from the campfire. Mack's.

"It's on a friend's refrigerator back in Manhattan. We were…never mind. She had a big sign taped to her fridge that said 'Violet is Level

Six—Start Where You Stand.' Never really meant anything to me, but I get it now."

"Well, I don't." He ran his hands slowly up and down her back and she could feel herself being soothed by the simple action. Feeling better with each moment. She wasn't some goddamn dog who wanted to be petted, but neither did she want him to stop.

"Violet is Level Six. It's completely meaningless. She kept saying that and I kept trying to read some meaning into it anyway. But now I can see that she meant it even if I didn't understand it. The whole point is that Level One through Five *are* meaningless. 'Start where you stand.' You can't change the past, so the past doesn't count. It's actually meaningless. Only how you react, only what you do about the future matters."

"And your future is so clear? Because mine sure as hell isn't."

"Kind of," Patrick leaned his cheek against her hair and rubbed it there the way a dog would. Except Patrick Gallagher was a deliciously strong cowboy, not some four-legged fur beast. "Clearer than it's ever been before."

"What is it?"

"I don't have much of it yet."

She could feel his sudden discomfort, but couldn't find the energy to pull away from his warmth and surety. "Give me what you have."

He rubbed his cheek against her hair a few more times. If he kept that up much longer, she was going to forget her question and have her first sex in far too long right here in the forest up against a tree.

"I—"

She could hear and feel Patrick's frustrated growl. She'd wager that it wasn't a sound he often made. She breathed him in. Horse and pine forest, yes. Honest sweat, too. But also a depth. A realness so wide and vast that it filled every one of her senses with him.

"I love this land. I'm just figuring this out today, though lord alone knows why. Slow learner, I guess. I've been out here most of four years and I can't imagine ever going back to the concrete jungle of failed dreams." His hands went still, one on her waist and the other wrapped around her shoulders. "Another lame movie analogy, but there it is."

An unaccountable sadness came over her. Patrick was absolutely right. He belonged here. It was easy to see in every gesture, every motion, even the way he walked and rode. And she belonged… nowhere. Would New York fit her any better than Fort Bragg or Afghanistan? She suspected not and *that* thought scared the hell out of her.

"But there's more… And I didn't just say that."

"You're on a roll, cowboy. Don't stop now." Because if he did stop, she might have to start thinking and she knew she wouldn't like the answers she'd be coming up with.

"Kiss me."

"I knew that was your secret agenda all along," she teased. "But don't think this gets you out of answering."

He leaned down and brushed his lips across hers.

Like last night's kiss, there was an unaccountable heat that rushed into her.

It burned hot, almost frantic.

Of their own accord, her hands dug into his hair, his neck, his chest. She'd never been a scratcher, but she dug her fingers into those beautiful pectoral muscles until it felt as if he could hold her up forever, as long as she hung on.

When her breath wrenched out of her, he breathed it in, consuming all that she was.

His hands—those big, wonderfully strong cowboy hands that had carried her so easily—were beneath her shirt, one down the tight back of her pants, forcing his fingers hard against her buttocks.

Lauren peeled off his shirt to get at his chest. Then she ran her own hands down his front and inside his jeans.

"Damn it!" Patrick groaned as she cupped him. "Damn it to hell!" his curse grew in energy but cascaded into a groan as she stroked him.

"What?" Lauren tasted his neck. His chest. She nibbled at his ribs.

"I didn't bring any goddamn protection."

She stopped. Holding him. Wanting him inside her. She wanted the mind-blanking relief of meaningless sex. He felt so soft and powerful in her hands. Vulnerable, willing, and tremendously male. His was a body designed to satisfy women. To satisfy this woman. Now!

"We can't," he gasped out.

"Spoilsport," even though he was right.

He slowly disengaged his hands from up her shirt and down her pants.

With great reluctance, she did the same, though not above appreciating the feel of him as she disengaged.

Before she could step away, he turned her lightly around and pulled her once more against his chest.

Lauren lay in the cradle of his arms and watched the night as her body buzzed with a need she'd never felt for any man. Stars shone brilliantly through small gaps in the trees. Some night bird called happily from high in a nearby tree: *chirr-woop*. An answering *chirr-woop* and fast wingbeats answered back.

She sighed and relaxed back against Patrick. The heat wasn't going away. The need wasn't dissipating simply because they'd stopped. But lying in his arms was a very nice place to be as well.

Patrick's hands ached for her. To touch, hold, caress. He'd watched all the good sex scenes as often as any hormonal student of film. The porns had never grabbed him, but whether it was Kelly McGillis in *Top Gun* or Malin Akerman in *Watchmen*, he'd certainly enjoyed watching the lovemaking scenes.

Now that he was in that true fantasy moment, a beautiful woman leaning back against him in the deep Montana wilderness, he again understood the problem.

He'd spent his life seeking the movie moment. The instant when the unreachable actress tumbled helplessly into his arms.

Except Lauren wasn't some fantasy or, worse, a disappointing fellow classmate wrapped up in her own angst. She was a beautiful, impossibly real woman who had been on the verge of giving everything to him. Well, maybe he could give that to her instead.

He started slowly. One hand about her waist, the other about her shoulder. Too fast and she'd shy away like a skittish horse. Too slow and she might have time to catch on to what he was doing.

Patrick leaned down to bury his face at her neck as he slid a hand beneath her shirt and over that soldier-flat stomach. A woman with six-pack abs. Strong, amazing. A smooth, straight flow onto her ribcage without an anorexic cavity or anything other than muscle beneath warm, smooth skin.

For some reason, when he finally reached his goal, learning that she wore no bra surprised him. Her figure didn't require one, but imagining her as a soldier in battle, braless, was an awesome image—the woman never lost in the soldier.

She slowly leaned her head back until it rested on his shoulder, her hands riding lightly over his. Her breathing built slowly until it seemed that she was the voice of the night, of the forest breathing in and out in wonder. At his hesitation, she guided his hand downward, inside her pants as her hand followed over the outside.

Her groan rose from somewhere deep inside. As far beneath the surface as the anger had been, but there was no doubting that these sounds had a different origin.

She let him have her. Gave herself to him in a way that he'd have thought impossible before tonight. It was as if she'd let go of any willful control.

"Lauren," he whispered her name in wonder and she moved harder against his hands. Her fingers clenching into his through the fabric of her shirt and jeans.

Her moan was like a wounded animal's as he led her upward. She removed her hand from over the one cradling her breast—a perfect curve against his palm—and latched it behind his neck. Exposed... Giving...

"I'll follow you anywhere, Lauren." For he had never held a woman like her.

"No!" It was little more than a choked sob as her release slammed into her.

Lauren tried to pull away, even though her body was not hers to command at the moment. Her knees were Jell-O and her brain mush.

Patrick had slipped past her defenses and found places that she'd lost. Places she hadn't even known about. What he did to her body was of almost no consequence by comparison.

To be cradled. Held. To be made more important than those around her was not something she'd ever experienced in her life.

"No." She'd been protesting something, but couldn't remember what. Heat rolled through her in overlapping waves. A scorching heat that didn't burn, but rather cleansed. How often had she wished for one good purge. Some thought, some act, some magic elixir (that always turned out to be just one too many shots of bourbon) that would let her mind rest for even a moment. That would let her feel clean of her past.

"Violet is Level Six." Some meaningless phrase as she kept Patrick's hand trapped within her jeans and pressed it harder against her. The waves inside her crashed together again, amplified by the man holding her, building until they exploded with more force that a Mark 84 bomb obliterating a city block.

When she finally came back to herself, Lauren was shocked to find that she was still inside her skin rather than blasted across the Montana Wilderness.

Somehow—as she clung to Patrick's arms, her only anchor in the wilds of her thoughts—she still held onto one word.

"No."

"No what?" Patrick's voice whispered against her ear.

"I don't remember. How am I supposed to remember anything after that?" If he could do this to her fully clothed, what would happen when they really came together?

"You're not exactly hurting my ego."

"I'll take care of that later," when she could do more than remain leaning back against him.

"It's a nice ego and I've become rather attached to it. Don't stomp on it too hard."

Teasing. He was goddamn teasing her. Without that hard edge of a fellow soldier asking the underlying questions: *How much can you take? Are you up to real standards? You are a woman after all. Not really Spec Ops.*

But Patrick was teasing her about...how strong she was. Which was totally backward. But it wasn't. That, too, felt good. As good as the low thrumming still rippling through her body.

"You said something." Her mind was clearing.

"I did? I say a lot of things." He wrapped his hands once more about her waist and shoulders, keeping them close rather than done and ready to leave.

"About belonging here."

"Maybe," Patrick conceded and she could hear his smile in the darkness.

"And..." she almost had it. "And... No!" This time she exploded from his arms and turned to face him in the night. The sliver of moon that had hinted at his features earlier was gone. He was now a dim outline against the dark bole of the tree.

"You said you would follow me anywhere."

"I did."

"Why don't you sound the least bit perturbed by that?"

"Because it's true."

"Patrick..." Lauren could feel her teeth grinding together.

"Would you prefer I lied?"

"About that? Yes."

"Tough!" He laughed. Now he was goddamn laughing.

"We barely know each other."

"Okay. What's your favorite color?"

"What?"

"Should I ask if you were into dolls or stuffed animals instead? I was a big fan of Hot Wheels myself. You know. The little cars."

"Yes. I know the little cars." And there wasn't a chance she was admitting to her Barbie- and Ken-filled past. Soldiers weren't like that. "What are you doing?"

"Look, Lauren," he reached out and somehow found her hands in the darkness. "I don't know how this works. I just know that my life became a thousand times better the moment you stepped off that chopper."

"It's a helicopter or a helo—sometimes an airplane even though it's rotor based. A chopper is a motorcycle. Don't...never mind. Just...it's not a chopper." Why she was trying to explain herself, now, she had no idea. "Besides, you fell into a mud puddle. That was supposed to impress me?"

"Yep! I don't do that for just any gal."

Lauren wished she could see him. Could think of something to say. Could understand...but she couldn't.

Violet wasn't Level Six, it was just a goddamn color.

She hadn't spoken a word as they made their way back to camp. In silent gestures, once they reached the outer edges of the firelight, Patrick tried to help her get put back together: tucked-in shirt, finger-combed hair, and such. She still looked deliciously rumpled but he was too dazzled to be able to see how to fix it.

To have...rumpled her the way he had was the best sex of his life. Which shouldn't be possible—since it had been all about her—but it was. So many things about Lauren were impossible, but that was fine with him. He was a Long Island film student turned Montana cowboy. And he had just made love to a topflight soldier, even if she hadn't exactly made love back. Anything was possible.

Gibson afforded Lauren just a single glance, then turned his baleful gaze on him. Patrick wondered if Gibson had been trained by Cyclops from the X-men and could melt the flesh off Patrick's bones with just his stare. It sure felt as if he could.

Mack offered him a cheeky wink, so obvious that no one could miss it.

Emily simply scooted sideways on the log she'd been sitting on and Lauren dropped down to sit beside her. Nothing more. No friendly arm around the shoulder. No murmur of question or commiseration. Just a place to sit and…

Shit!

A place to sit where Patrick had no reasonable way to sit beside her. Lauren now sat between Emily and the boulder. Emily's move had closed the gap between her and Mack where Patrick had initially sat. That left only the space between Mack and Michael Gibson.

He handed Mack back his rifle—half wondering if he should keep it in case he needed to ward off the colonel. Would a .30-06 be big enough? Sure, it could bring down an elk, but at the moment Gibson looked to be made of much tougher stuff than he had at first.

"Crazy rifle, old man," he spoke to Mack to have something to say. "I'd never get off a second shot."

Mack hefted it. "We're gonna have to fix that, Pat, my boy. Can't have you go through life shooting the wrong way round."

"I don't. I shoot right-handed like most civilized folks." Mack's Winchester Model 70 was set up with a very rare left-handed bolt. If shot from the right shoulder, it would be very awkward to work the bolt handle mounted on the wrong side. And it would have a tendency to eject hot metal directly into the shooter's face.

"May I?" Lauren spoke for the first time since deep in the woods.

Mack handed it over.

She rested it on her left shoulder. By how smoothly her hands moved about the stock and barrel, it was clear that she, too, was a southpaw. Well, now he knew something else new about her. He'd count that as a good day.

CHAPTER 7

The next morning, Lauren had been a long time getting over the discomfort of leading the track. She knew nothing about tracking wildlife. Hunting explosives or a human was different. The habits of a Taliban gunner or an al-Qaeda bomb maker were second nature.

"Don't look at me," Emily had protested. "I grew up in D.C. and made my living in a helicopter."

Michael had settled into some speechless state that was only a little more silent than his normal state of being. Since the man was completely unreadable at any time, it wasn't that much of a change.

"My knees are getting too old for skulking along, girl. You show us how it's done." And Mack had settled back into following and doing some harmless flirting with Emily.

Patrick came to her side cautiously, unsure of his welcome. Which wasn't fair after his incredible kindness in the woods. She'd signaled him forward, but while he gave her pointers, he, too, proved unwilling to take the lead.

They passed by an elk cow and calf. It was clearly a late-season birth. The calf would need a mother's guidance to survive the winter. She let them continue on their way.

By the end of the long morning, she was second-guessing that decision. They'd left the horses back at the camp and covered several miles of very rough terrain on foot. She'd turned their track an hour ago to make a big loop that would eventually lead back to the camp.

"See the break in the land," suddenly Mack was beside her, pointing at a feature close to a mile away. "That roll there to the west? They'll like the combination of sun, water, and refuge. Smell that bit of sulfur? Hot springs. Elk are partial to hot springs. Wind is from the north so you'll want to circle us around wide."

Around wide. Lauren looked up at the fierce peaks of the Flathead Wilderness. It was hard, steep country. Trees clung tenaciously, seeking a hold that could survive rockfalls and winter avalanches. To swing wide would take them over a sharp saddle that rose at least a thousand feet above their present position.

After a break for a quick lunch, it took her two hours to lead them there. Finding a good route over the terrain was hard enough. Then there was a wind shift, which would have sent them in a new direction except for the pile of still-warm scat she found nearly as big as her boot.

The ground was hard here, so it took her a few minutes to find a clean paw print.

"Black bear," Mack told her. "Big one, but he's a black. See how the toes make an arc around the pad? A grizzly's toes go straight across in a line."

"Well, I don't want to be chasing along behind a bear: grizzly, brown, or black."

"Me either," Mack agreed. After a little debate—it was hard to read the terrain from the thick forest—she struck off in a new direction to avoid bears but stay downwind of the hot springs.

Once they arrived, it showed Mack's guess hadn't been a guess at all. Instead, it was just as a skilled tracker would have expected.

They settled around the base of a group of larch trees close above a small pool, steaming slightly in the cool air. From their hideaway beneath its drooping branches, they had a clear view of the surrounding mountain slopes. Fall was already here in the Rockies—

the season of change. Quaking aspen were disco balls of golden leaves shining in the sun. Maples were hinting toward the darker reds. Even the larch were a startling yellow among the dark green of Douglas fir.

Close below them, wisps of steam from the hot springs rose into the cool, early afternoon air. It was odd, after all of the years she'd spent tracking and scouting, to learn something new. She felt a spark of joy she'd always taken from the mental challenge: spotting and understanding all of the signs. She'd never have spotted this place from their prior position, yet Mack had and she could now see how and why.

Maybe she and Patrick could come back here alone someday and make slow love in the warm pools. She'd slept last night like the dead despite the rough ground. Her emotions even more spent than her body. But she had very nice memories of just quite how her body had felt.

The five of them sat in companionable silence, occasionally whispering back and forth, but mostly just enjoying the passing day. By the map in her head, they were actually less than a mile from the camp where they'd left their horses. A much easier path, once they didn't have to worry about remaining downwind from their quarry.

As they sat, she began remembering some of the other things that Patrick had said last night. Other than his *follow you anywhere* nonsense. So not going to deal with that.

"Why are you really out here, Michael? If you won't tell us why you're on the ranch, why are you on this hunt?"

The colonel looked up at her from the branch he'd been idly whittling with his Cold Steel SRK knife. He opened his mouth, then closed it again.

"Okay. That was you about to say it sounded like fun. And I don't think that you're just birddogging me. I was only a dog handler, not some super Delta who now needs handholding. You and I were on barely a dozen missions together over the years."

Emily's eyes widened at that. She'd clearly been operating under the assumption that their close association was the real reason he was here, despite Michael saying he was on a leave of absence. Well, at least Emily could finally stop pretending that Lauren was somehow special. She could do with a little bit of settling into obscurity.

That would leave only Patrick that she'd have to figure out what to do with. An even less comfortable topic than facing down the colonel.

Michael appeared to be carving a tall skinny tree out of the branch. Though the piece of wood he was working was less than a foot long and two inches wide, it felt as if the tree he was carving was truly huge. He'd worked the name Nell into the base. His wife was Claudia. Was there some former lover? Or—

"Oh, no!"

"What?" Patrick and Emily asked in unison. She ignored them.

"You bastard," she faced the colonel. "That's why you wouldn't speak to your wife about it. You're just like other men."

"Who?" Gibson's brows knit together in confusion.

"Who! Who?"

Mack shushed her, then nodded toward the woods.

"How can you ask who?" She nearly strangled with turning her shout of rage into a whisper. She couldn't believe that the colonel was just another cheating, asshole bastard. Wasn't there integrity anywhere in the world? Did Claudia know? Or were Mark and Claudia doing it even now in some seedy Great Falls hotel and Emily didn't know? Lauren trusted Emily, but—

"I can ask because I don't know what you're talking about, Sergeant Foster," he remained completely unperturbed. "Therefore, I can ask again. Who?"

Emily's eyes were wide, but her face was grim. "Michael..." she drew it out like a threat. She clearly understood what Lauren had uncovered. Though Emily said it more like a question than a threat. What the hell?

At that Colonel Gibson looked less certain of himself. She'd never seen him unsure of anything, but facing Emily Beale's ire was apparently enough to chip through his facade of perfectly passive warrior. Okay, maybe Emily wasn't a part of whatever was going on. *That*, at least, tilted a tiny part of Lauren's world back toward rightness.

"Seriously. I don't—"

Lauren snatched the carving from his hand before he had a chance to hide it and tossed it to Emily. "Who the fuck is Nell?"

Rather than the fury Lauren had expected from Emily, she spoke softly. "Is that her name?"

Michael nodded.

"Whose name?" Lauren could only watch in befuddlement as Emily very carefully returned the carving.

Neither one appeared willing to speak.

Emily caved first. "It's the name of a redwood tree."

"A—" Lauren couldn't manage more.

Michael wiped it with his fingers, caressed it as if her touch had sullied it. "I fell in love with Claudia while climbing that tree with her."

"While climbing a tree," she could only echo dumbly. "Were you children together?"

"No. Nell is a redwood tree. Claudia and I were three hundred and eighty-seven feet up the tallest tree anywhere in the world." Michael didn't return to his whittling though he continued to stare down at it.

"A tree," Lauren couldn't imagine why someone would name a tree. "You're not out here looking for another tree and another woman, are you?"

"No," he glanced up, then tried to return to his whittling, but she ducked down to keep his gaze on her when he tried to refocus his attention.

"Then who put you on leave and why?"

He huffed out a breath. "Just like last time, I put myself on leave. And I came here because I'm thinking of quitting Delta." His unreadable face wasn't so unreadable anymore. It was distinctly grim.

"Holy shit." Emily's voice was barely a whisper.

Lauren couldn't have said it better herself.

* * *

Patrick had no idea what was going on, but it was clearly important.

Mack tapped him on the shoulder, but Patrick was afraid that if he even glanced away from the scenario unfolding in front of him it was just possible Emily, Michael, *and* Lauren would all somehow evaporate, or beam back up to the mother ship in a *Galaxy Quest* pod of trans-warp goo.

Mack tapped him again. "Boy," his excited whisper cut through Patrick's thoughts.

"What?" He turned to glare at the old man, but Mack wasn't watching him, he was pointing toward the small hot springs.

A small herd had gathered about the springs. A doe and a fawn almost as big as she was were settling into the pool. A magnificent male with a huge rack of antlers grazed on the far side. He was a prime, once-in-a-lifetime bull.

"Those aren't elk, they're caribou," Mack whispered. "Almost never see them this far south. But a bull like that, you don't see but once in a lifetime."

Patrick could only nod in agreement as he watched the grand bull with a massive and complex rack of antlers.

In between grazing, he raised his head and watched the surrounding woods vigilantly. A pair of young bulls milled slowly about—one of them making playful charges at the leader who didn't even deign to look at him. He was going to be trouble for the herd's leader someday soon though, especially if the two youngsters ever ganged up.

Patrick could hear Lauren gear up to confront Michael again.

He reached out to clamp a hand over her mouth.

"Whagheffek?" She snarled against his palm.

He turned her head until she was facing the herd of caribou by the pool. The big male was on alert and might be looking their direction at the moment.

Maybe not, though. Suspicious but not yet alarmed.

Her lips formed an "Oh!" against his palm, but she didn't make a sound.

Mack had his rifle up and ready, but hesitated.

Then he held it out to Lauren, "You take my shot."

"Hey," Patrick's whispered surprise didn't even get Mack's attention. They had tracked all morning and waited through much of the afternoon for this moment. And now Mack was giving away a clean shot on the biggest bull Patrick had ever seen.

Lauren eyed the gun carefully, then Mack.

"That's quite some prize for a young lady," Mack continued. "Besides, he's old. I expect he's slowing down or he'd have a bigger harem. Might be his last winter."

"Maybe he's just picky," she whispered back.

Patrick wasn't a collector of antler racks, but that bull could tempt him to start.

"Or take one of the youngsters. They're gonna be nothing but trouble," he winked at Patrick, which earned him one of Lauren's rare half smiles. "Putting him in the freezer would be a kindness to this elder. His brother, too, while we're at it."

"I don't—"

"Gonna live on the ranch, you should know how to hunt, girl."

Live on the ranch? When had she said that? Patrick wanted to shout with joy and to heck with the hunt.

"But I'm not—" Lauren protested.

Oh, Mack was making it up.

"Either take the shot, or we might's well head on home." Patrick had never heard Mack be so forceful about anything. What did the old man know that he didn't? Just that there was some reason Lauren had to take the shot rather than Mack himself.

Lauren still didn't take the weapon.

The tableau held long enough for the leader of the herd to take another mouthful of grass.

"Together," Michael said, unslinging the pump-action Remington Model 760 GameMaster that he'd selected. Funny, Patrick would never have pegged him as a traditionalist. Michael slid forward to sit beside Lauren. No lying on the ground for support or resting the rifle against a tree. He didn't even bother to raise a knee to rest an elbow on it. He simply sat at the ready, waiting. They had three licenses as a group, so that wasn't a problem.

Lauren slowly took and lifted Mack's Winchester Model 70 .30-

06, resting it against her left shoulder. She didn't use a knee prop either. How good were Delta shooters? Patrick supposed that he was about to find out.

"The best is a double-lung shot. Just above and behind their shoulder, broadside," Mack whispered.

"I have the young bull to the south," Michael spoke softly.

"Roger." Lauren felt her breathing steady. He was leaving the choice of the grand bull or the troublesome youngster to her.

Live on the ranch? It didn't make any sense. Yes, Patrick was here, but they barely knew each other despite what they'd done last night. Emily was here, which Lauren was starting to think was a good thing despite how humbling she was to be around.

She sighted on the herd.

But her life wasn't here.

Four hundred yards figuring five feet tall at the withers. The caribou's height on the reticle marks inside the scope confirmed the estimate.

"What's the rifle zeroed at, Mack?" Her life wasn't anywhere. She watched the bull caribou through the scope as he watched over the extended family. So easy to take him down.

"Three hundred."

He'd never know what hit him. Just as Jupiter hadn't known—the first blessing she'd found about the whole screwed-up situation. One minute he'd accepted her command to scout ahead and the next he'd been gone.

She raised her aim to compensate for the extra foot of fall the round would take in the additional hundred yards from what the scope was set for. And just a fraction more for the wind blowing the scent of sulfur and caribou directly downwind in their direction. They couldn't feel it here in the woods, but she could see the leaves near the herd flapping in about ten knots of wind. It ruffled the bull's fur as well. The cool and dry Montana air was so close to the reference temperature and humidity for bullet flight that no compensation was needed, especially on such a punchy round as a .30-06 170 grain.

A chance to kill the grandest bull of all. To take down the lead male just like she wanted to do to all of the asshole men of her past.

"On one," Michael said. Old Delta joke—Delta shooters were always ready. "One."

She fired, their shots cracking out together.

Half a second of flight time. By which time she'd worked the bolt and had another round chambered. Plenty of time to take out all three bulls.

But she didn't take the second shot.

Impact.

The two young bulls didn't even have time to be surprised they were dead. Two seconds of stillness, then they began falling.

A sharp bray from the grand male.

Lauren kept his shoulder clear in her rifle scope, leading him even as he ran away with the doe and fawn, chasing them into the safety of the trees. Even after they were gone, she kept watch through ten long heartbeats.

She lowered and safetied the weapon. Someone took it as she handed it off.

Two young bulls. Meat for the freezer. Hides to tan.

At least they all had a purpose—leading a herd, feeding others. Whereas she—

Lauren left the carcasses to Mack, Patrick, and Michael to prepare.

There was too much meat to pack out. So Emily radioed Mark, who flew out later in the afternoon. There was no place to land the helicopter, but he lowered a long line and swooped the cleaned and dressed caribou back toward the ranch.

The entire time, Lauren sat where the sun slipped beneath the verge of the trees.

Watching, yet not watching.

It was the first purposeful shot she'd taken in two months. Being Delta, even just as a dog handler, meant that shooting was a significant portion of her training. And of her service as well. She'd shot maniacs running at her waving a machete, bomb makers, poppy growers harvesting and refining heroin so they could buy more weapons, men and women with rifles who left their families and risked everything for the chance to kill an American soldier. She could account for seventeen kills just against those who had targeted her war dogs over the years. That was part of the deal. They protected her and she protected them—until she hadn't.

By contrast, shooting a caribou was almost a peaceful act. Hundreds of pounds of meat. A beautiful hide that would become a rug or coat or something.

"You're being even quieter than Michael," Emily sat down beside her after waving the helicopter aloft.

"What's up with him anyway?" Lauren's voice felt tight and rough with disuse. She had no interest in sharing what she was thinking… because she wasn't thinking. All she felt was numb. The aches in her muscles told her that she hadn't moved in at least an hour. It could have been two or three minutes for all she knew except for the stiffness.

"You broke the back of it. We'll find out what's bugging Michael soon enough. What's up with Lauren?"

She blinked as if coming awake. "Well, I found something useful to do. Even if it's just once per year. That's something, isn't it?"

Emily rested a hand on her shoulder and Lauren took immense comfort from that simple kindness. "It's just a beginning."

Lauren looked over at her. Emily was smiling that half smile of hers…the one that meant she wouldn't be explaining a thing.

Figured.

"Why didn't you shoot the older bull?" Patrick rode so close beside her that they were practically rubbing boots.

Last night she had sat at the campfire. No romantic forays into the night forest. No shared laughter around the fire.

Mack had told stories. He'd done his two years of service, but just like everything else with him, none of it had happened in any normal way.

"Out at the wrong end of a long training run, we were offered a ride back to base if we'd volunteer for KP. I never did mind kitchen work, so my hand was first up. Better that than a 10K hike back. Ended up in the cushy post of being a waiter in the Officer's Club for my last eighteen months. Can't say I had any real complaints. A darn sight better than going to Korea and facing off against the Chinese."

Patrick had added some film school stories of his own, but they seemed even more distant than Mack's separation from the military—which had been at about the same time Patrick's mom and dad were born.

Even Michael had told them about climbing the big redwoods.

Lauren had remained silent.

When they'd bedded down, he'd made sure that he spread his

sleeping bag near hers. His shock had barely been outweighed by his pleasure when deep in the night she'd scooted close so that they lay back-to-back in their separate sleeping bags. The bags were rated to far colder temperatures so it wasn't for warmth, but he'd slept little as he'd relished the contact.

She'd been up and tending the fire with Michael by the time Patrick had woken. The sky had gone slate gray in the night and the temperature was falling. Their plan to camp a couple more days—having the unlikely good fortune of bagging the caribou on the second day—was aborted. A September storm in the Flathead Wilderness wasn't worth the risk.

Lauren had appeared normal this morning as they rode back out of the mountains. Her silence no longer the texture of steel, instead it seemed she was back to just her normal state.

They'd descended several thousand feet as they crossed out of the mountains and back onto ranch land, but the chill clung.

She inspected the gray sky for a long time before answering.

"It felt vengeful to take down the big bull. He has figured out how to survive a lot of years. He earned his right to enjoy his last winter or two, fair and square with no hunter snatching it away from him."

Patrick wasn't quite sure why the answer surprised him, but it did. He'd led all sorts of hunters into the wild from first timers to seasoned lifetime hunters like Mack. He never took the shot himself, because that wasn't the point of being a guide. Three years' experience had taught him that, just like in real life, there was a fair spread from responsible hunters who valued the bounty as well as the hunt to ones who shouldn't be trusted with anything sharper than a broken pencil. Not a one of them would have left that big caribou behind.

"You're a curious woman, Lauren Foster."

"In what way?"

He coaxed Minotaur along to keep up with her fast-paced Colette. "You're never quite what I expect."

A glance back showed that the other three had fallen well behind as they ducked down into a low swale of trees.

"Whoa," he eased Minotaur to a halt at a small brook and let the horse drink.

Lauren stopped and did the same. "Is that a good thing, or bad? Because I'm never what I expect either and it's scaring the crap out of me."

"With you, trust me, it's good. And how can you not be what you expect?"

She studied him for a long moment. Again he was fascinated by the winter-brown eyes and couldn't look away.

Without a word, she nudged her horse closer to him until their knees were practically interlocked. Not letting go of the reins, she leaned in to kiss him. This time there was none of the fire of the porch nor the desperation of the forest. This time, she kissed him long, soft, and slow.

When she eased back, he found himself tipping more and more forward until he was at risk of dropping into the cold stream rather than a warm mud puddle.

"That's not like me at all," she whispered.

"What part of it?" Patrick was impressed he could connect the four words into a whole sentence, even if they were all small ones.

"I'm not supposed to feel so much when kissing a man," she eased Colette out the far side of the stream just as the others rode into view. A single glance showed that her move hadn't fooled anyone.

"Good feelings, I hope?" Patrick whispered to her, then wished he hadn't. If it was a bad review, he didn't want to know.

Again she watched him with that impossibly unreadable face. The others were close now. He could hear their individual hoof falls on the trail winding down to where the stream flowed beneath the trees—the off-beat *clip clop* of a horse trying to move slowly down the bank that was almost too steep to do so.

"Yes," was all she said, then she smiled at him. Actually smiled.

It was…a shock.

That was the word.

He was sure of it.

It was his moment. The one when a hero was supposed to speak. It definitely was; he'd gotten his cue loud and clear.

But that smile, no matter how brief, was unanswerable. It lit her eyes until they glowed with life, more vital than...than—some crappy scriptwriter he'd become—than possible.

He was glad for Minotaur's steadiness, because it was the only thing between him and an ice-cold swim.

"What?" Lauren suddenly felt terribly self-conscious. She wasn't used to telling her feelings to anyone other than her brother. And him only when he pushed.

But the connection from last night had been undeniable. She didn't know what she was afraid of, but she'd woken up filled with it in the middle of the night. Shuffling her bag over until she leaned against Patrick in the night had calmed her down. The simple contact had been as comforting as his previous night's attentions had been arousing.

She didn't like a man having that kind of power over her.

But as she watched Patrick sit there on his horse Minnie as if petrified into stone, she understood that the power wasn't one-way—she also had power over him. Was that what a relationship was?

She didn't like the idea of being in a one, even if she was starting to enjoy it.

It was all Patrick's fault. If he wasn't so...likeable, thoughtful, considerate, and such a great kisser, her life would be much easier.

He deserved some form of payback for that.

And the answer was right in front of her.

Emily and the others had entered the stream, making the small ford quite crowded with all four horses, three of them wanting room for a drink. Minnie wasn't a horse who liked being crowded.

That gave her an idea. It was an evil idea. But in her opinion, that meant it had merit.

Chelsea had been right, Colette was an exceptional horse. Over the last few days Lauren had honed a clear communication with the horse, borne out of the month she'd spent on horseback riding with the Afghan hill tribes. Uneven pressure of the knees, combined with a slight kick and a looser rein.

Colette spun and headed up the far side of the stream bank—fast.

Not to be left behind, Minnie followed.

Patrick might as well have been a puck on an air hockey table. Minnie slipped out from under him as smooth as silk. He went straight over the back of the saddle. Almost saved himself at the saddlebags, but didn't.

She caught Minnie's reins and twisted around to watch the show.

Patrick plunged down into the water with a huge splash that had the other three horses shying away hard. Emily and Mack kept their seats. Michael didn't, but landed neatly on his feet still holding his horse's reins.

Patrick simply sat there, waist-deep in the foot or so of water, and visibly sighed.

Mack set in to teasing him right off.

Michael actually cracked a smile.

Emily wasn't looking at Patrick, instead she was looking at Lauren. Waiting for something. Waiting for her to remember…

The mud puddle.

Claudia and Emily had said that it all somehow made sense that a skilled horseman had fallen in the mud puddle upon Lauren's arrival. And now she understood that it did. Somehow he'd been smitten the moment of her arrival. How was that even possible when she was a screwed-up bitch who had just played an awful prank on him?

She glanced down at Patrick.

He was answering Mack that he felt a need to cool off a bit—despite the chill day. Then he looked up at her and half tipped his hat as if acknowledging the success of her trick before he rose, dripping, to his feet.

She'd have been livid.

Patrick was…amused and perhaps chagrined as he joined her on the bank.

She led Minnie back to him and whispered a soft, "Sorry. I just couldn't help myself."

"It was good," he grinned. "Got me fair and square. Guessing I shouldn't try it on you, though."

"I had to make up for letting that big bull slip away," she said it as a tease. Which earned her a few uncertain laughs.

"Time to take down the king of the herd, huh?" Patrick understood, of course.

Now the others laughed.

Patrick shook his head like a wet dog, then pulled his hat back on and winked at her. He turned to his saddlebags to pull out dry clothes as the others nudged their horses away from the stream and continued along the trail. In moments they'd wound their way out of the small stream valley as they climbed back into the woods.

But he wasn't wrong. He might not see himself as a leading male, but she'd never met anyone like Patrick. Twice now he'd rushed to her rescue—when she fainted and when she ran into the forest. And she'd paid him back by...

"I'm not a nice person. How can you be attracted to me?"

He stopped with his shirt off and looked up at her over Minnie's withers. "How can I not be? That would be the better question."

"But I'm such a mess."

"Hello, Mess. Nice to meet you. My name is Disaster. C'mon, Lauren. You aren't even in the same category. I'm a privileged Long Island film student, playing at being a cowboy so that I can star in the movie running in my head. Yep, that's a wrap. For sure!" Patrick shook his head sadly as he returned to stripping down out of sight behind Minnie.

What Lauren had been seeing as amusing, Patrick saw as a fatal flaw. What she saw as a fatal flaw in herself, he saw as...trivial.

Down between Minnie's legs, she could see Patrick shucking his soaking jeans and underwear until he was standing barefooted on the grass beside the stream.

Hardly aware of what she was doing, she swung a leg across Colette's haunches and slid to the ground. She tapped Minnie lightly on the haunch and he walked forward a few steps to graze on a fresh patch of grass.

And there Patrick stood. Naked in the cool afternoon except for his cowboy hat. There was so much to appreciate about him physically, but there was also so much to appreciate about the man. His spontaneous kindness—it was just part of who he was. His knee-jerk savior mode—he neither hesitated nor thought, he simply acted. His self-awareness so much stronger than her own.

His humor.

She'd had humor once, she was sure of it.

Patrick stood, looking at her suspiciously, once again frozen in place.

A quick glance up the trail revealed that the others were already out of sight. Only a few miles to the ranch, they wouldn't worry if she and Patrick were delayed. She was about to step forward when Minnie swished his tail and slapped it hard against Patrick's bare skin.

"Yipes! Get along, you!" His slap sent Minnie ahead a few more steps, with what sounded distinctly like a horse laugh.

A horse laugh that Lauren found it almost possible to join in on.

"You okay, Lauren?"

She nodded. Did a near laugh look so painful on her face? But she nodded again. "Better than I've been in a long time, I think."

"Uh, good." Patrick still stood there, his wet clothes at his feet and his dry ones still dangling out of Minnie's saddlebag. He looked right and left, then of all silly things, the naked cowboy tipped his hat. "Wa'll… Howdy, ma'am," his John Wayne was back.

It was too much. His humor, kindness, and amazing body drew her across the last two steps. Rather than being cool, the skin of his chest was warm against her fingertips. She kept a hand there lightly as she leaned in for the kiss.

He stood there naked, but didn't grab or even drive into the kiss. Instead he gave her the gentleness one would expect from a long-time lover—not that she'd ever really had one to measure such things by.

When his hands moved tentatively to her light jacket, she again rested her hands on the backs of his to guide them along.

Never breaking the kiss, he stripped her down in such slow motion that she did indeed feel as if she was in a movie scene. A fellow soldier yanked off clothes, expected you to do the same, then tumbled into bed.

Patrick made it an endless time of exploration and discovery. As his hands uncovered and explored her body, so she did on his. When they were finally able to press their bare bodies together, they groaned in unison.

It wasn't funny. It wasn't ridiculous. But it was so unlike her that she couldn't help but laugh.

She felt Patrick's answering smile against her collarbone. After the second time his hat hit her in the face, she pulled it off his head and placed it on her own. It slipped most of the way down over her eyes, but she couldn't be bothered to fix it. Instead, she simply closed her eyes and allowed herself to feel.

For a brief moment, Patrick was gone and the cool air that she'd become unaware of wrapped around her.

He crossed to where their two horses grazed, then he was back with his bedroll and spread it on the grass. It was in a patch of afternoon brightness too weak to call sunlight due to the clouds, but warmer than beneath the trees. He took her hand and pulled her over to join him.

Patrick couldn't believe the vision of Lauren naked in the woods. A wood nymph grown into a mature and powerful woman. A beauty like he'd never known.

And her smile…

He'd throw himself in a thousand streams if he could see that smile each time. It sparkled as bright as the morning dew on the prairie despite the cool day.

She was all goose bumps by the time she lay beside him, and he pulled the unzipped sleeping bag over them.

"Are you sure, Lauren?" He didn't know why he was asking.

Because he was an idiot? She'd helped him unclothe her, for crying out loud. No hero in his right mind would ask the question, but still he did.

For a long moment she curled silently in his arms, then she nodded, her hair brushed over his face like a balm for where Minotaur's tail slap still stung.

At least he had protection this time. Last night there hadn't been a chance to dig down to where he'd hidden it at the bottom of the saddlebag, even if he'd thought of it before racing off into the woods. It had felt too presumptuous to carry it in his pocket. But not now.

"Yes," Lauren whispered. "Now."

"As the lady commands."

She actually laughed again. Short, breathy with need, but a laugh.

Patrick didn't hesitate. He'd known that he had been acting irrationally—"love at first sight" was for the movies and he was so very done with that.

And it wasn't love. At least not yet.

However, something had told him she was *the one*. Even casting aside all the movie clichés didn't make it any less true.

What really swept his feet out from under him was the combination of the stainless steel soldier and the vulnerable woman. Every fiber of his being wanted to protect her…and she probably needed less protection than any woman he'd ever met. But she showed him who she was. What she really felt. And that was a miracle.

When she rolled him on his back, sheathed him, and took him in, it was as if they were the only two people in the world. Warm inside the cocoon of the blanket beneath and the sleeping bag above, there was only them, their heat, their need.

The light leaked in each time she rose above him and blinked out each time she rocked back down against him. He was offered a stroboscopic view of Lauren Foster.

Her honeyed eyes watching him.

Sliding closed.

Her perfect breasts so filling his palms.

Her ribcage slender enough that his fingers felt as if he could hold her aloft forever.

Her back arching with a gasp.

Relaxing with a groan only to arch again when shadow returned.

And the connection. The raw power of the connection between them couldn't possibly be merely physical. Each of her moves made him reach deeper and deeper inside himself to answer it until he felt as if he was pouring his soul forth and pounding it into her body.

When the orgasm took them, she cried out. A soul-deep, searing sound that seemed to echo between them.

Even as her body thrashed with the power of the reaction, tears splashed down upon his chest. Tracing burning hot tracks across his flesh.

He couldn't tell when the throes of sex shifted to the throes of anguish, but soon she was weeping uncontrollably, holding herself stiff-armed above him.

He aimed a gentle nudge at the insides of her elbows. She collapsed against him and he wound his arms around her to hold her as she sobbed. Not knowing what else to do, he kissed her hair and held her tight.

Lauren slowly shifted from weeping to merely shaky breathing, and at long last to quiet.

He stroked his hands up and down her back. Somehow cowboy-rough palms didn't seem to be an offense to such wonderful skin when he felt the line of her deeper scars. For it wasn't the ones on her skin that mattered.

"I'm so sorry," she sniffled softly in his ear.

"Nothing to be sorry for."

"But—"

"I know. You're such a mess."

He could feel her nod.

"Would it be too weird if I told you that I enjoyed it?"

"No. What? Yes, it would be way too weird." She tried to push away but he held her in place and she didn't complain, soon settling back against him.

"I can't help but enjoy the vulnerability you just shared with me. I mean the sex was beyond awesome—definitely ruined me for even reminiscing about any past encounter. But that you'd trust me enough, feel safe enough in my arms to let down your shields. I can't help but feel horribly male and smug about that."

Lauren lay against Patrick's deliciously male and extremely comfortable body and wondered if she should be somehow offended or worried.

Yes, the sex had been beyond, well, what she thought sex was.

But the release?

When she'd wept over Jupiter's grave, those had merely been tears of sorrow.

This had been… She wasn't sure what.

"It's hard to find words when you aren't used to thinking about something."

"My problem is how to *stop* thinking," Patrick smoothed her hair into place and continued to hold her as if she wasn't some psychotic train wreck. "Though making love to you did a pretty amazing job of that."

"All I wanted was a good fuck," which sounded completely shitty, especially when she registered his "making love" comment.

Patrick didn't even tense or get offended. Instead he asked, "But?" and continued to stroke her. He *was* calming her like a goddamn horse and it was working.

"But…" Lauren wondered if there was a thesaurus anywhere handy. Didn't matter as she had no idea where to start. She felt a last few tears trickle down her cheek.

"But?" And this time she could feel that Patrick was beginning to worry.

This time she sat up enough to let a little daylight into their sanctuary beneath the sleeping bag so that she could see his face. It was such a good face.

"What are you doing to me, Patrick?"

"At the moment, nothing. But give me a few minutes and I'm glad to try again."

But he *was* doing something. If she left after today...she'd miss him. She'd miss his face. And his kindness. *And* the unbelievably awesome sex—the first kisses hinted that this wasn't some mere fluke. There was connection here at a level she'd never felt with a man before.

And the safety that, if she was being honest, she *had* felt in his arms. Felt for the first time since she didn't know when. She'd never thought about it. Maybe she'd never actually felt it.

But she certainly had now. In the thin light she could see the patches of moisture her tears had left on his chest and shoulder.

"I still think you're doing something to me."

"And I think you're avoiding whatever it is you're thinking about, Lauren Foster."

"It's not nice to point out the flaws in a woman's defenses right after she's—" fucked you so thoroughly. But that was wrong too. "After she's—" Lauren couldn't go to *made love,* "—so enjoyed what we just did together."

"Okay. Let's just write this off as something that we have to try repeating at the first possible opportunity."

"Yes. But not the weeping part."

"You can weep on me any time you want, Lauren."

She was leaning back down to shut out the light and kiss him again. A part of her also wondered just how soon Patrick's body would be ready for more.

But a sharp whinny sounded from one of the horses.

Loud. Close.

Then another. Alarm turning to terror.

In moments there was a crashing sound and thunder of departing hooves. For a moment she cringed beneath the blanket, wondering if she was about to be stampeded to death. But the two horses passed to either side and raced away.

She threw aside the sleeping bag and looked up in time to see Minnie's and Colette's hindquarters disappearing into the trees.

Another crash and she turned in slow motion in the other direction.

This time there was a deep roar, so loud that it could have shattered some of the trees. A grizzly bear stood not thirty feet away. It's head twisted sideways as it unleashed another unholy roar.

Patrick's attention went from Lauren's breasts, truly revealed in full daylight, to a pissed-off grizzly bear with a bloody eye. It looked as if he'd surprised the horses and earned a hard kick to the face for his mistake.

Now the horses were gone, leaving him and Lauren in the bear's sights.

And he was pissed.

Patrick's can of bear repellant pepper spray was still on Minotaur's saddle, though he'd bet that it wouldn't work in this case. This bear was far too angry to be stopped by something as simple as intense pain and temporary blindness that bear repellant caused.

Patrick had set his rifle close beside the blanket when he'd rolled it out—an unconscious habit from a hundred nights of camping out.

His hand was less than halfway to his weapon when two things happened simultaneously.

The bear put its head down to charge. Thirty feet was about three bounds for a big grizzly.

The other thing that happened was Lauren dove aside.

Patrick had the briefest flash of the old joke: the best way to survive a bear attack was to be a faster runner than anyone else with you. He was flat on his back, his muscles were Jell-O despite the adrenaline surging into them, and he had no leverage in this position. By the time he sat up, he'd be dead.

In the middle of her dive and roll, Lauren grabbed his rifle.

It seemed grossly unfair. Not only wouldn't he be able to defend himself in time, but he wouldn't even have a weapon to do it with.

Lauren's roll brought her to her knees with the rifle raised and pulled tight against her bare shoulder.

Oh, she was *defending* them.

"The nose!" Patrick shouted. "Aim for his nose."

One shot!

Two!

Three!

The hard cracks were lost in the beast's roar.

It put its head down ready for the final charge. And its head—with bared fangs that looked as big as Patrick's arm—kept going down.

Down until it plowed into the ground.

It seemed to stumble over itself. Patrick managed to roll aside—and back into the freezing stream—just as the grizzly performed a somersault and slammed back-first on top of the blankets and sleeping bag with a ground-shuddering slam. The sharp points of one gigantic claw, definitely bigger than Patrick's head, splashed into the water mere inches from his gut.

All he could focus on was the straight line of toes less than a foot away. Definitely a grizzly.

The small patch of woods was suddenly dead silent except for the rippling stream and the bear's slow, final exhale.

"Oh. My. God." No movie could capture such a terrifying, jumbled-up moment. This was definitely real life.

He looked over the bear at Lauren.

She now stood, Wonder Woman incarnate—naked without even the sexy uniform. She still held the rifle braced against her shoulder, aiming down at the bear's head. But he wasn't going anywhere.

"You're magnificent!"

Lauren looked up at him, then burst out laughing.

He'd thought her smile was amazing, but her laugh was right out of this world.

"You're wet again."

Patrick looked down. He was still sitting in the stream, so there was no way to deny it.

CHAPTER 9

"That's when we heard the hooves of Emily's, Mack's, and Michael's horses pounding back toward us." Lauren was enjoying herself far too much, but Patrick didn't know how to stop the story. So he decided it was the better part of valor, or at least avoiding total humiliation, to join in the telling.

Everyone was around the big Doug fir table in the back kitchen. They'd just finished wolfing down one of Nathan's bountiful Tex-Mex, build-your-own-taco meals. For the ranch operation, it was one of those quiet turnover nights. The last of the guests had left this afternoon and the ranch had taken no reservations this weekend because of the upcoming wedding. Only Mack had remained, but he was practically family. That and the storm currently lashing rain against the big darkened windows made a flight home out of the question.

Julie, a younger, smaller version of Emily with white-blonde hair, sat so close to Nathan that she was practically in his lap. Somehow his big brother had won the heart of the unobtainable cowgirl from next door. She now rode as an expert guide for Henderson's Ranch and also ran a small construction company specializing in ranch maintenance.

To add to the merry confusion, Mark Sr. and Ama were back from their cruise. Mark Henderson, Sr. had always been called Mac, without the k, but was old friends with Mack Bryson with the k. The two of them sat side by side playing it up for all they were worth. Mac this and Mack that.

"Now that's where the real unfairness started," Patrick cut in before Lauren could completely bury him in the story. "When it was over—and before you others could cover the half mile back to us—she yanks on her clothes faster than greased lightning."

"Combat training," Lauren crowed and even the taciturn Stan laughed.

"This," Patrick waved his hand helplessly at her. "This warrior princess looks at me all demure as I'm climbing out of the stream. As if she hadn't been standing naked with a rifle while taking down a grizzly mere moments before. Minotaur—"

"Minnie," Chelsea chimed in with a toast of her long-neck Budweiser.

"You need better taste in beer, Chels," but he kept moving so she didn't have time to sidetrack him. "*Minotaur* had run off with all of my dry clothes. My wet clothes from the first time Lauren dumped me in the stream..."

He offered a scowl and she returned a cheeky grin.

"...had turned into ice cubes. I'd rather still be sitting naked in that stream than wearing them."

"Well, you make a *very* fine sight not wearing them," Lauren clinked her Coors on Chelsea's Bud. She needed a beer education as well. Patrick toasted his Dos Equis toward Mark, who appeared to actually be drinking his this time. Mark looked back at him as if he'd lost his mind, which was no surprise to anyone.

"His brother's a fine sight too," Julie was only looking at her fiancé, and Nathan was definitely blushing. It was still weird picturing his big brother getting married, or even having sex. He was a big brother, not someone who would... It was like picturing his parents having sex. Patrick did his best to shake it off and return everyone's attention to the story.

"And there's seven hundred pounds of very dead grizzly lying on top of the only blanket in the neighborhood." Not even a corner scrap had been exposed for him to cover himself with.

"Then, just before Emily and all crested the bank..." Lauren grinned at him.

"She picked up my cowboy hat."

"It had somehow gone astray in, uh, earlier events."

She actually blushed a little when the others laughed. Another new discovery about Lauren Foster—that she even *could* blush.

"*Truly* exceptional earlier events," Patrick tried to prod more of a reaction. Instead it earned him a different kind of smile.

"Truly exceptional," she agreed softly. Her smile was the kind that a woman reserved for one special man. To have Lauren Foster look at *him* that way was the best feeling of his life. Well, almost as good as the moment he wasn't killed by a charging grizzly.

"Guess what she did?" Their three companions knew, of course, but no one else around the table did.

"What?" Mark asked.

"Instead of tossing it to me so that I could be at least a little decent..."

"I put it on," Lauren took the end of the story anyway, earning her another big round of laughter. "Your head is too big. I had to wear it practically on the back of my head so that I could see."

"Sure, so that you could see Emily laughing her head off at my expense."

"Michael and Mack were laughing too."

"Perfect." Patrick considered crawling under the dinner table to hide. "I'll buy you one in your size the next time we're in town."

"You know," Mark's deep voice of command drew everyone's attention, but he was staring at Lauren. "They say that a cowboy only ever lets one woman wear his hat."

Patrick opened his mouth to save her, but was too slow.

"What woman is that?"

Mark offered what Patrick had always thought of as his evil supervillain grin. Then he rested his left hand on the big wooden table and began tapping one finger. His ring finger. His wedding band made a solid, rapping sound against the hard wood.

———

"That's pure bulls—" Lauren tried to scoff in a throat suddenly gone dry.

Only one woman ever wore a cowboy's hat?

The men around the table were looking at her differently. As if they suddenly knew something about her that she didn't. As if…

"No way!" She looked to Chelsea for help, but she was looking at her husband Doug with a soft and dreamy expression. "Emily?" Lauren turned to her last resort…

No refuge there either.

"You all need to stop thinking things like that. I'm not…" But she wasn't quite sure what she wasn't. She certainly didn't want to say that she wasn't falling for Patrick, because she was and hadn't yet figured out how to stop her downward slide.

Unable to help herself, she slowly turned to face Patrick. If he was looking at her with puppy dog hope, she was gonna have to flatten him.

She'd never really known fear in the heat of combat before. In the heart of the fight—in those few crucial seconds of mayhem—a soldier was too busy staying alive to be afraid. Before and after was when fear had its chance to grab hold.

Lauren had felt raw terror down to the core of her soul when she realized that Patrick had no way to get clear of the bear's path. Never in her life had she taken a shot as important as that first one. She'd been able to see the bear die with the first round, but had pumped in two more because somehow that would drive back the monstrous beast just one more crucial inch to save Patrick.

The thought, the *fear* of losing Patrick so soon after she'd found him was all out of proportion to how she thought she felt about him.

Patrick offered neither smugness nor hope. Instead he offered her a friendly shrug of commiseration that indicated the saying was real and she was going to get teased for it. It was a friendly look. As if he was the only one on her side in this whole crazy situation.

Talk moved on to other topics, but somehow Lauren had lost her voice.

She sat a long time listening to the merry banter around the table. It washed over her, around her, but didn't touch her.

The hand resting lightly on her shoulder jolted her with surprise.

Patrick stood beside her. With the tiniest nod of his head, he indicated he was leaving and invited her to join him.

There was nothing to hide from anyone at the table. Nothing but the fact that she had fallen for a Long Island cowboy and fallen hard.

Emily was right. She wasn't big on fooling herself, so why should she try to fool others? Waste of energy, and to a Special Ops soldier, energy conservation was a key tool.

Lauren offered Patrick a nod of her own, then rose to her feet. It earned them nods and winks and teases, but they were kindly meant —more of a welcome than anything else. Certainly no hint of a hardcore military tease seeking to break down a "mere woman."

Patrick offered her a rain slick and led her out into the storm.

Her room was close by the kitchen, which would never do.

Patrick bunked with Stan, which definitely wasn't a solution either.

He took her hand and led her up the road toward the guest cabins.

"There's one cabin in particular I've always liked. I've been imagining you there since the first day."

She didn't know why she was surprised when he led her to the last cabin in the row—the small cabin tucked by itself in the trees.

Of course that's where Patrick would take her.

Patrick tried to understand what was happening as he lay in bed and looked at the woman sleeping in his arms. Firelight washed across her, adding hints of red to her light brown hair.

Somehow, the violence of the storm lashing the cabin had the opposite effect on their lovemaking. It had been slow, sweet, lasting for hours in front of the fire he'd lit.

And why had he never realized the wonder of simply holding a woman close after sex and talking about nothing of importance? They'd identified three different concerts that they'd both attended as teens. He'd only attended a few Yankees' games, but she was such a fan that they'd probably been there for some of the same games. Sitting in roughly the same section. It was hard to believe that he might have seen Lauren and somehow not known.

Her education in movies was woefully lame, which was something he'd definitely have to start fixing at the first opportunity. He had a mental list going in his head: *Casablanca, Citizen Kane, Star Wars...* How could she not have seen *Star Wars*, at least the original? And all of the New York films: *Moonstruck, Ghostbusters, Crossing Delancey.* Not even *When Harry Met Sally,* though she had eaten at Katz's deli, of course. His attempts to explain the "fake orgasm" scene—one of the funniest in film history—had her looking at him strangely. Maybe he shouldn't have tried telling it so soon after he had just survived a particularly spectacular real one that she'd said was very, very mutual.

Despite being New York familiar, she was also strange, even exotic. But she was also impossibly alive, warm, and when she lay in his arms, it was if it was the place she'd always belonged.

He now understood something of where she was from. But that wasn't what was scaring the daylights out of him.

"Where are you *going,* Lauren Foster?" he whispered it into the night, lit only by the soft glow of quietly crackling embers.

"I'm the last one to know," her voice was as soft as she'd been still.

"I thought you were asleep."

"This feels far too good to miss a minute of it in sleep."

He snugged his arm tighter around her waist.

It wasn't long before they were again finding ways to make each other feel even better.

But Patrick didn't forget his question and it nagged at him on and off all the next day. Though not that much as they didn't leave the cabin except for a brief foray to gather up a genrous picnic basket filled with Nathan's leftovers.

CHAPTER 10

The knocking on the cabin door jolted Lauren straight from sleep to wide awake. Soldiers, even ex-ones, couldn't afford the risk of slow transition times.

Patrick, on the other hand, lay half across her like a dead weight.

She slithered out and grabbed the first clothing that came to hand before crossing the cozy living room. They'd made extended use of the couch, some of the rug close beside the now darkened fireplace, and generally created an amazing number of good memories here. She wanted to stop and appreciate the cabin. It's interior had completely delivered on the promise of the exterior. Comfortable, homey, perfect if you didn't have a lot of belongings—the entire contents of her duffle wouldn't fill a single closet. A couple of bedrooms across the back, a luxurious tub, and a great room with a view that was Montana wide and Big Sky tall.

Through the big front window, she could see Emily stepping down off the porch.

She opened the door and called softly, "Morning."

Emily turned, then smiled radiantly.

"What?"

Emily scanned her eyes down Lauren to indicate what was amusing her. Lauren looked down as well.

"Oh." She was wearing Patrick's flannel shirt, and nothing else. With one button open, it had slid off one of her shoulders and the tails danced high on her thighs. "Yes, you found both of us." And she could feel that she was now sharing Emily's smile. It didn't feel strange on her face. It felt…right.

"I was wondering where you two had gone to ground."

Lauren pointed down at the two sets of muddy boot prints, definitely in his and her sizes, that had tracked across the porch and through the door to where their boots rested on the rubber mat.

Emily shook her head. "I always miss the ground clues. I spent my career in the air. I couldn't have tracked those caribou in a year, never mind an afternoon. Get dressed. And roust Patrick. He's best man today and his brother is already melting down."

"Best man?"

"Nathan and Julie are getting married today. Big wedding?" Emily was chiding her memory. It had been a major topic at dinner last night…two nights ago.

Lauren could only look at her wide-eyed. She had just spent a day and two nights in a love nest with Patrick. She'd never done anything like that before in her life but the time had slipped away so easily.

"I know," Emily nodded merrily before continuing back to the big house. "It's crazy when it happens to you, isn't it?"

"When what happens?"

But Emily was gone back into the thin rain.

Lauren grabbed a heavy jacket from the peg by the door and sat out on the porch bench. She needed a minute to get oriented to this new reality.

The air was cool on her legs, but it smelled so fresh that she didn't want to go back inside. When people said that rain washed the air clean, they hadn't understood about Montana. The air here wasn't merely clean, it was new-made. It smelled of rain and rich earth. It smelled of the tall conifers clustered around the side of the cabin and the white-barked aspen with leaves turned wedding-ring gold with the changing season.

Seasons. New York had them marginally, but the Big Apple insulated its residents from most of them. Afghanistan had two seasons: blazing summer when the fighting was heaviest, and freezing winter when the locals were too poor to purchase ammunition out of Pakistan—which was isolated in the winter by the snow in the Hindu Kush anyway. Somalia and Libya hadn't even had that, just heat.

Patrick said that the winters here were brutally cold, with frigid winds roaring down off the Canadian plains. But he also had talked about the beauty of the land coming awake in the spring. She wouldn't mind seasons. Not at all.

"Morning." Patrick leaned in the open doorway. His jeans low across his hips, his chest bare, and a blanket over his shoulders because she was wearing his jacket as well as his shirt. It smelled so like him. That, too, had added to the pleasure of the morning.

Lauren was getting to know his body, very intimately. Like his friendly personality, it didn't disappoint. Patrick was so…himself—no matter what movie script was going on in his head. She scooted over so that he could sit beside her.

He held out one side of the blanket and folded her against him as he sat.

"Nice legs," he kissed her on the ear. The blanket wasn't long enough to reach down. "I don't know if I've ever seen so many goose bumps in one place in my life."

She swung her legs straight out. Could see the scars that Jupiter and Max before him had left on her. And the goose bumps, but she didn't really feel the cold. She swung them across his thighs and he scooped her up into his lap.

"Emily came by."

"Oh?" Patrick nuzzled her neck.

"Your brother is coming apart."

"Doesn't sound like him," Patrick's attention shifted lower. Why men were so fascinated by breasts was one of the great mysteries. But Patrick had taught her to appreciate that fascination for the first time in her life. So many firsts with him that they wouldn't all fit in a single post-op debrief report.

She cradled his head and leaned down to kiss him on the ear. Now it was easy to imagine holding a child there. One who would be seeking life from her, rather than joy. Could it somehow be in her to give both?

"The wedding is this afternoon."

"Uh-huh," he mumbled against her breast.

Guessing what was coming next, she managed to move her head back just in time to not have her chin clipped as Patrick jolted upright. "I'm best man!"

"Emily might have mentioned that."

"I've gotta go," he jolted to his feet. She slid off his lap and her bare butt thumped down on the cold and wet porch.

"Eww!"

Okay, she hadn't been ready for that.

But he stopped and helped her to her feet, even though he was looking frantic. Still, he took the moment.

"Patrick," she rested a hand on his cheek to keep him from rushing off as soon as she was standing once more.

"Uh-huh," hurried and clipped, she only had half his attention.

She leaned in and kissed him.

That earned her his full attention.

And hers as well. In the cool Montana morning, rain misting the air, he wrapped his arms around her and held her tightly as they kissed.

She had let Patrick in much further than any man ever before. They had avoided speaking of the future—she still wasn't ready for that—but they had explored much of her past and he had merely taken it all in stride.

No. More than that.

He had done his movie story thing and shown her a different way to shoot the scenes. A better view. They had even talked about Jupiter. Yes, her dog had been murdered, but he had also lived. They had saved hundreds of lives between them, found innumerable explosives, and ferreted out terrorists. Patrick had showed her that her past had honor as well as tragedy and that there were no clean lines, only how they were viewed.

She finally buried her face against the base of Patrick's neck and breathed him in.

"I have to go," but still he didn't release her. Then one last squeeze and he rushed inside.

Lauren ran her hand over his shirt and jacket that she still wore. In his suddenly frantic state, she wondered how long it would take him to notice where they were. She considered not telling him, waiting for him to discover their location and then make him take them off her. She knew it was a temptation that would lead them back to bed rather than toward the wedding, so she headed inside to strip them off and shower.

She didn't want to. She'd lose the smell of him, as rich and real as the newborn air filling the Montana ranch. But she knew that she'd never be able to wash the feel of Patrick Gallagher out of her—not how he felt and not how he made her feel.

And she did need to get the mud off her butt.

"Lamebrain! Where the hell have you been?"

"Heaven," was the only reply Patrick could come up with.

"Yeah, right." Nathan was slicing strips off a big dark-red bear roast and feeding it into a meat grinder. Most of it would have been dressed, packaged, and frozen by now. But his brother was definitely in chef mode.

"What, there wasn't already enough food?" Nathan had been prepping the wedding feast for days even though there would only be a few dozen people on hand.

"Sure. But this is for breakfast tomorrow. I have a great Italian bear sausage recipe that I've been meaning to try and we ran out of pork and beef sausage the other day." He finished with the bear meat and began dumping black peppercorns and big seeds of coriander into the bowl of a KitchenAid mixer.

Patrick sighed. His brother might think he had his act together, but he was completely wrong. Patrick fished out a spice grinder and poured the spices out of the wide mixing bowl before his brother could add anything else.

Nathan barely noticed the swap out. Just started the grinder with an ear-shattering buzz. He held it on until Patrick reached over and pulled his brother's hand off the switch. Past ground and right over into powdered.

"You know you're supposed to be getting ready for your wedding this afternoon?"

"Don't remind me," Nathan tipped the grinder to dump the spices into the mixer bowl, then accidentally dropped in the grinder as well. Thankfully, neither machine was running. Patrick plucked it out of the mixer bowl and set it safely out of reach.

"What's next?" He was clearly going to have to lean into his brother's mania and make sure that he didn't accidentally poison the guests on his wedding day.

"Then we live happily ever after, right?" Nathan grabbed a bottle of sesame oil and Patrick plucked it from his hands before he could do something stupid with it.

"Sure. You and the bear sausage."

When Nathan reached for a jar of pickled red peppers, Patrick grabbed him by the scruff of the neck. There were advantages to being several inches taller than his big brother. Patrick dragged him, protesting, over to the table. He was still clutching a jar of mayonnaise that Patrick hadn't seen him get ahold of.

He shoved Nathan down into a chair.

And he popped back up like a jack-in-the-box toy.

Patrick shoved him down again, managed to wrestle away the jar of mayonnaise, and set it well out of reach on the table before sitting to face his brother.

"You gotta chill, Nat."

"I know. I know," he clenched his hands together.

Stan came in the back door. "Has he melted all the way down yet?"

"Pretty much."

Stan fetched a cup of coffee.

"I could use one of those."

"Uh-huh," Stan acknowledged from the stove. Then he strode over and sat across the table…with just his own mug.

"Asshole."

"Hey, I'm not the one who abandoned his brother to shack up with some hot dame."

"I didn't!" Well, he had, but he wouldn't think of it that way. Suspecting that Stan would be more than happy to keep messing with him, Patrick turned his attention back to his brother. "Nathan, don't you want to marry Julie?"

"Should warn you, Nathan," Stan sipped his coffee, which smelled so good. Too bad Patrick didn't dare leave his brother alone long enough to get a cup. "We'll both beat the shit out of you if you don't say yes damn quick."

"Of course I do!" Nathan's scattered attention was finally focused a bit by the heat of his protest.

"Then what's the issue? She's awesome and gorgeous."

"And loves you," Stan tossed in.

"And loves you for reasons that pass understanding," Patrick acknowledged. Is that how Lauren felt? Would she even say if she did? Wait, if she did, then how did he feel? "Whoa!"

"See?" Nathan was eying him sharply. "That feeling right there. Now multiply that times like a hundred thousand and you've got how it feels to be about to be married."

"What feeling?" Patrick barely managed to stutter it out.

Stan just shook his head. "Bro. It was clear on your face from the moment that dame stepped off the whirly bird."

"Huh?"

Nathan rapped his knuckles on the top of Patrick's head—hard enough to really hurt. He hadn't done that since they were kids. Not and gotten away with it. "It's called being in love, lamebrain."

"What is?" Something wasn't registering. Something about this moment. The moment when the hero realizes that there is only one woman in the world for him. He already knew that. But there was something more. Something he was missing.

"Give him a few moments, Nathan," Stan rumbled.

Nathan stood, picked up his jar of mayonnaise, and returned to his bear sausage, but there was nothing Patrick could do to stop him.

"No way," Patrick just couldn't keep up with what was happening.

Stan smirked.

Patrick turned to Nathan, who was looking at him slightly sad-eyed.

"What?"

"Just remembering, Pat. In about a minute, you're going to feel like a colossal idiot for not realizing sooner that you loved her so much. Then you're going to rethink everything you've done since the moment you met her, absolutely sure that you screwed up every single choice. Don't worry, you'll get over that soon."

"Are you?"

"Sure. Now I'm in the second-guessing phase of why someone as incredible as Julie would ever marry someone like me. You know what marriage is, Pat?"

He could only shake his head.

"It's making a blind bet. A gamble in which the stakes are life-sized but you have no way to know the odds. It's a wager that you can find a way to keep the most amazing woman you've ever met happy...for as long as you both shall live." Nathan whooshed out a breath and leaned back against the counter. "You think falling in love is scary, just wait until you're facing the vows."

"But I'm not..."

But he was. There was never going to be another woman like Lauren Foster. Complex, funny, soldier-tough and, at times, only for him, impossibly tender as well.

"But..."

"Here it comes," Stan declared, set his mug down, and interlaced his fingers with his hooks as if he still had ten of them.

But Patrick did know.

And it was the best feeling of his life. Except…

"There's a problem," and it stole his breath away.

"There it is," Stan practically crowed with delight.

"And *Bam!* there it is," Nathan agreed. "What if she doesn't love you back? Scary as hell, isn't it?"

Scary didn't begin to cover it. Lauren certainly had New York on her mind. They hadn't talked about it in the future tense—because they hadn't talked about anything that way these last couple days—but it was definitely on her mind. New York was impossibly far from Montana, a journey back that he didn't want to make.

"That's what's screwing me up today," Nathan looked at his hand, which held an apple corer for no apparent reason. "It doesn't matter how stupid it is. I know how Julie feels about me. But I'm going to be terrified until the moment she says, 'I do.' Until then…" he sighed. He dumped his half-finished preparations into plastic containers and began shoving them into the refrigerator. "Until then, I'd better leave well enough alone."

The door to the dining room and the rest of the house swung open.

"How long until the wedding?" Mack came into the room, offering one of his cheery smiles. "Fifty-five years with my Nancy. That's what you two boys have to look forward to. Best thing I ever did, getting that girl to take me on."

Patrick would be happier if Mack hadn't used the plural.

"Where's the bride?" Seeing Patrick head into the kitchen, Lauren had followed Emily's boot prints out to the barn. The rain, again on the increase, wasn't quite torrential enough to immediately erase her tracks.

"She's out riding with Chelsea," Emily fed a carrot to her horse Chesapeake, who began crunching on it loudly. "They're both horse crazy and ride at every excuse no matter what the weather is. We have more sense than that, don't we?" She addressed the last to her horse.

Chesapeake's snort might have been agreement, or frustration that there wasn't another carrot somewhere.

"Chelsea is maid of honor and all it took was a hint to her that part of her duties was to distract the bride from her nerves. Frankly they're both being so intense and cheerful about it that they were getting on my nerves."

Lauren was glad it wasn't her out there. She'd had her share of horrid weather during her military career and had learned not to be bothered by it, but she didn't think she'd make it a part of her civilian persona to go out and actively seek discomfort.

Leaning back against the open door of an empty stall, she watched Emily and her horse together. The blinding light of the legendary major had faded, but it hadn't revealed a great deal of tarnish either. Emily still shone like highly polished metal—metal forged in the US military.

That had Lauren looking at the upstairs secure office, the Tac Room, placed above the downstairs tack room filled with horse gear.

Emily had turned and noticed the line of Lauren's attention.

"Not yet," was all she said before changing the topic. "There's coffee in Chelsea's office. She usually has some yogurts and energy bars tucked away in there too."

Lauren crossed the wide center aisle and entered the neatly appointed office. It was part rustic ranch with a roll-top desk, comfortable chairs, and the recycled barn-wood walls covered in photos of happy guests with their horses. A large gun safe filled the corner, including a range of fine hunting bows.

"Who uses those?"

"Me, among others," Emily answered from the doorway. "I don't hunt, but I've always enjoyed the target work. Led the West Point team. Glad to teach you, if you're interested."

So Major Emily Beale was also one of the military's top archers—which sounded bizarre, but Lauren was past being surprised by anything Emily did.

Chelsea's office also had a high-tech aspect to it. A wall was covered with several large monitors acting as a single screen. They offered an easy view of the status and health of what Lauren could only assume was every horse on the property. How often they were ridden, diet, health issues, and a whole lot of things that she didn't get. Two names were in yellow.

Emily didn't even have to look to see what had caught Lauren's attention. "The yellow says that those two horses haven't been ridden in too long. That was Chelsea's ploy to get Julie to go on a ride with her. Truthfully, both horses were out on that ride with Patrick, but Julie couldn't resist the bait. Then they'll probably take their own mounts out for a short ride so that they don't feel guilty about riding another horse. They are two very sweet women."

Lauren scavenged a cup of coffee with sugar and cream (an atypical luxury in forward operations), and grabbed a yogurt and a banana for breakfast before sitting on the couch.

Emily selected a bottle of juice and turned the desk chair around to face Lauren before sitting in it.

"Very sweet, especially compared with two women like us," Lauren peeled back the lid on the yogurt.

Emily gave a half nod of agreement. "They never had to face the kind of things we did. It makes me grateful every time I look at them. Not that everything has been easy for them, but there's an unspoiled feeling about them."

"What doesn't kill you…"

"…makes you stronger," Emily finished the truism. "You have to be careful about becoming too strong."

"I think Patrick has been giving me a lesson in that these last couple of days." Each time she had unwound, even the least little bit, they'd somehow become closer, more intimate.

"The right man will do that to you."

"The right man," Lauren began eating her yogurt. "I'm not looking for the right man."

"Neither was I."

"Where is he now?" Because she certainly didn't want to get into the whole "right man" issue at the moment.

"Flying to Great Falls to pick up Nathan's parents from the airport."

"Nathan's parents," Lauren almost choked on a yogurt-softened blueberry.

"Yes," Emily was again enjoying herself far too much and drawing out the pain.

"That means they're also Patrick's parents."

"Yes. They are brothers, after all." If Emily ever smirked, she'd be smirking. But Lauren suspected that at heart she was too nice a person. She certainly wasn't the sort who'd tease a horse into a run to dump *her* man into an ice-cold stream.

"Patrick is about to introduce me to his parents."

"Probably."

"I'm going to kill him. I'm going to take him back into the wilderness and stake him out. I'm gonna cover his privates with bear bait. So help me god, I will."

"If it makes you feel any better, I doubt if he has connected those two facts yet: you and his parents."

"It doesn't," Lauren slouched lower on the couch and finished her yogurt. "Nothing ruins a good bit of revenge like an innocent truth. Cut it out, Emily."

Emily shrugged and drank some of her juice.

Lauren unpeeled her banana. She could only marvel at their changing rapport. This was the great Major Emily Beale. And Lauren was talking to her like…like a friend who was teasing her for the fun of it.

"I—"

A sharp whinny of surprise sounded from the barn. Then two more getting closer. Just as a man began cursing in the distance, Rip came trotting into the office as if it was something he did every day. The Malinois sat at her feet and lolled out his tongue as he offered her a big doggie grin.

"What do you want?"

He looked down at her banana, then back up at her.

Lauren broke off a piece and handed it over. He took it gently from her fingers, chomped on it twice, then swallowed and it was gone.

"That's all you get."

"Where is that dumb dog?" She heard someone grumbling out in the main part of the barn.

"In here, Stan," Emily called out.

The big man filled the doorframe and glared down at Rip, then sighed. "Well, I can't do a damn thing with him. The kennel is down-wind of the barn at the moment. The instant I let him loose, he high-tailed it in your direction. Maybe you can do something with him. He'll certainly never be an explosives dog with an attention span like that." Then, without giving her a chance to protest, he turned away and was gone.

Rip had craned his neck to look at Stan, but now faced her again.

It was hard, but you never disappointed the dog because it wouldn't understand. She forced herself to reach out and brush a hand over his damp fur.

Rip leaned into it and it felt good against her palm. Real. Too real.

"Down," she whispered it softly.

At her command, he lay down and curled at her feet with a happy sigh of contentment.

She broke off another piece of banana and popped it in her mouth.

"Ahh! Ick!"

Rip's head popped back up.

She spit the banana back out into her palm. The piece of banana, and most of her palm, were covered in strands of wet dog fur.

"I don't need a dog," she told Rip, who leaned against her calf and settled once more, appearing to go instantly to sleep.

"Now you have two men," Emily's tone was remarkably dry on such a wet day.

"That's two more than I need." But her opinion didn't seem to be holding much weight at the moment.

Patrick did his best to run into Lauren, but it wasn't working.

She hadn't come to the kitchen for breakfast.

He'd scooted up to the highest cabin. She'd made the bed, but there were no other signs that she'd even been there.

As he came back down the hill, he saw Michael in shorts and a t-shirt, heading out on a run as if it was a sunny summer afternoon. He knew from experience that Michael wouldn't be back for at least 10k and more likely twice that. No wonder the guy was in such amazing shape.

When Patrick passed Stan out in the main yard and asked if he'd seen Lauren, all he'd gotten in answer was a SEAL-mean snarl. Man needed another cup of coffee or something.

He might have waved his hooks in the direction of the barn. What could Lauren have possibly done to make him so angry? He was halfway there when he heard the ranch's helicopter. In moments, Mark was swooping down onto the main yard and settling in front of the garage. It was a much gentler approach than when he'd arrived with Lauren and Michael. That had been…wow!…just a week ago.

Patrick double-checked the area. He'd have to be careful; after yesterday's storm, there were mud puddles everywhere. He'd had enough of that. He braced himself against the blast of the rotor-driven wind.

Then he almost did stumble and fall into a mud puddle when he saw who it was.

"Mom! Dad!" He rushed up to open their doors and welcome them. They'd never actually been out to the ranch. "Sorry it's such miserable weather for your visit, but I'm so excited you're finally here."

He'd tried to get them to come sooner, but they were classic New Yorkers and rarely traveled west of the Hudson River. That, and they were always trying to convince him to move back to The City.

"Ha!" At their inquiring looks he just hugged them again. Every time he'd been home, Dad had launched a campaign of making sure to list every still eligible woman from his past. Another attempt to get him to return East. "Man, oh man, do I have some news for you!"

Of course, at the rate things were going, he just *might* be back in New York after all and they'd be the ones getting the last laugh.

Patrick really wished he knew where Lauren was.

He'd love to introduce them.

"You sure you don't want to go out there?" Emily had tipped her chair back enough to glance sidelong out the window of Chelsea's office. "They look pleasant enough."

"They aren't even human." Lauren wasn't moving from this couch even if a herd of elk arrived to prod her along with their pointy antlers.

"What do you mean?

"They aren't people. They're parents."

"Parents of your lover," Emily finally stopped looking outside through the window.

"Stop saying shit like that." Lauren tried to sink lower, but there was a dog sleeping on her feet.

"Shit like what?" Chelsea stepped into the office from the barn's main aisle. She was still wrapped in dripping rain gear with a set of reins in her hand. Her gray horse looked suspiciously over her shoulder at Lauren.

"Lauren is having a panic attack because Patrick's parents just arrived."

"Ooo! I didn't even think of that. You get to meet the 'rents, Lauren. That's so cool! It's like your affair, which is not what it is by the way, belongs to a thoroughbred racer zipping through the pack so fast that it's a blur. That happened to me. It was a couple Christmases ago. I came to babysit Emily's kid, met Doug, and bang!"

"What went bang?" Julie came up beside Chelsea. Now there were two women and two horses staring at her. The doorway was so crowded that Julie's horse had to use the office's inside window that normally offered a view of the barn's main aisle. It was a horizontal slider, and the half that moved was open. He stuck his head through the window and snuffled at her face from mere inches away to see if she was of interest.

Lauren really wished she wasn't, but between the three women, two horses, and a dog, she was becoming resigned to her fate.

"Doug and me," Chelsea held up her left hand with a simple gold and diamond wedding ring on it. "There I was, Ms. World Traveler, figuring I'd settle down in a decade or so and eventually find a good man to help keep my toes warm. I hit the ranch and never left."

"Cost me a good nanny," Emily groused. "Not sure if I've forgiven him for that yet."

"Good thing I'm better at horses."

"You were great with Tessa," Emily unwound enough for the sincerity to shine through. "You're going to be amazing when you have your own kids."

Chelsea, for once, was silent. But her face turned as bright red as her hair.

"How long have you known?" Lauren asked while Julie and Emily just stared at her in shock.

"Just a couple days. We didn't want to take away the thunder of your wedding, Julie, so we were going to wait to tell anyone. I guess I kinda messed that up."

Julie threw her arms around her. "No! It's perfect. Nathan and I want to start trying right away. Maybe we can have our babies nearly together. Maybe I already am. It's my time," she laid her hand on her belly. "So maybe…"

"This is getting completely out of hand!" Lauren was doing what she could to not hyperventilate.

All three women turned to her, but none spoke. There weren't even looks of sympathy or understanding. They were all simply waiting, as if they knew something that she didn't.

Even the two horses standing patiently behind their riders turned to share a look.

There was no way that her stray thought of a child this morning could show on her features. It. Wasn't. Going. To. Happen!

"She's stubborn," Chelsea finally sighed. "She's so like you, Emily. You're like cosmic twins or something."

Lauren could only blink at that. She was like Emily? Why would anyone even think to compare them? They weren't even on the same scale.

"I heard about the job you did on the caribou and the bear," Julie said thoughtfully. And suddenly the excited bride-to-be shifted aside and Julie became Henderson's Ranch's top horsewoman. "I know where Mack took you and that's some tough tracking. I talked to him and Mr. Gibson about it and they both said they couldn't have done better. And taking down a grizzly that fast and clean. Don't know if even I could have done that. We'll have to work on your horsemanship some before you'll make a great guide. I saw you come in yesterday and your basic instincts are very good." Julie turned to face her maid of honor. "Nice job on the horse selection, Chels. Colette is dead-on the right horse for her. Emily," Julie faced her across the office. "I bet I could have her ready by next year. Take some of the load off me so that I can fulfill a few of the construction contracts I've got stacking up."

Emily made a thoughtful sound.

"But I won't be here next year." Lauren would be two thousand miles away.

Again they all looked at Lauren as if waiting for something.

Well, it's true. She was going to be back in New York soon.

Wasn't she?

CHAPTER 11

Patrick still hadn't found Lauren, but at least he'd found Nathan.

He'd been sitting in the lodge's main room where the wedding would be held, since the weather outside kept getting worse.

It was a great, lofted space rising over two stories. It had towering windows at both ends, one facing the cabins and the Rockies, and the other facing the pasture and the Great Plains. Most of what was visible in that direction was Larson land—Julie's family.

The massive stone fireplace had been lit.

Deep leather couches and chairs had all been turned until they were lined up like pews. The altar was a simple wooden arch. A pair of potted roses, which had been growing on the sunny southern porch until this latest storm, were still full of white and red blooms. The room was so big that the baby grand piano was almost invisible in one corner.

Nathan had been sitting quietly in the middle of the room when Patrick had led their parents in.

"What are you doing, groom boy?" Patrick had called out, but Nathan didn't turn.

"Not much. Sometimes I sits and thinks, and sometimes I just sits."

"A. A. Milne," Dad called out and Nathan leapt up to hug his parents. Mom wasn't much of a hugger, but he held on to her especially long as she patted his back.

They settled in quietly with Nathan and simply enjoyed the late morning light and the fire's warmth. They talked of his parents' latest classes: Dad was working on a new Modern-Interpretations-of-Shakespeare seminar, and Mom said they were close to another prosthetics breakthrough in her bioengineering lab. Patrick would have to make sure she met Stan. He could have so much more than hooks, no matter how much he insisted he didn't give a good god damn. Maybe Mom could work out some kind of prototype and get grant money for Stan to get a new arm.

They'd been in the great room-turned-wedding venue for close to an hour when someone peeked in.

Julie yelped with pleasure and came running up the aisle. She hugged Mom and Dad like she was already part of the family, then she sat on the bench-high stone hearth, close enough to Nathan to hold his hand.

Dad sniffled and surreptitiously wiped at his eyes afterward.

Would Patrick be the mush of the relationship just as Dad was? When the other person in the relationship was Lauren, that was a given—anyone would be a mush in comparison.

"Patrick?" Nathan hit him in the shoulder.

"What?" Patrick might have hit him back except he'd wait until Julie wasn't sitting to his other side. He filed away a note for later retribution.

"Julie was asking you something."

"Oh, sorry. Wandering brain." Maybe he'd let his brother off the hook this time. It was his wedding day after all.

Julie leaned in. "You know that if you mess up with Lauren, you're going to have a whole lot people angry with you. Right?"

"Who's Loren?" Mom and Dad were looking at him strangely. Loren Maxwell was a fellow professor and a good friend of the family. *He* was also a sixty-two-year-old three-time divorcé.

"Lauren with an *a-u*, not an *o*. She's... Hold it. Who would be angry with me?"

"Me, for one. Emily, for two."

"Yo," Nathan raised his hand. "Seriously, bro. If you—cover your ears, Mom—fuck this up the way you usually do, you're toast."

"I'm not going to—"

"Then Chelsea, Mark…"

"Mack," Nathan continued. "Colonel Gibson. Did you know that he did part of Emily's wedding ceremony? She just told me the story this morning. The President was there and the colonel. Together they—"

"Whoa! Whoa! Whoa!" Patrick held up both hands. "We've only known each other for about a week."

"Suck it up and do it right for once. This time it counts," Nathan emphasized it with a knuckle punch on Patrick's upper arm that really stung. Retribution, as soon as he was clear of Julie, was definitely back on the list.

"I just wanted to introduce her to Mom and Dad. That's all."

This time Julie, the most pleasant-tempered person on any ranch except maybe Chelsea, actually leaned forward and cuffed him lightly on the side of the head.

"And you don't think that is scaring the daylights out of her?"

"What? Why would it?"

Dad sighed and shook his head. Even Mom looked distressed.

"What? You guys aren't scary."

"Son, *she* doesn't know that. If you want us to meet your friend, you should ask her first."

"I would. If I could find her!" This conversation just kept getting crazier.

"I can't believe you're one of our best guides," Julie groaned. "How do you track anything if you can't even find the woman you love?"

"What?" His parents practically shouted it in unison.

Patrick shrugged. He did love Lauren. "I guess this conversation could have gone better."

"Well, at least he's smart enough not to deny it," Nathan noted and Julie nodded in agreement.

"Better than either of us were doing at this stage," and they shared one of those melty movie looks.

"Hold it," Patrick felt as if he was being tag-team battered by this whole conversation. He kept having to stop it just to keep himself from stroking out at all the changes going on. "Just…wait a moment!"

And everyone did. Except Julie, who glanced aside and actually started to giggle.

"What?"

"I just had a conversation with Lauren that was a lot like this one. Different, but kind of the same as well."

"How did *she* take it?"

"No better than you," Julie's grin just kept getting bigger.

"Where is she?"

"Now that would be telling," Julie glanced away as if averting her gaze.

"I need to find her."

Then he more felt than heard something close behind him.

"In that case," Lauren leaned down and whispered. "You should try actually looking for me."

Coming through the kitchen and down the hall past her room—where she'd used a bath towel to get Rip at least moderately dried off—had let Lauren hear enough to prepare herself a little before she'd entered the fray. If bravery was what was called for, then bravery she would provide. Even knowing Chelsea was pushing her buttons intentionally didn't make it any easier being called a chicken—especially not when she started her crazy chicken dance again.

"Hello," she stepped around the chairs until she was beside Julie and facing the Gallaghers. "I'm Lauren Foster."

"Isleen Gallagher."

"Liam."

They both offered solid handshakes. They were both shorter than Nathan, making Patrick by far the standout in the family. Nathan had his father's features, but his mother's slightly more solid frame. Patrick was the opposite, his father's slim frame, but his mother's beauty transformed onto male features.

"So, why do you need to find me?" She sat on the hearthstone beside Julie, across the close circle from Patrick. Rip shoved his way into the middle of the circle, solicited a dog scratch from the whole circle, then curled up on the floor.

Patrick looked at the Malinois and then he looked at her closely.

"I know," she mouthed to him. She'd come a long way since Rip's first appearance had made her faint.

"Proud of you," he mouthed back.

It was about the nicest compliment she'd ever had. She closed her eyes for a moment to take it in and hold it close. A Delta Force compliment might be a "Well done" but not much more. Her parents might have noted her good grades, but that was about their level of positive reinforcement in her childhood.

Patrick's "Proud of you" made her heart pick up its pace, but feel as if her blood flow slowed and calmed at the same time.

"He was looking for you so that he could tell you he loves you," Nathan was clearly enjoying himself by his tone.

Lauren opened one eye to look at Julie, who nodded a confirmation.

She opened the other to look at Patrick, who had never lied to her.

He shrugged that it was true.

And just that fast, her calmness was seared away by the fire's heat and rushed up the chimney.

Patrick opened his mouth to try and explain why this was happening in front of everyone instead of quietly, somewhere romantic, just between the two of them.

Then he closed it again. Some things were a lost cause.

But Lauren's eyes just kept getting wider and wider until he was half afraid she'd turn into an anime caricature of herself.

He opened his mouth again but still didn't know what to say.

Not even if his parents, brother, and soon-to-be sister-in-law weren't there as well.

"I do," was all he could think to offer. "You're the only woman there will ever be for me, Lauren."

Her mouth dropped open to emphasize her impossibly wide eyes even more. Then she blinked hard. When she looked at him again, it was with narrow, honey-colored slits.

"Since when?"

He scratched at his head. "Since the moment I fell into the mud puddle, I guess. At least it sure feels that wa—"

"Julie!" Chelsea's shout filled the room as the front door slammed behind her. "You're getting married in two hours, girlfriend. Enough fooling around. Shower, hair, dress. It's time, and Ama is waiting. We are going to pamper you so good that you're going to want to marry us rather than that handsome hunk holding your hand. Come on." Chelsea strode right into the circle, grabbed Julie's hand, and dragged her away before she could even kiss Nathan on the cheek.

"Patrick," Chelsea called back over her shoulder as she led Julie upstairs. "Make sure your brother is at least dressed and moderately clean. If he's going to marry someone as amazing as my BFF Julie, he'd better get it together and do it now." She continued making sure everything was in order even as her voice faded away, then was cut off by the closing of an upstairs door.

"You okay for a sec, Nat?"

"Sure. I'm dying to see how you dig your way out of this, Pat. Should be a good show."

"Thanks. You're totally useless as a big brother, you know that, right?"

"And I'm proud of it," and Nathan leaned back in his chair to watch the show. "I need popcorn."

His parents looked bewitched, bothered, and bewildered, but Patrick couldn't remember the reference for that at the moment.

He looked at Lauren and his heart simply stuttered.

"I—"

But Lauren wasn't looking at him. She was looking up over his shoulder.

Patrick spun around to follow the direction of her gaze.

Emily and Michael were standing at the door. Emily was waving for Lauren to come join her. It had a very military look to it—a sharp jabbing point at Lauren, then an upswept arm with a flat hand.

She jolted to her feet.

"No. Wait."

Lauren looked down at him. He could see her need to go. She'd turned all stainless steel soldier military.

Another glance over his head, and he could only assume that Emily repeated the gesture.

Lauren squatted quickly, resting a hand on Rip's collar. "Be quick."

"I—" How was he supposed to be quick? Just dive in...he'd had plenty of practice at that lately. "I love you, Lauren Foster." He had no idea what else to say.

"Okay."

"Okay?"

She reached out a hand to brush it down his cheek. "Best I've got at the moment. But I'm not running away, if that's of any comfort. Surprises the daylights out of me that I'm not."

All he could do was nod. By the time he repeated the gesture, she was gone.

"What a strange young lady," his Dad said slowly. "I like her, but I'm not quite sure why yet."

Patrick turned to his Mom. First impressions had to count for something.

"What your brother said," she pointed across at Nathan.

"What?" He turned to Nathan. His brother was lounging back as if all of his wedding nerves had been sloughed off in the last few moments. He grinned.

"Don't fuck it up, Pat."

CHAPTER 12

"Michael could have handled this, but he insisted that this was the right test," Emily was speaking quickly as the three of them jogged across the main yard toward the barn. The rain was back, heavier, but she hadn't had time to grab a jacket.

"The right test?" She snapped her fingers and Rip fell in tight beside her in heel position. Stan had trained him up perfectly. If she spoke the word "seek" and signaled which direction with a hand gesture, she'd wager that Rip would do his duty and find any explosives or adversaries.

"This is a live action," Michael confirmed. "Not a training scenario. You will treat it with utmost urgency. I will be assessing your performance."

Lauren almost stumbled. Colonel Michael Gibson, Delta Force's top operator, was going to be assessing her in a live-fire scenario? She was so screwed. She hadn't run a 10k since her arrival at the ranch. Even trotting across the yard in the rain, she could feel it. That was one thing she'd be fixing starting tomorrow—assuming there was a tomorrow.

She wore no safety gear or sidearm. She'd seen Chelsea's gun safe in the corner of the barn's office—it was a Winchester Ranger and as secure as they came. It would take some serious effort to breach without explosives. Even with explosives.

But Emily strode right past Chelsea's office with the safe and raced up the stairs to the Tac Room.

Six-digit code, thumb print, *plus* retinal scan.

Damn!

Emily swung the door open and stepped inside.

Lauren knew she was being judged, but she had to stop briefly on the threshold to even understand what she was seeing, never mind assess it.

Her initial estimation about a military installation in the middle of a horse barn had been completely accurate and wholly misguided. She'd expected a couple of radios. Perhaps a secure terminal.

"Tac" clearly stood for Tactical. It was a high-tech command center more impressive than even the upper deck on Air Force One, which she'd only seen in pictures.

Out the two one-way windows ranged a bird's-eye view of the barn. Dozens of horse stalls. For some reason, this view, more than any prior experience this week, emphasized the scale of the Henderson's Ranch operation. As many stalls ranged in the other direction. A big skylight, also one-way she noted, offered a wide view of the pastureland.

The views only made what was inside the room all the more surreal. There were two command stations, because there was no other word for them. A rack of satellite radios separated the two stations. She recognized several of the frequencies and could only blink—Delta Force and Night Stalkers headquarters command. Each station included a half dozen computer screens arranged to act as either separate displays or a single combined view, a pair of keyboards, and, Lauren turned, a server array of impressive power.

Michael gave her a small push between the shoulder blades and she stumbled into the room. He closed the door behind himself and leaned back against it with his arms crossed over his chest.

Emily dropped into one chair and, at a loss for what else to do, Lauren sat in the other. Rip sat at her side. She released him from heel and he dropped into the doggy equivalent of parade rest. Attentive, ready at a moment's notice, but no longer vibrating with urgency. That was left up to her. She hated that Rip was now depending on her for giving him the right signals, but didn't see any way out of it.

Emily's station had pictures of Mark and her children. A team of grinning pilots with smoke-stained faces in front of a helo painted black with flames down the side. She saw the Mount Hood Aviation logo that said Emily hadn't merely flown firefighting helicopters, she'd flown with the best outfit anywhere. A similar photo, but this time more serious, a company-sized flight crew of men and women in full military gear ranged in front of a Night Stalkers lethal black-painted DAP Hawk helo.

Lauren looked at the empty spot behind her console. What would she have? Four photos of dogs and a hook to hang Jupiter's last leash that she still wore as a belt? What kind of a legacy was that in comparison with Emily's array of photos?

"There's a team on the ground in trouble," Emily started in.

Lauren shook off her morose thoughts. "Where?"

Emily glanced up at Michael, who showed no sign of moving ever again. Until he did, there was no escape.

"All or nothing," was all he said.

Emily nodded. "All classified, of course."

"Duh!" Lauren had figured that one out on her own.

"Sorry. I've been dealing with civilians for too long. Most of what I consult on is mission planning and post-action air tactics analysis. I almost never get live-action issues. Not supposed to get any, but this call actually came in to Michael despite his being on leave."

"For reasons we will beat out of him as soon as this is over," Lauren had had enough of no answers. Michael, her own future, Patrick… Enough already.

"Absolutely!" And Emily shared a smile with her.

They both ignored Michael's soft curse of resignation.

"The team is on the ground in France."

Lauren blinked. "France?"

"We got a track on a terrorist cell with a link deep into GIGN."

Lauren could feel the sheathed Glauca burning against her ankle. Their Number One dog handler, who'd given it to her, had worked for the French commandos of GIGN.

"So we sent in a Delta team…"

"Without notifying the French," Lauren didn't need to guess. "And now they're caught in the sandwich between GIGN and the terrorists, both of which are thinking that the undercover Delta are the bad guys."

Emily nodded. "The team asked for our help to achieve their objective and exfiltrate without being caught and making a political disaster."

"Who's the target?"

Emily hit a key on her console and Lauren could only gasp at the face on the screen. She could actually feel the blood draining out of her face.

"I don't see what the big deal is," Nathan was once again working on his bear sausage, though far less frantically.

"Because we're wearing our wedding suits, you idiot." Patrick had made him take off his jacket and don an apron, but it was still stupid.

"I wasn't talking about that. I was talking about Lauren."

"Telling a woman you love her and having her say 'Okay' isn't a big deal?" Patrick gave up even trying to assist Nathan and just hiked up to sit on the counter, well clear of the work zone.

"Well, this isn't the movies, Patrick."

"I figured that out on my own." No movie had ever communicated how Lauren made him feel.

"Simple question. Is she the woman you want to take the blind, life-long bet with?" Nathan didn't even have the decency to stop what he was doing, as if it was somehow a normal, everyday question— rather than one that was completely freaking him out.

"I…" Patrick had no idea what to say to that. He began fooling around with the jar of mayonnaise that still sat unused on the counter, just to have something to do with his hands.

"It's only been a week. Take time. Ask me again in a month, or three. Despite the movies, lightning-strike romance isn't the norm." Nathan was not being helpful.

"How long did it take you to fall in love with Julie?"

"In lust? Several seconds, maybe. In love?" Nathan shrugged as he continued running cold water through the inside of a long line of sausage casing. "I guess I was a little stupid that way. When I was in it, I didn't realize until it was almost too late. In retrospect, once I understood how I really felt about her, I'd been gone on her from the first couple minutes."

"I still don't—"

"You fell off your horse and into a puddle the first time you ever saw her."

And there was the several seconds that his brother had mentioned. He *had* been gobsmacked by Lauren from the first moment.

"Heard you turned down a hot camper that night."

"Clara."

"Uh-huh. When did you ever do that?"

"All part of the ranch adventure for the guests. Have a fling with a cowboy." Single women had certainly arrived often enough with that in mind and he'd been more than happy to reap the benefits...until that first night after he'd met Lauren.

But that meant...

"Oh, shit! I really have loved her since the first moment, haven't I?" He'd thought he'd just been...taken by her since then.

Nathan tipped his head one way, then the other, before he slipped the casing on the end of the sausage stuffer and turned on the mixer attachment. "Love is a tricky word." He dumped his sausage mixture into the top funnel and meat began squirting into the casing. "That takes knowing a person. I thought I loved Julie when I proposed to her, but that was just a shadow of how I feel about her now. In six months, who knows."

"Or in six years," Patrick couldn't resist.

"Or sixty!" Mark entered the kitchen and dug a beer out of the refrigerator. "If that thought doesn't shrivel a man, nothing will."

Nathan just glared at him. "I didn't need to be thinking about that."

"Glad to help, Nathan," Mark handed each of them a beer, but Nathan just nodded for him to set it on the counter. His hands were busy shaping the five-foot-long filled sausage casing into a large coil before starting on the next one.

Patrick put down the mayonnaise jar—probably a good idea before he dumped it on his suit pants—and took the beer.

"You know, Nat. They say that medical science is really going to be extending our lives. Could be way more than sixty."

"Which means a hundred years from now, you'll still both be useless pains in my ass. Oh joy." Nathan set aside the first filled casing and began filling the next. "The trick is that it takes time to get to know a person. How much do you really know about her?"

"Like what? I know more about her than…" Patrick didn't like where this was going.

"Than most women you've slept with. Doesn't mean much when you've been such a dog. I mean like what do you know about her past hookups? Not who she's slept with, but had actual relationships with?"

"Why would I care, if she's with me now?"

Mark just grunted at that.

Nathan shrugged and set the second filled casing coiled on top of the first. "Just saying. You never know what is going to suddenly rear its ugly head from the past."

Patrick thought of some of his pasts and didn't like the sound of that at all.

Lauren couldn't look away from the Tac Room screen.

"Sergeant Georges Marchand," she barely managed to gasp.

Emily twisted to look at her in surprise.

Then she felt the rage build inside her, build until she couldn't hold it in and it boiled over. "He's the traitor? That bastard! He—" She couldn't even say it. They'd had an affair while she and Jupiter had been doing training with GIGN's war dogs. It hadn't merely been fun, that week they'd spent together in Tunisia was the closest she'd come to loving anyone before... Before...

She sighed. Before Patrick.

And Georges was a traitor? Passing intel to some jihadist terror cell?

It was bad enough that an American general had betrayed her dog to its death. But that a lover and fellow dog handler—

"What is it with men?" She spun and turned her rage on Michael.

He was so surprised that he banged the back of his head on the door as he tried to jerk away.

"None of you can be trusted." Back to Emily. "Tell them to shoot the bastard and be done with it."

But "friend" Emily was gone. In her place sat Major Emily Beale—the chill, daunting presence of a topflight warrior. Screw that. She didn't care.

"What?" The bitterness burned in her throat and Lauren had to swallow hard to keep the bile from blasting forth.

"It's Commandant Marchand."

"Fine. Whatever." Equivalent of a major. "So he lied about that too. Lied about—" but she bit that off. It was too painful. After a splendid week in Tunisia, he had sworn on his dog's life—the French were always so dramatic, which was part of his charm—that he loved her and there would never be another woman for him.

Which was far too close to what Patrick had just said.

Well, to hell with him, too.

"Shoot the bastard and let me go home." Except she didn't know where that was anymore. "Let me go back to New York." And she wrapped her arms around her gut against the knot of pain wound so tightly there.

"Is that how you really feel?" Again, Major Beale was asking. But she also wondered if Emily might be in there somewhere, asking a different question with the same words.

Lauren wanted to shout out her certainty, but it wouldn't come.

Patrick's declaration had been sincere. Awkward, almost funny in that sense. She suspected that the moment would have made a great movie scene: him declaring his love in front of his brother and parents, and her saying a mere, "Okay." She'd imagined, however briefly, having children with Patrick. A life…as if a warrior could ever have a normal life.

There was *them* and there was *us*.

Chelsea and Julie and Patrick all stood on one side. And on the other side of the door: she, Michael, Mark, and Emily. They knew better. They knew that love was too easily betrayed.

Except she could see Michael's simple band of gold and remembered how hard it was for him to tell his wife that he loved her.

And Emily's ring shone. Black gold with a blue diamond.

"Night Stalker blue," Emily followed the direction of her gaze and brushed her fingers gently over the diamond.

"No. It's the color of your eyes."

Emily blinked in surprise. And that's when Lauren understood just how good a man Mark was. He'd given his wife a ring that was for both the warrior and the woman. What kind of man did that?

It wouldn't surprise her if a man like Patrick did something similar.

She looked back at the image on the screen. Georges Marchand. Sergeant or commandant—the equivalent rank to Emily. He, too, had been sincere. She hadn't understood that then because she had simply been enjoying the affair. It explained his attempts over the years to renew the connection, but Delta Force hadn't left much flexibility in her schedule. Their affair had devolved to a disconnected series of occasionally steamy phone calls.

"It's wrong," the words were out before she knew it.

"What is?"

"Georges wouldn't do that. It just feels wrong."

Emily consulted something on her screen. "Can you prove it in the next twelve minutes?"

Lauren thought for a moment, pulled out her phone, and hit her Favorites list. Georges was still near the top.

"I *was* helpful," Mark protested.

"Likely story," Patrick teased him and sipped his beer.

"Actually, he was," Nathan nodded as he filled the last sausage casing. Several large stacks of filled sausage were now piled on the counter in great coils. "I almost lost Julie when I flew back to New York to help a friend launch his restaurant. Mark came and straightened me out."

"No idea what I was doing, but it worked," he shrugged. "I guess we did okay between us."

"I'm here. It doesn't even have to be about a relationship."

Patrick didn't like imagining Lauren having any past relationship important enough to rear its ugly head. But with his past, he'd be better off keeping his mouth shut. But what if not just New York, but something in her military past got in their way? Or her military future. It didn't take a genius to guess where she'd gone, even if he couldn't begin to guess what was happening there. How would she make choices now?

"Sucks when it *is* past affairs though," Mark studied his beer with none of his usual bravado. "Or when you think it is."

"What are you talking about?"

"Emily. Had a big-time crush on the President. Scared the shit out of me. Still have no idea how close I came to losing her to him, but it was close."

Patrick had heard that Emily and the President were friends, but... "Major ouch!"

"Yeah," Mark agreed. "Worked out in the end though. And he's been a good sport about losing her. Even performed the ceremony, half of it anyway."

"You beat out the President of the United States for Emily's hand?"

"Yep!" And the Mark Henderson he knew was back, cocky grin

and all. "Best man won. So, who are you gonna be winning with, Mr. Best Man?"

"One guess," Nathan answered for him. He slid the sausage into one of the big fridges, washed his hands, and leaned back against the counter with his beer.

"Where is *your* bride-to-be?" Mark aimed the neck of his bottle at Patrick's chest, then at Nathan's. "Off with *his* bride-to-be?"

Bride-to-be.

He'd told her that he loved her. If she agreed, then that step was kind of inevitable. Closing scene of *Notting Hill, Runaway Bride, My Big Fat Greek Wedding,* and just about every other romantic comedy ever made.

"No..." Patrick remembered Lauren rushing away from him. "She's off with Emily and Michael. Probably in that Tac Room." He'd never seen the inside once Julie had finished building it, but the way they'd left in such a hurry, it was the only thing that made sense.

Mark looked toward the barn with narrowed eyes as if he could see through all of the intervening walls. "Why doesn't that sound good?"

"*Ma chérie!* This is not a good time. Very not. Not even to hear from you, my love."

"Don't hang up, Georges," Lauren had set the phone on speaker and set it on the desk so that Michael and Emily could hear as well. "On your life, don't."

"This is no ordinary call where we heat each other up but never make a date to come together, is it, my Lauren?" Georges voice was thick with regret. Had she never noticed that before? Or had she noticed it and dismissed it out of hand?

"I fear not," she tried to think of how to approach this. "You gave me a gift once."

"My Glauca. They were no happy that I *lose* such a knife on a training assignment."

"Why did you give it to me?"

"Now is the time to ask this question?"

"Now." Lauren didn't know why. She was running on instinct here.

"I give it to protect you when I cannot be there to protect you myself."

"I wear it every day."

"Oh, *ma chérie.*" His sigh was eloquent and spoke of dreams that she'd never shared. At least not with him.

She didn't even need to glance at Emily before deciding the next step.

"Georges. There is a traitor inside GIGN. Whoever it is has been feeding information to a terrorist cell. Somehow they left a trail that points to you. We have an undocumented Delta Force snatch-and-grab team closing in on you, but they've been caught in a trap between GIGN and the terrorist cell. I think the mole is at work, killing you and framing them."

Georges' curse was particularly vile. "Norman. Only he is in position that he can do this. Do you have contact with your team?"

Lauren glanced at Emily, who nodded.

"Yes."

"Okay, we must run this like that day at La Koubba."

"I'll tell them. We have," she glanced at Emily, who flashed up eight fingers, "eight minutes."

Georges didn't even waste time on a curse before breaking contact.

"La Koubba?" Emily asked as she contacted the team.

"In between..." two nights of particularly passionate lovemaking at a beachside villa. "Just...in between...we took our dogs for a run in the Parc du Belvédère in the heart of Tunis City. To make it more interesting for the dogs, I created a counterattack scenario for something just like this. La Koubba is a seventeenth-century pavilion atop the highest bluff and was the focal point of the scenario, but the logic is the same even if the terrain will be different."

Emily studied her for a long moment, then glanced up at Michael. "You were right about her."

Then, without explaining herself, Emily hit some command. Suddenly, all the information that had been displayed on her screens was now on the station in front of Lauren.

No time to hesitate. She hit the radio link to the Delta ground team and began guiding them out of the trap they were in.

"There is an alleyway sixty-five meters down the Avenue de Gribeauval. Send two shooters twenty meters down it between the gray armory and red-roofed offices of Satory Commandant du Camp. Next—"

"You can't get out of it, you know."

"I don't want to get out of being in love with Lauren." Patrick knew at least that much.

"Good," Mark echoed Nathan. Mark continued, "I like her. Be fun to have her stick around."

"That's another part of the problem," Patrick tipped back his beer bottle, but it was dry. He wanted to chuck it at something—hard. Through sheer willpower, he managed to set it gently on the counter. Still not trusting himself, he nudged it away until it was at the limit of his fingertips.

"Why is it a problem to have her around?"

"Because she's going back to New York and I'm going to have to follow her."

"Woman will do that to you," Mark agreed. "Thought I was in the military for life, probably 'til they shot me out of the sky. Emily made me think about family and having something else to live for. Led me here of all strange places," he circled his bottle in the air to indicate the ranch.

"I don't want to leave!"

"Well, then, I guess it sucks to be you," Nathan agreed.

Patrick saw what Nathan had meant about not being helpful, but didn't think complaining would help much.

"Why does it suck to be Patrick?" Mack and Mac came into the room.

Just like his son, Mac hit the fridge first and fetched a beer for himself and Mack.

"We've got to do something about your names," Nathan protested. "Mac, Mack, and Mark. Someone named Jack or Mick shows up and we'll never get anything done."

"How about Liam?" Dad walked in and accepted a beer.

"Or a dog," Patrick was thinking about Lauren with Rip curled up at her feet. She had faced and conquered her fears until she was completely at ease with him trotting out of the room at her side.

"A what?" His dad looked at him strangely. Patrick felt as if he was having a different conversation from everyone else around him.

"Dogs have names too. I knew an Australian sheep dog named Jack once." What fears did he need to conquer to be with Lauren? No. Erase that question. What did he need to conquer to make sure that Lauren wanted to be with him?

"Mack, Mac, Mark, and Jack," Mack agreed. "I need to get a dog when I get home and name him Jack. Just like the old Monty Python routine."

"What kind of python?" Mark asked.

Nathan just shrugged when Mark looked his way.

The two Mac(k)s and Dad groaned in unison. "These boys are just too young, I'm telling you. Nobody is bringing them up right."

"One of them's your son, Mac," Dad pointed out.

"He's the worst of the lot."

Mark raised his beer in a toast of acknowledgement. That's when Patrick noticed that for all that Mark had been drinking, the liquid wasn't even drained to the top of the label. It was like a break in the film continuity as a glass was refilled over and over again between takes. To Mark, the beer was a prop.

Patrick wished he'd done the same, rather than drinking the whole bottle so fast—especially on an empty stomach. It churned there like a lead weight.

"Bruce," Patrick offered, though his mind was only half on what he was saying. "Everyone in the philosophy department is named Bruce. Then a new guy joins. Everyone decides that having his name be Michael is too confusing, so they rename him Bruce as well."

Michael!

Somehow Michael was the key to Lauren.

He pushed off the counter. He had to find Michael. Maybe the austere colonel would unbend enough to tell him what he was doing wrong.

"Hey!" Nathan called after him.

"What?"

"Don't go too far. I'm getting married in half an hour."

"Uh-huh." Patrick headed for the door.

"What's up with him?"

If anyone made any guesses, he didn't hear it.

"Ah, *chérie.* You were *magnifique.* As you always are."

"Thanks, Georges. You were amazing as well." His face was bloody on the display, but it wasn't his blood, nor any of the Deltas'.

At that moment, Lauren saw Patrick enter the far end of the barn.

"Ah, I know that look. You have finally found him."

"Found who?" But Lauren suspected that she already knew.

"The one who owns your heart."

Patrick wore a suit that looked truly spectacular on him, except that it was soaking wet. She could see, framed in the door behind him, the downpour pounding out of the darkened sky.

"*Chérie?*"

"Right. Sorry, Georges. And..." She remembered his many kindnesses. How to thank him?

Patrick shook himself like a wet dog, then looked right at her, as if there wasn't a one-way window between them.

She pulled the Glauca out of her leg sheath and held it up to the console's camera eye. "You'll always be my protector, Georges."

"This time, it is you who has protected me. And I am guessing that task now belongs to another man."

Patrick walked the length of the barn, right past Minotaur's outstretched nose without noticing, until he reached Chelsea's office across the main aisle from the Tac Room's stairs. There he leaned back against the wall and folded his arms to wait.

A very Gallic sigh sounded from the comm gear.

"Sorry, Georges," Lauren turned back to the screen.

"I will miss our talks, *chérie.*"

Lauren did her best not to blush. Georges knew exactly what to do with that sexy French phone-voice of his.

"Me, too, Georges. Bye." And she switched off before she could embarrass herself further.

She turned to go to Patrick, but she only made it half out of her chair before dropping back into it. Michael was still leaning back against the door with his arms folded. Still no sign of movement. Time to deal with Colonel Gibson first.

"Why did you come here, Michael? What drew you out of Delta to come to Henderson's Ranch?"

He shrugged. "Not important. You gave me the answer to my problem already."

Lauren blinked, then looked over at Emily, who only shrugged.

"You do know that you're not getting out of here undamaged unless you explain that, don't you?"

Emily nodded her agreement.

Michael sighed, then shrugged. "Colonel James Andhauer has been promoted to the rank of Brigadier General. He is replacing someone who you'll be very glad to know was told to retire quietly to avoid a court martial."

"The one-star bastard who—"

Michael's nod stopped her tirade.

"Loss of grade?" Lauren would really like to see him punished.

"No, but no standard pre-retirement bump in grade to increase his pension either. He's simply out of the system where he can't hurt anyone else."

Lauren decided that it would have to be enough. And since it was more than she'd expected, it would be.

"Wait a minute. The commander of Delta Force was promoted?"

Michael nodded.

Emily put it together the same moment she did. Michael was the Number One Delta operator in the entire unit. He'd turned down promotions a half dozen times to stay in the field.

"They offered you command of Delta," Emily whispered a moment before Lauren could find her voice.

Again the silent nod.

"But you said you were thinking of quitting," Lauren remembered that clearly. "Oh. You didn't want to leave mission operations. Better to quit? Are you nuts?"

"I can see you decided to stay," Emily was taking this more calmly than Lauren could manage. "But how did Lauren make the decision for you?"

Lauren hadn't seen that. There was still a lot to learn from Emily.

"Seeing that I knew exactly who to put where. It saved lives today. I can't do that unless I'm the Commander of Delta. Well done, Lauren Foster." He held out his hand.

She rose to her feet before she accepted the handshake.

Then Michael headed out the door and down the stairs.

Lauren looked down at her still outstretched hand, then over at Emily.

"Praise doesn't get much higher than that," Emily acknowledged that what Lauren was feeling was real.

"Michael," Patrick addressed the man as he came down the stairs.

And walked right by him.

"Colonel Gibson," Patrick followed him several steps down the main aisle of the barn.

The colonel turned and inspected Patrick closely. If before he had appeared inscrutable and austere, he now looked imposing despite standing six inches shorter than Patrick did. Patrick wondered how he'd even dared to interrupt the man's thoughts.

You dared because of Lauren. He squared-up his shoulders and returned the colonel's assessing gaze.

After a long, silent inspection, Colonel Gibson spoke softly.

"You treat that woman," he nodded up toward the Tac Room, "with the utmost care. Do you understand me?"

"Yes, sir," Patrick couldn't even find air to breathe. The unspoken threat was more than sufficient, there was no need to give it a voice. Yet another use of silence.

Patrick watched as Michael spun on his heel, walked down the aisle and out through the door into the storm without even so much as tugging up his shirt collar. He turned right, away from the house, and disappeared from sight.

He heard the bright clicking of dog claws on wood as Rip descended the stairs from the Tac Room.

Patrick turned just as Lauren—whom he hadn't heard—stepped straight into his arms and wrapped herself around him.

He did the same, swearing to himself far more strongly than any promise to Colonel Michael Gibson that he was never going to let her go.

"You're all wet again," she mumbled in his ear, her voice shaky.

"Special just for you."

"You are," she answered and held on like she was never going to let go either.

CHAPTER 13

Lauren sat on the big couch beside Emily and Mark. The two of them were holding hands as they waited for the ceremony to begin.

She wished she had someone to sit with, someone to hold her hand—neither of which sounded like her. At least not the old her, but was definitely going to be a part of the new her. The person she wanted to be holding hands with was standing at the front of the seating area with his brother, awaiting the bride's arrival.

Patrick only had the one good suit—now completely rain-soaked. They'd attacked him, and it, with a half dozen hair dryers, but he still looked damp and rumpled. She didn't care. He could be sitting naked in the stream for all she cared.

The image in her head—the *images,* for there were so many—were mostly centered around his easy smile. Whatever life threw at him, he still came up with a way to see the bright side of it. She needed to learn to do that, but she wasn't there yet.

"Damn dog," Stan muttered at her from across the aisle.

Rip sat beside her, with his head resting on her knee.

"Hey, dog boy. No teasing my sweet pup."

"Sure thing, dog girl," he offered her one of his friendlier versions of grimace. "You know, my pack is still small enough that we can't support two handlers—even smaller now," he scowled at Rip, who ignored him. "But some of the exercises would be easier with two people." This time his stern face almost shifted into a smile. "I mean, you seem okay being around dogs again…"

"You mean I've stopped fainting dead away every time I see one?"

"Only so much I can expect from a girl, I guess."

It took her a moment to understand that from Stan it wasn't an ex-SEAL dodging the edge of harassment, but rather a kindly tease from a member of the ranch.

"Um… I don't know what's happening yet. But if I'm here, yes. I'd be glad to help. I think… Or…" Or maybe not. There was still a scar inside her, though she could feel Rip and Patrick both working to heal it.

"Give it time, Lauren. Just give it time." Stan's voice was kindlier than it had been since her arrival.

"Patience comes hard."

He nodded. "Now I know you were Special Operations."

"Were. That's the problem."

He merely nodded once more, the common ground clear between them.

Patrick shuffled foot to foot, but it didn't help. They squished. He had changed from the soaking, muddy disaster of his leather shoes into fresh socks and cowboy boots. But his pants continued to shed water. The suit pants were too narrow to slip over the boots, so he'd tucked them in where they funneled everything into his socks. His feet were cold. He squished. Under his arms hadn't dried at all. And…

"That does it!"

"What?" Nathan looked at him in alarm.

"Next time I go rushing out into the rain, I'm going to use a jacket. And I don't care who tries to stop me."

"What is it with you and water lately?"

Patrick could only shrug. He glanced at Lauren chatting so easily with Stan about her dog. It had taken months of living together before Stan did more than grunt at him, and there he was all dry and comfortable chatting her up.

"The shark in *Jaws* spent less time wet than you have this week."

"Shut up or I'll throw your ring in the fire," Patrick patted his jacket pocket to make sure the box was still there.

"Go ahead and try. It's the one ring to rule them all. Fire couldn't hurt the Hobbit's ring and it wouldn't dare touch anything that is holding Julie and me together."

"The One Ring belonged to Sauron. Dire evil, brother."

"Not this one. It belongs to Julie, or will soon."

"The first Gallagher brother to go down into the deep pits of matrimony."

"Any bets on how far behind you are?"

Patrick didn't like the sound of that and looked toward the back of the big room, but there were no signs of anyone coming down the stairs. "What is taking so long?"

"You're not supposed to be the one asking that. I'm the groom. I'm the one who is supposed to be all impatient."

"Why aren't you, then?"

"Superior breeding."

Patrick considered dumping a pitcher of water over Nathan's head, but figured that would only prove his brother's point.

"Which is all that's keeping me from stroking out at this point."

Patrick checked his watch. They weren't even running late yet, but he figured it was better not to tell Nathan that. Neither of them was holding it together very well.

Lauren leaned down to say something to her dog, then sat up and looked directly at him.

"What?" he mouthed to her over the tops of people's heads.

She pretended to tug on non-existent lapels with pride.

So he made the same gesture, putting on his best Mr. Cool, Colin Firth expression.

She clapped both hands over her heart and pretended to swoon, landing her head on a very surprised Emily's shoulder.

Silly!

Lauren Foster had the ability to be silly? When did that happen? He couldn't help grinning. Sure, it was a lifelong bet, but one that would be completely worth it, because with Lauren it was never going to get dull.

This! This is what being in love feels like. It was—

Mac came hurrying up the aisle and headed for the piano.

Lauren saw Patrick rest a hand on Nathan's shoulder, perhaps to make sure both of them stayed upright.

Then Ama Henderson came up the aisle. She was as Emily had first described her. Tall, Native-American tan skin, and a straight fall of black hair heavily streaked with gray that fell almost to her waist. She wore a traditional Cheyenne dress of soft hide with red-dyed patterns and intricate beadwork about her shoulders. Moving to the front of the room, she indeed looked the high priestess.

"Rather than getting one of those online minister licenses," Emily leaned over and whispered, "she went back to her tribe and was trained in all of the traditions of conducting a ceremony and has been certified with the state to conduct weddings. It is up to couples how traditional or Christian they are. With Nathan's catering, weddings are becoming very popular here at the ranch."

"Is there anything you don't do?" Lauren wasn't sure if she was asking about the ranch or Emily. Maybe both.

"Play the piano." Emily wiggled her fingers, answering the second question. "Mom tried so hard to bring me up properly, but I became a soldier instead."

As if taking his cue from her, Mark Henderson Sr. began playing the "Wedding March."

Everyone rose to their feet, including Rip. Though she whispered a "stay" so that he wouldn't think they were going somewhere.

Chelsea, her hair a bright red flow over her shoulders, came first up the aisle in a dress that was pure Western cowgirl, right down to the denim and fringe.

Behind her came a tall, serious-looking man she didn't recognize, but who must be Julie's father. Lauren would have thought he was leading his daughter to a funeral if not for the way he held her hand. He didn't only have the bride on his arm, but he had reached across his other hand and interlaced their fingers as they walked up the aisle.

Julie was also Western cowgirl, though reimagined. Her skirt had ruffles to echo Chelsea's fringes. Her cowboy boots were intricately stitched, wedding white. A denim bolero offset the lacework of the top. Her hair was up, tucked inside a white cowboy hat with a single fall of veil down to her waist.

Everyone else was applauding, and Lauren finally realized that she was as well. Julie simply looked that amazing. She was a beautiful woman, that was a given. But she was an astonishing bride. What would Lauren herself look like when it was her turn?

Who would be in Chelsea's role, leading *her* down the aisle when it was time?

She turned, and found herself trading smiles with Emily.

You? Lauren somehow asked the silent question.

Yes. Emily bowed her head just enough to communicate that it would be an honor.

Someday…

Lauren looked at Patrick, so incredibly handsome as he pushed his stunned-puppy brother that one step forward he needed to take to stand beside his bride.

Someday soon, Julie would be her sister-in-law. It simply felt right.

But Emily. The daunting Emily Beale would be her friend.

Lauren looked down at Rip in sudden shock.

She had a friend. She had a dog. She had a man she would be saying yes to, when he asked—though knowing Patrick, he'd wait too long and she'd have to do the asking, but that was okay as well.

She had a place to be. The ranch and the wilderness called to her.

She didn't need the pressures of Special Operations or the distractions of the Big Apple.

All she needed was a reason to be here.

Julie had hinted at her being a guide. Stan wanted help with the dogs.

But neither of those would hold her. She knew that much about herself.

So what would hold her?

Chelsea might dazzle and Julie might awe, but Patrick couldn't wait to see Lauren in a dress. She had changed at the last second after joining in the efforts to dry him off. He'd been looking the other way when she entered and sat, and he'd had no clear view of her during the ceremony.

After the ceremony, he couldn't find her at first. Then he spotted her brunette hair between the ranged shoulders of Julie's three older brothers. Matthew in the center with the twins Mark and Luke to either side.

As soon as he had slapped his brother on the back and hugged his new sister-in-law, he rushed to Lauren's side. Julie's brothers were a formidable trio of cattle ranchers and he knew from hanging out with them at fairs and socials that they knew how to spot a "fine heifer" when they saw one. They had done an excellent job of cutting Lauren from the crowd. The brothers didn't quite have her cornered, but they definitely had her well enough off to the side that she'd almost have to be rude to leave them.

"Lauren," he hurried up to her, swinging through the narrow gap Luke had left between himself and a conveniently blocking couch. "There you—" The last word snagged in his suddenly dry throat.

He'd seen her in a tight black t-shirt, barely clothed in his own flannel shirt, and completely naked indoors, outdoors, and armed with a rifle while she stood over a dead bear.

None of that prepared him for the vision of her. No wonder the Larson brothers had gone out of their way to corner her.

He knew it was one of Emily's dresses—it wouldn't surprise him if Lauren didn't own any at all. He made a mental note to make sure and buy her more…just like this one.

It looked custom-made for Lauren's taller frame. A blue sheath of clingy jersey, with an asymmetrical overlap of fabric. The neckline was only open to just below her collarbone, but the edging of the upper layer swept down between her breasts and curved to duck around her waist. The edging was dark yellow and drew the gold out of her honey-colored eyes.

Her extra inches turned it from above the knee to mid-thigh and she'd capped it off with dark red cowboy boots that he suspected came out of Ama's closet.

"You look…" Again he had no words.

"Yep! Looks real nice," Luke tried to nudge Patrick aside and almost succeeded in dumping him backward over the couch arm.

"A real cut above," his twin assessed from the other side.

"Pr—"

Patrick stepped between Lauren and Matthew, the eldest of the Larsons, and got right up in his face. "You say 'Prime Grade' and I'll take you down, Matthew. As god is my witness, I will." It might be from some movie, but he'd never felt such rage. He and Matthew were close to the same height, but Matthew was about twice as wide. And both of his brothers were there, which tended to egg on his male ego as the alpha male.

"Oh, really?" Matthew leaned in until they were nose-to-nose.

Patrick didn't want to bust up his brother's wedding with a fist-fight—and definitely not one he had so little chance of winning—but he was fast running out of options.

Then Lauren rested her hand lightly on his shoulder and pushed him aside just one step.

She and Matthew stood eye-to-eye in height, just a single step apart. "Really? That's the best ploy you boys have?"

"What do you mean?"

"I mean," and she turned just enough for Patrick to see her infinitesimal smile.

He couldn't imagine why she was having fun with this, but he knew her well enough to keep his mouth shut and just watch.

"You boys are looking for a fight that you don't know you've already lost."

"Is that so?" All three of them squared their shoulders and turned to face Patrick.

"Really. Would you like me to prove it?"

"I could wrap Pat there around my pinkie if I felt like it. I wouldn't. I like Pat. Just sayin' I could if I had the mind."

Lauren turned to him. "I thought cowboys were known for being respectful of women."

"Oh, he is," Patrick decided that he'd join in the fun, even if it cost him later. "He'd like to take you to his hayloft and show you just how respectful he can be."

"That's what I thought." She heaved a sigh, then snapped her fingers down by her hip and whispered, "Guard."

Rip popped to his feet and his hard snarl of rage silenced the room.

All three brothers looked down at the dog in shock.

Mark and Luke managed a step back, but Lauren snagged the front of Matthew's cowboy shirt. From somewhere in the form-fitting dress, she produced her Glauca folding knife. She flipped it open with a hard snap. She held its squared-off tip about an inch from Matthew's nose, making him cross his eyes.

"You might think about treating women a little more nicely in the future," then she shrugged. "It's just a suggestion."

She flipped the knife closed as she let go of Matthew's shirt so that he could stumble back to join his brothers.

Patrick realized that no one else but him and the three brothers were in position to have seen the knife.

Lauren whispered, "Sit." All three brothers looked down at Rip as he plopped onto his butt, though he didn't look any more friendly. Patrick was the only one who followed as she palmed the knife and slipped it beneath the jersey fabric between her breasts.

Patrick moved back in. "Boys might want to think about what she said. Now move along and go congratulate your sister on her wedding." He felt that he did a fair job of not gloating as they left to do that.

The room slowly returned to normal.

As the last person's attention turned elsewhere, she turned to him and silently mouthed, "That's a wrap."

His burst of laughter had several people looking back in curiosity, but he didn't care. He took Lauren's hand in his. Not a tremor. Of course she'd probably faced down plenty worse.

"That's a wrap indeed!" He loved that she'd used one of his phrases. "There's hope for you yet, Lauren Foster."

"That's good, I guess. Thanks for trying to defend me. It was crazy, one against three, which in a way makes it all the more impressive."

"Colonel Gibson made it fairly clear that he'd kill me if I let anything happen to you."

"No. He didn't really, did he?"

"He really did. Though I forgot that until just now. I was simply so angry at the brothers treating you that way, I had to step in. Probably made things worse by doing so, but I had no choice."

That earned him a kiss on the cheek.

"Where is he, anyway?" He looked around, otherwise he'd be the one crowding Lauren Foster into the nearest place that he could get her out of that incredible dress.

They both scanned the room.

"Do you think he just walked out into the storm and disappeared?"

"I wouldn't put it past him," Lauren sighed. "I wish he'd said goodbye."

"I don't know. I'm still quaking in my squishy boots. That man knows how to lay down a threat without many words. Six, maybe eight words. Wish I'd written them down. It was damned impressive."

Lauren had chosen a quiet corner of the living room to share a dinner plate with Patrick. He'd been trying to teach her the two-step, at which she'd been pitiful, and a couple of basic line dances, at which she had to rank as downright tragic.

But the waltz. She could have waltzed in Patrick's arms until she dropped. And she was nearly there.

Julie and Nathan were clearly sustained by the energy of their marriage as they simply floated about the room together, at the center of every single dance.

She and Patrick sat together in the same oversized leather armchair sharing from the same plate balanced on her lap. Some were still dancing, but most had been tempted away from the floor by the tantalizing smells of Nathan's wedding buffet.

"That was decent of Matthew," Lauren finally broke the comfortable silence between them.

"It was," Patrick conceded. "Didn't make it any easier to watch."

He'd come up to them both after the dancing was well started and politely asked her for a dance. As he'd moved her expertly around the other couples, he'd apologized to her. "Sorry about earlier, ma'am. I just took one look at you and don't know what came over me. I'll straighten out my brothers and you'll have no trouble. Wish they were smart enough to not follow my lead, especially when I'm makin' a big mistake like that. But they're my brothers and there's not much I can do 'bout that."

"You could try scaring them every now and then."

"I think you took care of that for a good while, ma'am. I'll be sure to let you know if they need a reminder."

It was easy to feel flattered rather than angry after that, though it would take Patrick a bit to calm down yet.

For now, they simply returned to eating in silence, tossing occasional scraps down for Rip. He was particularly partial to the pork-filled corn fritters. They peeled off the deep-fried bits and fed him bits of the interior.

Chelsea had gotten Stan to his feet, and he was proving that he absolutely knew how to dance with a woman. Mark's father and Ama also floated effortlessly across the dance floor.

"Where's Mack?" He'd been there for the wedding, but she didn't think she'd seen him since.

"He's gone. He slipped out as soon as the storm broke. Said he had to get home to Nancy right quick as he was, and I quote, 'missing her something awful'."

"What? Without saying goodbye?" Lauren felt a sudden burning in her eyes. That hurt. She'd liked the old man and it really hurt.

"He said not to tell you until you asked."

"And you listened to him?"

Patrick looked suddenly uncertain.

"Next time. Don't. You tell me anyway. Okay?"

"Okay," Patrick bent his head down and toyed with a breaded venison cutlet marinated in something she definitely had to eat again at the first opportunity. "I'm not sure how soon he'll be back, but he left you a present."

"What? That could make up for just leaving like that?"

"His rifle."

Lauren was knocked speechless by that.

"He said it was from one southpaw to another. He promised Nancy that he'd give up hunting because he's long since too old. I didn't know, but he's past eighty. Said he made this trip just hoping to find the right person to give it to. Guess he did."

"Oh, god!" The tears were streaming down her cheeks before she even had time to understand what had just happened. "Oh, my heart! Oh, Patrick!" She turned into his shoulder. She couldn't hide there, but she could let the pain out. He held her close and just let her cry. Yet another gift.

"What did you do to her?"

Patrick had been simply holding Lauren while she wept quietly against him.

Rip had sat up with concern when she started. Rested his head on her knee long enough for her to pat him on the head without looking up. Then used his long tongue to clear half of what was left on their plate in a single mouthful.

Patrick had set the plate out of reach and brushed any spillage out of their laps and onto the floor for the dog. Then he'd just let her cry.

"Well?" Emily was glaring down at him. Mark hovered close behind her the way he expected a deadly military helicopter hovered the moment before it killed you.

"When Mack left, he gave her his Winchester 70 rifle."

"Oh," Emily's face softened abruptly and she sat on a nearby foot-stool. Mark sat beside her and reached down to ruffle Rip's fur. It was clear that he didn't know what was going on but was taking his cues from Emily.

Patrick stroked a hand once more down Lauren's back as she took a final sniffle. Mark now made even more sense to him—of course he himself would follow Lauren's cues in the future just as Mark did his own wife's.

"Sorry. I'm sorry." Lauren sat up, wiping at her face with her napkin, then blew her nose. "I just can't believe he'd do that for me. His father gave him that rifle, but his kids are right-handers and never took to hunting anyway. My father…wasn't much of a father. Lived and died for Wall Street. Mom stayed with him for the lifestyle, I guess. And Mack—" She blew her nose again and leaned against him.

"Always liked that guy," Mark agreed. "Damned decent of him, even if he wouldn't stop flirting with Emily."

If Mack didn't come back to the ranch, maybe he and Lauren could go visit him on the Oregon Coast.

He and Lauren.

He was still assuming things. What if—

"Emily's got something to say to you, Lauren," Mark cut him off before he could even complete the thought, never mind speak it.

"Not now," Emily nudged her shoulder hard against his. "Where's your sense of tact?"

"Thumb on the trigger of a Hellfire missile. That's me." Mark reached over to Patrick and Lauren's plate on the side table and plucked up bacon-wrapped chicken liver with an injected jalapeño cream. Patrick decided not to warn him about the dog slobber.

Mark chomped down on it happily.

Patrick thought about offering him more, or pulling the plate closer in invitation, but decided that was too much. He'd just watch and enjoy with no one else the wiser.

"Yep!" Mark spoke as he ate and reached for more. "Nathan and Julie were a damn fine addition to the ranch staff. And Patrick, you were here while we were still firefighting, so you're just part of the ranch for us. Just awesome."

Patrick wished it was. But he and Lauren weren't going to be here much longer no matter how much he wished otherwise.

"Time to add another."

"Mark," Emily ground out.

"Do it up, Em." He picked up the plate and kept eating as if his job here was now done.

Patrick wondered if Mark was impossibly brave or impossibly oblivious. He was messing with far worse than fire if he was pissing off Emily Beale.

Emily sighed, "Maybe Mark's right. No time like the present."

That surprised Patrick no end. It was easy to forget that Mark had also been a highly-decorated major and had convinced Emily to marry him. The man's persona made it hard to remember just how smart he was. Patrick didn't go looking for a movie analogy. There was no need. Mark was sitting right here in front of him in real life.

In real life. He and Lauren. That's what mattered.

Emily glared at him.

Suddenly Patrick had a brand-new appreciation for just how brave a man Mark was.

"What I'm about to tell her, you can't tell anyone. Ever! Are we clear on that, Patrick?"

"Not even…"

"No, not even your brother."

Patrick thought about having something on his older brother even if he could never tell him. "Excellent! I'm good with that."

Mark got it, of course, and snorted out a laugh before thumping him on the shoulder.

"Lauren," Emily rolled her eyes and sighed before turning back to Lauren. "I have a contract that I can't fulfill. At least not without you."

———

"A contract?" Lauren was still trying to get over Mack leaving her his father's rifle. Whatever this new thing was, she wasn't getting it. "What are you talking about, Emily?"

"I'm a specialist in air tactics and air security. I need someone who can get me the same thing on the ground. I mentioned the idea a long time ago to Michael, then forgot about it. I guess he didn't. He brought me you."

"Colonel Gibson brought me to meet you?" The fog of the day wasn't lifting.

Emily nodded, but didn't speak.

Lauren groaned. "I can see in your eyes this is another goddamn test. Haven't I been through enough of those today?"

"You're right. Sorry," Emily looked chagrined. "I—"

"No," Lauren stopped her, finally intrigued.

And Emily nodded. Emily. The chance to work with her and learn from her was enough to fire Lauren's imagination any time, any place.

"Tac Room. Ground tactics and security." She began ticking off the connecting pieces on her fingers. "You and Michael going on the elk hunt with me, then making sure I was on point for the tracking. I know you couldn't have planned the bear, but that must have fed into your decision. Oh, my god, even the muddy tracks across the porch."

"What muddy tracks?" Patrick would of course be a step behind, but only because he lacked the military training. "Oh, ours up at the cabin? What do they have to do with anything?" Okay, not very far behind. It was easy to forget that behind his content and outward complacency, he was also a highly skilled guide.

"And then this afternoon. Michael said it was a live-action test."

"What happened today?" Patrick asked.

But Emily shook her head. "This is the part that will suck, Patrick. There are some things that she can't discuss with you. We'll see about getting you enough security clearance, but for the moment just know that she saved a lot of lives today, not just by who she knew but also by how she thinks."

"Planning scenarios that haven't happened yet, just in case they do." Lauren now understood that part of the test as well. Her planning the La Koubba tactic with Georges just to pass the time had been a key factor in Emily's invitation.

"Exactly," Emily agreed, proving her assumption.

"So how long is this for?" This. *This!* was something that Lauren could dig her teeth into.

Guiding was an interesting challenge. Be even more interesting with Rip's sensitive nose at her side. He'd have sniffed the bear earlier, perhaps in time to still scare it off.

And training the dogs was something she'd always enjoyed. She'd wager that, with time, she could again.

But ground tactics for protection and security... That was just freaking cool!

"Open-ended contract. It's a new concept. If it works, we'll act as oversight for an indefinite time." Government work, without being trapped in the grind that was the military service. Even Delta Force took its mental toll over time, often far beyond the heavy wear and tear on the body.

"How high are the stakes?"

"They don't get any higher."

That stopped her and made her blink.

"In or out?" Emily asked.

"You don't tell me anything else until I agree?"

Emily nodded.

She slipped her hand into Patrick's and he squeezed hers so hard it almost hurt. Her decision, but his grip was support, not warning.

"One more question."

Emily shrugged a maybe.

"Are we based here? At the ranch?" Lauren could feel Patrick's body go galvanic with shock. He'd missed that one.

Emily's smile grew until it shone brilliantly.

The wedding, which seemed to have gone quiet in the background, burst back to life with a fast dance number.

"Except for the occasional field trip, one hundred percent from the ranch. Why do you think I had them build me that crazy room?"

Lauren could see it. Could see the two of them working side by side. And she would have more to hang on the wall beside the second command station than dog photos and an old leash that had probably cut into her for long enough. There would be a photo of the man she loved.

"The ranch," she turned to Patrick, trying to understand what had just happened. "Maybe even the high cabin."

Mark's nod confirmed that as well.

"A chance to do something you already excel at," Patrick put in his vote.

"With you."

"With you," he echoed.

Rip poked his head up to see if there were any more scraps.

"And you," Lauren tickled the tip of his nose and he sneezed on Mark's shiny boots.

Patrick was working his mouth but couldn't seem to find any words to go with it.

She rested a finger across his lips, then removed it to kiss him lightly.

"When you figure out how to speak, Patrick, the answer is yes. Okay?"

He nodded fiercely, then crushed her against him, which was the only answer she needed. Mark pounded him on the other shoulder— again. He was going to be black and blue.

Emily pulled her from Patrick's arms for a big hug.

"We're going to be awesome together," Emily whispered in her ear.

Lauren nodded in agreement. This was going to be amazing. "What are we going to be doing?" Lauren whispered back.

"Setting up a secret security team, without even the next President knowing about it."

"A what?" Lauren pulled back, but kept her face close so that they could whisper while Mark and Patrick were busy congratulating each other about both being men, or whatever men did with each other at moments like this.

"A security team," Emily explained. "One charged with maintaining the security of the United States no matter what the politics or who's in charge. The outgoing President has mandated it."

"Your childhood friend Peter?"

Emily nodded. "But he's not telling Zachary. Truly apolitical."

"Where is it based?"

This time Emily's smile was enormous. "I'm going to call it the White House Protection Force. It's run by the White House librarian."

Lauren couldn't help but laugh. The joy was just too big to keep inside.

She and Patrick and Rip and her new friend Emily were going to absolutely be awesome together.

FINDING HENDERSON'S RANCH

Mac Henderson started out no more of a ranch owner than he did a Navy SEAL. Adrift on the post-college tide of the '70s, with no direction planned, he headed west to surf. But fate had other plans for him—beneath Montana's Big Sky.

*A broken starter motor during Cheyenne Frontier Days led him to witness **Ama's** traditional dance for her tribe. Since that moment, for twenty years, she has believed in his dream, inspired him, and given him a son (Mark Henderson).*

It was only when Mac retired that she found her own dream. Her reward? Finding Henderson's Ranch.

Mac Henderson didn't know whether to hate himself or the Top 40 station coming out of Cheyenne. In Wyoming it was that or country, so the choice of what to listen to wasn't hard. But the songs were insidious. How was it possible that he knew every word to sing along with John Travolta's *You're the One That I Want?* Mac did have to fake the high notes which perhaps implied he wasn't a complete "Lost Cause" his mother always accused him of. She said it with a smile, but still, it stung.

More importantly, how did Travolta get up there? Maybe it was those tight pants.

Wyoming. Could he get *more* different than Ohio? He'd left the lush greens of Oberlin right after graduation. Kissed Penny goodbye —nothing serious so no heartache—and headed west.

"Surfing?" She was an overachiever type and was joining the Peace Corps, headed for Africa with her honors degree in psychology.

"Sure. Get me some sun and surf."

"And surfer babes?" Penny didn't sound even a little hurt, which meant their time together had been less meaningful than he'd thought. *Chump!*

"Sure, why not? What else am I supposed to do with a degree in

French Literature?" He suspected that the defensive tone hadn't served him well.

"Have you ever surfed?"

"Now's my big chance."

"That's a pretty directionless choice, Mac." She'd shaken her head sadly, her Farrah Fawcett blonde curls wafting about her face. She was as fun as she was trendy and cute. They'd only been together for the last couple months of senior year though, now that he thought about it, she'd always given him the feeling that she was slumming a bit and mostly marking time.

He'd never been one for high goals. His dad had been a professor of French Lit at Loyola until he'd stroked out (in two ways) in a coed's arms at forty-eight. Mac had decided to follow in his footsteps, for reasons passing anyone's understanding—including his own. Even more disillusioning, he'd generally had better luck with the French Lit than the coeds. Penny had been the exception, not the rule. But even if he applied for the Peace Corps now, they'd be all out of sync. Not that he wanted to.

Wanted to.

For four years everyone—the entire college experience—had gone on and on about how they could all be anything they "wanted to." But for the life of him he couldn't figure out what that might be for him.

Travolta's "Oo-oo-oo" croon with perky blonde Newton-John gave way to ABBA's *Take a Chance on Me*.

The job recruiters had taken one look at his long hair, his mastery of Middle French literature, and his liberal arts school attitude, then looked the other way. No chance on him. *Oo-oo-oo!* Surfing was still the best bet he'd heard in a while. He'd delayed with some buddies who had a cabin on Lake Michigan—to work on building up some swimmer muscles, or maybe to have one last collegiate-style beer blast—and a week with his mom in Chicago. But it reached late July and he was missing summer in the surf. That had finally gotten him heading west again.

He pulled off in Cheyenne to study his road atlas as he chowed down on a Burger King Double Whopper and fries. Straight west or time to turn south? Holding west for Salt Lake could be a thing, not that he wanted to hang there, but it would be something to see. Or cut down to Denver then climb the Rockies. His Mazda pickup had been making some funny noises lately, so maybe the Rockies wasn't the best idea. Of course breaking down in the vast emptiness of Wyoming...

Turning the key, *Rocky Mountain High* blared out of the radio. Must be a Top Ten of the Past thing, but he'd take it as an omen. Denver it was. The randomness of his directionless life lived on.

Then he twisted the ignition the rest of the way and got that nasty ratcheting sound he'd heard lately. Except this time the engine didn't start. Again. No luck.

A cowboy, complete with boots and a big old hat, strolling by with his own burger bag, stopped and listened. "Yep! You got a cooked starter solenoid. Jason there can fix you up." He hooked a thumb at a service station across the street. "Need a push?"

Ten minutes later he was officially stuck in Cheyenne, Wyoming while they waited for parts. "Have it for you in the morning."

"C'mon, kid." Jason couldn't be more than a couple years older. "See how real people live." And he'd followed the cowboy back to his truck which was big enough he could have parked his Mazda in the back of it...if the starter had worked.

CHAPTER 2

Ama reluctantly followed her mother into the dance ring at Indian Village. The circle of white teepees had been erected for Cheyenne Frontier Days, just as it had for the last eighty years. Ten days every year that were the bane of her existence. Even private, tribal powwows boasted more RVs than teepees these days, but the truth didn't mix well with the stereotypes in people's heads. And RVs definitely weren't as photogenic as the line of white teepees on the Cheyenne prairie.

There were cowboys and farmers in the crowd, but there were far more tourists whose beer bellies conflicted badly with the newer, tighter fashions. Some women gave in to the mid-summer's heat with strapless tops, but many still had jackets so that they could wear their shoulder pads. The crowd sat or stood five deep between the circle of teepees and the grassy dance field.

Come for the show. Come see the redskin girl dance a blessing to the day —an importance you will never understand. After me, watch my cousin the hoop dancer. A great tradition tracing all of the way back to Tony White Cloud performing it in the Lucille Ball movie Valley of the Sun. *Yes, come see the least authentic powwow dance you can imagine, up next.*

Yet Ama knew better than to ever say or show such a thing. She was the good daughter. The youngest lead dancer since Great-grand-mother Swooping Bird. Her mother's scowl and her father's disdain were for her brother, never for Ama. Like the water that was her name, she flowed around problems, always quiet and level.

Watch me dance. I know every step perfectly. Not the modern ones, but the way that has been handed down directly by Great-grandmother from her great-grandmother. Leave this world for a moment and see how we tread the Great Plains when they still belonged to the Cheyenne, Crow, and Pawnee.

She let her vision unfocus as she found the rhythm of the drums and her feet hit the soil in traditionally short, hard steps. But it wasn't the shaking of the drums that called to her in the dance, it was the *tahpeno*—the cedar courtship flute. She'd never been able to resist its call and she could feel it capture her arms and let her float.

See the flight of the tiniest hummingbird greet the opening of the morning flowers in my fingers. Follow the robin and the dove in my hands. See the great eagle soar in my arms high above the family ranch. And watch the swallow swoop and play at dusk in how I float.

The tourists didn't matter.

The other dancers faded aside.

It was just the flute's call, the cycle of this day's bird-flight, and her dance.

In this moment, for this one precious instant, it felt as if she balanced between two worlds. Her life as a paralegal for a divorce lawyer had nothing to do with this dance, except when she was immersed in it, then it was the whole rest of her life that lost meaning.

As the swallow returned to her evening nest and the dance came to a close, the path of her feet—still stomping to the unceasing, unceasing rhythm of the drums—led her close to the crowd.

As Henry Morning Crow's flute ended the day with the first call of the *mista*—the great horned owl, the spirit of the night, *hoo-h'Hoo hoo hoo*—Ama came back into her own body. She planted her feet with the last beat of the drum and looked once more through her own eyes rather than the birds'.

The crowd's roar of approval and applause was, as ever, a harsh shock. She could never grow used to it. It was from the wrong world:

not herself or the dance, not her tribe. Instead it battered at her, hard and forceful.

A man stood directly in front of where her dance had led her. A man acting like no other in the crowd. He did not applaud; he did not even appear to breathe.

His looks didn't blend into the crowd either. He was her age and lean with strong shoulders; the sort of man who would never need shoulder pads. His collar-long hair, as dark as her own, framed his fair face. It was a good face, a strong one. His eyes were steel gray and seemed to see past the costume and the dancer. She knew her looks were a throwback to Swooping Bird, who had often been declared the most beautiful Cheyenne of her generation. But he didn't seem to see that either.

Men always saw her dancing or her beauty. Her parents saw the good girl. Her tribe viewed her as the granddaughter of a great Peace Chief and the great-granddaughter of a still celebrated dancer.

It was as if this man could see her as no one except the mirror ever had. As herself.

CHAPTER 3

Mac lay on his longboard, letting the swells roll beneath him. The chilly Pacific Ocean was actually pacific for a change. The waves had settled an hour ago and he was content to simply lie in the sun and wait as he was lifted and lowered by their lazy rhythm. This had become his favorite part of surfing. He could stand up and ride a wave now, but he doubted he'd ever be good.

"There they are again," Ama spoke lazily from the board beside him. She wasn't any better at surfing than he was, but at least she was far better looking while doing it. Also, her dancer's grace always looked so elegant that her lack of skill mattered far less than his own clumsy efforts. Her hair, a straight slash to her waist, now lay over the back of her wetsuit like a soft blanket. Her suit was the same sky blue as the deer hide dress she'd worn at the Frontier Days dance. Out of the wetsuit when ashore, the pure white bikini she favored high-lighted her dark skin—and completely scrambled his hormones. She'd taken to wearing dark sunglasses which only added to her mystery.

He was still unsure why she'd joined him for the drive to California. She hadn't volunteered her reasons and he'd been afraid to ask. For two months he'd had the most astonishing lover of his life in their little beach shack. They weren't broke, not yet, but this couldn't last and *that* troubled him. Unlike Penny, he'd be majorly bummed when Ama Dances Like Water left to return to her tribe. She'd given no hint of such a plan, but it worried him anyway.

September had seen the summer surfers retreat except on the weekends. Only the hardcore beach bums still remained afloat under the mid-October sun.

Ama didn't speak often, so when she did, he always paid attention. He followed the direction of her gaze.

Coronado Beach was no longer hazed by the heat as it had been since their arrival, but it was no less bright beneath the midday sun.

Mac propped his chin on his hands and squinted against the glare.

Navy SEALs. Only twenty remained in the group of men in green. There had been at least a hundred the first time they ran on the beach a month ago. They never ran where it was easy, down by the waves. Instead, they were always up on the dry beach where the heat burned and every step slipped and dragged in the deep sand. They sang as they ran. Four trainers ran with them. He'd seen the trainers haranguing their every step as their numbers dwindled—the sharp clang of a bell marking another grunt "ringing out" and quitting because he couldn't make the grade.

Today was different. Today the trainers sang with the running recruits. A team. Those who remained were becoming a team. In perfect unison, immensely fit, and dependent on one another.

He lay his head once more on his hands and contemplated the woman stretched beside him, rising and falling on the swells of the Pacific Ocean.

What would it take to make Ama *not* flow away from him? To not dismiss him with an easy shrug as Penny had. That struck him as being of desperate importance. Perhaps the first such thing in his entire life.

Had she pointed out the SEAL team for a reason? He had to think about that.

CHAPTER 4

Ama could only stare at Mac in surprise.

He had transformed past recognition without changing at all. Not a caterpillar turned into a butterfly, but rather a man transformed into a Man.

He was so much stronger now than even the surfing had made him; the physical power of his embrace utterly breathtaking in many ways.

But his eyes still saw her with Eagle's vision and he heard her with Coyote's sharp ears. Being with Mac had made her feel closer to her tribe and her heritage than she ever had back in Wyoming. He'd insisted that she return to the next Cheyenne Frontier Days to dance, and he'd been right. It was an important glimpse of her culture that she'd nearly lost all sight of in San Diego.

Over this year, his gentleness had faded, except towards her. In that he was as unvarying as the Great Spirit itself.

Living on the inside of his world, she could see how different he had become to the outside world. Mac had pulled on a shroud of power like a dancer who pulled the skin of Buffalo over his head and transformed into the beast.

All in white, Mac's uniform shone as brightly as the sun. And like a piece ripped from the sun itself, the golden SEAL trident shone fresh and new upon his left breast.

Other graduates of the year-long course were surrounded by their families or wives.

She found herself reluctant to walk up to Mac. He was so transformed that she half wondered if she still belonged in his world. Her dance had led her to stand in front of him. But had his dance of becoming a Navy SEAL led him toward her?

He often joked that he didn't believe in such things as something guiding her steps, but she'd had no other way to explain it. He *did* say often that "he wasn't complaining about the results."

And now?

He strode up to her, so tall and beautiful in his rugged way.

Then, without hesitation, not looking to see who of his new SEAL brothers were watching, he went down on bent knee before her. The silence rushed outward through the celebrating SEALs faster than a wave breaking on a reef until all attention was focused upon them.

"Now, am I finally worthy of you?" His words were so soft.

"Since the day my dance led me to you." And she must be worthy of him for he had come to her and that was all that mattered. For though he often said that he would be less of a man without her, she knew that she would also be less of a woman without her Mac.

CHAPTER 5

Mac lay face down and wondered if he'd ever breathe again. The heat drove into his body a thousand times hotter than any mere splash of the San Diego sunshine. Hotter even than Ama could still make his blood race after thirteen years together.

Why was it now, when they were ten thousand miles away that he could think of nothing but his wife and twelve-year old son? Ama had given him the gift of a son. It focused his thoughts. Even lying face down in the burning sand, so desperate that he wanted to give up or wither away, he knew one thing was true. Only by serving with honor and completing the mission could he face them. They were his strength and he needed to be theirs.

The dust of the Iraqi soil clogged every pore. Fifty kilometers behind Saddam's lines, his four-SEAL squad lay unmoving, covered in the sand, waiting out the midday heat.

Elements of the Iraqi Republican Guard were patrolling the area. A full platoon—ten times their number—and a pair of tanks. A T-72's treads had missed their hiding position by less than five feet, but if they'd so much as flinched, they'd have been gunned down before they could even raise a weapon. So they'd waited—and been lucky.

The Guard and their tanks weren't the real target. The targets were the Scud missiles they guarded. The ones that Saddam was firing at Israel and Saudi Arabia. The start of Operation Desert Storm was delayed for a week while Special Ops hunted and killed the Scud sites. The ones along the Jordanian border to the west and aimed at Israel were being hunted by Delta and SAS, but his SEAL team had been lucky enough to draw the short straw on the wasteland between Kuwait and Nasiriyah in the southeast corner of the country.

Lying low through the day, they'd gathered valuable intel, including talk of the three other sites hidden in the area. It was finally falling dusk. Come full dark, they'd pull back and pinpoint those other three—calling in simultaneous airstrikes against all four launchers.

This one—

Barty grunted.

"*Al'ama!*" A mild epithet by Arabic's typically pornographic curse standards. A Republican Guard, stepping off the path to piss, had stumbled on Barty Hughes—literally.

The guard struggled to keep his sidearm steady while grabbing for his rapidly sagging pants. He had Barty square in his sights. The hammer was already on the move.

Mac emerged from his hiding place just a step to the guard's other side. No other RGs nearby at the moment, but that wouldn't last.

He came up out of the sand with his KA-BAR knife already out of its leg sheath. Before the guard could react, Mac had rammed seven inches of steel upward through the guard's chin. With a twist, he sliced his brain's connection to the rest of his nervous system.

Just like the Vietnam vets who trained him had promised, the man's body shut down all at once without a single sound. His other teammates emerged from the sand.

He dragged the corpse—with the knife still in place to minimize blood flow onto the sand—back out of sight behind a thorn bush.

"Make a hole."

The other three scrabbled quickly in the sand. When it was a foot deep, he twisted the corpse around and flopped it in, yanking free his blade.

He watched while they covered it back up. It wouldn't hide him for long, but it didn't have to. By midnight, this site would be blasted to smithereens.

Night had fallen with a desert's abruptness and they faded away.

"Thanks, bro." Barty slapped him on the shoulder as they moved out.

It was the first real action either of them had seen. The '80s had been more about training and humanitarian missions. This whole Desert Shield / Desert Storm thing was new even to a SEAL with a decade in the teams.

"You get my back next time." But he couldn't find it in him to thump Barty back as they jogged off into the dark to find and pinpoint the next site.

He'd signed up for this and trained for it, but he'd never killed a man before. He'd *seen* death. Almost died himself during the disaster which was Desert One—the US' attempt to free the hostages from Iran in 1980 had ended in a fiery disaster. But he'd never dealt it before.

The next time he touched Ama, would he feel the mark on his hand? Would she?

Maybe.

But for the first time he finally understood just how fast a man's life could end. His own life as well. But he had a wife *and* a son.

As they ran through the darkness, he knew he was at a fork in the path. A decision. Did killing one man count as his lifetime quota and, if so, that would lead him back to…where? To their small house in San Diego? To surfing and bobbing on the waves without a purpose?

No. He wouldn't allow the death of an enemy to change the path of his life. He now understood what Ama had once said, that life's changes must come from the good, not the bad. *Let the Good be our guide.*

Ama had changed more than his life, she'd changed his world. And she'd given him a son who had had changed his heart.

He thumped his fist against Barty's shoulder as they ran side-by-side. Barty wasn't the only one who was thankful to be alive. Mac would stay in the SEALs. He would fight to keep his family safe despite the danger.

At least until he found the next fork in the path formed from joy, not death.

CHAPTER 6

Ama rode behind her beloved men. She had grown up riding horses, a skill she had almost forgotten but her body had remembered as easily as any dance. The two of them rode miserably, yet acted as if falling off would be the greatest possible wound to their manly pride. She was careful to reserve her smile for when they were looking the other way.

How had her life led her to riding across this lush prairie ranch while listening to her husband's and son's hearty voices, loudly reassuring themselves of their competence? How had her life led to any of the places it had?

She had followed a young boy with mystical eyes to San Diego against her parents' wishes. They had lived together on the beach as well as overseas when his assignments allowed. The nights apart she had slept curled around the phone, praying that each time it rang, it would be his voice on the other end of the line and not his commander's. For twenty years her prayers had been answered.

For twenty years she had worn the warrior's face each time he left —assured and proud. Each time he returned, she'd worn the wife's— thankful to the Maheo Sky Chief or any other power that might be listening for his safe return. And she had done her very best to hide her tears from Mark on all the nights between.

She looked at the open prairie beneath the vast blue sky. They were safe now, in this instant: her husband returned from war and her son not yet gone. This ranch had been another family's dream, and it was clear that they had struggled before they left. It would take a lot of work to bring the ranch back to life. But she'd never feared hard work and a SEAL knew of no other kind. It could be a home. Perhaps the one she'd always dreamed of.

Mac's dream had come complete the day he retired. His entire team had stood down together—those who had retired before twenty years had come to the celebration on the beach at Coronado. They had raised a glass to those who had fallen. The SEALs all agreed they'd been fortunate that so few of their teammates had died, but she had felt battered anew by each name that was called in that toast.

Later in the party, after her nerves had finally calmed down, Mac had taken her hand. Just as he had twenty years before, he'd gone down on one knee before all his SEAL brothers. There had been laughter among the team at the memory.

She had waited to see what he would ask this time.

"You have dreamed *my* dream long enough, my love. I think I found a way to help dream *your* dream now."

So she and Mark, who had come to the retirement party on a school break from West Point, had followed him here to this ranch nestled close against the feet of the towering Front Range.

Up to Wyoming. Past Cheyenne where she'd returned every summer to see family and to dance. North of Yellowstone and into the heart of Montana where the grasslands were alive with the yellow and purple of summer flowers.

She patted her horse on the neck and watched her two men riding beneath the shimmering blue sky. They were so excited with dreams of building a new home here, even if neither one had much of an idea about what that meant. Neither of them had ever lived in the country. She was shocked that they had yet to fall off their horses—though there had been many close calls.

But this was a dream *she* understood.

Mac had passed that certainty, that perfect clarity of self on to his son. A senior at West Point, he stood as tall and handsome as his father. His dark hair short for the training, had run long through the sunlit years of his teens—just as his father's had when Ama had first seen him. Mark's skin was closer to her tone than Mac's; his face so handsome he could have been one of the Cheyenne. Except for the eyes. He had his father's blue-gray eyes—soft when he was happy and like cold steel when angered.

They'd ridden deep into the ranch on horses borrowed from a neighboring cattle rancher. At a river that wound through the miles of Montana pastureland, she had taught them how to fish. They had planned on two days, yet stayed for a week, living off what they caught. She had snared a rabbit, pleased that she remembered the tricks to skin it and cook it over a campfire—lessons learned from her father so long ago.

Now they were returning. Across the rolling hills, they had climbed the high bluff that sheltered the main ranch buildings. A mile down the dirt road, the cattle ranch where their horses belonged could just be seen. The horses were anxious for their stables, but Mac and Mark were finally confident enough in the saddle to at least keep them from running off. That still didn't mean they knew anything about ranch life.

"Put up a new barn there," Mac pointed to a swale in the land that would be wet in autumn's rainfall, "and you could start a nice herd of cattle."

But it would be a fine place for a swimming hole with only a little work. Besides, cattle were smelly, rude, and not very rewarding to the rancher. She'd seen many of her father's friends broken by a bad season, a runaway disease, even rustlers.

"Sure," Mark had agreed with his father. "And build a bunkhouse for the hands up here on the bluff so they get a nice view. Treat your team well and they'll treat you well."

This place where the harsh north winds would run chill across the Canadian Plains and slam straight into them all winter.

There was a reason that the old ranch house down below had been built on the south side of the bluff. Ten years abandoned, it still stood square and strong with a long porch wrapping around three sides. Thirty miles to the nearest town, it had not been plagued by vandals and the weather had claimed only two windows.

Halfway between their perch on the bluff and the big house were several copses of Ponderosa pines. Sheltered from the north, their view was to the southeast, not of the ranch, but rather the neighbor's land that seemed to roll to the horizon. It had made the view of the mountains once over the bluff a surprise and a gift.

A few weathered cabins still huddled among the pines. A little clearing, a little fixing, and guests could come there. Their future happy voices seemed to catch on the breeze that washed over the tall grass much as the waves had when she would watch Mac just to see what he would do next.

The old horse barn and the ranch manager's house still stood strong as well.

She had lived so much of her life alone. First, with a tribe she had felt curiously disconnected from. Later, separated during tour after tour from the one man who had ever made her heart soar like the dance. And finally, after her son had gone to West Point to become the man his father was, she'd been completely alone. The last three years had been a time of holding her heart closed and waiting.

Well, that was done and she wouldn't miss it. Her heart could open now and soar like an eagle. She stretched her fingers out and let them feel the breeze trickling between them.

There would be people here, and laughter. She could already see them: riding horses, fishing in the streams, and eating good camp fare at the long wooden table they'd discovered still standing in the ranch house dining room. Mac could lead hunting parties or teach shooting on a range (over the other side of the rise so that guests didn't have to hear it). People would come here to escape, to discover happiness. It could work.

This Montana ranch wouldn't be just some step woven into the old, she decided. It would be a whole new dance.

CHAPTER 7

Mac kept an eye on Ama as they rode down the hill, past the big house, and along the dirt driveway.

He tried to read what she was thinking about the place. The verdict looked hopeful, but she'd always been hard to read. He was fairly sure he had it right, because when she was feeling deepest was when she was quietest. And she'd barely said a word since they'd left the high bluff lookout.

Even back at the retirement party, he'd been watching for her reaction but been unable to read it. Barty and his dad had approached Mac with an idea.

What to do after retirement had worried at him. A SEAL knew how to fight. A SEAL knew that nothing could stop him once he had a mission. Except, in retiring, Mac no longer *had* a mission.

"Thanks again for saving my boy's life," Bart Sr. had handed him a fresh beer.

"Served twenty years on the same team, seemed like the right thing to do," Mac had earned a laugh from them both.

Bart Sr. had been a Marine in Vietnam and understood. Barty had saved Mac's life a time or two as well over the years—though not so graphically. That's just how it worked on the teams.

"Got a place up in Montana," Bart had told him, while looking off into the distance over Coronado Beach and the Pacific. "Twenty thousand acres of the prettiest land you've ever laid eyes on. Former owners moved on a decade ago and I grabbed it. Needs tending."

Mac could only shake his head. "I saved some. Ama's good with money and I sent home all I could, but we can't afford a ranch."

"Not talking about selling it to you. If you'd like, it's yours and your kin's for as long as you tend it. When you're done, I'll buy it back for the cost of improvements. No risk. Go up there and take the family. Once you give it a good look over, I know you'll love it. All yours if you want it. Did I mention that I'm right grateful you saved my son's life?"

"Might have," Mac had agreed as he had looked over at Ama standing with a few of the other SEALs. People were drawn to her, but "social" wasn't how he ever thought of her. Ama and city life had never made sense. Not in Cheyenne. Not in San Diego. Not outside the Marine Corps base in Böblingen, Germany.

There were images, moments, that had pulled him through the worst of Hell Week when half the remaining hopefuls had rung out and quit because they couldn't hack it. Grown men, tough soldiers, had openly wept at their failure. But each time he'd had to dig deep, there were certain memories that had let him find the resolve to stick out the training or to survive when by all rights he should have died in some foreign hole.

He always remembered her lost in the dance—the tall beauty in sky-blue deer hide dress and boots. And he always remembered her floating out on that surfboard when the waves were too quiet to ride but too peaceful to leave. She belonged somewhere she could find that peace.

Bart's description had sounded completely on the mark. So completely that Mac had asked him to arrange one other favor. Once he'd asked, Bart had slapped him on the back as if they'd been comrades in the same war instead of thirty years apart on opposite sides of the world.

But now, here in Montana, it was only Ama's opinion that mattered and, as ever, she kept her thoughts carefully to herself.

His family rode three abreast down the ranch's drive. Looking ahead, he saw that the broken arch of the ranch sign had been replaced while they'd been camped back along the river. New and hopefully carved just as he'd asked of Bart. Mac truly hoped that he'd made the right decision in asking his favor.

The cattle rancher's daughter—a blonde sprite who couldn't be more than ten—galloped across the field toward them as if riding was more natural than breathing. She reached them just as they arrived beneath the sign, its message facing out toward the world.

"Would you like a picture? Pa said he thought you might like a picture." She flourished a Polaroid camera at them. "Saw you up on the bluff looking around and I guessed when you'd get down here. Guessed dead right." She was breathless with her own success.

Ama's nod was all Mac needed. He had no photo of her dancing. Nor of her long body in a sleek wetsuit afloat on the Pacific Ocean. But this time he would. His whole family at once, gathered under the arch of the repaired ranch sign.

Julie, that was the sprite's name, got them all lined up on their horses, then backed her own horse up without touching the reins as she peered through the finder.

"Whoa," she called softly and the horse whoaed. Maybe he'd have to hire her to give him lessons. Ama, of course, rode a horse even more elegantly than she'd ridden those long ago waves.

Julie snapped it and the square print churned out the front slot.

"Take another," he called to her.

She eyed him over the camera.

"Dollar apiece," he offered.

"Two for five dollars. I'm saving up for an entry in the junior rodeo at the fair." Not greedy, just ambitious. Something a SEAL always appreciated.

He couldn't help smiling and nodded for her to fire away.

She did, then walked the horse back up to him, flapping a photo in each hand as they developed while the camera dangled around her neck. He solemnly fished out a five and traded it for the two photos.

"Don't tell my dad," Julie folded the bill very small then tucked it deep into a jeans pocket. She grabbed her reins, spun about, and galloped off with her long blonde hair floating behind her.

Mac handed one of the photos to Mark. "Your copy, son. This is family. Keep it close." Mark's nod said that he understood, or thought he did. For now it was enough, he'd learn the rest when luck and love found him.

"Say, Dad," Mark had raised his sunglasses to inspect the photo as it developed. "It's a cool sign, but..."

Mac glanced at the photo he still held as Ama rode forward enough to look back and see the sign itself.

"Looks good to me, Mark. Let's see what your mom thinks."

If Ama had been quiet before, she'd now gone so perfectly still that she might as well be hypnotized by the arcing sign of new wood.

"It spells Henderson's Ranch," Mark continued, just a little bit oblivious to what was really going on. "Which is great. And I think you and Mom will love it here. But shouldn't it be plural with the apostrophe after the s, not before?"

But Mac was still waiting for Ama's final reaction.

She slowly lowered her eyes to look at him.

Just like that long ago day at the end of her dance. She had looked at him and a smile had slowly bloomed to life across her lovely features. Love at first sight was far too slow a word for her effect on him.

Until now, she had always lived his life. And it had been a good one.

Now he expected that he would be even more content living hers.

"It's *her* dream now, son. Her ranch. I can only hope you find a woman who makes you feel like I'm feeling right now."

Then he managed to nudge the horse forward until he could kiss his wife. They'd make a home together under the brilliant blue arch of Montana's Big Sky.

EMILY'S CHRISTMAS GIFT

Major Emily Beale (retired—mostly) keeps her hand in the Black Ops world remotely from the family horse ranch on Montana's Front Range. Her husband, Major Mark Henderson (fully retired), has settled comfortably into his new role as father and ranch operator.

Years ago, she helped rescue a young girl. But when Emily's childhood friend, the former President of the United States, comes to visit, he raises doubts about the girl's safety. No longer so sure of herself, Emily must reach deep into the White House's secret library to find the answers. Little does she know the true location of Emily's Christmas Gift.

CHAPTER 1

Emily watched Mark being as calm as could be and tried not to resent it. When the heavy Montana snowstorms of December kept them indoors at the main ranch house, he was content to slouch low on the couch and watch a Disney movie with the girls in the cozy family area off the kitchen.

If they wanted to build a fort—Emily always thought of it as a fort, though the girls kept insisting they were tents—Mark would reconfigure the family sitting area off the kitchen no matter what inconvenience it caused the adults.

Between the three of them, they made sure that each construction looked unlike any prior effort. A tropical paradise one time, decorated mostly with one of the ranch hand's awful Hawaiian shirt collection. Another time, a Cheyenne teepee built with Mark's mother's lovely weavings. She'd particularly liked that one. Being in Montana, and especially if Julie was around to help, Western themes were common, often with horse tack or some of her rodeo trophies for decoration.

In the summers Mark lived to fly tourists around in his helicopter and fish, but in the winter his one joy was keeping his girls happy.

That she herself was one of "his girls" always made their daughters giggle with delight. And she *was* happy. All she had to do was watch her daughters and she let their constantly bubbling joy wash over her. They might build their forts—*tents* with their father. But it was never considered complete until she had joined them for the final tour. Mark often left some final task for her to do so that she'd at least feel included. Then they would all lie in it together—Mark at the center with all three of "his girls" clinging happily to him.

Those were the best moments of her life. Perhaps a close second to waking in his arms on the long quiet winter mornings before Tessa and Belle sprang to life like a pair of Jill-in-the-boxes.

She'd known he was a good man and a great commander, but his daughters had never met "The Viper" who used to scare the shit out of everybody, including her. His steel gray eyes had rarely been revealed from behind his mirrored shades. He'd even proposed to her while wearing them—after dark. Which was perhaps the only thing that had kept her from turning into a complete empty-headed mush in that moment.

But his daughters only saw the sky gray that his eyes shone when he was happiest—and the mirrored shades were now worn only in the strong Montana sun. It was impossible for her *not* be happy while she watched the stern, taciturn, demanding Major Mark "The Viper" Henderson (retired) have no compunction about acting as the total goofball with his girls. He was a better father than she was a mother, but she didn't know what to do about that. When they were upset, it was her they came to, so she still had something. But it often meant she got the tears and Mark earned all the cheers.

Emily didn't resent it...much. She mostly just wished it was somehow different.

She turned to the fire and watched what she could see of the flames. They were partially blocked by a great bulge in this week's fort, which was huge by any previous standard.

This room was where the family lived during the day when they weren't out on the ranch. The high-timbered main room and the dining room with its forty-person pine table was for the guests. In the long, bitter, off-season months, it was also where all the locals gathered for the occasional party to break the monotony of winter.

That was for others. The family lived in the kitchen. The kitchen itself was a full commercial setup, decorated like in ranch-house warm timber and cool granite stone. At the near end stood a large plank table of Douglas fir where the family and the ranch hands ate their meals together.

This sitting area to the side had a big stone fireplace, and a scattering of couches and armchairs enough for the entire staff...or there had been until the kids started showing up. Once they graduated from lap-sized, they would have to squeeze in some more furniture. The bookcases that lined the river stone walls already had more shelves added to accommodate the girls' picture books.

Of course more furniture couldn't happen with their latest fort in place—she could only see half the fire from her favorite end of the couch.

It was like a mighty Christmas igloo, its walls built high with pillows raided from all of the guest cabins that were closed for the winter. Mark had waded out into the freezing dawn this morning to cut down and drag home a ten-foot larch to stand at its center. Now, with the tree up and their pillow-wall built, the three of them were madly working away inside. Only the tree's single uppermost branch was visible above the domed roof, like a wide smoke hole escaping the dome of pillows.

Whenever there was a newborn about, either Chelsea's or Julie's boy, their father was instantly abandoned without further thought—which made her feel a little better. Of course, then Emily had to keep a close eye so that the girls didn't smother the two infants with affection. How in the world she'd raised two such...*girls* was a mystery to her. At five, Tessa was an utter extrovert who had all the ranch hands completely wrapped around her tiny pinkie. Belle at three was the steadier one, but only by comparison.

Emily didn't pace when the heavy snow and the biting cold winds forced them to remain indoors, but she wished she'd taken up watching sports on television or something. But after a career of flying helicopters first to war and then to wildfire, watching a bunch of guys chase a football up and down a chunk of AstroTurf in little one- and two-yard spurts couldn't be called exciting.

"I'm absolutely hiring Mark for the next seventeen years," Chelsea plummeted down into the big armchair beside Emily's end of the couch, then had to drag her fingers through her long hair to toss it over her shoulder so she could see. Her cheeks were brilliant red after crossing the snow from where she and her husband, the ranch manager, lived on the other side of the barnyard. Maybe Emily should grow her gold-blonde hair as long, the way Mark kept hinting, but it had been chopped dead straight to her shoulders for her entire life.

Emily saw Mark now sitting on the braided rug with Chelsea's three-month old boy Christopher cradled in his arms—whose hair was already as red as his mother's. Tessa and Belle were leaning on his thighs from either side and reaching over to inspect the infant who watched with such wide, serious eyes. Her own fair hair hadn't been passed on to either daughter, having no chance against Mark's genes from his brown-haired father and Cheyenne mother.

"Or maybe I'll just knock you off and get two husbands, keep Doug for me and have Mark for the kid." Chelsea extended her feet toward the fire.

"I'm notoriously hard to kill." Emily's specialty had been black-in-black missions. Black ops so sensitive that they were talked about with no one, ever. And so dangerous that each one was a curse of its own. Mark accompanied her on or referred vaguely to four—she'd stopped counting as she neared ten.

"Oh, don't worry, Emily," Chelsea slouched lower. "I'd like, uh, get Julie to do it for me. She was raised a cowgirl and knows how to do the icky stuff."

"I'm a horsegirl now. And do what?" Julie settled very slowly on the couch beside Emily, careful not to wake Jared asleep in her arms. Like her own children, Jared had his father's dark hair and eyes rather than Julia's wheat blonde and blue. If he'd slept through the snowy trek down the hill from their cabin, then it would take far more than a small bump to wake him, but Emily knew better than to say such a thing to a new mother. She had to smile at her own worries about Tessa in the beginning.

She did scoop up Jared and hold him while Julie shed her thick coat and tossed it over a maple wood chair. Then she settled back on the plaid sofa and took Jared back, again with infinite care.

Like the toddler-magnets they were, Tessa and Belle appeared on either side of Julie. Tessa sat on Julie's far side, but Belle pushed and squirmed—with plenty of bumps that Jared never noticed—until she was sitting between Emily and Julie. Emily looped an arm around her daughter, not as if there was anywhere else to put it, and kissed her on top of the head.

"I need you to...uh," Chelsea glanced at the two young girls before answering Julie, "...*remove* Emily for me. Kinda permanently so I can have Mark as a full-time babysitter."

"Too late," Julie gently blocked Belle reaching over to wake Jared. Belle was completely enamored of Jared's big eyes and the two of them could stare at each other for hours. "I've already got dibs. Besides, I thought we liked Emily?"

"We do. But where has that gotten us?"

"They grow, you know," Emily decided it was time for a subject change to something other than her demise. "Far too quickly, I might add." She pulled one of Ama's Cheyenne blankets off the back of the couch—this one she'd loved from the first moment, so rich with warm golds and dark reds in a geometric pattern. Spreading it over Julie's and the girls' laps earned her contented smiles.

"See?" Julie looked over at Chelsea. "She knows things. I vote that we keep her."

"Well, she is out there ahead of us," Chelsea finally agreed. "So, what are the good bits waiting for us?"

"We're almost done with diapers."

"Oh God," the two women moaned in unison. "Can't happen too soon."

"Thankfully, Mark is okay trading off on that duty."

"That does it," Chelsea declared. "Sorry, Emily. We really like you, but you're *totally* toast."

"I've still got dibs on Mark." The threat didn't seem too serious as Julie was looking down at her sleeping son with a big smile on her face.

Mark was bent halfway over from placing the now-sleeping Christopher into Chelsea's arms when he finally clued into the last comment. He paused, inspecting all of them carefully.

"Why does this sound like a conversation I want no part of?"

"Because you are a very smart man who loves his wife above any other woman on Earth."

"It's true," Mark shrugged happily before stepping around the back of the couch and leaning down to kiss her from the side.

Emily could feel her internal compass slowly returning to True North. It wasn't often she flew off course, but with Mark's lips on hers, she managed to rediscover her rudder control.

"Oh man," Chelsea groaned in envy.

"Chelsea's right," Julie agreed. "You'd better watch your back, Emily. We're ganging up on you and you're going down. Soon."

"By Christmas."

Emily ignored them both as Mark drew out the kiss to tease them. No complaints from her.

"Where are *your* men?" Mark asked when he finally let her surface for air, leaving her heartrate up about Black Hawk rotor speed. "Two such beautiful women with babies in their arms shouldn't be sitting here unkissed."

"They abandoned us."

"Left us destitute."

"They may have mumbled something about feeding the horses."

"So here we sit."

"In our prime."

"Unkissed," they finished in unison and both aimed ridiculous puckers at Mark and batted their eyelashes. Well, Chelsea did. Julie tried but mostly looked down and blushed for being so forward.

"Feeding the horses, huh? I'd better go check on them." He didn't leave at a run, but he definitely used his best ground-eating stride.

"Ooo," Chelsea cooed loudly. "Looks good from behind too. All mine."

Mark double-timed it out as the three of them shared a laugh.

When he was gone, there was a long silence. Long enough for Belle to slip into a nap against Emily's side and for Tessa to yawn broadly before curling up at the end of the sofa and resting her head on Julie's thigh while Jared wrapped his tiny hand around her pinkie without quite waking.

"What's up with you, Emily?" Julie asked softly.

"There's something up with you?" Chelsea peered at her in surprise.

"Nothing." Emily ignored the slump that Mark had only temporarily lifted. She toyed with the blanket's fringe for a moment before she caught herself at it and tucked her hands out of sight. "Besides, since when can either of you tell what I'm thinking?"

"Since forever. We're your best friends," Julie spoke softly.

"Yeah. Maybe we aren't all experienced and old like you, but we know shit."

They'd both found the love of their life and reproduced in their early twenties. It had taken her until thirty to find love, then more years of service, finally the first kid…and that had been five years ago. Forty wasn't here yet, but it was incoming—fast. She closed her eyes. This was December. She'd been born in… Yep, really fast.

"Is forty bumming you out?"

Emily sat with it for a while. "No, I don't think that's it…"

"Told you something was up with her," Julie whispered to Chelsea.

"Of course, you two youngsters are enough to make a grown woman a little nuts."

"But you love us both anyway, huh?"

Emily looked at Chelsea and couldn't deny that truth.

"Like daughters?" Julie's voice was slightly wistful. Her family life hadn't been real fun. Just the hard life of a cattle ranch with a strict father, a silent mother, and three older brothers, but none of the joy she'd discovered when she'd fallen in love with the man who was now Henderson's Ranch's head chef.

"*Daughters?*" Emily winced. "Now you're just *trying* to make me feel old. How about younger sisters?"

Julie actually nodded fiercely. As if it was important.

Chelsea too was blinking hard. "If I wasn't afraid of waking this little terror, I'd come over there and give you major kiss."

Curiously, Emily caught herself in mid-sniffle, but managed to take a deep breath to cover it.

"It's just,,," She honestly didn't know.

"Pre-Christmas blues?"

"Year-end blahs?"

"Desperate need for a third child?"

That earned them a bark of laughter that made all four children stir in their sleep.

They all held their breaths until the kids had resettled and the only sounds were the fierce Montana winds struggling vainly to rattle the solid house.

"Not a chance," Emily kept her voice low just in case they weren't fully asleep again. "I don't think Mark would mind, but having your kids late means all sorts of strange things. I'll be sixty before this one graduates from college." She could feel Belle so warm and safe against her side. What would it be like when Belle was a woman grown like Julie or Chelsea and maybe with a child of her own? Out in the world where Emily couldn't protect her?

At Tessa's age, she herself had already had a crush on Peter Matthews—the perfect older boy next door. But he'd married and become President of the United States. She'd gone to West Point and become the first woman of the Night Stalkers. By Julie and Chelsea's age, she'd been flying helicopters on her second tour into war zones with the 101st Airborne.

"Sixty? Shit, you *are* old, sis."

"Go to hell, Chelsea."

"Not gonna happen. I've got you for a big sister, means I've gotta being doing something right."

Emily knew Chelsea had earned a laugh, but she couldn't seem to find it. She lay her head back on the couch and wondered what was wrong with her. Maybe it *was* just the season. Or that Night Stalkers helicopter pilots, unlike most Special Operations Forces, could fly well into their fifties—if they hadn't reproduced. It wasn't some rule that had kept her out. Instead, her own fears for her child's safety had cost her that finely-honed *edge* that made a true Spec Ops pilot. Maybe it was that…

Something was wrong, and she had no idea what.

She heard a soft gasp from Chelsea that made her open her eyes.

And looked up directly into Peter's. Mark and Peter were grinning at her—upside down over the back of the soft, brown-leather couch.

"Surprise, Squirt."

"You're supposed to be in Washington, D.C., Sneaker Boy." Her childhood nickname for the former President of the United States. Except he wasn't anymore. He was the Secretary of State. His nickname was still Sneaker Boy.

She heard a deep, guffaw in the background.

"Hi, Frank."

"Good afternoon, Major Beale," the head of Peter's Secret Service Protection Detail sounded as formal as ever. Yet another reminder of what she'd left behind.

Then she looked over at Mark.

"You seemed kinda down, Emily. So I invited Peter out for Christmas as a surprise. His wife, kid, and maybe a few others will be out next week."

"You're feeling down?" Peter suddenly sounded worried. Just exactly what she didn't need—the Secretary of State and former President flying to Montana in the middle of winter to hover. There'd be no point trying to explain it to Mark; he'd never be convinced he'd overreacted.

"You're what?" "What's wrong?" Apparently done with the horses, Chelsea's and Julie's husbands chimed in from somewhere out of view.

Emily sat up and looked at her younger sisters. "Don't bother killing me, just take Mark for yourselves, please. Now."

"Do you really change diapers?" Chelsea turned to Mark, who shrugged a yes.

"Dibs," Julie said again.

CHAPTER 2

"Seriously, Em. What's wrong?"

She'd led Peter through the bitter cold out to the horse barn, because no matter what Mark thought, the Secretary of State didn't fly to Montana just because a friend was feeling sad. Though she had to give Mark a few points for noticing how she *was* feeling when she'd barely realized it herself.

She stopped at Chesapeake's stall. The barn was warm with the scent of horse and hay. The light was dim beneath the blowing storm, making it feel almost as cozy as the kitchen—as long as you were wearing a jacket or a horse blanket.

She hadn't had the clarity of mind to remember to grab a treat from the house, but Chelsea kept a bag of carrots in her office and Emily had grabbed one as she walked by.

Breaking off a piece, she palmed it to her horse. The big chestnut mare lipped it off her palm and crunched it down. She leaned her cheek against the horse's and felt her chew.

"Mark's right. You are looking down."

"Which isn't why you're here."

"Well, not all of it, but—"

"Why are you here, Sneaker Boy?"

549

Peter laughed, then startled when Julie's black-and-white painted horse, Clarence, stuck his head out of his stall to see what was going on and almost knocked Peter over.

Emily gave him a chunk of Chesapeake's carrot as a reward.

"I don't know as I'd have come for either reason separately, but when Mark called to invite me out and…" he shrugged. "It's about Dilya."

She spun to face him, but he only looked concerned, not afraid.

"What about her?" Emily barely managed to keep her voice steady. Dilya was the war-orphan adopted daughter of her best friend Archie and his wife Kee, the first woman to qualify for the Night Stalkers after she herself had. That terrified and starved ten-year-old was now a lovely seventeen-year-old, living in the White House as nanny to the First and Second children.

"She's…" Peter's face showed that he really didn't know as he stumbled to a halt.

"Okay. Not sick. Not in trouble. What?"

Peter finally shrugged. "She reminds me too much of you."

"Of me?" She showed him how to hold some carrot to feed to Clarence before she fed the greens to Chesapeake. Why on earth would that be?

"Remember when we first met?"

"No. I think I was about three days old. My memory is good, but even I have limits."

"I mean when we re-met."

"You mean when I slammed the head of your Protection Detail onto his ass on the White House's main staircase?" She raised her voice enough to make sure Frank Adams could hear her as he returned from checking that there were no four-legged assassins lurking in the horse barn.

"Are we really back to this, Major? You just gotta keep bringing that up, don't you?"

"It *was* memorable."

Frank grumbled as he moved by to check the other end of the barn.

"Yes," Peter waited until Frank was again out of earshot. "I'd been following your career for some time by then. And I was horrified at the dangers you were going into."

"Because I was a woman."

Peter looked down and scuffed one of his perfect leather shoes at the dirty straw. For all his supposed sophistication, he was still a guy —which meant she'd never understand him.

"That," he admitted, "and because you were my friend. You were the little girl next door who was suddenly flying thirty-million-dollar helicopters straight into harm's way."

"What has this got to do with Dilya?"

"You know that girl's nose for trouble?"

"You don't know the half of it." In her first month after they'd rescued her, Dilya had identified two men so intent on revenge that they didn't care if it could start the next World War. Then she'd stowed away on a clandestine insertion deep into Uzbekistan to stop them. A detail that was never included in any action report.

"And I'm guessing I don't want to. But now? I'm getting worried for her, Em."

Emily glanced up at her secure office within the stable. Her Tac Room (short for Tactical) had been built directly over the Tack Room (filled with saddles and bridles). It had been finished with the same, aged wood, so that it didn't stand out at all. Its windows were dark— with special glass that appeared opaque even when lit from within. The only clue from the outside that it was anything special was the very sophisticated lock mounted out of sight from below. From there, at Peter's behest, she'd created the White House Protection Force. The WHPF had proven to be immensely successful, saving the new President's life on three separate occasions and averting any number of other minor disasters.

And despite Emily's best intentions, Dilya had several times ended up far too close to the action for comfort. The last time, nearly being shot down over Canadian soil.

"So, what do you want me to do? Scare her straight?"

She could see Peter's face brighten.

"You know that's not going to happen, don't you?"

And he looked worried again.

"She's an incredibly bright kid. And she's grown up with the elite Night Stalkers company for companions, a sniper mother, a strategic consultant father, and essentially unlimited access to your and now Zachary's White House. You think she was just being cute all those times she 'hung out' in the Oval with you? I guarantee you that Dilya was never an innocent child—at least not since we found her. Watching both your parents be executed right in front of you will do that to a kid."

Peter leaned sadly against the stall door. His idea of casual was a two-piece suit rather than a three-piece under his heavy black wool coat. Clarence snorted in his ear and made him jump away in alarm. Out of carrot, she made a point of scritching the horse's cheek with her fingers until he huffed out a happy sigh.

"If we can't keep her out of trouble, how do we teach her to judge when she's in too deep or at least to cry for help?"

Emily leaned back against Chesapeake's neck. Her childhood friend had been Peter, who was six years older than she was. Julie had been right, Emily knew things because she was out ahead of them… but Belle was two and Tessa was five. That wasn't seventeen. She knew nothing yet about anything after age five. Her only solution had been to treat Dilya as a small adult…one who wasn't so small anymore.

But it was a crucial question. Peter was right, Dilya's well-being depended on it. And she knew just who to ask.

CHAPTER 3

Convincing Peter that there were some things he didn't want to know had proved just as hard as usual, but Emily had practice at it. With Frank's help, she soon had him shooed back over to the main house.

Mounting the stairs to her Tac Room, she keycoded the door, offered her eye for retinal scan, then locked the door behind her.

The one-way glass gave her a long view of the horse stalls, their occupants lazing through the cold winter day, happily napping and munching on hay. Chelsea came into the barn at the far end of the stalls. She waved up as she always did in case Emily was watching, and headed into her own office. As the ranch's horse manager, she was meticulous in the care of her charges and the recent vet's visit to give all of them a checkup had probably left a pile of paperwork.

Emily liked the company when they were both working out here, even if they were isolated in separate offices. Chelsea didn't have the security clearance to ever be inside this room.

Emily had already done her check of the public world news this morning. Now, in her secure space, she flipped through today's briefing documents from the various agencies. No real surprises—hot spots were still hot, but nothing abnormal. She'd be paged if there was a real crisis calling for her attention, but it wasn't the sort of day where that seemed likely. The First and Second families were having their typical White House workdays without travel. Which also meant Dilya would be rattling around the White House.

She tapped in a coded signal and settled in to wait while she read up on that latest internal status reports from NATO.

Her Tac Room assistant, Lauren, had proved herself immensely capable when dealing with military contacts. But the other side of Emily's information network—the one that reached deep into the White House itself—no one knew about except herself. With Lauren honeymooning at Disneyland over the holidays, Emily didn't have to worry about shooing her out to place this call.

"Hello, my dear." Her central screen lit with the face of one of the White House Protection Force's primary assets. Her gray hair framed an ageless face. Sometimes it seemed she'd aged past old crone and gone straight on to wizened. At other times, her face was clear enough that the gray hair was a shock. Today, she simply appeared what she was—a beautiful woman in her seventies (probably).

Behind her ranged the most unusual library in Washington, DC —which was saying something. Emily knew from her one visit there that it wasn't large. Her office felt even smaller because every inch of wall space from floor to ceiling was packed solid with books. Also on display were some of the more clandestine tools of the spy trade, which the shadows hadn't afforded her a chance to study. It was also perhaps the most accurate library on spies and spy craft ever assembled. There were less than a dozen people who knew where it lay—behind the door of Room 043-Mechanical in the White House Residence's deepest subbasement. And the woman in charge had been one of the greatest spies, including undocumented ones, of them all.

A blurred red-and-green glow stood to one side of the camera's view—too close to be clearly seen. A desktop Christmas tree perhaps? What did a master spy's Christmas tree look like? Probably a cone of stacked red-and-green code books used over the last half-century.

"Hello, Miss Watson. How are you today?"

"Oh, I'm good my dear. Very good. Thank you for asking. Is there something amiss that I'm unaware of?"

"Not likely," Emily sometimes wondered if Miss Watson was helping her keep the White House safe or if she was helping Miss Watson.

Miss Watson offered one of her grandmotherly smiles, "I don't know that you've ever made a social call before."

And at Emily's wince, Miss Watson clearly understood that this one wasn't either.

It wasn't that she didn't want to, it was that she never thought to. Not a single one of those fine skills that her mother, one of DC social queens, had struggled to cultivate in her only offspring had stuck.

"Emily, dear child…"

She almost laughed. She now had two younger "sisters" and all of them had children, yet—

"Tell me the reason you called, then we can talk about why you should have called earlier."

Emily tried looking at the books behind Miss Watson. Was there a guide to mindreading tucked away somewhere on those shelves? Unsure quite what Miss Watson meant, she described Peter's concerns about Dilya.

"That child was never young. Such potential."

Emily suddenly wasn't sure that Miss Watson's influence on Dilya was a good thing. What little she knew of Miss Watson's exploits told of the immense risks a woman could take in the name of the Cold War. It had been inevitable that Dilya's natural inquisitiveness had brought them together. Unfortunately what happened at the White House was outside of her control. Emily could protect, but she couldn't control.

Instead, her skill had always been in locating and cultivating exceptional talent. The President's new driver, one of his dog handlers, and others she'd helped put in place kept the President safer far beyond anything the Secret Service would understand—or ever be told about.

The White House Protection Force did *not* include Dilya, and yet she seemed to end up in the center of every problem—even when those problems became life-threatening.

"The girl is so independent. Perhaps too much so."

"Too much?" Emily had always prided herself on her own independence. It was what had let her succeed in a male world—absolute self-reliance.

"Yes. She knows a great deal more about depending solely on her own judgment than even you, my dear child. Despite your deservedly decorated career. And don't we both know about some of the decorations you can never admit to."

Emily kept her best neutral expression on her face, but Miss Watson merely winked. No one, but *no one* other than the former President and the Joint Chiefs of Staff should know about her medals from black-in-black operations. Even Mark didn't know about those. No more than he'd know that she was technically still on active duty as a consultant.

"Dilya has carefully positioned herself to know more than everyone around her here at the White House," Miss Watson continued blithely. "I even hold a hope that someday she— Well, never mind that now. I believe that you've raised a valid question and I shall give it some thought. It is Christmas soon. Perhaps I shall give her a Christmas gift after all."

Emily considered what that might mean and suddenly wished she hadn't placed this call in the first place. Perhaps she should call Dilya and warn her away from Miss Watson. Actually, she could think of no faster way to drive Dilya directly into the fray. In that, she and Dilya were much alike.

Before Emily could open her mouth to protest or perhaps even try to call Miss Watson off, she continued so smoothly that Emily never managed a word.

"Now, my dear. Let's talk about what's troubling you."

"Nothing's troubling me."

"It isn't age," Miss Watson ignored her fib. "No woman as beautiful as you with two lovely children and such an exceptional husband can doubt that she is in the prime of her life."

She sighed.

"And I must compliment you on the fine job you did helping your husband transition to retired life. You are much better with people than you think you are. You picture yourself so austere and remote, yet people are drawn to you anyway."

Emily opened her mouth to protest, then closed it. She *had* just acquired two younger sisters this morning. Miss Watson couldn't know about them, could she? At least not yet? But she was right, the emotions on their faces had been no lie. Emily had always built team loyalty by being the best—no matter what it cost her. By being the best, she'd attracted the best. Yet it wasn't by outperforming anyone on the team that Julie had asked, *I thought we liked Emily?* And Chelsea had agreed, *We really do.*

"I remember such a time of reflection shortly before I died."

"You...died?"

"Oh yes, dear. Any number of times." She nudged a finger against the Christmas tree that was just a blur on the edge of the screen. It moved, so it wasn't books. Maybe it was better if she didn't know. "It is an easy way to cover your tracks in an on-going operation. But I'm referring to when I let the CIA believe I had died."

"How did they take it?"

"Oh, it was a lovely funeral. I have a star up on their wall, which is quite an honor in my business."

"And they still don't know about you surviving?"

Miss Watson shrugged, "There comes a time in a woman's life where one must move closer to the heart. We aren't men, after all."

Emily felt that was rather obvious.

"You'll want to think about that, child. You are a woman grown. You've fought for the right, and done the duties that a man does. For great achievers like us, struggling within a society not ready for us, we must now come to terms with being...ourselves."

"How did you do it?"

But Miss Watson's ghost of a smile demurred.

How had she done it? From what little Emily knew, Miss Watson might have always been in the White House subbasement. Yet apparently she'd also been a spy in the final years of the Vietnam War and had a Soviet two-star general as a lover. Emily, too, heard things.

She'd first met Miss Watson years before during her brief residence at the White House as the First Lady's personal chef. She'd thought nothing of it at the time—some elderly White House staffer she'd chatted with about the war she was fighting in Afghanistan. In hindsight Emily could see that things had changed for her from that moment. She'd— "Oh, I became *your* weapon."

Miss Watson offered her a slightly surprised expression.

"All those additional black-in-black ops. The toughest missions—"

"—Came to you because of your supreme confidence and exceptional abilities. Don't try to make me the wizard behind the curtain of your career, Emily. You are tactically an exceptional woman. It is the bigger picture that slips by you. Dilya is beginning to see her own bigger picture, which is why you worry about her—we fear what we don't understand."

"But—"

"Oh, my dear child," Miss Watson was gently shaking her head. "In the later years, you are still *yourself*. But the challenges are new. You must learn who you, yourself are. Rediscover or, if that fails, discover for the first time, the amazing woman you are."

"That's your advice?"

"The voice of experience."

Emily couldn't help but remember Julie leaning forward just this morning, *She knows things. I vote that we keep her.*

Man oh man, did she ever have them fooled.

"What did you—"

"Oh no, child. It would be cheating to tell. Besides, Dilya is far more my daughter than you are—at least in how she thinks. You must discover your own woman."

"Why doesn't that feel helpful?"

"Because you're still thinking as if you live in a man's world, challenging the status quo." Then Miss Watson shook herself lightly, glanced at her bookshelves somewhere out of sight, and suddenly appeared much older.

"Miss Watson, are you—"

"It is time I sent for Dilya."

"Miss Watson?" Emily could think of nothing else to say.

"Go see your family, dear." Then she was gone.

Emily sat in her small Tac Room and looked at blank screen, she tried not to feel sadder than before the call. Did the poor woman even have any family? Did she even have someone to spend Christmas with? Not that Emily knew of, and yet here she was dumping her own doubts upon Miss Watson.

She knew she could trust Dilya to Miss Watson's care and she'd hear soon enough what had happened. Emily had forgotten how much she liked Miss Watson and promised herself that her next call would be strictly social. Or when she needed a break from the Montana winter, she'd visit her parents in DC and arrange to drop in on the White House subbasement personally.

As for herself, none of it felt like a solution to anything.

CHAPTER 4

"What are you up to, babe?" Mark slid down on the couch beside her. He flipped up the edge of the big Cheyenne weaving she'd thrown over herself hours before while she'd watched the fire burn. There were only a few embers left, dying from lack of tending.

"What time is it?"

"Way early, but I missed you in bed." He pulled her into his arms and kissed her on the temple.

A week had passed and she was no closer to understanding any of Miss Watson's life lessons. Now she was out of time and simply had to shake it off.

Later today the ranch house would become much more lively. Vice President Daniel Darlington and his family had decided to fly out for Christmas along with Peter's wife and child. The local ranchers' potluck was going to get a big surprise tonight—for security's sake, no one would be warned ahead of time. Of course surprises were fair on both sides of the coin—she also hadn't forewarned the Secret Service just how many rifles would arrive tonight, hanging in the back windows of Montana pickup trucks.

The girls' pillow igloo fort would have to come down—or it

should. Knowing she'd lose that battle, she decided to leave well enough alone. Julie's husband Nathan and Mark's mom Ama would be awake soon and the three of them were planning to cook throughout the day. All week, Peter had practically taken over her secure Tac Room in the barn, doing Secretary of State things, so at least he'd been out from underfoot.

With the ease of long practice, Mark had eased her into his lap with her barely noticing until her head lay on his shoulder and his hand cradled her behind underneath the warm blanket.

"This isn't like you, Emily. Got me worried some." She'd always enjoyed feeling the deep rumble in his chest when he spoke.

"That makes two of us."

"You missing the action?"

She shook her head. At first the adrenaline-junkie withdrawal had been hard, but she'd expected that. Besides, she hadn't gone straight from Spec Ops to civilian—the years flying to wildfire and her occasional calls to consult had eased the transition.

"Sick of the cooking?"

No. She loved that. Mark's mother Ama had run the kitchen for over a decade, but cooked much less now. Nathan, a world-class chef who'd stumbled into love with Julie, had taken over the kitchen with such zeal that Emily could come play whenever the mood struck her, but she didn't have to worry when it didn't.

"Nothing about the kids?"

"I couldn't love Belle and Tessa more if they were part of me."

"They *were* part of you."

"Exactly my point."

As if on cue, the two girls appeared, still rubbing their eyes sleepily. In moments, they were all curled up together under the warm blanket. It was awkward, a little uncomfortable, and amazingly perfect.

"Not...us?" Mark whispered against her ear once the girls were settled. They were huddled under the blanket, mostly on her lap, whispering back and forth.

In answer, she managed to twist around enough to kiss Mark. He made it as thorough and perfect as their very first kiss—and she felt no desire to smash his face into an aircraft carrier's table as she'd done the first time.

"Then what?" Mark asked as she once more lay her head upon his shoulder and tightened her arm around Tessa's waist earning a happy giggle from beneath the big quilt.

For the life of her, she hadn't a clue.

CHAPTER 5

The mayhem had started even sooner than she'd anticipated.

Belle and Tessa, finally coming wide awake under the blanket, had found their father's one ticklish spot and completely undone him. To escape, he'd finally fallen off the couch. Turning it into a roll, he regained his feet and moved over to stoke the fire. The girls knew about not interfering around the flames. By the time she and the girls were dressed, Ama had breakfast on the table. Nathan was eating as he worked, assembling the ingredients for Emily's dry rub on the massive roast they'd planned for the potluck.

Second Lady Alice had arrived with their newborn, and Peter's wife Geneviève brought their little girl. At four, she had all the poise and elegance that her mother embodied and Emily's own daughters completely lacked. Belle and Tessa practically transcended on the spot with the additional playmate. She didn't know if she hoped her girls rubbed off on Adele Gloria—simply to harass Peter—or perhaps the other way round and her own girls might become more comprehensible to her. Either way, kid heaven had taken over much of the floor space in front of the fireplace with Mark often in the fray.

Her mood kept lifting through the day.

She'd never thought of herself as a particularly social or even approachable woman, but there were only so many welcoming hugs and joyous smiles that could be aimed her way before that belief became undeniably foolish.

Thankfully, the storm blew out and all that was left were achingly clear starlit skies and bitter cold. But Montanan ranchers had never yet been stopped by mere cold and soon the house was packed. The local ranchers soon shed their awe of the Washington elite—helped in part by all of the children in their pre-Christmas excitement. As more local children had arrived, they'd strained Tessa's and Belle's "dress up" wardrobe to the limit, but Christmas fairies and elves had abounded.

The big afternoon puppy-pile nap on the kitchen's couch had averted most of the exhaustion meltdowns.

And somehow, through the whole thing, the Christmas igloo fort had survived—no mere "tent" could have made it through the constant stream of children in and out of it. Of all the adults, only Mark had been allowed admittance.

As the evening wound down and the ranchers drifted back home through the chill darkness, the family and Washington guests slowly gathered once more in the kitchen. Chairs and benches were dragged over until everyone was packed in close to the fireplace. Hot cocoa, laced with brandy for the grownups, was served all around.

Emily could only look around the circle in wonder. Julie and Chelsea sat nearby with their husbands and babies. Her childhood friend Peter and his lovely Geneviève sat with her friend Vice President Daniel and his cheery wife. All around the room, there wasn't a person here whose life she hadn't touched, and who hadn't touched hers.

How had she not known this? Why was she just seeing it now?

These were her friends. Her family. Just as surely as the action teams of the Night Stalkers 5th Battalion D Company and the firefighters of Mount Hood Aviation had been her family.

She...belonged.

Is this what Miss Watson had been talking about? That somehow, this was her "woman's" role after having lived in the "man's" world for so many years?

Maybe it was. Maybe—

"I think it's time, girls," Mark called, loudly enough to silence all of the conversations.

With a squeal of delight, they launched to their feet in a mad swirl of excitement and fairy wings. Adele Gloria—Peter's and Geneviève's daughter had devolved only a little under Tessa's influence and Tessa had settled (a little)—was rapidly recruited and the three kids disappeared into the Christmas igloo fort.

"Now it's your turn, honey," Mark rose and held out his hand to her.

Emily was terribly conscious that everyone was watching her as she rose to her feet. She should have gone and locked herself in her Tac Room—nobody would dare to disturb her there. Then she certainly wouldn't be the center of attention.

Once she was on her feet, Mark knelt before her, something he hadn't even done while proposing. What was he—

"Up," he patted his shoulder.

"What?"

He hooked one of her knees and dragged it over his shoulder. "Climb aboard, Emily."

"No. I—" she resisted his attempt to grab her other leg.

"Here, Mommy," Belle came out of the igloo and handed her a package wrapped in Christmas paper before racing back in.

Mark took advantage of her momentary distraction and got her astride his shoulders. Then he stood quickly before she could escape. He faced the Christmas igloo and called out.

"Ready, girls?"

A high chorus of "Yes!" was their answer as she hung onto Mark's forehead with one hand and the wrapped present with the other.

"Go!" Mark roared out like commanding a fleet of weapon-laden helicopters into battle.

The igloo wavered as if hit from the inside. Then it wavered again.

The assembled crowd was absolutely silent in anticipation.

Another impact and one pillow fell off the top of the wall.

Then there was a shout of little girls joining forces in some supreme effort. The three of them, with their arms locked together, burst clean through the side of the pillow igloo, which fell and scattered in every direction.

Emily joined in everyone's gasp of wonder.

The larch tree, that had stood so long in hiding, was revealed. It had been decorated with hand-made ornaments, lights, popcorn-and-cranberry strings, and everything else that little girls and her husband could think of. People were pulling aside the tumbled pillows until a great mound of them had been piled up behind the couch and the tree stood fully revealed.

"It's beautiful," she barely managed a whisper but somehow Mark heard it through all of the applause and general chatter.

"Not finished yet."

"No, it's perfect."

But he stepped up to the tree, giving her the feeling that she was floating along in a helicopter once more. She considered tugging on his ears to see if they acted like rudder controls, or maybe a cyclic to get her down from here. But his big hands were clamped over her thighs, pinning her in place.

"Emily, open your present."

At a loss for what else to do, she unwrapped it as she teetered high in the air. And discovered a golden star.

The bare top of the larch, the only part of the tree that had ever shown above the pillow igloo, was right at eye level. By reaching out as far as she dared, she was just able to slip it onto the top of the tree.

A fresh round of cheers and applause broke out as Mark stepped back and helped her down to the pine floor. The tree was glorious with its wild decorations and brightly colored lights set off by the golden warmth of the fire's flickering glow.

With Mark's arm around her waist, and the girls' hanging on to either side, they all admired the tree.

Or at least Mark and the girls did.

Emily instead heard the joy and the laughter of her friends gathered around her. So many. So true.

"You're my star," Mark whispered—absolutely the romantic one in their relationship.

This right here, this moment was who she *truly* was.

And Emily could feel that gift all the way to her heart.

And don't miss the companion story: Dilya's Christmas Challenge, a White House Protection Force story.

DILYA'S CHRISTMAS CHALLENGE

A SPECIAL BONUS (ON LOAN FROM THE WHITE HOUSE PROTECTION FORCE SERIES), HERE'S THE STORY FROM DILYA'S SIDE

Teenager Dilya Stevenson's life at the White House is like no one else's. As the First Family's nanny and dog walker, her duties are sometimes light and always enjoyable. Which leaves her plenty of time to keep her eyes and ears open behind the scenes. Facing danger as a child, and even death has taught her to be a loner—too much so her elders fear.

Retired spy Miss Watson takes pride in trusting no one. But she keeps a weather eye on Dilya from her secret library in the White House's deepest basement. Both she and Major Emily Beale, an old friend, wish to save the girl from following in either of their footprints. Little knowing that all their lives will be impacted, they set Dilya's Christmas Challenge.

CHAPTER 1

Miss Watson had considered painting a giant spider web on her door. If it wouldn't draw undue attention, she well might have. Room 043-Mechanical in the White House Residence's lowest subbasement had nothing mechanical in it, at least nothing that a building engineer would ever care about. Good cover because the best cover was a bland one.

Her small desk had once belonged to Assistant Secretary of the Treasury, Harry Dexter White, who had run the Silvermaster spy ring for the Soviet Union for years. Her walls were packed with every biography or interview transcript from a spy going back to the early days of the American colonies. The rubbish about The Craft that consumed so much of the CIA's libraries—written by analysts and others even less informed—were not to be found within her four walls. She also kept a number of the more gruesome tools of the trade on display to remind her of just what horrors the human psyche was capable.

But even at her age, a woman wasn't supposed to feel like Moriarty —Sherlock Holmes' greatest opponent—curled "motionless, like a spider in the centre of its web, but that web has a thousand radiations, and he knows well every quiver of each of them."

She rarely left her office anymore, instead listening only to the information that flowed into her domain rather than gathering it. She allowed only a few bits, a very precious few, to flow back out. Maybe she'd paint the spider web in blacklight or some other ink that wouldn't show. But she'd know was there.

It always surprised her when a thread was activated that she hadn't anticipated. When the computer beeped she dropped a stitch in her knitting in surprise—a nice bit of double-sided colorwork scarf recalling a long ago sunset along the shore of the Black Sea.

Assumptions are dangerous, she reminded herself.

She forced herself to pick up the stitch and count to make sure that everything was put to rights before she answered.

"Hello, my dear." Her screen lit to reveal one of her favorite people. Major Emily Beale (retired—at least according to most official records) had a mind that worked so differently from her own. For that reason if no other, Emily would have been very useful to her. But as a force of nature in her own right, the immensely skilled and well-connected woman brought far more assets than most could muster.

However, she should have known a call was coming. It wasn't unusual for Emily to call from her Montana ranch, but it was strange that she herself had no inkling of what the topic might be.

"Hello, Miss Watson. How are you today?"

"Oh, I'm good my dear. Very good. Thank you for asking. Is there something amiss that I'm unaware of?"

"Not likely."

Miss Watson couldn't quite resist smiling at the compliment. "I don't know that you've ever made a social call before."

Emily's grimace communicated a great deal. It wasn't social, which was disappointing. But she saw in how Emily's eyes shifted to the side, beyond the breadth of the screen she'd be using, that Emily wished it had been. She was such a sweet woman.

"Emily, dear child..." Miss Watson merely said it to herself, but saw Emily react much more strongly than expected.

A laugh?

A hysterical one?

Major Emily Beale was not the sort given to hysterics.

"Tell me the reason you called, then we can talk about why you should have called earlier."

Emily nodded, "I'm worried about Dilya. She keeps placing herself at risk. I don't want her to create a situation that's over her head when she's too young to know what she's doing."

"That child was never young. Such potential." She regretted the last as soon as she said it aloud. She could see the sudden wariness in Emily's eyes—so protective of the teen, despite the girl being adopted not by her but by one of her teammates. That protectiveness was one of Emily's great strengths. Her own instincts were far more honed to self-preservation.

Dilya, as a seventeen-year-old war orphan, was much the same. She'd been afforded the best training imaginable: her deep involvement with the fighting elements of the Night Stalkers 5th Battalion D Company, who had rescued her originally. Her placement in the White House as a nanny and then the dog minder for the First Dog had placed her in the way of exceptional information. Her skills at passing through a room unremarked were truly exceptional. It definitely reminded Miss Watson of her own, long ago youth.

And most importantly, Dilya possessed the sharp mind to go with it.

That girl's mind… Yet Emily had a point.

"The girl is so independent. Perhaps too much so." How different would her own past be if she had learned to rely upon others? Even occasionally?

"Too much?" And there was Emily's limitation. Her definition of success was the survival of her team and the destruction of her target. She was terribly linear. Independence was a lesson that Emily only thought she had learned. She had been embedded in teams her entire life.

"Yes. She knows a great deal more about depending solely on her own judgment than even you, my dear child. Despite your deservedly decorated career. And don't we both know about some of the decorations you can never admit to."

Emily's bland expression would be a sufficient denial—to anyone who hadn't spent a lifetime surviving by studying human body language. She almost considered pointing out how easy she was to read for a professional, but decided that there were some things Emily would be happier never knowing.

Dilya's strength was in her covert gathering of knowledge. But oh, the price that was paid for such a gift. Miss Watson both envied and pitied the girl.

"Dilya has carefully positioned herself to know more than everyone around her," Miss Watson continued, more to herself than Emily. "I even hold a hope that someday she—"

Not yet. She didn't dare think that far ahead. Hope often hurt as much as it helped.

"Well, never mind that now. I believe that you've raised a valid question and I shall give it some thought. It is Christmas soon. Perhaps I shall give her a Christmas gift."

Emily looked relieved to hand off the problem. Miss Watson found that trust to be the nicest compliment of all, it actually warmed her old heart.

"Now, my dear. Let's talk about what's troubling you."

Through the rest of the conversation, Miss Watson wondered at how curiously innocent Emily was. She was one of the finest warriors Miss Watson had ever met, yet she was curiously unaware of what it meant to be a woman.

One thing Miss Watson envied her was motherhood. She herself had launched a hundred women on their careers in espionage, giving birth to their nascent dreams of adventure, danger, and intrigue. But she'd only given her own heart once—and the price that the Cold War had exacted upon her for that single mistake had been a chilly one indeed.

"No woman as beautiful as you with two lovely children and such an exceptional husband can doubt that she is in the prime of her life," she assured Emily.

There was so much she herself had lost.

Lieutenant General Sergei Kulakov of Soviet Union's KGB First

Directorate had unwittingly taught the United States more about the Soviet intelligence operations than any other man. As his mistress, she had siphoned away his secrets until it destroyed his life. Like a Stalinesque purge, he and his family were erased from history by the Soviet regime—from re-doctored photos to a "training accident" that had leveled his Black Sea dacha with a firebomb. To this day she didn't know where the leak had come that destroyed her best source and the love of her life in a single, vicious stroke. Whereas Emily…

"And I must compliment you on the fine job you did helping your husband transition to retired life. You are much better with people than you think you are. You picture yourself so austere and remote, yet people are drawn to you anyway." The pain swelled in her chest until she feared it really would kill her. As they had never been drawn to her. Except for that one time. There had never been a man for her like Sergei. "I remember such a time of reflection shortly before I died."

"You…died?"

"Oh yes, dear. Any number of times," Miss Watson shook off the memories. She was the reason they had bombed the dacha, to kill Sergei's mistress. Some instinct had sent her racing away across the Black Sea in a tiny open boat that stormy December night. That instinct had saved her life, if not her heart. She nudged her tiny Christmas tree on the desk, so bright and cheery—it didn't fully mask that old memory, but it helped. It was impossible to look at it without smiling.

"It is an easy way to cover your tracks in an on-going CIA operation. But I'm referring to when I let the CIA itself believe I had died." Because she desperately needed to stop thinking about her cherished Sergei.

"How did they take it?"

"Oh, it was a lovely funeral. I have a star up on their wall, which is quite an honor in my business."

"And they still don't know about you surviving?"

Not a chance. She'd die for real before she'd work for the cretins now in charge. The CIA was no longer about national security or even trade security. It was all about political gain, which she had no stomach for.

"There comes a time in a woman's life where one must move closer to the heart. We aren't men, after all. You'll want to think about that, child. You are a woman grown. You've fought for the right, and done the duties that a man does. For great achievers like us, struggling within a society not ready for us, we must now come to terms with being…ourselves."

"How did you do it?"

She'd been babbling. Now, having professed her evolved state, she certainly couldn't admit to lacking such. Instead she offered her best enigmatic smile.

"Oh, I became *your* weapon," Emily had thankfully jumped topics. Perhaps her thoughts were more creative than Miss Watson had previously given her credit for. "All those additional black-in-black ops. The toughest missions—"

"—Came to you because of your supreme confidence and exceptional abilities." Oh how she wished she could take credit for Emily's achievements, they were so very impressive. "Don't try to make me the wizard behind the curtain of your career, Emily. You are tactically an exceptional woman. It is the bigger picture that slips by you. Dilya is beginning to see her own bigger picture, which is why you worry about her—we fear what we don't understand."

Yes. Dilya. She was the important one, because she had the potential to be so much more.

"But—"

"Oh, my dear child. In the later years, you are still *yourself*. But the challenges are new. You must learn who you, yourself are. Rediscover or, if that fails, discover for the first time, the amazing woman you are."

"That's your advice?"

"The voice of experience." And perhaps she'd try to follow it someday.

"What did you—"

"Oh no, my dear. It would be cheating to tell," though she might, if she knew. She had grown to like Emily more than any woman in her past. "Besides, Dilya is far more my daughter than you are—at least in how she thinks. You must discover your own woman."

"Why doesn't that feel helpful?"

"Because you're still thinking as if you live in a man's world, challenging the status quo." And if she didn't help Dilya see that soon, the girl would walk the same horrid path she had. By seventeen, she'd already been recruited and embedded in the depths of the Vietnam War. JFK, such a pretty man, had asked what she could do for her country and she'd joined the CIA. For forty years she'd done the horrific and the unthinkable.

"Miss Watson, are you—"

"It is time I sent for Dilya." She needed to shift the girl's path—immediately. She could only hope she wasn't too late to turn Dilya from the fateful missteps she had made in her own long-ago youth.

"Miss Watson?" Emily sympathy was sweet but misguided.

"Go see your family, dear." She cut the connection and listened.

Not to the noises of the dishwashers flushing water through the pipes that ran along her ceiling. Not the low hum from the massive air conditioning units across the hall. None of her alarms were lit. In fact, at the moment even the laundry and the sub-basement usher's office were unpeopled.

Normally she liked it when she was the only person on this level. At the moment, it left her feeling cold and...old.

CHAPTER 2

Dilya had never been called by Miss Watson before. It was a strange experience.

She was in the curator's library on the White House Residence's ground floor. It lay down the hall from the kitchen, between the Secret Service room and the library. When the call came, she'd been poking through the records and trying to find out just how much trouble she was in for letting First Dog Zackie break the small antique table in the hallway outside the First Lady's secretary's office. Especially because she'd supposedly been over in the Residence that morning and not eavesdropping on the second floor of the East Wing.

She'd hoped it was a reproduction and not a 1789 Thomas Sheraton original, but the photo she'd just found in the curator's library wasn't encouraging. It was late at night, so the curator and his assistant had gone home hours ago, not realizing that Dilya had breezed in one door to wave hello and not breezed out the other on her way to the Chocolate Shop as usual. It was one of the advantages of creating predictable patterns, it made other people have assumptions.

Then the assistant curator's phone range.

She'd frozen in place for the three rings, then it stopped.

She knew that voicemail took over at four rings, so she didn't think anything of it...until the senior curator's phone rang three times.

On the third round of ping-pong between the two phones, she gingerly answered one.

There was nothing but silence...and the sound of dishwashers draining through overhead pipes.

All she said was, "Yes, ma'am." before hanging up the phone. The White House was quiet tonight, but she avoided the stairs by the kitchen. Instead, she slipped out the curator office's back door and down the two flights of steps—perhaps the least used in the entire White House. She circled twice around the elevator machinery space and ducked into the lone bathroom at the east end of the lowest subbasement.

Five minutes later, she stepped out. She'd long since observed that most people grew impatient after two minutes. Even most of the Secret Service agents would start looking around by three minutes. By five, almost everyone was bored out of their skull. They'd start moving about, making noise. When she stepped back into the hall, there were only the noises she'd cataloged in her thoughts as "typical" of this level.

Nothing changed as she found her way to Room 043-Mechanical and slipped in through the narrow opening before shutting the door behind her.

"Took your time, girl," Miss Watson sounded almost stern.

"You've never called me before. I decided that I'd better be cautious."

Miss Watson harrumphed thoughtfully. She was never the sort of woman who would grunt, but it seemed to carry meaning—but nothing that Dilya could interpret.

"Have a seat, child."

Dilya used to welcome that diminutive—most people discounted and thus ignored children—but at seventeen, she was finding it less than charming. Especially from someone close to her. But one didn't lightly correct Miss Watson.

She slipped onto the chair and idly wished Zackie was here so that she could scratch his head. He loved her without question or judgment and there were times she needed that. Even her parents would ask about school or boys…as if setting a trap without meaning to.

"What's that?" Dilya bit her tongue, but the little Christmas tree on Miss Watson's desk was very peculiar. Tiny rectangular boxes of red-and-green wire had been stacked up to make a foot-high cone. Miniature blinking lights had been woven through them.

"It's a lobster pot Christmas tree. And, yes girl, sometimes it is best to just ask the question."

It was one of the first things that Miss Watson had ever told her that didn't ring true—there was a strain in her voice as she'd said it. Dilya would have to keep an ear out for why. She also made a note to herself to look up more information about lobster pots. She'd seen lobsters arrive in the kitchen for White House state dinners and knew they'd never fit in these. The entire tree wasn't much bigger than a lobster.

"A gift from a friend."

She'd never thought about Miss Watson having friends, but she supposed everyone did. Of course, everything Miss Watson ever said contained a double or even a triple meaning. *Friend.* Did she herself have them? It was hard to tell. Her world was defined by the adults of the military and the White House, and by the President's and Vice President's newborns who she was a nanny for. Super busy when they were here. Time to observe things when they weren't. Though lately she'd come to appreciate that people observed the baby in a room, but not the person carrying her.

High school had garnered her no friends. The stigma of working personally for the First Family had marked her as an outsider from the beginning, even in the most elite school of Washington, DC. It had also taken her too long to understand that there was such a thing as competitive sports. Her life in war zones had taught her that only victory mattered—only survival. Her intensity didn't go over well in harmless games. She'd learned to temper that instinct, but not soon enough. She'd scared her classmates and they didn't forget that easily.

"That's nice," Dilya finally acknowledged that Miss Watson had friends. It would be nice to have one of her own, who was her own age. But she could count the number of seventeen-year-olds who worked in the White House on one finger. And the number of people who actually lived here on one hand: the three members of the First Family, the rotating watch officer with the Nuclear Football (the launch codes and radio that were never more than a hundred meters from the President), and herself when both her parents were out of town. Which was surprisingly often: her father Archie off consulting and Kee on a training mission, or a live one, with the Hostage Rescue Team.

She didn't mind though, not really. When she slept at the White House, she lived in the same small apartment that Emily Beale had occupied when she'd been a chef here a long time ago. Dilya had seen how good a fighter Major Beale was—even Michael from Delta Force had said the major was especially good. She so wanted to be like her: really smart and totally lethal.

Dilya had hated her looks in her early teens because short girls with Uzbekistani dark skin and riffled hair would never be tall and blonde and bright like Major Beale. Once she'd understood that it wasn't the appearance that mattered, she'd forgiven her heritage and focused on what else she could learn.

"You present a fascinating problem, child."

"I don't mean to." For half an instant she wondered if Miss Watson was referring to the broken Thomas Sheraton table in the East Wing, but decided that was silly. Not that she wouldn't know, but that she wouldn't care. Then Dilya was sorry she presented a problem, because it meant she was doing something imperfectly that must have come to Miss Watson's attention.

"What have you learned in your expeditions today?"

Fridays were generally quiet, especially in the weeks before Christmas. The decorators had been through at the beginning of December and turned the White House into a winter wonderland. How could everyone ooh and ahh over it? It reminded her too much of her freezing walk over the Hindu Kush Mountains of Afghanistan when she'd been a child of ten. She tried not to look too closely in case she imagined her parents' blood spattered on the snow as it had been when they'd been murdered shortly afterward.

Still, she thought of a few things to tell Miss Watson that she heard lately. In the beginning, she wasn't sure if she should share things with the old woman. But then she'd managed to eavesdrop on a surprisingly frank conversation between Miss Watson and Emily Beale regarding the risks of a new White House intern—who was dismissed almost immediately afterward. There were now few things she held back. Because if Emily trusted Miss Watson, so would she—mostly.

Miss Watson nodded in surprise at the passing remark between two of the cabinet secretaries about "coal futures." Yet another thing for Dilya to now research the meaning of the next time she was online.

"Let's have some tea," Miss Watson rose to her feet.

CHAPTER 3

Dilya knew which hidden trigger to press inside the bookcase's shelving to release it so it swing aside.

Miss Watson let her do it herself. The heavy cases were on silent rollers, but they still required force to move—something Dilya did so easily and that she herself now had to work at.

The bookcase folded aside, opening a doorway into her inner parlor. In sharp contrast to the outer library, this was a warm and cozy space. The rich Oriental rug, white-rose wallpaper covered with photos of history's greatest female spies, and the comfortable armchairs before the marble-mantled fireplace was often all that kept her morale up.

She eased into the armchair as Dilya went about making tea and setting out cookies that she herself had baked last night. It was her one solace, a skill she'd learned years ago. She'd learned to cook to endear herself to the men she was spying on, but she'd always baked for herself.

When everything was set out and served, they drank a while in silence. The Harvey and Sons chamomile from Egypt was very floral, but the taste was incredibly smooth and lulled her nerves after even the first few sips.

She looked across at Dilya and tried to think how to teach this girl the lesson that she needed, the lesson that she'd never learned for herself. Yet Emily had done it. How?

Miss Watson had become caught in a trap of her own making. Emily had appeared to take her advice to heart. So, to ask how Emily had learned what Dilya needed—how to value the team above independent action—would have undercut her own advice. It was crucial knowledge, she knew it by her own lack. She'd always undervalued the importance of people in her life as anything other than targets and potential threats.

When Emily accepted the amazing woman she already was, then she would truly step into her power. She hoped that Emily did it soon so that she'd still be alive to watch.

Yet Dilya needed…

"Tell me about your friends."

Dilya's face revealed no telltale expression as Emily's had. Dilya was almost perfectly unreadable. Not chill, but so self-contained that she didn't reveal anything of who she was. It was startling to realize that though she was so pretty, she wasn't beautiful. It was because the girl kept herself locked away so safe behind her mystical green eyes that her features appeared slightly lifeless.

Oh, she could appear animated at a moment's notice, but this blankness was her normal, silent self.

"You have no friends." Miss Watson didn't make it a question.

Dilya didn't argue.

And there was the difference between herself and Emily. Emily had garnered a team, a family, and a circle of friends so loyal that it might take her years to understand their true depths. The only reason that the wives of the White House's leaders—who were so dependent upon Emily—didn't become jealous, was because Emily Beale had won them over as well with her immense integrity. And as the coming years of friendship mellowed the awe they held her in, their true friendships would grow.

Her own friends? All except for a very select group of fellow librarians thought she had died fifteen years ago. And her closest friends might indeed be Emily—who she'd only met once in person—and this young girl watching her so carefully.

That was the different path Dilya must learn to walk.

"I'm sending you to school."

"I already go to school."

"Tomorrow."

"It's the weekend and my high school is closed, but you know that. Which school?"

"The White House kitchen."

Dilya actually let enough emotion through to blink at her in surprise.

"Saturday at nine a.m. And you aren't allowed to leave early."

Miss Watson was very pleased that she was able to finish her tea before Dilya even thought to take another sip of her own.

CHAPTER 4

Dilya had been in the White House kitchen any number of times, though not nearly as often as visiting Chef Clive in the Chocolate Shop.

Chef Klaus was terribly strict, far more likely to explode with German epithets than to deliver praise. She knew he tolerated her presence, but she'd failed to make him smile even once. He was a tall, spare man, far above her own five-foot five. He seemed to look down at her like a stooping vulture. His tall chef's hat often hanging directly overhead when he was scowling down at her.

This morning, he was in "a mood". She'd heard the pastry chef and soup chef making a joke that if Chef Klaus was ever not in "a mood" the kitchen would freeze over. Only when, three months later, she heard a cabinet member saying he would agree with a new policy when hell froze over, did she understand the chefs' joke. She also knew from listening to the others that he was immensely respected. Whether his kitchen created a plated five-course dinner for two hundred guests or a sandwich for the President to eat in the Oval, the kitchen ran with the same clockwork precision.

He was thumping down bags of flour and sugar. Crashing mixing bowls against one another so hard that she was surprised they didn't break, even if they were steel.

"*Es ist verrückt! Warum heute* must my pastry chef be sick? Someone tell me why?"

"He caught it from his son," Dilya ventured. She liked Chef Emile, who still slipped her choice pastries like she was a little girl. "He brought the cold home from his kindergarten class."

"Eh? Oh, Dilya."

"He must be very sick to not be here, chef."

"So. Today *you* are my assistant?"

"It was…" She didn't think that Chef Klaus would know about Miss Watson. "I heard there was school here today. I thought I'd come learn."

"What? Someone who acts as if I have something to teach them instead of just doing my commands? *Gut! Gut!*" He waved a hand at the pantry. "Bring me butter, five pounds. Molasses, cinnamon, nutmeg, allspice, ginger—crystallized, powdered, and fresh. Well don't stand their looking so surprised. *Schnell! Schnell!* And take them with you." He waved a hand over her shoulder. "Oh, *ja.* Eggs, we must have two dozen to start," he stomped into the walk-in refrigerator to fetch those himself.

"Don't forget the butter while you're in there," she called after him.

"Now she thinks she runs kitchen." At least that's what it sounded like. She didn't know enough German to be certain. She committed it to memory to look up later and see if she was right, "*Jetzt glaubt sie, sie leite die Küche.*"

She turned.

Four kids were standing in the doorway, frozen in place as if they'd been cast in ice like the rest of the White House's horrid winter wonderland nightmare.

Everybody in the school knew Trevor, he was captain of the soccer team. He was tall, with dark straight hair and very good-looking. He was standing just a little too close behind Kimberlee. She'd seen Major Henderson do it when he thought his wife needed protecting—as if Major Emily Beale ever needed anyone to do that.

Kimberlee made up for average features with a cheery personality —she was an Alabama senator's daughter with medium skin similar in darkness to Dilya's, but a very different hue. She'd dyed her wavy hair with a blonde so bright it was almost gold. It reminded her of the thin stripe of blonde that her adoptive mother Kee wore in own dark hair, to remember a dead friend. The color choice made her like Kimberlee even if she was one of the school's super-popular crowd.

She didn't really recognize the other two, though she thought she'd seen them around. A tall, serious blonde girl and a boy about her own height with messy brown hair that needed a comb. He was the one scanning the kitchen as if he was cataloging everything in the room against some internal image. He'd clearly done some research before coming.

"You run the kitchen?" The tall blonde asked.

Well at least she wasn't going to have to look up the translation of Klaus' comment.

"No, but I guess Chef Klaus needs someone to order around. Let's get moving; he doesn't like delays. *Nicht hier!*" She tried to imitate his gruff tone. It actually earned her a laugh.

She had their names by the time she'd shown them where the spices were, though she had to think to remember that the fresh ginger would be in with the other root vegetables.

Trevor, Mister Soccer, was indeed following Kimberlee around.

Kimberlee didn't seem to notice, though it seemed obvious. She was also head of the Debate Club that had just taken down George-town University's freshman debate team.

The quiet blonde was Valentina—"But call her Val," Kimberlee had stuck in. Once Dilya heard her name she remembered all of the details. Val was the daughter of the brigadier general stationed at the French embassy as the Defense Attaché. She was also the valedictorian who was taking every advanced placement class on the planet. Well, not every one, because she wasn't in Dilya's Government Affairs, American History, or Political Science. And if she was taking a language, it wasn't Russian or Mandarin. Val was a science-and-math nerd's science-and-math nerd.

"Trevor's the best cook," Val said in that soft voice of hers. She looked a bit like Emily Beale, but she didn't sound at all like her. Too gentle.

"Mom runs the kitchen at the Hay Adams Hotel. If you'd met my mom, you'd know I couldn't help but learn."

"Sound kinda defensive there, Trev," Kimberlee winked at Dilya. "But because Val's French, we made her be the president of the Chef's Club."

"The Chef's Club?" Dilya let her guard down for a moment. Miss Watson wanted her to spend the day going to school with a Chef's Club? She didn't even know that her high school had a such a thing.

"Yeah, the four of us are the whole club, unless you want to join?" Mr. Observant Jimmy made it a little funny. He was the misfit in this group of misfits.

"Ha!" Dilya figured that response would cover a lot of ground. Joining wasn't something she did. Of course she could cook. The chow cooks at the secret Night Stalkers base in Pakistan—where she'd lived after Kee rescued her at age ten—had been her source of food. As soon as she'd figured that out, she'd made friends with them and in turn they'd taught her to cook—and turned a blind eye whenever she secreted away a bit of dinner in case life went wrong again. She'd eventually managed to observe the food locker combinations and had no longer needed to hide food under her cot.

She'd also watched Emily Beale cook. Often, when there was no mission, Emily would make a special meal for her crew. Dilya had never helped, but she'd watched and done her best to memorize each step.

"King of war games," Kimberlee offered another of her asides, nodding toward Jimmy.

"Not war games. They're strategy games."

"Guns, tanks, spaceships with nuclear weapons?"

"Yeah," Jimmy admitted and tipped his face down just enough for a long chunk of wavy brown hair to slip over his eyes.

"King of the war games," Kimberlee summed up.

Kimberlee might not know the difference, but Dilya certainly did.

Her mother was a sniper, the ultimate in *tactical* warfare. And her father was a leading geopolitical global *strategy* consultant to the President and the Joint Chiefs of Staff.

"Why do you cook?"

But Chef Klaus returned from where he'd been called away to consult on a soup before Jimmy could answer her question.

"Today we're going to start with learning how to a sharpen a knife," Chef Klaus did his looming vulture thing over them. "Then if you somehow manage to master that task, I will teach you how to peel ginger."

CHAPTER 5

An hour later it seemed they were no closer to satisfying him than when they began. Trevor was the closest with Val as a near second—she finally had graduated to a mere sniff of disdain before he blunted her knife's edge on a steel and told her to try again.

"I never knew there was so much to just sharpening a blade," Kimberlee whispered sadly after her latest effort was blunted and returned with an outright scoff.

Then Chef Klaus focused his ire on her. "That's not a weapon of war you're wielding there, Miss Dilya Stevenson. It's a tool of art." And with a single stroke he wiped out twenty minutes of painstaking work. She'd had about enough of this.

"I'm sorry, sir," Dilya glared at him across the table. "My first knife was a KA-BAR 11-7/8" knife. But I was only ten and the leather-wrapped handle was too big for my hand. So my mother bought me a Cold Steel Recon 11-3/4" Tanto point with a black DLC coating over a VG-1 stainless blade. *That* is what I learned to sharpen."

Klaus stared down his long nose at her.

"*Es ist hier?*"

"*Jawohl.*" She'd heard Val use that as a strong affirmative.

With a tip of his head, he sent her to fetch it. On her return, she

591

considered doing many things, but common sense had prevailed and she handed it, still in its sheath, across the steel table where they sat lined up on their stools. The members of the Chef's Club didn't even pretend to be sharpening their knives, instead watching her avidly. She tried to ignore it, but wasn't having much luck.

Chef Klaus tugged the knife free—on his third try. It required a strong pull and it was easier if the sheath was strapped to a body part. When he glared at her, she was careful to show nothing.

After inspecting the blade carefully, he stepped to the cutting board and dragged it lightly across one of the overripe tomatoes they'd been trying to slice. It slid through the loose skin without a wrinkle and created a slice so clean that the tomato might have still been fresh and firm.

He wiped it carefully with a cloth, replaced it in the sheath and returned it to her. She made a show of strapping it onto her thigh over her jeans. It wasn't the sort of thing to be left lying about. She had a small combination knife safe in her room. The Secret Service had made her leave her sidearm at her parents' house.

"Do you know how to use that blade?"

"I've been trained by my mother," Dilya offered him her best smile. "But I haven't had a reason to use it…yet."

"I could almost like you, Miss Stevenson," Chef Klaus condescended before waving for them to return to their sharpening.

"Super cool," Jimmy whispered.

Which might be the first compliment she'd ever received from a classmate in the two years she'd been in the States and going to a real school.

"You really know how to use that?" Trevor asked as he once again began working his blade in a swirl of vegetable oil on the slab of black sharpening stone. It didn't sound like he doubted her, more like she'd surprised him.

"Her mom is a sniper on the Hostage Rescue Team," Val answered for her.

Dilya could only blink at her. She'd thought she was invisible at school—as invisible as was possible in such a group of DC's overachiever kids. School hadn't mattered to her, but it had been important to Kee and Archie, so she worked hard to get her A's...and to *not* be noticed.

"Oh, man," Jimmy groaned. "That isn't super cool, that's super wicked extra cool."

"If you think my mom is cool," Dilya couldn't help being pleased. Kee was an awesome mom. "You should have met her commanding officer before she retired. She was the first woman to fly helicopters for the Night Stalkers."

Dilya didn't know if they'd ever let her do that, but if they did, that was her dream. A sniper like Kee or a pilot like Emily. That would indeed be super wicked extra cool.

CHAPTER 6

They'd eventually graduated from knife sharpening to ginger peeling—by the end of which Jimmy was wearing a pair of bright blue Band-Aids. The lunch was a rich borscht and corned beef on rye sandwiches, big enough to satisfy even Trevor, served right there at the counter with the other chefs.

That was a welcome respite. All morning they had kept asking her questions—about her and about the White House. While it would be rude not to answer, she wished she'd managed to slip in more questions of her own. Except she wasn't used to speaking. She was used to listening. By the time she'd think up her own question, someone would already be talking again.

At least over lunch they started asking questions of the sous chefs instead.

Finally able to listen, Dilya realized that the Chef's Club had been doing this for a while. They'd ask to meet some elite chef—there were a lot of those in DC—and they'd go get a free class.

"I know the chefs at Pauley's Island. Would that help?"

"We didn't even dare try there." "Wow, really?"

One of the chefs was amused that the group had braved asking the White House for a visit, but not Pauley's.

"One of my mom's closest friend's family owns it." Actually, Tim was also one of her friends. He'd been there at the 5D's base since the very first day—doing his best to make her laugh when everything had been so different and terrifying. "I'm sure Tim Maloney would be glad to set it up. Wait, I don't know where he's stationed. I guess I could call his mom."

"That does it," Kimberlee declared.

"It absolutely does," Trevor agreed.

"Madame President?" Jimmy turned to Val.

Val thumped her soup spoon on the counter like a gavel with a bright ting, "You are hereby inducted as an official member of the Chef's Club. All in favor?"

The others all said, "Aye!"

"The ayes have it. Welcome, Dilya Stevenson."

Dilya didn't know what to do with that. She'd never belonged to anything. But she couldn't figure how to get out of it without hurting their feelings.

That question plagued her through lessons on: measuring flour (by weight, never by volume), grating ginger (never mincing), mincing crystallized ginger (never grating), sampling a dozen different sugars, and tasting butter (salted, unsalted, organic, English Midlands, and finally French butter from Brittany). They spent the whole afternoon on ingredients. There were only thirteen ingredients in gingerbread, including all the spices and everything, but they spent a long time learning about each one.

Did Emily Beale know all this? Dilya made a bet with herself that she did. So she paid extra attention and made sure to ask about anything that was unclear, even if it meant interrupting someone.

"Tomorrow, we will mix and bake," Chef Klaus announced. "If you learn very fast, we will decorate as well. Now go away. Get out of my kitchen, *Kinder*. I have a dinner that must be served to people far more important than you."

"I hate being called a child," Val whispered once they were well clear of the kitchen.

Dilya agreed completely. She also wasn't quite ready to see

everyone go. She was unsure why, but she'd learned to trust her instincts—or at least the ones that told her when to hide or run. Maybe she'd listen to this one too.

"You know, just down this hall, the White House has a Chocolate Shop. The chef is my friend." There was that word again. She'd always applied it to friendly adults: the former and current President, the Chief of Staff, chefs, pilots, gunners.

If they were friends, then what was she supposed to call the Chef's Club's members? What was their agenda for "inducting" her? Just to get into Pauley's? No, she'd already made the offer before they did that.

She'd always loved the amazing scents of the Chocolate Shop, almost as much as the treats themselves. Chef Clive Andrews teased her with funny looks about her silence. As if she'd ever known what to say. If the others noticed, they were too excited to comment on it as the chef explained the tempering of chocolate and pulled out a tray of holiday truffles he was developing.

She was no wiser by the time she escorted them back to the East Wing entrance.

CHAPTER 7

"Are you my friend?"

Emily tried to make sense of the question. Was the problem the question or because it was four in the morning?

"Who is this?"

"It's me, Dilya." Then there was a small gasp. "I'm so sorry. I forgot about the time zones. How far away is Montana?"

"Three thousand…" No. "Two hours. I think." She'd know for sure if she could wake up.

"I'm sorry. I'll go away and—"

"Wait! Just hang on, Dilya." She took her phone into the bathroom and shut the door. She'd accidentally left the ringer on and, thankfully, it seemed as if Mark had slept through it. "Now what was your question?" She sat on the edge of the tub, then stood to throw a towel over it before she sat back down. She pulled another one over her bare legs. It was only a little damp.

"It's stupid."

"Good. Because if it was a smart question, I wouldn't be able to answer it right now."

Dilya remained silent. Emily tried to remember the last time she'd received a call from the girl, and wasn't sure she ever had.

"You asked if I was your friend?"

"Yes," her voice was tiny.

"Well, you aren't my daughter, so I guess that's about the best word for it. Yes, I'm your friend." She had her own issues with that, but this call wasn't about her, so she shut them out. "Don't you want to be?"

"No. Yes. I... Oh pooh!"

Emily had to fight hard not to laugh. Winnie-the-Pooh was the first book Dilya had learned English from and Pooh's typical curse had stuck with Dilya ever since. Emily also remembered that odd negatives still tripped Dilya up sometimes.

"Do you want to be my friend?"

"Yes. I—" Dilya sighed. "I bet I'd make more sense if I'd slept last night. Is a kid supposed to have adults for friends?"

"Sure, why not? Besides, you aren't really a kid anymore." Especially not with the things she'd survived.

"But if adults are my friends, then what do I call people my age?"

"Hasn't this ever come up before?"

"No!" Dilya practically shouted. "My friends are Tim and Big John. They're White House chefs and the heads of Secret Service details. Don't know how to have friends!" Then she seemed to manage a breath. "I guess... Like at school and stuff."

Emily hung her head and tried not to think about the parallels in her own life. Friends were a new concept to her as well.

"I—" she started then stopped again. "I've always just had a team. Or at least for a long time that's all I had. I flew with your mom and dad, Connie, Lola, and all the others."

"But you're *Emily Beale*," Dilya protested.

Emily sat up and narrowed her eyes, until she saw herself in the bathroom mirror wearing a faded West Point t-shirt and a slightly damp bath towel. She closed her eyes again.

"What do you mean?"

Dilya sputtered in surprise. "You're...you! Everyone wants to be just like you."

"You want to be just like me?"

"Well, not the blonde and tall part, I've kinda given up on that, but the rest of it, absolutely!"

"Dilya," Emily had had many strange conversations, including the one with Miss Watson yesterday, but this was fast outpacing that. "I'm just a woman. I'm not even a pilot anymore."

"But you're Emily Beale!"

"Stop saying that. Please?"

"Well, okay… But you *totally* are!"

"Dilya."

"Okay. I'm sorry I called. I'm sorry I woke you up."

"I'm not."

Again her voice had gone tiny, "You're not?"

"You get to call me anytime you want. Day or night. I mean it."

"Because my mom was on your team?"

"Because I like you. *You* are my friend."

Dilya actually sniffled. "Okay…thanks." Another sniffle. "Emily?"

"Uh-huh."

"Is it okay if I still want to be like you, even though you're my friend?"

"How about you being more like *you?*" That definitely echoed some pieces of what Miss Watson had told her.

"I don't know. It's kind of…I guess…lonely being me."

"You'll find friends your own age, Dilya. It doesn't mean that the grownups are going to be any less your friends."

"Kinda like a team? Everyone always wanted to be on your team."

"Teams are different than friends."

"How?"

"It's four in the morning, Dilya. Give me a break." She'd forgotten about Dilya's insatiable appetite for answers.

Dilya always wanted to know.

"Okay," Emily tried to clear her head. "You lead a team. You have responsibilities for their actions, if not their lives. But you get to be yourself with friends."

There was a long pause before Dilya responded, "I like that explanation."

"I do to," she just hoped that she remembered it when she woke up.

"Thanks. I'm…no longer sorry I called."

"Anytime. Seriously," though she had to fight to keep a massive yawn silent.

"Emily?"

"Uh-huh?"

"I love you, Emily."

"Love you too, Dilya." The end-of-call tone came so fast, she wasn't sure Dilya had heard her answer. As far as she knew, Dilya had never told anyone except her new parents that she loved them.

The innocence of a child's love. Except Dilya was no child. She was a young woman who had seen an even worse slice of the world than Emily had. And if Miss Watson was right, she understood exactly what was happening to her in a way that Emily never had.

When she crawled back into bed, she didn't care if Mark was asleep, she just curled up against him. Without questions, he held her as she cried on his shoulder.

When she was done, she whispered to him softly, "I love you, Mark."

In answer, he just kept holding her tight. It was all she needed.

CHAPTER 8

Dilya had the kitchen set up, even before Chef Klaus came in. She had each of the ingredients aligned in an arc, including the ones they'd spent so much time preparing yesterday. She even prepared the cookie sheets with parchment paper—better for crispy edges and bottoms than silicone mats he'd told them. She tore off the correct lengths and tacked them in place with quick swipes of butter underneath the corners.

Chef Klaus looked surprised for only an instant when he came in.

He neatened the rows to make everything perfectly linear, orderly and symmetrical. She let him. As soon as he was done and had gone to hang up his coat, she moved everything back to the arc it had been. It would be easier to reach everything, radially from one position, the way she'd arranged it.

He stepped back into the main kitchen and stuttered to a halt just as the others arrived.

Without speaking, she simply reached out her hands to touch each item without moving from where she stood, rather than having them spread neatly down the length of the table.

The chef made a show of buttoning up his white chef's coat and pulling on his towering hat before he offered her a nod. He even made a grimace that just might have been a smile.

Through the morning they made numerous batches of dough. The variations to make hard sheets of gingerbread and soft ginger cookies. The difference between over- and under-beaten. Proper aeration of the mixture. Why different ingredients were added at different times. That was when quiet Val finally stepped into her own. She and the chef discussed baking soda activation, protein molecule deformation in the eggs, ingredient density, different mixing techniques to ensure even distribution of the grated versus the minced ginger…

Even Kimberlee's eyes were crossing by the time they were done with Val's questions. And Dilya suspected that it only stopped because Val finally realized how thoroughly she'd monopolized the chef. She wasn't a team leader the way Emily was—charging to the front and proving who was best, while beckoning others to try to follow. Val was simply one of the Chef's Club with her own interests and specialties.

Maybe these people didn't need a leader.

Maybe they *were* just friends.

She toyed with that idea through the rest of the day. They'd rolled out the dough perfectly evenly—done by placing thick rubber bands on either end of the rolling pins so that every spot of dough was exactly the same thickness.

"What should we make?"

A gingerbread house was out of the question. They'd all seen the framework of the massive traditional Christmas gingerbread White House taking shape in Clive's kitchen yesterday afternoon.

"Is there a game that the President likes to play? Maybe we could make a gingerbread version of it for the First Family." Jimmy was clearly picturing ray guns and spaceships.

"Yes there is." First Lady Anne Darlington-Thomas stepped into the kitchen. "My husband likes to think he can do *The New York Times* Sunday crossword. Which means every week my Sunday breakfast is about telling him the answers. *Two across. A seven-letter word for a fool.* Easy: *husband.* As in one who thinks he's doing the crossword on his own. I'm so glad that's now done for the week." Though her easy smile said she might enjoy the weekly ritual just as much as the President.

All the kids of the Chef's Club laughed despite their obvious awe at being in the First Lady's presence.

"Good morning, Dilya."

"Hi, Anne." The others looked at her goggle-eyed.

"Are you all having fun?"

There were a lot of mumbled, "Yes ma'am."

"Well, if Chef Klaus gets out of line, just sic Dilya on him. If anyone can keep Herman in line, she's the one. Now I have to go face him about the menu for next week's Residence reception for the Australian Prime Minister." And she breezed off into the back of the kitchen.

"Whoa!" Kimberlee whispered.

"Why did you use her first name?" Even Trevor was whispering.

"She asked me to. Besides, I'm nanny for her kid most days after school."

They all exchanged looks, but it was Jimmy who voiced the group's consensus opinion. "Super wicked uber-cool."

CHAPTER 9

Dilya's face and sides hurt.

She'd didn't get why, until Val made one of her dry French observations or Kimberlee teased Trevor.

Laughing and smiling. She simply wasn't used to doing that for a whole afternoon.

With Kimberlee, as head of Debate Club, leading the way, they'd mapped out a gingerbread crossword puzzle. *Christmas* down the middle; the First Family's names attached crosswise (though they had to use the First Daughter's middle name to make it all work—she actually had two of them, so she got to be in twice). Then they'd toyed with words until it was totally filled.

Chef Klaus had taught them piping and flooding techniques—requiring different mixes of royal icing because one had to stay where it was placed and the other had to flow to fill in the squares that needed to be white. Jimmy tackled the vast expanse of cookie that needed conversion into the puzzle. He was in nerd heaven.

Val had the best handwriting with a piping bag, so she took a large sheet of dark gingerbread and began writing humorous clues on it.

Dilya sat with Kimberlee and Trevor calling out suggestions for Val and making ornate letters on round, softer ginger cookies.

Whenever a cookie was broken or had its icing smeared past recovery, it was shared around, until they were all sick of them—even with tall glasses of milk. Kimberlee scrounged up a brown paper bag and started filling it with the broken bits and pieces.

All through the long afternoon, they sat together and worked on the ginger crossword. And all afternoon, Dilya could only sit in wonder. At school lunchtime, Kimberlee's table was always popular. Trevor sometimes sat with her and sometimes with his teammates. Val sat with a few other equally brilliant friends. She wasn't sure where Jimmy ate lunch.

Dilya ate with no one. Half the time, she didn't even go into the cafeteria, preferring to find a quiet corner. For this one great day though, her afternoon was filled with laughter and ideas.

As the day progressed, it became clearer and clearer where the members of the Chef's Club would end up.

Val was headed straight for the diplomatic corps—that was so obvious. She was too smart and too nice to do anything else. Maybe a science liaison or something.

Kimberlee could well follow in her senator-father's footsteps. Maybe she'd even end up in the White House someday.

Trevor was going to cook—it was clear that he was in the club for a lot more reasons than following around after Kimberlee. Dilya did wonder how long it was going to take him to ask her out. Kimberlee was going to be in for a big surprise, as she really was clueless that Trevor was hot for her.

And even in joking, she could sense Jimmy's clear grasp of how strategy worked. He could teach her some things about that, but he was weak in the real world. They'd have to talk about his strategy skills and what was actually going on globally—instead of inside some online game.

And she...was totally fooling herself. Why would they want her around? To get into Pauley's Island restaurant and the White House Chocolate Shop. To have a story to tell in the cafeteria.

She wouldn't fit in at any of their lunch tables. Everything they'd built this weekend was just about this weekend. Dilya wasn't dumb enough to believe there was a future here. She'd enjoy the day, but that would be the end of it.

They finished the giant crossword, scooting it onto a big silver platter she found in the butler's pantry. A shallow silver bowl with FDR's family crest stamped into the side was filled with the letter cookies while Val wrote "A First Family Christmas" across the top of the puzzle. In the bottom corner, she wrote "Thanks for having us." Below that they each signed their names with piped royal icing.

Dilya looked at the five names together. For a weekend they'd come together just like one of Emily's teams. She liked that. It gave her ideas for the future. Someday she'd have a team. More importantly, someday she'd have friends. Maybe like these.

It was hard leaving the kitchen. Chef Klaus actually did smile when he saw the finished project. He promised to make sure it was delivered this evening with after-dinner tea. He came around and shook each person's hand and gave them a personalized signed copy of his White House cookbook. Dilya peeked at her own, it simply said, "*Niemals aufhören!*" Thankfully, beneath that he'd written, "Don't stop!" As if.

When they neared the exit, Kimberlee slipped a brown paper bag to her. Dilya peeked inside; it contained all of the failed and broken cookies.

"I'm too nervous to try and smuggle it out through security. But you can do it. Everyone likes you."

Dilya looked down at the bag and back at Kimberlee. "I don't understand."

"They taste awesome. We can't let these go to waste. You smuggle them out of the White House tomorrow and we can share them during lunch."

Then with a wave, they were all gone.

Dilya stood inside the East Wing entrance as she weighed the cookies in her hand. There would be plenty to share at a lunch. It was silly, it was just a place to sit. A place to sit...with people. With *friends!* And she could feel the smile tug at her cheeks once more.

As she walked back through the White House, she looked upon the shining winter wonderland of plastic icicles dripping from high ceilings and fake snow sweeping under brightly lit Christmas trees.

Emily was right. There were teams and there were friends. And she'd make sure that her life was filled with both of them.

BIG SKY DOG WHISPERER

Petty Officer Jodie Jaffe brought her war dog home after they were both blown up on a SEAL patrol. But her dreams of a normal life are shattered by her dog's PTSD nightmares.

SEAL Team 6 dog-handler Stan Corman left his war dog's ashes and a part of himself overseas. For three years he's been training new dogs under Montana's Big Sky. Knowing he'll never be whole again, he hopes his dogs can save lives even if he no longer can.

But when Jodie brings her damaged dog to the ranch, Stan faces far more than he counted on...or knows how to handle.

CHAPTER 1

"This wasn't one of my better ideas."

Nikita's laugh over the phone drove Jodie even deeper under the covers.

"Fine for you. You're still on the inside, Nikita." And Jodie so wasn't. She considered switching her phone to her other ear so that she couldn't hear Nikita's laugh. Holding her phone in her left hand still felt wrong—but the blast that had taken both her and her dog out of action with the SEAL teams had left her right ear completely deaf.

"What made you think that moving back in with your parents made any kind of sense?"

"I like my parents."

"And you don't think that makes you weird?"

"Not being helpful, Nikita." Jodie pulled the covers over her face so that she couldn't see her room. She'd left home at eighteen to go into the Navy. She was back at thirty when twelve years of service was cut off as suddenly as a New York taxi cutting through a crosswalk. Her parents had left her room unchanged over the years so that she'd have somewhere to go when she was on leave.

Everything was familiar, known, safe. Eerily so after a decade in the war zones. Like some part of time had been frozen in this room. The posters on the walls still reflected every band she'd seen at Madison Square Garden as a teen. The shelf above her small desk held every dog book she'd found at used bookstores over the years, starting with *Go, Dog. Go!* and going to Cesar Millan's *Be the Pack Leader* that she'd bought new but never read because she'd joined the Navy a week later. The bed had the blanket that she'd gotten when she was twelve and Nanny had helped her redecorate from a small girl's room to a "grown-up" teen's. They'd gone a little mad at Macy's and she had a carpet the color of a tropical sea, a sunset bedspread, and walls painted in the palest blue of a beachy summer sky.

And here Nikita was, telling her that rather than being embraced by the room she was being *entombed* here—as if that was helpful information.

What better way to ease back into civilian life than sitting at the breakfast table as Mom and Dad prepared for their morning ride into the city? Mom would take the A or C train from Brooklyn to the New York Downtown Hospital where she'd been a nurse since college. Rather than taking the more convenient F train, Dad would ride with her, then stay on up into Midtown. He'd stroll along 42nd, buying a second cup of coffee before reaching his job as a librarian for NY Public Library. For all Jodie knew, that had been their invariable routine since the day they were married and first moved back into Pop Julius' brownstone.

About the time she went to high school, Pop Julius and Nanny had retired to Florida. Mom and Dad hadn't even moved into the big bedroom on the main floor, saving it as the guest bedroom. She, Mom, and Dad still lived on the second floor. The only thing that had changed was that her little brother, instead of living alone on the third floor, now had his wife and two kids up there with him.

"So, what's the problem, Jodie? You know reentry sucks. Everyone says so. Especially for long-timers like us."

Everyone says so. The insider's statement wasn't helping.

Being back in her childhood home might sound weird, but it didn't suck. She'd lost thirty pounds the day she got mustered out—

twenty of body armor; five of sidearm, extra ammo, and other survival crap; and the last five to unhunching her shoulders wondering if she'd die today. That last part felt pretty good. Though she still carried a combat knife in her small knapsack, she didn't feel the need for a concealed sidearm. Brooklyn wasn't a bit like Libya or Syria or…

"The problem…" Jodie hated it, because there was no way to fix it here. "The problem is Brandy."

"What's wrong with her?"

What *wasn't* wrong with her was the real question. Jodie could feel the heat against her leg of the pure black Belgian Malinois lying on top of the covers. Brandy was all nerves wrapped up in a bit of dog. Every sound made her twitch. The throaty diesel of a metro bus two blocks over on Smith Street sent a ripple along Brandy's haunches where they pressed against Jodie's calf. A horn honking at the corner of President and Smith was a flinch of shoulders against her thigh. A siren down their quiet residential street—*Shit!* The first one of those had given her war dog a full-blown panic attack.

During their years overseas together, Jodie had heard her dog make any number of sounds. A whimper could be anything from thirst to worry to knowing it would get her some extra attention. There'd been cries of pain—as Jodie pulled glass shards from the dog's footpads or held her while a medic stitched up a bad laceration from tangling with a feral dog and a length of razor wire. Sharp barks of warning, or excitement during play.

Not until Jodie had brought her to New York had Brandy ever made a cry of pure terror. It was the eeriest sound. High pitched. Like an incoming mortar round whistling down on your head that kept building until it was a pure howl. The sound made sense. It was a mortar that had almost taken both their lives, which made the accuracy of Brandy's imitation creepy as hell. Jodie had finally pinned the frantic dog to the carpet, lying on top of her until Brandy had finally calmed.

That she'd woken the entire family, who'd all tried to storm into her bedroom to see what was happening, hadn't helped matters.

Brandy, who'd always loved hanging out with her SEAL squad and all the attention it got her, could no longer deal with any kind of crowd.

Jodie wanted to go get a bagel with cream cheese and lox at Shelsky's. She wanted to bop over to Carroll Park, buy a Nutty Buddy ice cream cone from the cart vendor, and sit on a bench in the May sunshine watching the kids play on the swings. She wanted to take her dog for a run down the length of the Brooklyn Heights Promenade. Hell, she'd even thought about going back to synagogue to see if there were any answers for the devastation and cruelty she'd witnessed overseas.

Instead, they'd spent her first week home cowering in her ten-by-ten bedroom that would soon be stuffy with June's heat. It was already getting that way because of the need to keep the window closed to muffle any street noise. Even her two nieces didn't dare come into the room anymore after Brandy had snapped at them. Twice a day, Jodie forced Brandy outside; but she had to put on a full harness and muzzle, only daring to lead her out when kids were at school or so late at night that no one else was out walking their dog.

Nikita listened with sympathy. As one of the few other women to work with the SEALs, there was some understanding. Even though Nikita had gone all SEAL Team 6 while Jodie stayed with the Navy teams, they'd somehow stayed connected. Loosely, but connected. Out of desperation—this evening had been another bad one for Brandy and she was shaking now in her sleep—Jodie had called her. The two women were SEALs, about all that they had in common.

But PTSD happened to other people, not to people still on the inside, still serving. It was like an infectious disease, rarely discussed, "instant isolation ward" treatment from both active and veteran personnel as if it was a highly contagious plague—worse than being a dweeb.

It wasn't herself. Jodie felt fine. She really enjoyed just being home —the few times she dared leave Brandy alone and venture downstairs to be with the rest of the family. Davy Golding had even come by to pay a visit. They'd been hot and heavy for all of senior year of high school. He'd married and divorced, "Standard practice for us lawyers," he'd joked with a good laugh. He'd also matured a lot and she wouldn't have minded checking out the possibilities. But there were only so many times she could invite him to her bedroom—that probably smelled a bit too much of dog—to sit in the creaky desk chair and watch her hold Brandy, who cowered at his presence.

Brandy had always been the fun dog: quick to find explosives, glad to pal around with rest of the squad, tolerant of other war dogs, and a total goofball for a Frisbee or her KONG toy. They'd FAST-roped out of Black Hawk helos together, parachuted out of C-130s at thirty thousand feet while both on oxygen, and patrolled through more hell-hole towns than she could count.

Not so much fun after the explosion that had given Brandy half of her scars in a split second and had taken out Jodie's right eardrum just for the hell of it.

"You know," Nikita's voice slowed, "Luke mentioned this place once. Somewhere out west. Hang on."

Jodie listened as her friend moved about. She could hear her, leaving the apartment she shared with her SEAL husband Drake, wandering down the barracks hall, and thumping on someone's door. Some whispered conversation of which Jodie could only catch a few words: dog, out west, and that ultimate curse, PTSD.

"This is Commander Luke Altman. Who am I talking to?" His voice was deep and solid as a subway tunnel.

"This is Petty Officer First Class Jodie Jaffe, formerly with SEAL Team—" and her voice choked off.

Luke Altman? Like Mr. Legend SEAL Team 6 Altman? What the hell had Nikita just done to her?

Jodie bolted upright in her bed, heaving the comforter over Brandy. On her feet at full attention, she tried to think of what to say. One didn't talk to such highly decorated officers about such trivia as "my dog is unhappy." Especially not while wearing a Yankee's t-shirt that had been worn thin back in high school, white cotton panties, and not a scrap else.

Brandy shook off the comforter enough to look nervously over at her, but Jodie couldn't make herself move to reassure her.

"What seems to be the problem, petty officer?"

Jodie was going to kill Nikita. But that would have to happen later because it was never good to keep an officer waiting.

"I'm sorry to disturb your evening, sir. I was discussing my dog with Nikita Hayward just now and suddenly I'm on the phone with you. I'm not sure why, sir." Could she sound any stupider?

"Tell me about him."

"Her, sir." Yes, stupider was possible, but she wasn't going down that path to nowhere. So she told him. She'd been twelve years in, the last six with Brandy inside the SEAL teams—he'd know what a rare honor that was for a woman and just what it said about her and Brandy's competency. Hundreds, maybe thousands of lives saved. Service in the Dust Bowl of Afghanistan as well as Somalia, Yemen, and the unusual list of unmentionables.

"Deep in Syrian battlespace, we caught a bad hit—a mortar, so it wasn't her fault. After a lot of surgery and physical therapy, the vets gave her a clean medical and I did all the paperwork to get her home. But she's suffering badly, sir. Skittish as hell, which isn't like her. She was always rock steady under fire. I'm unsure how to help her."

There was a long silence. She'd spilled it all out in a single rush, the way officers liked their information. Everything relevant, nothing extra around the edges.

The silence stretched long enough that she checked the phone to make sure she still had it against her good ear. She did.

"Hard question first, Jaffe. You up for it?"

"Former SEAL, sir." An enlisted's way of telling an officer they'd asked a dumb-ass question.

"Would putting her down be a kindness?"

"Sir, no sir!" *That* was the kind of advice Nikita had found for her? Like discarding an old weapon? Might as well condone ethnic cleansing while they were at it.

"You willing to do whatever it takes to help her?" Altman moved on before she could say something nasty.

"Sir, yes sir!" She'd already spent two months overseas after her discharge, making sure they didn't put Brandy down before she was pronounced fit for release.

"Got a pen and paper?"

Jodie grabbed the first thing that came to hand, flipped it open, and grabbed a marker pen. "Ready, sir."

He gave her an address. Without realizing, she'd scribbled it across Davy Golding's photo in their old yearbook. Of course it had naturally opened to that page. He'd filled every bit of white space on the page with one of the hottest love letters imaginable—which she might have read more than a few times, so naturally the old yearbook flopped open there. She'd just obliterated whole sections of it with her Sharpie. Jodie wasn't going to read anything into that.

Then she looked at what she'd written across Davy's face and mash note.

"Montana?" She had trouble getting Brandy across the street. Getting her across the country sounded as unlikely as getting the Dodgers back to Brooklyn.

"Just write it down, Jaffe. If anyone can help you, it'll be Stan Corman."

***

"What're you doing out here on such a fine spring day, Stan?"

"Pissing myself. Go away." He really didn't need Patrick's questions at the moment.

"Sure thing," and Patrick slid down off his horse to come stand beside him. "What are you looking at?"

"At where I pissed myself." At the goddamn limitless Montana prairie where an unknown load of suckitude was apparently inbound.

Patrick actually leaned forward to look down at the front of Stan's jeans.

Stan swung his left arm into Patrick's gut hard enough to make him grunt—and mostly double over.

Odd. Stan didn't often forget that his left arm was made of metal from the biceps down. "Sorry, buddy. Been a bad start to my day."

"Expecting someone?" Patrick shrugged it off. From this bluff southeast of the ranch house and barns, he could see the first dozen of the thirty miles of dirt road to Choteau—the nearest town.

"Your wife and your mother. We're gonna have a three-way." The Larson cattle ranch spread for eighty thousand acres across the low roll of the Montana plains in a carpet of brilliant spring green. In another month it would be cooked-down brown. That land was a sharp contrast to this spread. Henderson's Ranch started at the dirt-road boundary with Larson's and straddled the more rugged foothills of the Front Range from this bluff, going ten miles back to the sudden upshot of the Rocky Mountains and the Flathead Wilderness.

"She's not my wife—not for two weeks yet. Besides, you try to tangle with Lauren, good luck to you." Patrick leaned back against his horse like it was a barn wall.

"Next you're gonna be plucking a piece of grass to chew so that you and your horse look even more alike."

Patrick did just that and grinned at him. He was wearing that goofy-guy smile. So besotted you couldn't even tease him none.

Stan turned back to watch the horizon. Pa had once said that women were a bottomless pit that men fell into and never recovered. As he hadn't remarried and had barely dated since Ma had run off with some insurance man when Stan was three, meant he probably knew what he was on about.

But Patrick sure looked to be enjoying the fall.

He was just as bad as his brother, the ranch's chef, who'd married the ranch's head cowgirl last fall. Six months and they still looked and acted like the honeymoon would never end. There was enough happy couple shit on this ranch to gag a guy. Just give Stan his training dogs and he was fine.

He and Patrick had shared a bunkroom for three years and all of a sudden Patrick was all Mister Luv. Stan had gotten to like living with Patrick—a naively optimistic goofball who'd also become a better-than-decent cowboy and trail guide. Stan missed him now that he'd moved into one of the cabins with Lauren. Of course she was hot as hell and a former war dog handler, so he cut her some slack for that.

Just like him, she'd also lost her dog in combat, which cut her a lifetime's worth of slack. She'd been lucky enough to make it out in one piece herself, but he knew that didn't make the loss any easier. Survivor's guilt probably made it harder in some ways, not that he'd ever ask. The memory of his dog was etched on his skin. And his metal arm.

But what was coming down the road today, he had no fuckin' idea.

His CO—or he had been back when Stan still had two hands to scratch himself with—had sent him a text just as chatty as ever.

Sending you a dog. Needs help.

He didn't like this shit at all. He raised and trained young dogs for Special Operations units. That was it. He could field-stitch a wounded dog, but he wasn't some veterinarian.

But you couldn't just say no to a man like Commander Altman.

That itch between his shoulder blades had only failed him once. Actually, it had been there—and he'd ignored it. And it was itching now. Last time he'd lost an arm, this time…

So, he had texted it anyway.

Hell no!

Altman had replied, *There within the hour.* Then he'd gone silent.

Asshole. Sometimes the truth just needed to be pointed out.

Still no response. If ST6 commanders used emojis, Stan could feel the smiley slapping into his forehead.

Then, weirdly enough, a smiley did appear. That new wife of Altman's, Zoe something, was definitely a bad influence. Stan had never expected Altman to fall, but he had. If Stan had Patrick's sense of humor, he'd probably be humming "Another One Bites the Dust." He wasn't Patrick. Thank God for small favors.

Altman had invited him to the wedding, but last thing Stan wanted was to hang with his old teammates who would stare at his metal arm like he was a fucking cripple. He already knew that shit and didn't need them to tell him.

That itch had made him to walk up here onto the bluff to watch east for an incoming transport. The only military base in Montana, other than a couple of National Guard units and a whole lot of missile silos, was Malmstrom Air Force Base over in Great Falls, a hundred miles east. So far the only black specs he'd spotted in the sky were a pair of high-circling turkey vultures.

Ain't dead yet, he thought at them. *Come to pick my carcass, you're gonna bust your beak on these steel bones.* Actually his arm was mostly aluminum and titanium, still didn't make him roadkill.

Patrick was talking about the upcoming wedding. Patrick's brother had gotten married last October during the winter's first big storm. Lauren was going to be a June bride. With Montana weather, who knew; there still might be a storm, but not too likely.

"Why'd you wait so long?" He asked to keep Patrick talking, as if Stan didn't already know the story. But he needed the distraction.

"Well, you know that Mom and Dad are professors at Stonybrook University in New York, right? They could only stay for a couple days for Nathan's wedding, but they really liked it out here. I figured if we waited until the semester was over and the weather was nice, they could stay a while and really enjoy themselves. You know that Mom still wants to talk about your arm?"

"Uh-huh." Yeah, like that was gonna happen. She might be some hotshot head of the nation's first-and-foremost biomed engineering school. Didn't mean that he wanted to be some sad-sack guinea pig. "Like my arm just fine the way it is."

"But—"

"Drop it, Patrick."

"Stan, seriously. I think—"

"One thing is damn clear, boy."

"What's that?"

"You were never military."

"Why *this* time?"

"What part of 'drop it' don't you understand?"

"All the parts," Patrick tipped back his cowboy hat to scratch at his forehead in confusion. "Don't you want—"

"Nope."

That finally stopped him.

"Well, it looks like whatever you're waiting for is just about here."

"What? Where?" Stan checked the sky again.

Patrick pointed down at the dirt road winding around the base of the bluff. A black Dodge Ram truck with a dog-sized cage in the back rolled along, raising a long trail of slow-settling dust.

That meant that Altman hadn't texted him until he was turning off Highway 287 onto the road out to the ranch.

Typical.

"Let's go down and meet him," Patrick gathered up his horse's reins and turned to lead the way.

"Altman's an asshole." What kind of a SEAL commander let his wife corrupt him into using emojis?

But Stan was out of options. After the pickup swung out of sight around the base of the bluff and toward the long ranch drive, he turned and followed Patrick leading his horse down to the ranch compound. Place always looked like a picture postcard from up here.

The sprawling log-cabin main house commanded the central yard from its place at the base of the next rise of land. Two long horse barns and the mother of all machinery garages lay across the broad parking area. The ranch manager's smaller house—the main house in miniature—nestled out beyond the barns. His dog kennel and training grounds lay in the low meadow around to the northeast past the bunkhouses for the hands. He'd had to argue with Mac, the ranch owner, so that they were way out of the action. The less he had to do with nosy ranch guests, the happier he was.

The guest cabins climbed the west face of the bluff on the opposite side of the main house, offering a clear view east and south, and well-protected from the chill northerlies that blew down off the Canadian Plains.

Beyond the cabins rolled the hills of the Montana Front Range. In the ten miles that belonged to Henderson's Ranch, the land changed from prairie to the abrupt edge of the Rocky Mountains that etched a rugged line into the Big Sky. He'd fought all over the world and even after three years here, it was still one of the most breathtaking places he'd ever been.

And then the black pickup rolled into the central compound and ground to a halt.

Time to go give Altman a piece of his mind. Though he wouldn't mind meeting that wife of his—had to be some serious kind of lady to match up right.

Patrick's horse trailed them as they approached the pickup.

CHAPTER 2

All Jodie could do was clutch the steering wheel and hang her head. It had taken everything she had to navigate the last thirty miles of washboard that Montana called a road. Of course, doing the whole trip in one pull from Brooklyn had taken its toll, too.

Brandy had hated leaving Jodie's room. Hated Jodie packing her bag before that—had tried to unpack it for her until Jodie shoved her off the bed. Hated getting in the truck even more. Jodie had spent her own share of time drugged out of her mind after she'd been shot four years ago in Mosul, Iraq, and couldn't face doing that to her dog even though she had the bottle of doggie-Valium in her pocket. Instead, Brandy'd sat quivering in the passenger seat for the whole trip across.

So, like any good SEAL, Jodie had simply leaned into it. Get going and get it done. They'd both suffered plenty over the last thirty-six hours, but they were here.

A sharp metal clank against her window made her jump. Brandy cried out, as she had a thousand times during the trip. Every semi-truck that had roared by them had nearly given the poor thing fits.

Not even having the energy to look up, Jodie punched the down button on the window, then returned to clutching the wheel with both hands.

"Where the hell is Altman?" The man's snarl sounded junkyard mean.

"How the hell should I know? Naval Air Station Oceania, Virginia? Bumfuck, Somalia?" At least, if the guy knew Altman, it meant she was in the right place. For the last thousand miles she'd been dreading that she'd somehow gotten the directions wrong and would have to turn back and drive over the endless damn Plains states again. Who knew that so much of the country was flatter than a week-old root beer?

The guy unleashed a string of curses as foul as any seasoned sailor.

The first thing she saw when she looked up was a pair of metal hooks where he ought to have a hand. Beyond that and the metal arm attached to them, the whole left side of his face—where it wasn't hidden by the curling fall of deep brown hair—was scar tissue. Burns. Long healed, but seriously bad ones.

He glared at her with eyes as dark as a dog's.

No, he glared past her.

"That the dog?"

"No. It's a camel. What do you think? That I drove thirty-six hours straight for my health?"

"Thirty-six hours," Hooks grumbled. He turned to the cowboy.

She didn't know there still were such things, but he had a saddled horse, a cowboy hat, even a plaid flannel shirt, so he must be one. Did they still wear spurs? She was too tired to look.

"Altman signaled me less than an hour ago. He is such dog meat." The scarred guy turned back to face her. "Who are you?"

"Who the hell are you? I'm looking for Stan somebody. *Commander* Altman said there was someone here who would know this was a dog and not a camel."

"My CO sent you?"

She just rolled her eyes at him and could feel them like sandpaper against the insides of her eyelids.

"You look like shit, sister."

"Thanks. And not your sister. You going to help me or are you just gonna stand there and use your hooks to keep playing with yourself?"

The cowboy snorted out a laugh. "Always wondered how you did that, buddy."

Brandy wormed her way under Jodie's elbow to bury her face against Jodie's belly.

Hooks looked in at them for a long moment. "Your dog?"

"No. She's just a total slut who does that to every truck driver she can find." Then she just gave up. "Six years together, four of that forward-deployed. In service with SEAL Team 8, technically on loan from— Aw, screw it."

Again the long silence that forced her to look up from comforting Brandy.

He no longer looked gruff. Instead he looked impossibly sad.

"Senior Chief Petty Officer Stan Corman, retired," he raised his hooks to explain why he'd retired. "I was a dog handler for SEAL Team…uh, 3. I don't know what I can do, but I'll try."

The cowboy didn't appear to notice Stan's overlong hesitation about being in SEAL Team 3, but even one-eared Jodie heard it loud and clear. A hesitation long enough to think about what teams were stationed with hers at Virginia Beach and then to pick one of the other ones, based in Coronado, California. No SEAL ever admitted to being a part of the top-secret DEVGRU, commonly known as SEAL Team 6. But if Altman was his former CO, that meant Stan had also been Team 6. Hard not to respect that.

The cowboy actually punched him in the arm, well above where the armature strapped in. "First thing you can do is get her some food and somewhere to sleep, you doofus."

"Uh, right. Patrick, can you handle that for me?" Then Corman walked away as if she and Brandy no longer existed.

"He's a sweet guy," the seriously tall cowboy leaned down to explain through the open window.

She gave him her best deadpan expression.

"Okay. Maybe he doesn't show it or even know it, but he really is."

At this point, all Jodie cared about was shower, food, and sleep— with sleep being her top priority. If Brandy's nightmares would let her.

Stan stood in the dog kennel building and looked down the line.

Twelve cages all down one side so that the dogs didn't face each other. This way he didn't have to worry about some dog that was in a foul mood ticking off another dog just because he could see him. The eastern wall had generous windows so that the morning sun could help warm up the place quickly on cold winter mornings, but not overheat it on hot summer afternoon. The heaters were off for the spring and it wasn't yet hot enough for AC, so the windows all down the side were open wide to let the fresh morning air flow through.

Each gate opened into a generous six-by-eight-foot cell. Comfy dog bed, water bowl, and a chew toy. Seven of the cages were still occupied. This class, his first class, had started with ten dogs. There'd been five drops and two late starts.

Of the five failures, one had gone to a local rancher, three had enough potential for regular forces and he'd shipped them down to Lackland Air Force Base for training, and one had attached himself to Lauren—Patrick's intended. It was strange, Rip acted as if he barely knew Stan anymore. Instead, from the first day, he went everywhere with Lauren like it was love at first sight. He'd been on the verge of flunking out anyway—well-behaved, but he just didn't have that essential hard-driven nature of a good military war dog—so his weird fascination had solved a placement problem before it became one.

Of the seven remaining, all were set to graduate. He had a group of Spec Ops handlers coming out for final evaluation and pairing next week.

The various teams had promised at least ten candidates, because sometimes there just wasn't a good match for a dog so you needed more handlers than dogs.

Only Bertram, his very first dog here at the ranch, had noticed his arrival in the kennel. Bertram lay with all the perfection of a canine sphinx—front paws together, head up, rabbit-sized ears perfectly erect. The ears were smaller than a German Shepherd's, but so was the head, making the ears just as ridiculously oversized. He was as fine an example of a Malinois as Stan had ever seen. He was the only animal that ticked all five boxes with top scores: obedience, tracking, agility, herding, and physical conformation.

War dogs were all about the first two boxes.

To qualify for Spec Ops Forces with Delta or ST6, they had to tick the first three with top marks.

Herders went to ranchers. Physical conformation went to show dogs.

Bertram could round up stray cattle as easily as he could dive between the slats on a fence line at a full sprint.

"You know how beautiful you are, don't you?" He whispered to the dog.

An ear twitch acknowledged his speech.

Damn, he was going to miss that dog. But he knew what was needed out past the line, that place in hell where SEAL teams lived. Exceptional wasn't good enough; it was just the starting point.

He trained young, healthy dogs to get ready for war. Wasn't a dog in the room who couldn't pick out all of the most common explosives and a lot of the rarer ones. Not a one who'd do more than glance aside when a machine gun fired from ten paces away. None of them would hesitate for an instant to take down a two-hundred-pound aggressor in a massive bite suit.

Stan moved down the line, popping open the cages. He went in and greeted each dog, gave them a good morning scritch and rubdown. Timmy had already come through, brushing and then feeding them. The old man had been around horses for all of his seventy-plus years, but was glad to help him with the dogs after a bad fall last year had limited his ability to ride. The guy was game and a great help. Though even that was becoming a strain for him.

After Stan greeted the last of them—Tiger, whose coloring had formed rough stripes down his flanks—he slapped his thigh and called, "*Strecke*." He'd shortened it because *Hindernisstrecke* (obstacle course) was just too much of a mouthful in German, the dogs' training language.

The seven dogs leapt from their cages and raced out the door headed for the obstacle course. He'd built it up over the last couple of years and he and Timmy had made even more improvements this spring. What had started as a few planks, a fence line, and an abandoned pickup truck, would now match any training setup short of Lackland Air Force Base. He'd been out to visit the Secret Service's course at the James J. Rowley Training Center near DC. They had a big simulated urban center, the body of an airplane, and a few other things he didn't, but their primary dog course had nothing on his.

Of course JJRTC was in a carefully wooded compound so that no one could observe Secret Service training methods. Out here, with only five other ranches within ten miles, crowds coming to watch wasn't an issue. Sometimes ranch guests lined up along the fence, but as long as they left him alone, he didn't care. The area had only one decent shade tree—a thirty-foot Ponderosa pine—which four of the dogs lay under awaiting their turn.

He began running the first trio through their paces, just loosening them up. Up the steep ramp to the narrow plank five meters in the air. Run along it, then jump off the far end into a water tank to simulate an ocean deployment out of a helicopter. Climb out and, after a good shake to clear the water, duck low and race through a twenty-meter twisting black-plastic sewer tube that was half the height of the dog.

Out the far end and up to a split in possible paths.

He'd done that to teach them to listen for his commands or watch for his hand signs. Sent to the right, they'd slalom through vertical slats. To the left, jump down into a grave-deep hole, then climb out through another section of sewer pipe that he'd buried at an angle. If signaled to proceed straight ahead, they'd launch themselves in through the open passenger's window of an old pickup and place a hard bite on the mannequin driver until told to release.

The dogs never knew the order of the obstacles and he'd made several of them so that he could change their configuration quickly. They'd learned to always look to him for guidance.

After two years of training, they were to the point where he could have three at a time in the course, each watching for their separate commands from him. The ones under the tree watched their teammates attentively, eager for their chance to run. He no longer needed to leash them to a stake. Once told to *Blieb*, they stayed like rocks until he issued any number of release commands: Go, Come here, Attack, and so on.

He signaled the first group over to the sidelines and turned for the second group.

The woman was standing there. She was leaning against the fence that had once made this a horse paddock. The fence wouldn't keep his dogs in, especially not these dogs. But it did keep any dumb horses from wandering into his training course and falling down a hole.

She leaned on the top rail with a fat burrito in her hand. No sign of the dog that wasn't a camel. Damn woman cracked him up.

Out of the truck, she wasn't much of a thing: five-six, maybe one-twenty. Camo pants, black t-shirt, and lace-up boots said that she was fresh out of the military. Plenty of muscle and no padding looked good on her. Her light-brown hair—or did they call it dark-blonde… dishwater…who knew with women—fell from her Navy ball cap to her shoulders in a tousled disarray that said she didn't care how much of a mess she looked. It hid much of her face from view.

He waved the second trio forward. The first trio lined up to watch —panting heavily with their tongues lolling out. After any workout, Malinois always made it look as if they'd done some massive task and could never be bothered to move again. Given the least chance though, they'd happily bound back in for as long as he was willing to run them. During training, they'd been through a whole series of twenty-four- to forty-eight-hour hikes together, ending with an explosives test. Every dog in this class had massive endurance, they just liked pretending they didn't. Maybe it was the ever-so-casual attitude of a seasoned SEAL warrior.

Once they were fully involved in the course, he signaled Bertram forward. On a whim, he sent his prize dog to run the course counter-direction. It only took knocking one of his classmates unexpectedly into the water tank for Bertram to get the idea.

He glanced back at Stan.

Stan sliced a flat hand twice—once at each of the other two dogs on the course. In moments, Bertram was giving them a hard lesson in surprises from unexpected quarters. The best comedy show he'd seen in a while, he couldn't help laughing.

Something made him glance over his shoulder.

The woman was walking away, just turned and on the move. Half of her burrito lay in the dirt. What the hell was up with that?

CHAPTER 3

Jodie had tried sleeping in the bunk they'd given her. She had her own room with a two-tier bunk sporting clean sheets and lovely Native American woven blankets. Small sink and bathroom down the hall. She'd settled in just fine.

But sleep wouldn't come.

Overtired. She was just overtired from the long drive.

Still nothing. She lay there long enough to watch the moonlight shift across the bare wood wall that had seen dozens of seasons of ranch hands come through. When it lit her jacket on the back of the door, she took the hint, pulled it on, and went out for a walk.

Her ears—her ear—actually popped as she stepped out beneath the light of the half moon. The silence was so deep that it was an assault on her senses. No Navy barracks. No hospital or vet sounds. No constant rumble of Brooklyn outside. She waited to feel the tiniest vibration as an F train passed by fifty feet under her bootheels. Nothing.

She actually had to snap her fingers lightly to make sure her hearing was working at all. It was. Montana wasn't. How could there be a place that made no sound?

As if in answer, she heard a set of wingbeats. Having no directional sense for sound with only one ear, she had to scan the whole horizon to spot the big owl before it disappeared over the bunkhouse roof. The thing was huge. Good night to not be a mouse.

Except for a porchlight in front of the main house, the only light was the setting half-moon's. She checked her watch, zero dark thirty —just like the title of the bin Laden takedown movie. But no SEAL team, loaded for bear in a pair of stealth Night Stalkers helicopters, came roaring over the rooftops. They'd attacked Osama's compound in the dead of night. In their number was a military war dog. Cairo had become famous in that moment—even meeting the President.

Brandy, on a far less illustrious mission, reported by no one except her commander on some official post-mission briefing document, had become a basket case.

Jodie pulled her denim jacket more tightly around her though the night was warm. The air smelled of grass and flowers. Of the distant horse barn and...

She found the kennel more by body memory than any conscious thought, the shining starlight enough to see her way. Her body actually buzzed with exhaustion and her brain felt like it was still back in the endless stretches of South Dakota. She planted one foot in front of the other until she reached the building, never once certain that she felt the ground as she stepped on it.

At the threshold, everything started to make sense. The kennel might be better built than the typical concrete-block and tin-roof structures the military threw up for field cages, but otherwise they were much the same. The hint of wet dog permeated the structure. A sharp tang of antiseptic salve spread on some dog's cut reached her through the ever-present whiff of Clorox bleach used to scrub every surface. The lingering musk of canned dog food served hours ago was as familiar as boot leather. It was all a reassurance that these dogs were well cared for.

Tiny noises followed her down the aisle. A click of claws on concrete, as some dog rolled over to watch the shadow walking past their cages. One of the dogs huffed out a question in a low, explosive release of a breath—so that he could draw in fresh scent through that ever-so-sensitive nose.

Supposedly a thousand times more sensitive than a human nose, what did they smell? Unleaded fuel from filling up her truck in Great Falls? Drive-thru burgers because she hadn't dared leave her dog in the car alone in Billings or Bozeman or Butte—one of those B towns that seemed to be everywhere in Montana? Maybe the sack of onion bagels her mother had placed in her hands as she'd set out into the night less than twenty minutes after her call with Altman?

Past the seven occupied cages and the four empty ones, she reached the last one in the row.

This time the whine was one of eager greeting. She'd unloaded Brandy in here, coaxing her out of the truck. At her frantic pacing, Jodie had managed to lever the big portable dog cage from the back of her truck into the caged area. Brandy had dived into the security of familiarity like she'd just escaped a Navy drown-proofing exercise.

Unable to face the pain, Jodie had followed Patrick to drop her own gear in a bunkroom. While she'd showered, he'd fetched her a break-fast burrito. If that was how they ate on ranches, she should have come to one sooner. It had tasted awesome and her body had been wolfing it down automatically as she'd explored the ranch. Wandering past the kennel and out to the field where Stan had been training the dogs.

Brandy whined again in the dark, so Jodie undid the latch and stepped into the cage with her. Brandy plunged into her shoulder so hard that she was slammed back against the wall. Once she recovered, Jodie sat down on the dog bed and Brandy swarmed her lap. She'd never been able to train her that once you hit fifty pounds, you were no longer a lap dog. Brandy curled up, and after a few quick nuzzles, collapsed into an exhausted sleep.

In moments Jodie's legs were going numb. It was comfortingly familiar and she stroked her hands deep into the dog's fur.

As numb as she supposed she'd been this morning when she'd found the guy with the hooks, Stan, working the dogs through the obstacle course. She had leaned on the fence as she had a hundred times at other courses. Not her turn, she'd watch the handler running the dogs through their paces.

This was actually earlier in the process than she was used to seeing. Usually, it was dog-and-handler pairings working a course. A military war dog went through initial selection at about three months: basic intelligence, situational awareness, able to learn commands, and not afraid of bright lights and loud noises. Then they were typically fostered out for at least a year with frequent check-ins. Lackland AFB ran a whole crowd of families willing to foster incredibly active Malinois puppies. They had to live within three hundred miles of the base outside San Antonio, Texas, so that they could bring the dog in for monthly assessments.

If the dogs passed through fostering well, then they received six months of rigorous testing and training before being paired with a handler. And that was regular MWDs.

Military war dogs for Special Operations Forces like SEAL Team 6, Rangers, and Delta Force all came from private contractors.

Jodie had watched this training with fascination. Brandy was good, as good as she and the Lackland trainers could make her. But these dogs had been doing something else entirely.

She could work Brandy on- or off-leash—not all MWDs could be trusted off-leash.

This guy worked them in teams of three completely off-leash. And just like a team, he deployed them to separate challenges and different tasks. Leaping straight up from sitting to grab a ball dangling six feet in the air. Commanded to take out a bad-guy pop-up mannequin high atop a fifth-wheel RV trailer, a dog had circled to jump on the pickup's hood and roof, making a clean bound across to the fifth wheel to put on the bite.

Scenario after scenario, all done by hand signal and voice command.

It was an impressive show. Half the commands were hand signals and half in German—the standard language for most American war dogs. It cut down on confusion in a crowd, such as a dog triggering when someone said, "When I get back to the office, I'm really going to *attack* that."

Then for just a moment the trainer had turned and looked at her. The sunlight caught his scarred left jaw. His dark eyes had inspected her and found her...lacking? He was pissed off at...? Hell if she knew or cared.

Then he'd waved in the last dog. In moments, the precision of the exercise was blown to hell. Like he'd sent in a saboteur—a sleeper-agent terrorist. Dogs yipped in surprise as they lost their balance or missed the mark. They tried to return to the course, but the rogue agent blocked their every attempt.

Mr. Hooks had started laughing like a madman, delighted to destroy the perfect precision he'd created.

This wasn't some...joke. This was military war dog training. Nothing could be more serious.

Yet he laughed at dropping a dog-shaped bomb in their midst. Just like some bastard Syrian militia had dropped a mortar round on a US advisory team patrolling through the middle of a marketplace. Bombing their own goddamn civilians in the process.

She'd felt the explosion all over again. The searing, icepick-deep pain as her right ear was silenced forever. And the pure agony when she opened her eyes and saw Brandy where she lay, blown twenty feet through the air to crash land in a tomato vendor's stall. For a moment, she'd thought all the red was squashed fruit. Then she'd seen the wetness of Brandy's blood welling up from a dozen places under her black fur. Only the Kevlar vest and doggles—sand goggles for dogs— had saved her dog's life and vision.

Jodie didn't know what she'd done next after that memory slammed into her.

She'd "come to" nowhere near the ranch's obstacle course. She'd hiked up on some high ridge and been walking toward the sharp peaks of the Rocky Mountains. She hadn't even known which direction she'd gone or where the ranch lay from here.

But she never blanked.

Ever.

That was part of PTSD and that was *not* her.

There'd been a hawk's cry and the rustle of wind through the bright green grass reaching up to her knees.

Her left side was sun-warmed, so she'd been walking west. She had then turned east and began trudging back. She'd originally arrived at the ranch in the morning. By the time she'd come to, the sun had been well past due south and headed to west. She must have walked for hours.

It had been coming on to sunset and she'd begun to wonder if she'd have to sleep wild tonight when she saw the first signs of life. A group of horses and riders trotting down a hillside about half a mile away. In the vast silence, she could hear their excited talk drifting down the wind. The kind of talk that came as the end of a long patrol neared.

She changed her angle to intersect their track. Half an hour later, beneath a blood red sky so vast that it seemed to go on forever, she stumbled upon the ranch. She'd come at it from an odd angle: behind the main house, between the guest cabins to the right and the bunkhouse to the left.

Jodie had gone straight for the latter, drunk as much water as her gut could hold straight from the tap, and plunged into the bunk to lose herself in sleep, just as she'd lost herself on the prairie.

Except she hadn't.

She'd lain awake remembering every mission she and Brandy had walked together. And imagining every mission they'd never walk in the future. Dreading the body count racking up every day because they weren't out there doing their job.

Now, sitting in the cage with Brandy curled up in her lap, at least this one, single thing was right. Through long practice, she shifted Brandy's weight to the side without waking her. By clutching an arm tightly around Brandy's chest, they were both mostly on the dog bed.

Stan looked down at the sleeping pair. He'd gone looking for the woman once he had the dogs bedded down but hadn't found her anywhere. He hadn't knocked on her door at dinner, figuring after that long drive, she just needed sleep.

After that, he'd spent a while watching the dog, what little he could see of her. She'd hidden herself deep in the portable cage's shadow. When he tried going into the cage, she hadn't snarled or snapped. Instead she'd cowered even deeper into shadow with a whimper of fear.

Unable to bring himself to face that, he'd backed away until he could track down the handler and find out what the fuck had happened to make a dog do that.

Well, he'd finally found her.

Somewhere in the night, she'd come to the cage and curled up with her dog. It felt voyeuristic to watch them sleep. How many nights had he and Lucy slept curled up together like that before she'd been blown to hell? Shredded along with his arm and two of his team by a little boy the Taliban had wired up with an explosive and sent over to "pet the doggie." Ten-thousand-dollar reward for killing an MWD, twenty if you got the handler as well—a fortune by Afghanistan standards where the average per capita income was four hundred dollars a year. Apparently that was also the price of a kid's life.

Something about the sleeping pair pissed him off. And something about them made him wish it was him curled up with the dog instead of her.

At least she still had her damned dog. What right did she have to be upset when her dog was right there beside her instead of blown into a thousand pieces in Afghanistan?

The dog woke first, saw him, and bolted from the woman's arms into the portable cage with a yip of fear.

The woman jolted upright, slapping for a sidearm she wasn't wearing.

He envied her even that. He'd been lefthanded and couldn't have slapped instinctively for a weapon even if he was wearing one.

"Morning."

She eyed him, glanced over at her dog cowering in the portable, then back at him.

Blue. Her eyes were an intense blue, dark-blue here in the shadowed cage.

"Morning, I guess."

"Spend the night here?"

"No, I spent it in Kansas." She shrugged as she scrubbed at her face as if trying to wake it up. It was a good face. He hadn't really noticed yesterday, when her eyes had been bloodshot holes with dark rings beneath. Then she'd looked…just like any SEAL strung out at the end of a hard mission. "Couldn't get to sleep in the bunk. Too quiet."

"You want some chow first, or do you wanta just start?"

She glanced at Brandy hiding in the shadows. "Let's just start."

"You got a name, sister?"

"Yeah. So does my dog."

"I'll take either one."

"Brandy," but she didn't bother telling him if that was her or the dog.

Sass. He liked that in a sailor.

It wasn't until Jodie had coaxed Brandy out of the portable that she noticed that the guy had moved into the cage. He'd done it so smoothly and quietly that there was no doubting he was a SEAL. Stan Corman, SEAL Team 6. This must be the guy.

He had the attitude to prove it as well. Supreme arrogance.

Only when he was sitting so close did she see how big he was. Despite the loss of an arm, he was one of those guys you could easily use as a substitute for an M1 Abrams battle tank. But his very stillness made him unthreatening despite the harsh scars on his face and the garish arm. It wasn't some pretty, cosmetic prosthesis thing. Instead it was all exposed steel and wires right up to the nylon socket for his stump.

She liked that he did nothing to hide it.

Here I am. This is me. Deal with it.

Okay, she'd deal with it. She just hoped her dog could.

"This," she stroked a hand over the dog's head as she had again moved into Jodie's lap, "is Brandy. And yes, 'she's a fine girl,' and no, please don't sing the goddamn song. I'm Jodie Jaffe, most folks call me JJ."

He nodded to her, but kept his eyes on Brandy as he said, "Hello, *fine girl.*" He made it feel as if he was talking to both of them. At least he had some sense of humor.

Brandy eyed him carefully.

Unsure what to expect, Jodie waited.

So did Stan.

And Brandy.

Jodie almost asked what he was doing, but he gave her the tiniest shake of his head. So she waited and watched him.

The burn scars on his face pulled slightly at the corner of his mouth. It didn't make him appear to be smiling, but more as if he was laughing at some joke only he understood. Or perhaps the best joke of all was that he was laughing at himself. It made the right side of his face the more serious side. There, she could see that he'd once been lady-killer handsome; might still be if he ever really smiled.

He didn't strike her as the kind of guy who smiled much.

Had she been? She no longer remembered. Twelve long years of service might have knocked that out of her.

Jodie felt the change beneath her palm resting on Brandy's head.

Brandy had extended her nose toward Stan, perhaps just a half inch, but toward him. And then she'd taken a deep sniff.

At Stan's infinitesimal nod, Jodie whispered a soft, "Good girl."

"You can't!"

Stan groaned. It had already been a long morning.

Timmy was working the dogs, not the coursework they should be doing, but that was beyond the old cowboy's skills. But he could run the ball tosser to exercise them. One of the ranch hands had cobbled it together for him. On "days off" the dogs got to play. The tosser launched tennis balls high and hard. The direction was made unpredictable by a loosely attached exit tube. The dogs chased their assigned balls, retrieved them, and dropped them back in the hopper at the base of the machine. Timmy just had to point at the next dog up and hit the launch button.

His own morning had been a constant battle of wits with a freaked-out dog. And an almost equally freaked handler.

Brandy would sniff Stan but wouldn't let him touch her.

She'd walk on the lead with Jodie, if that belly-scraping near crawl could be considered a walk. Still knew how to swim, but the dog was weak as hell. Probably hadn't gone for a decent run since being blown up two months ago.

The handler wasn't in all that much better shape. Steady, and knew how to dig deep to hold it together. But he recognized in her how tight that hold was. Knew it like a second skin.

He'd tried JJ on for size, but didn't like it. JJ sounded like a guy on the team—probably the joker of the patrol. Jodie might be wearing fatigues and boots, but she was very definitely a woman. Overprotective, but that was part of being a dog handler.

And now that protectiveness was becoming a major pain in his ass.

For a last test, he'd loaded them in the back of his truck and driven out to The Urban. It was group of old ranch buildings, maybe a branding camp from when they used to run cattle decades ago. He'd fixed it up as an "urban experience" training area. Hidden traps, explosive hides, and all the other challenges he'd been able to build in. It was still one of the weakest areas in his training setup, but it was the best he had.

The Urban also had the advantage of being out of hearing range from the ranch. Horses and weekend cowboys were notoriously skittish around live rounds and explosives. But he had to go through war indoctrination with the dogs.

"Absolutely not!" Jodie clutched Brandy so tightly it was a wonder the dog could breathe.

If the dog had been in good shape, she should have bristled at him, picking up on Jodie's anger. Instead, the dog had become so used to having her emotions protected that it was getting hard to separate what was dog and what was overprotective woman.

All he'd pulled out was a lousy .22 single-shot rifle. The dog was just watching him, but Jodie was definitely losing it.

"It's not like I'm going to shoot her, for crying out loud."

Jodie kept her arms wrapped around Brandy's neck. "No, Corman. Just no."

"My pa used to say that you've gotta know your limits before you can push them. I haveta know how bad she is, okay?"

"Like I'm supposed to trust your pa?" Jodie bit her lower lip way past white. If she kept on like that, she was going to draw blood.

"Look, Jodie. Just chill. All we need to know is—" And he pulled the trigger, dropping a round into the big log corner post of the farthest storefront.

The dog totally freaked.

Tried to bolt.

Jodie swept Brandy's legs out from under her and the dog landed on her side with a hard-enough thump that it looked like she *had* been shot. Jodie lay down on top of her. Pinned, Brandy lay there and just howled. Howled like the sky had fallen and the world had ended.

Not even in his worst nightmares had Lucy ever made a sound like that. He safetied the rifle and tossed it back in the truck.

"Shh, girl. Shh. It's okay now," he knelt and stroked the dog's head past the crook of Jodie's half-nelson hold around Brandy's throat. "Shh. Quiet, fine girl. Quiet now." It hadn't even been a supersonic round with its characteristic crack, just a quiet .22 short. How in the world was he supposed to help a dog this bad off?

Slowly the dog came back from whatever hell the single shot had sent her to. He kept his hand steady on her head as she quieted, then finally calmed. If dogs could weep, she'd probably be doing just that.

Close by his ear, he heard the softest whisper, "You fucking bastard."

Then Jodie pulled Brandy against her and struggled to her feet.

She went to the truck, carrying fifty pounds of sack-of-potato Malinois, and struggled into the back seat. Once there, she sat looking straight ahead as if Stan no longer existed, unable to close the door because it would mean letting go of her trembling dog.

Stan closed her door. Setting the rifle over onto the passenger seat, he climbed in behind the wheel to drive them back to the ranch.

Definitely not his best day's work.

Shit.

CHAPTER 4

Jodie gathered up her gear from the bunkhouse.

She didn't care if Commander Altman was SEAL Team 6—she was going to kill him for sending her to this madman.

She tossed her duffel in the back of her truck.

And how she was ever going to speak to Nikita again after this, she had no idea.

Driving over to the kennel building, she prayed that Stan-fucking-Corman stepped into her path. She'd run him over like a rabbit in the road if he did.

Her luck was holding—all terrible. Corman was nowhere to be seen.

She almost skidded into the building on the gravel. Driving way too fast in the compound. No MPs to threaten her with meaningless tickets—like that was the best thing to happen to her since getting here. If not for the fact that there might be dogs inside, she would back up and ram his precious building for real.

Instead, she went inside. No Corman. The red fury was so thick that she could barely see her way as she stalked down to the last cage in the row and began struggling with Brandy's big portable. As soon as she had it loaded, she and her dog were gone.

All she could see was her dog's scream. The only sound was her mortal cry.

Patrick had helped her load it into the cage, but he wasn't around either. Getting it out by herself wasn't so easy. She knocked over the water bowl, which she somehow slopped into her left boot.

Jodie's role had placed her where she'd had to shoot any number of hostiles—walking point on patrols had placed her first in the way of fire. But never before had she been so consumed by the desire to hurt a man.

The portable jammed in the width of the gate designed for a dog and handler, not for a Malinois-sized cage. How the hell had they gotten it in here?

She wanted to kick it. Beat on it until she was black and blue. Until even half of her fury had been spent on destroying—

The cage moved suddenly and slid out the door.

Jodie fell forward into the sudden vacuum and hit the concrete floor hard enough that her knees were definitely going to be showing bruises for a while. She'd also planted one hand firmly in an untouched bowl of wet dog food. *There* was a stench that wouldn't be going away fast.

She sprang to her feet, ready to clobber one Stan Corman.

"Hi!" A cheery woman with long red hair and dressed in full cowgirl gear including electric-red boots and a bright pink Stetson greeted her. "Looked like you needed a hand. Sorry. Should have warned you before I freed where the cage caught on the gate's latch. You sure weren't going anywhere until I did. I'm Chelsea, by the way. I manage the horses here. I heard there was a new woman on the ranch."

Jodie tried to figure out what to do with the sudden flood of information. "Uh, new woman?" was all that she could unearth. Maybe she should have just turned a deaf ear—literally.

"Go ahead. Tell me that you're here on the seven-day package with five riding lessons, three trails rides, and an overnight campout by a trout stream."

Jodie couldn't quite resist the woman's cheery smile. "Yes. I am.

Absolutely. That's why I smell like dog food, my favorite perfume when I sign up for seven-day packages with five riding lessons, three trail rides, and an overnight campout by a trout stream." She waved her dog food-smeared hand to make her point. "It also made me very popular on the Caribbean cruise ship last week."

Chelsea laughed brightly and tossed her a clean hand towel over the portable cage still resting between them. "I knew it. We don't get new additions to the ranch very often. I can't believe that Stan was keeping you all to himself. Though I can see why he would. Bet guys go crazy over you."

Jodie wiped her hand as clean as she could, even rinsing it in the little bit of water she hadn't knocked out of the water bowl.

Did guys go crazy over her? Sure, since she was the only woman on any SEAL platoon she'd ever served in. There was only one other women among Team 8's hundred and thirty combat-qualified SEALs, so of course the guys gravitated to her. Didn't count for anything. And she and Davy Golding had history going back to kindergarten, so he didn't really count either. She hadn't had much other experience with men.

If guys were going to go crazy, it was over the tall, slender redhead with her easygoing manner and effortless cheerfulness—two traits that Jodie had never been known for.

Chelsea picked up the other end of the portable, "Where are we going with this?"

"Out to my truck," Jodie picked up her end—then dropped it.

Chelsea lost her grip too and it banged to the ground loudly enough to hurt Jodie's one good ear.

"Where the hell is my dog?" Somehow, she'd been so blindly furious with Stan Corman and so focused on getting the portable out to her truck that—

Fuck! She was really losing it.

She spun around to look in the cage as if she'd somehow missed seeing Brandy. She was half way to checking inside the portable before she caught herself—then she checked anyway. Both were as empty as her head.

"Oh, I saw Stan out taking a dog for walk. All black? She's beautiful. Is she yours? What's her name? I keep trying to get Doug to get a dog but he says that seventy-five horses and a redheaded wife are enough trouble for him. He's the ranch manager here at Henderson's and—"

"Stan-fucking-Corman is taking *my* Brandy for a walk?" Jodie tried shuffling the words around in her head, but there were too few of them to mix up the meaning. Since the explosion, no one had been able to get near Brandy. Jodie *always* had to be there. Even the trained Navy veterinarians hadn't been able to handle her solo without scaring the poor dog half to death.

"Sure. I passed him going the other way," she waved vaguely toward the hills beyond the ranch compound. "Then I saw you driving over here and thought it would be a good chance to meet you."

"Which way did he go?" Jodie shoved against the portable, kind of knocking Chelsea aside, so that she could escape the cage. She raced out the back door and ground to a stop. Everything was so big here. The curving ridgeline that wrapped around two sides of the ranch made a giant protected bowl for the compound. In the other direction, the view stretched on forever. The midday sun had climbed high in the achingly blue sky, a color she certainly never saw in Brooklyn.

Chelsea came up beside her. "Well, I saw him heading up the main trail there," she pointed up the road leading past the guest cabins. "Over the top it goes a bunch of different ways. There'd be no way to tell which trail he took."

"I'm gonna kill him if he hurts my dog."

"Stan wouldn't hurt a flea."

Jodie gave her a "you gotta be shitting me" look.

"Seriously. Have you seen him with his dogs? He trains them hard but treats them like they were his favorite children the rest of the time."

"Stan has children?" There was something impossible to imagine.

Chelsea giggled. "That would be a sight, wouldn't it? Though he's awfully sweet with my Cristopher and the other ranch kids. Hey, are you hungry? It's about lunchtime." She momentarily cupped one of her own generous breasts. "I can bet that Cristopher is hungry, that boy would stay permanently attached to my breast if I let him. If I'm this sore after four weeks, what are they going to feel like in six months before I can start weaning him? Doug likes them this size, but I want my body back."

Jodie had no idea how to answer any of that. She couldn't seem to catch her breath around Chelsea. Thankfully, her silence didn't seem to bother Chelsea. So, after loading the portable into the back of her pickup and taking one more look at the empty hills, she followed Chelsea toward the big ranch house.

Brandy had finally stopped casting worried looks behind her for Jodie. Instead she was bouncing up in alarm at every little surprise.

A couple of sparrows landed on a trailside larch sapling. When they flitted off, Brandy jumped several inches straight into the air. She watched a large blue butterfly for several tentative seconds before deciding that it wasn't going to explode. A mountain cottontail rabbit, young and small enough that it could have sat just fine on Stan's palm, bolted across the trail and almost caused the dog to stroke out.

It was a long, slow amble up to the lake, so Stan did his best to just enjoy it. It was hard. Walking along with a dog like this, out in the open beneath the spring sky, would be wonderful—except it wasn't his dog. It was Jodie's dog, who had lived to come home from war. She was such a lucky bitch and didn't even get that—

Brandy whined and looked up at him.

Dog gets your emotions right down the leash. The Number One rule Pa had ever told him when he'd given Stan his first pup. Other trainers had repeated it any number of times, but he always heard it in Pa's voice.

Forcing his thoughts away from how lucky Jodie was without appreciating it, Stan focused on remembering a lot of long summer evenings. Pa slouched in a tattered folding chair under one of the fifth wheel's awnings with his nightly beer. He'd sit there calling out things for Stan to try with his dog. Stan'd eventually made a lot of pizza money doing obedience training with other RV park dogs. He and Pa were always on the move, so there were always new customers.

Stan let himself think about all those good times and hoped that Brandy, who winced as a bumblebee zipped by mere inches from her nose, could feel some of those times down the leash.

Thankfully, the lake was unoccupied at the moment. In another month, when June's heat started slamming down, the ranch guests would spend a lot of time up here when they weren't on the horses. For the moment, it was all theirs.

Mac Henderson, the owner, had seen the natural swale just on the backside of the ridge. A little work with a bulldozer and he'd carved a couple-hundred-foot lake. There was a kiddie swimming area formed by a log wall that reached from the bottom to one log above the surface. A central float offered a slide and a diving board for the bigger kids. A gazebo perched well out over the water was so picturesque that most of the ranch's weddings were held here.

He led Brandy to the kiddie pool area, but she showed no interest in going in. Stan wasn't sure if he'd ever met a Malinois who didn't like to swim.

With a sigh, he went through the steps to unlace his boots and remove socks and trousers. Three years ago this would have taken him half an hour of intense frustration trying to get his hooks to do what he wanted. In the early days he'd come close to pissing his pants any number of times while trying to get them open. Now he hardly gave it a thought—wouldn't have if he wasn't thinking that this dog was as much of a mess now as he'd been back then.

Down to his underwear, just in case a ranch guest happened along, he led Brandy into the water. His arm wouldn't fare well in salt water, but in fresh, it would only take minimal cleaning tonight for it to be no problem.

At first Brandy tried to walk in it by lifting her paws fully clear with each step.

He led her in deeper—knee-deep for him, chest-deep for Brandy.

She was cowed enough to not complain or even look up at him in question. If this was another burden she had to bear, she'd take it. At that, he almost turned her around. But that would be about him and his empathy, and not about what was best for the dog.

He splashed the water with his hooks.

Didn't seem to bother her. He slopped some over her back. No twitch. Just zero excitement.

After about ten minutes, he led her from the kiddie enclosure out into deeper water, up to his waist, forcing her to swim. She remembered how just fine, but within minutes he could see that it was exhausting her.

Malinois liked to work out hours per day. They were a seriously high-energy breed. Lucy used to come back from an eight-hour patrol that kicked every single SEAL's butt including his own. And the first thing she'd do in camp was fetch a ball or Frisbee and drop it into his lap so that she could play.

Brandy looked as if she hadn't left her dog cage in months. Definitely have to talk to Jodie about that.

He was leading Brandy back to shore when he heard a wolf whistle.

Patrick and Lauren were sitting up on their horses—Lauren was doing the whistling. Rip, the Malinois that had adopted Lauren the minute she arrived on the ranch, sat happily near the horses. Stan flashed a stay signal when Rip started to rise; he didn't want Brandy feeling pressured when she was so tired.

"Damn, Corman. You keep displaying yourself like that, I'm gonna start thinking I'm marrying the wrong man."

He looked down—his soaked boxers might as well have been tissue paper for all they were hiding. "Your choice, lady. Never could figure why you hooked up with Patrick in the first place when you could have had a real man." Lauren was six-foot of long, lean brunette who looked magnificent up on a horse.

"Don't worry, Stan. I'll make a real man of him soon. I promise."

Patrick groaned but wasn't dumb enough to argue.

Just to tease him, Stan stepped ashore and shucked off his wet underwear before pulling on his jeans commando. He did turn aside, but he didn't make a thing of it.

"Wow! Maybe I *did* choose the wrong man."

"Don't worry, honey," Patrick leaned over far enough to kiss her, horseback to horseback. "I'll show you tonight that you absolutely made the right choice."

Lauren made a deep, happy "Mmm" sound before breaking off the kiss. "We need to get you a woman, Stan."

"Why do you married people always think that?" He squeezed as much water as he could out of his underwear and stuffed them in his back pocket.

"Hey," Patrick looked up in surprise. "What about that Jodie girl? She's seriously cute."

"Who?" Was Lauren even aware of the possessive tone in her voice?

Stan wanted nothing to do with any woman thinking she owned any part of him. As if. His fiancée, Marybeth Anne, had Dear Stanned him sight unseen while he was still en route back from Afghanistan with one less arm than he'd gone over with. Women didn't want half men like him.

"The one I told you about. With the dog."

"You didn't tell me she was cute."

"Really cute. About five-six and nice dishwater blonde hair to her shoulders. Very nice curves, too. She has that whole warrior-muscle, super-fit thing going on. I think— What?" Patrick finally caught a clue that he was pissing off Lauren. Or at least she was pretending that he was.

Stan was glad to see that spending three years bunking together had been a bad influence on Patrick.

"Oh, sorry. Don't know what I was talking about." Though not too bad an influence. Patrick was too nice a guy for it to really stick.

"Better forgive him quick, Lauren. Otherwise he slips into this whole sulky puppy-dog mode."

"Don't I know it." Then she grabbed Patrick by the front of his shirt and hauled him in until they were nose to nose. "Remember which woman you're supposed to be looking at, buster." Then she laid a kiss on him that could boil the water right out of the lake.

By Patrick's dazed expression at the end of it, he wouldn't be thinking of any other woman for a long time to come.

After they rode off, with Rip trotting happily beside them, Stan was surprised by the tightness in his jaw. When was the last time a woman had tried to warp his mind like that? Long time. Last he could think of was that little Asian midshipman—Jasmine? Jana?—on the aircraft carrier USS *Harry S. Truman*. She'd given him several lessons on just what could be done in a small shipboard cabin with sufficient agility and imagination. Different person. Different lifetime.

"You got a boyfriend, Brandy?"

The dog just looked up at him without even raising her head. She'd laid down the moment after she'd shaken off the lake water. Too tired to even startle at the arrival of the two horses, though they had been at least ten meters away. He'd have to test Brandy's perceived threat perimeter. Another day.

"Come on, girl. I'm not going to carry you back."

On the walk, she seemed to be doing better...until they spooked that damn cottontail again.

Jodie stumbled through the back door of the ranch house and ground to a halt. Impressions slammed in from a dozen directions.

Her family's brownstone had been built two hundred years ago. Each of the four floors was one room wide and two rooms deep, and they weren't big rooms. The windows were big enough to let in a cozy light but small enough to keep out the cold, back before they knew how to make double-paned glass.

Here she'd come into a commercial-grade kitchen that could probably feed an entire SEAL team all at once and it was in full swing. Streams of platters mounded with fried chicken, tureens of coleslaw, pitchers of iced tea and lemonade...all were being moved out through the swinging door to feed the ranch guests who were in some nearby dining room. The kitchen had lofty ceilings and big windows open to the climbing ridge behind the house. Even though it was on the back of the house, sunlight filled the space.

One side of the vast kitchen was a comfortable seating area of well-worn couches and armchairs surrounding a big river rock fireplace. To either side of it were tall bookcases. The lower shelves sported a wide assortment of games and toys down at kid level.

Close by the door was a Douglas fir table that could probably seat twenty. The people gathering there were clearly the ranch's working hands—not a bit of Gucci leather or Donna Karan silk among them.

Even over the amount of happy noise they were generating, Chelsea's cry was easily audible.

"There's the love of my life!" And Chelsea rushed away, leaving Jodie awash at sea. Chelsea dodged through the crowd to race up to a rugged-looking cowboy, one of those guys that probably looked more handsome with time, but the first impression was all about skill and competence.

Chelsea snatched the baby from the man's arms and made it clear that she'd been referring to the baby, not the man.

"Hey!" At the cowboy's protest to her tease, Chelsea spun once more around with the newborn cradled in her arms before leaning over to kiss him. It wasn't some passing idle peck either. There was heat and love in it. And no one took any notice.

Jodie's own family was about as demonstrative as a, well, a SEAL team. She didn't doubt that her parents loved each other, but they weren't about steamy kisses in the kitchen either—not even without a crowd around.

She wondered what Stan thought of this scene. She could almost see him, sitting at one end of the table, just watching everybody with that scowl he wore as easily as a black t-shirt. Luckily for him he wasn't here so she wouldn't be splattering the slate flooring with his blood.

"Do we know you?" A tall woman with a dark, Native American complexion and aquiline nose stood before her. Her thick fall of straight black hair was tinged with steel gray. She was perhaps the most impressive woman Jodie had ever seen. There was a...peace about her. A steadiness that seemed to radiate in all directions. Yet somehow, it made Jodie feel even more off balance.

"No, you don't, ma'am. I'm Jodie Jaffe. I—"

"Hey, Ama. She's the one who brought that dog for Stan to work with," Chelsea reappeared at her side with her child. "Neither she nor her dog are real happy at the moment. It's kind of sad. You need to cheer up, kid." And she was gone again. The fact that Chelsea was at least five years younger than Jodie made her hope that Chelsea had been addressing the last to the baby in her arms. Not likely, as the kid was happily suckling beneath a towel Chelsea wore over her shoulder.

Without another word, Ama guided her over to the table when all she wanted to do was escape and go find Brandy. Ama sat at one end, placing Jodie at her right. In moments she was crowded in with several other women: a tall blonde in her middle years, an immensely pregnant younger version of her that had to be her sister, and Chelsea.

Her need to escape redoubled, but she couldn't bring herself to duck out under Ama's watchful eye.

"Hey," Chelsea's rugged kissing cowboy called out. Doug the ranch manager? Maybe. "How come all the women are sitting down at one end of the table?"

The stretch of the table was on her deaf side. Chelsea could override it because she sat so close, but she had to guess at what others were saying. SEAL training had included basic lipreading, so she got along okay.

"Grab a clue, Doug." A big guy wearing mirrored aviator shades dropped into a chair one down from the other end of the table. "New woman on the ranch. We poor men don't even get her name."

"Nope!" Chelsea replied cheerfully, then turned her back on them and spoke to Jodie pointing at the lovely blonde seated to Ama's other side. "This is Emily. She says she's from DC, but I think the Army just manufactured her when they needed somebody who's way too perfect to be real. She and her husband—the guy in the shades—are ex-military. Helicopters. What were they called again?"

"The Night Stalkers," the middle-aged blonde spoke softly.

"Right, that's it."

Before Jodie had a chance to be shocked at meeting a pair of Night Stalkers in Nowhere, Montana—especially a female one—Chelsea pointed to the younger version of Emily.

"Julie's our token local."

So, not sisters.

"She grew up on the cattle ranch across the road and is like this total champion horse racer and the best rider on the ranch. She's also our local builder—she built that kennel for Stan."

"Nice work," Jodie managed to get a word in edgewise that earned her a radiant smile from the pregnant cowgirl.

"She married this lug," Chelsea hooked a thumb at the man delivering two big platters of fried chicken to the table. It looked magazine-ad perfect and Jodie suddenly realized just how hungry she was. "Nathan was like a twenty-star chef before Julie kicked his feet out from under him."

"No, it was two stars. Michelin only goes up to three, Chels. And I think the feet kicking was mutual."

"Ignore him. A Michelin star is like, worth ten normal ones. Makes you twenty stars. Go away, Nathan."

"Whatever you say, Chels," and he headed back to the kitchen after planting a kiss on top of his Julie's head.

"You think he'd have figured that out by now. Men can be so slow about some things. Anyway, Julie totally rocked it on the feet kicking front. You've met Ama. Her opposite number is Mark's dad, Mac, up the other end of the table."

Jodie didn't get to do more than glance to see the older version of the man in aviator shades. White hair and lighter complexion, but just as broad-shouldered as his son. She'd already lost half the names, but that didn't slow Chelsea down for a moment.

"All that's missing is Lauren and her Patrick, I think they're out trail riding somewhere—or busy celebrating their upcoming marriage in some luscious midday way—so tell us all about you." And Chelsea grabbed two pieces of chicken and passed the plate, then grabbed the bowl of potato salad before Nathan even set it on the table.

In the sudden void that appeared at the end of Chelsea's breathless introduction, Jodie didn't even know where to begin. Opening with, "Does anyone know where Deadman Corman took my fucking dog?" didn't seem appropriate.

"I'm Jodie. I'm from New York."

"Patrick and Nathan are too," Chelsea offered with her mouth full. Jodie glanced around the table as more ranch hands, both male and female, drifted into the kitchen and joined in at the table. Thankfully Chelsea didn't feel some need to add more names for Jodie to forget. She remembered Ama. That one she knew. And she didn't dare forget Emily.

Apparently the others were comfortable with Chelsea doing most of their talking for them. Or perhaps they just couldn't stop her.

"That's where Nathan's restaurant was before Julie convinced him Montana was *so* much better."

Julie was...the pregnant cowgirl who had come from... She gave up and just let the names flow around her.

"Lauren was from New York too. What is it with you people and big cities? I've traveled all over the place and just do not understand big cities at all. Give me the outdoors any day. You and me, kid," she looked down at the baby now snoozing off his meal in the sling across her chest, "definitely going back to the Himalayas again. Awesome hiking. Just awesome!"

Over half of the people who'd been named were ex-military. What was this place?

Jodie decided that was a topic she didn't want to explore any more than the Big Apple. Not with how badly she wanted to be sitting at Sal's having pizza with her brother. And definitely not with how badly she wished she was already fifty miles down the road away from goddamn Stan Corman who had better not be scaring her dog again.

"I was a SEAL dog handler for three tours, conventional forces for three tours before that, until a mortar took Brandy—"

"That's her dog," Chelsea chimed in and served herself another piece of chicken. "I'm eating for two, you greedy little gullet," again that soft smile down at her newborn.

"—took Brandy and me out of the action," Jodie managed to squeeze in the words while she could. And tried not to feel as if her insides had just been shredded.

"Former SEAL, huh? That's like Mac Senior—he's actually Mark Senior which makes Mark, Mark Junior, but that would get confusing —and Stan, right? Lauren did dogs for Delta Force. That's different from SEALs, right?" She turned her attention to the new arrival who must be Lauren as she strode in and sat down beside Julie the blonde cowgirl. Lauren was tall, lean, and very brunette.

"What are we up to?" Lauren started filling a plate.

"About five foot six," Jodie offered in her driest tone.

Lauren barked out a laugh. "You must be the new gal Patrick was telling me about. Hi!" She leaned in to reach right across the table and Julie's lap to shake hands.

"She's Jodie. She ran dogs for one of those SEAL teams. I thought they were all about swimming, but Stan was a SEAL too, which shows what I know. Why are there so many SEALs in Montana."

It was...Emily, the austere older blonde, who spoke next. "Now shut up, Chelsea. You've utterly steamrollered Jodie."

"She's the quiet type. Can't seem to get more than five words at a time out of her, so I was just trying to be helpful." But Chelsea didn't look the least bit chagrined when told to be quiet.

"You came in yesterday. How long are you planning to stay?" Lauren waved a chicken leg at her.

Jodie shrugged. *Twelve seconds after that asshole Corman returns with my dog,* wasn't something she could say to the people feeding her. Maybe they even liked Stan. Apparently her shrug didn't hide as much as she would have liked.

"Ooo, Stan got under your skin, didn't he?" Chelsea was practically bouncing with delight. "You know that means—"

"Be quiet now, Chelsea," Ama's steady voice silenced her instantly. Even the irrepressible redhead wasn't up to arguing with Ama though she spoke far more softly than Emily had moments before.

Jodie hunched her shoulders, waiting for the probing questions that would be sure to follow anyway.

Instead, with an unexpected kindness of understanding, Emily turned the conversation to Julie's pregnancy and Chelsea's newborn.

It let Jodie focus on eating. The chicken was the best she'd ever had —not that New York was a known mecca for fried chicken. But SEAL Team 8's base in Little Creek, Virginia, boasted plenty of utterly amazing fried chicken joints. But eating this didn't make her nostalgic for a platter of BoBo's fried with sweetened iced tea and her former squad crowded around the table. In the future, if she ever hit BoBo's again, it would make her nostalgic for this.

"Ranch-raised chickens," Ama said to her softly. "Nathan uses my recipe for the breading. I'm glad you like it."

Jodie could only nod as she was busy chewing. "It's incredible," she finally managed.

"I'd say that you have to excuse Chelsea, but it's who she is." The rest of the conversation had turned to children and for the moment it was just her and Ama.

"Not a mean bone in her body," Jodie agreed. That much was obvious. She could hear Chelsea's "sage" advice to Julie about what was waiting her for during birth—being way too graphic for a lunch table conversation. Of course Jodie had heard a thousand times worse over meals with her squad and was immune to it. It didn't appear to bother any of the women. But the men who sat just down the table were looking a little squeamish and Jodie could hear them struggling for a topic that would block the women's images from their thoughts.

"There isn't a mean bone in Stan's either," Ama's voice remained so even and calm that it attracted no attention other than her own.

Jodie nearly choked on a flake of the crunchy crust. She could only look at Ama in disbelief. There was no way she was that transparent. And how could Ama be so wrong? He wasn't just mean. That would be fine, as she'd served with many mean SEALs who'd made damn fine fighters. But Stan Corman also had a streak of cruel like a black mark upon his soul.

Ama's ghost of a smile said that she was reading thoughts that Jodie would never admit to having, at least not in polite company. She wasn't some Jewish princess bitch nor an asshole sailor. She was a dog handler who was worried sick about her animal.

Brandy! That's where she should be, finding her dog and getting gone. But Ama's calm spread like a warm blanket over her and made her reluctant to move.

Ama continued eating quietly. Her dark-eyed gaze didn't feel as if it was imposing on Jodie, but neither was it easy to look away from. The sheer neutrality of it made it impossible to read what the woman was feeling. Compassion? Amusement? Understanding? Goddamn telepathy, reading all of her thoughts and feeling pity at the maelstrom she could see inside Jodie's head?

Unable to stand it, Jodie broke the spell and pushed to her feet. "If you'll excuse me? It was a pleasure meeting you." Twelve years in the military hadn't completely wiped out her civilian manners. For eighteen years her family had a sit-down dinner every night, and probably still did though she'd been gone. *Please pass the salt. May I have another slice of roast beef? What interesting topic did you bring to the table tonight, dear?* Manners that had devolved into the grunts and slagging among the SEALs. *Shut your yap long enough to give me some salt. That ain't a bad yarn, but didja hear the one 'bout the stripper and the raghead horde?*

Ama's nod agreed with her polite words. Whether or not she believed them, there was no way to tell.

Jodie used all of her skills to slip away unnoticed. Neither Chelsea nor the pregnant cowgirl were aware. But Emily, the ex-Night Stalker, tracked her easily. It made her feel like a blip on a tracking radar as she scuttled across the kitchen floor.

Out the door and not wanting to meet anybody, she took a sharp turn to the right around the back of the log ranch house onto the narrow walkway between the building and the low stone retaining wall of a kitchen garden.

Head down, she managed one hurried breath and ran square into Stan Corman.

CHAPTER 5

The impact was too solid.

Stan had no options except grabbing Jodie or going down hard on his ass. But her forward momentum was too much and all grabbing her with his good arm did was to take her down with him. Reaching back with his left, his hooks just skidded on the stone pathway. Then, because he hadn't let go until she crashed down on top off him, he was slammed down doubly hard. Pain shot up his arm, not just from where his stump fitted in the socket, but from the elbow he no longer had. His nerves told him he'd just snapped his nonexistent wrist.

Then the pain really hit.

It felt as if he'd just dipped his nonexistent hand in a cauldron of fire—as hot as the day it had been blown apart.

"Goddamn it!" Jodie cursed and rolled off him.

He let her go.

He was past speech. Or caring.

All he could do was curl into a ball and clench his good arm around his missing one. His instincts didn't care that he was holding onto a metal and wire armature, they just held on as he gritted his teeth to not scream at the pain firing up his nerve endings.

"What the hell, Corman? Where's my dog?"

He could hear the words but couldn't make any sense of them.

Pain. Blinding red behind his eyes. Flame. The Afghan boy exploding in a ball of light from the IED strapped between his legs. Lucy taking the brunt of it, seventy pounds of Malinois shredded in an instant. Her blast shadow protecting most of his body. Most—but not all.

"Breathe! Goddamn it, sailor. *Breathe!*"

He managed a gasp.

"Again!"

Another stuttering breath.

It was hard.

It hurt.

Like something had rammed him in the solar plexus.

Something had.

He managed to open one eye and see the blur of someone kneeling over him.

"No," he barely got the word out. Not again. He hadn't lost his arm. Not again. He'd been conscious after they killed Lucy. His team dead: two in the explosion, two more machine-gunned down.

The hard buzz-saw bark of a heli-borne Minigun chewing up the attackers. Too little. Too late.

A medic who FAST-roped down despite the ongoing firefight. No room for the helo to squeeze in to the narrow streets.

The medic kneeling over him to put out the fire still burning on the left shoulder of his uniform—it had started to burn his face. Telling Stan to breathe as he put the tourniquet on and then slammed a morphine ampoule into his upper shoulder.

"Not my arm. Not my arm." It was all he'd been able to say then. It was all he could manage to say now.

"Shh. It's okay. Nothing looks bent." The medic was female this time.

"Put it out," he begged. "Put out the fire."

A cool hand slipped onto his upper arm. The cool spread like a balm, easing the pain. Like cold water on a hot day, the fire went out of his nerves until he was finally able to see Jodie squatting over him. Her hand, resting cool on his stump just above the socket for the prosthesis.

"Fuck," was all he could manage. He felt like he'd aged ten years. The nightmares had always scared him awake, though it had been a long time since he'd had a bad one. A year maybe. But the nightmares had never hurt like wildfire.

Finally she dropped back on her heels, then rocked too far and collapsed back against the log wall of the ranch house with a hard thump.

He missed her hand the moment it was gone.

"You okay now?"

"Uh. Don't know. Three years since it was blown off. Never felt anything like that." He sat up slowly. The sharp knot in his solar plexus was easing. Must have been her elbow or shoulder. Thankfully she didn't weigh enough to do serious damage in a simple fall.

He forced himself to look at his mechanical arm, which still hurt like hell, but only the parts that still existed: stump, upper biceps, deltoids, and shoulder. The skin inside the socket felt particularly raw. He put the armature through the movements. Hunch his shoulders apart in an Incredible Hulk motion to tighten the cross-back strap. It flexed the elbow, a left-arm shrug to lock the elbow joint, another spread of his shoulders and the hooks dutifully swung open. When he relaxed, the rubber bands pulled them back together. Once more he shrugged, releasing the elbow lock. No visible signs of damage.

"If you had a real hand still, you might have broken your wrist the way you went down. Or at least scraped the shit out of yourself."

"Hadn't planned on going down at all." Exhausted by the impossible pain, he managed to prop himself against the stone side of Nathan's garden bed. It smelled of...he wasn't sure what. Herbs and shit: sweet, tangy, soothing. He and Pa were more burger and chips guys. On Sundays, they'd grilled a steak.

"Where's my dog?"

"I'm fine, thanks." He was a long way from fine. The phantom pains might be gone, but the scale of them had left him shaking and with a chill that rippled over his whole body. Adrenal letdown. How long since he'd ridden out one of those? Slow and steady is what got him through every day.

"Good. Where's my dog?" Jodie was SEAL relentless. He liked that about her.

Her Navy ball cap lay on the walkway between them, but he couldn't find the energy to toss it to her. Her hair was a mess. Her face grim. But Patrick had been right, seriously cute. No, seriously pretty. Brilliant blue eyes, wide open even when angry. Very nice shape, pure female warrior. Slimmed down in the way that happened to the ultra-fit, but still screaming her gender. The inside of his good palm still remembered the feel of all the muscle in her shoulder as she'd strained for a moment to try and prevent their fall.

"My dog?"

He sighed. Okay, trying to prevent *her own* fall. By her tone, he could fall over dead and she might not blink. Or maybe she'd do a cheer.

"Your dog is asleep. Back in the kennel."

"What did you do to her?" Jodie fired her questions just like a Minigun, fast and hard.

"I took her for a walk and a swim."

"You..." That finally seemed to stop her accusatory tone.

"She's in awful condition."

"Hello, might have driven all the way from New York for that reason."

Stan shook his head and struggled to his feet. "She's a Malinois. Yet she barely had the energy for a ten-minute swim and a quarter-mile walk each way. Skittish as hell, yeah. We'd already figured that out. But also incredibly weak physically."

Jodie was looking down at her propped-up knees.

He had to wait her out for a long time before she spoke. So softly that he could barely hear her.

"The vets had her caged and sedated for most of two months. I got her back to New York, but..." she waved a hand helplessly. "You've seen the way she is. I could barely get her out of my bedroom. Out the front door was ten times worse. And I live in a quiet neighborhood, even by Brooklyn standards."

"Look, I'm not saying it's the whole solution, but she needs to get some strength back. That should help her mental state too. Maybe. But, yeah, exercise. As much as she can take."

There was a sudden noise. The kitchen door banged open and the ranch hands streamed out. None of them looked over their shoulders to see him and Jodie slumped down just around the back corner of the house.

"You get any lunch?"

Jodie nodded without looking up. "Some."

"More than I got," he pushed to his feet. "Come on, Jodie. Let's see what we can scare up. I missed breakfast with your dog."

<hr>

And in that instant, Jodie remembered exactly what he'd been doing to her dog this morning instead of eating breakfast—scaring the shit out of the poor thing with that gunshot.

No way was she breaking bread with Stan-fucking-Corman.

But she couldn't bring herself to slice at him either.

She'd seen the blind panic, the pain far too great to bear. The pain and fear combined so badly that they'd made him go fetal and beg her to not take his other arm. The fact that he was sitting there, talking to her rationally, said just what a tower of strength he was.

Had she done any better than Brandy? She'd gone back to Brooklyn and tried to curl up back inside her old life. Tried to wrap it around her as if the twelve years since her departure hadn't happened. Twelve years of kill or be killed. Of turning herself and three separate dogs into living explosives detectors.

No, she hadn't done so well. But she was going to do better for Brandy, starting right now.

"Not hungry. You go ahead without me."

"You sure?"

"I'm sure," she kept her voice carefully neutral.

In her peripheral vision, she could see him shrug. He bent down and snatched up her hat in his hooks. He handed it off to his meat hand and tugged it down on her head.

Her peripheral vision was blocked by the brim, but she could see his boots departing. She heard him greeting and being greeted by the stragglers coming out the kitchen door. They obviously knew him... and the idiots sounded as if they liked him.

When the strangling silence of Montana had once more settled over her, she rose to her feet. She moved fast, keeping carefully crouched below the kitchen windows until she was well clear.

Past the back of the house, past the ranch hands' bunkhouse, and out to the dog kennel where she ducked inside.

Nobody in the first cage. Or any of the others. They must be out with Timmy for exercise.

She almost stumbled on the Malinois lying in front of the last cage.

Not hers. It was the dog Stan had sent out to disrupt the exercise for the other dogs, a massive and beautiful dog. He was strongly black, but with some soft tan on his chest and belly that kept him from looking like an unholy terror.

He popped his head up to look at her but didn't move.

No leash. He was simply lying there.

Beyond him, she could see Brandy on the dog bed. She was curled up as tightly as an anteater. Or an armadillo. Or whatever animal it was that did that curl up thing. Hedgehog? The tip of her tail lay over her face making a complete circle of fur with no nose or eyes. Only the two large ears sticking up to either side of the tail definitively marked the position of her head.

As Jodie moved closer, Stan's dog jumped to his feet, turning to face her. It wasn't some submissive, lowered forebody posture eager for play. Nor was it an easy stance with a lolling tongue, inviting a pat on the head.

The dog's legs were stiff and straight, his head lowered, and his teeth ever so slightly bared. It wasn't his attack position, but it was telling her in no uncertain terms that he was on guard duty.

God *damn* Corman. There was only one reason he'd have set his dog here: to keep Jodie away.

The tiny bit of sympathy she'd been feeling for him flickered out faster than a rifle's muzzle flash in broad daylight.

She backed off carefully until her back bumped into the kennel's opposite wall less than ten feet from the bristling dog. She let her back slide down it. After her butt hit the cool concrete and she showed no other sign of moving, Stan's dog lay down again. He kept his body along the full length of the cage door so that there was no way for Jodie to get by him, even if she dared try.

Not a chance.

She'd seen how exceptionally well-trained this dog was out on the course. He was also an amazing specimen, way at the upper end of Malinois size. He was seventy-five, maybe eighty pounds of intensely fit and dangerous war dog. Half again bigger than Brandy, he embodied lethal fighter.

Out of options, Jodie readied herself to wait.

That was a skill built into every SEAL's soul, the patience of being in position and waiting for the op to actually begin. Layer by layer, she built herself into readiness. Her knife shifted on her thigh to its optimum angle, her hand lightly on the hilt. Her legs positioned so that they wouldn't go to sleep no matter how long she sat in the one position. Her position would allow her to spring from perfectly still to full attack at a moment's notice.

Then, with Stan's damn dog still watching her, she did what every top fighter did before a mission. She slept.

CHAPTER 6

S tan spotted her the moment he stepped into the kennel.

Bertram to one side, lying down but in an alert position.

Jodie sitting directly opposite. Her head back against the wall and tipped slightly to one side, exposing a nice length of neck. Clearly asleep, he was once again taken by her face. Without the aggressive scowl, she really was lovely. Some women looked innocent, even childlike when they slept. It was something he'd noticed any number of times as he'd carefully slipped out of a bed and left.

Marybeth Anne had been like that. Maybe that's what had kept him in her bed, watching that impossible innocence in such a seriously built body. Long enough to become engaged. But the girl with three first names hadn't acted so innocent and kind once he'd been injured.

Jodie wasn't like that. Asleep, it was somehow easier to see her inner strength. The raw drive it must have taken to make it up to the SEAL standard as a dog handler. It was a kind of beauty he wasn't that used to seeing on women. Emily had it, and Lauren. But it was damn rare in his experience.

He wanted to go and squat down in front of her. Study that face. Watch her wake.

But he also understood her physical position: ready for instant battle.

Stan knew that waking her accidentally could be a fatal mistake.

What could have so pissed her off that she'd take such a position? He tried to see it, but even squinting down the length of the building didn't make it any clearer.

He looked down at the box lunch Ama had handed him after he'd eaten his own. The box had chicken, slaw, a cookie, and a can of soda. In her typical fashion, Ama hadn't said a word but she'd made two things clear.

One, Ama had befriended Jodie and the woman didn't do such things lightly.

Two, Jodie hadn't eaten much despite saying she'd had enough.

Seeing Jodie asleep, without anger darkening her features, he also understood why she hadn't come in to lunch with him. In her sleep, he could now see that she wore no mask of fury. That must be for him alone.

Now the scenario before him made perfect sense.

He'd left Bertram outside Brandy's cage so that the dog wouldn't wake alone.

But Jodie's position said that Bertram had taken his guard duties too seriously and hadn't let Jodie near her own dog. And Jodie would see that as his doing. As if Stan was trying to keep her away from Brandy. As if he didn't trust her near her own dog.

If that's what she thought, he was surprised she hadn't come hunting him, blade drawn. He'd kill any bastard who tried to block him from getting to Bertram.

He flashed a signal.

Bertram rose to his feet. With a single glance into the cage as if reassuring himself that Brandy was okay, he padded silently over to Stan.

Stan set the lunch box in the middle of the aisle where it would be clearly visible, then headed out with Bertram, leaving Jodie to awaken alone with her dog.

Jodie came fully conscious at the scrape of her knife clearing its sheath as she drew it.

The afternoon shadows lay deep on the cage area.

Brandy whined again, the sound Jodie's subconscious had registered to awaken her.

Nothing else moved.

The big Malinois who'd been guarding Brandy's cage was gone.

A glance down the row showed all of the cages still standing empty. A small box sat in the middle of the concrete aisle that ran the length of the building.

Her instincts screamed IED even as her brain knew that was ridiculous here. There was just enough light to see the ranch's running-horse logo on the sky-blue box. Maybe Ama had sent her a box lunch, but hadn't woken her because she thought Jodie was sleeping from exhaustion rather than waiting to kill a man. That sounded a little extreme—maybe just maim him. Except he already had been maimed.

Before her mind could spiral completely out of control, she sheathed her knife and pushed to her feet. Four hours, her body told her by its stiffness. Brandy wasn't the only one who needed more exercise.

In the cage, Brandy greeted her with an eager tail thump and actually rose to meet her at the gate. Jodie opened it and knelt. She hugged Brandy's neck with one hand and did the automatic rubdown check with her other. No injuries. The lumps of thick scar tissue all down one side except where her doggie Kevlar vest had protected her internal organs. No whine as she checked over legs and tail.

But Stan was right. Jodie could feel every rib and every knob of Brandy's spine despite the thick coat. Each leg was a study in skeletal structure, not the heavy muscle of a willing and able war dog.

"We've gone through some changes, haven't we, girl?"

Brandy leaned her head into Jodie's chest.

No wonder Stan didn't trust her with a dog. She would never trust a handler who let their dog get into such condition. Jodie did her best to look at Brandy objectively. Despite a good daily brushing, there was no shine to her coat. Her fur didn't even lie flat.

Unable to stand looking at her any longer, Jodie just wrapped her arms around Brandy's neck. Willing Brandy to forgive Jodie for her blindness.

Blindness?

Self-absorption?

Denial?

She didn't know which of them was the worst. But the Malinois lay her muzzle on Jodie's shoulder just as she used to out in the field despite all of her mistakes.

It was all the way back in boot camp that Jodie had learned not to cry. The drill sergeants attacked any sign of weakness. They attacked it with vitriol, ridicule, and a thousand other weapons they kept in their arsenal. After the end of her first 10K run in full gear, she'd collapsed at the finish line, weeping with the pain. Her time had been good, but the pain was unlike anything she'd ever known. The verbal and emotional abuse they'd heaped on her had been far worse.

"Fucking Jewish princess" had only been their starting point.

She'd almost gone seeking an Entry Level Separation. Instead she'd dug in and buried all emotion as deep and hard as she could. Never again was a drill sergeant going to have that kind of power over her.

No man ever did.

She'd never hardened her heart to her dogs, but neither had she ever cried again—not even at seeing Brandy's horrific injuries.

Now, this poor, sweet animal who had depended on her and trusted her had no idea how badly Jodie had let her down.

"Never again, Brandy. I promise, never again." She turned her face into the dog's neck fur.

When Brandy leaned into her, it almost broke her. The unhesitating trust.

"I'll make you better. Somehow. I'll do it."

Fighting down a sniffle, she pushed away before she wept into the dog's fur.

She snagged the leash that had been hanging outside the cage and snapped it on.

Brandy looked at her doggie bed.

"Only going to get better if we push ourselves."

Reluctantly, Brandy fell in at the heel position and Jodie led her out of the cage. Brandy snuffled to the box lunch but didn't trigger and sit to mark it as an explosive. That was good, but no way could Jodie eat anything, not with how her stomach felt knotted up. Stan must have brought it or the big Malinois would never have left his guard post. If the box lunch was a peace offering from Stan, he could just go to hell.

The dogs' training course lay to the northeast, the ranch house to the west, and the horse barns southwest. Jodie turned southeast and headed for the driveway. She'd thought to be many miles down this road by this time.

She hesitated at her truck, but where could she go? Brandy would be miserable in Brooklyn. Was Jodie supposed to settle in someplace like Little Creek? It would have the familiarity of the base where… Where every single member of SEAL Team 8 would look at them both with that mixture of pity that they were now on the outside and horror that it might ever happen to them.

"We certainly couldn't find any place more nowhere than here, could we, girl? The nearest pizza is over thirty miles up this road." She led Brandy down the driveway toward the road.

At the first curve in the driveway, the ranch disappeared from view behind a high bluff. She could feel the pressure ease.

"Maybe we'll just keep walking until we reach that pizza. Get us a double pepperoni. What do you think?"

Brandy just kept her head down as she shuffled along.

At least she was moving. Both of them. Moving forward.

That was a good thing.

Wasn't it?

It was past time to feed the dogs and bed them down for the night. It had been a good day of training. Timmy had run them hard all morning, then Stan had sent them repeatedly through the full obstacle course until they were actually slowing down, which was hard to do to a Malinois. That's when he ran them out to the explosives course—making them race the two miles behind his truck to grind them down even more.

They'd still hit high scores, though only Bertram had nailed the elusive DET cord in every location. It was the dog whistle of smells—so marginally detectable that it was more of an itch than an actual sensing for a dog.

They all got a free ride home in the back of his pickup for a job well done.

In the shadows of the evening light, he didn't see Jodie's truck at first. A panic sweat made the steering wheel slick against his one palm that could still sweat.

"No," he whispered it at first, but then it built within him. "No. No. NO. NO! You did not just leave and take your dog, you bitch. You didn't—"

Then he saw her pickup, the black truck hood emerging from the shadows.

He blew out a breath—hard—and was glad that the only one in the cab to see his stupidity was Bertram. Timmy had headed to the horse barns after lunch, so it was just him and the dogs.

But in the kennel, the last cage in the row was empty, its gate swung open. The leash was gone. He hurried to shoo the dogs into their cages and almost tripped on the box lunch. It sat there in the middle of the aisle, untouched.

"What the hell does that mean?"

He settled the dogs in record time, just dumping food in each bowl without bothering to measure. No added protein powder tonight for their glossy coats. Food. Water. Latch the gates. Done.

Still no sign of her or where she'd gone.

"Think, Corman. Think. Her truck is here, she isn't."

He strode down to the last cage, but it was barren.

Her truck. He hurried outside, but the portable cage in the truck bed was empty.

Stan stood where she must have.

What had she seen? They had the same training. How had her mind worked in that moment?

The woman was a goddamn mystery to him, how the fuck was he supposed to know? Let her sink, swim, or go to hell—or Brooklyn. She wasn't his problem.

But the dog.

Jodie had made the dog his responsibility.

He looked at the truck in the half light. It was a typical SEAL truck: solid, American, heavy-duty enough to move a SEAL fireteam and their gear while towing their insertion boat, even if it would never have had to. Probably five or six years old, but in perfect condition except for the road dust from crossing the country. SEAL POVs— personally owned vehicles—spent most of their lives parked in a stateside garage while their owners were overseas, so low mileage, maybe even the original rubber despite its age.

Get in her head.

Jodie would have stood here next to her vehicle because it was a natural place to stop coming out of the kennel.

Think like a SEAL.

Again, who knew how she thought.

He pulled out a penlight and squatted down to shine it low across the dirt.

Boots…and there, a dog print.

Stan scooted forward, keeping his eyes on the dirt. Southeast. Headed like an arrow toward the driveway.

Had her truck broken down and she was going to *walk* her dog all the way back to Brooklyn? While he wouldn't put it past her, he guessed that she'd gone out for a walk, but for some reason hadn't come back.

He clicked off the light. Even that little bit of delay had been too much. The sky was shifting from blood red to nighttime deep blue.

No way could he follow her visually. Thankfully he didn't have to.

Hurrying inside, he opened Bertram's cage. Stan led the dog down to Brandy's spot and directed Bertram to her dog bed.

"Verloren." *Lost.* Generally a tracker dog and an explosives dog received two very different sets of training, but Bertram had clearly been getting bored about just finding explosives and Stan had expanded his lessons to include tracking scents on the fly. It had been a challenge because Stan's own training hadn't involved much tracking. It was the teacher just one step ahead of the dog the whole way. He'd consumed any books he could lay his hands on and had spent hours on the phone with different trainers. Now to see if it paid off.

Bertram huffed eight or nine breaths at Brandy's dog bed in as many seconds, then looked up expectantly.

He then led Bertram out to the tracks by the truck and hoped they weren't too old. There was only a gentle breeze, so maybe the scent hadn't been wholly erased.

"Such." *Seek.*

Bertram sniffed the air, high-and-low, then side-to-side.

Then he set off at a light trot. His first line was straight out the driveway, which fit Stan's guesses…and fears.

He followed close behind.

Jodie had to roust Brandy soon for another stretch of road but didn't know if she was up for it herself. Maybe they'd spend the night here, curled up in the deep grass along the dirt roadside. She could do worse, but not much. Her jacket was in her truck, and while it wasn't cold, yet, the temperature had started falling with the setting sun. That had been a while ago and she didn't know how low it would go beneath the clear sky.

Brandy had drunk some water before leaving the cage, but Jodie hadn't and her throat was so parched that it hurt to breathe.

The last of the light had revealed nothing and she'd been too exhausted on the drive in to remember one stretch of nowhere dirt road from another. There was a barbed wire fence and miles of grass on the other side of the road. The only difference on this side was that the ground rose so she couldn't see anything. She definitely didn't have the energy to climb the roll of land to see where she was—which would be pointless since it was black as…well, night.

She considered phoning for help, but she didn't have the number of anyone at the ranch. She'd have to call Nikita, who'd have to go find Altman, to whom she'd have to explain how she'd totally fucked up once again. Then Altman would have to call Stan to come rescue the helpless female. Not a chance it was going down that way.

Besides, her phone was in her jacket pocket. That there probably wasn't any signal out here anyway wasn't much of a self-soother at the moment.

It was her own damn fault that she hadn't been thinking. Without noticing, she'd walked Brandy right out to her limits, leaving her with no reserves for the walk back to the ranch.

Which meant it was up to her to carry her dog. Dog carry was a standard part of training. It was also one of the reasons that the Belgian Malinois were favored over German Shepherds—they typically weighed fifteen to twenty pounds less. While it was a big difference out in the field, it wasn't helping her so much right now.

But Brandy was shattered—not going to sleep but just flopping onto her side the instant Jodie set her down each time. Even after numerous long carries, the dog could barely stand up on her own. She was way past any chance of walking. Anyone who did this to a dog should be taken out and shot. Not an instructor in the military who wouldn't boot her ass for this.

Well, her ass was very thoroughly kicked.

Brandy's convalescence had enforced a convalescence on Jodie as well without her really noticing. Her muscle tone and endurance were shot to shit. Carrying Brandy across her shoulders was something she could manage only in short stints, and starting the next carry wasn't going to happen anytime soon.

It was so dark that the starlight was all that showed her the road. She'd done enough night patrols out beyond the fence in countries that couldn't afford electric light to know how bright the stars could be. But she'd never really noticed it in the US before. Brooklyn wasn't exactly the star-watching capital of the country. Here they were bright enough to see the road but, unlike the Southern Hemisphere with its broad band of the Milky Way shining in the night, the Montana stars weren't bright enough to show the potholes. Every third step was a hard jar as she stumbled into yet another hole and fought for balance with fifty pounds of Malinois across her shoulders.

"There," she pointed out to Brandy. "Orion and Canis Major, that's *big dog* like you, are just setting. Canis Minor, which so isn't you, will be down soon. It's not like you're a military war Chihuahua. I'd like to get to a bed before the little dog rises again. What do you say? Want to try walking yourself for a bit?"

She knew it was pointless to ask. Not only was Brandy out past even her Malinois limits, but she also didn't speak English and wouldn't have understood a word.

"It would really help if you could understand. Then I could explain how sorry I am. How sorry for…everything."

With one hand buried in Brandy's fur where she lay beside Jodie, she used the other to pull her knees up close so that she could rest her forehead on them.

"We get out of this, I promise to never fuck up again. Honest." Regrettably, reality sucked and getting Brandy to a bed with food and water was Jodie's sole priority.

She sat there wondering why her training in how to dig deep in extreme situations had never covered this particular scenario. Montana wilderness. No radio. No traffic—ground or air—to signal for help. Just her and a hoot owl somewhere in the distance. Not as if the owl had bothered telling her how close she was to the ranch. It could be around the corner or another two miles.

Something. She looked up. The only other sound—

"Yipes!" A huge shadow appeared just inches away. The shadow sniffed loudly at her once, then sat abruptly.

Moments later a big man-shaped shadow moved in behind the dog. She didn't need to see the starlight shining through the gaps in his arm's structure to recognize Stan.

"How did—" No. How he found her was obvious by the big dog snout still inches from her face.

Stan complimented the big Malinois lavishly in that high, happy voice that all dog handlers used unabashedly, in public or not. It actually sounded just fine to her ear, even coming from as macho a dude as Stan Corman.

"*Why* did you find me? You're not gonna convince me you were worried about me."

His shrug outlined against the stars was eloquent. "What happened?"

"We wanted to get away by ourselves and do some stargazing. Now go away."

Stan's silence was even more eloquent than his shrug.

"I was stupid! Okay? I screwed up. I do that. Just ask my parents. 'Navy, dear. What ever gave you such an awful idea? Oh no, that will never do.' I'm a professional screwup. Again! You happy now? I was trying to get Brandy a second round of exercise for the day and I forgot about getting back after hitting her limits. I've just walked my dog into the ground and now I feel dumber than shit—which isn't very smart stuff to begin with. So bring it on, Corman. Tell me how else I fucked up. Go ahead. Set your dog to guard against me ever getting near Brandy again." She finally bit it off because her voice was shifting dangerously close to a scream. Which also made her parched throat hurt like hell now that she'd stopped.

He let the silence of the Montana nighttime sky fill the air for a bit before asking, "How far?"

She looked back up the road and couldn't remember. "Ten carries. Maybe fifteen. I started at a couple hundred meters per. I barely hit a hundred on the last one." And she could feel every inch of it as a throbbing in her legs and shoulders. Two klicks or close enough.

"Okay if I carry her for a bit?"

Jodie wanted to shout no. *She* was the one who'd screwed up and it was up to *her* to fix it. And Stan Corman being solicitous? No idea what the hell was up with that.

He must have taken her silence as consent.

In moments he'd coaxed Brandy to her feet. Then he scooped up fifty pounds of Malinois one-handed and draped her across his shoulders in a fireman's carry as if she weighed no more than a winter scarf.

He hadn't let himself go to shit. Even three years out and missing an arm, Stan was in incredible condition that was reflected in every move he made. Rubbing in even worse what a failure she'd turned out to be.

When he started off, Jodie tried to follow, but it wasn't as easy as it looked. Her muscles had seized up from sitting too long at the roadside. When she did reach her feet, the stars took a vicious spin as her crashed blood sugar almost plowed her back to the ground.

"You okay?"

"Go to hell, Corman."

He sighed. Then he whispered, "Bertram." She hadn't known his dog's name. Stan moved his arm, but she couldn't follow the signal in the darkness.

Apparently Bertram could as he moved into the heel position on her left side and leaned into her thigh. With his steadying reference, her body finally decided which way was up and her head stopped spinning. When Bertram moved forward, to a signal she hadn't seen at all, she moved with him. He was big enough that she could rest her hand on his head without bending at all. So she did and gave him a pat of thanks.

Fifty, seventy-five, a hundred. She'd taken to counting her steps to force herself ahead. At two hundred she asked, "Need me to take a turn?"

Stan snorted out a laugh. "Lady, I'm surprised you can carry yourself.

When was the last time you ate? More than the two bites of chicken at lunch."

"Breakfast."

"No, you were with me this morning. Testing Brandy—" *Yeah, real smooth mentioning that, Stan.* He'd been busy scaring the shit out of her dog. He could still feel the eerie sound of Brandy's howl creeping up his spine. "Uh, this morning."

"Breakfast *yesterday*. Brandy and I got some drive-thru at a place named Billings around dawn. Five hours from there to the ranch, I guess. Couple bites of a burrito. Half a chicken leg at lunch today."

"And you just did a two-klick carry of a dog that weighs half as much as you? That's SEAL tough, lady." Something he hadn't really expected from the woman, whether she served on a SEAL team or not. He'd assumed that they'd taken her on to the team just for her dog, but clearly she'd lived up to the standard.

"Would be if I hadn't first been JG stupid."

Stan had to laugh. Nothing dumber than a lieutenant junior grade —fresh-minted out of school and thinking he knew shit. "Nobody out here gonna hold that against you."

He liked this. Walking along, just talking. He didn't do it much. When he and Patrick had been sharing a bunkroom, he'd at least had someone to tease. Ever since Patrick had moved in with Lauren, Stan realized he hadn't talked to much of anyone. But clearly it was going to be up to him to keep the conversation going. Not exactly something he was good at.

"What do you miss most?" Seemed like a safe topic.

"About being inside or about home?" Her voice creaked. Next time he staged a rescue, he'd grab a water bottle and an energy bar before heading out. Hell, he hadn't even paused to grab a med kit. Not like him. Thank God neither of them was bleeding out.

"Either. Home."

"Sal's Pizza. Family place in Brooklyn. They sell it by the slice, each as big as your head. Anything you want on it, as long as it's cheese, and sausage or pepperoni. Enough grease that it will leave you stained to the elbows. The best red sauce in all of New York. Two slices will leave you bloated like that camel I mentioned and wishing you had room for a third. How about you?"

"Pa's steaks. He grilled a mean one. Nothing fancy. Salt and pepper. Sage butter and grill sauce. Miss them still."

"What happened to him?"

"He was a boiler welder—pretty specialized and high demand in the welding world. Means we traveled a lot. Just lived out of the RV and rolled to wherever the job was. I think my record was seven different schools for fifth grade, but we were solid. Real close. While I was overseas, he got into something bad. No one's sure exactly what happened. They think a junior welder bled some acetylene onto a copper feed pipe, then torched it off. Burned up the hose and back to the tank, which blew apart and killed all four guys inside the boiler."

"I'm sorry."

"Not you're doing. Besides, he had asbestosis from work he'd done as a kid for a shyster building contractor. At least he went out fast, 'cause the cancer was sure gonna take him slow and ugly." Didn't mean Stan didn't miss him. Or his steaks. "Your old man still around?"

"Yes. He's a librarian in New York. And Mom's a nurse. I still live in the house Mom was born in. My little brother lives upstairs with his wife and kid. Grandparents in Florida."

"You've got family. They're close. That's good." Stan ignored the fact that after Ma ran off, there'd only ever been him and Pa. If there were grandparents anywhere, Pa had never mentioned them.

Brandy shifted restlessly on his shoulders. He slid his good hand up to pat her on the side behind his head. Her head was over by his hooks, so he couldn't do much to comfort her from that side. All across her flank, he could feel the scars.

"How did it go down?" No need to explain that question to another SEAL.

The night grew colder as the silence stretched out—stretched out a long way.

He finally glanced over to make sure Jodie was still beside him.

"My dog didn't screw up," she finally growled.

"Never said she did." Neither had his. *He* had been the one who'd screwed up and gotten his Lucy and his team killed. They'd walked into the jaws of a trap, but he'd had point. He should have known. "Look, let's talk about someth—"

"A mortar," Jodie snapped it out. "Dropped right in the middle of the marketplace we were patrolling. Brandy was off-leash—well ahead of me on point. It landed right next to her, blew her through the air nearly ten meters. Killed six civilians and injured another twenty. Single shot, our teams never found the raghead killing his own people."

"Shit. Ugly. But it wasn't anything you could have fixed."

"You think I don't know that? That's not why I stayed overseas for two months after they gave me my DD 214 medical discharge. I did that to make sure Brandy came home on her own four feet instead of inside an ash urn."

"Medical?" Wasn't a thing wrong with Jodie Jaffe that he could see.

"Eardrum and most of the little shit behind it. The mortar blew out my right ear," she grumbled it out like it was a stain on her character. "Can't serve without directional hearing."

"Thought they had implants for stuff like that."

"And would you be willing to have the VA carry out a hundred-thousand-dollar operation to dig into your brain and hook electronics straight into your nervous system? Because if you say you are, I'm going to call you a lying asshole. Otherwise you wouldn't have that old pair of hooks instead of a modern prosthesis. I'm not saying that they can't do it. I'm just saying that it isn't my first choice by a long shot. I function just fine. Still have my balance, which surprised the docs."

Stan mused that it was yet another thing they had in common. Patrick's mom was all set to wire him up like a goddamn cyborg. What was left of Stan was all him, except for a few titanium plates and a fistful of screws. When he took off his arm at night, all that was left was pure Stan and that let him sleep just fine at night, except when the nightmares used to kick his ass.

He shifted Brandy a little to make sure she stayed comfortable—or as comfortable as possible during a shoulder carry.

Jodie fell silent as they turned into the driveway. It would have been shorter to cut over the bluff—she'd been sitting directly opposite the ranch house, right where he'd first seen her truck arriving. But he'd chosen the flatter route along the road and up the drive because he wasn't sure Jodie could negotiate the hill in her current condition.

By the faint light that reached this far from the cabins and main house, he could see the look on her face. He knew it well. She was deep in The Grind. It was the place out past the breaking point, except SEALs didn't break.

Stan knew that he hadn't been nearly that strong when he'd come home and eventually come here to the ranch. He'd dug in because you didn't say no to people like Luke Altman or Mac Henderson. Not because he cared for shit in those first months. There'd been days when he hadn't even crawled out from under the covers.

Not Jodie Jaffe. Pale as the light from a crescent moon, she still placed one boot in front of the other.

Half his size and twice the guts. What would he have done if he'd been like her?

He'd joined the Navy to get the college education that Pa couldn't afford. Pa had said it was the way out, but Stan had never made it past the first semester. Too damned boring. He'd turned down several "suggestions"—that were closer to orders from multiple commanders —to apply for OCS. Hitting Officer Candidate School would have meant leaving the dogs. He'd never aspired to more and turned them down cold. Pa had been fine with it when Stan told him why.

Jodie had educated parents, but had chosen the Navy and dogs herself. How strong had she been to go against her family's wishes? Damn strong. She was clearly a driven woman.

At the cages, he eased Brandy down. She drank water and wolfed down about half the dinner he set out before she collapsed onto the dog bed. The dog was asleep before she'd done that characteristic curl up of hers with her nose under her tail.

When he went to guide Bertram down to his cage, the dog looked at him askance.

"You want to keep her company, boy?"

Wouldn't hurt anything.

"Okay with you?" He turned to Jodie, but she was out on her feet. With how tightly curled up Brandy was, the dog bed was big enough for two. It was also clear that the dog was too far out to care as Bertram settled beside her. He lay downand rested his muzzle on Brandy's back, looking set for the night.

He swung the gate shut, then wondered if he needed to get Jodie up in a shoulder carry to get her settled too. He put a water bottle in her hand. Some automaton part of her training kicked in and she raised it to her lips. Once she started, she knocked the whole bottle straight down. Still weaving, at least she showed some signs of consciousness.

"Food first," Stan decided.

He tried to take her elbow to guide her, but misjudged. He'd reached for her with his left hand and the hooks closed on thin air rather than his fingers coming to rest lightly. That was twice in two days he'd forgotten his arm was mechanical. Very weird. He was always conscious of the hooks that had made him half a man.

Apparently his motion was enough and Jodie headed out of the cage under her own impetus.

He led her past the bunkhouse and up to the main kitchen. Dinner would have been done long since, but Nathan always had enough leftovers around that he could scrounge up something. It was one of their first weeks with full staff and full guest cabins, so everyone should have dispersed by now. He often waited until after everyone else had gone off to relax or bed down before coming up here.

The kitchen was quiet except for Ama standing at one of the counters. She'd turned over the bulk of the ranch cooking to Nathan, who was assisted by Ama's daughter-in-law Emily, but she still kept a hand in.

"Hey, Ama."

His simple comment evoked a whirlwind of responses. Chelsea popped up from one of the big armchairs by the fireplace like a Jill-in-a-Box. Emily emerged close behind her. In moments all three women had surrounded Jodie, herding her to the big Doug fir table more effectively than a whole pack of sheepdogs. Once a full meal was placed in front of her and Jodie had started eating, Chelsea came to plant herself in front of him.

"What did you do to her, Stan?" She actually looked pissed, a very rare expression on her face.

"Nothing. I—"

"She's more skittish than her dog. And you drove her until she's like that?" Chelsea stabbed a finger in Jodie's direction.

"But—"

"Get out of here, Stan. Before someone hurts you."

Jodie could hear Chelsea getting it all wrong, but couldn't find the energy to stop her. It took keeping her elbows firmly planted on the table—her mother would be horrified—to keep from falling sideways.

All that had kept her from putting her head down on the table and going to sleep had been Ama setting the dinner plate squarely in the target zone before she was even fully seated. A fresh grilled burger with mashed potatoes smothered in a gravy so rich and thick she could use it as skin cream. There was something green too. Roasted Brussels sprouts still crispy around the edges. She slathered on some butter to hide the flavor, then wished she hadn't—they tasted surprisingly good.

All the food did.

Maybe it was just her body's hunger. She was halfway through the meal before she became aware of the women grouped around her. Once again she'd landed to Ama's left, with Chelsea to her other side and Emily across from her at Ama's right.

"Where's Stan?"

"I sent him to bed without supper," Chelsea proclaimed defiantly.

"He—"

"Don't worry. We won't let him near you again. Do you want to talk about it? I mean if you don't, I understand. But you really should because—"

"Chelsea," was all Ama had to say.

It still took Jodie a conscious effort to batter her way through the barrage of words even after they'd stopped. "He didn't do anything. He carried Brandy for me." *After I totally screwed up.*

"He shouldn't— Wait. What?" Chelsea cut herself off. "Then who kicked your ass? 'Cause you sure look ragged, girlfriend. Who do I have to kill?"

"Me, I guess. Did it to myself," she was able to slow down enough to taste the last bite of the burger. Top quality beef—maybe from the ranch. Light pink in the middle, crunchy on the outside. Salt, pepper, and just the perfect dash of barbeque sauce. Just perfect. She regretted not tasting the rest of it.

"You did this to yourself? Are you crazy?"

Thankfully Chelsea didn't wait for an answer because Jodie knew where her own vote would land.

"Oh no! Really? Oh, man! I'll go fix a plate and take it to him. Do you think some chocolate or something for an apology? I'm always putting my foot in it. You think I'd learn someday but *no-o*, not me. Crumbs!" Apparently Chelsea's idea of a foul curse. She rushed away to the stove.

At her soft exclamation of surprise, Jodie turned to see Chelsea peeking into a box lunch container sitting on the counter.

"Oh, thanks, Ama. I'll just deliver this. Don't anyone go anywhere before I get back. No, wait. It's almost Cristopher's beddy-bye time. Gotta scoot. Bye. Stop doing things like this to yourself, girlfriend." And the whirlwind that was Chelsea headed out the door so fast that her long red hair was fluttering behind her.

Girlfriend. Jodie hadn't had a lot of those in high school. Bedford Academy had been academically demanding and brand new—she'd been in the first class through. The girls who weren't husband hunting had all been brainiacs who were out to become overachievers. She'd fit in with none of them.

Being one of the few female jocks, the coach had made her volleyball setter and softball first base. That had made her even more of a stranger there than she'd been in her own family. The other girls didn't like being outperformed by one of the few white kids in the entire school. Her "Princess" nickname—short for "the fucking bitch Jewish Princess we wish was dead"—had stuck like glue through all four years. Of course the Jewish Princesses of her neighborhood wanted nothing to do with the girl going to school in Bed-Sty. She still had no idea how she'd ended up way over there. Bedford Academy was over twenty blocks from Frontiers High where all the local Jews went.

There'd been no girlfriends once she joined the SEALs either—because there weren't any other women in her squad. That had been fine with her. Nikita had been more acquaintance than friend before making it into ST6.

Emily laughed softly. "That's our Chelsea. She's right. I better go check on Tessa and Belle. Mark will give in to their begging for more stories all night if I let him."

Jodie was startled when Emily rested a hand on her shoulder, making her look up to where Emily had circled to stand beside her.

"The transition back is never easy. It's a long road." Then she was gone.

Jodie didn't know whether to scoff or...what? She couldn't seem to connect the majestic blonde Night Stalker with a husband and two children to anything that could possibly be relevant in her own situation.

Now the peace of the kitchen settled over them like a warm blanket, only she and Ama remained.

"Way better than the cold and foodless prairie I thought I'd be sleeping in," she said to break the ice.

Ama didn't make her nervous, but her silence was of staggering dimensions.

"I took my dog for a walk. Forgot how weak she is. How weak," Jodie swallowed it like a bitter pill, "we both are." After all, she deserved it. "I walked out until we had nothing in us to come back with."

"Yet you came back anyway."

"Most of the way, but I didn't know that."

Ama nodded. She'd sat the whole time with her hands folded on the table, her stillness so deep that it drew attention to the soft crackling of the dying fire as the only sound aside from Jodie's own heart.

"Yet you kept walking."

Jodie shrugged, unsure how to answer.

Ama's dark eyes finally shifted to look at the ceiling, but not as if she was actually seeing it. When she finally spoke, it was very softly.

"For twenty years I kept walking. I loved a man who loved being a SEAL. For twenty years I walked mostly alone, wondering each day if he'd come back to me. He did. And now we walk together. But I know about the hardship of the long walk."

Then all of Ama's focus shifted to her, and Jodie couldn't have moved or spoken if her life had depended on it.

"My daughter-in-law is wiser than she knows. It *is* a long road. But I see you have the strength to walk it."

Jodie managed not to laugh, poking her fork into the last Brussels sprout roasted to crunchy sweetness.

"You don't believe it. For now," Ama opened her hands palm upward, "I will hold that belief safe for you until you are ready to take it back." Then she curled her hands closed before holding them tightly against her chest.

Jodie closed her eyes against the image.

The only people who had ever believed in her were her fellow SEALs—and being female in a male world, that acceptance had taken years.

Even her family didn't. They loved her, she didn't doubt that. But it was love without understanding. Their daughter was as much of an enigma to them as an Al-Shabab terrorist would be.

"Why—" But when she opened her eyes, her empty plate was gone, as was Ama.

CHAPTER 7

S tan was squatting over Brandy when he felt Jodie come up behind him. Midmorning, so she must have finally gotten some sleep. He'd already run all of the other dogs through the obstacle course for a couple of hours. She'd stopped behind him and didn't come any closer.

"What? No knife in the back?"

At the continued silence, he turned to look up at her. She was biting her lower lip.

"You've got something stuck in your craw. Any chance of you spitting it out?"

She shook her head, then offered him a half smile of chagrin. Even that partial change was transformative. The SEAL-fit woman, who was somewhat off on her conditioning, had shifted aside. In her place stood a lovely woman with a sharp intelligence and a sense of the ridiculous. "If I do, will you be throwing it back in my face?"

"Chances are good. You know it's SEAL rule 543, never let a straight line go by untrammeled."

"Figures," she took a breath to steel herself.

He wished she was wearing a jacket so that his attention wasn't struggling quite so desperately to travel downward. Jodie's tight t-shirt offered a lot of nice shapes to look at and it *had* been a damn long time. Stan hadn't really missed it much until Jodie Jaffe rolled onto the ranch, but now…

"Thanks for last night." She kicked a boot at the kennel's concrete floor.

"Oh, was it good for you too?"

"Oh, yeah, sailor. You sure know how to show a girl a good time. Carry her dog and everything," then her smile went out like a light switch, but he wasn't going to forget about it so easily. "Sorry Chelsea went after you."

He shrugged, then grinned.

"You made her grovel," Jodie didn't make it a question.

"Not too much. The dinner smelled too good and I was hungry." Time for a subject change. "Your dog is sore, but not as bad as I feared. You did good carrying her back last night. Need to go easy today."

"Easier than yesterday anyway." He could hear Jodie beating herself up for it. She was a dog handler who'd overstepped her dog's resources, so no surprise there. He'd be deep in self-recrimination too.

"Couple of local walks and another swim. There's a small swimming lake back behind the cabins over the ridge. Gets campers in the after-noon, but mornings are pretty quiet what with classes and trail rides. Go up the main path and you'll see a sign just after the cabin named Aspen."

"You fed her?"

At his nod, Jodie slapped her left thigh.

Brandy rose to her feet and did more of a shuffle than a trot over to Jodie.

"Oh girl," Jodie knelt to greet her in squeaky dog voice. "My poor girl with the crazy handler. I'll make it up to you. Yes I will. I will. I will." She went higher with each repetition.

Brandy was wagging her tail happily at her handler's obvious excitement. At least obvious to a dog.

Stan did his best to keep his smile to himself.

First, Jodie the seriously tough warrior. Then, Jodie the majorly contrite dog handler. Now, just too damn cute for words.

What next? The moaning lover?

He blinked hard at the thought. Where the hell had that image come from? Though it was hard to deny it was a good one. Then he started wondering what that reality might actually look like and decided he was in deep shit. So wasn't going to happen with a half-man like him.

"You want to join us?" Jodie's soft question surprised him. And made it worse. Picturing that t-shirt soaked from a swim so that it clung—

He opened his mouth to say yes, but the dogs' graduation was less than a week away. That's when he'd find out if everything he'd done for almost three years was for nothing. Mac Henderson had taken him on when he was a seriously bad bet. Stan *needed* this to work. Needed to prove to Mac that his faith hadn't been in vain. At $40,000 and up for a dog trained to Special Operations' standards, these dogs would also go a long way to paying back all Mac had invested in Stan and his dream.

"Gonna have to pass. I want to work these guys hard today."

She simply turned to go.

"Jodie?"

"Yeah?" She looked back at him over her shoulder.

"Thanks for asking." Damn but he wouldn't mind spending a little more time with her. His body was definitely giving signals that it was thinking about it in other ways, too.

"Okay."

"Maybe a run later?"

For the briefest instant her glance slid over to his artificial arm.

Normally he'd be pissed. He'd certainly taken some of the ranch hands down a few rungs for just as little. But Jodie didn't slam his anger switch.

"It weighs about half of my meat arm. Caused me some balance issues early on, but those went away fast." If anything could be said to be fast about the healing process followed by learning to use the prosthetic. "I actually had to wait for the amputation by IED to heal before

I added the arm, so the half-original weight felt more natural than none at all."

He never talked to anyone about his arm. Even bunking with Patrick for three years, they'd mentioned his arm only once or twice. And never how he'd lost it. Why had he thrown that in? To test and see if she *could* be pushed away? If he repulsed her?

"Okay." She didn't react one way or the other.

Most women shied away from even looking at the entire left side of his body. He'd seen Chelsea's pity and saw Lauren doing the standard ex-military thing of not looking and being damn glad it hadn't been her. Neither Ama nor Emily had ever made a thing of it, making them his ideal standard for women. His fucking fiancée sure hadn't passed the test—dumping his ass sight unseen. That was why he'd refused a cosmesis. If people needed a cosmetic arm to be comfortable around him, they could go suck on a howitzer.

Jodie treated it like it was just a fact of life. Even all that time rooming together, Patrick had never quite managed that.

After she and Brandy were gone, he went down the row, letting the dogs out and getting them moving—an easy task with a Malinois as they were the Energizer Bunny of dogs. When they were arrayed around him for the run over to the shooting range, he realized that he only had six dogs.

Where the hell had Bertram gotten to?

He checked the whole kennel, including Brandy's cage.

He was nowhere in sight.

Stan stepped outside and squinted up at the low ridge behind the cabins. Right where the trail crested the ridge before heading down to the lake, there were three tiny figures. A woman, her dog, and...*his* dog.

What the hell?

Jodie could feel it in her legs from climbing the little hill. It wasn't bad, but it wasn't good. She should never have noticed it as the ridge was less than fifty meters high. Barely a bump.

Bertram padded along silently beside Brandy.

Stan must have sent him to keep an eye on her. He really was unbelievable. Like what was his spy dog going to tell him?

Oh, that Jodie. She's such a bad person. Do you know that she ate pork when she was overseas? What kind of a Jew eats pork? And let me tell you how little she flossed when she was on patrol. As to how she treats poor Brandy, I can tell you...

No. Bertram wasn't there to tell Stan anything. It was just a threat: *My dog is watching you. If you mess up, he'll know.*

Some part of her had to wonder how he'd know, but she didn't doubt that he would.

Bertram wore only his dog collar. No war dog Kevlar vest with a top-mounted infrared camera and GPS sending signals back to his handler. She actually checked the collar, but it was just a standard nylon strap with a break-away buckle. If it caught on something, the dog could snap it rather than be trapped. No embedded micro-cam.

"Fine, Mr. Corman. Glean whatever knowledge you feel you can get from your dog."

For a moment she wondered if Stan had sent him just to keep Brandy company, but such thoughtfulness seemed unlikely.

And what was up with his offer to go for a run together? Like she needed a babysitter to make sure she got back in shape? A SEAL survived by never, ever repeating a mistake. Making up new ones? Sure, in the highly dynamic situations SEAL teams fought in, there was no such thing as perfect. Mistakes were how you learned—unless you made such a bad one that it was fatal.

Anyway, it had been a mistake to let herself and Brandy get so out of shape. It hadn't killed them, so she'd learned, and now it was time to fix it.

When they crested the low ridge, she had to stop and stare. From here, out of the protective bowl in which the ranch nestled, the world seemed to expand outward forever. She hadn't really stopped and looked at it during her semi-demented walk that first day. Now she could only stare. The foothills rolled away to the north and west. Then, like God had personally created these mountains on the Third Day in between making dry land and gathering the waters together in Seas. They soared aloft with a permanence that made New York seem like an ephemeral blink in time.

Closer to hand, the "swimming lake" was a lovely location completely worthy of the fine style that marked everything here at Henderson Ranch. The still water that reflected the brilliant blue sky lay in a broad swale of neatly mown grass. There was a kiddie pool, a middle float, and the prettiest gazebo perched on pylons just off the shore's edge. There were plastic bins of water toys and even one of little-kid life preservers.

And best of all, Stan had been absolutely right: there was not a single soul in sight.

When she waved the dogs forward, Bertram raced toward the water. At the water's edge, he gathered himself for a great leap—one moment all bunched muscle, the next high in the air stretched out to his full length. He splashed into the water in a great spray that shattered the sky reflection into a thousand shards of sunlight and was already swimming as he surfaced.

With his lead, Brandy went in as well. With far less flair, merely walking into the water, but soon she too was swimming.

Jodie looked. No one around to care.

She stripped down to her sports bra and underwear to join the dogs. They swam back to meet her. When she snagged a head-sized plastic ball from the convenient toys bin and heaved it high and hard, they went nuts chasing after it. Malinois were easily entertained, even the smartest of them.

The water was sun-warmed, feeling just refreshingly cool.

She swam out to the dogs, batting the ball as far away as she could as she swam. They chased after the ball and tried to put the bite on it. It was too big, but that didn't diminish their ardor for a moment. Every time they chased it anywhere near her, she batted it again. In between, she swam laps from the kiddie pool wall to the gazebo and back. She counted strokes across three times and ran the math in her head—roughly ten laps per kilometer.

No goggles, but this wasn't some chlorined-up pool, so that was fine. No flippers. Well she wasn't doing an infiltration, she was just swimming.

About the time she hit five laps, Brandy was flagging. Jodie took a moment to coax her out of the water. She lay down on the shore but kept her head up on alert, so apparently not overtired.

Bertram continued chasing the ball through the water.

Jodie continued her laps, changing them up with each lap. Freestyle, rarely used by SEALs, but she'd liked being able to measure herself against Olympic swimmers. She'd never matched their times, of course, but she'd like the competition. Then a lap of breaststroke to change up muscle groups. Finally, the combat swimmer stroke.

Without fins, it wasn't the fastest stroke, but any self-respecting SEAL could do it for hours if necessary. A sideways scissor kick, driving her forward and underwater. A long glide with arms extended. When the shoulder started to ride high, she turned it into a sidestroke dig. Complete the roll and take a breath. Dig in with the leading arm to keep moving. Fire another scissor kick and back into the long glide.

It was low energy, and because most of it was underwater, it made the swimmer that much harder for an enemy to spot.

After ten laps, she shifted completely over to the combat stroke. When her shoulders and legs began to burn with the effort, she started to smile. Twenty laps and it went from burn to sizzle.

Even Bertram had abandoned her, chasing his ball to shore and lying down next to Brandy with the ball resting between them.

At lap twenty-three, the cramp hit. It punched into her calf like a hot knife just as she was rising to take a breath.

Out of air, she curled up into a ball under the water. There was out of air—and *out of air*. SEAL training had taught her the difference, and for the moment, the only thing that mattered was relieving the pain in her leg.

She grabbed her calf with the fingers of both hands, gritted her teeth, and plunged her thumbs into the knot of the muscle cramp. No time to be gentle about it, she kept squeezing until her vision was tunneling from the pain, never mind the lack of oxygen.

Her lungs actually bubbled out some air they'd scraped up from some uncharted depths. It was her signal to get air soon.

One more punch with her thumbs, then a wild flail to the surface while her leg remained twisted up tightly. She grabbed a breath and went back under. It still wasn't letting go. Pulling on her toes to stretch it out was only making it worse.

As she snatched another half breath, she glanced quickly around, then assessed her situation as the cramp pulled her back under. Now her side just below her left ribs was getting in on the game of *Let's Drown Jodie.*

Halfway between the central float and the shore. Twenty yards, maybe thirty, either way. With a double cramp. Even doing a drown-proofing SEAL float was going to be tough. She went under and pounded a fist against her calf muscle, but it wasn't letting go. Digging her palm into her side wasn't helping either.

She knew she could swim through it, but it would be excruciating.

Out of options, she managed to surface for air but didn't get any.

Instead, she got a faceful of wet fur.

She grabbed on. Then got kicked from the other side by another dog.

Reaching out as well as she could, despite the side cramp, she managed to hold on to both dogs. In moments they dragged her from the edge of desperation to kneeling on the muddy bottom.

As soon as she had her breath, she flipped over and sat. Now able to massage the leg cramp more slowly, it finally let go enough for her to move without wanting to cry or scream.

After a group hug, the three of them crawled onto the grassy verge and collapsed.

Brandy licked her face.

"Thanks, that really helps."

She did it again.

Jodie grabbed her muzzle, holding it closed, then kissed her dog on top of her head. "Seriously, that's enough." She scritched Bertram on the head so that he wouldn't feel left out. "Good boy. Amazing boy." She'd wager the rescue had been his idea.

She flopped back on the grass and ever so slowly stretched out her leg. The last of the cramp let go in stages. The one in her side was being far more persistent so she just lay there to wait it out.

"Well that was fun, wasn't it?" she told the big, blue sky.

At long last, between the warm sun and the comfort of the two wet dogs lying against either side, the second cramp let go as well.

She turned her head to face Bertram. "You make a lousy spy."

But he wasn't looking at her. Instead he was looking across Jodie. But not at Brandy, rather across her and up.

Jodie followed his line of interest. By tipping her head back far enough, she managed to get an upside-down view of Ama on a majestic black beast. Her horse had a definite king-of-the-herd attitude. He was definitely pretty enough to be. His long mane was as dark as storm clouds and as smooth as a fall of silk. His tail reached most of the way to the ground.

"Are you okay?"

"Sure."

Ama looked at her for a long moment, then slid from her horse as gracefully as if she'd ridden her entire life. Jodie wasn't sure if she'd ever been this close to a horse. The family had done the occasional summer vacation up to Saratoga Springs. The big outing of each trip had been to Saratoga Race Course. Dad always gave her and her brother each twenty dollars, enough for a two-dollar bet on each of the night's ten races. That, a good dinner, and some friendly family competition on who came out best made for a good memory. After a dozen years overseas, she didn't know if her family even still did that. But horses in her experience were always at a distance.

"Is your dog comfortable around horses?"

"I don't know that she's ever met one. Donkeys never bothered her." Jodie held onto Brandy's collar as Ama led the big black closer. The horse and dog sniffed each other and then both appeared to lose interest. The scent of horse and hay nearly overwhelmed her own senses it was so rich, but if Brandy decided it was okay, then it must be.

Ama loosely knotted the reins over the horse's neck and let go of them. The horse bent down and began cropping the lush grass. Ama pulled a towel from a saddlebag and handed it to Jodie before sitting to Brandy's other side. Brandy sniffed her, then licked her hand, something she did with very few people. She certainly hadn't with Stan Corman, which was a good thing or she and her dog were going to have words.

Jodie looked at the towel and then at herself: a wet sports bra and underwear.

Ama wore brown-and-gray cowboy boots that showed elegant stitching and years of wear. Her calf-length gored denim skirt had enough volume that she'd been able to ride the horse. A simple white cotton blouse and a flat-topped cowboy hat—cow*girl* hat. Apparently cowgirls still existed too—and they didn't have to be all red and pink like Chelsea's outfit. Ama's attire was simple, but elegant.

Jodie did what she could to dry herself off as Ama gazed out over the lake. She got to her feet to go fetch her clothes and tried not to limp. The back of her calf was already turning black-and-blue from where she'd dug at the cramp. A glance at Ama's back, and Jodie stripped off the bra and panties before slipping back into her t-shirt, camos, and Army boots.

The moment she sat down between the dogs again, they rolled back against her legs…and her jeans were instantly wet through and would now smell of dog fur. "You two are more trouble than you're worth. You know that, right?" But she didn't say it in squeaky-high dog voice, so they ignored her.

Ama might have smiled as she continued gazing out across the lake.

"Did you ride out looking for me?"

Ama shook her head, her hair moving as silkily as her horse's mane. "I ride every day that the weather isn't too harsh. My husband joins me on many days, but he has meetings today."

"I'm glad he didn't today." Jodie might have lost most of her modesty as a SEAL, but a Montana ranch wasn't a SEAL team barracks.

"I am as well. Sometimes I need to hear the peace of the land."

Silence. Ama's silence wasn't uncomfortable, as it would be at her family dinner table. It was…simply silence.

The wind cooled her skin. A screech, far away, had her searching around—one-eared tracking just totally sucked—finally following Ama's pointing hand skyward. A big hawk soared on a thermal with its wings well-spread. Ama's horse snorted softly, then the sound of more tearing grass. The wingbeats of a Steller's Jay zipped by her as the black-headed blue jay flitted and perched, then flitted again to perch elsewhere, then again. It moved along the shore of the swimming lake in stops and starts. Sometimes tilting its head as if listening intently.

"Can they really hear worms underground?" She heard that once and never believed it.

Ama nodded.

"Wild." Jodie didn't doubt Ama.

The more Ama waited, the more aware Jodie became of sounds. It was different from her SEAL training, which was all about listening for shifts in patterns and calculating what was a threat and what wasn't.

Here the sounds simply…were.

The richness both made her incredibly aware of the silence to one side, but also seemed like another layer to the land as if it brought it into brighter and sharper focus with each passing moment.

And if she spent any longer listening to them, she'd start analyzing all of the smells. Then maybe she'd kneel on all fours and taste the grass to see what Ama's big black horse found so satisfying about it.

Then while she was kneeling there, she could go looking for her mind. Because she'd certainly lost it somewhere along the way.

CHAPTER 8

S tan's training had been off-kilter all day. Each time he sent a signal for Bertram, and he wasn't there, it was as strange as his missing limb.

The other dogs didn't notice and he was finally able to suppress the additional signal.

But it didn't make him feel any more normal. His neck actually hurt from the number of times he'd craned it around to look for any sign of his dog's return.

When Bertram finally came back, he missed it. One moment he wasn't there, and the next moment he was.

A glance up and he spotted Jodie walking back toward the kennel. Again, walking away from him.

Before he could think, he sliced a hand in her direction, *"Bringen."* *Retrieve.*

Bertram shifted from sitting facing him to sprinting away at full speed in a single twist of pure power. His sprint was so graceful that it was mesmerizing.

Mesmerizing, until Stan realized that he was about to take down Jodie with a full-body blow.

"Nein!" he shouted it out, but it was too late.

Bertram cleared the top rail of the four-foot fence without even tapping it. He hit the ground once, then twisted sideways as he made his final gallop. He slammed sideways into the back of Jodie's knees. It was a technique of his own design for taking down an escaping enemy. Up until this moment, Stan had been rather proud of it.

Jodie's cry of alarm as her feet were swept out from under her was high. The grunt as she landed flat on her back in the dirt was low with having all of the air knocked out of her, but he heard it clearly enough as he sprinted over to her. A cloud of dust enveloped her.

Bertram then grabbed the thin material of her t-shirt in his teeth and tried to drag her toward Stan. The material shredded.

"*Nein!*" he shouted again. "*Sitzen!*"

Bertram stopped as he was shredding the other shoulder of her t-shirt. The dog glanced at him as Stan was vaulting the fence, then with the equivalent of a doggie shrug, he sat on Jodie's chest.

"Goddamn it," Jodie's voice was little more than squeak with eighty pounds of war dog sitting on her diaphragm.

"Bertram. *Fuss!*" Stan slapped his left thigh and Bertram pushed off Jodie's chest and came to stand in the heel position, literally "foot" in German, as in by-my-foot.

"What the hell?" Jodie groaned.

"*Gute hund.*"

"Good dog?" Jodie managed to push herself upright as Stan knelt beside her. "You're complimenting your dog for attacking me? What kind of an asshole are you, Corman?"

"Are you hurt? And Bertram didn't know he was doing anything wrong. He did it exactly as trained. So I had to reassure him. Dogs don't understand it when you delay the feedback for an action. You know that."

"The action of flattening me? You *asked* your dog to flatten my ass? What is wrong with you?"

"Uh," Stan didn't have a good answer for any of that. He'd seen Jodie walking away and responded without thought. All he knew was he hadn't wanted her to leave. "Are you hurt?"

He began inspecting her. Her eyes were clear, so she probably hadn't banged her head. She was rubbing her ribs, but it was a generalized motion, not protecting a particular area. The t-shirt…

The right shoulder was completely gone except for the collar. Not a single toothmark on the front of her shoulder. He reached out and turned her to see the back of her shoulder. Just the lightest of red marks where Bertram's lower canines must have raked across her skin as he gathered up a mouthful of cloth.

She twisted free of his grasp and turned back to face him.

That's when he really focused on her shoulder as more than a potential location for an injury. The loose flaps of the material had fallen away. No bra strap crossed the clear skin. A few lines of old injuries—the inevitable bite and claw marks that were the badge of any MWD handler. The swell of her breast was a smooth rise. The torn fabric barely hid—

The punch caught him hard just below the jugular notch in his collarbone. He tumbled backward. He tucked his arms in tight against his chest. Better a concussion than hit his bad arm again. And he landed on his own back. He felt a thick linear lump under his ribcage.

Bertram yelped as Stan landed on his tail. He caught Stan's ribs with his rear claws as he launched away. The dog's snarl of surprise pulled the other dogs off their Stay. They'd been trained to respond to each other. MWDs didn't often work together, but Stan had wanted them to be able to.

Now, six alarmed Malinois vaulted the fence in unison.

"Platz!" Jodie shouted out.

Much to his surprise, all six dogs jerked to a stop as if they'd hit the end of a heavy chain. Then they lay down abruptly.

He'd had little chance to make sure they'd respond to others as well as they did to him, but Jodie had just proved that his training wasn't about their bond with him, but rather about what they had learned.

He rubbed at his throat. Stan supposed that he deserved it, but hoped that she hadn't just broken his collarbone. If she hadn't, it wasn't for lack of trying. It hurt like hell and he definitely wasn't up to speaking yet. One of her knuckles had caught him right in the vocal chords.

"You do *not* get to stare at my breasts after your dog attacks me."

Stan nodded. And half caught himself going there again.

"Then cover them," he croaked out softly. Reaching for his back collar, he hauled off his t-shirt and tossed it in her face. Women weren't supposed to be as attractive as Jodie Jaffe sitting in the dust.

She tugged it on over her head. It fit her like a tent dress, which was good, because without a bra, his imagination had begun firing badly. She rose to her feet.

This time when she turned to go, he didn't send Bertram to fetch her back.

But he considered it. Yes sir, watching her walk away with his shirt hanging half down her thighs and sliding off her shoulders (and imagining her in nothing else), he definitely considered it.

Jodie checked her shoulder in the mirror and could only look in surprise at the lack of damage. As Bertram's massive jaws had closed over her shoulders, all she could think was that the nearest hospital was thirty miles away over rough dirt roads. Her chances of survival were almost nil. Instead, she could only see the faintest of marks, which were already fading.

She pulled on a dry bra—goddamn Stan Corman to hell—and one of her own t-shirts. She was a SEAL with a dog. Not some babe for ogling.

Then she looked away from the mirror so that she didn't have to see the heat rising to her cheeks. Stan might be missing a wing, but there wasn't a thing wrong with the rest of him. There were burn marks, knife scars, and a myriad array of dog marks—including the pair of livid scrapes along his ribcage from Bertram's launch that must have stung.

There'd also been exquisite pecs, major abs, and big broad shoulders. Still sitting on the ground, surrounded by seven exceptional war dogs in their prime, he made a truly stunning image. He might be shy an arm, but there was no questioning that Stan Corman was pure warrior.

Her phone buzzed.

Hey Jodz! Want to go dancing tonight?

Jodie had to stare at the screen for a moment before she could even make sense of the words. She used to love going out to the clubs, but how did anyone here know that. She hadn't told Stan or Chelsea. And she and Ama had exchanged so few words that her ear still rang with the depth of Ama's silence that wasn't silence at all.

Jodz. Only Davy Golding had ever called her that.

She hadn't told him she'd left Brooklyn.

She'd just…left.

He was the reason she used to enjoy the clubs. He had a sense of fun that had never been one of her strengths. And he made dancing almost as intimate as sex. He'd taught her the basics, then they'd made it up from there together. He'd kept joking that they should enter one of those dance competitions—but she'd gone into the Army and he'd headed off to college, then law school.

Love to. But can't tonight. Yeah, dancing with Davy was a near future she wouldn't mind at all.

Tomorrow? Or is your dog still sick?

Sick. Was PTSD a sickness? Antibiotics couldn't fix it. No painkiller would touch it. Was it a condition? Or…the label didn't matter.

Part of her wanted to be angry because Davy was blaming her saying no on poor Brandy. But he was also being considerate enough to ask how her dog was doing—even if he didn't understand that PTSD didn't just go away like the common cold.

Love to. But I'm in Montana.

Seconds later the phone rang and Davy's name flashed up on her screen.

"Montana? Jodz, please tell me that's just a Brooklyn bar I don't know about." Davy's teasing made her want to laugh.

"Actually, it's a new Disneyland ride. Brandy and I are gonna do the Pirates of the Caribbean next."

"Just make sure you hit Sleeping Beauty's Castle and get your princess costume. Wow, Jodz Jaffe in a princess costume. There's an image. I'll catch the next flight out and join you."

"Don't *you* start."

"What?"

Jodie bit her tongue. Stan's gaze said that he was seeing far more than a little bit of exposed skin on her shoulder. She'd glanced back sideways through her hair just as she turned the corner of the kennel building. He'd still been sitting in the dirt, magnificently bare chested and surrounded by his war dogs. "Never mind."

"So what's in Montana?"

"A dog doctor."

"We don't have any vets here in Brooklyn?"

"Military war dogs are different, Davy. Brandy's…"

"Pretty screwed up. Yeah, I saw."

"…hurting." But Davy was right. Her dog was royally screwed up. At least her own problem was just being out of shape.

"Montana. That's like *The Horse Whisperer* country, right? So did you find yourself a dog whisperer?"

"More like a dog asshole." She was starting to feel all the abuse her body had taken today. The hard swim, the cramps, the hard slam of Bertram hammering her to the ground…it all added up to more pain than she'd felt since her last patrol almost three months ago.

"Want me to come out and beat him up?"

"Yeah, that would be good." She tried to keep the laugh inside, but it wasn't working. Six-foot-plus of human tank vs. five-seven of Jewish lawyer earned him an unintentional giggle.

"You sound good, Jodz."

And just that fast, that too was slammed out of her. She was a fucking train wreck.

Stan Corman still topped her personal shit list—and he'd been staring at her like she was some answer to his lustiest prayers. Brandy *was* screwed up and all Jodie had done so far was make it worse.

She glanced in the mirror…and she finally saw what was wrong. Had she looked at her own eyes today? Since getting home? Since the mortar attack?

Today she and Ama had said almost nothing. They'd just sat and listened to the silence until Jodie had felt as if she was the Black Knight in *Monty Python and the Holy Grail.* Bits and pieces of her lost along the road until, armless and legless, she stood on her leg stumps shouting for them to come back and fight—she'd bite them to death.

Why had the silence been so loud that she'd wanted to scream?

She didn't show anything, of course. Not to Ama. Not to the dogs.

When it had built to the point that she was sure she was going to fracture into a thousand pieces, she'd grabbed a ball and thrown it into the lake for Bertram. He'd happily chased it in magnificent leaps and bounds, followed by powerful swimming. She'd gotten to the point where she could reliably bounce it off the central dock, getting far more distance. Bertram, being a Malinois at the height of his training, had chased after every throw with an exuberance that Brandy had once had but they'd both forgotten.

Jodie had thrown it and thrown it until her arm burned. And her eyes.

Ama had left, and still Jodie had heaved that ball until the pain was all in her arm and no longer in her chest.

Then, down at the training course, Bertram had taken her out at the knees. Knocking her on her ass as effectively as the mortar that had blown her and Brandy aside.

In the mirror Jodie watched her eyes getting wider and wider. Her breathing— Her heartrate— Her heart!

There was some kind of buzzing in her ear. A noise she could make no sense of.

Words.

A tone of worry.

She hung up the call and set the phone down carefully on the battered old dresser.

When another call rang in, she didn't dare touch it.

What could she say to Davy? How could she explain?

What if it wasn't her dog?

What if it was…*her?*

Emotion travels down the leash.

Was she unloading her own shit on her dog? Was that why Brandy was such a mess?

Her dog's world had been shattered and Jodie had no idea how to put any of it back together.

"The only easy day was yesterday." The SEAL motto.

If this was tomorrow's easy day, one thing was absolutely clear: she was totally fucked.

CHAPTER 9

Stan had stopped in the bunkhouse hallway outside Jodie's room. It was a long corridor with bunkroom doors down its length, five to either side. The scarred wood marked the passage of hundreds of ranch hands on thousands of nights over the decades.

Tonight the passage, which he'd never really noticed, felt...wrong. Something wasn't right.

Yeah, took a real genius moment to figure that out, Corman.

It should have been funny. Bertram had swept her off her feet like a cartoon. She obviously wasn't hurt. But every time she was near Stan himself, her reactions were off the charts, like chaotically bad. But when she didn't know he was there, her expression always said she was totally chill—that she had it all together.

Maybe she did. But he was starting to suspect that maybe she didn't.

Or maybe it was just his fault. Chelsea seemed to think Jodie was completely wonderful. Ama too. Was it because he was a trigger of some sort? Or was it because he was a fellow SEAL that she didn't need to hold it together so hard when she was near him?

Now that he thought about, he knew where he'd seen that kind of overreaction before.

With a wry smile, he remembered a poor asshole fresh out of the service who'd squatted for an entire winter in one of Mac Henderson's remote fishing cabins. Stan had been slowly turning himself into mental shreds until Ama had ridden out in the middle of winter to deliver a Malinois puppy. Bertram's arrival had been his turnaround point.

Yet ever since Jodie's arrival, Stan had been begrudging Jodie her own dog. Her dog was alive and his was dead.

But how could Jodie move on when her dog was so damaged? He glared at Jodie's door. Might it have been a mercy that his Lucy hadn't survived the attack?

Stan had planned to ask if she wanted to go for a run; he'd been looking forward to her noncommittal "okay" all day. But now he wasn't sure if he was up to facing yet more of her chaos. Though if it was more than just anger at him, he really should try to help and—

Going 'round in fuckin' circles, Corman. He turned to continue down the hall when he heard the scream. It shot through the thin door like a knife.

He tried the handle—locked.

He went to crash the door in with his shoulder but, thinking better of it, he stepped back and kicked it in.

Jodie was standing in the middle of the room, another scream erupting from her lips.

It wasn't fear—it was anger. *Fury!* And pain.

She was bent half over, pounding her fists against her knees as if what she most needed was a target.

There were times for asking.

And there were times that weren't.

He shifted his mechanical arm to a right-angle bend and locked it in place, then he took the two steps in and wrapped his arms around her.

She transferred her anger from her thighs to his chest, but he held her so close that she couldn't get much of a strike. Which was good because, for an out-of-shape woman, she was damn strong.

"Stronger than a gator with a hard-on." *Thanks, Pa. Real helpful.*

Jodie fought his hold, but he just pinned her against him—meat hand around her shoulders, mechanical across the small of her back. She thrashed and groaned. As if she wasn't even aware what she was doing.

Pure rage.

He'd seen it in survivors whose teams had been blown to shit. They held it together while it mattered, but at some unpredictable moment it blew up on them. This must be Jodie's moment.

He just held on. He hadn't been this close to a woman (other than when Jodie had fallen on him yesterday) in a long time. Oh, there'd been the occasional crassly adventurous ranch guest who'd been open to a tumble with a one-armed man, but he'd grown bored of that type of woman, which had left him hanging out to dry as no one else came close.

The scent of Jodie was overwhelming. She smelled…female. Like… a fresh day and a warm night stirred together.

She began pounding her forehead against his chest.

Out of hands, he pressed his cheek down onto her hair, which seemed to calm her. He'd forgotten how much softer a woman's hair was than a Malinois'. It was like a miracle against his skin.

Finally she went quiet, just resting her forehead and hands against his chest. Her heart rate eased down. Her breathing following.

She finally pushed back enough to look up at him.

"You okay?"

"Yeah, there's the dumbest question of the day. So not." Then she rubbed her hands over his chest in a patting motion. "You might have put on a shirt first."

"Uh," he'd been headed back to his room to do that. Then stopped at her door. Heard the yell.

"Here," she held out the t-shirt he'd given her earlier.

He tried to pull it on, but got himself all snarled up.

"Let me." And before he could stop her, Jodie straightened out the fold that had snagged on his elbow joint and he was able to finish the job. No one since the physical therapists at the VA had been allowed to touch his arm. And not them as soon as he got control of it. Even the most adventurous women hadn't wanted to. Jodie hadn't given him a choice, nor made an issue of it.

"Better?"

Jodie patted his chest once again before nodding, but she didn't look up.

"Gonna tell me what that was all about?"

She shook her head.

Jesus, but he'd had enough of this woman's messed up shit. "Fine. Wallow in it, then. Just keep it away from your dog."

Jodie watched Stan's back as he walked back out her door. He tried to slam it, but the shattered latch and splintered shreds of the door frame made it just swing back open. By the time it did, she was staring out at an empty hallway.

He got a good slam out of his own door though; it echoed right back to her with a vengeance.

Nothing out there to see but two dark walls of aged wood no one had thought to hang a picture on.

How was she supposed to explain what was going on inside her to a blank wall? Or to Stan? She couldn't even explain it to herself.

She was the broken one. It had taken her three months out of the military and a trip to Montana to figure that one out.

Brandy was weak and had massive PTSD. But how much of that fear was something Jodie had suppressed in herself and was sending down the leash to her poor dog?

As much as she hated to admit it, Stan was absolutely right—she had to keep it away from her dog. All this wasn't his fault, it was hers. Maybe if the mortar had hit Brandy they'd all have been better off.

Maybe if it had hit her, they'd all be...

Despite all of that, Stan had held her. Held her close as the awful truth threatened to crush what little was left of her soul. She'd felt safe, curled up ever so briefly against his chest.

As if!

There was no "safe" against Stan's chest, no matter how amazingly good it was.

If Brandy had any chance, it was here in Montana, not in Brooklyn.

It was with Stan.

Not with her.

She didn't know how long she stood lost in the chaos of her own internal disaster. Long enough for Stan to slam his door again and storm down to the exit at the far end of the building so that he didn't have to pass by her room again.

Jodie tried listening to the silence. All she could hear was the building's old wood creaking as it was unevenly heated by the sun or brushed by the wind. All she could taste was the acid in her mouth that she really hoped wasn't fear.

In some weird state of slow-motion that might have taken minutes or hours, her hands dumped the few items she'd set out on the dresser back into her duffel. She dumped the shredded t-shirt in the small garbage can, grabbed her duffel and keys, and walked out.

Her truck was still parked by the kennel.

Jodie circled around the backside of the building. If she faced Brandy, she wouldn't be able to do what was best for her. Jodie had done plenty of hard things for her dog. She'd stayed overseas and fought the veterinarians and the bureaucracy to make sure the Malinois made it home. She'd bunkered them down in her childhood room. She'd even driven to fucking Montana and faced down Stan "Asshole" Corman.

The fact that he was right just made everything that much worse.

The last thing Brandy needed in her life was a fucked-up handler like herself.

The only easy day was yesterday.

She could do this. Hadn't she already given everything else? What did the last piece of her heart matter?

She chucked her duffel into the pickup's passenger seat.

No dog? Then she sure as hell didn't need a portable cage. She hadn't strapped it in earlier, so it only took a moment to dump it off the side. She barked her shin hard on the metal edge seam between the top and bottom half. Didn't mean she couldn't drive even though she could feel the slow, hot trickle inside her jeans leg. She wore socks —they'd soak up the blood just fine.

Once inside the truck, the engine offered a throaty diesel roar as she hit the gas too hard. Yanking it into drive, the tires spun on the dirt and gravel. With a hard fishtail that almost *did* slam her truck into the building, she was moving. Jodie wrenched for control, then aimed down the driveway.

A rider with long red hair was just exiting the horse barn as Jodie roared past. The horse reared up high. In the rear view, Jodie could see that Chelsea had kept her seat and was looking after her. Thankfully the turn in the driveway blocked out the rear view—which Jodie had been watching too hard—and barely avoided putting her truck in the ditch.

Back under control, she did a four-wheel drift where the driveway reached the road and gunned the engine hard. Diesels were made for power, not acceleration, but with no load they did just fine. In moments she was jolting over the washboard roadway at a teeth-jarring fifty miles an hour.

Every minute and twelve seconds was another mile away from that ranch. Away from Brandy. Away from Stan Corman.

Jodie didn't need to get away from herself.

This was the right thing to do.

For Brandy.

Jodie Jaffe was just fine.

Just fine.

She turned on the radio to prove her point.

Toby Keith came on singing *How Do You Like Me Now?*

Jodie punched the radio display as hard as she could. The glass fractured. But Toby didn't shut up. She punched it again and relished the pain shooting up her hand. Again, she left bloody knuckle prints. Again and again until the pain in her hand was worse than the pain of Toby's question.

Jodie finally fisted the power button, which sent pain rocketing all the way up her arm.

Oh brother, was she *ever* "just fine."

As she sucked on her knuckles, the truck launched over the next rise and she almost plowed into a cow. At least she assumed it was a cow—nearly as big as her truck and with horns as wide as an aircraft carrier.

Her long skid ultimately twisted her sideways before she ground to a stop. The monster cow eyed her uncertainly through the driver's window from mere feet away. It looked at her from one big brown eye as if Jodie was insane. Then it did the same with the other eye before meandering out of the road to crop grass on the other side.

Jodie popped the lid on the center console to haul out a couple of Kleenex for her bloodied hand. Her whole hand stung, so she just grabbed the first thing she could feel.

She hauled out a plastic baggie of dog biscuits.

Brandy's dog biscuits.

The seat beside her was empty. No overeager dog whining for a biscuit. She no longer had a dog.

Brandy was Stan's problem now...wasn't she?

Yes.

Yes! She was.

Jodie was done.

She was so fucking done.

She rolled down the window and heaved the biscuits out onto the road for the cow to find. Again, she dug around in the deep console bin for some tissues. She'd take an oily rag at this point.

This time she brought up Brandy's favorite KONG toy—three rubber spheres of decreasing size melded into a six-inch rubber snowman shape. Every Malinois went nuts for the unpredictable way that KONGs bounced. That was their true reward for finding explosives. Dogs didn't care about TNT, C-4, or Methylammonium nitrate. They cared that they got to play with the KONG toy each time they detected some. She tossed it onto the floor in the back of the crew cab so that she didn't have to see it.

She leaned over to stare down into the dark depths of the console. Doggie med kit. Another baggie of biscuits. Two more KONG toys. Her life had become synonymous with her dog's.

No longer. She was going back to New York.

To hell with the dog. And with the tissues. And with her bloody hand.

She slammed down the console's cover, backed the truck until it once again pointed down the road.

She was going to eat pizza, bagels, and every other unhealthy thing she could lay her hands on.

Unable to ease her foot up once she'd started off again, the truck was soon running over fifty again.

Jodie was going to track down Davy Golding and screw his fucking brains out. Just for old time's sake. She was going to keep doing it until she'd purged Montana, SEAL Team 8, Brandy, and Stan Corman from her brain.

Maybe she'd never stop.

That's what every guy wanted, wasn't it? A woman who could never get enough?

Because some part of her knew that no matter how often she did something to fill the space, a piece of her had now been left behind and she'd never be whole again.

Gripping the wheel tighter and tighter against the pounding of the road didn't help anything, but she couldn't stop. She finally realized that there were plenty of bandages in the doggie med kit that would work fine on her hand, but she couldn't unwrap her fingers to grab it.

Despite the desperate strength of her grip, when she hit the asphalt, it was such a jarring surprise that it almost ripped the wheel out of her hands. Where the thirty-mile ranch road hit the T-intersection with the two-lane highway, she left black rubber as she took the turn. She didn't even care which way, so long as it was away.

There was traffic here. Not much, just the occasional pickup, but it was a step back toward civilization.

Now on smooth pavement, she became aware of the blood still dripping from her knuckles onto her jeans. Blood wasn't an issue. It was all part of being a SEAL, right? Picking up a buddy's arm. Riding in the back of an evac helo as a medic struggled to staunch a sucking chest wound and sprayed blood all over everyone aboard in the process. Brandy's blood on her hands as she'd fought to save her dog. *The* dog. No longer hers.

She was immune to the civilian horror of blood.

Blood happened.

Flexing her hand, which hurt like hell, proved that at least she hadn't damaged it.

Wouldn't it just be life's joke if she ended up with hooks for a hand like Corman, but have it be all her own fault.

It would serve her right. Whatever gave her the idea that she could save a dog as badly damaged as herself? The blind leading the blind.

And her shin?

Who cared?

Not her.

She was too busy being fine.

She flexed her hand again but didn't allow herself to hiss at the pain.

At least now some tiny sliver of her own massive internal damage was visible on the outside.

"What the hell do you mean, she left?" Stan's ears were ringing.

"I saw her in her truck." Chelsea had ridden out to The Urban to find him. Snowflake was panting, which meant that Chelsea had pushed her horse hard to get here fast.

"Maybe she just wanted to go to town?" Didn't sound likely even as he said it.

"She was spinning wheels and way out of control. She must have been doing thirty by the time she hit the driveway. Spooked Snowflake pretty badly."

Stan knew that the gray was an incredibly steady horse. To spook her, Jodie must have been doing something pretty drastic.

"I stopped to check. Brandy's in her cage."

Stan started to relax. "That's okay, then. She'd never leave her dog."

"And the portable cage is upside down in the dirt next to where her truck was parked."

His skin went cold at Chelsea's news. He'd been regretting the last words he'd said to her—*Just keep it away from your dog.* It was an awful thing to say to a handler. If someone said it to him, they'd find themselves in a world of hurt.

Whereas Jodie—

"Where is she now?"

The dogs, who'd been lined up for the next run through the course, eyed him at his tone. He couldn't seem to rein it in, but he gave them a Down, then a Stay signal. That would keep them out of trouble.

"Like I'd know," Chelsea glared at him. "You're the one who's been hogging her since she got here. What did you do to her?"

He hadn't been hogging her. He'd just— But there was no point trying to explain any of that to Chelsea. Hauling out his phone didn't do him any good. He didn't have her goddamn phone number. He had Altman's.

Punching that number dumped him straight to voicemail without even the four-ring pause of an ignored call. Bad sign. That only happened if Altman's phone was off, which he'd do only if he'd been deployed on a mission. SEAL Team 6 missions could be three days or three months. There was no way to know. Stan didn't bother leaving a message.

"Where's the helo?" He called Mark's phone even as Chelsea shrugged. Despite being some kind of hero pilot, Emily flew only rarely. Mostly it was Mark who flew the ranch's Bell JetRanger, ferrying high-paying guests to and from the Great Falls airport. Taking them on back-country heli-fishing trips and the like.

"Hey there, Dogman. What grand occasion warrants a call from our resident alpha dog?" The whine of distant jet noise over the phone told Stan that Mark and the helo were fifty miles away at the airport.

"Jodie bolted."

"Who's Jodie? Oh, that new chick."

"Yeah, that new chick."

Chelsea was scowling down at him. He didn't have time for one of her lectures on how hopelessly backward men were and what was and wasn't PC. As if he gave a shit. He turned his back on her but could feel the heat of her glare burning into the back of his head.

"Bolted you say?" Mark was trying to make one of his jokes. "Is she a horse? Must admit she looked like a damn fine filly to me, not that I got a chance to talk to her."

Why didn't women get that guy-speak wasn't always disrespectful? For some guys it was just…their speak.

"Mom really took a shine to her."

Ama had taken a liking to Jodie? That wasn't the sort of thing that Ama did lightly.

"Saw her and Jodie with a couple dogs up at the lake when I was flying a group on a heli-tour of the backcountry." The million acres of the Flathead National Forest that started on the backside of Henderson's Ranch was very popular as an add-on package. As a SEAL, Stan had crossed enough mountains humping a forty-kilo pack for a lifetime and didn't really see the attraction.

Jodie and Ama? What did that mean? Was that why she'd left? Nope. That didn't pass the bullshit test. Odds on, it had been his doing.

"Let me tell you just how little she was wearing. She was a fine sight in just—"

"I need you to track her." Stan cut Mark off. He really didn't need be thinking about a mostly undressed Jodie.

"I've got guests running about twenty minutes late. I'll be airborne in half an hour, but with a full load. I can look as I go, but don't be holding your breath. Have Emily trace her phone—she can do one of her GPS things with it."

Stan ground his teeth. "I don't *have* her goddamn number. My only contact with her appears to have deployed overseas."

"Not giving me a lot to go on, Alpha Dog. What's her ride?"

"Black Dodge Ram 1500. Late model."

"Got a license plate?"

"Why the hell would I have that?"

"A black 1500? That's like the national truck of Montana. Unless I stop every rancher between here and Bozeman, I'm not gonna find her. So just chill the hell down, Dogman." And Mark's tone was suddenly sharp enough to remind Stan that Mark had also been a major with the 160th SOAR Night Stalkers. Not a man to be messed with.

But he didn't feel like chilling.

"Shit!" He ended the call and stuffed the phone in his pocket.

There would be no tracing her with Bertram this time.

"Where the hell would she go?"

"Home?" Chelsea asked. He'd forgotten she was even there.

Brooklyn? Stan didn't know squat about Brooklyn.

"Wow," Chelsea's whisper of surprise made him turn to look at her.

"Wow, what?"

"Someone finally got under the skin of Stan Corman the Metal Man." Chelsea started singing some song about a chrome-plated heart as she turned to ride away.

If she wasn't a female and a friend, he would have flattened her. Though he'd be damned if he knew why.

CHAPTER 10

The tapping on her truck window woke Jodie.

"Go to hell, Corman!" She shouted, then pulled the blanket over her head. But it reeked of dog and that reminded her of Brandy which reminded her of—

The tapping repeated.

"God damn you to hell! I gave you my dog. Wasn't that enough?"

She flipped away the blanket. She was stretched out on the bench seat in the back of her crew cab.

Yanking out her knife, she sat up and—

Was staring into the business end of a Glock 17—barreled for the .45 ACP by the look of it—with a very pissed-off state trooper holding the business end.

"Drop the knife."

She did, then cursed as it sliced the edge of the seat. Just the kind of cut that was now going to look like shit forever.

"Ease out slow."

"I'm sorry, officer. I thought you were an asshole named Stan Corman."

"Ease out, *now!*"

Jodie sighed. Hell of a start to a new morning. She eased out slow.

"If you let me pull out my ID, I can show you that I'm US Navy recently retired."

"Hands against the truck."

Really crappy start to the day. She looked around and blinked. Scrub desert. Couple places in Afghanistan looked like this. Iraq was wetter, Syria was drier. Then she spotted the "Welcome to Arizona" sign to one side of the dusty two-lane. She remembered stopping here last night, but it was about all she remembered. Her truck was pulled over onto the sandy shoulder and already she wished for her shades against the blinding morning light.

How in the world had she gotten to this piece of hell? She had no idea how she possibly could have reached Arizona or why—it was nine hundred miles from the ranch and nowhere in the direction of Brooklyn.

Staring at her hands, she saw that while one of them was caked in blood, at least it was dried blood. No fresh bleeding.

The trooper, who stood at least as tall as Corman if not half as wide, fished her wallet out of her pocket none too gently, with an ass grab that would have gotten him flattened if he didn't have the Glock against her back. He fumbled with her wallet one-handed.

"Navy SEAL? Yeah, right. Gonna take you in for forgery, too. What kind of name is Jaffe?"

"Jewish."

"Never had me no Jewish princess. Never seen one in Utah before. What have you got other than that knife?" He chucked her wallet into her truck, then slammed her against the side panel and began running his hand down her body. They were both out here alone, so she didn't see any point in protesting.

When he grabbed her between the legs and squeezed hard enough to make her want to scream at the surprise and pain—she triggered. Hundreds of hours of training made the motions pure instinct. As a SEAL, she'd probably done more hours of hand-to-hand combat training than any state trooper had done training—total.

The essential factor in taking down an armed opponent was absolute control of the position of his weapon.

Jodie leaned hard into the truck, pinning his entire left arm with her body. Then she rolled into it. Their closeness forced him to turn with her. That brought her right shoulder up against the back of his hand holding the weapon as her other shoulder twisted out of the range of fire.

She continued the turn, bringing her hands down from the side of the truck.

Double flat palm on his weapon arm, pushing it farther aside.

Sliding her right hand down his arm, she felt the contact of the weapon—metal against her palm. Grabbing the barrel, she guided it wide of her body.

She slammed her left hand from his elbow down to his wrist.

He jerked the trigger the moment before she caught his wrist. The scorching heat of the muzzle flash blasted into the right side of her face.

The kick of the weapon, cocking his wrist back just as the edge of her left hand impacted the back of his, snapped the wrist bones. Using her right, she ripped the Glock out of his right hand and rammed it up against the underside of his jaw.

He began shouting.

"You do *not* do that to a woman, you bastard. Do you understand?"

He cried out again.

She pulled out her phone and hit record.

"Repeat after me. I will never again attempt to sexually abuse or rape a female I have stopped."

"Hot! Hot! Hot!" He made a nod toward the gun barrel pressed up against his skin.

She eased it down and saw a small red circle the shape of the end of the barrel. "Sissy. Now, repeat what I said."

He did, after a little prompting.

"Then you're going to confess to your captain about every woman you ever abused. Right?"

The cop nodded rapidly.

"Say it!"

He did.

"Now repeat the part about you 'never had no Jewish Princess before' and were getting set to rape me."

"Bitch!"

"Close enough." Jodie quick-walked him over to his cruiser, stripping him of his backup piece—a SIG Sauer P226 Blackwater Tactical with a twenty-round mag and a laser sight. How small was this guy's penis anyway? She popped the cruiser's back door and shoved him in.

He tried to grab the door flange with his broken hand. It didn't work and he collapsed back onto the seat.

Jodie picked up his legs, stripped the Colt .380 Mustang out of his boot—three handguns, each with a different caliber. No ammunition sharing was just brick stupid. She shoved his legs in and slammed the door against his scream as he finally noticed his dangling wrist.

At least it didn't sound like one of Brandy's mortar attack noises. Now what she was supposed to do? The Utah-Arizona border looked as if it was forever from anywhere.

She opened the front door and asked the trooper through the wire mesh dividing the front and back seats, "Where's your station?"

"You broke my wrist, you bitch."

"I noticed. Where's your station?"

"My wrist."

"Your station."

"I'm gonna make sure that you never get anywhere near fresh air again in your life, bitch."

"Names, names, names."

"The only light you're gonna see is when my guard friends come at night and use you until you wish you were dead. Then you'll—"

"Blah. Blah. Blah." Jodie stopped listening as his rant shifted back to a whimper. She spotted his traffic stop book sitting on the dashboard. Flipping back to the carbon copy of the last stop she saw that he'd filled in Hurricane, Utah. A moment with her phone's mapping app showed that it was twenty miles north.

Jodie sagged against the outside of the cop car. She didn't want to turn north. She had no idea how she'd gotten all of the way to

Arizona, but she didn't want to turn back toward anything to do with Montana. Not even twenty miles' worth.

She blinked at the sun. The desert sun was already scorching down despite sunrise being less than an hour ago.

Two vehicles, one driver.

Leaving the asshole here to cook sounded like a good idea to her. Well, maybe not a good one, but at least it had the credit of being an idea.

Towing the cruiser back to his station and dumping the trooper's sorry ass on his captain's desk seemed like a better idea, even if it wouldn't be as much fun. At least the day couldn't get any worse.

After turning the cruiser around, she rummaged through his trunk until she found a towing cable and hooked it to the car's front bumper. Jodie went to get her truck so that she could tow the cruiser.

The front seat of her truck was covered in glass. The trooper's round had shot out her driver's window and windshield.

Perfect.

He liked that Jodie's parents were cautious over the phone, but this was getting ridiculous.

Maybe if he hadn't started babbling like an idiot.

"I know Jodie." "I'm a former colleague." "We fought together." Except none of that was true and Jodie's mother must have heard it in his voice.

He didn't know Jodie. How in the world could she walk away from her dog? *Because you told her* she *was the problem, asshole.* Okay, he could respect that. It took a kind of strength he didn't know if he had himself, to walk away from a dog for the dog's own good.

Colleague? Yeah, right. Might be the first time in his life he'd used that word.

Though they'd definitely fought together—with each other.
Shit!
"I'm really worried about her, ma'am. I just want to make sure that

she's okay." *And drag her back here so I can wring her neck before she gets any farther under my skin.*

"I will call her. And if she wants to speak with you, she can call you."

"I'd appreciate it, ma'am." Stan sighed and gave her his number.

He didn't appreciate it at all. He needed to know she was okay and he needed to know it now.

Realizing he was in no condition to work with the dogs—who knew what kind of shit he would be sending down the leash today— he turned them over to Timmy and stalked out of the kennel.

He was halfway across the yard when a baby blue BMW almost plastered him.

The guy who rolled down the window looked smooth and unruffled. His dark hair was as neatly trimmed as a recruiting officer's though a bit longer. He had tanned skin and a two-day beard that looked like it was on purpose.

"Sorry about that," he climbed out of the car. Five-nine, one-seventy, and one of those shirts with the little yuppie logo on the left chest. Were yuppies still a thing? Stan had no idea, but this guy sure looked like one. He stared wide-eyed at Stan's arm for a moment before he caught himself. To his credit, he recovered faster than most folks did.

"Guest check-in is up to the main house," Stan started to walk on by.

"I'm looking for Jodz. Sorry, Jodie. Jodie Jaffe? I was told she came out this way. Do you know where I could find her?"

Stan froze in his tracks and turned slowly until he was facing him. "You know Jodie?"

"Sure. Since forever. You know her. That's great! Do you know where I can find her?"

"You were *told* she came here?"

"Her mom told me. Jodz sounded upset on the phone last night. I'm between big cases, so I dumped my little ones on a first-year and came out to surprise her."

Stan was feeling a little slow—perhaps because he hadn't slept a single instant last night—but his brain finally coughed up the key piece of information.

"Phone number. You have Jodie's phone number."

"Sure, I—"

Stan's own phone rang.

"Corman," he snapped out without looking at it. He didn't want to look away from the new arrival for fear he'd evaporate.

"I couldn't reach Jodie."

"That's okay, Ms. Jaffe. I've just found her number."

"That's the problem. Her phone was answered by a desk sergeant in Hurricane, Utah. It seems that Jodie is under arrest."

CHAPTER 11

J odie considered taking down the two sergeants who came to get
her out of her cell. It was doable, even with the cuffs. But that
would leave her stuck in the depths of the land of assholes.

She was angry enough to do it anyway.

Then they could lock her up and throw away the key with good
reason. At least then she could stew in her own juices in peace.

Before she could decide just how truly masochistic a day she
wanted this to be, the two sergeants guided her into an interrogation
room.

There was the police captain who'd had her thrown into a cell the
instant he saw his officer. She had to blink several times before she
could make sense of the others waiting there.

Stan Corman, last man on the planet she wanted to see, looked as
pissed as she felt. Maybe the two of them could take down the
sergeants and the captain and whoever was behind the one-way
mirror that ran all down one wall just for fun. It looked like she and
Corman were in the same mood for once—a foul one.

Next to him stood one of the guys from the Henderson's Ranch
lunch table. Owner's son or something like that. Mirrored aviator

shades, he was almost as big as Stan. Oh, Night Stalkers officer, but she couldn't dredge up his name.

The last in the room was—

"Davy? What are you doing here?"

"See, that's the thanks I get for flying you two all the way down from the ranch," Mark, that was his name, smiled beneath his aviator shades.

"Hey, Jodz. You sounded so down on the phone that I flew out to cheer you up. But you weren't there. Instead you're…here?" He looked around in bewilderment. Davy did family law and had probably never sat in the utter blankness of an interrogation room before.

She glanced at Stan, but he said nothing. Just stood there with his arms crossed over his massive chest. She could see that the wire-tension of the muscles in his meat arm were just as taut as the actual wires in his mechanical one.

"What's with all the blood? What did they do to you?" Stan was the first to break the silence. He wasn't pissed, he was furious. Great, just what she needed.

"What blood?"

His eyes tracked: shin, thigh, hand. Two large splotches of dried-blood-brown on her jeans, and her knuckles were still an untreated mess.

"Uh, did those to myself. What do you care?"

"And your hair?"

"My hair?" She reached up and felt the short ends all down the right side of her face. "I guess it was burned by the muzzle flash when that trooper tried to shoot me." Now that he'd pointed it out, she could smell the burnt hair stench. It was something she hadn't noticed in her six hours in lockup.

"Whole side of your face is red—first-degree burn. Dried blood in your ear, too."

Jodie rubbed at the dry flakes on her ear. "Didn't notice. Good thing I was already deaf on that side."

"Was that before or after you broke his wrist?" the police captain snarled.

"About half a second before."

"You broke a policeman's wrist?" Apparently that was too much for Davy Golding and he dropped into the chair that had been meant for her, the prisoner.

Mark and Stan were military and they didn't even bat an eye. They weren't her problem and she'd deal with Davy's civilian sensibilities when she had time.

She looked at the police captain. "In front of these witnesses, I'll speak without a lawyer."

Davy was staring hard at her bloodied ear. Right, she hadn't told him about the deaf ear either. He finally blinked hard for a moment and tried to push back to his feet but his knees weren't up to it.

"I'm a lawyer. Don't, Jodie. That's legal advice."

"That's the advice of a friend who isn't licensed to practice law in Utah. Now be quiet, Davy."

He looked unhappy, but knew better than to argue. He might be the lawyer, but she could debate him into a corner any day of the week and he knew that.

"Where's my phone?"

After a long glare, the captain nodded to one of the sergeants, who came back with it in moments.

Jodie played the recording, complete with the trooper's confession and his scream as she shoved him into the back of his own cruiser. She hadn't remembered to turn it off until after he'd threatened her with life in a black hole decorated with rape.

"Threatening an officer," the captain snapped out.

"I woke with a knife in my hand and dropped it when he asked me to."

"Resisting arrest."

"After he grabbed my crotch."

"Checking you for weapons."

"Hard enough to leave bruises on me?" She'd seen the livid fingerprints when using the toilet. At that the captain blanched, then tried to rally. The look on Stan's face made her wonder how many more seconds the captain was going to live if he persisted. The arresting officer was lucky he was still at the hospital getting his wrist set.

She'd suffered worse in the Navy a number of times before the SEALs taught her how to really defend herself, though never a full rape. This time just pissed her off. It was overseas that was supposed to be dangerous, not an American highway, especially not from a law enforcement officer.

"We still have you on possession of a forged ID."

"Assholes won't believe I was a SEAL. And I wasn't going to open my goddamn mouth on anything without a lawyer present."

"There aren't any female SEALs," the captain snapped out.

"Did you bother to check?" Mark was still doing that half-smile thing of his.

Again the captain hesitated, which was all the answer any of them needed.

"A woman," Stan spoke for the first time. His voice was lethally soft. "*Any* woman recruited from another branch who is good enough to serve with a SEAL Team for six years can call herself any damn thing she wants. She is routinely issued an ID like that to *save* her trouble—not cause it." Stan's tone left a threat hanging in the air that actually silenced the room until Jodie broke it.

"They wouldn't have seen anything but my Navy rank anyway, even if they had checked."

"Enough of this." Mark pulled out his phone, dialed, and put it on speaker. It was answered on the second ring.

"Hey, Mark. When are you coming to DC to play some poker?"

"Be a while, we're headed into our busy season. Maybe you come out. I know Emily would love to see you. In the meantime, sir, could you do me a favor? Could you do a look-up on the code-classified military rosters for one Jodie Jaffe, tell us what you find, and then state your title and name?"

"You've always got the strangest requests," the voice said from the phone's speaker. Whoever he was, he didn't sound in the least put out by it. There was a quick rattle of keys. "Petty Officer First Class Jodie

Jaffe. Dog handler for SEAL Team 8 transferred from…oh, well." He didn't finish the sentence.

She'd gotten involved in being on loan to a Black Ops CIA team, which was what had ultimately brought her to the SEAL's attention. She'd had the only available dog on short notice when the CIA was poking around just days before the Benghazi embassy was taken down. She and her dog had flown out only hours before mortars killed two of the team she'd been with—an attack that ultimately led to the riots that took the US ambassador's life. Whoever was on the phone could clearly see that and knew enough not to repeat it aloud.

Stan and Mark both glanced at her for a long second, then looked casually away. They'd both understand the kind of thing that silence meant.

"Hey, she's cute." Subject change over the phone, if not a smooth one. "Should I be telling Emily about you and her?"

"She's standing right here, sir," Mark warned the caller.

"Oh, hello Petty Officer Jaffe. Sorry about that, but you're very pretty."

The only thing that Jodie could thing to say was that she was a bloody mess, so she kept her mouth shut.

"Besides," Mark answered for her, "she and Emily have already met. Though it's Ama who seems to have taken her under her wing."

"Ama? Really?" There was a low whistle of surprise that Jodie didn't have time to wonder about, but he sounded impressed. "Twelve years in, whole list of honorables and decorations. Medical retirement a couple months ago as Petty Officer First Class. Her CO noted that he was really upset to lose her. She okay?"

"She tangled with a Utah Highway Patrol that has less common sense than a turnip and the attitudes of a cave dweller who should have been fed to a saber-tooth tiger. Would you mind stating who this is?" Mark finished.

"Oh, right. Secretary of State Peter Matthews. Two-term President and Commander-in-Chief. Did that fix your little problem?"

Everyone turned to look at the police captain, who had gone sheet white and looked way past speech. For her own part, Jodie managed to keep her mouth shut, which wasn't hard with how tightly her jaw had been clenched since waking up at the Arizona border.

"It seems to have," Mark's tone was droll. "Thank you, Mr. Secretary."

"Sure thing, Mark. Just remember to be that respectful the next time you're taking my money at the poker table."

"It would be my pleasure, sir." Mark's half grin turned into a true smile for a moment. Not avaricious, but as if he was truly good friends with Peter Matthews.

"I'll give Ralph a call. I'm sure the governor will want to be in on making sure this gets fixed all the way. Actually I'll see you out there next week. I've got some meetings along the Pacific Rim and we're going to be able to attend Patrick's and Lauren's wedding on the way back. But be sure to let me know when you do hit town—I'll talk Zack into joining us and we can scalp a little Presidential cash. I can't wait to see how your kids have grown."

"Yours too. My regards to Geneviève. See you next week, sir." Mark hung up the phone and returned it to his pocket still wearing the smile that had varied only the once from what she now recognized as a very dangerous threat. She'd wager he'd been a formidable officer.

"You just called the Secretary of State for me?" Who the hell *was* Mark Henderson? Someone who played poker with the Presidents, past and present.

He nodded, "Just seemed like the easiest way."

Night Stalkers... Mark and Emily...

"You...and your wife...5th Battalion D Company." They were the most famous fliers in the most elite helicopter unit in any military anywhere. She should have put it together sooner, but they'd left the service about the same time she hit the SEAL teams.

This time Mark's smile went completely genuine as he bowed. "At your service."

And she'd sat at a table with them talking about babies and ranch life?

Now Jodie wished that she'd been the one sitting down.

Stan couldn't seem to unclench his arms.

The captain couldn't get rid of them fast enough. The governor's call had removed him from duty pending an investigation. Troopers from the Governor's Security Detail—the elite of the Utah Highway Patrol—flew down to arrest the officer who'd harassed Jodie. Finding out he was the captain's brother-in-law had only put another nail in both their coffins.

They'd given her a full medical and cleanup in Cedar City while a Dodge dealer replaced the truck's glass and stereo system. A GSD trooper, who'd commandeered a car to follow them, paid for it all. He'd been instructed to escort them all the way to whatever border she chose to depart by. Once they'd heard and copied the recording on her phone, nothing was too good for Jodie Jaffe—except killing the bastard who'd touched her.

Which was good, because Stan wanted to be the one who did that. But he never saw him. Probably all that saved Stan from getting arrested for murder himself.

Jodie was cleared through medical minutes after he returned with the repaired truck, with the seat moved way the hell back. He and Davy were leaning against the truck bed when she came out. He signaled Davy to sit in the back, then held open the passenger door for her.

"No, you're going back to Montana with Mark."

"He already left." When she didn't move, he picked her up and dropped her in the passenger seat.

"*I'm* driving. I'll take you to the airport because I'm not going anywhere near that ranch."

He planted his hand on her shoulder to keep her in the passenger seat, which didn't stop her struggling.

He readjusted the angle of his left arm, then he reached up and caught her nose between his hooks.

"Ow! Hey! Dat hurthz!"

He was half tempted to call her a sissy just as she had the trooper on the phone recording. Damn but the woman could handle herself.

Figuring he had only seconds before her counterattack, he buckled her seatbelt and let go. She set her jaw and stared straight ahead. It gave him a chance to study the right side of her face before he closed her door. She'd obviously had a professional haircut courtesy of the Utah Highway Patrol. The burnt ends were gone and her face, typically half-hidden by the comfortable disarray of hair, was now fully exposed, revealing lovely features. The incredibly smooth-looking skin was barely red anymore, except for her ear, which was still bright pink and shiny with salve.

"Testing one, two, three," he whispered.

"Go to hell, Corman." Jodie didn't turn.

"Thought this ear was deaf."

"Other one works just fine. Acoustic bounce off the inside of the driver's window. Besides, where did you learn that was a whisper? Holland Tunnel?"

As he closed her door and circled the truck to the driver's side, he pondered why he'd done that. The idea of whispering soft nothings into Jodie's ear? He almost liked the image. Holland Tunnel? He couldn't imagine what she had been doing in The Netherlands.

"Airport," she declared as he climbed into the driver's seat, moved the seat way the hell back, then pulled out of the hospital parking lot behind the GSD trooper.

"Ranch." No way was he leaving her on her own anywhere near Utah.

"I don't need your protection."

"No shit. Mighta figured that out for myself. You took down an armed trooper twice your size and you did it barehanded."

She was silent for a long time before she mumbled something softly to herself.

"What?"

"Nothing."

But there was nothing wrong with his hearing, only his body. She'd said, "And I thought this day couldn't get any worse."

CHAPTER 12

Trapped by the implacable vortex that was the silent Stan Corman, Jodie leaned her seat back enough that she could talk to Davy where he sat behind Stan.

His hands were tightly pinched between his knees as if it was the only way he could keep them from shaking. All signs of the smooth, confident man who'd sat in her bedroom with Brandy just last week were gone.

"You really flew out because you thought I sounded sad?"

Davy nodded, shrugged, and nodded again. "I suppose that I did. You don't show your feelings very often, Jodz. So I decided that since you had, maybe you needed…" he hesitated and stared at the back of Stan's head for a moment, "…a friend."

She didn't know why Stan's presence made him change what he was going to say. Nor did she know what to say to his innate generosity. In a strange way, Davy just might be her only friend. At least the only friend from the past. She supposed Chelsea was also her friend, though Chelsea was the kind of person who was friends with everyone. And there was Ama, if that could be called a friendship. Jodie tried to find another word to fit there, but couldn't come up with one.

A *Bekannter*—Germans had a word for that state between acquaintance and friend, literally *known*. But that didn't fit either.

"Did you really lose your hearing?"

"Yes. On my right side only. The mortar that wounded Brandy also destroyed my right ear. Think of the loudest sound you can imagine—a firetruck ripping down Bond Street or the squeal of the F train's wheels at the York Street curves—and make it five or ten times bigger. But that doesn't cover it, because it's all at once. A single massive thump that blocks out the screams of the injured and dying afterward just with the shock of it. That's not counting that it throws you to the ground hard enough to make a whole side of your body black-and-blue."

Again, she'd gone too far. It was painted on Davy's face in wide eyes and a series of near-compulsive swallows.

"Sorry. I keep forgetting that you're civilian."

Stan glanced partway over at her, then turned back to the road.

That small gesture only emphasized the difference. He'd been through war. He understood completely what had happened. The noise, the destruction, and the horror all wrapped together, then overlaid with the need to continue to perform or die. Bloody, battered, and deaf in one ear (which had still hurt like an ice pick to the brain at the time), she'd saved Brandy's life. She'd also bound up a pair of injured teammates. After she'd finished binding one's arm, he'd put a bandage over her bloody ear while she'd packed gauze around an embedded piece of shrapnel in her commander's thigh, immobilizing it until the medics arrived to take over.

To Stan this was automatic. A known and a given.

His half-glance...

Had it been empathy? If so, did she want that? Which would be easier? At Henderson's Ranch she'd rarely have to explain herself—to most of them, military service was a fact of life. Even Chelsea had married a retired Navy helicopter pilot. Back in Brooklyn, she would have to explain everything she said or did, or leave it all behind. Forgetting about those years didn't sound like such a bad option.

Except it was *everything* she'd done since high school. Twelve years of service, of growing and becoming who she was, couldn't just be ignored. Or could it? All it had done was make her a basket case unable to help her own dog. Or apparently make a coherent decision about the course of her life.

Unable to face Davy's worried gaze or Stan's silence, she turned to look out the passenger window as Utah rolled by. Snow-capped mountains lay to the east, climbing above the desert. Compared to back East, they were towering and impressive. Compared to the breathtaking drama of the Rockies from Henderson's Ranch, they were barely bumps on the horizon.

She was only vaguely aware of when, hours later, the trooper escort popped his siren at the Idaho border and circled back to the south.

Stan watched, but Jodie didn't stir once in the long hours across Idaho and most of Montana. To reach Arizona, she must have driven through most of the night. But Stan couldn't tell if she slept or was just staring out her window in some semi-catatonic state.

He'd seen soldiers go there. Wide awake, but they wouldn't eat unless you told them to. Wouldn't shoot at someone firing at them without having the weapon placed in their hands and being ordered to fire. Once they had, they might not think to fire again or they'd dump the whole magazine at once and then not think to reload.

How far had Jodie been pushed? His desire to wreak mayhem on that bastard officer rose up in him until he was surprised that he didn't crush the steering wheel with his hand.

Stan didn't like feeling helpless, but he didn't know what else to do other than drive. He glanced in the mirror. Davy appeared to be asleep, slouched in the back corner. No help there.

Who was Davy to Jodie? He hadn't really had a chance to think about that until now. Lawyer, Brooklyn, and squeaky clean. Old friend, she'd said.

How friendly?

And why did he care?

It wasn't any business of his, but he still didn't like the guy being here. On the long flight down on the ranch's helo, none of them had been much in the mood for talk. Mark had tried, but he knew as little about New York as Stan did and Davy knew nothing else. So the flight down had included little more conversation than a sightseeing tour for Davy. *That's the Idaho River of No Return Wilderness.* Which looked just like Montana's wilderness areas. *There's the Great Salt Lake.* Big whoop. *There's a bunch of arid desert filled with coyotes and Mormons.*

The drive back had been stone silent. Stan had stopped once to fuel up. When he'd shrugged off Davy's offer to drive, the man had gone into the station and bought them all coffee. Jodie's still sat in the holder, now stone cold.

Stan had spent much of the last hundred miles wondering if he should have turned aside to take her to the Fort Harrison VA hospital over in Helena's west side or the big one over in Missoula—the only one in Montana big enough to make adjustments on his arm.

Not a word as they jounced over the thirty miles of road out to the ranch into the amazing light show that was a Montana Big Sky sunset.

As he turned into the driveway, Jodie suddenly jolted upright and screamed.

"No!"

Stan slammed on the brakes, sliding to a halt directly beneath the carved arch of the Henderson's Ranch sign.

"I can't!" Jodie's voice rose to a shriek.

Stan ignored Davy's startled babbling of "What's wrong? What's wrong?" Instead, he turned to face Jodie and waited. They locked eyes for a long moment, then she collapsed back into the seat and stared down at her clasped hands. Still he waited.

Davy finally caught on that it wasn't all about him and shut up.

"I—" Jodie hands were clenched white in her lap. "If I go back, I won't be strong enough to leave my dog again. And you said I should. You're the one who told me to keep it away from my dog. Why do you think I left? I can't go back. I just can't do it, Stan." The desperate pleading in her voice was more than he could bear.

He reached out to brush a hand on her cheek. He was surprised by the tears he felt there; Jodie didn't strike him as the sort who cried very often.

"I'd take those words back if I could."

"But—"

"Look," Stan became aware of Davy and removed his hand from Jodie's cheek. "Yes, Brandy is a mess. And other than being the strongest woman I've ever met—which is saying something on this ranch—you are too."

"No. I'm—"

"We just found you on the Arizona border after breaking a state trooper's wrist, then towing him and his car back to his brother-in-law's station."

Jodie grimaced.

"I still think I was right that you've got to keep your shit away from your dog. But there's no way in hell that animal is going to recover without you here to help her. She puts up with me because I'm the alpha dog, but you're the one she's bonded with."

———

"And what am I supposed to do with that?"

At Stan's shrug, Jodie could almost laugh, except she knew it would be a hard, bitter sound if she let it out. So she didn't.

"Is that why you came all the way to southern Utah to bail me out?"

Again that shrug. This time it seemed to indicate that he didn't know the answer to that one either.

"The crippled leading the deaf."

"About right," Stan agreed with military-typical graveyard humor. "Just a pair of once-upon-a-time dogmen."

"Woman."

"People."

"Aliens," because that was certainly what she felt like. She didn't belong here any more than she belonged in Brooklyn.

"Space oddities," Davy offered. And though it was appropriate, it somehow killed the moment and Jodie found herself staring at her hands once more. She'd never felt so small in her life.

Still Stan waited with unexpected kindness as she struggled with her thoughts.

"Do you really think I can help her, Stan? Help Brandy without making her worse?"

"Yes."

"But how can you know?"

"Because you're the only chance she's got and SEALs don't know how to fail."

"I've failed plenty."

"Name one." Stan made it a flat challenge.

Each thing she thought of, she could hear his counter in her head.

I let down my dog in the field.

No, you saved her life. The mortar was out of your control.

I left her and drove blind for nine hundred miles.

He'd already answered that, telling her that even he wasn't strong enough to have done something like that. Strong or—

It was just a psychotic break. And it kind of had been.

And she could easily imagine his sympathetic half laugh.

Yeah, we're just two crazy-as-all-fuck SEALs willing to leave a chunk of themselves stuck in Death's door to stay alive.

Stan snorted out that knowing half laugh exactly on cue.

She didn't need to look at Davy to know that none of it made sense to him, especially not the twisted humor.

Jodie could feel Stan's smile as if he followed her train of thought. It wouldn't show on his face if she looked, but she could feel it anyway.

Summoning a strength that was all the harder because she wasn't rushing away in a panic, she nodded infinitesimally.

Stan put the truck in gear and eased the last quarter mile up the driveway to the ranch. He didn't pull up to the bunkhouse, but rather beside the kennel building. Brandy's portable still lay upside down in the dirt.

Climbing down, she entered the darkened building.

"Hey," she heard Davy's soft exclamation as Stan stopped him from following her.

The last hint of red from the fading sunset was enough for her to see her way down to Brandy's cage.

When she opened it, Bertram padded out and sniffed at her, then he trotted down the aisle, probably looking for Stan.

Jodie stepped into the kennel, more than half fearing what she would find. What she already knew was true.

The moment her knees touched the dog bed, Brandy swarmed into her lap with a happy whine of purest joy. She hooked her chin over Jodie's shoulder in the equivalent of a doggie hug.

Jodie held Brandy tightly and let the tears she'd been fighting for nine hundred miles come out on a soft sob.

She finally knew a truth, all the way down to her core. Jodie would never go anywhere without her dog for a single day of whatever remained of Brandy's life.

CHAPTER 13

Stan had taken Davy with him to wake Jodie. The guy had come a long way to see her and it seemed only right. He didn't like it for reasons he wasn't going to think about, but it was the right thing to do.

"She's in the cage?" Davy looked at him in confusion.

Stan looked down at him and managed not to offer a "Where else would she be?" Didn't the guy know anything about her? After waving Davy down to the last cage, Stan stopped at Bertram's cage to start the morning ritual of brushing and feeding the seven dogs. A whispered *Ruhig—Quiet*—silenced the dogs' usual morning noises of excitement to start the day.

"You slept here?" The tone of Davy's shock carried easily along the line of cages.

He couldn't make out Jodie's reply, but it was notable for its brevity.

"Why would you do that?"

Stan smiled at Tiger as he gave the dog a morning rubdown. Tiger was the strongest and most willful dog other than Bertram. "Such a good boy," Stan whispered in squeaky dog voice. Tiger wiggled happily. Stan bet himself that Tiger would win himself a place on a Delta or ST6 team.

"Are they making you sleep out here? Just tell me who I have to talk to and I'll get this fixed right away," Davy's lawyerly bluster was almost cute.

Stan could feel Jodie's smile—both amused at the response and perhaps saddened at how little Davy understood about what it meant to be a military war dog handler. It was obvious that there was something between them, or had been. But Davy sure didn't know the woman she'd become.

"You *chose* to sleep in a cold cage on a dog bed?" Poor guy just didn't know when to let it go. He was like a new puppy faced with a full-on MWD obstacle course—flat out bewildered.

It was getting a little painful to listen to, so he called down the kennel, "Breakfast in about ten minutes up at the house." Then he called out *Gute Hund* to the dogs, who returned to making a normal level of noise—which over breakfast was just one step below utter mayhem. One of the happiest sounds there was and a great way to start any day.

If there were any happy sounds from the farthest cage, he didn't want to hear them.

"Seriously, Davy. Why are you in Montana?" As if she didn't know. But Jodie wondered if he knew.

She tossed a ball into the kiddie corner of the lake and Brandy went in after it—which was an improvement. Her plan to do another swim was shot down because she didn't have a bathing suit. And while stripping down to bra and panties wouldn't bother anyone from the ranch, she knew that Davy Golding would make a thing of it. Especially since she hadn't bothered with a bra under her t-shirt when she'd changed and showered before breakfast. She had chosen shorts because of the warm day, but still, the whole swimming-with-Davy-watching thing didn't sound right.

So she sat at the water's edge and watched Brandy nudge the ball around. It wasn't very energetic, but at least she was willing to go in the water on her own. Another ball floated out in deeper water, where Brandy apparently wasn't interested in venturing on her own. A soft breeze rippled the surface. At times it brushed the ball toward the far shore, only to turn and ease it back out into the middle. The wind had no more direction than the three of them did.

"I came out here to see you. You sounded so sad, and that was *before* you were arrested."

"Hard to believe that I spent twelve years defending our nation so that assholes like him could prey on women." Not any longer. Whatever mental aberration had launched her down the road had at least taken out that one bad egg.

"I still can't believe you broke a state policeman's wrist."

Jodie pulled up her knees and propped her chin on her hands. It wasn't a question of having enough power to break his wrist. The challenge had been holding back her training enough to not shatter it completely, then crush his windpipe and leave him to choke to death.

A red-tailed hawk cried once. She squinted up at the blazing blue sky trying to spot it. There, in front of a puffy cumulus cloud in the shape of a bagel—complete with the hole. Hawk and cloud drifted across the sky, their distorted shadows danced across the prairie grass.

"So, what's next?"

The hawk circled away, but Jodie continued watching the cloud and its shadow.

"Jodie?"

How in the hell was she supposed to know? She hadn't had a chance to think about it. Up until this morning, every waking second had been about Brandy, not her. How many nights had Jodie slept outside her cage, first in Kabul, then Ramstein in Germany? Most of two months.

Davy flagged his hand in front of her eyes. "Hello? Anybody home?"

She slapped his hand away.

"Ow! Crap that hurts." He tucked his hand under his arm and squeezed it against his chest.

"Sorry." She was, but couldn't seem to put any more energy behind her apology than she had behind the soft slap on his hand.

"I don't get what's up with you."

Jodie couldn't find the energy to explain even if she knew. She'd already exchanged more words with him than she did with her entire SEAL squad on a typical day. In that cage: unable to accept that *of course* she'd slept with her dog. On the way to breakfast, during, and after. On the walk up to the lake…

She knew more about Davy Golding, his law practice, and his divorce than she knew about herself.

What Jodie had wanted to do was relive Chelsea's enveloping hug and whispered thanks that she was safe. She'd wanted to see Emily's fleeting smile of acknowledging the hard transition back from the war zone.

And most of all she wanted sit with Ama. To apologize for running from herself. She'd set out to run from her dog—for Brandy's sake. But waking up at the Arizona State Line, with no idea of how she'd gotten there, told her it went deeper than that. Somehow, Brandy wasn't the key.

She half-listened to Davy expostulating theories about what she was feeling. The other half of her remembered Ama's promise to hold onto her belief in Jodie's strength until Jodie was ready to take it back.

So not.

The morning breeze had tired of playing with the ball in the deep water, and now left it merely bobbing out near the central diving float. Adrift with nowhere to go.

And if she kept thinking that way, she was on the road to nowhere.

She turned to Davy, cutting him off about some neighborhood gossip. "Seriously, Davy. Why did you come here?"

"I told you. You sounded sad."

"You asked me what's next. What do you think happens from here? Sex on the prairie? Me tucked into your Brooklyn condo bedroom?

Happy ever after with one-point-three children and a PTSD-ridden dog? What?"

"Jesus, Jodz. It's not like I have our future all mapped out." Davy looked aghast. "Sure, all that sounds good. Except for your dog having PTSD, but you're gonna fix that, right?"

Jodie had thought she was making a joke. Apparently her and Davy's sense of humor had diverged wildly over the last dozen years.

"I'm not trying to jump the gun here, but we were really good together senior year. Is it so crazy to think that we could pick up where we left off?"

The bagel cloud had followed the hawk off to some distant land. Brandy had wearied of playing with the ball and emerged from the water to shake and then lie down next to Jodie. "Not much of a workout, girl. We'll do more later, I promise."

"I drop the question about our entire future and you talk to the dog? I don't understand what's happening here." Even frustrated, he still kept that lawyerly calm as if they were talking about whether to get pastrami or corned beef on their shared Katz's sandwich.

"Our *entire* future?"

"Okay, I shouldn't have said that." He dug his hand through his hair and she remembered how soft it had felt and how she'd enjoyed toying with it after they'd made love. Now it was too short to do that.

"A lawyer should know that once you've said something, there's no backsies."

"Crap. I'm sorry. I never should have… Crap!"

Somewhere along the way his sense of humor hadn't changed, he'd lost it entirely. Sure, hers had been honed toward the ridiculous as a survival mechanism, but at least she still had one. If Davy was taking everything so seriously, he'd probably actually meant that he'd expected they could pick up where they left off.

In a strange way, she knew exactly who Davy was. He was the safe choice. He would provide for her and their family no matter what. He'd be a good man.

And she'd go insane inside of two years. Because while she might not know who she was anymore, she knew for certain that she wasn't the woman Davy was so sure he loved.

"Davy."

"Look, really. I'm sorry. Sure I'd like to have you back in my life and we could—"

She leaned over to place a finger on his lips to silence him. For old times' sake, she replaced her finger with her lips and allowed herself to sink into his fantasy for just a moment. It was a good fantasy. He'd been a kind lover, if somewhat predictable. His kiss was as familiar as an old pair of boots.

When she eased back, his eyes had closed and he appeared to be barely breathing.

"Thanks for coming to my rescue, Davy. It's probably the nicest thing anyone has ever done for me."

"Of course. It was my—" She silenced him with her finger on his lips again.

Jodie waited until she saw the realization finally sink in that this was it. The sadness struck at him and she wished she could change her decision for his sake. She didn't know the road ahead, but she did know the next step and it didn't include anything except her and Brandy.

Finally he offered her a half smile. "I guess this means—" but the words choked out on him. He truly cared for her, as if there'd ever been a question.

"Say hi to my family for me. Okay?" Because there was no way that any of them would understand her turning down Davy Golding. She was fine with letting him take the first round of heat for that.

"Okay," he looked sadder than an abandoned puppy.

She kissed the tip of his nose, which earned her half a smile.

Then she shed her boots and knife before turning toward the water and slapping her thigh. Brandy followed her in. Jodie made a point of swimming very slowly to the far side of the lake. The cool water washed away the remains of yesterday's...lapse. She'd call it a lapse.

When she turned to come back, they were alone at the lake.

She could only pray that she'd done the right thing.

Stan and Bertram had crested the ridge to look down on the lake just as Jodie leaned in to kiss Davy Golding.

He froze. Only a quiet snap of his fingers kept Bertram from charging ahead.

The kiss lasted far too long to be casual. Or merely friendly.

He'd been wondering what they were to each other and now he had his answer.

Even after the kiss ended, they sat nose to nose far too long to leave any doubt.

Then as casually as could be, she shed her boots and walked away from Davy and straight into the lake like some mythic water sprite beckoning men to their doom beneath the waves. Jodie Jaffe in shorts had definitely given him problems this morning. How someone only five-six could have legs that long was an absolute mystery. And now, picturing the shorts and that tight t-shirt wet from a swim, all he could—

Stan turned away before he had to watch Davy strip down and follow her in.

Goddamn it to hell. She'd never once indicated that Stan was anything other than a reviled dog trainer. Actually, she had. There had been the moment she'd thanked him for carrying her dog. The moment after she'd raged against his chest. And last night in the truck, stopped under the Henderson's Ranch sign, they'd had that...moment. He needed a goddamn thesaurus.

Davy had badgered him after they got out of the truck at the kennel building.

I'm a lawyer. I know there was a subtext there. What is it I'm not under-standing? He wasn't quite that blunt, but it was close. He'd thought his territory was under threat from Stan and was trying to piss as far and wide as he could to mark it. Now Stan knew why.

But it was so...*wrong!*

All of his training told him it was wrong. Davy didn't understand a single thing about Jodie. Not her strength. Not her determination. Not even the passion with which she attacked life. Jodie Jaffe only had one mode: full-tilt. Sometimes she needed a GPS course correction, but she was more determined than most SEALs—even his former Team 6 mates. It was humbling...and awesome.

But whatever he'd thought, she'd just made it clear that she belonged to Davy Golding. She'd heal her dog and be gone back to Brooklyn faster than a A-10 Warthog jet on a close-fire strafing run.

Fine. He didn't have time for her anyway.

Dog graduation.

Forty-eight hours.

What had he been thinking, coming up to the lake in the first place? He had just forty-eight hours until the dog handlers arrived to tell him if he'd just wasted three years of his time and a bunch of Mac's money. Mac had taken a risk on a blown-up, one-armed vet on no more than Altman's say so.

Now it was up to him to prove that the old man's trust hadn't been misplaced. It would kill him to let Mac down. He'd become a second father in so many ways—just as gruff and carelessly kind as Pa had been. Always glad to lend a hand, but just as happy to leave you to flounder a while if you wanted to figure it out yourself.

Stan hit his bunkroom and changed from boots into runners on his way out to the kennel.

"Ready to sweat a little today, team?" Stan called it out as he went down the row popping open the cages. Being young Malinois in top form, they bounded out of their cages and gathered around him.

"*Trinken!* Drink up, boys and girls." Good advice. He grabbed a water bottle and knocked it back. As they doubled back to hit their water bowls, he went down the row snapping on vests. They were fabricated out of old horse blankets rather than Kevlar, but the shape and weight were close enough for training. Each one had the lifting loop on the top of the harness and he'd done what he could to simulate parachute drops, with them dangling by those loops. He desperately needed a jump tower. He slipped supplies into each of their pouches: med kits, foldable water bowl, a liter of water, and a packet of food.

He pulled on his own pack, with the special cutout so that it didn't smash his harness into his back as he ran. What would it feel like to run without that? Without the harness, without the arm? To feel as if he was whole again?

It wouldn't make any difference to Jodie, but someday it might make a difference to someone just as special. Except he didn't have two arms and the red lines of his harness felt permanently marked into his skin. Branded: arm, face, and body.

At least he had his dogs.

"Let's hurt a little!" Figuring he'd warmed up enough on the walk to the lake and back, he started out with the fast trot that any Spec Ops warrior with a full pack could maintain for half a day—a whole day if needed.

The dogs raced and galloped around him for the first few hundred meters. But they settled soon enough and strung out in a line tight behind him except for Bertram running in the point position. He clicked a long-long-short with his hooks—a G for Good boy. It made very little noise compared to their running as they began climbing the first ridge to the north. Only Bertram would understand the signal, and by the sudden swivel of his ears, he knew his dog had heard him.

Damn he was going to miss that dog.

Without Bertram, what the hell was he going to do?

Without Jodie—

CHAPTER 14

"You're all wet, girlfriend." Chelsea met her at the top of the trail. Without even pausing for a breath, she turned to the line of ranch guests coming up the trail. "Here's the lake I told you about, folks. As you can see, the water's just fine."

Standing still under the heat of the midday sun, Jodie couldn't agree more. Brandy gave a nervous shake, spraying water over a group of children who screamed in delight. Brandy made sure to stay on the far side of Jodie after that as Chelsea managed to entice the kids toward the water. Once it was just the three of them, Brandy relaxed a little. Not much, but Jodie would take anything as a good sign.

"Yep. Wet through," she squeezed water out of the hem of her t-shirt, which released even more water despite her having already done it twice. "Occupational hazard. Where my dog goes, I go."

"Does that mean that you're going to explain your solo road trip to Arizona any time soon?"

"No, and I didn't go to Arizona. I stopped at the border."

"Will you spill if I bribe you with brownies?"

"No, but I won't turn down the brownies if you want to try."

"Deal!" Chelsea declared with one of her electric smiles. "Provided that next time you do a road trip, you gotta take me. Actually, we'll get Julie and Lauren. And we just gotta take Emily, too. I'm sure she needs a break. Besides, she's a pilot. We can take the ranch helo, go dancing together, and mercilessly tease men in a Missoula cowboy bar. What do you say, is it a date?"

Another group of ranch guests came up the hill. Jodie would have to remember that afternoon was a good time to be nowhere near the lake. A number of the men looked her over and more than a few of them aimed inviting leers her way despite their families moving along close beside them.

"What's their problem? It's like they've never seen a woman before."

Chelsea giggled. "Could be my lovely red hair and awesome ass." Her back *was* toward their line of approach. "Or it could be how sheer your t-shirt is over what are clearly a truly superlative set of breasts."

Jodie looked down and groaned. She stretched out the lower hem to make a tent out of the front of her t-shirt, but it was still age-worn and wet. She was really, really glad that Davy didn't see her like this. She surveyed the ranch, which was spread out below them. No sign of the blue BMW. She hadn't swum to cramping, but she and Brandy had both done well. Apparently long enough for Davy to be headed back to Brooklyn.

"What's the sad look, girlfriend? You trying to destroy the chances of all the other women here? The wet look *and* the lonesome-puppy-dog look? That's a lethal combination. Not a Y-chromosome within fifty miles could survive it." Chelsea took one last glance toward the lake where the guests now all appeared to be enjoying themselves. They'd know that they could get back by just walking up the clear trail to get back to the ranch and didn't need Chelsea anymore. Then she tucked her arm through Jodie's and arm-in-arm they walked down the hill toward the ranch house.

It felt strange. The only people she'd walked arm-in-arm with during the last decade had been wounded civilians in need of support or a drunken SEAL in need of guidance back to his bunk. To walk along companionably was as foreign as...her being at a ranch in

Montana. Except it didn't feel foreign. In a weird way, it felt less foreign than her all too familiar childhood bedroom.

"Were you just thinking about Davy? The cutie in the zoot suit?" Chelsea leaned in to whisper her question confidentially even though they were the only ones on the trail back to the main ranch house.

"He wasn't wearing a zoot suit. What is a zoot suit anyway?"

"Got me," Chelsea shrugged. "But even if he wasn't wearing it on the outside, he certainly was on the inside. It showed all over him. Total city boy. You two looked like Dr. Jekyll and Ms. Hyde. Or is it Ms. Jekyll and Dr. Hyde. I can never remember which is which. I like your hair better this way, can really see your face now. Either way he's as un-country as you're un-city."

Chelsea continued to chatter happily as Jodie tried to digest that statement. She and Davy should have been a great fit. Sal's Pizza, the corner bagel shop, the new gourmet ice cream outfit down by the Gowanus Canal—one of the original Superfund sites and still pretty much the most polluted water in the US. They were all things she'd been wanting to do. She'd been both born and bred in the best city in the world. But instead she was out in the middle of Nowhere, Montana.

If she'd chosen a different direction the night before last and headed for New York, would she have stopped? If she hadn't, and had reached the city without running off the road from sleep deprivation, she might not have come back to Montana so easily. Or would she?

"Where did he go anyway?" Chelsea paused and managed to coax Brandy out of her hiding place on Jodie's other side and give her a pat on the head. It gave Brandy a chance to rest, which she realized was exactly why Chelsea had stopped. Another reason to like her.

Somewhere she'd lost the thread of what Chelsea had been saying, "Who?"

"Mr. Zoot Suit."

"Oh. Davy is headed back to Brooklyn."

"Is he coming back anytime soon?" Chelsea's sideways glance was filled with innuendo.

"One-way trip." And she still hoped it was the right thing to do. "Where's Stan?"

"*Now* you're asking the right question, girlfriend!" Chelsea squeezed their arms together tightly to match her happy chirp.

"What? No! I'm just asking because I don't see his dogs out on the course." No way was she ever going to be taking up with Stan Corman.

"Maybe in the kennel. Or he might have them out at The Urban. No. There's his truck." Chelsea pointed to a black Dodge Ram 3500—the testosterone-laden version of her own truck. Even from here she could see that it was fully tricked out with rear duallies, running boards, roll bars topped with a massive light bar, and probably every other gewgaw he could find. So not her sort of rig.

Chelsea's phone rang. "Perfect timing!" She answered the call but handed the phone to Jodie.

"Chels?" Stan asked. No mistaking the voice or the no-nonsense tone.

"Corman?" Jodie returned in kind.

"Jaffe?"

Chelsea started doing a happy dance.

Jodie tripped her onto the grass before Chelsea could do something even more obnoxious, then sat on her butt just as Bertram had sat on hers. She kept humming some goofy, happy song until Jodie bounced on her a little, which earned her a very satisfying "Oof!" and blessed silence.

Brandy got in on it and lay down over Chelsea's shoulders.

"Hey, dog! Get off! You're all wet." Her voice was muffled by the phone over Jodie's one ear.

"She only speaks German," Jodie flashed a Stay sign to Brandy. But she did put Stan on speaker so that Chelsea could listen in...and she could hear Chelsea. Half deaf was a major pain.

"Was wondering if Chels could do me a favor."

"Chelsea's tied up at the moment," or soon would be if she didn't behave. "What's in it for me if *I* do it?"

"I was thinking that I *did* carry your dog back to the ranch."

"Oh sure. You're going to hold that over my head the rest of my life. I got her most of the way back myself, you know."

He grunted very satisfyingly at her tease.

"Might've also flown down to bail you out."

"No. Mark did the flying, he told us so himself. I never did thank him; have to fix that soon. And you didn't have to bail me out. Again, Mark, the Secretary of State, and the Governor of Utah took care of that nicely, thank you very much."

"Give me a fuckin' break, Jaffe."

"Oh yeah, swearing at me is going to completely help you in your cause." Jodie could feel Chelsea giggling happily. Jodie slid off to sit beside her in the grass but signaled Brandy to keep her pinned down.

"Seriously, I bunged up my ankle. Could you get my truck and come fetch me?"

"I'd ask again what's in it for me, but you'd probably just throw driving all the way back from Southern Utah in my face. Or maybe how you've been taking care of Brandy."

"Nah, I'd never make no skin off a dog's poor luck."

"Poor luck? Like having me for a handler?"

"You said it, not me, Handler Girl." She could hear his delight at scoring the point.

"Not helping your case, Alpha Dog. You do know that, right? So where are you?"

"Casper Creek. Follow the ranch road about three miles north. When it goes from one lane dirt to cow trail, it'll be just over the next ridge. Wouldn't mind if you hurried."

"Chelsea and I were just going to get our hair and nails done. One of us will be out right after that, unless the masseuse has an opening."

His growl was very satisfying. She hung up in the middle of it.

"Way smooth!" Chelsea huffed out a slightly breathless cheer. "Now can you please get your dog off me?"

"What's in it for me?" But she signaled Brandy aside.

"Eternal gratitude and everlasting friendship," Chelsea pushed up onto all fours, then flopped over onto her butt. She had muddy paw prints on her back, her butt was wet from Jodie's shorts, and she had grass stains down her front. Her long hair was definitely going to need a good brushing.

"Everlasting friendship, huh?" For a woman who had just sent her one and only friend hustling back to Brooklyn with his tail between his legs, that was a hell of an offer. Yet from Chelsea, it was actually believable. "I guess that depends."

"On what?"

"On whether being eternal friends means I have to tell you about Brandy's paw prints all down your back."

"You two may just be more trouble than you're worth," she scratched Brandy's head to show that there were no hard feelings. "But it's a deal."

They shook on it solemnly.

"I think you got the worse end of the deal, Chelsea."

"Why's that?"

"I'm guessing it might be hard to find a friend better than you."

Chelsea blushed brightly and transferred a few grass stains from her hands to her red cheeks.

"Also, you're now stuck with me as part of the deal."

"Oh no. That's an absolute winner for me. Friends for life—totally worth it. You'll see," Chelsea jumped to her feet with a confidence Jodie didn't much share. Down the hill, Jodie turned for her truck.

"No, you better take his like he said."

She looked her question to her new "friend for life."

"It's rough country out past the cattle guard. You'll want the dual-lies on his truck. You always need at least one truck like Stan's on a ranch for hauling a dead bear away for butchering or something. See that big dent in the fender? That was a moose that decided it wanted to bust up a camp. And more than one hard horse birth has been done under those lights." She pointed at the light bar that most jerks would use for illegal night hunting.

Why the hell couldn't Stan ever be what he appeared to be? She'd know how to deal with some asshole ex-SEAL. But one who kept insisting on being decent? That was just too weird for words.

Chelsea turned toward the horse barns.

"But I don't have his keys."

Chelsea unleashed one of her merry giggles. "Hon, you're thirty miles into the countryside in a state where every truck has a gun rack and most folks are carrying. It might be in case we run into a bear, but we're still armed when we go wild," she nodded toward the mountains. "Tell Stan to make sure you get outfitted. Don't forget the bear spray."

"Why? Do they have smelly armpits?"

"No, silly. It's Mace, in bear-sized quantities. The keys are where they always are in Montana, in his truck. I'd go with, but—" she cupped one of her breasts "—I'm betting someone's hungry again."

Jodie headed over to his pickup and wondered just what rabbit hole she'd fallen down, because this place sure wasn't anything like Brooklyn.

Stan heard the low growl of his truck's 6.7-liter Cummins diesel as it took the stiff climb up the far side of the ridge.

"*Geh weiter.*" He told Bertram to *Go ahead* since his sharp ears had also picked up the sound. In moments, he bounded away. Even without being told, the other six dogs remained lying beside him, vigilant but patient. He'd taught them the difference between individual and pack commands.

His truck nosed into view just as Bertram crested the rise. He could just make out Jodie leaning out the window to look down at the dog. Bertram did a twenty-pace trot toward Stan, then stopped to look back at her.

Jodie tracked in his direction...and finally raised an arm in greeting.

He couldn't hear her, but she must have called out *Geh zurück! Go back.* It wasn't a typical command taught to dogs, but apparently Jodie knew it and Stan had made sure all of his dogs did. Bertram bolted in his direction. Down the hill, he splashed through the stream—running thick and fast with glacial melt—swimming briefly, which swept him twenty feet or so downstream, then came ashore, racing up to Stan and shaking right in Stan's face. Stan barely noticed as he wiped the chill spray from his face.

Jodie climbed out of the truck. Brandy followed her out. Together they inspected the slope between the ridge and the stream that he sat on the far side of. The water was only thigh deep, but he felt it was safer to sit on the grassy bank on the other side than try to cross it with only one foot.

Jodie flagged a "vehicle" hand sign—a raised fist rocked side to side —but it looked like a question.

Stan held up a closed fist for "freeze in position" in response. As much as he didn't want to try crossing the creek, then climbing the hill, he'd rather not get his truck stuck down in the steep-sided gully.

He watched for it, but if the Brooklyn lawyer was in the truck, he wasn't getting out. Jodie rummaged around in his toolbox, then strolled down the slope with her dog at her side as if it was a lazy Sunday in the park.

She made Brandy sit and stay on their bank, then waded almost hip-deep into the stream and out on his side, doing her water-nymph-fantasy thing. Damn but she was a looker. At first all she'd shown him had been the fear and anger, mostly the latter. But this time she actually smiled, not caring in the least that her boots were soaked and she was dripping wet from the waist down.

"Fancy meeting you here."

"Nice day. Got me some good company," he waved to the circle of attentive dogs. "Didn't really have anywhere else to be."

"Well, I've still got that gorgeous masseuse waiting for me back at the ranch. So if you don't need anything..." Jodie made a partial turn to go, her smile not dimming for a second.

"Christ, woman. I can't even walk. Give me a break here." He really didn't need to hear about her goddamn Brooklyn masseuse.

Without further comment, she squatted at his feet. He prepared himself for pain, but her fingers were gentle on his ankle. She clamped a hand over the toe of his sneakers. "Wiggle the toes for me."

He did.

She grasped either side of his foot and made tiny movements side to side and flat-foot to a slight toe-point. The second time she did a greater range of motion and he hissed as she did the toe-point. Two more tests up the ankle and he'd be damned if he didn't feel better each place her hands rested.

"My best guess is a bad sprain, not a break."

"You the medic on your squad?" Every squad had one.

"Dog handler and nurse's kid." She rose in a single lithe movement and wandered off into the streamside scrub brush. He watched it wave and rustle, then he heard a sawing sound. In a minute she came back into view whittling shoots off the sides of a long branch. Using the saw on the back edge of her big knife, she chopped it into four pieces.

Kneeling over his bad foot, she laid two to either side, then yanked a couple of dog leashes out of her back pocket. That must be what she'd been looking for in his truck. In minutes she'd lashed together a very respectable field splint.

While she was doing it, Stan couldn't help but notice the woman. He was looking down on the top of her head, her trimmed hair sliding neatly over her ears and cheeks. The long line of her back from good shoulders down to her slender waist. She smelled of spring air and fresh prairie grass. Somehow the air around her was warmed until it was lush. God help him, the woman was going to be the death of him. He hadn't wanted a woman the way he wanted her since… Damned if he knew. Marybeth Anne had certainly never fired his imagination this way and he'd almost married her.

"I'm certainly never running in sneakers again," he had to say something to distract himself.

"There's a reason the Navy issues boots," she agreed as if he'd said something relevant. When had he lost that attitude? He'd been out three years and at some point he'd gone civilian.

"There, that should do it." She glanced up and caught him staring.

How was he supposed to look away from those deep-water blue eyes? She was a SEAL's wet dream in every way.

Jodie hesitated for a long moment, long enough for him to become aware of his own breath running short and sharp. Then she shrugged to herself and rose to her feet. He'd give a lot to know what that shrug meant but didn't want to ask. She was another man's woman and he'd never mess with that.

"So, are you going to sit there all day? Or are we going to try and walk you out of here?" Her smile was half tease and half challenge.

"Bring me a fresh grilled burger, a beer, and a bucket of fries and I'm good just sittin'."

"The Man didn't make me a waitress."

No. "The Man" of the military had made her a goddamn SEAL.

As he pushed off the ground with his meat hand, she reached out and grabbed his hooks. "Can this take the strain of a pull?"

"No problem," he managed to grunt out as he bumped his bad ankle on the ground and pain shot up his leg. No one touched his metal arm. Certainly never as if it was a normal thing to do.

Jodie ducked under the curve of it and hauled it over her shoulder. With her right arm around his waist, she fit against his side as if she'd always been there. He could feel her from his hip up to mid-biceps. He wished he could feel the rest of his arm across her shoulders and where her hand held his hooks, but that wasn't ever gonna happen.

"We good?"

He suppressed the first dozen comments that came to mind about just how very good. "Let's give it a try," was the best he could manage.

They stepped into the stream and the cold was a hard slap against his bad ankle. Chilling it would be good for the swelling, but barely above freezing stung. They were halfway across when he remembered the dogs all waiting on the bank.

"*Hier.*" Come.

In a moment they were stormed: seven dogs from behind and Brandy from the opposite bank where she'd been watching her mistress impatiently. He tried to brace himself, but one foot and Jodie just weren't enough support.

In moments they were down in the water, a tangle of two humans and eight dogs.

"Oh my *gawd!*" The cold slapped her so hard that all she could do was scream out her curse.

"Voraus!" she shouted at the dogs and they all bounded out of the water and over to the truck's side of the stream. They gathered there, racing about and barking, eager to see what happened next. They followed along the bank as she and Stan were tumbled well downstream before she managed to get her feet under her. Emerging from the water was almost worse than being in it because once she hit the air, she knew just exactly how cold she was.

"Stan!" Jodie still had a hold of his hooks and tugged on them.

He emerged a moment later, shaking his head to clear his long hair from his face, spraying most of the water into her face.

They made it ashore more in a desperate crawl than a planned stagger.

Both on all fours, they knelt on the muddy bank and were once again stormed by the dogs.

"You sure that you've actually trained them?" Jodie called out as she was tumbled into the mud. At least the sun-warmed mud was warmer than the stream water.

"I thought so. Now, not so much." Then he called out, *"Sitzen."*

"No—" but it was too late. Brandy sat squarely on Jodie's stomach. The others decided this was a grand idea and soon they were both buried in sitting or sprawling dogs.

Stan grumbled, "Someone should smack whatever asshole trained these animals."

Jodie tried to laugh, but couldn't get a breath with Brandy sitting on her stomach.

After a few moments, Stan had them cleared aside. "You okay?" He loomed above her, leaning on one elbow. His hair was thick with mud, and smears of it covered much of his face and body. Reaching up with his hooks, he brushed the tips along her forehead, shifting her slimed hair out of her face with a shocking gentleness.

How many minutes ago had she told Chelsea that there was no

way she'd ever do anything with Stan Corman? And now she lay beside him in the mud, soaked with glacial melt that she was half surprised didn't flash off her in steam with the sudden heat she felt. Stan's t-shirt lay like a second skin on his exquisite chest and rippling abs. The concern in his dark eyes was—breathtaking.

She could see now that it had always been there, from that first moment when he'd stood by her truck's window to standing like a vengeful god in a Utah police station.

He was—

"Jodie?"

"I'm fine," some self-preservation mechanism answered. It was also the answer she'd given after being struck by the mortar and slammed back against a stone wall so hard that it had stolen her breath and bruised her whole side. It's what every Spec Ops said in such moments.

"Okay then," Stan blew out a hard breath that was warm on her cheek. "Okay. Let's try this again without their help." He ordered the dogs out of the way and they both struggled to their feet.

Once they were upright and the steep slope was ahead of them, Stan looked down at her for a long moment.

"Christ, woman." Then he stared fixedly ahead.

Jodie glanced down at herself. Slathered in mud. Dog fur all over her soaked t-shirt. She was a two-legged disaster area.

Each step up the slope was a laborious task, and she could see Stan's jaw clench tighter with the pain.

She tried to make sense of what was happening as they struggled along.

He'd clearly been admiring her as she'd bandaged his foot. But he'd given no other sign of what he'd been thinking. For half a moment she'd been tempted to kiss him just to see what the formidable Stan Corman would do with that, but she'd shrugged off the idea as foolish.

Then he had lain beside her in the mud and touched her with an impossible gentleness despite it being his hooks. Again, he'd done nothing.

Another step, she could feel the strain all along her arm where it lay across his fabulously sculpted back muscles.

Then he'd taken one good look and cursed her.

Right. Because who would want a fucked up mess like her?

It was a good thing she *hadn't* tested that brief impulse to kiss him. She didn't know if she'd be able to take the rejection on top of everything else that was wrong with her.

CHAPTER 15

Stan waited out behind the kitchen for her after lunch.

She'd been strangely distant and silent once they'd reached his truck. He'd almost teased her about sharing a shower but thought better of it at her stonewalled silence.

During lunch, he'd dropped in on Doug. He was the closest thing they had to a veterinarian on the ranch. He even had a small x-ray machine, more suited for horse legs than human ones but it worked. Doug had confirmed the sprain, given him an Ace bandage, a bottle of ibuprofen, and a pair of crutches he had lying around. Then they'd had a couple of sandwiches and sodas out by the barn just shooting the shit and watching the horses laze around in one of the corrals. He'd have to remember to do that more often.

Stan now sat on the stone wall of Nathan's herb garden where he and Jodie had collided so hard a few days before. No way was there such a thing as love at first sight, but now he could see—looking back at that moment where Jodie had been so solicitous after he jammed his arm—that she was a woman well worth falling for.

Of course she loved someone else. Which so completely sucked that it was beyond imagining. Not taking her right there by the muddy stream, dogs and sprain be damned, had been one of the hardest things he'd ever done. Then seeing her prize-winning wet t-shirt contestant look had been like a knife in his gut. He'd pulverize Davy Golding if he didn't get how lucky he was.

Chelsea came out first and spotted him.

"My hubby got you all fixed up?" She came over and plopped down on the wall beside him.

"Bound and drugged," he showed her the bottle of Advil.

"Ooo, he gave you the heavy stuff. You must have really screwed it up."

"Bad enough," he nodded toward the massive wrap job that Doug had done. That's when he realized what a pain that bandage was going to be, with only his hooks. Doug stocked some premade braces for ranch guests who bunged an ankle or wrist, but none were big enough to make it around his calf muscles.

Didn't plan on having to treat a goddamn human Clydesdale, Doug had grumbled.

Good enough to haul a Budweiser wagon.

Not on that foot. You even put it on the ground this week, I'm gonna spank you.

Stan had laughed.

Go ahead and laugh at me. I'll get Chelsea to do it for me. Which wasn't a bad threat because she just might pull it off, so Stan had given him the win.

"So, did you and Jodie…you know?" Chelsea wiggled her eyebrows at him.

"No!" He should have pretended that he didn't know what she was talking about. Or at least said no as if he was a little surprised by the idea. Instead it came out as a growl so hard it hurt his throat.

"Why not? Why do you think I didn't go with her to your rescue? I told her Christopher needed to be fed, but it was his naptime."

He kept an eye on the others coming out the back door. Still no sign of Jodie.

"Stan?"

"Even if I wanted to—" so bad it hurt worse than his ankle and no painkiller was going to touch that "—she's with someone."

"Who?"

He didn't even bother commenting.

"Davy Golding? You didn't take Jodie down and kiss the crap out of her because of a man named Davy Golding? Did you know that's his real name?"

Stan's teeth hurt where he ground them together.

"Oh, Stan." Chelsea rested a hand on his meat arm, suddenly all thoughtful and kind. "Davy's gone."

"He'll be back."

"No. She sent him home."

"For now."

"Are men always this stupid?"

Apparently. But he kept that thought to himself.

"Okay, let me translate to man-speak." She lowered her voice, trying to sound gruff—as if. "She booted his ass."

"I saw them kissing, Chelsea."

"Kissing him goodbye."

"Didn't look like that even a little."

"Trust me."

Stan snorted. Chelsea was such a dreamer. She might manage an entire ranch's worth of horses, but she had a naive, romantic view of the world that he'd never understood. Pa never had either. Ever since Ma took up with that insurance guy, they both knew better.

"Ask her yourself."

Not a chance. But some part of his SEAL brain kicked in. *Never reject new data, no matter how sure you are of a plan.* What if? What if Chelsea was right and Davy was gone? Did that mean something different had happened this morning than he'd thought was happening?

Part of him wanted desperately to believe that her silence during the drive back to the ranch had been because... It was almost there, but he couldn't quite connect the pieces. Because he *hadn't* kissed her when he had the chance?

"Whoa!"

The Jodie who had waded to him across the freezing stream had been inviting, friendly, teasing. Even lying in the mud she'd been like that. But something had changed climbing that hill. He remembered only moments of it as anything other than a hard grind through blinding pain. But there had been flashes of Jodie's beauty, and her strength as well, that stood out as clear as the sun high in the sky.

"Finally!" Chelsea leaned close enough to kiss him on the shoulder. "Now are you going to go ask her?"

"Where is she?" The lunch crowd had all gone back to work and there was still no sign of her.

"She and Brandy went up with Ama after lunch," Chelsea nodded toward the second story of the ranch house. "Don't think you want to mess with that. I know I wouldn't."

Stan glanced upward at the high windows and knew exactly what Chelsea was talking about. Nobody in their right mind interfered with Ama.

"Oh!" It was all that Jodie could think to say. The ranch house had been built on a grand scale. The immense kitchen, the airy dining room with its massive Doug fir dining table, and the vast living room with a huge river-stone fireplace and vaulted ceiling with vast glass walls facing the sunny plains all combined to create a commanding showpiece right out of *Architectural Digest.* No ranch guest could be daunted by the sheer grandeur of it because it was also so welcoming.

The upstairs was a different matter entirely. At the head of the sweeping stairs, a long corridor clearly led to the family's private rooms. But at this end was a single room that was both large and cozy without the cathedral ceilings and fine architecture of the downstairs.

Ama stood in silence as Jodie tried to take in the room, but even her SEAL training couldn't take it in as a single gestalt because there was so much to see.

High windows along the north wall filled the room with a soft light. On the shining oak floor stood four large floor looms and a number of smaller ones. Several of the looms had complex works in progress on them.

Motion drew her eye to one of the southern windows that would be warm with the winter sun, but long eaves now made cool with the late spring shade. A flock of black-capped chickadees and nuthatches descended on a line of bird feeders with a constant flutter of wings, and a lively twittering that filled the room with birdsong through the open windows.

The ivory walls were adorned with Native American weavings. From small squares to large rugs. They had mind-bogglingly intricate geometrics that were oddly soothing to study despite their complexity. White, black, gray, and a dusky red predominated.

"These are all traditional colors, the ones my ancestors could make on the Plains as they followed the bison: sumac, bloodroot, alder, rabbitbrush," Ama spoke before Jodie could think to ask the question. And yet Ama's silence allowed her to continue her study.

At some time that Jodie couldn't quite pin down, perhaps while she was inspecting a piece made of three shades of gray that reminded her of the beauty of the Rocky Mountains, the sound of one of the big floor looms joined the birdsong.

The soft clack-clack seemed to fill empty corners that Jodie hadn't realized were there. For a time, she watched Ama sitting at one of the big looms. Sliding the shuttle wound with a reddish-brown yarn from right to left. Pulling the tamping bar toward her, then working the dozen foot pedals without even a glance down. Each pedal she pressed shifted the vast array of white or black threads up and down, then she slid the shuttle left to right and tugged the tamping bar again.

"I teach classes on the looms. Many of the guests also pay for the finished work I make during the quiet winters. Though very few have the patience to learn the traditional methods, I teach those as well." Her hands never stilling, she nodded toward a vertical loom that appeared to have no moving parts. The intricate pattern was clearly being built in tiny sections of varying forms—triangles of black melded with squares of red and yellow-brown in the most intricate pattern of them all.

The big loom kept thumping away.

Jodie had never seen anything like it. Something about the precision of it, all the pieces moving with a sense of purpose to create something as beautiful as the rug section rolled below the tamping bar, made her want to learn to do that. Not some three-afternoon long, ranch-guest-dilettante introduction after riding horses or swimming in the lake. She could picture long winter evenings spent in this room—just her, Ama, and Brandy.

She looked down at her hands and wondered what that would feel like. For twelve years she had worked with dogs and uncovered explosives. She'd also fought, killed, and survived with those hands. She could field strip thirty different rifles blindfolded—the sort of things SEALs practiced for fun at night. What would it be like to create something beautiful instead?

Much to her surprise, Jodie saw that Brandy lay at Ama's feet, close by the foot pedals—as close as she could be without being trammeled. The really surprising thing was that she was fast asleep. Not as she'd been ever since the mortar attack: twitching with suppressed energy and ready to leap away at any moment. No, she slept with the absolute depth she'd always had before that attack.

Was it the rhythmic sound? The vibration? Just...Ama?

Puddle Dog. That was what the squad always called her when she was in this state. She looked more as if she'd been poured upon the floor than lying upon on it. Head tipped over backward until the top of her nose rested on the floor and her ears splatted out to either side. One front leg pointing up into the air with the paw flopped over as if she'd fallen asleep in the middle of waving good night. It was completely different from the coiled ball of fur hiding beneath the tip of her own tail.

Jodie didn't know what to make of it. She looked almost...normal.

She'd behaved reasonably well around the other dogs when they'd gone to rescue Stan. Of course on the drive home, only she and Bertram had been allowed into the back seat; the rest of the dogs had to sit in the truck bed. The kids at the lake had certainly freaked her out and she'd always been careful to stay on Jodie's far side from Davy.

Ama she appeared to trust absolutely. Or perhaps it really was the rhythm of the clacking loom.

Not wanting to risk ruining the moment, Jodie returned to inspecting the wall hangings. At a turn in the room was a space that would easily be missed unless actually inspecting the wall hangings one by one. It was a small alcove, yet it felt spacious with light. Two utterly breathtaking dresses were all that hung there.

"It always surprises me how few people find these," Ama spoke softly from close by. The loom had stopped. Neither she nor the sleeping Brandy had noticed.

"Perhaps they can only see what they expect to see." A great deal of SEAL training had been about seeing what others don't. And that was before the dog's nose taught how to see what was truly hidden.

Ama smiled at that and nodded agreement.

Jodie turned her attention back to the dresses before she could see the question that she knew would come next in Ama's eyes: what was Jodie *choosing* not to see? Nope! No way did she want to be answering that one.

"The robin's-egg blue of the buckskin is not traditional," Ama let her off the hook. "Blue dye came with the white man's invasion across the Great Plains. At first the indigo from South Carolina was new and precious and was allowed only in ceremonial clothes. This dress design I made especially for the Dance of the Day. My father claimed its proper name is *Éta-no'keéno'e,* or 'It's been one day', but that is not how my grandmother taught it to me. Besides, it is a woman's dance, not a man's. This dance has been handed down through our family for longer than anyone can remember. But each dancer has designed and made her own dress."

Ama brushed a hand over the fine beading work of the elaborate collar. It was echoed at the wrists, waist, and hem. A yellow shawl with multi-colored fringes that seemed to rain from the lower edge was mounted behind the dress like brilliant angel's wings.

"I would bet that you were breathtaking in it."

Ama laughed softly. "The first time Mac ever saw me, I was performing the Dance of the Day at the Cheyenne Frontier Days festival. I am quite sure he completely forgot to breathe even after I was done. I still go and dance every year, though no longer this dance. It is a young woman's privilege. I have a niece who now carries on the tradition of that dance."

At Ama's indication, she turned to look at the other dress. It begged to be touched; Ama nodded that it was okay. The natural ivory buckskin was so soft that it felt like silk under her fingers. The long fringes had no vibrant color like the winged shawl, but they felt somehow complete—as if the colored one was a thousand notes and this undyed one a complete song. The neck and shoulders were unadorned. Instead, a blonde-gold inlay of rawhide hinted at a winged bird taking flight—a powerful bird.

"This dress is very traditional. I hunted and skinned the deer myself. Then I tanned the hide in the old ways. This was my wedding dress forty years ago. Mac wore his Navy SEAL dress uniform. Oh, he was so handsome that I'm surprised my heart didn't break that day just looking at him."

Jodie could only marvel at the history represented by these two simple garments.

Her family had left Poland four generations ago, just before World War I, and landed in Brooklyn with little more in their pockets than their names. They'd settled, and nothing much had changed since. She knew her grandparents and about ten stories of her great-grandparents, though that was all.

That's the past, Pop Julius would say when she asked. *We only look forward. The past? Feh! Cossacks trying to kill us? Who wants to remember that? If they had waited, the verkakte Germans would have done it for them.* Then he'd finished with a proper Brooklynism that just confirmed his opinion, *Fuhgeddaboudit.*

Jodie had no past like Ama, ranging back who knew how many generations like Ama's dance. Her own past right now was about one dog deep.

"You would look lovely in one of these yourself."

Jodie turned to face her. "I'm Jewish, not Cheyenne."

"And my daughter-in-law is English. Julie is eighth-generation mostly-Swedish farmer. Chelsea is our Scottish-German melting pot. All of you are my daughters, but they are all fair. With your hint of olive-coloring and your light gold-brown hair, it would be striking."

Jodie could only blink at her in surprise.

Ama's soft smile as she faced the two dresses was both happy and sad. Happy to lay claim to so many fine women and sad at…having no daughter of her own?

Jodie had never thought about children, not really. She had her squad and she had her dog. But now she had done her duty and once again the choices were hers.

For the last months, she'd only thought of Brandy's future. Jodie glanced over, but Puddle Dog still sprawled by the big loom.

If the future was Jodie's, then…what?

Stan wanted to kick himself, except his foot hurt too damn much to kick anything. He *still* didn't have Jodie's phone number. Despite all that madness, he'd never gotten it. Once he heard she was arrested, all he could do was pray that she was safe and get there as fast as he could. A strung-out Special Operations warrior under police arrest was never a good combination.

Jodie was right, Stan owed Mark big-time for straightening it out so easily—on top of what he already owed Mac for changing his own life.

He'd been all ready to send the text before he realized that problem. He still had no number to send it to: *I need to ask another favor. Please find me ASAP.*

Now it had been hours and he didn't have hours.

Enough was enough. Doug had told him to keep his foot up, so Chelsea had parked him in one of the armchairs off the side of kitchen. That had been good for about five minutes.

Then he'd crutched his way down to the dog yard, which was a hell of a lot harder than it sounded. Crutches sucked over rough terrain. The steel arm wasn't a problem once he set it to the right position and clamped the hooks around the handle. But the heads of the crutches pinched the arm's harness badly where it passed around either shoulder. And if he leaned into his left side too hard, the crutch pulled the release wire on his hooks, which opened unexpectedly and the crutch dropped to the ground.

But after watching Timmy play with the dogs—he knew nothing about training them, just how to exercise them—Stan knew he absolutely needed Jodie's help. So he crutched his way back up to the main house. This wasn't a time for the dogs to play: only thirty-six hours before the handlers started arriving to assess his dogs and his program. Not enough time for anything.

He made it into the house without killing himself, but the long, switch-back flight of polished wood stairs gave him pause. Nobody had told him how to do stairs with crutches. Sticks then feet? Feet then sticks? Throw the damn things in the fireplace and walk on the pain?

Digging out several ibuprofen, he chewed them to get faster intake of the drug. Tasted like shit, but sometimes you needed the dose.

Just as he was bracing himself to try the stairs, Jodie turned the corner of the landing and descended toward him. A goddamn vision. Still in boots, shorts, and that paper-thin t-shirt with nothing underneath. All dry now, but...

He had to cough as his body remembered to breathe...and sucked down a lungful of powdered painkillers.

"You okay?" She stopped on the last step, placing them almost eye to eye.

Managing a nod, he cleared his throat one last time. He didn't recognize the expression on her face. "How about you?"

"Ask me some other time when I actually have a clue. How's the ankle?"

"Okay. Doug confirmed it's just a sprain. Though I might be willing to kill myself to get off these crutches and it's only been a couple hours. I need your help." *Real smooth segue, Corman.*

"Wow! Two favors in one day? You're really racking up a tab there, Stan. You okay with that, Alpha Dog?" She was so close. He could just reach out a hand and it would be on her waist. Then they'd—

"No," he snapped out and wouldn't think about which one of them he was answering—her question or his libido's. "Don't like owing anybody. But I owe Mac more than I've owed any man in a long time. More than Altman. Maybe anyone since my Pa. Payback is in thirty-six hours and I can't…fucking…*walk!*"

"Easy, Stan. Easy. Sure I'll help. I'll extract my pound of flesh later."

"Already gave at the office," he shrugged his mechanical arm, then wanted to kick himself for slapping her back down.

But instead of being offended, Jodie laughed. "Know the feeling," she tapped her ear. "What's up?" As if he needed a reason to like her more.

"Can we sit somewhere?" Because if he stood face to face with her for five more seconds he was going to do something he'd be bound to regret later. That and he could feel his pulse pounding like a jackhammer in his ankle.

Her shrug was simple assent.

He turned, but the huge living area was too daunting. Stan only entered here for the big parties and hardly those. There were couches in lazy groupings, a puzzle area, some poker tables, a small bar, more conversation areas. Forty ranch guests could be here on a rainy night and not feel the least bit cramped. In the winter, sixty or more would come over from all the local ranches about once a month. He always just felt lost in the vast space.

Out the front door, he spotted a couple of Adirondack chairs on the front porch and leveraged himself into one. Jodie lifted his bad leg with a gentle hand and slid a footstool under it.

"Thanks."

Jodie waited for more, but Stan wasn't exactly a word guy. He had that military fast sense of humor, which she liked. It was familiar. But he took time to form his thoughts. Was this favor something he'd just realized he needed because he'd bunged his ankle or had it been burning somewhere deep since the long silence of the drive back from Utah?

Though at the time she'd been thankful for it as she had enough to consider while trying to come to terms with her own actions. She could have ended up raped or dead for being so stupid. Wouldn't that be the ultimate joke: survived Syria and Libya, dead in Utah? Driving a dozen hours in the wrong direction without even noticing what she was doing wasn't something a normal, rational person did. Especially having no memory of the long miles.

Her grand conclusion? Only some pretty messed-up handler-girl did that kind of thing—which placed her and Brandy in the same category. The whole drive back and she still hadn't come to terms with that. Her...PTSD...maybe. More than maybe?

Rather than push, she sat beside Stan in silence, as Ama was teaching her, and looked out over the ranch.

A beginner's ride was just departing one of the corrals. She didn't know anything about horses, but watching the guests' faces and seeing pride raised as a flag to mask fear reminded her too much of new recruits landing in a war zone for their first time. Entry shock was always a wake-up call.

On cue, an advanced trail ride came cantering into the other side of the yard. Their bedrolls strapped behind their saddles, they rode like seasoned veterans—though none as smoothly as Patrick in the lead. One of Ama's "sons," or did she only count the "daughters" and her own Mark?

Ama's simple statement was unquestionable in its sincerity, and incredibly touching. It placed no valuation. There was no price tag of "she's our daughter, but she never went to college." "We had such hopes for her, but..." and a sad sigh. "Her brother is a very successful stockbroker now," implying everything their daughter wasn't. By tomorrow, her parents would know that they could add, "She had a chance to marry a very handsome and successful lawyer, but..."

From Ama there was no judgment. No sense of obligation. Jodie was simply "one of her daughters." Jodie added that to her growing pile of "no idea what to think about that." A pile that was fast becoming a mountain of dog shit that was going to tumble down and bury her all too soon.

"First time I sat in this chair," Stan tapped his hooks on the wooden arm, "I was about as dumb as a brick."

"Team 6 doesn't recruit stupid." The warriors in the very top units like DEVGRU were among the smartest in the military; they had to be to excel in the harshly dynamic situations they were inserted into. Every one of them had several languages and libraries of culture-specific knowledge, above and beyond any fighting, survival, or espionage skills.

"Same thing I thought at the time. That's before I chose to spend a winter fixing up an uninsulated fishing cabin," he waved an arm toward the western mountains. "Afterward, I sat here, in this chair, with Bertram beside me. Little more than a puppy. He was four, maybe five, months old when he saved my life during a freak spring blizzard just a few weeks before. Old Mac sat in the chair that you're in."

"All we need are a couple beers to complete the picture," Jodie could almost see it.

"You got that part right, young lady," Mac came out through the screen door holding three beer bottles. He handed them around and settled slowly to Stan's other side. He might be a long generation older than Stan, but she could see how Stan would age to be much like the man and his powerful presence. "Telling her about the day we started all that?" Mac waved a hand toward the dog area.

"I was. But you should tell it."

Mac's smile said he was never averse to telling a good story. "Three years ago this boy didn't seem all that much older than his pup, gotta say. Had me an idea and I'd been thinking to myself that Stan was the right sort to make it happen. Ama had already placed her vote when she rode out to give you Bertram just after he was weaned."

"The morning she came out to the cabin, I'm bucked naked, freezing cold, and wondering if I can find a way to throw myself into the woodstove," Stan sketched a square smaller than a microwave in the air with his hooks. "There's a knock and Ama walks in with the pup wrapped in one of those amazing blankets she makes. Just set it on the table and walked back out with hardly a word."

"Hold on, boy." Mac pushed himself upright. "You never said a damned thing about being naked in front of my wife." His voice was gruff but his eyes were twinkling with humor.

Stan's laugh was sharp and bitter. "I coulda been painted bright green and I doubt if she'd have noticed. No woman's ever going to look at me like the way she looks at you, Old Man." He glared out at the ranch compound.

Mac smiled across at her and winked—though Jodie had no idea why—before he continued, "Thought that training up some war dogs would make a nice income. Also give handlers a place to come after their service was done. For a time I thought Lauren might team up with this guy, but Emily snatched her up for her operation. What about you, girl? You willing to take them out for a spin?"

"Take who out for a spin?" Or was Mac trying to matchmake her with Stan? As if. He would barely look at her. She'd stood inches from him on the stairs and all she'd been able to see was pain. A pain so deep that she felt it herself as well.

"Why the dogs, of course." He didn't need to actually wink this time for her to feel that he did.

"That's the favor I need," Stan cut in as if trying to stop Mac from saying anything else. "I've been training these dogs for three years. Day after tomorrow, I've got Spec Ops handlers from several units coming out to assess them. I can't do all the things I need to do with them while I'm on crutches."

"You want *me* to run *your* dogs in front of Spec Ops? Are you *insane?*" Stan trained his dogs in ways she'd never seen before. Except...in the field. "Holy shit, that's what you've done?"

"What?" Mac and Stan both asked in unison.

"You were a Team 6 dog handler."

"Uh-huh."

"You guys and Delta, there just *aren't* any more complex field situations for a dog. You found a way to bring that training back out of the field." Dogs were just like their human counterparts. The first time they hit real battle, it was nothing like their training. A number of dogs washed out right there despite all of the simulations they'd run through. If they stuck with it, again like men and women, then the harsh real-world lessons only an actual war could teach were integrated into their trained skills.

Stan was squinting at her. Mac's eyes were narrowed with assessment.

She started to laugh, she couldn't help herself. Couldn't *stop* herself either. Stan had done something truly magnificent and had no idea that he'd done it.

As she laughed, Ama stepped out through the door with Brandy at her side. Brandy checked in every direction, then slipped up beside Jodie's chair, pausing only for a moment for Stan to pet her absent-mindedly.

Ama offered Jodie one of her serene smiles, then leaned down and kissed her on top of the head like a Jewish mother's blessing for safety before continuing down toward the horse barn. It was ridiculous, but a Jew being blessed by a Cheyenne out here in the Montana wilds felt more important than a thousand similar ones her mother had planted all through childhood. Maybe it was because Mom's all belonged back in childhood. Ama's belonged to Jodie the woman.

"Day after tomorrow?" Jodie managed to recover her breath before either of the men.

Stan nodded.

"Then why are we sitting on our asses here?"

"Uh—" Stan obviously didn't have a quick answer.

But Mac didn't hesitate. He toasted her with his mostly full beer, "Yep, you definitely are a SEAL."

CHAPTER 16

By sunset, Jodie looked as exhausted as the dogs.

Stan would lay better than even money that if he hadn't stopped them all, nothing else would. Even Brandy had done a few of the obstacle course drills until her physical limitations had caught up with her. She was a long way from agile and definitely didn't have the strength to clear the tests where power was needed. But she threaded through the pipes and took the jump off the high walk into the dunk tank several times.

However, she was as merciless as Jodie when a dog didn't make the mark on any element of the course. The least little deviation from "best action" and they were as likely to have their hindquarters nipped by Brandy as to be sent back through to try again by Jodie. Even Bertram wasn't immune to her corrections, which he took with surprising meekness. Not submissive, but rather, *Oh, right. I get that now. Sorry. Won't happen again.*

Stan had started out sitting near Jodie to prompt her on best ways to use the course, but soon she was out on the course herself. Stan would issue a command, but Jodie would knock out a brace just as a dog was crossing and force them to find another way through the problem. They'd jump for an attack and Jodi would whip the target aside. Those that didn't compensate fast enough weren't given another try; they were given five more repetitions *after* they finally got it right to her satisfaction.

By the time he made her lead the dogs to the kennel, he'd started having some ideas about what Mac had said earlier.

At first he'd thought Mac had been all about trying to find Stan a girlfriend—which meant he and the old man were going to have to have a serious talk about backing the hell off. He'd had enough of the adventure-seeking fucks and the pity fucks and all the rest of it.

But now it was clear.

Working together, for even just the few hours they'd had today, they'd been able to challenge these already exceptional dogs in new ways. He began planning what to do with two trainers at the same time out at The Urban (though he'd make damn sure to leave Brandy behind for that). He didn't want to ever again hear Brandy's mortar attack cry.

With Jodie's help...With Jodie doing all the work while he did a piss-poor job of hiding how much he hated not doing it himself, the dogs were soon fed and put to bed in their cages. When Jodi was slow to depart Brandy's cage, Stan crutched over to Bertram's and popped the latch. He didn't even need to signal for Bertram to trot down to the end of the row.

Less than a minute later, Jodie stepped out of the cage and latched it behind her.

"Bertram is very protective of her. Like he worships her or something." Stan had never seen his dog like that with any of the others.

Jodie scoffed as her silhouette made the long walk toward him, doublechecking each cage's latch. "Your dog's *in love* with my dog."

"No way."

"Get over it, Corman. Anyone with eyes can see that."

Well that was gonna suck for both of them. They'd get the next day together, then *Pffft!* Just like his Pa, there one moment and gone the next. There hadn't even been anything much worth burying after that six-thousand-degree acetylene explosion had passed through.

Jodie might not be his to lose, but the day she left, he was going to be as bummed out as Bertram would be when he left the ranch for war. Unable to bear how much he was going to miss that dog, he crutched his way out into the yard.

They walked and hobbled up to the main house together as the gold sky bled to deep red.

"Nathan always leaves something around for those of us trying to scrounge up a late meal."

"Is that all you have to say?" Jodie swung to a stop in front of him and he almost spiked her toes with his crutches.

"What?"

"How about good job? How about well done? How about thank you so much for the help? How about—*Argh!*" She spun on her heel.

He reached out and, grabbing her shoulder, spun her back. "Go on. Say it!"

"Go to hell, Corman!" She swatted at his wrist, but he wasn't knocked aside that easily.

He could just see her by the light of the darkening sky. He could see the frustration. And the hurt. The first would be easy to yell at. The second he didn't stand a chance against.

Unable to help himself, he dragged her against him in apology. He almost whimpered like one of his dogs at how good she felt.

"What the hell are you doing?" Her voice, despite being muffled against his shoulder, was harsh. Though she didn't push away.

"Can you shut up with the questions for just one, single minute?"

Much to his surprise she did. She only jumped a little when his right-side crutch fell away and thudded to the ground. He pulled her a little closer and she turned her face so now her cheek was on his shoulder rather than her nose. Her hair was softer on his cheek than a Labrador dog's ear. He became so aware of her. Each breath expanding his hold on her, each release tightening the circle of his one-armed hug. Her body pressed against his, thankfully slightly to one side or this would become embarrassing incredibly fast.

She slipped her arms around his waist and then tipped her head back enough to look up at him.

"Stan?"

"Uh-huh."

"Your 'just one, single minute' is up now. So are you going to explain what's up with this? Not saying it doesn't feel good, because it does. But what the hell are you thinking is going to—"

Out of patience, and with no more words than he'd had sixty seconds ago, he kissed her. It would probably be his only chance, so he made the most of it. She tasted of... He wasn't some goddamn poet. She tasted good and he wanted more. As the kiss deepened she hummed happily deep in her throat, more like a cat's purr than a dog's happy play-growl.

Her left arm remained pinned around his waist because he had clamped his good arm across her shoulders to support her head in the crook of his elbow as she tipped it back. But her right hand slid up his chest, his neck, and onto his cheek. Beneath her cool hand, he could feel every hot scar of his burned cheek like it was etched in fire.

"Jesus!" He yanked back. No one touched him there, ever. Not even the most thrill-seeking bitches. He tried to back away. Except he'd dropped one crutch and the other was at his side. Bracing back on his left foot, his weight landed hard on it and he yelped.

Jodie grabbed his mechanical arm and leaned back hard, managing —barely—to keep him from toppling over backward a second time. Once she was sure he was steady, she bent down to grab his second crutch. When men did that, they bent at the knees. When women did it, they just sort of folded in half at the waist. He hated himself for staring at her ass as she did. No, he didn't hate himself. Instead he filed the image securely away for later admiration.

None the wiser, she tucked his crutch in under his arm.

"Now that you're steady on your pins, do you want to explain that?"

"Nope!"

"Asshole," but this time he could hear the smile though he could no longer see it in the darkness. Maybe because he was too dazzled by her.

"Psycho." After all, who counted seconds during a hug that felt that good?

"Says the man who tried to fall over backward to end a perfectly good kiss."

"Uh…why did you kiss me?"

"You mean kiss you back? Because you're definitely the one who kissed me first, I remember that much." He barely did. He just remembered how she'd felt, tasted, and how much he wanted more.

"Okay. Care to tell me why you kissed me back?"

"To quote someone I know, or at least thought I did…Nope!"

"Asshole," he countered.

"And you called *me* psycho? Are you hungry yet?"

Hungry? Give him half a chance and he'd devour her. "Yes!"

"Tough, shelve that. I'm talking about food." And he could see her shadow moving off toward the kitchen entrance at the back of the main ranch house.

It was dark enough that he indulged himself in a smile.

"Stow that smile and come get some food."

He followed, but he had no intention of stowing the smile.

Jodie walked up the path, picturing a quiet and maybe slightly intimate raiding of the fridge in a dimly lit corner of the silent kitchen. It was the sort of thing that she'd sometimes fantasized about being able to do in her own home, because she sure couldn't do it living with her parents. There was always someone underfoot in the Brooklyn brownstone.

With his success, Davy probably had his own place by now. She hadn't thought to ask and now it no longer mattered. She'd burned that bridge. Oh, he'd probably take her in happily if she showed up, but it hadn't been the right choice this morning and it wasn't now.

And that wasn't even considering Stan's kiss. Talk about a SEAL who put a hundred percent of his focus on the task at hand. Her body still vacillated between shivering and burning up from pure animal heat at the thought of that. She'd admired his chest earlier; his t-shirt had been just as wet as hers on the river bank and he was gorgeous. A woman could get lost in a chest like that and take a week to find her way back out, even with a tracking dog.

It had *felt* even better. She'd been counting the beats of his heart automatically, an instinct from tracking how many steps she'd gone from the last known safe point. And lying with her good ear against his chest was way more than sixty beats into the danger zone. As if to prove her point, he'd backed up that chest with a kiss that—

She almost did a face-plant when she pushed open the kitchen door. As she was gaping at the crowded room, a small girl slammed into her knees hard enough that Jodie might have gone over backward if Stan hadn't placed a hand against her back.

"Tessa," Emily called from across the room, sounding exasperated.

The girl giggled and tried to bolt off in a new direction—just like a dog taking a game too far. So Jodie scooped her up in a clean sweep, tucked her under an arm so that her legs dangled to one side and her head and arms to the other. The giggles escalated as Jodie trotted her across the room to Emily, with a galumphing gait like a playing dog, sometimes spinning in little circles just to add to the excitement.

"No, please," Emily held up a hand to fend her off. She already had her two-year-old on her hip. "Give her to Mark. No, better yet. Keep her. Forever. With my blessing." To belie her words, Emily tickled her elder daughter's exposed ribs close by Jodie's arm. And then leaned down to blow a raspberry there. "Welcome to the evening zoo," Emily whispered before she turned away.

Indeed it was.

The very pregnant Julie was slouched on a couch, well-buffered with pillows and earnestly talking with Patrick about how to tell if a ranch guest was capable of a certain wilderness trail. Lauren was leaning against a kitchen counter, teasing her soon-to-be brother-in-law Nathan about a stew pot he was stirring. Mac and Ama sat in side-by-side armchairs with big mugs of tea, chatting easily with Mark like the lord and lady of the castle they were. Chelsea sat tossing comments into any conversation that caught her whimsy as she breast-fed Christopher.

"Did you ever see anything like it?" She whispered to Stan.

"Not before I moved here. Pretty amazing, isn't it?"

She leaned back against his chest for just an instant in acknowledgement. Then Tessa flailed again. Jodie swung her up until they were nose to nose, then rubbed their noses together. The girl seemed to like it as much as a dog would—at least Tessa didn't try to lick her face immediately afterward. She looked as blonde and perfect as her somewhat harried mother normally did.

"Would Tessa like a cookie?"

"No sugar!" Emily called out.

"Too late. She's in the hands of her evil Auntie now. I claim my constitutional right to spoil any child who isn't mine."

Emily grimaced, "That can't be a constitutional law."

"It must be," Stan answered for her. "Because she's solemnly sworn to uphold it."

Jodie stuck her tongue out at Emily. She didn't get the expected eye roll. Instead Emily was eyeing Stan speculatively.

Stan appeared oblivious to the look.

But Emily nodded to herself and turned to Chelsea. "I didn't believe you, but you were right."

"Told ya," Chelsea's smile was electric.

Jodie figured her best course of action was to pretend she didn't hear them and carry Tessa over to the table where there was a large plate still sporting a few Toll House cookies—the last remains of the meal they'd missed. She really didn't want to know what Chelsea had been right about. It was easy enough to guess, knowing the way Chelsea's mind worked, but having Emily confirm it made Jodie really, really anxious.

Even as she and Tessa sat, Nathan delivered a small glass of milk for the girl and a big bowl of stew each for her and Stan. "It's really for tomorrow. The flavors will develop more overnight, but it's all I have hot at the moment."

"The way it smells," she took a deep breath and sighed, "I'll gladly eat it twice in a row."

He squeezed her shoulder in thanks before returning to tend his pot.

Tessa sat happily with her cookie and milk. Jodie kept one hand casually around Tessa's waist so that she couldn't escape unexpectedly.

"You're good with kids," Stan tasted the stew. "Oh, last fall's venison. That is so good."

Jodie poked at the meat carefully; she'd just assumed it was beef. She tasted a small bite and the flavor filled her mouth. It was richer and...deeper than beef. It tasted a little wild and a little mysterious. After a second spoonful she decided that she *would* be glad to eat it again tomorrow, though she couldn't imagine it being more flavorful.

"I don't know much about kids. My brother was only a year younger, so I don't have much of a reference. But I know what makes a puppy happy."

"Chocolate chip cookies," he offered a lopsided smile. She'd been right all that long time ago: when Stan finally smiled, he was the dictionary definition of lady-killer handsome.

"No, that's me who loves cookies," and she stopped eating her stew long enough to grab one and bite off half all at once. She leaned down and shared a nose-to-nose "Mmm" with Tessa.

Stan did the same and they exchanged that greedy smile she'd been able to feel aimed at her back in the darkness just moments ago.

"You look good with a kid," Stan persisted.

Jodie looked down at Tessa in surprise. Done with her cookie and milk, she leaned against Jodie's side and looked ready to drift off to sleep. "Never thought about them really. Certainly not my own."

"C'mon. All women think about that like mad. I mean just look." He waved a hand to encompass the happy families scattered about the room.

Jodie just shook her head. "Seriously no. Not saying I don't want them, just never really thought about it. Too much else to do. What about you?"

Stan fooled with his stew for a moment, then spoke without looking up. "Used to. Back before..." he waved his spoon toward his left side and face. "Before this. Had a fiancée and everything."

"What happened?"

"Dear Stanned me. After."

"Bitch."

He shrugged.

"No, seriously, Stan. Total bitch. What kind of a teammate doesn't stand up when it counts? For a fiancée to not be willing to stand up for her man—that's obscene."

Again the uncertain shrug. He still didn't look up.

Tessa lay her head in Jodie's lap and she took a moment to get the girl settled.

"One thing for damn sure…" Jodie waited until Stan finally looked up at her.

"What?"

"She wasn't a SEAL."

His soft grunt of agreement was slow to turn into a smile, but it got there eventually.

Stan had lost track of Jodie a dozen times before the evening was over, which had made him crazy every single time. But one moment she was there and the next she was carrying Tessa off to bed close behind Emily. How long did it take to read a twelve-page picture book to a child anyway?

Then Mac, who'd been a Coronado SEAL, wanted to hear what she thought of her station at Virginia Beach. When Mark had started telling war stories, Chelsea had taken Jodie off in some other direction. She and Julie bonded over something else until finally Stan was going mad with how friendly all the ranch women were being to Jodie.

He wanted Jodie.

To himself.

And he wanted her now.

His attempts to be subtle didn't work. She missed the military hand sign for "rally point"—a pointed finger circled above his head. Rather than her coming over, Doug spotted it while he was at the fridge. He delivered Stan a fresh beer and started asking questions about the upcoming assessment of the dogs. Christ, somehow, after worrying about it all day, dogs were the furthest thing from his mind.

Jodie had touched him. Had touched his face. Not as if it was some scarred disaster (which it was) in need of pity (which it wasn't). As if it was…his face. It had been such a shock. Yet he could still feel the outline of her cool fingers as if the fire's heat had only now been eased after all these years.

He wanted more of that.

Instead, he was talking about his damn dogs.

They were halfway back to the bunkhouse before he finally realized it was just the two of them and he stumbled to a halt.

Jodie laughed, "And I thought SEALs were observant. What took you so long to get away from everyone?"

"Me? God damn it, woman. Your female pals weren't letting me near you."

She poked a finger into the middle of his chest. "Aw, is da big bad SEAL afwaid of widdle women?"

"I'm *not* Tweety Bird."

"No, Tweety is way cuter."

"Like you."

"I'm not cute, I'm—"

"The hell you aren't!" Stan couldn't believe he was having this conversation. And Jodie sounded as if she could go all night. All night. *That's* how he wanted her. That wasn't going to happen in a bunkhouse filled with ranch hands and thin walls. Taking her in the dog cage, however appropriate for the two of them, wasn't exactly decent.

He smelled the night air. It was warm and thick with the growing grass, sweet silverberry, pungent sage, and Ponderosa pine. Montana's notoriously fickle spring had issued a lovely night beneath a shining half-moon. *That* was how he wanted to see Jodie.

He turned and headed back the way they'd come.

"Wait. Where are you going?"

No way was he going to explain himself. Something had to be

done to keep the woman even a little off balance. Besides, if he tried to explain, she'd just shower him with more words.

Stan listened, but never heard a step. He finally turned to see if he'd misjudged and lost her, but she'd come up close beside him without making a noise. Former SEAL. She'd have made a damn good one even without her dog, except for weighing little more than a deep-field mission pack. Thirty pounds of gear when they had to move fast and light; sixty when going in heavy-duty; and when going deep into the field for a long-duration, complex mission, that could easily break a hundred pounds. No woman her size could meet the requirement of carrying that for a week at a time.

She walked beside him in silence, probably guessing where he was leading her.

Up, past the darkened guest cabins and out the path to the swimming lake. Tricky with the damn crutches and he had to concentrate. Jodie's hand brushed his forearm a few times in guidance over rough sections and it was all the steadying he needed. At a small, weatherproof hutch, he grabbed a couple of the big beach towels that the ranch kept stocked there for guests who forgot to bring one from their cabin.

"Might have been useful to know about that," Jodie remarked as she took them and they continued down to the lake's edge side by side.

"It says 'Spare Beach Towels' on the side," he teased her.

"Damn it. Mom was right, I should have learned to read. Too late now."

He couldn't wait any longer. Dumping his near-side crutch, he reached for her, but he didn't have far to go as she was already moving into his chest.

"You aren't going to jackrabbit away from me this time, right?" Her breath was a whisper on his cheek.

"Wild horses. Not even."

And once again she lay her cheek on his chest, her good ear, and the world went quiet. The darkness was rich and thick, like the Congo jungle—without the humidity and psychotic warlords.

"Are you just going to hold me all night? Not that I'm complaining," her whisper barely reached him.

"Just hold you," he whispered back and leaned down to kiss the top of her head.

"What? Goddamn it!" Jodie pulled back and hit his nose, thankfully not too hard—he saw only a few more stars than were painted across the sky. "Sorry. I can either listen to your heart or to you."

"I can either hold you one-armed or one-armed. Deal with it."

She thumped her forehead a couple times against his head. "I was better off when I was just listening to your heart."

He shifted his hand to place her cheek once more against his chest.

"Yeah, got the message. Not the time for talking. Except I am. You sure about this, Corman? I'm a total and complete basket case. No, don't answer. I won't hear you if you do. Squeeze once for yes, twice for no, and three times for I'm a total lunatic. Isn't that the rule? It's just nerves, right?"

That gave him pause. She was nervous? He was more in the land of utter disbelief.

Unsure what else to do, he just kept his good arm around her and held her close.

Jodie didn't know why she was freaking. Whatever this became tonight, her body wanted it. She wanted it.

Turn off your brain. Just turn it off and feel.

When was the last time she'd just *felt*?

While being slammed to the ground by a mortar blast? While holding her dog as Brandy screamed in terror? Maybe they'd both screamed and she'd never known.

Shut it down!

Block it out!

That's what she needed.

"Now, Stan. Take me!" Jodie pushed away and hauled off her t-shirt.

Remember nothing.

Feel nothing.

Just purge.

"Whoa. Slow down, Jodie."

"No! Now!" Pants to the ankles.

Boots.

Goddamn boots.

A good set of boots can save your sorry-ass life. Some stupid chief petty officer in Navy boot camp.

Wrong! They were killing her right now.

She sat her bare butt on the cooling grass, yanking her pantlegs up enough to reach the laces. Broke an already short nail digging at the knot. She sucked on it with one hand while tackling the knot with her other.

Double-knot that sucker, seaman recruit.

Goddamn Chief rules.

Finally free of the boot, she shoved it, her sock, and her pantleg all off in a single push. But her underwear somehow wouldn't slide free. Because of the bunched pants around her other foot. She found her knife, pulled it out and sliced away the side of her underwear.

"Jodie."

She began dragging at the other pantleg, hauling it up to get at the other boot's laces.

"Jodie!"

No time to untie them. She grabbed for her knife again, just as an arm clamped around her arms and ribcage from behind, just below her breasts.

"My boot!" She struggled to reach it, but the arm trapping her was almost as big as her waist and might as well have been made of steel even though it was flesh.

Helplessly pinned against his chest, she vaguely heard the soft click as Stan reset his artificial arm. Then the cool of his metal arm slid across her stomach.

All she could do was hang there, naked except for one fully-clothed foot.

He whispered something close by her ear.

"Wrong damn ear, Corman."

"Yeah, because you can hear me in this one."

She wilted, "It's never going to be okay."

He held her tighter. "Been there. Done that. No promises that there's an okay, not sure there ever was. But it gets better. Gets easier." He hugged her more tightly for a moment. "It even gets good."

"Good as in holding down a naked psycho so that she doesn't do something really stupid?"

"And what stupid thing were you going to do?"

"I was going to fuck you."

She felt the blow of her words slam into him. He tried to yank his arms away, but she trapped them against her.

"I was going to use your body to wipe my goddamn mind, Stan. I wasn't going to know or care if it was you or not. I was just going to use you until I couldn't feel anything anymore."

His attempt to pull away stopped. But he didn't pull her back tight again and she needed to feel that.

"I don't want to be…"

"Yourself," Stan declared with such simple understanding that it shocked her to stillness. "Bad news for you, Jodie. You're stuck with being you for the rest of your life."

"Damn it! I want a refund."

He kissed her on her good ear and somehow it was okay.

"Now what? You just going to keep holding a semi-naked woman all night?"

"Pretty naked from where I'm sitting," he slid his hand up over one of her breasts, then the other. She could feel the sudden tension in his body.

Tension? More like a fiery heat in hers. She raised her booted foot with its pants leg and sliced underwear anklet to make her point.

Stan let her go and shifted, with a small grunt of pain, until he was sitting by her knees and facing her.

"You're all clothed. I'm naked, except for…" she waved her booted foot again. "Something's wrong with this picture."

"Moonlit Montana spring night. Naked, mostly, woman sitting in front of me. Not a damn thing wrong with it from where I'm sitting." Then he rested his hand on her foot. "You want help putting it on or taking it the rest of the way off? I've got my vote."

"You'll take me any way you can get me."

"Damn straight, woman. Any man willing to walk away from you without a fight doesn't deserve the name."

She felt a chill and wrapped her arms over herself to ward it off.

"Which…oh shit. Your Brooklyn guy didn't even try, did he? Sorry. That's gotta suck."

"No," Jodie tried to understand. "He did. In his way. It just didn't do him any good. He's who I was and not who I am."

"And that is…" She could see his growing smile, pulling against the moonlit scars of his left cheek.

"The crazy bitch who's about to take you down, Alpha Dog."

"Bring it on, sister."

She didn't bother with her boot before launching herself at him.

His instinct was to ease the impact with his left hand.

Instead, he rammed the rounded backside of his hooks into her gut.

Such minor considerations didn't faze a fighter of Jodie's caliber.

Her attack flopped him down on his back.

With a growl, she grabbed the mechanism's wrist and had it pinned down awkwardly above his shoulder. He couldn't even get the angle on his shoulder so that he could release the angle adjuster to ease the tension. In another moment, she had his other hand under one of her knees.

Wouldn't take much to flip her aside, but she kissed him before such thoughts had a chance to go anywhere. The kiss was anything but a savage attack. It picked up exactly where the kiss they'd shared behind the main house had been before he'd cut it off.

No longer pinning his metal arm, her hand slid up his chest, his throat, then, pausing just long enough for him to stop her—as if—onto his battered cheek. Slowly, so slowly that he could think of little else, she traced every line of those scars with her thumb. No one had ever touched him that way.

He freed his meat hand and began to explore her body. His hand could span the small of her back. Her butt was as amazing a handful as her breast had been a palmful. And when he placed his hand on her shoulder and pulled her in so that her breasts pressed against his chest, she hummed happily.

"Stan?" She rocked back to sitting, giving him access to her chest. If ever a man needed two hands, now was that moment, but he worked with what he had. Her wet t-shirt had promised plenty, and her naked body delivered on that promise more than twice over.

"What is it with you and words?"

She slid a hand behind her and rubbed it down over the crotch of his pants, "I was raised in a Jewish household, so sue me."

"Which means what?"

"Oh," she began rubbing him with her palm in an almost absent-minded way that was gonna make his blood pressure set Olympic records. "Everything is either a debate or a learning opportunity—usually both. Word usage, Dad's a librarian. Medical knowledge, Mom's a nurse. National and international markets, I think my brother traded his first stock while still in the womb—he probably sent Morse code to Mom as if she was a ticker tape reader."

Still sitting across his waist with her hand behind her, she unzipped his pants, slipped her hand through the opening, and wrapped her fingers around the thin cotton.

"And you?" He managed to gasp out, hoping that if she kept talking, she wouldn't stop what she was doing to him. Unable to help himself, he swung his metal arm around and rested it on the long line of her thigh just so that he could feel any of her motion that was conducted up to his biceps stump.

She didn't even flinch in surprise. "Me? Total black sheep. My family has always been a cat family. Not me. By nine, my after-school income was from dog-walking, not something respectable like babysitting." She withdrew her hand, but shifted down to sit on his thighs as she undid his belt and pants. The grass was cool and prickly against his butt and back as she stripped his shirt up and his pants down to his knees. For a long moment she looked down at him, then up at his face.

"What?" He'd earned compliments for his build before from other women. But Jodie wasn't other women.

"How do you feel about clichés?"

"What? Are you kidding me?"

Then she grinned at him, glanced meaningfully at his crotch and the prominent evidence of how badly he wanted her. "Ooo, *sailor!*"

He couldn't help but laugh. Then he had a horrid thought. "Oh no! No! No! No!"

"What?" Jodie froze in place.

"I didn't think. Not in a hundred years. The nearest condom is back at the bunkhouse."

"So not." Jodie leaned back to where her pants were still around her ankle, completely exposing herself to the moonlight in the process.

Damn but she was beyond stunning. Even out of shape, he could see the muscle rippling along her arms and down her slender frame.

She pulled a string of three condoms out of her pants pocket and lay the strip on his chest, "Emily."

"Emily gave you—"

She laid another pair next to them. "Julie."

"I love those women. Gotta remember to tell them that."

"Then, of course, there's Chelsea," she hesitated for a long moment before dramatically pulling out two long strips of five each, which she lay on his chest.

"Are there any more?" It came out a little more weakly than Stan intended as he tipped his head up to look at the vast array on his chest.

"Nope, but I'm wagering that Lauren will be kicking herself that she didn't think to pull me aside during dinner and add to the collection."

"Umm…"

"Wondering where to start?" Jodie traced her finger along his chest between each foil-wrapped packet in the collection.

"No." He slid his hand up her thigh where it had come to rest. "I know exactly where to start. I'm just wondering if we can get through all of them tonight."

Jodie didn't even blink. Setting all but one aside, she twisted it back and forth in the moonlight. Without a word, she opened it and sheathed him so slowly that he was shuddering with need by the time she crouched over him.

She lowered herself onto him as she leaned down to kiss him. The moment before their lips met, she whispered in a soft sigh of pleasure, "One."

CHAPTER 18

For pure sex, Jodie had never had such a night…or morning. The predawn glow was chasing the last of the stars from the sky as she lay inside the curve of Stan's good arm while he slept. A small pile of beach towels had kept them close enough to warm through the night.

If they'd been just teenagers, last night would have made some sense. A contest to see how many times it was possible to screw in a single night. As grown adults, not so much. They'd done it on the grass and again as soon as they could recover.

After she'd taken off his mechanical arm, which had really disturbed Stan until she'd kissed him on that shoulder, they'd gone for a swim. She hadn't brought a condom out to the central float, but they'd found other ways to entertain themselves.

His missing arm was less of a problem than she'd feared. They'd celebrated the moonset in each other's arms, Stan propped himself over her one-handed, blocking out the stars themselves until her whole world had become him. They'd talked about it as they spooned together with her head resting on his stump—though it took her a bit to get her ear shifted so that she could hear him speak. Not the most comfortable position, but she was adjusting. Kind of.

"Haven't been truly naked with a woman since…before."

"Thinking it made you less of a man?"

His shrug had spoken volumes.

She'd curled up enough for him to take her from behind as they lay side by side. But it wasn't his hand pulling her hip tightly against him that had almost unbalanced her. It was the ever-so-tentative brush of his stump down her neck and over her shoulders.

In the darkness of the starlit night, with vision of anything more than outlines and shadows taken from them, a freedom and trust had formed between them. The latter had been easy. SEALs lived by trust. Trust your team. With the implied: trust no one else. Not exactly the best training for cross-team missions, but it definitely had its place. Somehow, with the removal of his arm, the trust had been the most natural thing.

The freedom, the unexpected collapse of the inhibitions and rules that had always bounded her life, was a much less comfortable feeling. Uncomfortable or just unfamiliar? She rolled her nose closer to his skin and breathed him in. Letting herself simply enjoy the moment—without worrying about the consequences, implications, what her parents would say, or any of that—was incredibly liberating. That alone was increasing her pulse.

That and knowing the encroaching daylight was fast bringing their night together to an end.

"Choice time," Jodie whispered to herself. The next moments would set the tone of their morning-after. Would it be distant or sexy?

She looked down from the last of the stars to inspect the man she lay against. Distant or sexy? That was such a dumb question that she didn't know why she'd even thought of it.

Brushing aside the towels, she eased herself up, then did an abrupt face-plant in the middle of his chest.

Stan went from fast asleep to wide awake in a moment.

"Oh, Cassandra," he moaned happily.

"Cassandra?" Jodie pushed up to glare down at him.

"Wasn't that the great beauty of Greece or some such?"

"No. Cassandra was a true prophetess, but no one would ever

believe any of her predictions. You're thinking of Helen of Troy, which I'm so not."

"Awkward. Why wouldn't anyone believe her?"

"She'd been cursed by the gods. Man, do I know that feeling."

"Really awkward. So, if you *are* Cassandra—and I called you that, so I'm guessing you must be—what are you prophesying at the moment that I won't believe?"

"Oh, you'll believe it by the time I'm done with you."

The sun was cracking the horizon by the time she finished delivering on that promise.

They were both grinning like idiots as they made it down the slope to join the others for breakfast, not that either of them cared.

CHAPTER 19

Stan watched Jodie working the dogs, just as he had through the long day. Each gesture evoked a memory from last night. Watching her arch back to toss a ball, he could almost feel her hips pressing hard against his as she did so. She talked to the dogs as much as she did during sex, which was so damn cute. The simplest sideways glance— Hell, just the sound of her voice as she called out commands sent shivers of memory through him.

They'd spent the morning at the obstacle course. With Brandy exhausted, they'd left her in the cage to sleep it off and come out to The Urban. The whole afternoon had been working on advanced techniques that were so hard to do alone. His favorite was with Jodie as a victim in standard body armor. Stan was able to have the dogs take turns dragging her to safety while he returned live fire over their heads. He had the dogs drag her time after time until she couldn't stop laughing about it.

He could spend a lifetime listening to her laugh.

That thought hit him square in the gut and he actually lost count of how many rounds he had left in his current magazine.

"Crazy talk," would be Chelsea's phrase for it, at the same moment going all dreamy-eyed because she *was* Chelsea. Was that what the women had been talking about last night at dinner? He'd registered that Emily had told Chelsea she was right about something, he simply hadn't understood what they were talking about.

But now?

Was it really that obvious how gone he was on Jodie? And that had been before last night.

Pa had always said, "You'll know when you know." Stan knew that for the first time, he finally understood what Pa had been talking about.

Christ, he'd almost cried like some sniffly chick when she'd kissed him on his bare stump. No woman had ever even seen that, or ever wanted to. To Jodie, it was like he was more himself without the prothesis than with it. As if he was somehow whole rather than broken. She'd made no distinction between bracing herself against one of his shoulders or the other as she unraveled above him. Having her curl up against that side, with her hair as a soft cascade that seemed to coat the stump's skin with pure light, hadn't been a surprise —it had been a goddamn miracle.

But a lifetime?

He knew he'd never find anyone else like her. Driven, stubborn, lovely, and totally mad about dogs didn't just happen along every day of the week. That she didn't see him as broken he flat out didn't understand.

Stan sent Bertram over to knock her down from behind. Again that laugh as she tumbled to the dirt and was dragged over to him.

When she was close enough, he just grabbed her by the lifting ring on the front of her armored vest and picked her up. Without hesitation, she wrapped her arms and legs about him. He had enough blood in his brain to remember to safety his rifle before he dropped it and his crutches in the dirt. Then he grabbed her ass and pressed her up against the side of one of the old buildings, balanced on his good foot.

He could feel the handle of her thigh-sheathed knife pressed against the inside of his wrist. Could feel where her arm crossed over the boundary of flesh and prothesis as if it wasn't there. The heat of her kiss seared his flesh as he felt the pressure build where their hips were pressed together.

"Christ, woman!" He could barely groan as she shifted to nibble at the side of his neck.

"Wrong ear," she mumbled but didn't stop. Indeed his mouth was near her bad side.

He leaned back enough to break off her attack on his jugular, then swung up his mechanical arm and used the backs of the hooks to nudge her chin up so that they were looking at each other. "Don't you ever shut up?"

"Nope!" Her eyes sparkled as blue as the Montana sky.

"Someday I'm going to make such love to you that I'm gonna leave you speechless."

"Dare you to try. I'll never give in. I'll fight you to the last, you cur. Why, I'll—" she stopped on a strangled sound. "What did you just say?"

"I'm going to make you feel so goddamn good that you lose the power of speech."

"No, not that. And just for reference, I'm definitely looking forward to that part of it. Or at least to you trying."

Stan had to force himself not to take her right here and now, even with the dogs all gathered around. He forced himself to review what he'd said. He'd...

Oh! He hadn't even heard it go by himself.

"Oh, yeah. I'm seriously talking about *making love* to you. With you."

"Uh, okay. I'm having a hard time with that phrase too, but that's not it either."

"Then what are you talking about, woman? Maybe now might be a good time to try out some of those words of yours. Or maybe I'll just go ahead and use your body until neither of us can remember the question."

"It was..." Jodie tried to look down, but he kept the curve of his hooks under her chin so that he could see her eyes, "...the part about *someday.*"

"Why is that the problem?"

This time, when she went to put her head down, he let her. But he didn't lower her to the ground. Last time he hadn't been paying attention, she'd driven a thousand miles before he'd caught up with her. That definitely wasn't happening again. Instead, he kept her pinned between him and the post and kissed her forehead, as much to calm himself as to calm her. That seemed to unleash her words.

"I don't even know what I'm doing tomorrow. *Someday*? Really, Stan? I can't think that far ahead. I'm kind of in the place where I'm just glad not to have had a nervous breakdown in the previous hour. *Someday* is just way too scary."

"So…it's okay if I make love to you until you lose all your words as long as you don't have to commit to shit?" What was wrong with him? He should be jumping at an offer like that, but that Jodie could even *think* of leaving scared the shit out of him more than his first firefight in Mosul, Iraq.

The even-toned anger in Stan's voice had Jodie jerking back suddenly enough that she banged the back of her head hard against the log doorpost Stan still held her pinned to. His good hand still cupped her behind. In fact, physically there'd been no shift between them—her own arms and legs were still wrapped around him.

But her world had just shifted. And not for the better.

Even the dogs alerted to the change in tone. They'd been lounging in the building's shade, panting from the long day's hard workouts. Now they all sat at alert, dead silent and waiting for a command.

"Stan, seriously. I…" What? "I told you I was a bad bet in the beginning. Psycho lady, remember?"

"And last night was just—"

"Was," she cut off his acid tone, "the best sex, the best," she swallowed hard, "lovemaking I've ever been a part of. I want more. I want you now and I want you tonight. But tomorrow? That's scary land. I have no way to even think about something like that, never mind *someday* as if we have forever."

"Don't you *want* forever?" At least his tone went from acid to only mortally wounded. Which was somehow even worse.

"I don't know what I want. If you'd asked me last week, I wanted a healthy dog and a slice of really great pizza. Yesterday, before you bunged your ankle, I was kind of down to hoping for no repeat of the psychotic break that sent me down the highway. By the way, any future with me can never include returning to Utah, just so you know. Last night was like…a glimmer of hope. The way you can made me feel, Corman, I've got no previous calibration for how to even think about that. That was an amazing gift." She kissed him on the nose to confirm it.

"So, the sex was good, huh?" Stan grunted like a Neanderthal.

"Sex. Good. Yes." Jodie grunted back.

"You really are psycho."

"Warned you."

"Okay, I'll take that as an answer for now. But you've got to promise me something."

She wanted to argue. She wasn't in any shape to make promises to anyone, including herself. But he was being so damned decent that she offered him a tentative nod.

"You feel the need to run again, you come talk to me first. Not Chelsea. Not even Ama. Me!"

"Or else what?"

"Easy. Never gonna put you down."

Jodie didn't know whether to laugh or cry. Or both. She rested her forehead on his shoulder and let herself just be there for a moment. The joy of being held. The moment that he laid his scarred cheek against her hair, she knew she was in trouble. How could she ever walk away from this?

Walking away from Stan might be even harder than walking away from Brandy had been, which had almost killed her. The only way would be if she didn't have to agree to see him first. Stan knew that. He was SEAL smart and knew he'd trapped her if she agreed to his demand. Just being held like this for eternity didn't sound like such a bad option though. Maybe she could somehow never answer *and* never let go. She could just—

"Thought it was her *dog* I sent to you."

Jodie startled at the deep male voice. She peered over Stan's shoulder and spotted the oddest couple. The compact woman, with black hair and the bluest eyes, was even shorter than Jodie and model slender. The other, a blond-haired man who was built on as big a scale as Stan, loomed protectively beside her.

Stan glanced over his shoulder, so that for a moment he and Jodie were cheek to cheek, then he turned, stepped on his bad foot, and dropped her without ceremony.

It was too sudden.

She couldn't recover.

Jodie planted her butt in the dirt and slammed into Bertram's side, taking the dog down with her.

Stan collapsed on her with a yelp of pain.

The big guy glared down at them all piled in the dirt, but the woman burst out laughing. "Well, we have no question that we found who we were looking for. Hi," she offered Jodie a hand to her feet. "I'm Zoe, he's Luke and—"

Jodie twisted to look at the man, then snapped to attention. He must be SEAL Team 6 Commander Luke Altman who *had* sent her here.

Stan was still cursing on the ground and holding onto his bandaged foot.

Finally he shot out a salute without getting up. "Thanks, asshole. You totally destroyed the moment."

"My pleasure," Luke didn't smile, but deadpan might just be his only expression. "Which one of these is yours, Jaffe?" Luke was eyeing the attentive line of dogs.

"None, sir. She's at the ranch's kennel. She still hasn't recovered enough to be near live fire. but she is doing better with Stan's help."

"Glad to hear he's good for something." Then he looked down at Stan. "Does surprise me some, though."

"Same to you, asshole," Stan muttered.

At that, Luke smiled broadly, proving he did have more than one expression. He gave Stan one of those manly handshakes as he helped him to his feet. Jodie gathered up his crutches, then recovered the M16 rifle they'd been using for training.

Zoe made brushing motions at her hair from out of Luke's view.

Jodie finger-combed her hair as casually as she could.

Zoe shrugged that it hadn't helped much, but then made it okay with a smile.

"They ready for tomorrow?" Again Luke was inspecting the dogs.

"Tomorrow, as in when we were expecting you to show?" But Stan didn't wait for an answer. "Jodie, take a walk."

Zoe and Luke looked at Stan in surprise, but Jodie just sighed. She absolutely knew what was coming.

He let her get far enough away to wonder if she'd misread the situation and Stan really did want her out of the way. There was no sound at all, even though she was listening for it: Stan's command, the dog's racing feet, nothing. She was just debating turning back—because there was no way Stan was going to just dismiss her like that—when both Bertram and Tiger took her feet out from under her.

They clipped her so hard that she actually flipped over backward to end up lying on her stomach. By the time she'd rolled onto her back, they had her by the shoulders of her vest and were dragging her through the dirt as three-round bursts of 5.56 mm bullets whistled by close overhead. Redoubling their efforts, the dogs dragged her through a muddy patch that she'd stepped around on her outbound journey. Dogs didn't care about such things.

They released her, covered in dust and mud, at the feet of a SEAL Team 6 commander.

"Thanks, guys," she told the dogs. Tiger barked happily, then the two dogs sat on her. "Goddamn it!"

Stan laughed aloud. "She's the one who taught them that trick."

"*Aus,* you crazy dogs. *Verschwinde!* Get off and go sit on someone else." Even shoving at them didn't get them moving. Then she spotted Stan's flat-palmed Stop signal. "Corman!"

He grinned, then finally released them with a *"Gute Hund"* and a head rub they totally deserved.

"Nice to meet you, Petty Officer Jaffe." Apparently Altman's idea of high humor. Zoe's smile confirmed that estimation. So, his wife was the window to Altman's moods.

"Likewise, sir," she said from the dirt. Was Stan the window to her own emotions? Did he somehow know her better than she knew herself, with his demand to come see him first if she felt the urge to run? She didn't belong here, but she was starting to suspect that she didn't belong in Brooklyn either. Even without Brandy. Too many thoughts, she pushed herself to her feet.

"We were done for the day, sir. But we can put them through some paces if you'd like."

Luke shook his head. "Sounds as if they've earned their rest. Right now I'm more interested in hearing how PO Jaffe and her dog are doing."

"Nikita's been worrying at him for a full report," Zoe explained why he'd care before Jodie even had time to be surprised.

"Had to send her on a mission back in goddamn Honduras to get her out of my hair," Altman groused. Jodie knew that's where she and her husband had gotten together. But that's all she knew—Nikita had been very careful to never talk about it—which meant it had been on some seriously hairy and very Black Op.

"If you're still here, she promised that she and Drake would take their next leave here at the ranch," Zoe patted her husband's arm.

Jodie tried to imagine that. Still here? As in Stan's *someday*? Still here, as in this was where Nikita expected she'd be? Jodie desperately needed to find the speed dial on her life so that she could spin it to Slow-the-Hell-Down. Better yet, a big goddamn Emergency-Stop-Rip-Cord.

"I'm willing to commit to being here through tomorrow anyway." She offered the comment lightly to Zoe. After all, working with the dogs had been such a joy. And she wanted to see them through their selection process.

Stan heard it go by, though. Tomorrow was one more day than

she'd been willing to commit to even a few minutes ago. He nodded his acknowledgement. No smile of triumph. Not a hint of smug. Nor was it relief. Instead, she knew that he understood how major that simple statement was for her.

She, in turn, nodded her appreciation.

Jodie knew two things in that moment. One, she'd just agreed to Stan's terms of promising to talk to him if she again felt the urge to run. Two, that maybe, just maybe, with everything else aside, Stan Corman might be worth staying for all on his own.

Back at the kennel, Bertram trotted down the line to check on Brandy.

Stan let him go until he heard a loud whine of panic. Jodie raced down to the cell faster than Stan could even turn on his dumb crutches.

"Where's my dog? Who the hell took her this time, Corman?"

"Not me. I—"

"Well someone did. I'm gonna hunt them down and…" Her voice tapered off when Stan pointed at the dog bed. It was now covered in one of Ama's weavings done in russet and black.

"That's where your dog has gone." It reminded him of the blanket Ama had delivered Bertram to that remote fishing cabin and given him hope. In fact, he still had the blanket across the foot of his bed and he saw how perfectly the two weavings would go together. Ama was always a tricky one.

Luke and Zoe had come down to look into the cage with them. "Well, certainly can't fault the accommodations. Pretty piece of work."

Stan only had eyes for Jodie as she knelt and brushed her fingers over the weaving. For a woman who was never at rest, she appeared suddenly calm and peaceful.

"You okay, Jodie?"

She nodded uncertainly. "I don't know what this place is doing to me, but it's okay. I think."

"Someone want to explain what's going on?" Luke didn't sound angry, just puzzled.

"My dog," and Stan caught the subtle edge of humor in Jodie's voice, "is at the ranch house learning about Cheyenne weaving."

Luke and Zoe looked at her askance.

"Let's get these dogs bedded down, then I'll go and introduce you."

It didn't take much to settle the dogs. They might be in peak form, but they'd been worked hard. Dinner and a quick brushing, most of them were asleep before the humans were out of the cage.

Stan didn't know how to read the situation. He puzzled at it as they walked up to the ranch house, but it made him no wiser. Altman wanting to check on Jodie's dog made only a sham's worth of sense. *Coming here a day early?* Stan hadn't expected him to come at all. He'd been looking for ten or twelve handlers to show up for assessment and pairing tomorrow, not his former CO tonight.

And Zoe? All he'd heard was that Altman had married, but she looked like no more than a plaything. Next to her, Jodie appeared tall and powerful. Next to Altman, Zoe was...what? He didn't know a thing about her. She hadn't cried out in alarm when the dogs had taken down Jodie. Nor flinched at the firing of the M16. But she looked so insubstantial that a strong breeze might have knocked her over.

That's when he noticed the odd fold in her pants leg. Not her boot catching, nor was it the right shape for a handgun.

"What knife is your carry?"

"Boker Plus Anti-Grav." She smiled up at him like he'd just won a door prize. Slim profile, ceramic blade, carbon fiber handle—basic and lethal. "I see you still carry the Winkler G-10 you got in ST6."

"Lady knows her knives."

"Know a lot more than that, sailor. You might try remembering that."

"Jodie might be teaching me a thing or two on that subject."

Zoe rapped her knuckled against his metal prosthesis, surprising him almost as much as Jodie did. "Keep that in mind, big guy. None of us are quite who we appear to be."

"And who are you?"

"The woman in love with Luke Altman. Care to ask me *what* I am?"

Stan didn't know if he dared. Zoe had said it so easily. So matter-of-factly. He glanced ahead at where Jodie and Luke were chatting as they led the way.

In love with…Jodie Jaffe? Making her promise that she wouldn't run from him again was certainly well down that path. Asking her questions that included words like "forever." What was up with that?

Zoe's laugh drew his attention back down to her.

"I know that look. Just picture your life without her in it. Your question isn't *what* I am. Your real question is how the hell can Luke be with someone, with anyone. Trust me, he was just as sure as you are that he'd be a solo act for the foreseeable future."

He tried to imagine a day waking up without Jodie beside him. No teases. No tussles beneath the stars. No incredible synchronicity co-training the dogs. No soft smile when they had reached their unspoken agreement. It had been one of those he-knew-that-she-knew and he-knew-that-she-knew-that-he-knew moments about all the layers of meaning behind that promise. There'd been no need to say any of it aloud. He understood the battle she waged inside herself. Hadn't he fought it every damn day since he and his dog had been blown to shit on the battlefield?

He'd come through it. In pieces, but through it. At least that's what he'd thought until Jodie had somehow convinced him that he'd come through it pretty intact. Despite his missing arm, scarred cheek, stupid-ass crutches for a week until his ankle healed… Despite who he *knew* he was, she'd convinced him that he was whole.

But to be complete? Again he found himself watching Jodie's easy stride, already more comfortable with Altman than most SEALs were after a year on his team.

To be complete *required* Jodie. He didn't just want her; he'd be less without her. Less of a man, less than whole in an entirely different way.

"Whoa!" The breath rushed out of his body.

"Yep! Hit me that way too. Quite the surprise, isn't it? Don't bother answering. I'm guessing your brain needs a subject change before it shorts out."

"Big-time."

"*What* I am, in addition to being Luke's wife, is Night Stalker Chief Warrant 3 Zoe Altman, 160th SOAR 5th Battalion E Company. I'm an Avenger drone pilot."

Subject change? That was a full-on, head-slamming change of direction. "You're what?"

She just grinned up at him as they reached the steps at the front of the ranch house. She looked like a happy twelve-year-old who'd just managed to tease an older sibling. Except those eyes said just how a grown-up woman lived behind that angelic face.

Stan hadn't even known the Avengers were aloft. Three years ago they'd still been in the someday-maybe category of prototyping. And this bit of a woman piloted one? For the 5E, who were the best of the best in the Spec Ops helicopter world. That at least explained how Altman had met her. He'd heard about Luke's first mission into China with them shortly before Stan was blown off the team. Couldn't really credit they were that good.

"How long have you flown with them?"

"Formation day."

"There from the beginning."

She nodded. "I was copilot until recently. My commander fell in love with an X Games freestyle skier, lucky bastard. Sofia was awesome, even if she was so ridiculously gorgeous that she made me ill just to look at myself. He's pretty drop-dead too, so their kids are gonna be a-maz-ing! She retired to be a mom—already caught with her first one. They'd already been hot and heavy for a year but were keeping it all quiet so that some X Games paparazzi didn't compromise her career."

"Now she's gone and you're pilot-in-command."

"Yes!" Zoe did a little happy dance. "Been in the field a couple of times, but I love the drone flying too much to give it up. And with Luke's team and ours pretty much embedded, we're not apart that much." Her smile went wicked and wiped out any hint of the smug twelve-year-old, replacing it totally with the smug twenty-something. Actually, to make CW-3 she had to be at least thirty, which was hard to imagine. She wasn't kidding about not being who she appeared to be. How much more was Jodie than she appeared?

Stan's head was still spinning.

Luke and Jodie had disappeared inside. He managed the front steps onto the ranch house's front porch, but didn't feel like tackling the big flight upstairs. He dropped into a chair and propped his aching foot up on a stool. He waved Zoe inside, but she sat down in the next chair over instead.

"So, back to figuring out that you're actually in love with her. I mean, it's like written all over you. You know that, right?"

Stan sighed. What was it with relentless women, anyway?

"See, here she is." Jodie had found Brandy in the same Puddle Dog pose beside Ama's loom.

Brandy jolted awake and looked around, startled for a moment. Then, eyeing Luke carefully, she slipped up to Jodie for a hug, keeping Jodie between her and the stranger. Jodie knelt down to reassure her.

Ama allowed the loom to come to rest and turned to face them.

"And this is Ama Henderson. She's one of the owners of the ranch."

"Hi, Ama, how have you been?"

Ama rose and stepped up to hug Luke.

Jodie didn't know why she was surprised. Luke had been the one to send her here after all.

"I'm wonderful. And you? You look so very good, Luke. We haven't seen you since the wedding. Where is Zoe?"

"Downstairs with Stan, I guess. We'll have to rescue him soon."

"No," Ama tipped her head for a moment as if somehow she could hear them out on the front porch. "No, I think we'll leave them be for the moment."

Then she smiled down at Jodie, who was still holding on to Brandy in case she didn't take well to Luke.

"Luke was Stan's commander. And Mac was Luke's."

"Took me under his wing back in the regular teams. You want a model SEAL, talk to Mac Henderson."

Coming from Luke, that was quite a statement.

"That's how you knew about this place."

He nodded.

"You sent Stan here after he was wounded," she could see the pieces fitting together in her head.

Then they clicked. *Altman the Matchmaker?*

"You, asshole!"

Brandy was suddenly on her feet, a hard growl echoed about the room as she faced off with Luke. Jodie grabbed her collar.

"Well, Brandy hasn't *completely* forgotten who she was," Luke said coolly, but Jodie noticed that he was being very careful to make no sudden moves.

Jodie had to reinforce her call to sit with a sharp smack on Brandy's butt to get her attention. Still, the low snarl sounded past her bared teeth.

Ama was smiling at her. Smiling again as if she alone understood some joke.

A joke of...*Thought it was her* dog *I sent to you.* That's what Altman had said when he'd found her in Stan's arms. *Okay, overreacting again, Jodie.*

"So...you didn't send me to fix Stan." As Jodie calmed, so did Brandy. She petted the dog's head, actually glad to see that Brandy's defensive attitude had overcome her own fears, even for a moment.

"Didn't realize he needed fixing." He squinted at Ama. "What did I miss? *Does* Stan need fixing?"

"Not anymore," Ama said softly.

Jodie sat down abruptly on the hardwood floor. There was no mistaking Ama's smile now. Stan *had* been broken. Then Jodie had been sent in, perhaps by chance, perhaps not—the jury was still out on that. Certainly in bringing her dog here, she'd also brought herself. Whatever had been broken in Stan, Ama now perceived as healed.

What about her? So much was broken inside her that she still couldn't see the tree for having her face smashed up against the bark. Forest? What a laugh. There was no such thing.

No…

"Wait a second…"

"You—" Jodie looked at Altman, but he hadn't even realized how much pain Stan had been in by thinking he was less of a man. Even though he was such an *amazing* man.

"You—" She turned to look up at Ama.

"Yes, my daughter?" Ama made it a question, but it wasn't.

Somehow Ama had met her over the lunch table and simply known. Known what? That Jodie and Stan were going to become lovers? Jodie supposed that after last night, it was the only word for it. They'd left mere sex behind the moment they'd slid together for the first time. Sex *never* felt that incredible. And then it had started getting so much better.

And why was she figuring this out in front of an ST6 commander.

"Uh, okay. I'm letting you both off the hook for now. But I'm warning you. I find out that one of you is behind whatever the hell is happening to my life, I'm going to have Brandy pee in your favorite boots."

"Deal," Luke nodded.

Ama's reaction, Jodie was far less sure about. She'd never lead one of her "daughters" astray…would she?

CHAPTER 20

Stan had never been much of a joiner. There was the ranch life to one side, with him and his dogs on the other. And now he wondered why he'd been that way.

Here he was, sitting on the ground to one side of the campfire circle. Jodie sat between his legs and leaned back against him as if it was the most natural thing. A beer in his hooks and a woman in his arm. It was so…normal.

Luke and Zoe sat much as he did. Patrick was over with the remaining ranch guests on the other side of the fire. It was changeover night, so any one-week guests had left this afternoon and only a handful of multi-weekers remained. Chelsea was over there, as well as some of the other hands. Lauren and Emily were sitting comfortably nearby as a buffer on his other side.

Sparks were dancing up into the night skies like a thousand fireflies. The fire's toasty heat kept back the descending coolness. Nathan squatted by the fire making another batch of his gourmet salted caramel s'mores.

Thankfully, Stan wasn't someone the guests had any chance to bond with so they always ignored him—even the ones who didn't shy aside at the sight of his arm.

But with the others from the ranch, he could actually get used to doing this a little more often.

The stars were just starting to show. He tapped his bottle to Jodie's in a toast, then tipped it up toward the sky. She looked upward, then nodded before leaning back against him harder for a moment. Last night, at this moment, they'd been making love for the first time. Now they were—

He considered his conversation with Zoe and decided that now was definitely a good time to keep his trap the hell shut.

Mac stepped up out of the darkness and eased himself into a lawn chair on Luke's other side. "What do you think about a one-week, in-residence obedience course?" He jumped right in.

Stan was trying to figure out how to not say *no*, but rather *Hell no!* When Jodie chimed in.

"Like training SEALs how to use their words and behave like human beings?"

Zoe snorted out a laugh. "I can think of a few Night Stalkers I'd like to sign up for that course too. Tell you what, Jodie, we'll run a test class on these two," she hooked a thumb at Luke behind her. "I'll get them here and you can beat them into submission."

Stan traded a look with his former CO. Luke shook his head just enough to say, "Do *not* be dumb enough to get into it." As if he would. Definite no-win scenario.

"You ladies," apparently Mac was a braver man than either of them, "appear to already have them pretty well in hand."

Jodie tipped her head back enough to offer Stan a great view down her front. Instead he was looking at how the firelight caught her eyes. That was a new one.

"Heel," she said to him.

He went for a noncommittal, "Woof."

"She's got you, Stan," Luke was enjoying himself far too much.

"Oh, like you didn't put a ring around Zoe's finger the first moment she let you."

"Hey," Zoe twisted enough in Luke's lap to look at him. "Don't besmirch the smartest thing he's ever done just because you're a coward."

"Because I'm…what?"

"Jodie, hold out your left hand." Zoe held out her own hand as an example, the diamond and delicate gold band catching the firelight.

When she didn't, Zoe took her hand and hauled it out into view.

"See. No ring. Coward."

Jodi jerked her hand back as if it had been burned. "We've known each other about two days."

"You called Luke over a week ago, Jodie. I know. I was there."

"Took me a day and a half to drive here."

"And then you spent another day—" Jodie's elbow in Stan's gut cut off his comment about her other road trip.

"How long did it take *you* two to get together?" Stan fought for a leg up.

"The length of the Dakar Rally, plus a little."

"The Dakar what?"

Zoe snarled, just like one of the dogs only cuter. "World's biggest car race. Duh! What planet do you live on? Can't tell you the story, a Black Op."

"Shouldn't have even said that much," Luke grumbled.

"Oh, like that part of it wasn't all over the news," Zoe shushed him. "You should definitely check out the videos of this really hot blonde racer named Zoe DeMille. She's a serious cutie. Just totally awesome." She batted her eyelids like a 1930s Hollywood starlet.

Luke just grimaced as if he was in serious pain.

"Though I'm not sure he ever said the actual words to me," Zoe mused more quietly.

"What words?" Luke looked puzzled.

"See?" Zoe turned to Jodie. "See what you're going to have to put up with?"

Then Mac smacked Luke on the back of the head like he was a new recruit—he probably had been when they'd first met.

"What?" Luke rubbed the back of his head. It had been a pretty solid connect.

"Tell her that you love her, you damn fool," Mac sighed. "Thought I trained you better than that."

"But she knows—"

Mac smacked him again.

Stan was hard pressed not to laugh in his former commander's face.

Instead Luke bent forward far enough to kiss Zoe on top of her head. Stan was just close enough to hear the whispered, "I really love you, Zoe Altman."

Zoe's reaction was electric. She jolted out of his lap and spun to squat between his knees and stare at him. Stan could see tears already coming to her eyes, then she threw herself at Luke.

Stan had to turn away from the look on his commander's face. Some things weren't meant for other people to see and Luke's impossible tenderness as he held his wife was one of those things.

Instead, he looked down at the top of Jodie's head. Was he supposed to say something like that? Was that what he was feeling? Life without Jodie was unimaginable. But life with words in it like love? Marriage? *Children!* How was he supposed to use words like those? Could he tell Jodie that he loved her?

"Don't, Stan," Jodie whispered softly enough that it was only for his ears. "Just don't go there."

He pulled her in a little tighter with his good arm. He considered asking why but knew it wasn't the time.

"I just couldn't deal with it."

Surprisingly, he realized that he could. Being in love with Jodie Jaffe sounded real damn good to him. "I'll...wait."

She nodded her thanks against his chest.

"Just don't make me wait too long."

In answer, she thumped her head back against his sternum hard enough to hurt.

———

The words.

Jodie had seen the words slam into Zoe. She'd already married him. They were one of those crazy close couples. Not like her parents or her brother and sister-in-law, who were…comfortable together. Zoe and Luke were obviously as close as any at the ranch.

Yet the words had sent Zoe flying into his arms and she still hadn't surfaced. She'd curled up in Luke's lap and he'd wrapped his arms around her and rested his chin on her head until they'd practically morphed into a single being.

And Stan had just offered to say those same words to her? Did he even understand what they meant? It didn't seem likely.

But neither did it seem impossible—which it damn well should.

That worried her more than anything. What if he came to understand them and she never could?

Mac had watched the whole thing calmly. He smiled at Luke and Zoe like a beneficent father. That was fine. It was Ama's smiles that were too all-knowing.

Time for a subject change before Luke decided to pass Mac's slap on the head down the line to Stan.

"Obedience school?" Jodie grabbed on the first thing that came to mind.

Stan groaned and whispered something about tenacity near her deaf ear. She ignored him.

"Well, sure," Mac took the bait. "I saw right off Stan was good people, so I knew I had to have him on the team. Old Marcinko himself taught me that back in the teams before he formed ST6. *Get the right people first and worry about finding their slot later.* Took a bit of puzzling what to do with Stan once I got him here, but bringing that Malinois litter aboard solved it neat as a pin. You gonna do us proud tomorrow, Stan?"

"All in, all the time," Stan responded and Jodie found herself echoing the vow familiar to any SEAL. If he failed, it wouldn't be for lack of putting his entire heart into it. That was something a SEAL did better than anyone.

And she couldn't believe she was sitting here in his arm and thinking about the power of his heart. If he really had set his sights on her... That was a damned powerful thing when it was done by a SEAL.

Mac nodded with an "of course" feeling. He expected no less, and no more. He wasn't demanding success, only that Stan give it his all.

Jodie understood that kind of emotion. Her family didn't. Davy didn't. He'd left even more meekly than he'd arrived. If she'd really felt about him the way he *thought* he felt about her, nothing on Earth would have chased her off.

"Obedience school," Mac picked it back up and this time he made it clear he was looking at her. "Been watching you, Jodie. Been watching Ama watch you. You've got something special. People like you. They trust you from the get-go. Bet you could make a kick-ass obedience class. Maybe spread out at a couple animals a week. Maybe a couple of intensive weeks where you take over the whole ranch. You start thinking about that, missy. Get back to me once you've had a chance to mull it for a while."

He tipped his beer bottle at her, winked, then rose to his feet and wandered off. And still she couldn't think of what to say.

"Not a half-bad idea," Stan spoke softly.

"Not a—" Jodie could only sputter. "And you think if 'someday' scared the shit out of me, something like that wouldn't?"

He put his lips on her hair and she could feel his silent chuckle.

"Asshole."

"Psycho." Sadly, she had no good answer to that truth.

Stan considered going after Mac and kissing the old guy, but she felt too good in his arms to let go. Whether or not she bit on the idea of teaching obedience courses, he knew that Mac was firmly on his side trying to keep her here. It was clear that the women had adopted her as well.

And the dogs.

What she'd done with the dogs today had been nothing short of a miracle. If tomorrow's handlers did even half as well with the dogs as Jodie had right out of the chute, it was going to be a huge success.

"Proud of you," he made sure he was speaking into her good ear.

"Why?"

"Because," a voice spoke from just to Stan's right.

The man was unremarkable in every way, except that Stan could swear there hadn't been someone there. Couldn't be, without triggering his SEAL situational awareness training. Yet he was, undeniable in the flickering firelight. It made him feel a little better that Jodie also startled at his sudden appearance.

"Because you have proven yourself to have exactly the qualities that any smart commander looks for."

"Michael," Emily said from his other side. "Where did you come from?" She was even harder to surprise.

The man's smile was enigmatic.

"Right, almost as silly a question as when did you get in." Instead she hugged him. "Is Claudia with you?"

"Tomorrow."

"Colonel," Luke's greeting was unreadably deadpan as he reached a hand across in front of Stan and Jodie.

"Commander," the Michael guy answered in kind as he shook it. Then he seemed to pull back into himself and Stan wondered if the guy would disappear if he looked away.

Then Stan recognized him, "Colonel Gibson. Good to see you, sir." He half wondered if the guy would recognize him. He'd visited the ranch a number of times, but always arrived and departed with a minimum of fanfare. They'd spoken only once or twice. He was the master shadow, the commander of Delta Force, and before that their Number One field operative for almost three decades.

"Senior Chief Corman. And how is Bertram?"

"He's," Stan really should know that the guy missed nothing, "he's doing great. We hope to show you something special tomorrow." Not that Stan had expected him to come, but he did his best to fight down the sudden case of nerves now that he was here. An infinitesimal twitch of Gibson's lips said that he'd absolutely pegged Stan's reaction.

"This is—"

"Hello, sir. Your reputation precedes you," Jodie had sat up without his noticing.

"You would be Petty Officer First Class Jodie Jaffe. Emily mentioned that you had a dog in some trouble."

"Yes, sir. I'm not sure why she mentioned it, but Brandy is improving since our arrival last week. A long road," she glanced over and Emily rewarded her with a nod, "but we're walking it."

"Wouldn't expect anything less." Michael scanned the circle around the fire.

Stan followed his gaze. The guests had long since faded away and gone to bed. Now it was only the long-term staff. Even the summer staff had gone to bed.

How long had Michael stood outside the light, waiting until that happened? If a guest had stayed until the end of the fire, would anyone even know Michael was here before tomorrow? One never knew with this guy.

"Yes. This ranch is a good place to be. My wife is partial to the desert. I myself am partial to the redwoods. But we both find a certain peace here."

"Which may be the longest speech you've ever made," Emily teased.

Michael shrugged in reply.

For the rest of the evening, Jodie had struggled very hard not to be impressed.

The talk had turned idle, almost meaningless. It was simply friends who enjoyed being together. And she'd been included as effortlessly as if she'd always been there.

As she and Stan headed back to the bunkhouse, she kept her hand on his where it held the crutch handle.

"Is it always like this here, Stan?"

"Tonight? Wouldn't know. I've always sat on the outside of these kinds of gatherings. But no, I think tonight was pretty special."

"No, I mean… I don't know what I mean. I get that the company was special. But I feel… I don't even know what I feel."

Stan paused and they were holding hands in the moonlit main yard. The barns were silent with sleeping horses, though the scent of hay tickled the still night air and mixed with the lingering woodsmoke. The sole light was on the ranch house's porch. She could feel the emptiness of most of the cabins that would be filling up again tomorrow.

"Try," his question sounded both merely curious and terribly urgent. Such conflicting emotions must be coming from somewhere inside her.

"I told you that, as a kid, I was the black sheep because I was interested in the dogs."

"I remember."

"In the military, I was a woman. Sure, the Navy has twenty percent women. But I had a knack with the dogs, especially the high-end ones. I could get them to do things no one else could. That pushed me into forward positions: part of advance teams for beach landings, deep-penetration assignments, my dog and I would be first off the helo to check for sign of bombs."

She held more and more tightly to his hand because it was all that seemed to anchor her in place.

"Eventually the Teams noticed me. A lieutenant commander pulled me for a high-risk op when his team's dog was down with an injury, and they never assigned me back. I was embedded with Team 8 for six years. War zones, hellholes, and the usual we-were-never-here places. I became an adrenaline junkie just like every other warrior at that level. But I was always the only woman."

"You don't mean they—"

"No. Nothing like that. Nothing even as bad as that stupid Utah trooper once I reached the Teams. No, I was theirs and they guarded me as if their lives depended on it."

"Which they did if you were their dog handler." And Stan understood that as well. The dog team was always at the point of any patrol.

If a SEAL team was the "Tip of the Spear," the dog and handler were the foremost honed-to-a-needle point.

"But I was always *other*. I was the woman to be protected. To many I was the Little Sister. For some I was even the protective mother, but never once did I truly belong. I've made an entire life of not belonging. And tonight…"

"Tonight," his prompt was as gentle as his thumb brushing over her knuckles.

"Tonight I did. Lying in your arms. Chatting with Luke, Zoe, Mac, Michael, and Emily as if I knew them. Understood them. And they understood me. They treated me as if I was one of them. You all did."

"Because you are."

She turned and placed her face against his shoulder. All she could do was shake her head in disbelief.

"Mac was right about you. People see you so fast. Chelsea said Ama sat you next to her at that very first meal."

"Sure. I was a guest."

"There's no *sure* about that. And that's not why she did that. She did it for Emily, of course; she adores her daughter-in-law. She's never done as much for Chelsea or Lauren. For Julie she did though. Apparently she and our resident cowgirl go back twenty years to the day Ama and Mac took over this property. When Julie came to work on the ranch a couple years back, I thought they were both going to die of happiness. Some one of Ama's cycles had come complete and she couldn't stop smiling. Ama did that again from the moment she met you."

"Why?"

"You'd have to ask her."

"Oh, like that's going to happen."

Stan shrugged and they resumed walking through the moonlight.

"I think we're too tired to do anything, but I'd like to sleep with you tonight."

"I don't leave much space in a bunkhouse bed."

"I want to sleep with you tonight." It wasn't desperation, but it was more than just a whim. She wanted—*needed* the anchor that was

Stan's embrace. Because that had been the true miracle of the evening.

For a woman who had never belonged anywhere, belonging in his arms had stolen more than her breath.

It just might have stolen her heart.

The predawn light of Test Day pinked the sky outside his bunkroom window.

Nerves. SEALs had nerves, especially pre-mission nerves. They'd just trained to the point where they felt less nerves about a mission than tossing out a pick-up line in a crowded bar.

"Will she, won't she" felt no different from "HALO jump from thirty thousand feet, take out Viktor Roskoff and any guards in your way, gather intel, and hike five klicks to extraction point alpha."

But still the nerves were there.

Despite all his training, Stan's nerves had been building throughout the week. Would he let down Mac? Would he disappoint the Teams? And what the hell was up with him and Jodie?

This morning he woke just as he'd gone to sleep. His back against the bunkhouse wall, Jodie spooned back against him with her head on his stump, and his meat arm around her waist. And in that instant, all the nerves became meaningless.

This was a pre-mission moment. All the prep was done. Weapons checked and rechecked until all that was left to do was wait. Any seasoned Spec Ops warrior with his ass stuck on a pre-mission flight slept. By that time, they were to the point where planning no longer mattered and all that remained was action. Nerves washed away and a good nap was called for—whether it was a thirty-hour jaunt to a war zone or a thirty-minute helo ride into hell.

Having Jodie in his arms, asleep and trusting, shifted that entire world. It wasn't ignoring pre-mission nerves, she simply washed them away. He'd had a good life, with only a few brief exceptions. He and Pa hanging together most every night of his childhood, the willing women, making ST6, and even Henderson's Ranch despite being half broken.

Waking with his face in her hair and her dressed in nothing but one of his t-shirts that had gathered around her waist in the night made everything okay. *Everything.* And how could it not? The words he'd been ready to say last night were as nothing.

"I love you" was easy. Women wanted to hear it, so it was easy enough to give because everyone knew it didn't mean anything.

Not to Zoe. It had changed her world. As if the words had meant more coming from Luke than "I do."

The surprise was, he *did* love Jodie. For real. If love meant that he'd die without her and he'd gladly trade his life to save hers, then he loved her like no woman before. He knew she wasn't ready to hear that though. So, as he had the night before, he'd wait. SEALs were good at waiting. Waiting for the right intel, the right moment to attack, or the exfil moment when you were still wondering if the helo would show before the enemy patrol.

But a man didn't wake with a woman like Jodie in his arms and just ignore the situation.

He slid his hand up over her t-shirt and cupped a breast. That perfect balance between athlete and woman, generous enough to make a man greedy yet small enough to not be an issue if she chose to go braless. She released a soft sigh in her sleep as he slowly rolled a circle with the flat of his palm.

Down her length, ribs, hip, thigh, then back up the inside.

Now half awake, he was able to coax her legs apart and cup her. Just hold her there. He'd done similar things with women before to arouse them and make sure that they enjoyed the moment as much as he did.

But with Jodie, it was the most intimate thing he'd ever done. She lazily shifted, closing her legs once more, pinning his hand in place. She seemed ready to fall back into deep sleep with his hand pinned against her.

He wished for his other hand so that he could bring it around her shoulder and cup a breast at the same time, but it wasn't going to happen. Instead, he angled his stump down so that it half-pinned her shoulder against his chest, then he went back to waking her up with his meat hand.

Her transition from asleep to awake was slow and smooth. Rather than jolting up, or trying to jump him as she had yesterday at the lake, she simply shifted more strongly against his palm, turning her face down into the remains of his biceps.

When her hand slid up over his and rode lightly on the backs of his fingers, he felt as if he could do no wrong. She didn't guide or direct. It was simply her hand, feeling his hand as he softly massaged her body to life. He retraced his way up to her breast, and her touch floated on his as he traced and retraced the amazing shapes there. Back down, she groaned so softly even he could barely hear it, yet it was as loud as an old stair creaking during the last moments of an infiltration before all hell broke loose. It sounded like some long-abandoned part of her was being forced open for the first time in years.

Once, she tried to turn to face him. But this wasn't about him, this was about her. He didn't know why. Showing her how much he wanted her? Or maybe demonstrating how she made him feel?

No. This was about giving something to her that was all about Jodie. It didn't sound as if much of her life had been that way. The black-sheep daughter—not rejected, but definitely not understood or supported. The SEAL who wasn't a SEAL. She'd given so much to others. He could see that in Davy Golding, now that he thought about it. Sure, he'd been a good guy to come out to Montana because she was feeling down. But Stan knew that Davy had also come because of how he'd seen Jodie fitting into his life, not his life fitting into hers.

So, Stan pinned her in place with his hand until she stopped trying to turn and finally let herself just feel.

Not once did she turn her face from his sad excuse for a left arm. Instead, the hand that had been curled under her chin in sleep reached up and took his stump as if she was holding his hand, pinning it between her cheek and palm. She hooked her upper leg back over his, offering him greater access that he gladly took advantage of.

Jodie rode her way up against his palm. He could feel muscles clenching in anticipation. Her breathing rapid, then ragged where her back pressed against his chest. The pulse pounding in her throat as he leaned in to kiss her there. Her fingers hung on to his left arm, digging in as she struggled to hang on. And when the slam of her release took her, it was almost violent. The tighter he pinned her in place, the harder the shocks slammed through her, through them both.

Stan could only watch in awe.

Jodie kept her face buried against Stan's left arm. Her hold there and her hand riding on the back of his were all that kept her anchored in this world. The rest of her body rode on a storm-tossed sea like none she'd ever known existed.

Storm-tossed sea? How damn cliché was that—except for a Navy SEAL. Maybe it was a SEAL cliché. Maybe she really needed to have the word part of her brain excised.

The night before last, up at the lake, that had been about sating their bodies and even their minds. This… *This* had been about stripping those away. Barriers she hadn't even been aware of had been torn down, not by some blast of raw power, but by the kindness behind them. By the man who held her through the night and woke her like this.

The releases had been awesome; the only word she could come up with for it. Them. Whatever.

But the miracle was Stan's strength. His steadiness. He had held her so close that fear couldn't get to her. That doubts weren't allowed. Being a good Brooklyn Jew—other than dodging Hebrew school and synagogue whenever she could—meant that she worried about everything.

Not in Stan's arms. He made it so clear that he wanted her. That he thought she was…magnificent. Magnificent? Not any Jodie Jaffe that she knew.

Yet here she was, her legs once more clamped around their joined hands as her body slowly calmed. His strength, even in what remained of his arm, let her hang on there. The smell of his skin, the feel of it.

For perhaps the first time in her life, she felt as if she was enough—just as she was. Somehow Stan had given her that gift. To glimpse it even for a moment opened a whole realm of possibility. If she could be whole in this moment, could she possibly learn to extend that feeling, knowing it wasn't merely possible but undeniably real?

As the last long wave rode all the way up her body from his hand anchored against her to where she still kept her face pressed into his left arm, she could feel the heat of tears. Rather than fighting them back down, there was no need to be other than who she was in Stan's arms, so she let them run.

"Whoa," Stan twitched when they spilled hot on his skin.

She didn't let him go. One hand clutching his left arm against her cheek, the other pinning his right hand exactly where she wanted it.

"I didn't hurt you, did I?"

"Only my heart, Stan," she managed despite the flowing tears. "You are such a gift."

He grunted in surprise at that. "A gift?"

"Sure," she sniffled and turned just enough to plant a salty kiss on his skin and then lay her damp cheek back on it. "Pretty wrapping paper," she rubbed the back of her shoulders against his chest. "A really nice bow," she rubbed her behind against him (something she'd have to take care of soon). "And Patrick was right."

"Patrick? What's he got to do with this? Spreading rumors and lies?"

"That first day he said that you're a really sweet guy, you just didn't know it. I laughed, but he was right."

"Lies. Complete and total." Yet he gave her a hug even as he spoke by squeezing his upper arms together across her shoulders. "Boy is just trying to undercut my obvious manliness because it shames his wimpy little ass."

"Can't say as I noticed his ass." She totally had and it was a good one. "Should it worry me that you have?"

"Only one ass I'm interested in. Now or ever."

Her heart skittered across the next couple beats as she tried to catch her breath. There was that long-term thing again. But the worry was different this time. Rather than fearing *ever*, Jodie was fearing that there *wasn't* ever. Because if it felt like this, lying in the safe circle of Stan's arms, *ever* actually made some kind of sense.

There were soft sounds in the bunkhouse. A shower started down the hall. A door slammed open and boots treaded down the hall.

"How quiet can you be?"

She could feel Stan's smile where he was kissing the point of her shoulder.

"That quiet?"

He let his silence be an answer.

There wasn't much room on the bunk, so she had to improvise.

But true to his word, he was SEAL silent as she took him down.

They gave the dogs a light workout—just enough to make sure they were awake and feeling agile—then shut them back in with their breakfasts. They then spent an hour reconfiguring the obstacle course in ways the dogs hadn't seen before.

Afterward, Stan tried to leave his crutches behind, but Jodie threatened to lock him in Bertram's cage and throw away the key. Because he more than half believed her, he used the damn things.

Following Jodie up the path, watching the unconscious sway of her hips that must have nearly killed her squad to ignore as they kept an eye out for unfriendlies, Stan actually blessed the changes that had sent him here. Not that he wouldn't give anything—short of another arm—to get his arm back. But that he was here, now, with Jodie. Whatever screwed-up path got him to this moment was paying off better than any VA benefits for service and loss of limb.

At breakfast Jodie, of course, got swirled up by the women. With the additional guests and all of the hands in for the meal, there wasn't enough room at the big kitchen table. Jodie, Zoe, and Emily were soon seated together on one of the couches with their breakfast plates balanced on their knees.

"You don't want to be messing with that," Luke, half through a massive plate of French toast of cinnamon swirl bread, sausage, and real maple syrup, waved Stan over to a spot at the table that a ranch hand had just cleared. Nathan dropped a loaded plate and coffee there for Stan since he couldn't fend for himself with the crutches.

"Probably right." Stan eased down across from Luke and cursed his crutches and his ankle for the hundredth time—just today.

"How bad?"

"One week crutches, week or two of light duty."

Luke nodded, acknowledging that it was going to be nothing more than a pain in the ass.

"What is it with you and…?" Stan tipped his head toward Zoe.

Luke glared at him narrow-eyed for a moment.

"No," Stan cut him off. "Didn't mean that. You gotta already know that you and Miss Five-four-and-a-hundred-pounds-soaking-wet make a hell of an odd couple. But what…" He wasn't even sure what his question was. "How…" But that wasn't it either.

"Looking for why?" Luke grimaced and went back to eating. "Damned if I know. One day she was this crazy butterfly thing flitting off to the side. The next we're deep in a mission and I'm the one following her lead."

"Her lead?" He glanced over, but couldn't imagine it. She was petite enough to fit *inside* a SEAL's mission pack.

"Hers. Proved it wasn't a fluke on another mission a year later.

Then I wake up one day with no idea how I ever lived without her. You want advice?"

Stan shrugged.

"Never assume."

It was an old SEAL grind. Never assume anything about a mission, because if you did, you'd be wrong and it would kill you.

Luke sipped his coffee, making it clear he was done.

So Stan offered him a thoughtful, "Huh."

Never assume that he knew what Jodie was feeling or thinking unless she told him—and maybe not even then. Never assume that just because he was in love with her that she was in love with him. Never assume that she *had* to be psycho to want to be with him.

"Huh!"

Luke grinned, "See? Damned if I know what that little woman sees in me, but I'm not filing a complaint with any review board. I can tell you that much."

This time, Stan looked over at Jodie.

She glanced his way and shot him a smile that sizzled and reminded him all over again what that woman could do with her lips and hands.

"Dogmeat," Luke remarked drily.

"Huh?"

"Exactly."

Stan decided that maybe his CO *was* a wise man. Jodie could do anything she wanted to him and he'd happily agree. "Not a bad way to be," Stan finally decided.

"Nope. Not bad at all," Luke mopped the last of his maple syrup with the end of his French toast.

CHAPTER 22

J odie wasn't enjoying the audience.

The last two days of working the dogs had been mostly just her and Stan. That was the way she liked it. Now half the ranch staff—everyone not involved with a guest ride—was standing out in the pastureland beyond the dog training course.

At least for the moment, the attention wasn't on her; but it soon would be. Instead everyone was looking aloft as the big twin-rotor Chinook helicopter swung into view. She'd been expecting a truck or maybe a Black Hawk from Malmstrom Air Force Base to the east. Instead it had been a pitch black, Night Stalkers Chinook MH-47G from the west. The only base they could be coming from was Joint Base Lewis-McChord in Washington, a three-hour flight away.

A glance over her shoulder showed that the horses in the corral were so used to Henderson's Ranch's small five-seater Bell 206 JetRanger that they didn't even bother watching. The Chinook could lift ten JetRangers and had an internal capacity for fifty-five fully kitted troops.

Stan just shrugged when she looked his way in question. What were they going to be doing with such a big bird? Stan had said he expected ten candidates for his dogs, not fifty.

It settled with the perfect grace of a Night Stalkers pilot, then the rear ramp folded down. The first thing off was a pair of tan ATVs. But not just any ATVs, they were Polaris MRZRs (m-razors), each designed especially for moving four Spec Ops soldiers fast and quiet over rough terrain. Then came a dozen Deltas and SEALs. Last down was the Chinook's five-person crew.

They lined up like troops ready for review, except for the Chinook's pilot. He'd exchanged his helmet for a white cowboy hat and moseyed toward the ranch group—he actually moseyed. No one in New York would believe her that cowboys weren't totally passé.

Then she eyed Stan and tried to picture him in a big Stetson hat and couldn't help laughing.

"What?"

"You. Cowboy hat."

He rolled his eyes.

"Definitely black. Like Bad Bart black." Chelsea's snort of laughter—the only other one to hear—said that he just might be stuck wearing one in the near future. Jodie vowed to help.

"Howdy, y'all," the pilot's accent was thickly Texan and sounded completely authentic. "Hear you got some dogs for us to meet up with. Hey, Zoe. Why are you still hanging with that big hoss when you could be gettin' all cozified with me?"

"Because, Captain Roberts, Kara would kill you if she even heard you say that."

"We are so telling!" A woman crew chief crowed with delight.

"Keep it shut, Carmen, or I'll be telling Danny a thing or two."

"Huh, what? Telling me what?" The copilot looked over when he heard his name.

"Worth the risk. Besides, she's probably up there right now, watching you."

They all glanced skyward, but Captain Roberts shook his head. "She's busy flying somewhere south of here it's better not to mention." Kara must be a drone pilot like Zoe.

That's when it really sank in. Jodie could only look at Stan a little wild-eyed.

The colonel in command of Delta Force, a SEAL Team 6 commander (which was just a single rate below the colonel but in a different branch of the service), a Night Stalkers Chinook crew, and a whole bunch of hopefuls with some serious equipment.

Jodie scooted over behind Stan.

———

Stan almost went to the ground when Jodie shoved him forward. He barely swung the crutches ahead in time to brace himself.

There wasn't time to scowl. And with Luke and Michael Gibson watching, there wasn't even time to be tongue-tied.

"Hi," he addressed the lined-up operators. "Welcome to Henderson's Ranch. Who here has handled dogs before?"

Every hand went up. That made his blood run cold. He hadn't expected to have to satisfy seasoned handlers. Stakes had just gone up another notch.

"Are you all—"

"That's *y'all*," the cowboy Chinook pilot offered with a broad smile.

"—*you all*," he ignored the cowboy's pleased chuckle, "Special Operations Forces?"

The carefully blank looks gave him the worst answer. They weren't just SOF, they were all Delta and DEVGRU—not a Ranger or standard SEAL team among them. These were the military's most elite fighters.

"What the hell?" Stan turned on Luke and Gibson.

Luke looked at Gibson (who unsurprisingly didn't say a word) before finally speaking himself. "Michael told me what a bang-up job you did with the training. We didn't want to waste your time."

Stan tried to remember how to breathe.

Stakes times a hundred.

The SEAL training pipeline was about a year long—ST6 was two more years past that. From 75th Rangers to Delta was similar. These guys were the end result of that and had all been in the field long enough to be ready for a second dog. Sometimes dogs were injured out, but it was more common for them to age out. Counting from training to retirement, four years was good, six years like Brandy was truly exceptional and said as much about the amazing handler Jodie had been as it did about the dog.

"Uh," really needed to breathe soon, "we've trained them on ATVs. Though the ranch ATVs are nothing like these." And he probably hadn't done enough of it. Ultra-high mobility for elite forces had definitely been on the increase and he hadn't really thought it through.

"We'll have our lead dog, Bertram, show them how," Jodie spoke right up with absolute faith in his dog. "Once they see him do it, there won't be any problems."

The urge to kiss the crap out of her right on the spot was almost overwhelming. But he resisted and did the rest of the introductions, particularly Mac.

"He's the one who believed in this project from the start. We've got seven dogs available for evaluation today. So let's get start—"

"You mean six," Jodie cut him off.

"Seven. I know how to count."

Her eyes went wide. "No, Stan. No way in hell!"

He could feel everyone watching in curiosity. "This is not the time or—"

"If you'd mentioned you were an idiot sooner, we could have done this before, but you can't be that dumb." Clearly Jodie didn't care crap about who was witnessing this.

"Jodie..."

"No way in hell are you letting Bertram go."

"He's the best dog I've got."

"He is. And he's a hell of a lot smarter than you." That earned her some chuckles that Stan would rather not have heard.

"These guys need the best," he forced himself to keep his voice even though he wanted to shout her down. "You know that. Better than most people here, you know how badly they need the best."

"So you're going to rip out your heart in the service of your country, again? Is that it?"

"Yes! Yes, I am, goddamn it. And you've got no place telling me otherwise, Jaffe."

———

Jodie kicked out his crutch and gave him a hard shove. He didn't stand a chance and slammed down to the ground.

"Cheap shot, Jaffe."

"All you deserve, asshole. *I've* got no place? *Me?* If I don't, then who the hell does? Tell me that one." She didn't know if she'd ever been so angry in her life. This was his idea of being in love? Because she knew he wanted to say it. Love was telling her that her opinion didn't even have a place when he was so wrong it was unbelievable? He'd *die* without his dog. She knew what it was to walk away for a single day. But to walk away for a lifetime? Knowing Bertram was in mortal danger almost every day? He'd goddamn *die.*

"Six dogs," she put her fists on her hips and faced Luke and Michael.

Luke put up his hands palm-out in self-defense. Michael had just a hint of a smile like Ama sometimes did. Jodie knew how to read that now. Partly amused but absolute approval. She offered him a nod of acknowledgement but didn't wait to see his response. She turned back to the smirking operators.

"Six dogs, you assholes, and wipe those goddamn smiles. You've never seen dogs like the ones Stan has trained. It won't be a question of whether they're good enough, it will be a question of whether you are—or *not.* We're going to start on the obstacle course. This way."

As she passed by him, she kicked Stan in the butt hard enough to hurt.

"Don't you *dare* tell me my opinion doesn't matter. Not after—" But she couldn't say it. *Not after the way you made love to me. Not after you made me feel like the most important thing in the world.* Instead she kept walking.

CHAPTER 23

"Well, I'm thinking that didn't go to mission plan." Luke offered him a hand up as Jodie led the operators away.

"What the hell land mine did I just step on?" Stan looked around and only Luke and Mac had stayed behind. The Chinook crew were securing their helo. Patrick and most of the other ranch hands were headed over to the obstacle course corral. Michael was walking hand in hand with a blonde. One her other side, Emily had linked arms with her. The three of them were strolling across the pasture like it was a Sunday afternoon in Paris. The blonde must have come in on the helo, but Stan hadn't noticed her. Maybe she'd done one of Michael's teleport maneuvers.

"Big damn land mine," Mac chuckled. "And son? You didn't step on it, you jumped in with both feet and your crutches as well. Haven't seen sparks like that in these parts for some time." He made a show of looking around his feet. "Nope, no fire, though I'll be damned if I know why. Fine show for the folks. Real fine show."

"You talk a hell of a lot for a SEAL."

"Spent twenty years in the teams and spent over thirty out of them. Mighta learned a few things along the way. A few more than you apparently."

Stan looked over at Luke. "Did he talk this much while he was training you?"

"Hold your focus."

Stan felt the slap down and almost balked at it. He was out of goddamn DEVGRU. He could focus on any damn thing he pleased. But Luke did have a point. It was *his* dogs that were about to be shown off and he was standing out here in the field yammering.

He took his hooks off the crutch handle long enough to point them upward as if giving Luke the finger before heading toward the kennel.

Dogs first. Then he was gonna have to argue some sense into Jodie. Bertram belonged on the front lines no matter what she said.

Why did he think that wasn't going to be fun? Because he knew that he didn't stand a chance?

By the time he came even with the obstacle course, Jodi already had the dogs trotting out of the kennel building. He just couldn't seem to keep up with her.

He wasn't going to miss the damn crutches. In fact, there were a whole lot of things he wasn't going to miss... And a couple things about which Jodie was dead right. He'd miss Bertram like ripping off another piece of his body. Five months old, the dog had saved his life. He had the best instincts Stan had ever seen in a dog. Since Patrick had moved in with Lauren, Bertram had spent most nights curled up at the foot of his bed.

He stopped just inside the course fence and leaned back against it.

Jodie didn't look at him once.

If he somehow chased her off, that would be losing a piece of himself that he *really* might not survive.

She set up the dog / handler intro dance. Every one of them knew to get down to the dog's height and use the high, squeaky, happy voice when addressing the dogs. Jodie ran them through a quick rotation. Take each dog out on a leash for a hundred-meter run—fifty out and fifty back.

It was smart and revealed right away that two of the handlers thought they were the ones in control, as if the dogs were servants.

Finally, Jodie glanced his way. He flashed up three fingers, then five. She nodded. The third and fifth handlers to make the run had already earned places at the bottom of the pecking order.

She ran Bertram through the course flawlessly to show off the challenges. Half hand signs and half voice commands.

"They respond to either," she announced clearly. "All in German, of course. Stan also created what he calls the Spec Ops Add-on Pack. These additional commands beyond the basic thirty phrases include," and she listed off another twenty commands by rote as if she'd always known them.

Yesterday—was it just goddamn yesterday?—Jodie had been startled by the list. Today she had it down cold and didn't miss a one. And as she went through them, she had Bertram running them for her.

"Each has an associated hand sign, in case you're in a high-risk scenario and need the dog to move in silence. Bertram has an additional set of phrases that only two of these dogs are close to having down. The phrases will be on their turn-over sheets if you want to keep working on them. Those are Tiger and Ralphie. There is one command that is quite new but they all have it. It's hand signal only."

Stan considered flashing it to Bertram to take down Jodie—the dog kept glancing over at him. But his hesitation lost him the opportunity.

Candidate number seven had turned to chat with the operator next to him, to tell some joke—probably about Jodie. Jodie signaled two dogs, then flashed the sign—flat hand shot straight out, clenched into a fist, then yanked back. Within seconds, the guy was facedown in the dirt being dragged to Jodie by Tiger and Tanya as he yelled imprecations at the dogs.

When he rolled onto his back, both dogs sat on him. He raised a fist to batter them aside.

Jodie knelt and put the blade of her KA-BAR knife tight under his chin. "You touch one of my dogs because you can't pay attention and I'll cut you."

"Bitch!" The guy cursed.

Stan didn't know the last time he'd moved so fast. In moments, he'd brushed Jodie aside, signaled the dogs to full alert, and clamped the twenty-five-year-old SEAL's windpipe in a vice grip with his good hand. The hard snarl from the dogs would tell any idiot he was within seconds of being ripped apart.

"You even so much as *look* in her direction and I'm going to rip your goddamn throat out before my dogs can. Are we clear?"

The guy's eyes widened as he tried to breathe. But instead of getting afraid, he got angrier.

"Fuck you, cripple," the guy managed to choke out.

Before Stan could just snuff the bastard, Luke spoke softly.

"Petty Officer Second Class Jamieson. I'm sending you back down to the Teams. Your official record will reflect the recommendation to never let you near a dog again. You also just lost a rank, and the reasons will also be reflected in your record. If your new CO wants to discharge you from the Navy, the senior chief and I will be glad to testify in support of that action. Personally, I think you should save yourself the humiliation and quit now. Are we clear?"

Stan remembered now why he'd liked serving with Altman so much. Not once had he raised his voice.

"Are we clear, Jamieson?"

He squeaked.

"Let him go, Senior." It was a title of great respect. Senior chiefs were the upper backbone of the enlisted Navy. There were two enlisted ranks above that, but they were practically officers and far rarer. It was the chiefs who ran the Navy and the senior chiefs who showed them how it was done. Somewhere along the way, Stan had lost sight of the fact that he had achieved that too. That hadn't been blown up along with his arm. *He* had done that.

Stan let Jamison go.

He did the standard choke-and-gasp thing. "You were a Senior?" came out on a gag.

Stan didn't bother answering.

"Get off the course, Jamieson. You can wait for us somewhere else."

"I can get my boy to dump him at the nearest airport," Mac spoke up. "Don't know as he'd survive the flight back." The rest of the candidates clearly wanted nothing to do with him. Falling off a team as elite as DEVGRU for a disciplinary reason was a black mark on a service record that could never be erased.

"Thank you, Master Chief."

Jamieson spun to look at Mac.

"Dumber than a damn brick," Mac muttered, then pulled out his phone to call Mark.

Once Jamieson had left a pile of the gear he couldn't take on a commercial flight and was sent to wait in the ranch's main yard for Mark to fly him out, Stan looked over at Jodie.

She was watching him and he couldn't read her damned expression. Perplexed? Pissed? He had no idea. But he knew one thing, she had earned the right to be respected by the dog handlers gathered here and there was no way he was taking that away from her.

He nodded for her to continue, then hobbled back to where he'd abandoned his crutches. At the fence, he leaned back and surreptitiously pulled out a couple of ibuprofen and chewed them down dry. Christ on a crutch, his ankle hurt.

It had been one of Pa's favorite expressions and he'd gotten it dead right.

Jodie began running the handlers through the dog's drills. Some of the pairings were already becoming obvious.

Mackie, a Delta Force operator, and Rex were a good match in temperament—the former rock steady and the latter overeager. Rex had clearly needed someone to temper his natural enthusiasm.

ST6 Francis and Ralphie looked as if they might be another pair for exactly the opposite reason—Ralphie's mild-mannered attitude was offset by Francis' gung-ho approach. As soon as Francis had heard that Ralphie was one of the more highly trained dogs, he'd instantly set about winning the dog's affections.

Jodie ran them all hard for a solid two hours without a break. It was no push for the high-energy Malinois, but it might be for the handlers and she wanted to see that. It wasn't. These were all ST6 and Delta operators and they ate it up.

Only when she'd called a break before heading them out to The Urban for shooting and explosives work did she let herself think about what had happened.

Jamieson was just another asshole and she dismissed him from her thoughts.

But Stan, despite being so fucking stupid that he thought letting go of Bertram was in any way a good idea, had come to her rescue like an avenging angel.

Except she hadn't needed rescuing. He'd known that.

No, he'd simply been so furious about anyone calling her something as mild as a bitch (hadn't she heard that one a thousand times before—sometimes even as a friendly endearment on the Teams), that he'd almost strangled the man. Then, when he'd backed away and turned the training over to her once more, she hadn't known what to think.

She still didn't.

These were *his* dogs. Their magnificent training had all been his doing. All she'd learned in the last thirty-six hours was how to get the dogs to do what Stan had already taught them. And he'd just clearly indicated that he respected her abilities. And her decision. He hadn't ordered Bertram into the standard rotation though she could see that he was still as angry as hell about it.

Couldn't he see that Bertram was so much like him? He was the trainer. He was the one the other dogs looked up to and did their best to match. He was the ultimate alpha dog and if this was going to be more than a one-time school, Stan *needed* Bertram.

But there was no time to talk.

The operators were using the break time to quiz her and Stan for best tips in the worst environments. Some had served desert time like her, others had tropical experience. Stan quickly turned it into an open discussion on what the challenges of each environment were.

"In humid environments, smells hang much longer in the air. The scents latch on to water molecules with a drastically increased hangtime, which will make a dog think the explosive is closer than it actually is. The real danger is going the other way, a jungle dog into the desert. He may practically sit *on* the explosive because of its lower air-concentration making him think it's farther away than his jungle experience has taught him it is."

As the discussion continued, Jodie could see Stan cataloging some of the same tips she was to add to the next round of training. These were some of the US military's best dog handlers and their shared knowledge base was huge.

***

The more Stan watched Jodie, the more he respected her. It was one thing to believe that she was a top dog handler; it was quite another to see it in action.

He'd stepped away because he needed to get away from the handlers before he did some damage. But he hadn't moved back in because he saw that Jodie—despite having only been in the regular SEAL teams—was teaching new tricks to top operators. Her loss must have been devastating to her squad because replacing her would be next to impossible.

"Why didn't DEVGRU ever pick her up?" He asked Luke, who was leaning on the fence nearby.

"There are over a thousand combat-duty SEALs. So give me a fuckin' break, Corman. Didn't know she existed or I damn well would have," Luke sounded ticked.

Deploying the dogs from the ATVs was a non-issue. Racing over the lumpy pasture at forty miles-an-hour, the dogs gladly launched straight from the ATV to take down a bite-suit-clad handler who was pretending to run away. For a while, the group tested and developed techniques on what was most effective for both handler and dog.

Out at The Urban, they dropped another handler—a Delta named Varkov—except this time it was voluntary.

"I thought I was good, had it down with a dog, until I met these guys," he nodded toward his fellow candidates. "These hounds are into next-level shit. I'll be a target or whatever, but I'm gonna let these dogs go to guys who are good enough to match them."

Stan made a point of using him as an assistant because that must have been tough for the guy to admit. Between the two of them, they took over stashing the explosives in places that would be a true challenge for the teams to find. And while each team was on its run, the two of them had a great time offering the distractions of live fire and small flash-bang explosions. It was a far more realistic challenge than he'd been able to simulate before, even with Timmy's help, but the dogs had proved unflappable.

By the time they finished, the teams were pretty well coalesced except for three guys all working with Tiger, who hadn't settled yet.

When they got back to the ranch, Nathan had one of his big chuck-wagon lunches set up near the helo. The fixed-up prairie schooner, complete with a red-and-white checked canopy, was rolled out by Chelsea leading her dapple-gray mare Snowflake in the harness.

Soon they were all elbow-deep in barbequed ribs and potato salad. Nathan had sent out operator-sized quantities. And with Chelsea at her most charming, the guys were half in love with her before the meal was over.

Half in love?

No way was he "half in love" with Jodie. She was… He'd run out of goddamn words. That was her specialty anyway. Magnificent. Fantastic. Lovely. Kind. And so goddamn competent. Also stubborn, obnoxious, and several other adjectives that he'd think of some other time, but he liked even when they were pissing him off.

It still bugged him watching the three operators vying for Tiger and here he sat tossing treats to Bertram. All three guys were seriously good and would know how to really use a dog like Bertram. Just as Jodie had deserved a dog as exceptional as Brandy. They'd brought her out of the cage for lunchtime and she lay beside Jodie. She wasn't showing any nerves over all of the new faces, but neither had she moved more than six inches from Jodie even once. Definitely getting better, even if she had a long way to go.

"You observe, but you must also remember to see." Colonel Michael Gibson squatted close beside him—once again teleporting in from outer space or wherever he lived.

Stan looked around the gathering more carefully, but he didn't get it. "Okay, what am I missing?"

"Things we were never trained to see."

Stan ran through the list in his head: threats, opportunities, weaknesses, strengths. Thinking about it, it was obvious that Daggert was the right match for Tiger—he was the kind of guy who could grow up to be a Luke Altman someday.

"He still doesn't see it," the blonde he'd seen with Michael before knelt slowly to Bertram's other side and rested a hand on the dog's head.

Bertram looked at her in surprise, as if he hadn't noticed her approach either.

"What don't I see?"

Her smile was frustratingly enigmatic. She was lovely. Taller than Michael, but perhaps only a little younger. She was also pregnant. Not as big as Julie, but definitely showing.

"Captain Claudia Casperson-Gibson, 160th SOAR." She held out a hand and he shook it with all the energy of a Pavlovian response by a dog. Imagining Colonel Gibson married had simply never entered his thoughts. Seeing Gibson with a kid on the way...that was just too weird.

But then he looked across the gathering and watched Jodie in earnest conversation with Ralphie's handler Francis. Jodie with a kid —a girl who talked too much and never slowed down long enough to take a breath. A boy who didn't know how to be anything but as fearless as his mother. Jodie had faced Stan down over Bertram in front of an entire group of alpha-male operators.

Had she been right?

He dug his fingers into Bertram's coat. In response, his dog twisted enough to lay his muzzle on Stan's thigh and closed his eyes in contentment.

Somehow, he could see it all falling apart if he insisted Bertram go.

Brandy's recovery, the training program, Jodie would leave, and the whole dream that had felt so solid when he'd held her this morning would slip through his fingers like trying to scoop sand with his hooks. Is that what Jodie saw? Had she somehow seen so much in that single moment?

Couldn't the damn woman have just said as much instead of kicking his ass in front of ST6 and Delta?

Did she *need* to drive it in with the force of a sledgehammer to get it through his thick skull?

Maybe.

Shit.

"Now he sees it," Claudia said softly. She petted Bertram on the head once more.

He scanned the crowd and wondered what else wasn't he seeing?

Nothing, because all he could see was Jodie.

As usual, Stan wasn't exactly sure when Michael and Claudia moved off to the other side of the group.

"Our jump program is only about a fifteen-foot drop," Stan replied to a question from Varkov. It was one of the few real shortcomings to his training program.

"Really?" The force of Varkov's surprise made sure they suddenly had everyone's attention.

"Thought you were my buddy, buddy," Stan whispered to him.

"I am. But no jump training? How can tha—" Varkov caught on a bit too late.

"No time like the present," Roberts hooked a thumb back toward his Chinook. "We brought us some chutes and a dog harness or two."

Stan glanced at the shadowed interior, saw the pallet of chutes, and felt ill. Everything had been going so well, but there was no way to predict how a dog would react to a parachute jump. He'd tried to get them prepared with the high-ramp jump down into the dunk tank he'd set up on the obstacle course, but it was all the facility he had.

There was an old windmill well pump on the property that he'd thought about converting to a jump simulator with at least a zip line, but it was still far down his list of projects.

"Why no parachuting? You have a helo. We saw it taking Jamieson out of here," Luke was in on it now too.

"I'm no longer jump qualified." Each word hurt as he ground it out. Stan hated that his ankle was sprained so that he couldn't risk a parachute landing even if he was still qualified. Hated that his arm was a goddamn piece of metal so that he couldn't trust to handling both a chute and dog if it panicked. And he hated looking at all the twenty-something-year-old operators lined up in the peak of their health who looked at him like he was old and broken. "You know that," he whispered the last.

Luke looked deeply chagrined. Which didn't keep Stan from wanting to pummel him for pointing it out to everyone.

"*I'm* jump-qualified," Jodie stepped forward and Stan could only blink at her in surprise. Of course she was. "My own dog is still recovering from…injuries."

She managed it with only the smallest of hesitations, which just made him prouder of her. Her dog having PTSD would label her as suspect in all of the operators' eyes. But that wasn't the point. Her absolute belief that Brandy just suffered from "injuries"—whether physical or mental—and not permanent debilitation was the path to healing her. Maybe to healing them both.

"I'll jump with our lead dog. Where he goes, all the others will follow without a problem. After their first jump, they'll be fine."

Stan wished he was half as confident.

She hurried over to Mac, and after a whispered conversation, he took one of the ATVs and raced away.

Before Stan could ask what was going on, Jodie strode up the rear ramp into the cargo bay of the huge Chinook helicopter. He followed close on her heels.

Stan fussed. He knew he was fussing, but he couldn't help himself.

Jodie resisted, "I can rig my own harness."

He wanted to shake her. "What makes you think that you can jump with a dog that weighs eighty pounds?" Stan checked that the rig was set to the right width for her narrow shoulders. "You can't weigh more than a hundred pounds."

"One-thirty, Stan. I'm five-six, not four-ten."

"Well, Bertram still weighs eighty pounds. He's right at the top of the Malinois weight range." He pushed her around to check the straps around her thighs, tugging them tighter.

"Goddamn it, I need blood circulation to my legs, not a tourniquet."

He eased it a quarter inch. She slapped away his hands and eased it over an inch.

"And Brandy, plus armored vest, plus weapon and munitions, weighs about as much. I'll also be jumping without a field pack."

"When was the last time you jumped?"

"This isn't a combat jump, Stan. We're not HALOing in to the Russian Ukraine."

"That's not what I asked." His skills went rusty in a month, though she was right. For a daylight practice jump, the honed edge was less critical. She'd be fine if she just—

"Goddamn it! I don't care." He abandoned his right crutch, grabbed the two front straps across her chest, and dragged her out of the helo where the rest of the operators were gearing up. Leading her around the side, out of the sight of everyone, he shoved her back against the Chinook's pitch-black hull.

"Jesus, Stan. Get a grip."

Was he freaking over the risk to Bertram or to Jodie? Or himself if he somehow lost both of them?

He pulled her an inch off the hull and slammed her back against it. What sledgehammer could make Jodie hear him?

"I'm warning you!" Jodie slid her hand onto the butt of her knife. He didn't care.

"How the hell are we supposed to spend the rest of our lives together if you kill yourself on a jump?"

"How the hell are we *what?*" Jodie laughed right in his face.

Jodie could see the hurt as it slammed into him.

"Goddamn it, Corman. If you propose to a girl, it's not supposed to be while you're manhandling her."

He stopped cold but didn't let go of her. She put her hand on his face, felt the slick skin of his scars against her fingertips.

"Stan. Hello. You in there somewhere?"

His dark eyes, which had gone black with fury, slowly eased in their intensity. He finally grumbled, "Maybe."

"I've done a lot of jumps with Brandy, okay? Deep insertions far behind the lines. Emergency missions on a zero-slack timeline. I know how to do this."

She could see him taking that in.

"Feeling stupid yet?"

"Maybe," he offered one of his lopsided half smiles.

"Good. That makes two of us. I never should have confronted you about Bertram in front of the other operators."

"Glad you finally—"

"But there's no way you can slam common sense into someone like me. Besides, you asshole, you should never have even thought about giving him up. He's your trainer for the next litter."

"The next what?"

"Stan. Start thinking ahead. You've done something amazing here all by yourself, starting with nothing. These operators are going to be in such high demand for what they can do with these dogs. You did that. Now let go of me and I'll finish proving it to them." She pulled him in enough to kiss him, then ducked out under his arm when his grip on her harness eased.

Because there was no way in hell she was going to answer that last question.

Spend the rest of our lives together?

She wanted to kill Patrick for being right. Stan Corman might not know it, but at heart he was a damn sweet guy. Not once had he questioned her skills. Instead, he was fighting for her in ways that Davy

Golding could never have imagined. After a dozen years patrolling in some of the worst disasters that humanity could create, having someone who cared so deeply about her safety was…humbling.

Stan humbled her. This program and what he'd achieved doing it. His thoughtless kindness in rushing to her aid in Utah—because there was no question who had actually flown to her rescue, dragging the others along in his wake—and the long trip back as she'd tried to make sense of her old life versus…she hadn't known what.

Now she did. She could see her new life. It wasn't formed yet, but for the first time in years, it didn't merely feel safe. It felt good. Really good.

Not that she was ready to tell Stan that.

In moments she was back in the helo, calling Bertram over to be fitted with a war dog vest. It was the full kit from K9 Storm in Canada, which were about twenty grand apiece. The Kevlar wrapped over his back, down the sides, and around his belly, protecting most of the vital organs.

It had an infrared light and camera sticking up above the spine high enough to see over his head—the pictures could be transmitted to a small wrist unit so that an operator could see what her dog did. The stalk also folded down in either direction in case the dog had to get in or out of a tight space.

The comms package, which was new since she'd served, offered her remote control of the camera and light. Varkov showed her that it also let her silently issue basic commands directly to the dog with the press of a button even if they were at a distance. "Press this and a small speaker on his harness will say *"Platz," Down,* to get him out of the way of incoming fire. And this…"

"You good with this, Bertram?" she asked once she had him fully strapped in. He wagged happily in response to her squeaky dog voice.

There was a pair of lifting rings the size of her palm along the vest's spine, one near Bertram's neck and the other near his tail. They matched up with a pair of clips at her waist.

Snapped in, she stood, careful to lift with her knees rather than her back.

Bertram looked up at her in surprise as his feet lifted off the helo's steel deck.

"Oof! We gotta put you on a diet, kid." He ignored her normal human voice because there were no commands in it. She turned around slowly so that all of the other dogs could see Bertram dangling from her harness with his feet several inches in the air.

Then she folded down one of the seats mounted on the side of the long cargo bay and settled into it as the helo lifted and the ramp closed. Soon, all six handlers and their dogs were fully rigged and sitting in the seats with her. Ralphie made a fuss about the vest, but his new handler calmed him fast enough.

The helo circled aloft. And kept climbing. And climbing.

"How high are we going?" Jodie asked the crew chief when she came by carrying a sack.

"Commander Altman said he wanted a full HALO simulated. Ground here is four thousand feet and we top out at eighteen thousand. Fourteen-thousand-foot drop."

"But—" To do a High Altitude, Low Opening jump—one of the most dangerous types—was the extreme limit of parachute jumping. "For their first test? Are you guys fucking nuts?"

"I just take the orders, ma'am. Don't like it, take it up with the man."

"Where is he?"

In answer, the woman leaned over and looked out the round window in the side of the cargo bay. Jodie turned enough to see Luke driving away in the second ATV with Michael and his wife, and Varkov. Stan sat on the small rear cargo deck with his legs dangling off the back and his crutches clutched to his chest. His face was turned up as he watched them climb, as if he could see her despite the small window and shadowed interior.

"Oh, that's a big help."

"We aim to please. Here, you'll want these. Though don't start them yet." The crew chief handed her a cylinder as long and slender as Jodie's forearm with a short hose and a mouthpiece attached—auxiliary air. She knew the model. Sixty breaths, about four minutes if she remained dead calm. About thirty seconds if she thought about what Luke had ordered, so she wasn't going to think about that. She secured the cylinder and dangled the hose by her chin.

She slipped the second oxygen tank into the sleeve of Bertram's vest and let the muzzle cup dangle loosely.

"You're going to love this, boy!" Jodie squeaked for him. *Hopefully.*

As they climbed, she decided the orders were up to her, even if they were all still in the service and she wasn't.

"Exit is eighteen thousand," she shouted above the pounding of the twin sixty-foot-diameter rotors and the pair of Lycoming turboshaft engines currently pumping five thousand horsepower apiece into the drive train. "Open chutes at seven thousand, ground at four. I want to see nice, tight, flying formation on my lead. Roger that?"

She checked to make sure she saw six thumbs up.

"All know the landing target?"

Again a round of thumbs up.

Then they all pulled on black full-head woolen face masks that covered everything except eyes and mouth. Fourteen thousand feet above the ground meant the air would be seventy degrees cooler at altitude than on the ground. Even with a hundred and twenty miles per hour of wind chill during freefall, the mask wasn't a necessity; but if this was out of the back of a C-130 at thirty thousand feet, it would be a life-or-frostbite necessity. For a true HALO—a hundred and fifty degrees cooler than ground and ninety full seconds of freefall—she'd have a full-face mask, but it wasn't necessary here. But better safe than sorry. She pulled on her jump helmet and made sure it was strapped tightly enough that she could flex her jaw, but not too far. Then her own goggles over the mask.

She slipped Bertram's doggles over his eyes. Stan had made sure that all of the dogs were well used to these and there were no complaints.

"Crossing fifteen thousand," the crew chief called out. "Air up."

It would take them two more minutes to reach the profile altitude. And thirty seconds to freefall the first ten thousand feet. Four minutes of air was plenty.

She bit down on her mouthpiece and reminded herself not to inhale through her nose. Hitting the release on the regulator, she felt the cool flow of richer air flow into her lungs. She'd always liked the slightly euphoric moment of that sudden boost.

"Let's do it, Bertram." She slipped the clear plastic cup over his snout and strapped it behind his head before he could react. The dogs were, of course, used to muzzles—war dogs were rarely transported without them. But the solid air mask would be new.

He tried to shake it off. Then he clicked a paw against the outside, which she slapped aside so he'd know not to do that. A muffled woof of surprise acknowledged the start of air flow. And then everything began happening too quickly for him to have time to complain.

The wide rear ramp lowered down until the entire back of the cargo bay was exposed to the sky. As the jump lead, she stood and waddled to the rear, glad they hadn't loaded her down with a full mission pack and an M4 rifle.

In line, the crew chief moved quickly down the queue, checking parachute and dog harnesses. Jodie was careful to keep her good ear turned toward the crew chief. Technically she wasn't jump qualified, having never been tested without her hearing. But if Stan's program was to be a success, she had to cover that for him. Doing a HALO jump—the most dangerous one of them all—after three months out wasn't exactly what she'd been counting on when she'd claimed she still was.

"Five," the crew chief shouted as she returned to Jodie's side and gave a thumbs-up that everyone was ready.

Jodie held up five fingers and waggled her hand so that everyone behind her could see it.

Four.

Three.

She hooked an arm under Bertram's chin so that she was cradling his head in the crook of her arm.

Two.

She started down the ramp.

One.

She stepped off the end of the ramp, twisting at the last second to fall backward so that Bertram would have the momentary comfort of feeling as if he was lying on her.

She rolled to belly-down, still cradling Bertram. He was looking around like it was the ultimate ride with an open car window in a convertible. He wiggled as he looked about, but he didn't struggle. She hoped the other dogs were doing as well.

Seventeen thousand on her altimeter and they were flying clean.

It seemed that all of Montana lay spread out below her, even though she knew her altitude gave her a horizon of only a hundred and forty miles. Its beauty was startling from up here. The mountains hard and jagged in the distance. The entire sweep of the foothills that she had yet to see. Great swaths of it were wildflower blue. They reminded her of the patch of bluebells in the Brooklyn Botanic Garden. Except instead of covering half an acre, they covered hundreds.

She and Stan would have to get out among those flowers. It had always been one of her favorite spots in the gardens, the bluebells of spring. Of course she didn't ride a horse and she didn't know if he did. Probably couldn't ride one with a sprained ankle anyway. Maybe they'd take out one of the ranch's ATVs. Maybe she'd start riding lessons with Chelsea while she was at it.

Fifteen thousand.

Jodie flexed an arm and a leg to turn them in a slow circle. Mountains west, rugged foothills north, the small town of Choteau thirty miles to the northeast, vast prairie east and southeast, finally turning back into foothills to the south. At first she'd thought it was a terribly stark land, but it had a real beauty as well.

Spend the rest of our lives together.

That implied here. Thirty miles from a town, most of a hundred from a city—a city that had nothing to do with being Brooklyn.

Twelve thousand.

Stan cursed himself for not having binoculars. The Chinook was little more than a black dot three miles up.

He cursed himself for not being the one jumping.

And for how he'd yelled at Jodie about them spending the rest of their lives together.

Didn't women want shit like that said sweetly over some fine meal?

Instead he'd had her pinned against the side of a Night Stalker's Chinook. Of course, for Jodie, maybe that was the right circumstances.

But damn it, he hadn't even told her he loved her yet.

He started laughing as he watched the period-sized dots of the jumpers. If he could see them, they were already most of the way down.

Jodie would be first, of course. Not just because she was showcasing the jump with Bertram, it's simply who she was, even in front of Delta and ST6 operators. She couldn't be any different and he wouldn't want her to be.

Love her?

That didn't *begin* to cover how he felt about the woman. She was his conscience—when she could convince him to hear it. She was his right hand—even though it was a left one he was missing. A life without her? Wasn't gonna happen.

Screwed up psycho, lovely mess Jodie Jaffe was what he'd spent his whole life never knowing he wanted.

Well, he knew it now as she fell out of the sky.

Ten thousand.

The whole ranch laid out before her. She spit out the supplementary air mouthpiece and removed Bertram's muzzle cup as well.

Eight thousand.

Course correct and shift her wrist so that she could keep a

constant eye on the altimeter. No need to watch the other operators, they'd be in tight formation.

Seventy-five hundred.

Seventy-three.

Two.

One.

Pull.

The chute deployed with a hard, crotch-slamming snap. In a single instant she went from a hundred and twenty miles per hour to fifteen. She released Bertram's head and reached up for the control handles.

A glance down. Bertram was perfectly calm, just busy trying to look everywhere at once.

A glance up. Six chutes in a tight, staggered stairstep formation above and behind her. All seven, including hers, looked clean with no snarls or twists. She didn't expect any less.

Two minutes to landing.

Jodie turned through a wide circle. Partly to fly out over the ranch and look at it from a few thousand feet up. There was so much here. It might not be the city she was used to and had planned to return to, but it would be impossible to be bored. Horses, dogs, and a master chef who could maybe be bribed to teach her how to cook something more advanced than frying an egg or opening an MRE packet.

There would be friends here. And there would be family. Not only Stan, but a ranch run by Ama and Mac couldn't be anything but family.

She completed her circle and lined up on her objective. The dogs were used to a water dunk tank, so the lake had made perfect sense as an objective. Mac had raced away in the ATV to move the central float ashore to make as much clear space as possible for seven landings.

Now, the lakeshore was crowded with people. Tourists holding their phones aloft taking videos. Seven military war dogs parachuting into the lake was definitely going to go viral. Next time she'd make sure to have a Henderson's Ranch sign that she could fly below her as she descended.

Next time? No chance to think about that now.

Five hundred feet.

She picked out the clustered ranch hands, partly by the banner of Chelsea's long red hair flashing in the sunlight as she jumped about like a cheerleader gone mad.

Two-fifty.

And there was Stan. Standing slightly apart, leaning on his crutches and watching her descend like a tracking radar.

At fifteen feet above the shore, she eased down on the toggles to achieve level flight. With her feet skimming just inches over the water, she stalled the chute and plopped into the water as if stepping off a dock. She'd kept just enough air in the chute for it to drag backward so that it didn't cover her.

She yanked the release on the rings that linked her to Bertram, and he floated beside her. She grabbed the back lifting-loop on his harness and let him drag her to shore.

Once there, and after he'd had a good shake, she signaled him to sit and stay before turning to recover her chute and watch the others come in. In neat precision, another handler and dog splashed in around the circumference of the lake every two to three seconds. In under sixty seconds from her feet first hitting the water, they were all standing ashore with their chutes rammed into a stuff bag and their dogs beside them.

Not a single complaint from any dog in the pack. A very neat infiltration.

A big round of applause sounded from the ranch hands and guests. Dozens of cameras were aimed in their direction, recording every moment.

That was a problem she hadn't anticipated. None of the operators would want their faces photographed. There were bad guys who would hunt SOF operators and their families if they could identify them.

As they rallied up around her, she flashed a Hold hand sign to them.

She spotted Stan in the crowd, but there were a lot of people between him and her. How could she ask him—

He pointed upward.

That's when she became aware of the Chinook descending above them.

They traded thumbs-up.

Except the helicopter didn't come to land or even hover near them. Instead it stopped fifty feet up, then dumped a rope out the hellhole—a small bottom-side hatch in the center of the cargo bay. It was a SPIE rope—Special Patrol Insertion / Extraction. It had D-rings threaded through the rope at intervals.

She and the other operators quickly reharnessed the dogs to the front of their rigs. Lining up to either side of the rope, they snapped a safety line from the front of their harness onto one D-ring and a second one to the ring above that. As they each finished, they held their arms straight out to the sides to signal they were ready.

Moments later, the thudding roar of the Chinook increased and they were lifted aloft to dangle at intervals along the rope.

The crowd went nuts as they were flown over the ranch back toward the dog compound.

Extracted from the crowd, they floated along, fourteen human feet and twenty-eight dog feet dangling from the sky.

CHAPTER 24

S tan needed something to hang on to; thank God that Jodie was close to hand.

The last week had been such a whirlwind that his sense of balance was gone. He was half-tempted to start using the crutches again even though he'd so despised them.

For the moment, they sat side-by-side holding hands in the last row of chairs lined up along the side of the lake. They were alone, but it wouldn't last long. The rows of chairs faced the lake-edge gazebo where Patrick and Lauren would be married shortly. The only way he and Jodie had been able to get a moment alone was to come here early to sit and watch lovely afternoon sunlight sparkle off the lake's surface.

Spring rains had shadowed most of the week and there'd been talk of moving the wedding inside. But it had cut off two days ago and the June sun had struck down like a blessing. The entire prairie seemed to have burst into bloom. All of the early summer flowers had gone mad in vast carpets of reds, yellows, blues, and purples.

In the dog compound, a new class of the cutest puppies imaginable were frolicking in their cages. Seven Malinois, four German Shep- herds, and a chocolate Lab named George that Jodie fawned over ridiculously just because he was so cute. His paws were still bigger than he was; George would be a big dog if he could stop tripping over his own excitement. With all twelve cages filled, Bertram and Brandy had moved into the bunkhouse with them—which hadn't worked at all.

"Thank goodness we're out of there," Jodie was, as usual, reading his thoughts.

Just last night they'd finished remodeling the kennel's office that Julie had insisted on adding when she'd originally designed and built the place for him. He'd never used it, so they'd converted it to a bedroom big enough for a king-sized bed and a pair of dogs. Not much else would fit, but it was plenty for people like him and Jodie. With their lack of culinary skills and the ranch house so nearby, they certainly didn't need any kitchen gear more than a coffee pot. Jodie hadn't shown any inhibitions about the dogs being so close, but he'd shooed them out onto a bed in the main corridor of the cages before he had his way with her.

"I'm so proud of Brandy," Jodie reached out her other hand to scratch her dog's head where she lay on Jodie's right side.

Stan liked the symmetry of it. His right, meat hand holding her left also placed him on the same side as her good ear. It would have been awkward the other way around.

"She's totally mothering those puppies already. We're going to have to watch that she doesn't get carried away or too attached." Jodie tickled Brandy's ears, making them twitch and flick.

"I wouldn't worry about that. She'll be distracted soon enough."

"But I do. Did you see that she's—"

"Pregnant."

Jodie turned to him wide-eyed. "She's…what?" She pushed Brandy over on her side to run a hand over the dog's belly—the first sign of a pregnant dog was already evident.

Stan fought for his best deadpan just to tease her. "War dogs through Lackland Air Force Base are typically neutered. But Brandy coming straight into Special Ops apparently wasn't, and I was planning to breed Bertram someday, so I never had him fixed."

"You sly devil, you," Jodie leaned over to squeaky-voice down at Bertram snoozing against Stan's left leg. He didn't raise his head, but he did twitch his ears her direction and wag his tail. "Smug. That's what he is. We're going to have to expand the kennel building."

"Give us a chance to add a second room to our place while we're at it."

"Getting ahead of yourself, Stan Corman."

"Once you marry me, there are definitely kids in our near future, Jodie Jaffe."

"You haven't even proposed to me."

"What part of 'spend the rest of our lives together' didn't you understand?"

"The part where you haven't proposed to me. That isn't a proposal, is it Mr. Secretary?"

Stan twisted to see Secretary Peter Matthews and his wife Geneviève, a tall and stunning brunette of French-Vietnamese extraction, sitting down to Bertram's left. Not far behind them stood Frank and Beat, their Secret Service detail. They were playing catch with a little girl who was already as breathtaking as her mother.

"No, it's not a proposal," Secretary Matthews sided with Jodie—of course. Everyone did. "Heard that you two did a bang-up job last week. Top reports coming from both Michael and Luke. Didn't have a chance to mention it when we got in last night."

"The top reports were because they earned them," Michael and Claudia sat down in the row just ahead of them, but turned to face back. They'd left but oddly come back again. Stan hadn't thought Michael was close to either the bride or groom and wondered what they were doing here.

"Had a chat with the Secretary of Defense," Matthews continued. "He's very pleased. He wants more, of course, so you just let him know what you need. I told him that you weren't set up for a jump program so he's already found you a Little Bird helo to do jumps from and all the chutes and harnesses you'll need."

Stan blinked. "We don't have a certified Little Bird pilot here at the ranch." That would be far better than the rickety old windmill he'd been wondering how to restore and rig with a zip line. "Though I guess Mark or Emily could cross over easily enough."

Claudia raised her hand briefly. "Twenty years as a Little Bird pilot, most of it for the Night Stalkers. With the arrival of this little tyke," she rubbed her hand over her belly, "we've decided to retire here. I'd be glad to fly for you anytime you need it."

Stan looked at Michael in surprise.

"Oh," Claudia answered for him, "he'll be joining Emily and Lauren's little military-security consulting team. I'm hoping that will keep him out of trouble. Mac wants him to take over the shooting range instruction as well."

"Not sure quite what a life looks like without Delta, but Claudia convinced me it was time to find out." Michael shrugged.

Stan decided that the ranch was about to get a whole level more serious with Delta's best operator teaching range work.

"Survival school," the idea just popped up and Jodie spit it out before even thinking that she was addressing a full colonel. She'd seen people look less excited about retirement, though she couldn't imagine when.

Michael actually looked interested, so Jodie let her imagination run despite being convinced it would end up sounding foolish before she was done.

"There's a million acres of Flathead National Forest right over there," she waved at the rocky backdrop to the fast-approaching wedding. "It's some of the roughest country around. You could run week-long courses into there that would make SERE look like child's play. But maybe just the survival portion. If you're anything like me, that's plenty. If I never have to evade, resist, or escape again, I'll die happy. But survival skills. I could see doing that with you sometimes."

"I do miss that," Stan agreed. "And we agreed, no escaping. Right, Jaffe?"

"Right, Corman," Jodie was aghast that she managed to respond with a straight face. A week ago, giving a promise to not run away had been impossibly hard. Now she couldn't understand why she'd ever even thought such a thing. "There you go, Michael, two part-time assistants. And does anyone run a decent tracking school anymore? We could expand the dog school to include tracker dogs as well as explosive dogs."

Michael looked thoughtful, but Claudia's glowing smile said that Jodie had just slammed a home run in the last inning of the World Series. The Yankees would be proud.

"Lauren is also an exceptional tracker. She's Delta, but I suppose," Michael said in what she finally understood was his droll tone of highest humor, "that if I had to put up with a couple of SEALs, you two might do the job." That tiniest slice of a smile completely gave him away.

This is what it feels like. Jodie repeated that to herself. *This is what it feels like when you're in the right place at the right time.* Here, with Stan and Michael. It was as if this was what she'd been working toward her whole life rather than the Teams. Training dogs. But no longer having to face the armpits of the world where there was a price on her head because she was a dog handler or a SEAL or an American or simply a woman. Teaching survival to any who wanted to learn just what nature could offer.

"There's a catch," Michael spoke with an actual smile.

Jodie was glad it was aimed at Stan—Michael Gibson actually smiling was a little disconcerting. Maybe even a little scary.

"I heard Patrick's mother last night. You're going to have to let her give your arm an upgrade."

"Like hell!" Stan dug in.

"Mr. Secretary," Michael said very respectfully, completely ignoring Stan's reaction.

Jodie didn't know how she felt about that. She'd gotten to know Stan just the way he was and she wouldn't change him for anything—not even getting the Dodgers back to Brooklyn. Though maybe for a bagel and lox stand on the ranch.

"Oh, right. I forgot. Part of the package the US government is giving you includes full recertification at the Army Airborne School.

You can't do that with a pair of hooks. But by tapping into your still-existing nerves, you'll be able to use the new arm just as you always did, by just using it. Mrs. Gallagher assures me that not only do they have individual finger control and pressure sensitivity now, but their newest arm will be capable of sensing temperature. They just pick up your cut-off nerves and your finger will actually feel like your finger. If you do that, they granted authorization for you to go through Airborne again."

Jodie expected Stan to look up at the sky and the dream of jumping again. It was one of the best parts of any mission—except for the chance of being shot dead while still in the sky.

But he didn't. Instead he looked at her. She could see into those dark eyes and what she saw there surprised her. Since when did Stan Corman fear anything?

Actually, he'd shown her plenty of fear. A fear of connection that ran so deep that he'd built up a wall against his feelings. He'd made it so high that he'd almost shut out his own dog by giving him away. Fear that he was less of a man because of his metal arm. He was still as jittery as a "fresh-meat" SEAL shipped to the line for the first time whenever she touched it. She knew it wasn't her, it was the relationship he had with his arm.

"Stan," Jodie didn't know quite what to say. *You aren't your arm?* He wasn't, but she didn't think it would help to tell him that.

"Uh huh."

Maybe… "Just say yes, Stan. It's the right decision. We'll leave figuring out how to live with the decision until later."

For another long moment, he studied her. Then he simply said, "Okay."

It earned him a bark of laughter from the men, but both Claudia and Geneviève looked as if they were going to start crying happy tears even before the wedding began. Claudia took Michael's hand and held it tightly. He returned the gesture, even if he didn't seem to understand why his wife was suddenly holding his hand.

That deep level of communication, of feeling, that could only happen between husband and wife. Was she—

"There's a catch there, Jaffe."

"And what's that, Corman?"

"I get a new arm, docs are going in on your ear."

"So that you can tell me I'm a psycho from either side?"

"So I can whisper sweet nothings into it." Then he blushed at his own answer. Stan Corman actually blushed.

Again, he'd totally trapped her. There was no way she could turn him down after that.

Personally, Jodie found it to be a little daunting that he'd agreed at all, never mind so easily. Stan believed in her so deeply. No one outside her squad had ever done that. Actually, because they didn't really understand the handler-dog relationship, they believed in Brandy like she was the magic talisman that kept them safe all on her own. They didn't *dismiss* Jodie as the handler, but they didn't *believe* in her either. Not really.

Stan did. And that was…breathtaking.

"So," Stan looked at her with a degree of caution that surprised her. "You're going to stay…here?"

"That totally depends, Corman."

"On what?"

Jodie laughed, but it was Geneviève who answered for her.

"On whether you ever propose to her or not, you silly man." In her lovely French voice, there was no way not to be charmed and apparently that even included a SEAL-tough man like Stan.

"I—" Then he turned to her. "Jodie—"

"Not now," she cut him off.

"Why not?"

"It's not nice to steal someone else's show."

Stan looked up and saw that while they'd been talking, Patrick's wedding to Lauren was almost underway. The groom was standing at the step up to the gazebo in a dark blue suit that looked pretty damned fancy since all he'd ever seen the boy in was cowboy gear.

His brother Nathan stood beside him. Patrick had been apologetic about not choosing Stan and it had been up to him to talk Patrick down. Though it hadn't been that hard. "Patrick, he's your brother and you like him. We're good. Done." Then he'd walked away leaving Patrick still in mid-sputter.

It was exactly the same tone Jodie had used about his getting a new prosthetic arm.

What had finally tipped the scales wasn't Patrick's mother or the carrot of Airborne School. It wasn't even that Jodie had she said it was "the right decision" the way she did—though he'd learned to trust her judgment over his. He leaned down to scratch Bertram's head with his hooks and blessed Jodie again that she'd made him keep his dog.

It was because she'd said, "We'll figure it out later."

We.

He hadn't been a "we" since he'd been blown out of DEVGRU. On the ranch he'd been the loner. Friendly, but no real friends. He'd been the outsider who worked with the dogs.

Until Jodie.

He'd always respected Michael. Working with him on a survival and tracking course would soothe an old itch that went all the way back to Pa. That had been their weekends together. They'd take a pair of bedrolls, a canteen, a knife, and not much else other than his dog, and hike out into the Blue Ridge Mountains or wherever Pa's current job led them.

Sometimes getting away gets you closer to yourself.

And sometimes, Pa, getting there with the right person makes all the difference. Maybe that's why Pa had never remarried; he'd already had the right person—at least right for him if not for her. Stan wished he was still alive to ask, but then realized he didn't need to. His father had found his one true love and had drifted through life after she'd left; lost at sea without her.

We? Damn straight he'd agreed when she hit him between the eyes with the "we" word. Two letters to make him feel better about himself than probably any time since Pa had shaken his hand at SEAL graduation and told him, "Go kick some ass, son!"

Ama came down the aisle in a Cheyenne dress of whitened buckskin with the mustard-yellow of rawhide worked around the neck and long fringes. She had become a certified minister in order to perform the weddings on the ranch. She stopped for a moment beside Jodie and rested a hand on her shoulder. She looked astonishing.

Her height and natural majesty were emphasized by the dress. The shot of gray in her dark fall of hair didn't detract, instead it made her seem taller and prouder of bearing. She might be sixty or more, but she was still a knockout.

Without a word, she continued looking at Jodie as if the two were communing. Brandy rubbed her muzzle against Ama's rawhide boots.

Then Ama cupped her hands together, holding them filled with nothing toward Jodie.

Jodie nodded. Uncertainly once, then again more strongly, before she held up her own cupped hands. Ama poured her nothingness into Jodie's. Then Jodie closed her own hands together.

Ama continued her walk toward the gazebo and the waiting groom as if she'd done no more than say good morning.

"That was her wedding dress," Jodie whispered.

"And she still fits in it like a glove. Mac is one lucky bastard. What was that all about?"

"She's so beautiful," Jodie was actually sniffling.

"Ceremony hadn't even started yet, psycho." Then he leaned over to kiss her temple. "You're gonna knock them out when you're a bride. Best ever."

"That's what Ama just told me. She gave me back just what she promised when I found the path for the long walk back to myself."

"She didn't say a word. And what are you talking about?"

"She didn't have to. I didn't think I was ready…but she believes that I'll find my path. She gave me back my belief in myself, something I've been missing for a long time."

"Well, duh, psycho. Didn't need her to tell you that." But maybe Ama's empty gift wasn't so empty after all. Whatever it was, he could see that it had touched Jodie very deeply. He brushed aside a tear that rolled down her cheek.

"You still haven't asked me, Alpha Dog." Definitely a better nickname than asshole. Though the way she said that one too, it was hard to mind. Jodie sniffled again. "Now be quiet."

And Stan was. He kept his silence through Lauren coming down the aisle in a long sheath dress that matched her trim six-foot frame—her dog Rip, of course, trotting happily at her side. He kept it through the ceremony and all of the congratulations afterward.

His foot wasn't up for dancing yet. Jodie took a few turns on the grass—enough to make it clear that he'd definitely need lessons if he was going to dance with her at their own wedding.

He waited until the sky had turned red gold and the bride and groom were off to honeymoon for a week in Vegas. They'd left a very distraught Rip in Timmy's care. Unable to ride the horses anymore and with Jodie helping him with the dogs, Timmy had thankfully found a place as the nanny for the growing population of ranch children. They ate up his decades of Montana cowboy stories and he ate up their unconditional love. It was a perfect match. Some day his and Jodie's kids would hang with Timmy until they were old enough to help work the dogs. He liked the sound of that.

For their own honeymoon, Stan would get Jodie to take him to every single place in New York that she'd talked about. See the dinosaur bones in the museum and eat pastrami sandwiches and pizza. They'd go to Ground Zero and see where America was forever changed, launching the wars that had reshaped both of their lives.

He waited until he could feel the future rippling through their clasped hands. No matter what she was thinking, he could always feel it in her just as accurately as she could read him.

Emotions getting transmitted down the leash.

Except, like his dogs…*their* dogs, there was no need for any leash.

The ranch hands and guests still lingered. Not because they were holding on to the party, but because they genuinely liked each other. They enjoyed sharing their lives with this family made up of friends.

As he shifted out of his chair to kneel at her feet, a silence settled over the crowd. At a snap of his fingers and a point, Bertram trotted over to sit beside him facing Jodie.

"It seems unfair, you know," he muttered to her. "You're the one who always has all the words."

Her smile grew along with her silence. Words were never his strength, but he knew what he wanted and oddly her silence let him say it.

"Marry me, Jodie. Not for today or tomorrow. Marry me for the rest of our lives. Because I'm lost without you."

Without a word—for once—she nodded yes and leaned down to kiss him. When Bertram planted a cold nose against both their cheeks, she didn't even flinch. Instead, she simply put a hand on the dog's head to match the one on Stan's cheek.

The Secret Service dogs of the White House Protection Force, exclusively at: www.buchmanbookworks.com

OFF THE LEASH (EXCERPT)

(WHITE HOUSE PROTECTION FORCE #1)

"You're joking."

"Nope. That's his name. And he's yours now."

Sergeant Linda Hamlin wondered quite what it would take to wipe that smile off Lieutenant Jurgen's face. A 120mm round from an M1A1 Abrams Main Battle Tank came to mind.

The kennel master of the US Secret Service's Canine Team was clearly a misogynistic jerk from the top of his polished head to the bottoms of his equally polished boots. She wondered if the shoelaces were polished as well.

Then she looked over at the poor dog sitting hopefully on the concrete kennel floor. His stall had a dog bed three times his size and a water bowl deep enough for him to bathe in. No toys, because toys always came from the handler as a reward. He offered her a sad sigh and a liquid doggy gaze. The kennel even smelled wrong, more of sanitizer than dog. The walls seemed to echo with each bark down the long line of kennels housing the candidate hopefuls for the next addition to the Secret Service's team.

Thor—really?—was a brindle-colored mutt, part who-knew and part no-one-cared. He looked like a cross between an oversized, long-haired schnauzer and a dust mop that someone had spilled dark gray paint on. After mixing in streaks of tawny brown, they'd left one white paw just to make him all the more laughable.

And of course Lieutenant Jerk Jurgen would assign Thor to the first woman on the USSS K-9 team.

Unable to resist, she leaned over far enough to scruff the dog's ears. He was the physical opposite of the sleek and powerful Malinois MWDs—military war dogs—that she'd been handling for the 75th Rangers for the last five years. They twitched with eagerness and nerves. A good MWD was seventy pounds of pure drive—every damn second of the day. If the mild-mannered Thor weighed thirty pounds, she'd be surprised. And he looked like a little girl's best friend who should have a pink bow on his collar.

Jurgen was clearly ex-Marine and would have no respect for the Army. Of course, having been in the Army's Special Operations Forces, she knew better than to respect a Marine.

"We won't let any old swabbie bother us, will we?"

Jurgen snarled—definitely Marine Corps. Swabbie was slang for a Navy sailor and a Marine always took offense at being lumped in with them no matter how much they belonged. Of course the swabbies took offense at having the Marines lumped with *them*. Too bad there weren't any Navy around so that she could get two for the price of one. Jurgen wouldn't be her boss, so appeasing him wasn't high on her to-do list.

At least she wouldn't need any of the protective bite gear working with Thor. With his stature, he was an explosives detection dog without also being an attack one.

"Where was he trained?" She stood back up to face the beast.

"Private outfit in Montana—some place called Henderson's Ranch. Didn't make their MWD program," his scoff said exactly what he thought the likelihood of any dog outfit in Montana being worthwhile. "They wanted us to try the little runt out."

She'd never heard of a training program in Montana. MWDs all came out of Lackland Air Force Base training. The Secret Service mostly trained their own and they all came from Vohne Liche Kennels in Indiana. Unless... Special Operations Forces dogs were trained by private contractors. She'd worked beside a Delta Force dog for a single month—he'd been incredible.

"Is he trained in English or German?" Most American MWDs were trained in German so that there was no confusion in case a command word happened to be part of a spoken sentence. It also made it harder for any random person on the battlefield to shout something that would confuse the dog.

"German according to his paperwork, but he won't listen to me much in either language."

Might as well give the diminutive Thor a few basic tests. A snap of her fingers and a slap on her thigh had the dog dropping into a smart "heel" position. No need to call out *Fuss—by my foot.*

"Pass auf!" Guard! She made a pistol with her thumb and forefinger and aimed it at Jurgen as she grabbed her forearm with her other hand—the military hand sign for enemy.

The little dog snarled at Jurgen sharply enough to have him backing out of the kennel. "Goddamn it!"

"Ruhig." Quiet. Thor maintained his fierce posture but dropped the snarl.

"Gute Hund." Good dog, Linda countered the command.

Thor looked up at her and wagged his tail happily. She tossed him a doggie treat, which he caught midair and crunched happily.

She didn't bother looking up at Jurgen as she knelt once more to check over the little dog. His scruffy fur was so soft that it tickled. Good strength in the jaw, enough to show he'd had bite training despite his size—perfect if she ever needed to take down a three-foot-tall terrorist. Legs said he was a jumper.

"Take your time, Hamlin. I've got nothing else to do with the rest of my goddamn day except babysit you and this mutt."

"Is the course set?"

"Sure. Take him out," Jurgen's snarl sounded almost as nasty as Thor's before he stalked off.

She stood and slapped a hand on her opposite shoulder.

Thor sprang aloft as if he was attached to springs and she caught him easily. He'd cleared well over double his own height. Definitely trained…and far easier to catch than seventy pounds of hyperactive Malinois.

She plopped him back down on the ground. On lead or off? She'd give him the benefit of the doubt and try off first to see what happened.

Linda zipped up her brand-new USSS jacket against the cold and led the way out of the kennel into the hard sunlight of the January morning. Snow had brushed the higher hills around the USSS James J. Rowley Training Center—which this close to Washington, DC, wasn't saying much—but was melting quickly. Scents wouldn't carry as well on the cool air, making it more of a challenge for Thor to locate the explosives. She didn't know where they were either. The course was a test for handler as well as dog.

Jurgen would be up in the observer turret looking for any excuse to mark down his newest team. Perhaps teasing him about being just a Marine hadn't been her best tactical choice. She sighed. At least she was consistent—she'd always been good at finding ways to piss people off before she could stop herself and consider the wisdom of doing so.

This test was the culmination of a crazy three months, so she'd forgive herself this time—something she also wasn't very good at.

In October she'd been out of the Army and unsure what to do next. Tucked in the packet with her DD 214 honorable discharge form had been a flyer on career opportunities with the US Secret Service dog team: *Be all your dog can be!* No one else being released from Fort Benning that day had received any kind of a job flyer at all that she'd seen, so she kept quiet about it.

She had to pass through DC on her way back to Vermont—her parent's place. Burlington would work for, honestly, not very long at all, but she lacked anywhere else to go after a decade of service. So, she'd stopped off in DC to see what was up with that job flyer. Five interviews and three months to complete a standard six-month training course later—which was mostly a cakewalk after fighting with the US Rangers—she was on-board and this chill January day was her first chance with a dog. First chance to prove that she still had it. First chance to prove that she hadn't made a mistake in deciding that she'd seen enough bloodshed and war zones for one lifetime and leaving the Army.

The Start Here sign made it obvious where to begin, but she didn't dare hesitate to take in her surroundings past a quick glimpse. Jurgen's score would count a great deal toward where she and Thor were assigned in the future. Mostly likely on some field prep team, clearing the way for presidential visits.

As usual, hindsight informed her that harassing the lieutenant hadn't been an optimal strategy. A hindsight that had served her equally poorly with regular Army commanders before she'd finally hooked up with the Rangers—kowtowing to officers had never been one of her strengths.

Thankfully, the Special Operations Forces hadn't given a damn about anything except performance and *that* she could always deliver, since the day she'd been named the team captain for both soccer and volleyball. She was never popular, but both teams had made all-state her last two years in school.

The canine training course at James J. Rowley was a two-acre lot. A hard-packed path of tramped-down dirt led through the brown grass. It followed a predictable pattern from the gate to a junker car, over to tool shed, then a truck, and so on into a compressed version of an intersection in a small town. Beyond it ran an urban street of gray clapboard two- and three-story buildings and an eight-story office tower, all without windows. Clearly a playground for Secret Service training teams.

Her target was the town, so she blocked the city street out of her mind. Focus on the problem: two roads, twenty storefronts, six houses, vehicles, pedestrians.

It might look normal…normalish with its missing windows and no movement. It would be anything but. Stocked with fake IEDs, a bombmaker's stash, suicide cars, weapons caches, and dozens of other traps, all waiting for her and Thor to find. He had to be sensitive to hundreds of scents and it was her job to guide him so that he didn't miss the opportunity to find and evaluate each one.

There would be easy scents, from fertilizer and diesel fuel used so destructively in the 1995 Oklahoma City bombing, to almost as obvious TNT to the very difficult to detect C-4 plastic explosive.

Mannequins on the street carried grocery bags and briefcases. Some held fresh meat, a powerful smell demanding any dog's attention, but would count as a false lead if they went for it. On the job, an explosives detection dog wasn't supposed to care about anything except explosives. Other mannequins were wrapped in suicide vests loaded with Semtex or wearing knapsacks filled with package bombs made from Russian PVV-5A.

She spotted Jurgen stepping into a glassed-in observer turret atop the corner drugstore. Someone else was already there and watching.

She looked down once more at the ridiculous little dog and could only hope for the best.

"Thor?"

He looked up at her.

She pointed to the left, away from the beaten path.

"*Such!*" Find.

Thor sniffed left, then right. Then he headed forward quickly in the direction she pointed.

Clive Andrews sat in the second-story window at the corner of Main and First, the only two streets in town. Downstairs was a drugstore all rigged to explode, except there were no triggers and there was barely enough explosive to blow up a candy box.

Not that he'd know, but that's what Lieutenant Jurgen had promised him.

It didn't really matter if it was rigged to blow for real, because when Miss Watson—never Ms. or Mrs.—asked for a "favor," you did it. At least he did. Actually, he had yet to meet anyone else who knew her. Not that he'd asked around. She wasn't the sort of person one talked about with strangers, or even close friends. He'd bet even if they did, it would be in whispers. That's just what she was like.

So he'd traveled across town from the White House and into

Maryland on a cold winter's morning, barely past a sunrise that did nothing to warm the day. Now he sat in an unheated glass icebox and watched a new officer run a test course he didn't begin to understand.

Buy now to keep reading this completed trilogy.
Available exclusively at:
www.buchmanbookworks.com

ABOUT THE AUTHOR

USA Today and Amazon #1 Bestseller M. L. "Matt" Buchman started writing on a flight south from Japan to ride his bicycle across the Australian Outback. Just part of a solo around-the-world trip that ultimately launched his writing career.

From the very beginning, his powerful female heroines insisted on putting character first, *then* a great adventure. He's since written over 60 action-adventure thrillers and military romantic suspense novels. And just for the fun of it: 100 short stories, and a fast-growing pile of read-by-author audiobooks.

Booklist says: "3X Top 10 of the Year." PW says: "Tom Clancy fans open to a strong female lead will clamor for more." His fans say: "I want more now...of everything." That his characters are even more insistent than his fans is a hoot.

As a 30-year project manager with a geophysics degree who has designed and built houses, flown and jumped out of planes, and solo-sailed a 50' ketch, he is awed by what is possible. More at: www.mlbuchman.com.

Other works by M. L. Buchman: *(* - also in audio)*

Thrillers

Dead Chef
One Chef!
Two Chef!

Miranda Chase
*Drone**
*Thunderbolt**
*Condor**
*Ghostrider**

Romantic Suspense

Delta Force
*Target Engaged**
*Heart Strike**
*Wild Justice**
*Midnight Trust**

Firehawks
MAIN FLIGHT
Pure Heat
Full Blaze
*Hot Point**
*Flash of Fire**
Wild Fire
SMOKEJUMPERS
*Wildfire at Dawn**
*Wildfire at Larch Creek**
*Wildfire on the Skagit**

The Night Stalkers
MAIN FLIGHT
The Night Is Mine
I Own the Dawn
Wait Until Dark
Take Over at Midnight
Light Up the Night
Bring On the Dusk
By Break of Day

AND THE NAVY
Christmas at Steel Beach
Christmas at Peleliu Cove
WHITE HOUSE HOLIDAY
*Daniel's Christmas**
*Frank's Independence Day**
*Peter's Christmas**
*Zachary's Christmas**
*Roy's Independence Day**
*Damien's Christmas**
5E
Target of the Heart
Target Lock on Love
Target of Mine
Target of One's Own

Shadow Force: Psi
*At the Slightest Sound**
*At the Quietest Word**

White House Protection Force
*Off the Leash**
*On Your Mark**
*In the Weeds**

Contemporary Romance

Eagle Cove
Return to Eagle Cove
Recipe for Eagle Cove
Longing for Eagle Cove
Keepsake for Eagle Cove

Henderson's Ranch
*Nathan's Big Sky**
*Big Sky, Loyal Heart**
*Big Sky Dog Whisperer**

Love Abroad
Heart of the Cotswolds: England
Path of Love: Cinque Terre, Italy

Other works by M. L. Buchman:

Contemporary Romance (cont)

Where Dreams
Where Dreams are Born
Where Dreams Reside
Where Dreams Are of Christmas
Where Dreams Unfold
Where Dreams Are Written

Science Fiction / Fantasy

Deities Anonymous
Cookbook from Hell: Reheated
Saviors 101

Single Titles
The Nara Reaction
Monk's Maze
the Me and Elsie Chronicles

Non-Fiction

Strategies for Success
Managing Your Inner Artist/Writer
Estate Planning for Authors
Character Voice

Short Story Series by M. L. Buchman:

Romantic Suspense

Delta Force
Delta Force

Firehawks
The Firehawks Lookouts
The Firehawks Hotshots
The Firebirds

The Night Stalkers
The Night Stalkers
The Night Stalkers 5E
The Night Stalkers CSAR
The Night Stalkers Wedding Stories

US Coast Guard
US Coast Guard

White House Protection Force
White House Protection Force

Contemporary Romance

Eagle Cove
Eagle Cove

Henderson's Ranch
Henderson's Ranch

Where Dreams
Where Dreams

Thrillers

Dead Chef
Dead Chef

Science Fiction / Fantasy

Deities Anonymous
Deities Anonymous

Other
The Future Night Stalkers
Single Titles

SIGN UP FOR M. L. BUCHMAN'S NEWSLETTER TODAY

and receive:
Release News
Free Short Stories
an awesome collection

Do it today. Do it now.
www.mlbuchman.com/newsletter